ewal
nterne
erson
hone

PENELOPE'S
WEB

ALSO BY CHRISTOPHER RUSH

NOVELS
A Twelvemonth and a Day
Last Lesson of the Afternoon
Will

SHORT STORIES
Peace Comes Dropping Slow
Into the Ebb
Two Christmas Stories
Venus Peter Saves the Whale

MEMOIRS
To Travel Hopefully
Hellfire and Herring
Sex, Lies and Shakespeare

POETRY
A Resurrection of a Kind

BIOGRAPHY
With Sharp Compassion: Norman Dott, Freeman Surgeon of Edinburgh

AS EDITOR
Aunt Epp's Guide for Life: A Victorian Notebook
Alastair Mackie: Collected Poems 1954–1994
Selected Poems of Felix Dennis
Felix Dennis: The Four L's: Poems of Love, Loss, Life and Laughter

CRITICISM
New Words in Classic Guise: An Introduction to the Poetry of Felix Dennis

SCREENPLAY
Venus Peter

WORDS AND PHOTOGRAPHS
Where the Clock Stands Still (with Cliff Wilson)

TRANSLATION
Young Pushkin (with Anna Rush)

Christopher Rush

PENELOPE'S WEB

Polygon

This edition published in Great Britain in 2015 by
Polygon, an imprint of Birlinn Ltd
West Newington House
10 Newington Road
Edinburgh
EH9 1QS

www.polygonbooks.co.uk

9 8 7 6 5 4 3 2 1

ISBN: 978 1 84697 309 3

Copyright © Christopher Rush, 2015

The publishers acknowledge investment from Creative Scotland
toward the publication of this volume.

ALBA | CHRUTHACHAIL

British Library Cataloguing-in-Publication Data
A catalogue record for this book is available on request from the British Library

Typeset by Studio Monachino
Printed and bound in Great Britain by Clays Ltd, St Ives plc

For little Sam
and with a low sweeping bow
to Adam Nicolson
and a long libation
to the divine Bettany Hughes

CONTENTS

PROLEGOMENON
The Grand Plan

PART ONE
Before the War

PART TWO
The War in Troy

PART THREE
The Homecomings

PART FOUR
Ithaca

EXODE
The Last Voyage

ACKNOWLEDGEMENTS

In my Dedication I have picked out the two scholars and explorers of the Ancient World who have inspired me most in recent years: Adam Nicolson and Bettany Hughes. I stand on their shoulders and see much further than I did before. If in places I have also leaned too heavily on either of them, I beg of each: grant me absolution.

In the editorial process I have been borne along by Sarah Ream, an editor so watchful and all-knowing I think she was sent by the gods, though I know she was hired by Neville Moir, my rod and staff at Polygon, together with the rest of that splendid team.

Turning back the page half a century and more to my school days at Waid Academy Anstruther, I want to thank two teachers in particular. Buggie Brown (I never discovered his first name) cheerfully taught me Greek for fun in the little steam puffer that chugged us to and from school each day between St Monans and Anstruther. 'Never fear the Greeks,' he used to say. 'Homer is their greatest gift to the world.' For relaxation he brought out the Greek New Testament.

I owe another huge debt to my English master, Alastair Mackie, poet and translator, who first inspired me to read and write about Odysseus. We shared translations, and our mutual musings bore fruit in a number of dramatic monologues, one of which forms the basis of Odysseus's last words in this book.

It is a book which has taken me five years to write, and which kept me from my family: Anna and Jenny, and more recently Sam. To them I apologise for the long hours spent with Odysseus and with those who have written about him and his world: Kazantzakis, Tennyson, du Bellay, Umberto Saba, Aeschylus, Rupert Brooke and all the usual suspects, not least Homer. At last it's over and I'm glad to be back in Ithaca. I hope the reader will think the voyage was worth it. Read and perpend.

Christopher Rush
MAY 2015

AUTHOR'S NOTE

Penelope's Web is the story of Odysseus, one of the heroes of *The Iliad* and the eponymous hero of *The Odyssey*. *The Iliad* is narrated throughout in the third person, the impersonal voice of Homer. So is *The Odyssey*, apart from a slender middle section in which Odysseus himself brings a listening audience up to speed on his adventures. Other Greek writers, ancient and modern, have followed Homer's example. In the present book, I have reversed this technique, allowing Odysseus to tell his own story in a blunt, soldierly, first-person voice that echoes the realities of war and peace, while Penelope re-invents her husband's experiences, drawing on myth, legend and Greek literature, to portray him as the hero who overcomes impossible odds – and a series of women – to return to her and to his home in Ithaca. Arching over these two accounts is that of the omniscient narrator, the invisible author, who sees all.

The constant voice-shifts are indicated by symbols – the Odysseus and Penelope icons, which represent him and her, and the Greek key icon, which represents the impersonal narrator. Penelope's is the voice not of the woman herself but of the myth-making weaver spinning on her loom the web of lies – and truths. Odysseus's voice is that of the soldier and sailor, finding his way in the field, charting a course through the sea of life, the aftermath of war. He is the man on the ground, as opposed to the stuff of myth. And yet Odysseus also dips in and out of myth and by his own admission is a slippery teller of the truth. Moreover, the voices sometimes merge and blur as truth shimmers like a mirage. The symbols are intended, therefore, as a general guide. I hope that the reader will find them helpful in the re-imagining of these old stories for our time.

C.R.

PROLEGOMENON

THE GRAND PLAN

From time to time the population of the earth becomes too much for it to bear, so certain methods are employed to thin out the density of its peoples and reduce numbers to a safe and acceptable level. Some say these steps are taken by nature, wisest of nurses. Or else human instinct is at work on an inscrutable level, a self-regulatory strategy scribbled deep into the genes. The religious sort say that the problem is addressed not by mortals, who are incapable of controlling themselves, but by the powers above us. Whichever way you look at it, it's a survival tactic for a human race too clueless consciously to look after its own affairs. Neutral nature or the benign and merciless gods: they're the same thing, really. It just depends on your choice of terminology, and that's naturally determined by your beliefs.

Let's go with myth then, for the moment. Let's occupy the ethical and imaginative high ground. Let's leave reason aside.

Once upon a time, as they say, there was a great race of men, a god-like race, a race of heroes. They were called Greeks. And there was another race, almost as illustrious, called Trojans. And these mortals, though separated by a wide and unpredictable sea called the Aegean, thronged the world to such an extent that Zeus, in his wisdom and his pity, hit on a plan to deliver the all too fruitful humans from themselves. That plan was war, an effective means of easing the squeeze on population. Specifically, the Trojan War, in which vast numbers of both Greeks and Trojans were killed, nature triumphed, the gods' will was done and the earth's burden was considerably relieved.

True, that's how some saw the war. It's how some people will always see a war – as anything other than what it is: blind, brutal destruction. The men who fought it knew different. Soldiers in the field always know different, and better. I was a soldier. On the ground we knew precisely what caused the war: greed. Wars are always about ideology or greed. Or both. And in spite of all the hot air, it was no ideology that took us to Troy.

But it's always tempting to imagine a grand plan, even to believe in one. Penelope liked the idea of the grand plan. And under her cunning hand, the gods saw the problem and reached for something they had kept hidden. That something was a woman. And there she lay, naked and smirking in the lap of the gods, biding her time. You can see her in the opening scene of the web, wearing that salacious smile, the one that loosened so much sperm, so many nerves, knees, lives. She was the argument, the agent, the exterminating spark. She was the excuse. She was the weapon of mass destruction. And we were sent to Troy to find her.

PART ONE
BEFORE THE WAR

When I got back to Ithaca from a long tour of duty in Troy, plus other inconveniences I hadn't bargained for, you might think I'd have done what every soldier supposedly does after a long campaign and a hard homecoming – get stuck straight in between my wife's spread legs and smash pissers with her for an hour or two before the nightmares start up and the blackheads surround me for the hundredth fucking time in a three-sixty attack. The dreams of war. You might think that. And you might think that for all soldiers there's nothing like I&I, intoxication and intercourse, to put the war behind them. For as long as the Lethe limbo lasts.

If that's what you think, then you've never been a soldier – at least not in Troy. And you know nothing about what war does to a soldier, how it strips him of himself. It has to, if the chain of command is to operate effectively. There can be no individuals, no identities, only numbers. You're not there; inside that armour you don't exist. It's the anonymity that lets you kill, and every time you kill the more anonymous you become and the further away from home. The tide pulls you away from your wife and kids, your old folks, while the emotional undertow inside you is always trying to suck you back to what you left behind, what you hunger for in your heart of hearts. Or so you think.

Sometimes it works, the undertow. And sometimes it doesn't. Sometimes you're left feeling that only the dead have identity – they're always returning to us, after all – and that you'll never regain your own self until you too are gone. Somebody once said it: call no man happy until he is dead.

But that's another fucking lie. As the great Achilles found out. Home turns out to be as cruel as war – normal life has been put on hold at best, destroyed at worst, and things are what the ordinary soldier calls FUBAR. Fucked up beyond all recognition. Or repair.

You come back with a divided, displaced, dislocated feeling, a disquiet as loud as fucking thunder in your head. Your chest is never at rest. You've come home but you know you'll never feel at home. You know that in spite of what they say about the hell of war, life will never be as rich again, you'll never feel as close to anyone as you did to your comrades in the field, you'll never feel the adrenalin kick in, the buzz of action that made you so intensely aware of being alive. Never again. You know that from now on there will be no hell like home.

That's not all. You know you've been brutalised and that you have to try to separate the killing instinct from the survival instinct. You also know for a fact that the two are inseparable in a soldier, yes, even though the brutality existed only to protect peace and defend civilisation – if you want to believe what your leaders have told you. The thing is, it's still there, the blood-lust is still there, you need it, you need to keep going over and over in your mind the actual enjoyment of enemy casualties, the kick and thrill of killing up close with blades, boulders, bare hands, anything, the sheer satisfaction of knowing that you rained fucking devastation on the bastards.

You know something else too. You know you'll never trust anyone like you did before, not even your wife. For months, years, you've relied on the man next to you, your comrade, your best friend, looking out for you as you looked out for him. And you've relied on yourself, on your wits, on your weapons. On discipline. And on your determination to overcome the enemy, and to survive. And now all that's gone. And all that's left is a big fucking empty.

A BFE. Even the remote and utterly worthless locations you've served your country in start to look like Elysium compared to what you've come back to. Even bumfuck Egypt calls you back. And you'd go like an arrow.

There are other ways of putting it. Our army docs, with nothing but a handful of herbs to combat it, refer to it as the peace adjustment syndrome. Peace is now your enemy. Or, with some humour, I suspect, and half an eye to the sexual difficulties encountered by returning soldiers, they call it the re-entry problem. Re-fucking-entry. That's a polite way of looking at your wife's fanny. The ordinary soldier naturally puts it more graphically: WABHAC. War's a bastard, home's a cunt.

Cunt, by the way, was the last thing on my mind when I got home and slaughtered the bastards who'd been offering to screw my wife in my absence. And cock wasn't high on Penelope's agenda either. What was she supposed to think, let alone feel, as she stood in her room, under orders, and a butcher walked through the door? Even without the blood on me, even ignoring the fresh stench of lopped body parts, I was hardly her husband, was I? What was I? A salt-bitten stranger from the sea. A war-torn wolf with the madness hard in his eyes, still glittering from the recent killing spree. I could have killed her next.

I could see her thinking it, her hand clutching her chest, breathless, terrified, wondering what the fuck I was going to do, what I was going to say, a soldier from the war returning, blood on his beard, from a hard campaign, a long bastard of a tour. Long? It had been fucking years.

Later she lied about it, as she lied about most things. Said she'd looked me over and that when I checked out and she was happy I was still her old fuck-stick, she'd lain back and we'd gone at it all night as we talked the stars round the sky till morning. The star thing was her very expression – not verbatim, not even made of words, but an image, among the first of hundreds stitched into her web. Art gets away with murder, the things language can't always handle, including lies, and there were plenty of lies in Penelope's web.

Not that I can talk. I've lived by lies. I've survived by them. And survived them. But to be clear about the stars – yes, there were stars by the thousands. Maybe a million. But sex? No, I didn't want it, didn't want sex with the wife I hadn't seen for years, not as we stood there staring at one another on either side of that white unbroken bed. What normal man would? And I wasn't even normal. Nor was she. How could she have been?

So we didn't break the bed. We had a lot of ice to break first, a whole frozen ocean. And we both knew it would take months to melt, maybe years. Maybe never. Maybe talk was the best first thing. That much was true. We did talk. We talked the stars round the sky, and when dawn fingered the east we were still talking.

I've known soldiers who can't talk about war, their war, after they've come home. They don't utter a word. They only scream – when the nightmares come. I've known men who can talk about nothing else. They're still talking, years later they're still talking, when they die, still talking. Mostly to themselves. The ones who can't talk and the ones who can't stop talking have one thing in common. They're all well and truly FUBAR.

And the wives? Each to his own, I suppose. Mine wanted to talk. And why not? Conversation is a first step to sex, unless it's rape you have in mind. Nothing much the matter with rape, as a weapon. Nothing much the matter with conversation either, as a weapon, so long as it stays in hand. It's when it gets out of hand that it becomes an end in itself, an endless prevarication, and you both have to admit that you don't want sex anyway. Not because you're strangers, but because you're strangers who used to be close. Big difference. You're strangers who used to be man and wife. And so now you do the only thing you can do. You talk.

Talk's easy, talk's cheap.

What to talk about? Can you guess what she wanted to know most? Did I still love her?

No.

I don't mean no, I didn't love her, I mean no, that's not what she wanted to know most. What she wanted to know most of all was what she was like.

'What was who like?'

'Who do you think? Helen, of course, the cause of it all, the be-all and the end-all. Helen of Sparta. Helen of Troy. What was she like?'

I said it would take a century to tell her.

'Take your time,' she said. 'We have the rest of our lives.'

'Not long enough,' I said.

Right now I wasn't even sure what the rest of our lives would amount to.

'But there's one thing about Helen that might surprise you.'

'What's that?'

'She was like you in one way at least – she spent a lot of time at the loom.'

'The loom? That bitch-whore?'

'Whoring never stopped a woman from weaving, did it? Or weaving from whoring?'

'Hard to imagine.'

But she managed to imagine it when she set up her own web, her version of the war, its causes and effects. In Penelope's web, Helen sat in her apartments in Troy weaving a vast tapestry of her own life. The purple traders trod the seas for her, the fishermen spent years harvesting the sea-snails, carting them in tons to the city walls and into the palace, and the slaves dissected them and boiled them up in their own urine. They pissed and art prevailed. The snails gave up their essence for it. Into the weft went the dark red dye, staining her creation the colour of death with a blush of power. Around her the endless bloody struggle continued, stallion-breaking Trojans and Argives armed in bronze, coughing up their lives for her in the same colour while she wove on, depicting their suffering, tracing their tears. And her own. Don't forget, it was all for her.

'And where is that web now?'

'Nowhere. It's ash, my girl. It's dust. It's the dust of fucking Troy.'

Penelope's eyes were glittering slits. 'A pity. But it doesn't matter. I'll make my own web. I'll tell it my way. I'll unravel that slut-work.'

'Why bother?'

She looked hard at me, the smile cold on her mouth. 'I think you know what it's like, not being able to stop what you've been doing for years. Neither wanting to stop, nor even wanting to want to stop.'

I knew just what she was talking about. No man better.

'So now,' she said, 'tell me about Helen. Tell me about Troy.'

Troy and Helen. Was there ever a time when I could think of one without the other? If there was, it's been wiped from my mind, it's been so long. It seems there never was a Troy without a Helen. She was built into the walls. She was the heart of the citadel. Her abduction was eternal.

It's not true, of course. Troy invited attack long before Helen. Look and see. A glance at the map is all it takes. Agamemnon was telling the truth for a change when he addressed the army at Aulis, whipping up the hysteria, appealing to bellicosity, patriotism, piracy, selling us the war.

'The bastards are begging for it,' he said.

In that respect at least he was right. Troy was of no global consequence, little more than a local power, but regionally it was a peach of the east, standing strategically between two great seas, two worlds, east and west. The Trojans could have controlled all shipping between the two, and suppressed access to the Propontis and the Black Sea, except that they didn't even have a navy. Not a single fucking ship. Before Paris came to Sparta, he had to have one specially built. Amazingly, the Trojans weren't seafarers, they were horse-traders. They were also allies of the Hittite shites and therefore enemies of us seafaring Greeks. And they were straddling the trade routes into Anatolia from the Med.

A commanding position. One to die for. As many did. A plain sliced by two rivers, a citadel on a hill, and a lower city of six thousand, half of which were desirable females. Troy waves to traders, sailors, soldiers. It beckons to textiles, metals, merchandise, men wanting women, slaves. They might just as easily have hung out a flag on the walls. They might as well have bellowed out the message across the Aegean: come and assault us, we're here to be taken, kick our arses. Agamemnon just couldn't believe his luck when he was handed it on a golden plate, the golden excuse for responding to the call. So the truth is that Troy didn't need Helen to draw us east. Troy was her own reason for war. Troy was always going to be fucked.

That didn't suit Penelope's web. She wanted a scapegoat. And there was never a scapegoat like Helen. She was the bad girl, she fitted the part. She carried the war crimes of the world tucked tight between her legs.

And it's true that she collected most of the blame for the war. Everybody cursed her, especially soldiers' wives. And the soldiers. The brave lads had to have their say about Helen.

That slut has a cunt like the Hellespont – the whole world goes through it!

Understandable. But a sweeping exaggeration, and a slur. She stuck to the man who abducted her. The trouble is, she deserted the man she was married to. The abduction was no myth. It happened. And you won't have trouble telling fact from fiction in this report. I tell it as it was. Penelope tells it as it could have been, maybe even should have been, if life were art, or legend, or if life were fair, or moral, or beautiful, or all that stuff. So if myth is to your taste, listen to Penelope, follow the golden thread. It's all there in the web. But for now, let's stick with what's real.

Paris arrived in Sparta, long-haired, close-shaven, clean-jawed, his hairy medallioned chest matted with oil, his ears and fingers glittering with rings and trinkets. A right fucking mummy's boy he was, and an easy charmer. Easy with his arrow, easy under a leopard skin, easy at a distance, easy on wheels, easy with the women. An Anatolian archer, a battlefield butterfly, a gutless funk. He boarded his trim ship, newly fitted out, and homed in on Helen, scenting Spartan fanny all across the Aegean.

What really brought him to Sparta? If you want the truth he was a messenger boy. His father, Priam, sent him on an embassy to inquire after Paris's aunt, Hesione, who had married Telamon of Salamis. And it was in Sparta, at the court of Menelaus, that he met Helen. He was entertained in Sparta for nine days, and for not one of those days could he take his eyes off her. Everybody saw it, except Menelaus. But then he never saw much that wasn't up his own arse, which is where his head was most of the time. The rest of the time it was up Agamemnon's. That pair were true brothers, united by rectal cranial inversion, mutual and interchangeable. On the tenth day a message arrived for Menelaus. His mother's father, Catreus, had died in Crete and his presence was required at the funeral.

'I'll be back,' he told Helen, 'as soon as the obsequies are over. While I'm gone make sure you look after our guest. Carry on with the entertainment.'

But Menelaus had been set-up. When Paris swanned in, the Spartan leader had seen at a glance a pretty boy from a culture that made his palace look like some shack. That's what he was made to see, meant to see. Priam had primed his son and he'd oiled his way in with gifts beyond belief: golden bowls, razors, goblets, golden beds inlaid with ivory, mirrors, earrings, necklaces, dresses, weapons, chariots. There was even a fucking monkey. All of which he stole back again when he left. Except for the monkey. He said he'd left that to save Menelaus looking in the mirror – which was just as well as he hadn't left a single one.

A sharper man than Menelaus might have suspected another agenda than a mere state visit. Priam was up to something. Whether Helen was really on the agenda is another matter. But the sweeteners did the trick. Trojans were not exactly allies but if they could pull down pearls from Olympia – and it looked as if they could – then they had to be sucked off. And Paris was a young man well worth sucking off. So Menelaus had had no qualms about leaving his clever queen in charge of state affairs while he buggered off to his funeral in Crete. She had been ordered to lay on the sparkling wine, the roast boar, the charm, the lot. Up to the hilt.

Up to the hilt. So to speak. They later claimed that they hadn't actually desecrated the bed of Menelaus – they'd waited for the nearest convenient island, Kranai, as it happened, to consummate their passion. An offshore lust, if you like. The maidservants told it differently. But they kept their mouths shut at the time. And the sentries were out for the count. Helen had spiked the wine that night. She was a dab hand at that device. So they got out of the palace unseen. And laden with loot.

The Spartan spears would have whistled past their arses if they'd been spotted. She dropped a sandal on the mad dash. It was all her husband had left of her to chew at in his fury. But it hadn't taken too much nerve, not on Paris's side at least. He was a spoiled little tosser who just assumed things would always go his way. And that night they did – long before the big bronze bell began to clang and the shit-scared guards came to. They knew Menelaus would slit their throats, once he'd finished spitting.

Which is exactly what happened.

'Fucking hell! I go to bury my grandfather, and my wife walks out of here under your fucking noses – and with the Trojan fucking ambassador between her legs! Take them out!'

He spread it about that it was an abduction, but privately he admitted the opposite to Agamemnon and his closest friends.

'Every cunt from Tiryns to Troy knows she fucked off with him.'

It didn't matter. Abduction or elopement, it was still politically an abduction and an act of aggression.

'We don't have to declare war on the bastards,' he said, 'they've declared it already.'

Agamemnon grinned at him. 'What are you talking about, brother? Declaration? Of course you don't have to make any fucking declaration, you just fucking turn up! And if the bastards are unprepared, so much the better!'

Well, that was the Greek way. And there was nothing unusual about abductions either. We lived by acts of aggression. We took women away from their homes all the time. So did the other side, whoever the other side happened to be. The Phoenicians came to Argos and abducted Io, the king's daughter, took her off to Egypt. We retaliated by abducting their princess Europa. We abducted the King of Colchis' daughter, Medea. Paris abducted Helen from Sparta. Though you could say he broke the rules. The others were all unmarried virgins and fair game. And they were only princesses.

'Helen is a queen, for fuck's sake!' roared Menelaus. 'And my fucking wife!'

Paris upset the status quo, but the truth is, nobody much cared about the status quo. The Myceneans certainly didn't: they were keener on war than peace. And Agamemnon was a Mycenean, true bred. This was how things were. It was the scheme of things.

THREE

And in another scheme of things entirely, as Penelope has it in the web, Zeus lusted after the loveliest of the Nereids, the sea-goddess Thetis, and was all set to impregnate her until he found out from the Fates that the son of this sea-nymph would grow up to be more powerful than his father. Prometheus confirmed this under torture, chained to his rock. It took Zeus a thousand years to extract the information, but it was well worth the wait.

As soon as he knew what destiny had decreed for Thetis, Zeus lost no time at all. He married her off to a mere mortal, Peleus. It wasn't a random choice. Peleus was more than an admirer: he was a hero. He'd sailed with Jason and the Argonauts. He'd been on the famous quest for the golden fleece. So the even stronger son, sprung from such loins, was sure to prove a superhero, as destiny demanded. But at least he'd be no trouble to Zeus.

Understandably, Thetis had no wish to be matched with a mortal man. She had her own lusts, principally for Poseidon, and Peleus had quite a struggle to net and keep her. But he succeeded. And to pacify the nymph, Zeus threw a huge wedding party. All Olympia was invited and they all brought spectacular gifts. The celebrity guest list contained only one omission. The entire panoply of gods and goddesses was welcomed, except Eris. Nobody wants strife at a wedding.

'There's enough to follow,' said Zeus, 'in married life. Let them have their first day without it.'

And all Olympia shook with dutiful laughter at his joke. All except Eris, who came anyway, angry at her exclusion and ready to do what she was designed to do: sow discord. She brought along her own special gift, but not for the happy couple. It was a golden apple, inscribed 'For the fairest'. Simple words calculated to trigger cosmic disruption. Even so, it's hard to imagine those words causing so much suffering. But there were reputations at stake, the pride and vanity of three Olympian females: Hera, Pallas Athene and Aphrodite, three powerful players, and each one of them claiming the right to the apple. No sooner had Eris lobbed it into the nuptials, sending it rolling among the sandalled feet of the immortal guests, than all hell broke loose.

There's no hell like a cat-fight, and Zeus had three squalling cats with their claws out bitching blue on Olympia. They were all beautiful, naturally, but Hera pulled rank, Aphrodite argued that she was the official embodiment of beauty, and Athene claimed there could be no true beauty without wisdom, which she had in spades. Wisest of the gods, Zeus stayed out of it and ordered the contestants to be conducted to Mount Ida, where he would appoint the Trojan Paris to be judge of the greatest beauty contest of all time.

Why him? Why Paris? An obscure mountain shepherd and strummer. A son of Priam certainly, but Priam had fifty sons. He was short on bravery and not well endowed with brains either. All he had were his good looks. And he was an athlete between the sheets.

There was one other thing, though – he had a reputation for fairness and objectivity, attributes that had been put to the test when his favourite bull, a magnificent white specimen, had entered a contest with another. Paris himself had awarded victory to the outsider, which, unbeknown to him, happened to be none other than the god Ares, got up as a bull. So impartial Paris already had a good reputation among the gods. The fact that he was a flawed character didn't matter much to the Olympians, who were not exactly acclaimed for their morality.

That was the way Penelope liked to play it – to badmouth Helen and excuse Paris at every opportunity. The whole Paris history unfolded. His mother the queen had a nightmare just after he was born. In her dream, the child rushed through Troy like a Fury, setting it ablaze and pulling down its proud towers. When she woke up, she told her husband about her dream. Priam heard it with considerable alarm, called in his advisers, and immediately gave the baby to a servant, whose task was to expose the infant to die on Ida, near the den of a bear. If he didn't starve or freeze or shrivel up he'd be mauled and eaten.

Five days later the servant discovered the infant alive and well among the bear cubs. The boy was obviously destined not to die. So he brought him up as his own son, hunter and herd, and a handsome stripling too. The nymph Oenone fell in love with him and they married and had a son called Corythus. All three lived in a mountain cave, not far from the man Paris called father.

It was during that time that Ares took part in the prize bull affair. Priam happened to hear of the big white bull on Ida, and one year he sent up the mountain for it when he was holding the annual funeral games in memory of the son he still believed to be dead. The beast was to be brought down as one of the prizes in the competition. Paris was heartbroken – the bull was his pride and joy. But the king wanted it, so he had no choice but to let the animal go with the old servant, who drove it down to Troy. The son still didn't know the king was his father. Paris didn't know he was Paris.

Angry, sad, but also curious, he followed the bull down the mountain, and on impulse and in the hope of winning it back, took part in his own funeral games. He won the chariot race, the foot race and the boxing match, open to all-comers. The real Paris couldn't punch his way out of a bathrobe, but this Paris, Penelope's Paris, swept the board and won the laurel crown. He was the man of the match. Every time. Two of his brothers, Hector and Deiphobus, were so furious at being outrun, outdriven and outboxed by this unknown Arcadian upstart that they drew their swords on him and would have hacked him down. But at that point the old servant flung himself at the king's feet and told all.

There were tears of joy all round – except from Cassandra, who wept tears of doom instead and foretold Troy's ruin. But she had been fated never to be believed and Paris was duly reinstated. Cassandra was right. He survived to fulfil both her prophecy and Hecuba's dream. To his credit, however, he still enjoyed spending time on Ida with Oenone and their son and his adoptive father, and the gods liked that. Such a man could surely be counted on to do the right thing, unswayed by self-interest.

'Furthermore,' said Zeus, 'he's handsome. Some say he's the most beautiful man alive. Who better qualified to assess the loveliest of the goddesses?'

The logic may have been bent, but Zeus hoped it would straighten out the quarrel between the famous three. They were all sent off to Ida for the contest.

In a beauty contest, each of the competitors is expected to say something, to prove that nature has bestowed on her more than mere looks, even if what she says is some subtle attempt to sway the judgement. There was nothing subtle said on Ida. None of the three had any qualms about the bribe she was offering.

Hera, goddess of Olympia, went first. She didn't say much. As the wife of Zeus she assumed she didn't have to.

'Choose me and you'll enjoy unrivalled political power. I'll make you lord of all Asia, Greece, give you power greater than any king.'

Paris looked at her and saw the beauty of sway and dominion. It was enough to kindle the ambition of any man – if he had any to kindle.

Athene read his eyes and weighed in.

'I'll give you wisdom. Kings will come to you for counsel, world leaders for your advice. That's real power, believe me. With this wisdom you will enjoy invincibility in the field. You will conquer and rule, and no one will question your right to do so. Complete military and intellectual supremacy is what I offer. Just think of it.'

He thought of it.

While he was thinking Aphrodite left the line of goddesses and stood in front of him, her breasts almost touching him.

'Forget power, politics, wisdom, war. What do you really want? What does any man really want? Choose me and I'll give you every man's dream, the world's desire. I'll give you the most beautiful woman on earth, as beautiful as myself. Well, almost. I'll make her want you. Look at me. She'll be yours. I'll be yours.'

What a choice. Political mastery, military impregnability, mind control, ultimate power. Or the perfect woman.

How long was the adjudication period? How long did it take him to reach a conclusion? He could have asked himself why a mountain shepherd would want to dabble in politics, why a contented countryman needed global influence, statesmanship, reputation, power. He could have asked himself why he'd want to leave behind his wife and child, his prize bull, leave a life of bucolic bliss, to go to war. What war? What war could he possibly want to wage, let alone win? War was something Paris never even dreamed of, until the day the Greeks kicked the door in . . .

'Are you looking at me?'

He couldn't take his eyes off her. Which was hardly surprising. Her garments were spun by the Graces and dyed in the flowers of spring, in crocus and hyacinth, in the shy violet and the rose's alluring bloom, narcissus and lily buds, redolent of heaven.

And her voice was soft and thrilling.

'The woman in question is my representative on earth. In taking her you are taking me. Take me and turn your back on cruel wars and the harsh cares of state. Who wants them? Forget the heavy staff, the flaring torch, the cold bronze. Who needs them?'

He could have said . . .

But he wasn't given the chance to say anything.

'Take me – and take these.' She let fall her robe to the waist, baring her famous breasts.

He stared open-mouthed.

'Take me – and take this.' The robe dropped all the way to the flowery ground. She stood naked among the rumpled embroidery.

Outrage from the other two.

'Swindler!'

'Slut!'

She'd cheatcd by showing all, clouding his judgement.

'This is your prize. It's what you will enjoy. I once destroyed a man simply by letting him see me like this. It wasn't even his fault. He didn't mean to. Oh, you are not just one of the chosen few, you are the man, the only man. Perfect beauty. This is what she is like. And she's all yours. Go on – taste and see.'

Paris drops to his knees in front of her, reaches out and holds her by the flanks, cups his trembling hands around her buttocks, buries his face in her bush.

The contest is over. The others turn away, disgusted, and two hot hates go storming back to Olympia. From now on it will be war, total war, and Troy is already a doomed city. Never mind that Paris never stood a chance. He was a pin-head, a peasant, an ignorant boor. She'd rigged it and he'd fallen for it. She places her hands on his handsome nuzzling head and suddenly she's in love with him herself. Her eyes close, her mouth opens.

'I will endow you,' she sighs, 'with irresistible sexual allure. She will see you and she will want you, only you. Nothing else in the world will satisfy her. She is yours and you hers. It's decided. You will take her home with you to Troy.'

History is written. Aphrodite has her apple, Paris his prize. He will launch his ship for Sparta. Nobody knows it yet, but the Trojan War is under way.

FOUR

'It's a date that will live in infamy!'

Agamemnon bawled out the words across our heads.

'The day I went to my grandfather's fucking funeral!' yelled Menelaus, not quite matching the rhetoric.

'An act of treachery!'

'A stab in the back!'

'And one which will never be forgotten, brother. Or forgiven. Be assured of that. It cries out for retaliation.'

Agamemnon was addressing the assembled army at Aulis. Crouched beneath Mount Messapion, overlooking the Euboean Gulf, Aulis was a good port, the best in Boeotia, halfway between Mycenae and Phthia, between Agamemnon and Achilles. The perfect meeting place. It had taken weeks for the task force to muster, and now that mobilisation was complete, Agamemnon was busy telling us all why we'd come, why the offensive was justified.

He didn't mince his words.

'What the fuck? Did they think we'd let them get away with it? Did they simply fail to understand the scale of the consequences? The incredible suffering it would bring on their own people? The huge dust cloud that would mushroom up from so many pyres, so many burned bodies? All that ash. Was it a failure of the imagination? Or a catastrophic misunderstanding of the kind of people we are? Did they even think at all? And afterwards, the opportunities for peace were there, but they never took them. They opened up the skies instead to the inevitable annihilation that will now rain down on them – the destruction of an entire city. Destruction that will be followed by years of misery, generations of mourning. Why? They had their chances. They could have sent her right back. They could have given her up to any of the embassies.'

Agamemnon had a habit of grinning stupidly when he was in full rhetorical swing. He also had a habit of lying. He couldn't help himself. At this point, in fact, there had only ever been one embassy to Troy. Although it had been a high-profile affair. Agamemnon had gone in person on his brother's behalf and he had taken me with him.

The other leaders had insisted on an embassy to give the Trojans a chance to avoid war. Only Agamemnon wanted war. Big ugly fat warmongering, Chief Motherfucker in Charge. Even Menelaus would have settled for just getting his wife back.

Nobody mentioned that Agamemnon had abducted the three daughters of King Anius of Delos who were famous vine-growers and kept the Greek army supplied for years. They supplied a lot more than wine, in fact. The story went that they escaped and, when overtaken, prayed to Dionysus, who turned them into doves, sacred thereafter on Delos. A nice story. Truth is, Agamemnon fucked them two at a time while the third one served the wine. Then they changed shifts. That's how high the moral ground that Agamemnon occupied on the matter of abducted women happened to be.

The two of us crossed to Troy in three days, long before Paris and Helen even got there, we were told. They'd gone off course, made detours, and right now were fuck knows where. According to reports, they could be in Egypt. That's what Hector said, standing in for his father, who was unwell at the time. Apparently.

Agamemnon sniffed the air suspiciously.

Hector sniggered. 'Look, cunt-sniffer, I've told you, she's not here. Look for yourselves. You're welcome to search. And even if she does turn up, are you going to make such a fuss about one missing wife who's spread her legs a little wider than the rest? What's wrong with your brother? Doesn't he have other wives? Concubines? Aren't there enough whores in Sparta?'

'She was abducted!' Agamemnon interrupted loud and clear. 'Against her will!'

'I know what abducted means, thank you very much. And you're talking bollocks. She wasn't forced: she eloped.'

'How do you know that if she's not even here to ask?'

'I know. We have our messengers. And what about all the Anatolian women you Greeks have abducted? What about Medea? What about my own aunt, Hesione?'

'Now you're the one that's bollocking. Hesione was promised to one of ours. And Medea wasn't abducted – she was hot for Jason.'

'And Helen was hot for Paris.'

'Helen was taken against all the laws of hospitality, politics and civilised behaviour – things for which you easterners show scant regard.'

'Get this fucker out of here!'

The embassy was over. The guards shouldered us to the door, Agamemnon still shouting over his shoulder.

'And if she did spread her legs as you say, she spread them right across the fucking Aegean!'

'Go and fuck yourself!'

'Other way round, boy! They're your legs she's spread. And now all of Greece is going to come and fuck you!'

'I'm shitting in my sandals,' laughed Hector.

The first embassy to Troy had not been a success.

And now we were stuck in Aulis without a wind. We'd been stuck for weeks. That's why Agamemnon was haranguing us. Morale was low, the men lay about bitching and beefing and there was a lot of buggery about, some of it unsolicited. Juicies were in short supply as Agamemnon had said we wouldn't take whores aboard, not on a three-day crossing. He wanted the men to arrive in Anatolia with an edge on them.

'Happy shaggers don't make an effective landing force,' he said. 'Hag-shags banned on every ship. No exceptions. Got it?'

Got it, Chief Motherfucker.

'They can have their pick of prostitutes on the other side, not to mention all the other ladies we'll introduce them to. Let them earn their pussy. Fight first, fuck later.'

And now they'd turned to buggery. Brawls broke out over the bum-chums, the latrine queens, the dice, the rations, any excuse. There were desertions before each dawn, deaths before every sunset. The army at Aulis was an angry one. And Agamemnon was reduced to repeated speechifying, bullshit and lies.

The lies came first.

'This is a war of liberation. It's not about occupation or acquisition. We find what we're looking for and we leave. It could be over in days.'

That soon shaded into an all-important admission.

'Liberation is the object of our attack. But the object of our attack is no more important than the principle behind it: the act of revenge. Revenge not only makes us feel good, it makes us look good. Foreign powers don't fuck with us. If they do — they feel what it's like when we fuck them back!'

Roars of approval, huge round of applause.

It didn't last long. Agamemnon sounded convincing, except that there was still no wind. Not a breath from heaven. The venture stood still. Days passed. Windless weeks.

Then Boreas blew. The god of the north frigging wind. He blew all fucking summer, his cheeks puffed out. He never paused for breath, the bastard, just blew and blew, made the riptide roar, keeping us holed up. Then he stopped. But he didn't hand over to the other winds. He just finished his shift and buggered off. That's gods for you. The air was heavy again with silence and flies and unrest. The latrines reeked. Our skins itched and prickled. Our skulls were bursting. Low-level mutiny rumbled among the tents. Agamemnon had to work even harder to keep our boys up for it.

'Troy has rich pickings, more than enough for each leader and plenty left over to share out among the men. I saw what that bastard Paris brought to Sparta – and took away again, the cunt! They're stinking rich, these Trojans, and every thing they've got is going to be ours.'

'What about Helen?'

'Fuck Helen!'

He clapped a big hand over his brother's mouth.

'Helen goes without saying. We're going to suck the bastards dry. If they've got lice, we'll skin them for the tallow. We're leaving them with fuck all. Troy is history.'

Still no wind. The sea stood like a bronze dish, polished, empty, flat. Agamemnon stood up again to speak to the whole army. He let himself go. You could read the greed in his little piggy eyes, the quick, busy glittering, the truffling brain. His ancestry was thick with it, greed. A breed of grabbers. His language echoed it.

'Listen lads, you could own tripods, teams of Trojan horses, whole bevies of beauties, juicies for the journey back, the apples of Anatolia. You reckon you can fuck? You won't have to! They'll do it for you, these women. You've no idea what sex is till you've had an Anatolian cunt milking your dick. I was there on embassy, remember? Just wait till you see the legs on these women, the thighs. They grip like . . .'

He'd no idea what they gripped like because he'd been bundled out of the door so fast he'd never even smelled an Anatolian woman.

'Like . . . like nothing on earth!'

Like nothing. Nice when you run out of words.

It didn't bring the wind. Not a wrinkle on the sea. Word went round the ships. That's it, lads, fuck it, we've had enough, even the leaders agree, we're giving up, we're going nowhere. We're going home.

And home we'd probably have gone, if it hadn't been for Iphigenia.

FIVE

Calchas was the one who first came up with the idea that the impasse at Aulis was down to Agamemnon himself. Our great leader in his great wisdom had killed a deer sacred to Artemis, and in her anger the goddess had asked Poseidon either to lull the sea-winds or to make Boreas blow. And Poseidon had obliged on both counts. That was the official holy story according to the seer. Army god-freaks aren't expected to meddle in strictly military matters, but this had nothing to do with combat. Calchas hated Agamemnon and never missed a moment to tip him in the shit. Not that a sacred deer ranks high on a soldier's bad-news list. Agamemnon would have shagged Artemis herself if he could have got away with it, let alone bump off a deer. No fucking finesse – everybody knew that. And it wasn't exactly a stoning offence. But right now the troops needed somebody to carry the can, and when you're well and truly pissed off, there's nobody better to take it out on than your old commander. Calchas landed him in it nicely. He'd fucked with the gods and the Greek fleet was consequently going nowhere.

Not unless there was a sacrifice.

And not just any old animal either. That became obvious. Sheep, goats, boars, bulls – we slit their throats daily. We were sick of spilled bowels stinking up the ships in the heat, sick of breathing in the greasy air. Nothing that fed the flames made a god so much as fart. The sky sat on the sea day after day. You could slice the air. Agamemnon felt Troy's gold sliding through his fingers, slipping away from him like water. Until Calchas came right out with it at last, gave it to him straight, the thing that was expected of him, the ultimate sacrifice.

Picture a young girl, a virgin, and a priestess too, riding a mule eastward from Mycenae to Aulis, no small journey, and thinking all the way that she was being ushered to her wedding. She'd been spun the story that the great Achilles had refused to sail to Troy with her father unless he had a beautiful bride to come back to. And the bride he wanted was the father's daughter, Iphigenia.

But the great Achilles knew fuck all about it. The great Achilles was married already, if truth be told. But truth was not told. Not strong on truth, Agamemnon, not if slitting a fourteen-year-old girl's throat could swing the wind his way, save his skin, and make him rich. Not even if that girl happened to be his daughter. So truth was twisted. The trap was sprung instead.

And Clytemnestra walked into it too. The proud mother came down to Aulis in all her glory, accompanying her daughter, the gorgeous bride . . . only to be greeted by an empty altar, no bull to be seen, not a heifer either, not even a sheep, not as much as a chicken in sight, not a cheep, and certainly no sign of a bridegroom. She saw it clear: her chick was the one that was going to cheep. There wasn't going to be any wedding. There was only going to be this. She ran screaming at her husband, her white fists battering at his big chest as the girl gaped. It hadn't dawned on her yet. She thought the garlands they had decked her neck with were bridal wreaths.

They were her funeral flowers.

'You bastard!' Clytemnestra spat in his face, wrestling with him.

'You see my position,' he bleated. 'It's ugly for me either way. If the Trojans go unpunished all the other motherfuckers will think they can do the same. Every cunt under the sun will cross the Aegean to steal our wives and screw our daughters!'

'It's a lie, and you know it, you piece-of-shit coward!'

'If I don't do it I'm fucking sunk! My name's mud with the men already. And their blood's up. They're primed to kill. They want to murder those barbarians! I can't hold them back.'

'You mean you want them to help you get rich!'

'That's got bugger all to do with it. I can't control things beyond today.'

'Then step aside and let somebody else fill your boots. Let Menelaus lead them. It's his quarrel, not yours.'

'No, it has to be me.'

'Why? Because you're still wiping your little brother's arse?'

'It's got nothing to do with him either — it's in the lap of the gods, I tell you. If I don't do my duty I'll end up dead in Argos anyway. I won't even have to go to Troy for that. And you'll be slaughtered too — you and all your children.'

'Can't you do better than that? You'd take an innocent girl's life as the ransom for a slut? Your own child! A priestess for a whore: that's your filthy exchange. You'd spend what we love most to buy what we most loathe! How? Why? We both know why. It's greed that drives you, nothing else. We don't need this war. You're going for gold, and for your brother, not for us.'

'Wrong. I'm going for Greece. My country is greater than one private sorrow. I'm leading my people.'

'Well, may you lead them all to hell! And may you all rot there! That's my curse on you!'

Agamemnon threw the shrieking woman from him and gave her to the guards. 'Enough said. No more. Let's do it.'

The force of destiny.

Away back in time they come, appearing over Pelion, the Pierides, with their long golden tresses and sandals, dancing to the strains of the harp, the piping reeds and the song Hymenaeus calls up on the Libyan flute. They are coming to the wedding, the marriage of the nymph Thetis, daughter of Nereus, and Peleus, son of Aeacus. The centaurs' haunts ring with mountain melodies and the woodlands of Pelion rejoice. Loveliest of settings, and everyone ravishing in their beauty. Even Ganymede is there to mix the wine in golden bowls and pour libations, and Nereus's golden girls dance on the gleaming white sands.

Achilles is the fruit of that liaison, and that far back he is promised to Iphigenia – so the Aulis wedding is a story which, after all, contains a seed of truth. But Achilles' head is fated for a helmet, and Iphigenia's tresses for the brindled heifer's wreath. The force of destiny. They crown her like a queen and ease her out of life to ease the Greek fleet out of Aulis.

The ships there are a sight for any woman's eyes. The fleet's right wing is commanded by the Myrmidons: all the armaments of Phthia in fifty flamboyant vessels, Nereids at the sterns, the insignia of Achilles. These are the sweet honey of the fleet. It is a spectacle like no other, a spectacle to die for.

Agamemnon slashed her throat, slicing deep, almost taking her head off with his huge brutal cut. He wanted to make it quick, so he saw to it himself, but he was always heavy-handed with a blade and botched it. The girl struggled and gurgled as the blood gushed and spurted over her wedding dress, but it was brief. Clytemnestra's eyes were a cold flame.

'You murderer!' She almost whispered the words.

The father turned his head away from the dying girl. But not out of sensitivity or regret. A wind was already ruffling the Greek sails, lifeless for weeks.

'Who says the gods are not on my side?'

Iphigenia's last thoughts are of a snow-clad valley in Phrygia, deep in a haunt of Ida, where another child was once sent to die – the infant Paris, also plucked from his mother, then torn by wild beasts, though there are no beasts like men. He lived instead, survived among the roses and hyacinths and the fountains of the nymphs, and so grew up, and later came to Sparta to claim his illicit bride, Aphrodite's bribe.

And for this . . . for this I die, dreams the dying Iphigenia, for something that happened far away from here and has nothing to do with me. Why is it always like this? Why is death such an irrelevance? Why is war so strange? And the winds will blow all these lads to Troy, blown by my last breath, also to die, for a cause they care nothing for and which touches them not.

They pile up the cypresses for her pyre. The singing wind strikes the flames, sings in the sails that flutter under the breath of gods. She burns on the beach, a slip of a girl, not much of her to burn. Her scent goes up to the sky.

We were blood-brothers now with Agamemnon, partners to his ploy, his ruthless intent on Troy. And we were murderers. It would take many a sea to wash off Iphigenia's blood. It had begun: Iphigenia, Agamemnon, Clytemnestra, Aegisthus, Orestes, the Furies. Helen had unleashed a universal mad dog, a blood-cycle without end. You could read it all in Clytemnestra's eyes as she followed her husband in her head, the future in the instant, all the way to Troy and back, to the bloodbath she planned for him. Agamemnon was a dead man. The troops stood and cheered a corpse as he gave the order for the fleet to leave.

We took different routes to Troy, but we all went up the channel between the Greek coast and Euboea, then eastward to Imbros. After that it was a mere twenty miles to Troy, and though there was no navy to intercept us, we fanned out anyway – south by Lesbos, north-west near Sigeum, or as I did with Achilles and Patroclus, along the

Thracian coast, approaching Troy variously. The bird-beaked galleys massed again by Tenedos: thirty-five-footers, ninety-footers, fifty-oared penteconters. Over fifteen thousand men left Aulis. And not many of them came back. But nobody thought of not returning as the heroes hurtled across the surf, and certainly not of the untended crops they'd left behind rotted and dying. That would be the fate of the heroes too, most of them, rotted and forgotten in other fields, foreign fields, far from home.

SIX

For Helen.

They all died for Helen — so lamented Penelope. Heroes for Helen's sake, dead on both sides, and in terrible numbers, casualties of the quest. She was Agamemnon's secret weapon, his human shield, hiding his greed, or so he thought — but not from his wife. Helen fulfilled a need, the eternal itch of the Middle East.

Who was she? What was she? This weapon of mass destruction. What made her?

Swan-rape made her.

Picture her mother, Leda, a famous beauty — married to Tyndareus, King of Sparta — bathing by the banks of the Eurotas, ringed by Lacedaemon's lovely hills. In the centre of that ring of hills she stands naked in the enraptured eye of the great god Zeus, who swoops down from Olympia, turning, as he descends, into a giant swan and rapes her.

Or does he?

See her in the web, Leda, bent over on the riverbank in the act of washing, and the god taking her from behind, biting her nape before making for the vulva, his long neck probing like an enormous phallus, and Leda's hand reaching awkwardly between and behind, fumbling with the beak . . .

Swan-rape?

That's how it started. But what is she doing now? Is she protecting herself or guiding the way? Preventing him or helping him in?

Look at the next scene. She has wrenched herself round to face her attacker and the beak is thrust in her mouth like the bright tip of a penis. Thrusting or sucking — which is it? Her legs are forced apart and are wrapped around the feathered rapist. Her behind is high off the ground, her heels dig in. Bucking or struggling? Agony or ecstasy? It's hard to interpret the expression on her face, but it appears that what began as rape has turned into entirely another affair, one of lust picking up on lust, not an enforced impregnation but an unexpected congress of appetites, human, avian, divine. Helen will emerge from it to excite men to lechery, abduction, war. And more rape. Rape will breed rape. Brutal, ambivalent, murky lust. That is her genesis.

It's not all. Go back to the first scene again and look closer. As she bends double, either in pleasure or in pain, the belly is already bulging, sagging close to the grassy bank, almost touching it. She is already pregnant to Tyndareus, so the god's is an additional impregnation. Impossible in life, easy in myth, achievable in art.

They turned out to be quite a brood. Helen's half-sister was Clytemnestra, who murdered her husband, who'd murdered their daughter, and who was murdered in turn by their son, avenging his father. Two brothers, Castor and Pollux, were preordained to be famous rapists. They raped two sisters, died young, never made it to Troy. And they all came out of a clutch of eggs.

That's Penelope's version. An alien embrace, a swan's thrust, a shudder in the loins that engenders all the rest: the thousand ships, the toppled towers, burning, murder, rape. Achilles, Hector, Paris, Agamemnon dead. All dead. All dead for her. And that shudder was repeated over and over. Every time the Trojan women saw her, they passed her with that same shudder. Breast, back, belly and in between.

The eggs lay low among the Spartan hills on the lower slopes of snow-capped Taygetus, wooded with pear and juniper, wild with woodbine and irises, scented with myrtle, rosemary and thyme, danger nestling snug in an idyll. A shepherd stumbled on them and, because of their abnormal size, carried them carefully to the palace, where Helen was hatched.

Like a plot.

She emerged as white as the shell that had held her and needed no white-lead to beautify her skin. Already she stood out like a pearl in an oyster, ashen, immaculate, alabaster, blanched and wan as a goddess, offspring of a swan. Look at her – she walks right out of the web, vibrant and alive. The teeth are ivory, the tresses gold, the neck like the divine father's when he swanned on the Eurotas. Her hands are like snow, her cheeks like shrouds. She stands in a field of crimson poppies. Or is it a field of blood, streaming around her feet?

Equivocation, ambivalence, right from the start, before even the beginning. The most beautiful woman in the world. Yet even that is only a half truth, as she is only half woman. She comes to Paris gift-wrapped in ambiguity, shadows of doubt, a dubious prize. Even the identity of her mother is in question – Danaë perhaps, or even Nemesis, and not Leda at all. But for Penelope it's Leda, and the swan is the perfect parentage for Helen. She comes not out of a womb but, like a serpent, out of an egg.

Helen is damaged goods. And she will be further damaged long before Paris sets eyes on her, long before the competition for her hand. She will be damaged before she even grows up, she will be sexually impaired, and her spoiler will be the great hero Theseus, King of Athens, now however a wreck of his former self. He'd killed the Minotaur, punched it to death bare-fisted, crushed its skull. He'd sailed to Colchis with Jason and the Argonauts to bring back the golden fleece. He'd hunted the Calydonian Boar, defeated the Amazons, saved Athens.

But the years don't always confer wisdom. In his old age he turned cruel and desperate and hit it off with Pirithous, King of the Lapiths. They formed an evil partnership and swore to help each other to abduct the daughters of Zeus. Pirithous chose Persephone, and the two ravishers entered the cave at Taenarum and set off for the realm of the dead. Pirithous never made it back out of Hades: he remained stuck to the terrible seat near the spinning wheel on which his father, Ixion, was tortured. Theseus would have suffered the same fate, but Heracles begged for him and he was released, only to end his days wretchedly and in exile. He never became King of Athens again.

In this disreputable old age of his, Theseus went for Zeus's only daughter by a mortal. White Helen. He saw her while she was worshipping in the temple of Artemis in Sparta, abducted her and took her back to Athens, where he repeatedly raped her. But the Athenians revolted, sickened by his behaviour, and he carried her to the nearby castle of Aphidna, closely guarded and attended by his mother, Aethra. There he carried on raping her.

Rape ran in the family — Helen's. Conceived by rape, with rapist brothers, later to be raped by Paris — politically, if not enforced — this child-rape was part of the larger picture in which Theseus merely played his part. Penelope was always ready to excuse anybody who'd hurt Helen, always eager to illustrate the extenuating circumstances, assuming there were any. If they didn't exist, she made them up.

Observe. Theseus was a recent widower, sunk in his sorrow, poor old man, and Helen was prancing and dancing in the sanctuary, stark-naked on the riverbank where her mother had been raped years earlier. He was consumed by sudden lust, so struck with longing he knew that no matter what his past greatness, life was no longer worth living without her. He had to have her. And the ultimate intimacy was all that mattered.

His intimacy took an interesting form. He buggered her. And he did it from the purest of motives — to keep her a virgin. Observe the expression on her face as the king comes in carefully from behind. The eyes are tight shut, the mouth wide open. He seems to be giving her pleasure. But it's costing him. He's puffing and blowing and has to stop for breath before he recommences his sodomy. She waits for him to continue his assault. It's her first time. She almost looks sorry for the poor old stick.

Artemis could have stepped in and saved her, but the chaste huntress fails to appear, and Theseus goes unpunished. Penelope makes no attempt to illustrate his sexual history. In fact, he was far from unpractised in the art of raping virgins, after first killing their fathers. He once raped fifty in a day, out-raping Heracles. He abandoned Ariadne, slept with Hippolyta, attempted Persephone, assisting Pirithous, taking on Hades. But none of that appears in Penelope's web. And his abduction of Helen is a mere footnote to that history.

On the other hand, her brothers, the Dioscuri, who came to rescue her, are made to look like the villains of the piece. They liberated her from her prison in Aphidna. Practised raiders and rapists, they could have stormed the fortress, taken her, and left. Instead they ravaged Attica and took their revenge on Theseus by capturing his old mother, Aethra, raping and enslaving her and making her empty Helen's chamber pots.

'Our sister's piss is better than your blood,' they told her. 'Handle it with care.'

Some say they made her drink it.

They raped her in spite of her age. Or because of it. And they congratulated one another on their achievement.

Rape and counter-rape. As old as the hills. As for the territorial incursion, the violation of a religious temple, the assault on a princess, little is made of Theseus's crimes. In the web Helen herself appears at the heart of the conflict – dancing naked, flat on her back, bending over, bent double, legs in the air, from the tenderest age she's always there. Even in the womb she's there.

So Theseus raped her.

How old was she at the time? Twelve years old? Ten? Or even seven? The stories differ, according to the version of the legend you hear, or want to hear.

Or see.

Penelope's is multiple myth. Helen is seven. And ten. And twelve. And all ages in between. She is Theseus's prisoner and he abuses her whenever he feels like it. Over years. She grows up buggered. Literally.

The abuse is constant. But the seven-year-old Theseus saw in Sparta is still a virgin, if you accept anal intercourse as an emblem of the inviolate. Ravish the arse and venerate the vagina: it takes some imagining, but it worked for Theseus.

How long he might have kept her in this arguably immaculate condition remains an imponderable. When he hears that the brothers are finally coming to rescue her, he rapes her from the front. She is old enough now for her belly to swell, and she later gives birth to Iphigenia, who is bundled off at once to her aunt Clytemnestra to be sheltered from disgrace. By this time the brothers have razed Aphidna, raped and enslaved Aethra, and brought Helen to Sparta, to her father Tyndareus, who decides it's high time his daughter should be married.

SEVEN

A god-almighty roar went up as the first of the assault ships left Aulis. They must have heard the cheering in Anatolia. Hundreds followed. And the thousand ships supposedly launched that day, a catalogue, to be precise, of one thousand one hundred and eighty-six vessels under forty-four leaders, all of them named, present and correct in Penelope's web? Averaging fifty hands per ship, that would have given the Trojans a Greek fleet of sixty thousand men to meet and match. If they hadn't actually shat themselves, then with the many nations coming to their defence, not to mention the allies fighting on both sides, it would have engendered an epic conflict, as epic as anybody's imagination could have made it.

And Penelope was not short on imagination. She exaggerated the timescale as well as the numbers – her figures were fictitious and well off the map, a fabrication. All the same, she conveyed the spirit of the enterprise accurately enough. Troy was no backwater scrap. For the men who fought it, it was the motherfucker of all wars.

The biggest cheese in Greece, Agamemnon had ensured that anyone who was anyone had turned up at Aulis with ships and soldiers, and that nobody outnumbered his own contribution. Menelaus himself came nowhere near his brother, and my own twelve ships seemed modest, even for a small island like Ithaca. But other leaders had done the expedition proud. Philoctetes had come from the heights of Pelion and Ossa, where he was a famous archer. Diomedes' troops were there in strength from Argos and Tiryns. Both Ajaxes had arrived commanding large numbers – Big Ajax, big on brawn, short on brain, and Little Ajax, short on both, an utter thug with a murderer's mentality, and fast on his feet. We called him the Runner. Tlepolemus was another murdering thug who'd killed his great-uncle, as it happened. Bad to his friends, worse to his enemies – that was his motto, and he lived up to it. The decent and entirely amiable Idomeneus had come from Crete, and Achilles from Phthia with his Myrmidons. The latter were the crack troops of the Greek army, the elite, the death-squad. And every one of them was ready to die for their leader.

Not that Achilles wanted anybody to die for him. He made that message come across CFB, clear as a fucking bell.

'I've no desire to cross the wine-dark fucking sea to fill up Agamemnon's treasure chests,' he said.

Or, for that matter, to put Menelaus back where he belonged between his wife's wayward thighs. I had to agree with him there. We'd both done what we could to avoid active service but excuses had proved useless. Even if you'd lost an arm or a leg you were expected to turn up just to piss on a Trojan. Or fuck his woman.

'Your dick still works, doesn't it? Bring any weapon you like, but come to the party. Everybody's expected.'

Agamemnon. Your head would have to be missing before he'd even consider scratching you off the list. Even then, he'd just tell you to stick it back on again and do your bit.

As the old story goes, when they came to Ithaca to enlist me I tried to get out of it on medical grounds. There was obviously fuck-all wrong with me, so I argued a mental condition. And Penelope wove a good yarn out of it. The recruiting officers arrived to find an Odysseus who'd gone stark raving mad. I was busy trying to plough the beach – with an ox and a donkey yoked up together. And I was sowing the sands with salt.

'You see how he is,' shrugged Penelope. 'What can you do with him?'

They seemed convinced, and it looked as if I'd got away with it. Nobody needs a madman in an army, they said, at least not on their side. The leaders were mad enough for the whole force.

'Leave the poor bastard be, lads, and let's get going.'

But one of the officers, Palamedes, was on to me and one step ahead. He took my infant son Telemachus from his mother's arms and set him down right in the path of the plough. I swerved to avoid killing him, of course, and neatly revealed my sanity. Palamedes had called my bluff and I'd get the bastard back for that in Troy, when the time came.

As a matter of fact, Palamedes did play his part in my enlisting but it was a whole lot less dramatic than that. He just kept on his bastard rasping in my ear and yapping up my arse till I concluded it would be a lot less wearisome to go to war. But there's not much of a myth in that, is there? It just doesn't show the lengths I'd have gone to stay at home with the wife and son I loved so much. What would any soldier do in my place? That was Penelope's point. And, like all myths, it was true.

She told an even better one about Achilles. His goddess mother, the sea-nymph Thetis, had heard a prophecy that if her son went to Troy he'd be killed in action. Her husband Peleus heard this too, and although they'd split up by then, they acted together to try to thwart fate. The plan was to disguise Achilles as a girl and hide him among women. So he was sent to Skyros, where he was dressed up as one of the daughters of King Lykomedes and given the name of Pyrrha.

In fact, Achilles did go to Skyros and spent a lot of time with the women of the court. But he was a man all right, as one of the women, Deidameia, found out when he knocked her up. That's what happens in the real world. What also happened is that Calchas made another of his amen-wallah pronouncements – that the war would be lost unless Achilles joined up and brought his Myrmidons into the field. Otherwise Troy would never fall.

Agamemnon wasted no time. He sent me to Skyros see if Achilles really was holed up there.

'You're an old fox, Odysseus,' he said. 'If anybody can find him, you can.'

I said I'd do my best and asked if I could have a partner.

'Who'd you like? Take anyone you fancy.'

I said I'd take Diomedes.

So the pair of us turn up in Skyros, but in disguise ourselves, as merchants. We're laden with bales of beautiful fabrics and ready-made dresses, among which I'd concealed a number of necklaces, pendants, earrings and bracelets – and a weapon. A huge sword. The women went wild over the finery and the sudden finds, all except one, who went straight for the sword, and handled it with obvious interest, not to say skill. At that point, Diomedes organised a commotion just outside the door: a trumpet-call, a clash of arms, a fake attack. And all the girls screamed and ran about. All apart from Pyrrha, who swung the sword and stood ready to fight.

I put my hand on his shoulder and gave him a sweet smile and a kiss.

'Nice to meet you, Pyrrha. You can take your dress off now, sweetheart. It's time to hit the sea-road. To Troy.'

Anybody who didn't know Achilles would reject this one out of hand as a ridiculous story, even for a legend. How could a big sweaty squaddie wear a dress and expect to get away with it?

In fact, Achilles was an amazingly beautiful young man with a fantastic figure, slim and graceful. You couldn't work out where his strength came from, though it was easy to see how he was so fleet of foot: he was built like a gazelle. And with his long muddy-blond hair and green eyes he could easily pass for a woman – one you might even go to bed with if you didn't look too close. Or stroke the blond stubble.

In the real world, Achilles would probably have killed me for pulling a stunt like that. In the real world, we were both unwilling conscripts in Agamemnon's war. We waved to one another from our respective decks. There was only fifty feet of ocean between us as we hissed along east, a bright jabble on the sea. We were an army on the move, carrying light and heavy infantry, charioteers, archers, spearmen, slingers, sappers, standard-bearers, scouts, spies. We were a moving city too, a town dancing on the waves, an entire community of cooks, carpenters, cattlemen, priests and medics, shipwrights, wheelwrights, bakers, blacksmiths and slaves. The latriners were all slaves. So were the whores. Agamemnon had relented in his euphoria and a good supply of ship-shags had been carried ham-strung on board, spitting and snarling, sea-hags, cats on poles, official army-issue arse to relieve the crossing in the event of unforeseen delay — east from Aulis can be a mere seventy-two hours with a stiff wind at your stern, but three days can easily stretch to nine, or nineteen. They can stretch to weeks.

I dropped my arm. Achilles gave me a mock salute. I could read the green eyes easily. He was thinking the same as me. We were off to fight a war nobody wanted, not unless they were bored stiff with living, as he put it. It would extend no borders, yield no territories, further no causes — other than revenge and greed. Remove these and you were looking at a stupid and utterly pointless campaign.

'One led by a crude bully and a ridiculous cuckold — the world's biggest.'

Could Agamemnon's greed be excused? You could say that Menelaus couldn't help having a slut for a wife, but what about his brother? Certainly a leader is always under pressure. In Agamemnon's case, he had to sustain Mycenae and maintain his own standing as king of men to keep the Greek leaders and all his followers on side and smiling. It's a hard thing to make every bugger smile all at the same time. And the things that do it are hard to come by too: food, wool, wine, cattle, slaves, land, women, booty, bronze. They have to be worked for, fought for. The Trojans were famous for their horses, their wheatfields and fishing grounds, their yarn, their golden temples, their golden girls. Juicy pussy is not low on the list of reasons to go to war. You could argue that Agamemnon needed war; he didn't have to find a moral cause for it. But with a cause and an excuse, war becomes almost inevitable. The Trojan War was almost inevitable.

EIGHT

So we sped across the Aegean, Agamemnon bent on wealth, Menelaus on repossession.

You couldn't blame the poor bastard. He'd spent a fortune to net Helen, and Agamemnon had chipped in way above what could have been reasonably expected of a big sibling. Not because of brotherly love: he was determined to see Sparta in the family. It was also a matter of prestige. Helen may have been damaged goods, but she'd been buggered not by a nobody but by the man who'd buggered the Minotaur. The damage was a sacred wound, almost enhancing her. Add the looks and the land, and the raped babe and child bride was no ordinary catch. Unsullied or not, she was still a stunner and a prize.

They queued up to compete for her hand, a long line of hopefuls, invited by Tyndareus from all over Argos to strut their stuff. Fathers boasted they were sending their sons to Sparta – it was an honour just to be in the running, even with no hope of winning. Just being asked was something. Slim-ankled Helen was the ultimate trophy, and in quest of her, and with their heads held high, hordes of eager-beaver heroes descended, every one with an erection.

They didn't come unattended. The bigger the retinue, the better the impression, the greater the odds of winning. Servants, cattle, slaves. Huge herds were driven in by the thousand, sweeteners with horns and hooves, tits and testicles. There was a saying at the time that it was snowing in Sparta, snowing in summer. The countryside turned white with the flocks of sheep that crossed the hills and plains. Not to mention the silver and bronze and lapis lazuli. And the gold. Sparta glittered blue and gold and the air stank of big randy sweaty males.

It was quite a line-up. Diomedes was there, both Ajaxes, Teucer, who was Big Ajax's half-brother and always ran to him for protection in the field. Menestheus had come from Athens, Philoctetes from Pelion, and Agamemnon from Mycenae, though everybody knew he was there only to support Menelaus. To look at the little brother you wouldn't have said he stood a chance. He was a redhead who kept pigs, often slept with them, and occasionally fucked them. You could always tell a fuckpig by his smell, so the other contestants sniggered, holding their noses and fanning the air in his wake as if he'd farted. Such spite. But this affair wasn't about red hair or body odour or sexual preferences. It was about precious metal. And real estate.

All sorts of shit surfaced about that competition. Years later, the word went round that Achilles had turned up and had been rejected. He didn't. And he couldn't. Because at the time he wasn't even old enough to be getting hard-ons let alone contemplating marriage. His balls probably hadn't even dropped. Storytellers screw around with time. But I know who was there and who wasn't, because I was there myself. I was a contender.

Not a particularly hopeful wooer, I have to say, but a curious one nonetheless – intensely curious to see who'd come and what they were offering. I myself offered nothing to speak of, because I already knew who'd win and why. I also knew that if you were a loser you wouldn't leave Sparta with what you'd brought, and I wasn't about to waste a single decent drinking-cup on the girl whose chosen husband would scoop the lot and leave the rest of us with our arses swinging in the air.

I was also curious to see the Spartan stunner for myself. And my curiosity was more than satisfied, well above and beyond the slim ankles. Tyndareus was determined to leave nothing to the imagination. He paraded his daughter stark-naked in front of the assembled suitors, exhibiting her like a prize cow. What you see is what you get – tits and thighs, backside and belly. And the ankles. The only rule was no touching, no feeling. He was strict on that point. Otherwise you could assess exactly what you were buying, and comment openly on the purchase.

I'll pass over the comment – there was plenty of it and the tone takes little imagining. But I'll admit that when I first clapped eyes on the nude Helen I had to agree she was something special. Eyes, breasts, neck, belly, bum – just those ankles made your groin tingle as you imagined them linked about your loins. Yes, she was worth wrestling for, boxing for, running for, driving the horses for, hurling the javelin for. We had to do all that. This was a high-profile wooing. We were even expected to sing and debate.

'I've shown you her attributes,' said Tyndareus. 'Now you have to show her yours.'

Fair enough. I scored high in rhetoric, but the beauty didn't seem to take much interest in my debating skills. And in the end, her father told us, the choice would be hers and hers alone. 'You may be faster, higher, richer, stronger, but the winner will be the one Helen likes best.'

I didn't believe him.

Some of the others seemed uncertain in the presence of that nudity. Menelaus appeared oddly embarrassed, Agamemnon angry. I looked at the Ajaxes. Little Ajax had rape in his eyes. He was a lecherous bastard.

'And one last word,' said Tyndareus. 'There have been some wild words whirled about among you, some coarse and drunken talk, such as whoever wins her hand won't live to feel it cupping his balls, he'll lose them first, the losers will see to that. Oh yes, I've heard you all, threatening to slit each other's throats. And that's why I'm invoking an oath.'

An oath. Fuck. Now there was a passion-killer. Never a popular scenario, an oath, to swear to keep your word about something that probably didn't much appeal to you in the first place. And the Tyndareus oath consisted of several clauses. No falling out, no reclamation of gifts, winner takes all (just as I'd suspected), and, to avoid future bloodshed, all contestants were to respect Helen's decision and support the man of her choice in any situation of dissent or dissension whatsoever. Specifically, were Helen ever to be abducted or suffer an attempted abduction, or were harm of any sort to be offered to her or her husband, separately or together, each competitor was to come to their aid and with full force of arms. On our honour and in the presence of the gods. A binding promise and a sacred oath. Agreed?

Agreed. Tyndareus's sword flashed, a stallion fell gasping to the ground, and the sacrifice sealed the pact in hot steaming blood. We were all Helen's men now.

I didn't leave Sparta empty-handed. Tyndareus's brother, prince Ikarios, had come to view the suitors. He'd brought along his daughter Penelope, possibly hoping that one of the big losers would want her as a consolation prize. Not one of them did.

But I thought she had a good head on her shoulders, that Penelope, and what was beneath the shoulders wasn't all that bad either. Not that her father thought much of his small fry, prospective son-in-law, or of rocky Ithaca as a rough pillow for his daughter's fair head. But she took a fancy to me, and I liked the fact that, unlike Helen, she enjoyed hearing me talk. I was always a great talker. And she turned out to be the cunningest of weavers. I spun her stories out of my head and she spun them at the loom.

We were a good match. We left Sparta together, man and wife.

Menelaus left with Helen. Beauty had chosen the beast. The pig man. The losers ate sour grapes. There were plenty of pig jokes.

'Let's hope he finds the right cunt on his wedding night.'

'Or at least fucks the lady first.'

'Do you think he'll get it up?'

'Without bristles on her fanny? She'll be lucky!'

It didn't matter what was said, the jibes and curses. In the end the House of Atreus had prevailed. Agamemnon had seen to it. He'd opened his coffers and piled it on.

'Grease her crack well enough, and you'll slide in easy.'

Such brotherly advice. And subtle. You can see how he'd have gone far as a diplomat. A statesmen of incomparable eloquence. In the end, the good old-fashioned gold spoke the lingo it always does. She went for him. Or rather, her father did. And all the rest of us went home.

Agamemnon didn't go empty-handed either. To strengthen the alliance – Tiryns, Sparta, Mycenae – Tyndareus gave him his other daughter, Clytemnestra. Little did each glad bridegroom know that one brother had been given a murderess, the other a whore. The whore was to leave her husband. The murderess would kill hers.

Penelope and I stayed on briefly. I wanted to watch the nuptials.

They turned out to be fascinating. At first Menelaus found himself to be something of a footnote to the entire affair. Twelve fresh young virgins wound young hyacinths into their hair and took charge of Helen, removing her from her bridegroom, and spent the night dancing naked and massaging her and one another, their firm young flesh glistening with olive oil.

Meanwhile, the bridegroom got stuck in – not to his bride but to a big dinner. We all did. Lentil soup spiced with cumin and coriander, grilled beef, roast boar, duck and deer, fish and fruit stews, and wine charged with enough resin and rue to knock your head off.

I watched him be carried to bed heavily doped. The thirteen girls approached the chamber door, heard the snores and giggled. One of them had no virginity to lose. One by one, they took her in their arms, each girl miming what was in store for her when her husband finally did get stuck in. The little innocent knew more than all twelve put together.

They left her with twelve kisses on her lips, and she slipped in quietly beside her dozy snoring husband, a bag of farts. She slipped out again. He'd get his oats the next night. And, in due course, Paris would get his, the cuckold would be on his way to Troy to bring her back again, and we'd all be trailing in his wake, according to our oath.

'Like the fucking chumps we are!'

Big Ajax.

He was right. Helen had us all by the balls.

NINE

We suffered only one casualty en route to Troy. When we sacked Tenedos, the bowman Philoctetes got bitten by a snake as he was standing in a river, just about to pull off a peach of a shot. The bite didn't kill him, but it fucked up the draw and him too. The poison left the poor bastard so maimed he couldn't bring himself to go back home and show himself to his wife.

'To beg my bread at the town's end, sat on my arse all day, with a bowl between my heels. Fuck that.'

The leg smelled to heaven and looked certain to come off, whether by gangrene or surgery. Either would probably kill him. He insisted on continuing with us, but Agamemnon ordered me to maroon him on the nearest island. We left him on Lemnos with one of the whores who'd taken a fancy to him.

'He can still shoot his arrow,' she laughed, 'and if he can't, I'll fire it for him. Don't worry, I'll get him going again.'

We sailed on without our best archer.

As the fleet neared Troy, Nestor proposed sending a second embassy, prior to hostilities. I advocated more raiding instead, attacking the surrounding cities and settlements, stocking up on grain, beasts and women. Nestor was insistent.

'We should give diplomacy a chance,' he said.

'Raiding is diplomacy,' I told him. 'Don't hit the bastards straight away, hit their allies first, let them see what you're capable of doing to them, show them what you're made of, make them think about it, know what I mean? And give them the chance to avoid a fucking drubbing. All they have to do is surrender.'

'Do you think they'll surrender?' asked Agamemnon. His little piggy eyes narrowed to slits, lost in his stupid frown.

'Not a chance,' I said. 'Hector won't let them. He'll never kneel to us, never. But don't let them think we're in any fucking hurry here. Let them sweat. And if they get nervous enough they may even ask for an embassy. Give up the whore.'

Snorts from Agamemnon. 'Has your memory failed you, ambassador? Have you forgotten the first embassy? I was there, remember? That cunt Hector told us to go and fuck ourselves.'

'So he did.'

'So how do you reckon our chances next time?'

'About zero. But let's go through the due process of the thing, after the raids. Just imagine if the Trojan War should turn out to be the most bloodless campaign in history – and you still get Helen back. What a coup, eh? Can you really afford to pass up that opportunity? Would you want to pass it up?'

Of course he would want to pass it up. Peace was the last thing on that bastard's mind, the latrine bottom of the Agamemnon agenda. But he had to submit to the logic of the thing. And he was always up for a raid.

First we sacked Skyros, where Achilles had hidden himself among women – or, to be accurate, had hidden six inches of himself in one of them. Wick-dipping was the extent of his concealment on Skyros. No great disguise.

It was no girl who attacked Skyros either. Or Lemnos. Or Tenedos. We butchered their males, raped their women, slaughtered their cattle, stole their grain, drank their sweet red wine. The best girls weren't raped; they were taken as bed-slaves for the high command, spoils of war to be kept unspoiled until the proper selection was made.

Achilles always liked to do things fairly, and the men liked him for it. They called him Blondie, reflecting that fairness perhaps, as well as his dirty blond locks. They called Patroclus 'Blondie's bit'. The two were seldom apart.

It was Achilles and Patroclus who led the next raid. After Skyros, they sacked Thebe-under-Plakos, where Achilles captured the queen and killed the king, Eëtion, father of Andromache. He gave the royal corpse a respectful funeral and even burned the king's armour instead of stripping and keeping it. That was simply his way. Rank mattered to Achilles. He ransomed the rich and slaughtered the scum. Most kids were brained, others enslaved. He inspected the females personally, Patroclus always at his elbow, earmarking the blue-blooded beauties for the beds of the glory boys like himself, the heroes. There was a certain decency about Achilles that made him almost vulnerable.

Though vulnerability would not be what struck you about Achilles if you saw him coming at you in the field. After the killing and the prizes, he did his best to ensure that the high-class women ended up as – let's be honest about it – high-class whores, mistresses or even wives. Those without looks or status served as army issue, forced to shag the lowest of the low and deliver blowjobs to fuck knows what rotten monstrosities stood up for attention and tender loving care.

That particular raid yielded a whole lot of treasure. He shared it all out but kept the king's lyre for himself. He played it in the evenings, Patroclus his only audience, Achilles' fingers stroking the trembling strings, Patroclus's hand in Achilles' throbbing crotch.

He emerged from his tent one morning and ransomed the queen to Hector and Andromache.

But it was too late for her.

There she lies in the web, the queen, an arrow of Artemis coming in through one of the smoke-vents in the roof, making its way to her heart. Penelope has put a happy smile on the sad old face. A nice touch. The bereaved old queen has nothing left to live for. All that mattered to her is ash. Sometimes a heart attack can come as a good friend.

A day's walk from Thebe-under-Plakos is the city of Chryse. On the day Thebe was attacked, a visitor from Chryse got caught up in the raid. She'd been seeing a friend in the city and ended up as part of the spoils. Wrong place, wrong time. She was Chryseis, daughter of Chryses, the priest of Apollo in that city and an important man.

Important? Counts for fuck all in war. She was taken back to the camp and ended up in Agamemnon's bed. Achilles had fancied her and reckoned he had earned her, but he let Agamemnon have his way.

'He cuts that cunt too much slack,' complained Patroclus.

Like all wives, Patroclus was a nag. Achilles seemed to like it.

The pair of them then proceeded to sack Lyrnessus. This time, Patroclus insisted Achilles take what was due to him from the spoils, though it was mostly the usual story, the males butchered or sold, the women raped or penned, then sorted out as weavers, water-carriers, bed-warmers, whores and slaves to the soldiers who'd killed their husbands, brothers, sons and now fucked them whenever they felt inclined. They did much the same thing as before, but with a different man in a different place, speaking a few words in a different language. Words for water, food and fucking you can learn in half an hour.

That's what happened to Briseis. Achilles killed her three brothers, and their sister had to sleep with their killer. She was lucky. Achilles treated her well. Not everybody who met him in the field came off well – not unless you commanded a fat ransom, or if you were a girl with a nice belly and breasts like Aphrodite. Achilles' decency did not include any sentimentality. His Myrmidons were merciless.

But Agamemnon was simply rapacious. He always took the lion's share, even if he'd done bugger all to earn it. The men called him 'the jackal'. Seldom in at the kill, he was always quick and keen to clean up. He was no fucking lion, they said.

So bad blood was brewing. After the raids came the distribution of the loot and the pussy-booty, with the inevitable grumbling in the ranks. Except that on this occasion even the leaders were pissed off with Agamemnon. Nestor, sensing trouble ahead, called a meeting. Discontent can spill over into the combat zone and fuck things up. The meeting on Lyrnessus, Nestor said, was to clarify the rules.

They were rough and ready but clear enough and didn't need any sorting out. You'd have to be a complete moron not to understand and respect them. Or an arsehole. Agamemnon scored high on both counts, but Nestor patiently went over everything, determined to send a message to the top.

You kept what you'd taken from somebody you'd killed or raped. It didn't matter who that somebody was or what you'd taken – weapons or armour stripped from the corpse, a necklace torn from the neck of a wife become widow, a ring ripped from her finger – that was yours for keeps, whether you were Agamemnon or the lowly sod who filled in his private crap-hole. But the captive in question was not yours until or unless the allocations were approved. If you wanted a spear-wife or a bed-slave you had to wait in the queue. If they were aristocrats, the leaders wanted them for concubines or for ransom. You'd never even smell them. The same went for the pretty boys. Ugly slags or social shit became camp slappers. All being fair in love and fucking war. Clear?

CFB

'And let me remind you of the principle that still applies,' said Nestor, looking at Agamemnon. 'The best prize goes to the best fighter, the army's top soldier. And we all know who that is.'

An enormous roar for Achilles. Agamemnon had placed him second by awarding himself Chryseis.

'This is what has mainly caused the trouble,' Nestor went on. 'It was a flagrant breach of manners.'

Another huge roar, this time an angry one.

'Actually a breach of discipline,' Nestor added.

Agamemnon gave his fuck-you snort.

'Of *moral* discipline.' Nestor emphasised the adjective with his usual quiet clarity. 'Specifically,' he said, 'Chryseis should have gone to Achilles.'

We all looked at Achilles, wondering what he'd say. He said nothing. He was waiting for Agamemnon to drop himself in the shit. Which he duly did.

'Well, he got Briseis, didn't he? I didn't even ask for her.' He was red in the face.

Big round of laughter.

Idomeneus came in mockingly. 'He didn't even ask for her! That was odd, wasn't it? After all, Achilles killed her father and her brothers, all three of them, and the Chief Motherfucker didn't even put in a fucking claim for her even though he'd obviously earned her, by doing fuck all, as usual. Didn't even ask for her! What the fuck were you thinking, man?'

'Go and fuck yourself!'

Everybody turned back to Achilles. He smiled his cold smile of contempt but still said nothing. His look said it all. Agamemnon was a pathetic cheat and a greedy swindler and everybody knew it. Such was the high command. Nestor's attempt to clear the air had made it stink instead. An insult is a silver-plated turd, silence is pure gold. Achilles' silence was eloquent and spoke volumes. The disillusionment with the leadership had already set in. Nestor made one final effort.

'Achilles, are you happy?'

Patroclus shook his partner's elbow and made exasperated faces at him but Achilles ignored him.

'I'm happy with Briseis,' he said.

'And you, Agamemnon?'

An opportunity for an apology.

Agamemnon said he didn't give a fuck for Anatolian farm girls with their sunburned breasts and their big unsunned arses – they were cheaper than sheep. He cared about something called class.

Uproarious horselaughter. As if, the soldiers sniggered, refinement oozed out of Agamemnon's every pore.

'That's why we can hear you farting on the job every night!' Thersites lobbed his shitty witbit into the debate and made everybody laugh even louder.

'Shut the fuck up, you!'

But the men encouraged him, egging him on with shouts and applause. The rank and file especially liked him, because although he was well-born, you wouldn't think it to look at him. He was a smashed arsehole of a man, a deformed lump with a foul mouth that ran like an open sewer.

'Go on, Thersites, let him have it!'

Thersites grinned and spat. 'Come on, lads, you've got to admit it, you can't hide breeding. Look at me, for example. And our Big Chief

Motherfucker there is fucking full of it. That's why we're so short of pussy, don't you know? He suffocates the fleas and gasses the whores! That's not farting, that's fucking class you hear — and smell! Sleep with that bag of class and you're fishbait by the morning! It's a fucking death sentence! Class? Class my arse!'

Universal hilarity and prolonged applause. The whole army stood up and cheered. Thersites was as coarse as they come, but generally he knew when to strike. Nobody could improve on him. Agamemnon went purple.

'You scabrous rat, I'll fucking kill you!'

He knew he couldn't, but he didn't have the wit to realise that Thersites inadvertently had done him a huge favour. The meeting broke up in laughter and more jokes, much to Nestor's relief. Agamemnon's inequity was forgotten.

For the moment.

TEN

It's a great scene on the web. Helios is riding high in the sky, clothed in gold, his horses galloping unstoppably, drawing the flaming sun through the upper blue. He glances down at the blue sweep of the sea, remembering how Heracles had once looked up at him from his ship, crazed by the glare, and had tried to bring him down from the sky. Heracles was on his tenth labour at the time, charged with bringing back the cattle of Geryon from the island of Erythia, and when he passed the straits separating Europe from Asia, he set up two stone pillars at Gibraltar and Centa, the Pillars of Heracles. Helios had been so tickled by the audacious attempt to topple him that, instead of annihilating the man who had tried to oust him from the air, he gave him a golden goblet with a lion skin for a sail. Heracles sailed it to Erythia, Geryon got an arrow through each of his three throats, and the cattle were driven overland all the way back to Greece.

'Ah, the age of heroes,' sighed Helios. 'There are precious few of them left on earth these days.'

Then he looked back again, more closely this time, scanning the huge blue ploughlands of the ocean.

What did he see?

South of Samothrace, between Lemnos and Imbros and Tenedos, the sea is blackening with ships. The Greek fleet is approaching the straits. The sailors don't yet see what Helios can see – the plains of Troy, where fates will be decided, glory won, lives ended. The Trojans know we're coming, though, and already they're defending the beachhead, where the first casualties will occur. Men who never gave a thought to the gods will suddenly start praying to them, might even begin to believe in them. Nerves are strung out. Our mouths are dry. Our chests hurt.

'Keep a tight arse, lads!'

Agamemnon encouraging his troops.

'Don't let the blackheads sniff your shit! These raids were just a fucking warm-up! Get ready to win your laurels!'

Helios hears him, smiles and shrugs, looks ahead again, gripping the reins to bring the Greeks to Troy on schedule, dragging time blindly behind him, drinking the blue air.

As we neared the beachhead, the men kept looking at us, their leaders, sifting our faces, hoping to read in them somehow an assurance of survival, however fragile, however false. It's what leaders are for: they look after their men, they keep them safe. So if you were a leader, you looked at your men to reassure them, and you saw all those eyes, fixed on you, riveted, staring, the whites wide, depending on you. And you wanted to look away.

The men looked away from Menelaus. He was a shit leader. They could see it; anybody could see it, the certainty that he'd lead you straight to your fucking demise because he didn't give a shit about you or your family as long as he got his revenge and got back his good name. The good name he never even had.

And his wife. Got back his wife. Most of his followers thought he was a dumbo to go to war just because she'd spread her legs for a Trojan. So what? She was a receptacle for sperm anyway, wasn't she? A bed-warmer. Why did he have to make such a fuss about it? Why did he care so much? But he knew he'd be left without a face either if he didn't hit back. And then there was the treasure. She'd taken the dowry – and a lot more that had accumulated during their ten years together.

The fact is, he did care about her, and it wasn't just about status. Yes, he'd landed on his feet when she'd opted for him, and to find himself suddenly the Spartan king when Tyndareus died was a huge coup. He was cock-a-hoop at the time, up to his balls in clover. Even after she'd left him, they couldn't take that away from him. He'd always be King of Sparta.

And yet he was distraught. Some of his people thought he'd go mad. Some thought he'd lost it already. He looked at the sea, promiscuous among the pebbles of the beach, and saw her nude body laid out like water, sunning itself, spreading the practised thighs. She swarmed with ships. Night fell, the full moon slid out of the sea like one of her white breasts. Or the crescent hung high over his head like her ivory comb. She took it off and shook her hair, scattering stars. The bawdy sea-breezes stroked her belly, the shadow of the poplar stole slowly up the bed, between her legs. He saw it all, the whole cosmos having her. By all accounts he could neither eat nor sleep, pacing the moonlit columns, the darkened corridors, sitting with shadows, staring out to sea, saying her name at first light to the hungry palace dogs, to the stray stars of dawn, turning over and over in his mind the whole sordid affair, reliving it as if he were a fly on the wall of his own bedchamber, watching it happen, letting it fester.

As it festered now, right behind those eyes, and we neared the beaches, and the far-off lines of surf glinted like snow along the shore. So far still. And yet so near.

Had she ever really wanted him? Or did her father decide? Had she wanted his children? Why did she have only the one? And was Hermione even his? She had her mother's looks all right, the golden-haired Aphrodite looks, but there was nothing of her father in her — if he even was the father. Why? He was fertile. All the slave-girls had got big-bellied eventually. He'd even impregnated one of them before Helen. But his wife never conceived again. Fucked up by Theseus? Or was she just clever with her cunt — fuck the slut! — applying acacia and cedar juice and oil and vinegar, all held nicely in place with honey, whatever these bitches did to guard the gates of the womb, any old honeycap, anything to avoid a litter of little pigs.

Naturally he must have wondered, he must have fretted over the years, though he wasn't the type to insist on an intimate examination, a little squeamish for that, and still proud of his catch, poor bastard, and inclined to indulge her, till one day he indulged her a fuck too far — and suddenly we were all contributing to history.

Except Menelaus. Even though history was today, history was this moment, history was the sound of seagulls, the swoosh of oars, the sudden taste and tang of tangle. Everybody knew it except Menelaus. We all knew it, knew there was a rain of arrows waiting to fall on us, to hit us hard, ready to rub us right out of time in one split second and into the terrifying dark.

History gives you the shits. But Menelaus was stuck in the history of his own four walls, the stained sheets, the crumpled bed, and the blue air of morning pouring in to light up the place where the two had lain. Had they planned it all in his presence, under his nose, before he'd even left for Crete? Did they itch for one another even as they ate? Did they shag with their eyes? Did they pass notes?

Of course they fucking did. Look at the table where they all sat down to dinner, see the secret messages spilled out from the tipped drinking-cups, scribbled out in the spilled blood-red wine that he was too drunk to read, to decipher. They're there on the web, those messages, incontrovertible, and in Aphrodite's handwriting. *I want you. I want you too. I'm hard for you. I'm wet for you.* All arranged by the amorous goddess, artful at each elbow as the chuckling cuckold across the table sank into a dribbling torpor.

They longed for him to leave. The gooseberry fool. The pudding.

And when he did, and started snoring, who approached whose chamber door? Aphrodite had made Paris irresistible from the moment he turned up in Sparta, bright with barbaric charms, and now she was whispering in Helen's ear.

'He's younger, fitter, prettier – and he doesn't snore, and he doesn't stink of pigs. What are you waiting for? Go on, fuck the handsome bastard!'

And although the handsome bastard was only a glorified cattleman – the cunt! – the cattleman took her from the pigman, took her from reedy Eurotas, his Aphrodite bribe, looted the place, and left. Fucked off.

And now he's fucking her, fucking my fucking wife, the fucking whore!

Menelaus broke out into one of his sweats. The crew glanced askance at him again and averted their eyes. Their leader wasn't even there, the fucker. He wasn't with them. He'd emigrated inside himself. They'd have to look after themselves.

⌐⌐

Once clear of Sparta, Helen had relaxed. They could have made it to Troy in three days, but they felt confident enough to meander. She was sure Menelaus would follow her, but not in a skiff. He'd bring a fleet and that would take time. Plenty of time. Paris picked his way among pirates, traders, bought her expensive weaves, Sidonian women for her handmaids. The pair were high on henbane and laurel crushed and roasted, breathed in heavily and babbled out in dreams. They lay naked and entwined night and day, the slim Spartan ankles looped around his neck, the adulterous buttocks thrusting with the bucking ocean – in Menelaus's mind.

They reached the Hellespont. And Troy came into view, the coastline uninteresting, almost ugly, with its indifferent hills and long, indolent beaches. The city was still a few miles off, but already its coarse sounds and acrid scents were strong on the sea air. It was a city that didn't know her and didn't want to know her. She sensed it already. Her heart sank. The sounds increased as they rode inland, the smells intensified, she picked out the details, the shitty shanties of the lower town, the pungent aroma of horses, the stink of the stable, the rich reek of dung, mingling with iris and coriander, cumin, frankincense. The whole town was thigh-deep, elbow-deep in its sweaty work. People stopped and stared at the beauty in the cart trundling upwards, and the women spat three times across their breasts. Another new bitch for his bed.

But as she moved up through the town, she could see it was bustling and prosperous. The citadel Pergamos soared a hundred feet above the surrounding plain, protected by walls the height of ten men and equally thick. Impregnable. Menelaus would never storm a fortress like this, even with the help of his brain-deprived brother. She was safe. She breathed more easily. Up here near the citadel, in spite of her tilted head and jolting bones, she noticed how the air had improved, and she was met by people who needed to smell better and could afford to. She knew she was coming to a country where women were better treated than in Greece and had more standing, more respect. They could even make decisions for their husbands, rule in their absence. All this, at least, Paris had assured her of. From the very first night.

Even so. Even so, as she gazed back out across the sea she had crossed to get here, stared out across the swampy malarial plains, she felt a twinge. For Menelaus? No. For her daughter? No. But for lovely Lacedaemon, Sparta. She and Greece were strangers now, enemies even, enemies forever. What did Troy really have to offer her? What did she have to offer Troy?

'Doom!' howled Cassandra, the priestess, Priam's daughter. Her prophecies of doom were doomed to dismissal. From the walls of the citadel she saw her coming, saw it coming, the whole catastrophe. She tore her face and her hair flew out.

'Don't let her in! Keep her out! Send her home! Away with her!'

But the palace people were used to the lacerated face and the flying hair fluttering from the battlements. Cassandra was the most ravishing of Priam's daughters, but she was the skeleton at the feast. Nobody wants it, the skeleton, and she was fated never to be believed. She'd have done better to have kept quiet, and Troy could have made up its own mind. But she wailed her prophecy. And her words were thrown to the winds.

'To hell with her,' said the citadel-dwellers. 'Death and destruction are well worth the risk, and it's a slim risk to have such a creature as Helen in our city. Paris has done us proud. He's brought us a real prize, the beauty of the world. Here she stays. And we'll never give her up.'

Another bad decision.

Helen's wide eyes widened even more when she was escorted into the palace and swept into her scented bedchamber, vaulted and spacious. Her surprisingly kind father-in-law came to greet her. Well, he wasn't exactly her father-*in-law* – it was still illicit – but Priam was a nice old man and things suddenly felt good again.

Of course Priam knew he'd be living on borrowed time. He knew the long arm of Menelaus could reach easily across the Aegean and overshadow his city. He knew the Spartan king's rivals would see him as a weakened entity. He'd been humbled, gulled. And he would need to rescue his reputation. His brother would be number-crunching already, working out his share of the wealth, well beyond the dreams of even his ruthless avarice. Agamemnon's reputation went well before him.

There were few options. Sending her back was not one. Priam could have arranged for her to divorce Menelaus, allowing the elopement, or even the abduction, some semblance of legality. Then the brothers' justification for invasion would have been slender, and Helen would have earned herself a better reputation in Troy and in Greece. Women had been executed for a lot less than she'd done. But Priam indulged her. As men always did. Bad decisions all round. And the Greeks crossed the Aegean.

Priam may have clung to the possibility that in the end Menelaus simply wouldn't bother. Or that he wouldn't find the support. Crossing the sea for an adulteress is one thing: launching an entire navy to bring her back is another. Would wife-stealing justify the phenomenal effort, the expense, the terrible probable cost in lives?

But if Priam reckoned as much, he reckoned without Agamemnon's greed. Plunder was in the air. And the delectable scent of foreign women. Wherever there's war, there's always women. And these were dark women with the allure of the east in their eyes. Agamemnon's was an easy argument. If Paris had carried Helen to some barren crag, no one would have lifted a finger to bring her back home, or to help Menelaus save his face. Not one breast would have been beaten, not one tooth gnashed. Not a solitary sail hoisted. Not a single oar picked up. Even the oath might not have held. But Troy was a treasure trove and the gateway to other treasure troves. So with trembling bowels and beating hearts and itching fingers the Greeks found themselves on the riptide of history, speeding to the beachhead.

ELEVEN

We didn't have rams fitted to our ships, but we hit Troy at ramming speed. The speed was the thing – exciting, except that it was shit scary. Windy Troy – proverbial and accurate. You could feel the wind up your arse as well as in your ears. But the tide was roaring for us, a real ripper, bringing us through the surf and onto the beach at a terrific lick. Sand, grass, a plain cut by two rivers, a city and citadel high up in the air – all a blur.

But the enemy was no blur. We couldn't take our eyes off them; there were so many more of the bastards than we'd expected. The beach was packed with archers and spearmen, drawn up in long lines, ten, twelve, twenty deep, maybe even thirty at some points, we couldn't count, we were coming in so fast, and they were massed so tight and the formation ran back so far. It was a terrifying defence. And they were waiting specially for us, all eyes on us, all ready to release their missiles in one devastating fucking burst. That's when you saw that you could be seconds away from sudden death, you personally. And every other fucker under your command. What could you tell your men? What could you say to them?

Absolutely nothing. An amphibious assault. Every cunt knows what that means. You're not the arrow, you're the target, you're utterly vulnerable and you know it. It's not the best of perspectives. We tore across the surf, blackening the beach with our hulls, and still waiting, waiting for what we knew was coming, waiting for it to fall, the terrible iron rain.

Protesilaus didn't wait. The Trojan spearmen ran into the surf to meet us with their arms thrown back, poised for the first covering fire of their archers over their heads. But Protesilaus vaulted over the prow of his ship with a whoop and crashed into the swirling water, landing up to his waist. He was King of Thessaly and eager for action, with a dash of glory and a display of leadership. He had youth on his side. He was also still pissed from the night before. Stories had flown round the fleet that the first Greek whose feet hit Trojan soil would be the first killed. A Calchas prophecy for sure. Achilles had been expected to lead the charge with the Myrmidons. He was anything but a coward but he was also superstitious and held back. Protesilaus was untroubled by superstition. He'd placed a bet that his would be the first feet to hit the beach, the first man on Troy, and that he'd kick in the head of the first Trojan who got in his way.

He'd shouted from the prow. 'I piss on prophecy! Up Thessaly! Follow me, lads!'

And then he'd jumped.

He took the first hit from Hector, who led from the front. The next five spears came from all angles and struck him almost simultaneously, making him jerk like a puppet. The last spear went right through the throat and out the back of the neck. He went down like a porcupine, and the surf boiled white and red about him. He won his bet but never collected it. The undertow sucked him back among the ships. He was submerged and dead as a nit but you could follow the progress of the corpse by the bronze spears stuck like flags in his flesh, swinging above the sea's white thunder.

'Fucking arsehole!'

Agamemnon's epitaph for the King of Thessaly. He'd drawn the Trojan spearfire – their archers hadn't gone yet – and we were a leader down before we'd even got our feet wet.

'There goes the first glory boy!'

The Trojans gave a huge cheer. But they thought more of Protesilaus than Agamemnon did. First blood to them. And Thessaly without a king. Now their archers fired.

And the rain fell.

You could hear the order for it, Hector's order, bellowed out over the din, and then that cold moment of quiet when both sides suddenly stopped breathing and listened. Five thousand arrows left their bowstrings in the same split second and sang their song of death. The sky went black. It was like the longest, biggest strings of geese you'd ever seen crossing over, and the combined whistling sound was bloodcurdling. I'd never heard anything like it in any raid I'd ever been on. This was a beautifully disciplined assembly of men, and the message they were delivering was lethal.

Screams. So many screams all at once.

It's inevitable when you think about it. With that number of bowmen, even if just one in every twenty-five arrows finds a soft target, you have two hundred men suddenly screaming out, telling you that they're wounded and dying and in terrible pain, all in the exact same instant. It's a sound you don't want to hear. Not on your side, at least. It freezes you. Just for a second. But it's enough for the other side.

The spearmen cheered and hurled their javelins. Scores found their targets. Then the archers fired their second round, only seconds after the first. Our dead toppled from the ships, and as we beached and jumped out into the surf we found ourselves stumbling over floating corpses all the way to the shore. The sea around us seethed and ran red.

'Archers, fire!'

Hector again.

We were near to closing with them, but we were out of the shelter of the ships and their third volley halted us. We crouched behind our shields, waiting for the spears to stop.

If you were lucky, you heard the clang of bronze on bronze and you thanked the gods or your shield for your protection. If you weren't so lucky, your protection didn't work, or your god was somewhere else at the time, and the arrowhead pierced bronze and bone and reached softer places inside you, places you'd never even thought about till now, but you thought about them now, and it was the thought as much as the agony that made you add your own private scream to the others.

Or you made a mistake. You lifted your shield just a fraction to check the opposition, but you lifted it too early and before you'd even registered it you had one in the eye and out the back of the skull. You were lucky. You didn't even have time to take in the good news. No more hardship, no more fear, no more pain. For you, the war was over.

It was over for hundreds of us and the Trojans not a man down. Not a single trooper. When we did raise our shields, we saw them turning and running back up the beach. We stood there dumbfounded, thinking it was a manoeuvre, a ruse to suck us into some trap. But they just kept on running. And it got through to us. The bastards were retreating. They'd achieved exactly what they wanted. They'd shown us that they weren't going to be intimidated. We'd landed, but we'd lost heavily. They'd inflicted maximum damage at no cost to themselves. They'd also demonstrated the effectiveness of their archery. They'd be no pushover.

It was too much for Achilles, who had nothing but contempt for archers and archery. That was playing at war, he said. It was theatre but not the theatre of war. You weren't a real soldier if you weren't in the thick of battle, fighting with sword and spear at close quarters. Not swanning about with a fucking bow in your hand like some lyrist and keeping a safe distance.

'Gutless cunts!' he yelled after them. 'You might as well stand there with your finger up your arse!'

An arrow sang past his ear, and instead of getting his shield up he looked to see where it had come from. His eyes blazed. A big tall bastard called Cycnus had held his troops on the beach, covering the Trojan retreat. I knew him. He was one of their allies from Colonae on the west coast, opposite Tenedos. A crack archer, he was bringing men down at will, loosing off arrows like lightning. Even after he'd ordered his troops to join the retreat he stayed on to let off a few more. He made it look like target practice.

That's when I saw Achilles' famous speed for the first time. He simply ran at this bitch, taking arrows all over his shield. When Cycnus saw he'd no time for his last arrow, he turned and ran. But it was like a lion after a kid. Achilles was up to him in seconds. He grabbed him from behind by the helmet straps. Cycnus struggled and tried to turn round, but Achilles jammed his knee in the small of the man's back and just kept on twisting and wrenching at the straps until he'd throttled the bastard. Then he let go and Cycnus crashed on his back with his tongue out. Achilles picked up the bow, cracked it apart and flung it contemptuously into the water. Anybody else would have kept it. I would have. It was a stunner of a bow. But for Achilles a bow was no trophy. The riptide ran right up the beach and took Cycnus out to sea to join our dead.

Later, a story did the rounds that Cycnus was an old-time hero, invulnerable to ordinary weapons, and that this was why Achilles had to strangle him with his bare hands. Achilles smiled slightly when he heard that one. The plain truth was that he enjoyed the physicality of killing. Even weapons kept you at a distance from your enemy, he said. Nothing could beat the feel of a neck cracking in your hands, flesh and bone giving way, giving up, submitting to your strength.

There was another story, and Penelope used it to great poetic effect. Poseidon had taken pity on Cycnus and turned him into a snow-white swan, after his name. You can see him on the web, wafted gracefully away on the waves, a swan destined for a star. Or you can watch him as I did, on his back, wallowing in the water swollen-cheeked with his tongue stuck out purple and his dead bloodshot eyes bulging out of a blue bloated face.

Afterwards, somebody told Achilles about the swan story.

'Really?' he laughed. 'Well, that swan stuck his long neck out too far.'

And that was all he said.

His death hardly mattered. We'd been humped and we knew it. We'd landed but at a price. Already there were hundreds of wives and mothers who'd be paying that price. They didn't know it yet, but it would be for the rest of their lives, and till the day they died they'd be saying it was a price that was too high and that should never have been paid at all. Still, Achilles had downed us a king for a king. A grain of honour had been satisfied. And we'd taken the beachhead.

Our foot was in the door.

PART TWO
THE WAR IN TROY

TWELVE

🔲

Most men are driven mad in Aphrodite's bed. Even at the moment of bliss, when the sperm releases and the soul is sucked sweetly from the supine self, melting from every pore – even then men feel sadness and pain, and lose their reason.

Why? Why must Aphrodite lead to this?

It's what she was born for. It's how she was born. Go back to the beginnings, if you will, if you wish to find out, go with Penelope, go back and see.

Chaos, Tartarus, Gaia, Ouranos, the earth below, the starry skies above, sprung from her, partnerless, spontaneous. The stars long to shoot their spears, to penetrate the earth, and the earth yearns for it, the infiltration, the stab of satisfaction. The rain pierces her, and in time she conceives under the dew of the hymen – flowers, herbs, cattle, men. For now, however, she sleeps incestuously with her own son, producing hills and seas, monsters and Titans. Cronos.

Ouranos fears the monsters and keeps on copulating with his mother to trap the awful offspring within her womb. She lies flat and receptive. Her knees in the air are Assyria and Spain, her feet are in Africa – Libya, Egypt. The Great Sea is her huge opening. Ouranos pumps and plunges, and his mother's capacity for intercourse appears to be endless. But secretly Gaia wants to free her brood and, with the help of Cronos and a golden sickle, dismembers her son during the act of copulation, slicing off his erect penis and testicles.

The swinging balls and the stiff, foaming prick, spouting blood and semen at either end, are hurled into the ocean, and out of the bloody spume arises Aphrodite, beauty and bitterness born of the sea's vast vagina, salt silt in her pubic hair, still tasting of tangle the pert pudenda, the impudent tits . . .

There's her heredity, her parentage, displayed: her father the erect cock and balls of an incestuous shagger, her mother the bloodstained sea.

The sea clears. She stands for a moment in the bland campus, the crashing waves, squeezes the last drops of brine from her hair and steps ashore on Cyprus.

And so love is born, out of incest, treachery, violence, pain, sperm, gore. She walks naked through the world. Or provocatively, scantily clad, dragging behind her destiny, death, strife and sleep. Sweeping the earth, she leaves her scent on the air, filling men's nostrils with corruption and decay, like the sweet-sour musky stench left in the wake of whores.

War has its own stench. The first thing a soldier does when he occupies a piece of ground and knows that he'll be there for the next three days at least, and possibly even the next three years or more, is dig.

Digs the fucking crappers, as he says, and digs them with one nostril to the wind and half an eye to how long he reckons he'll be invited to stay on this alien scrap of earth.

'Hey, don't go so fucking deep! A month of turds and we're off.'

'Don't be so sure of that, bum-chum! Our crapper's a six-weeker. And we're digging four of the bastards. We're here for half a year, depend on it. And don't come crapping all over us when your thunderbox is shut!'

'Six months! You funny old cunt, how do you work that one out?'

How. How did they work it out, the latriners? Maybe it was something to do with the walls. The more you looked at them, the deeper you dug the crappers. They were fucking formidable. No one had seen walls like them. They said the gods had built them, principally Poseidon, whom the Trojans then neglected to pay for his labours, and so he became their sworn enemy.

That was just a story. But it said something to the men about the treacherous Trojans and about the scale of their fortifications. The Scaean Gate flashed its bronze at us, a glint of contempt. Even its hinges, the first scouts reported, were taller than Ajax. And the walls sent a clear message to all rams and catapults.

They had no toeholds either, and even if they had, you would have to be insane to attempt a climb with reliance on night and negligence and fuck-all else. The famous frown furrowed Agamemnon's stupid face as he stood and gaped at the town he'd boasted he was going to walk into at will and walk out of with all its treasures – without the loss of a single man. Vain crazy bastard. He'd remembered nothing from his embassy visit. Now you could see the idea starting to penetrate, even into that solid fastness of a skull. He swore at his latriners to dig deeper and put their backs into it. He was finally embracing the suck, getting a hold on it. GOFO – grasp of the fucking obvious. At last. And it took the walls of Troy to do it.

But walls at least stand still, unlike the Trojan allies – more than we could ever have imagined: soldiers from Abydos and Arisbe and Zelein, from Mysia and Phrygia and Paphlagonia and Maeonia, and from Caria and Lycia, plus the inevitable fucking Hittites. And still they kept on arriving. It was an awesome alliance, a multi-ethnic force. Priam had greased scores of royal palms with lapis lazuli and gold. And arses with whatever it took, brownjobs all round. He'd filled up their stables with prize horses, their cellars with fine wines, their beds with young girls. Beautiful horses and beautiful women speak the same language to leaders, no matter what the tongue. When the tongue's out, as they say, it's not what you say with it that counts. Agamemnon simply hadn't counted on Priam forming such a huge coalition. Together with the sheer strength of the city, it was a bummer beyond his worst nightmares, and Agamemnon wasn't good at hiding his feelings. When a big jaw sags, it's all too obvious. It was bad for the men's morale to see their Chief Mother Fucker standing there stroking that big stupid chin of his and asking himself the ultimate too-late question: what the fuck have I done?

Nestor came quickly to his rescue, addressing the depressed soldiery.

'All right lads, so we don't possess the required attacking ratio – anybody can see that and I'm not going to try to hide it from you. An attacking force in this situation should outnumber the enemy if possible and clearly they outnumber us. But equally their weaknesses are clear. They're archers and horsemen, none better, but they're not spearmen, not like us, that much was obvious on the beachhead, and our infantry is second to none. You all know that without my telling you. They won't stand up to the phalanx.

'So far so good. Plus, we're just as well disciplined and cohesive, highly cohesive. And we're a lot more mobile. Our flexibility is our strength. Yes, the landing was hell and we took a bad first hit, but what did you expect? Now we're in, and we'll hit back, in other parts of the country, in the deserted homelands, whose fighting men are all here, remember. We'll continue to make raids, as Odysseus has advised, just as soon as we're properly dug in. These people, they've never been attacked by a Greek fleet of any size, coming at them through the surf, right on their doorstep. We're the steeds of the sea. Our ships more than match their horses. And they can't bring their chariots to the beaches. We'll soon have the allies crumbling when they see the big-beaked birds coming at them, the terrible red stems, eh? It's what your fathers did before you, for centuries; it's in your blood, it's what you're for, bringing terror to the enemy straight out of the sea. Meanwhile, the main force stays here and starts to squeeze. Don't worry – they'll soon be begging us for an embassy.'

Nestor had the advantage of looking the exact opposite of Agamemnon. The sculpted cheekbone, eye of eagle and nose of hawk gave him a profile of piercing intelligence. It was actually an illusion, but it had the look of truth. And apart from his age, there was his figure: there wasn't a spare scrap of flesh on him. With his tanned old hide topped by a flowing white mane, he was composed of two colours, sand and surf. He seemed to have grown up out of the sea-bleached sandy strip of Pylos over which he ruled, and he also looked as if he'd be going back there after the war, the look of a veteran on whose watch you'd be safe. You could count on him. He exuded endurance, durability, victory, success. The applause wasn't ecstatic, but it was enough. Agamemnon was off the hook again. He cheered up.

THIRTEEN

She is Aphrodite incarnate. And she sits in Aphrodite's lap, between the divine breasts. She holds her own breasts in her curious hands, examining them, apples of love. The goddess touches Helen's cheek, lightly, turning her face to look at something . . .

Eros is entering the room at one of the doors. He is stark-naked, his huge penis glistening, erect. He is leading a lamb to the slaughter. You can see he is a shepherd by his staff. The lamb is Paris. Coming in at the other door is Desire, full-breasted, her nipples hard and enlarged. One hand is hidden between her legs. Aphrodite beckons to Paris and signals, indicating that the girl in her lap is all his. Eros and Desire will see to it. And the Graces. One by one, they too enter the room, followed by Ares and Hermes, Aphrodite's lovers, the god of war and the guide of the dead. The web is becoming crowded . . .

But there's room for more. Half hidden in one corner, stashed among shadows, Death stands and gloats, his grin hideous, his cloak embroidered with bones and skulls. And in the other corner the sea-nymph, Nemesis, looms.

Beauty and revenge, love and war, desire and death, they will all haunt Helen. And Paris. And all will marry in an instant. The intertwining is inescapable, unshunnable. Helen rises from the divine lap and stands naked before Paris, as she did when she rose from Menelaus's desecrated bed and her skin burned his eyes. All Troy will burn for her. She is primal fire, Prometheus stuff, born to set cities and men ablaze.

Menelaus lifts his eyes from the freshly dug latrines, each one pristine. He glares up at the citadel, glittering in the sun.

'I'll bring her down,' he hisses to himself, 'as low as excrement! I'll bring her down off that hill!'

The plains of Troy lie empty before him, yet already they are strewn with bones, and dogs are chewing them, and in the eye of Penelope the canines are all bitches, all bearing tits, all swollen-bellied, all feeding their lusts on fallen soldiers. Helen presides over this holocaust, this field of human losses. At one end of the field she is a big-bellied pregnant bitch with the face of the Spartan queen, the queen of carnage. At the other end she is herself, but with the face of a mad dog. Each of the faces, dog and diva, drips and salivates at the sight of the dead men, gnawed and lacerated by crunching canine teeth. She is far from indifferent to the mass extermination she has caused. On the contrary, she laps it up.

Menelaus laps up his revenge. 'I'll kill the bitch! I'll rip her to pieces!'

Anchises on Ida took Aphrodite on his bed, strewn with the skins of wild beasts, took her and didn't know who he was taking, the golden child of the bloody foam. She'd done herself up as a demure but nubile girl, *virgo intacta*, ripe for cock. Decked with gold, she'd made her way through the woods to his lowly lodging, where she heard the lyre thrill to his fingers. She wanted to feel those fingers rippling her nipples, thrumming her vertebrae, playing wantonly on her spine, his singing lips plucking out her tongue.

She walked in. He looked up. The fingers faltered on the strings, and stopped. The dress she had invented for the occasion was so flimsy she was scarcely wearing it at all. But when she dropped it he stopped breathing . . .

Afterwards, she revealed herself for who she was and Anchises was terrified. He knew that the terrible beauty of goddesses can kill. She was love and death and undecaying life. She was the rage of madness and she'd taken him in. He'd been inside her, the black goddess, laughter-loving, shy-eyed, penis-loving, sly-eyed Aphrodite, out of whose impregnated womb came Aeneas, out of whose desires came death, Helen, Paris, Troy. And from flaming Troy, Aeneas carried old Anchises on his back to a better life. A life free from the curse of Helen.

Running from the doomed city, running naked from her bed, clothed only with her breath, Helen leaned panting against Ilus's tomb, slid slowly down into the labour position, opened her legs wide, and gave birth. But not before Penelope opened up her belly for the web, exposing everything that was within, what was germinating there, waiting to be born. The Trojan women crowded round to assist at the birth. They looked, and their hands flew to their faces. The bitch was pregnant with all their beloved dead. Her belly held the bones of the city's fallen. She screamed and delivered them – not stillborn but past life, dead on arrival. The bones strewed the plains of Troy, pouring out through her vagina.

If they brushed shoulders with Helen by accident, they shrank away, passed her by with that shudder. It happened rarely. She avoided the lower town, dreading the ugly alleys, even with Paris's guards protecting her steps wherever she went. She stayed up on the hill, a prisoner of the citadel, bemoaning her lonely lot, her unbelonging, regretting lovely Lacedaemon . . . and sometimes even the husband who, if he couldn't match Paris in looks and graces, or in bed, was at least no coward, and he'd brought all of Greece to her doorstep. He looked up at the citadel every day. And the anger never left his eyes.

'I'll bring her down!' he raged. 'I can take her off her hill! I will. I'll take her down. And when I do, I'll fucking kill her!'

Nobody believed him.

And after a while nobody believed either that the Trojans were going to request a second embassy. They were ready to meet us beard to beard, the bastards, and beat us backwards to the sea.

But still Nestor wanted to talk. 'What will you tell all the widows and the old folks when we come back without their husbands and sons and they learn that we never even negotiated for them, never gave peace a chance?'

Agamemnon groaned. 'Same old fucking tune! Play another one. We gave it a chance – and fucking Hector waved his dick at us, didn't he? He didn't give a toss about peace.'

'Then you must show yourself to be the better leader. Men won't follow a leader who doesn't act like one. Of course there must be another embassy!'

'Embassy my arse!'

Agamemnon saw his dreams of riches draining down the old latrine.

'It's climbing down!' he wailed. 'It'll show loss of nerve. It'll make us look wet and weak.'

'The very thing they themselves won't wish to appear,' said Nestor, 'which will make them grateful to us that we took the first step. Then the negotiations can begin.'

'They won't fucking budge, I'm telling you.'

'Then at least you'll have given them one last chance. And ourselves too, by the way.'

The embassy went ahead.

I went with Menelaus, who insisted on coming, against all advice. He needed to get close to the scene. But Priam was sensitive enough to have us conducted to Antenor's house instead of to the palace, where Menelaus would have had to stand and ask for his wife back in the same building where she was being shagged by one of the king's sons. Too much of a humiliation.

An Assembly in Antenor's house, on the other hand, was no disgrace. I partly knew the man, a decent sort. His wife, Theano, was a priestess and Antenor himself was an elder statesman who happened to be well disposed to Greeks. As soon as we said we'd come to ask for the release of Helen without further bloodshed, Antenor stood up in the Assembly and supported us, not only in our request for Helen but in our demand that she be returned with all the treasures she and Paris had looted from the Spartan palace when they left.

'So fucking abruptly!'

That was Menelaus's subtle contribution to the diplomatic efforts. Antenor nodded sagely, as if Menelaus had just said something wise.

'The minute my fucking back was turned!'

Antenor nodded again and put up a pacifying hand, adding that in his opinion we should even be compensated for the insult and for the enormous cost of the expedition. This went down well with some of the greybeards, who'd no desire to see the skies of Troy go black and greasy with the smoke from their sons' funeral pyres.

It didn't go down well with Antimachus. The bastard stood up and glared at us and at the Assembly.

'So that's your idea of a solution, is it? These two swan in here and ask for this cunt's wife – who came here not in chains but of her own free will, let me remind you all. And we're supposed to say yes, certainly, have her back, and all the gold she brought as a dowry. And while we're at it, let's load them up with gold of our own to repay them for their trouble. Nobody asked the fuckers to come here, did they? We didn't invite them. And how do you think we're going to look to the world after that, eh? Like tossers, that's how!'

Antenor tried to interrupt, but Antimachus held the floor.

'I'll tell you exactly what will happen next. Every tin-pot king from here to everywhere will come and hump us. Troy, they'll say, yes, let's all head for Troy, the city which not only opens its gates to invaders and lets them through to take whatever they fancy, but tops them up with more, just for the inconvenience of getting here, and all the trouble they've gone to, having to come and fucking ask! It won't be horses and chariots and archery we'll be famous for in future – Trojans will be proverbial for poltroons! We'll be poorer than piss! And all those allies out there will melt away like snow in fucking summer. We'll be left defenceless. It'll be the end of us. Is that what you want? Are you all stark raving mad?'

Antimachus's speech caused an uproar. He'd swung the meeting quite the other way. Antenor tried to shout above the noise.

He was drowned out. Antimachus seized the moment. 'Listen, friends, to what I propose. Not only do we politely refuse to return the wife of this poor fucking cuckold here, I suggest we put an end to this impending war by putting an end to the cuckold himself. Let's kill the bastard right here and now!'

Sudden silence. I saw Menelaus reach for his sword. I laid my hand on his wrist.

'That's what he wants,' I whispered. 'Don't rise to it. Stay cool.'

We stood our ground, composed. The abrupt hush continued as the enormity of Antimachus's suggestion sank in. Antenor stood up and took the floor.

'This man has been bought by Paris, can't you see? It's perfectly plain he's been bribed to rig the Assembly. That's one thing. But to propose that we butcher an ambassador? It would be unbelievable were it not for the fact that it's Paris talking – that much is obvious.

'Doesn't matter who's fucking talking!'

Antimachus scented blood.

'It makes perfect sense. If she's got no husband to give her back to, there's no point in fighting for her, is there? The whole fucking logic of the war would be lost, don't you see? And we can even go one better while we're about it, by chopping down this cunt Odysseus too! They start off two leaders down, one of them the plaintiff, the cuckold himself, and the other a known troublemaker. They might as well show us their big white arses and go home. There'd be fuck all left for them to do!'

'And,' I said, speaking very quietly, 'the name of Troy would become a byword not only for cowardice and treachery but for total lack of respect for civilised behaviour between nations. Is that what you want – to be despised by the civilised world? Clearly Antenor is correct. This man has been bought over. Would an honest man make a suggestion so outrageous it flies in the face of all decency, let alone diplomacy?'

Much muttering in grey beards, much to Antenor's relief. He took the floor again.

'Of course it would be an outrage, as Odysseus has said. And one that Priam would never condone. In the circumstances, I propose we move the meeting to the palace right away and settle this matter in the open and at the top.'

So we were taken to the palace, where we were well wined and dined while Priam got ready to receive us.

I knew exactly what it would be: another bend-over-here-it-comes-again episode, one more pointless colloquy before the inevitable. Priam was polite and to the point, however, and I rather liked the old man.

We'd come for Helen, he said. But Helen hadn't asked us to come. In fact she particularly wanted to stay. She had no particular female or political need pressing her at this precise moment, no need to return to Sparta with her husband. Had she felt such a need, then naturally the situation would have been different. But she didn't. And so if we had no other pressing needs ourselves, we could take our leave from the palace. And from Troy.

'Is there nothing you can offer?' I asked. 'A face-saver of some sort? Anything at all?'

Priam smiled sadly and tried to look cheerful.

'Well now, how about a substitute for Helen? There's Polyxena, for example. Or Cassandra – though she's a bit wild. You can have the pick of my unmarried daughters. Together with a suitable dowry, of course. How would that suit you, Menelaus?'

'I only want my wife.'

Priam sighed and spread his arms.

'Yes, I thought so. I understand. But you see my problem. I'm an old man, old-fashioned in my ways. You won't blame me for that, I'm sure. When a little bird has flown to me for protection, I feel duty-bound to keep it under my wing. It's the least I can do. It's also a matter of honour. Do you understand?'

Menelaus stayed tight-lipped, looking at the ground. Priam turned to me.

'Understood, Odysseus?'

I bowed slightly. 'Absolutely understood. And I'm sure you equally understand our problem. Helen is still married to Menelaus. They didn't divorce. She belongs to Sparta, not to Troy. She's property. We simply can't leave without her, I'm sorry. If we can't take her by agreement then we must take her by force. And we will.'

'You are of course welcome to try.'

'So we're understood, then? It's war.'

'Regrettably.'

'Regrettably, yes. It is regrettable. But thank you for listening.'

'Of course. And I'm sorry, by the way, about Antimachus's little outburst. He'll be reprimanded, of course.'

'Thank you, my lord. I hope to be reprimanding him myself – in due course.'

A nice smile from the old king. And another sigh.

'Oh, and thank you for the splendid meal. I'd like to reciprocate sometime, on Ithaca, if we're still talking to one another. A humble island, Ithaca, but my own.'

'Every man values his own, though I don't think I'll be making it quite that far.'

A sadder smile. And a heavier sigh.

I returned the smile. 'No, I don't expect you will, but I hope you enjoy the rest of your old age.'

We left the city without the treasures and without Helen, but with our lives. Agamemnon was thrilled.

'That was a predictable waste of fucking time,' said Menelaus.

'Not entirely,' I said. 'Now I know one man in Troy I'll particularly enjoy wiping out.'

And so we got on our battle-rattle and went to war.

FOURTEEN

A woman, an apple, and a rape. Enough there to bring down a whole civilisation? Enough there to bring down gods from the skies, if that's the way you care to see it.

Or you can forget the woman and the apple and take a look instead at two proud powers and the conflict between them, the rivalry between a successful trading Troy and an insolent aspiring Greece that raped the sea with ships.

Fact or fable, there's one common factor: rape. You can have the rape and the rivalry without the apple, or you can have the rape and the gods without the rivalry. You can even have the rivalry, the gods, the woman, and the apple thrown in. But the one thing you can't avoid is rape.

Rape is the constant. If you're a seafarer or a warfarer or both, rape is inevitable. The sea is female. Thalassa. She's there to be raped by all and sundry. For the soldier, cities exist to be raped. It's what they're for. They're spread out for it, in the sun, always waiting, always expectant, in some cases maybe even half hopeful. Rape is better than routine, isn't it? The barbarism of war better than the boredom of peace. Not that I've ever heard that confirmed by any particular female in any city I've ever taken. Still, it's a theory, one to which I will return.

Sacker of Cities is a euphemism, by the way. I'd prefer Raper of Cities. It was my profession and it's closer to the mark.

How do you rape a city?

In much the same way as you rape a woman. You can take her by sudden storm, by slow siege or by stratagem. You knock down the city walls or you starve the motherfuckers out. If the first two fail, then you use deception. And deception usually takes one or both of two forms: somebody on the outside pissing in, or somebody on the inside pissing out: traitors, mercenaries, spies. A wooden horse is not an option. In the end, we had to employ the usual forms of deception. It wasn't the old heroic way, the Achilles way, but by that time his opinions were ash. As was he. Sometimes you have to take the only way that's left to you.

We did try siege tactics at Troy. You wouldn't believe how we tried. We tried for ages. But in the first year we found out, to our underdog cost, that strategically it was impossible to encircle the city and cut off access to the outside world. The Trojans' allies were everywhere. Eastward, they were invincible; they had too long an arm – it stretched all the way out among the sand-niggers and the Habeebs and even further, past the ragheads and the razor-faces to the ends of the earth. Out of our element. We abandoned the blockade and had a go at assaulting the walls.

Another clusterfuck. As a result of which we suffered heavy losses on the first effort and even worse ones on subsequent attempts that should never have been made. The outer walls' palisades and trenches were just too wide to traverse, and Agamemnon's skull just too thick to get it. Even a horse couldn't fucking jump them, and they were deep enough to trap you, allowing the blackheads ample opportunity to use you for target practice once you were in the pit. That's if the fall hadn't disabled you anyway. Or if you hadn't been impaled.

All this meant you couldn't bring siege-towers or rams up to the walls – only to the gates, where the Troads themselves needed access. And the gates were defended by monumental towers that rained down Hades, absolute fucking demolition: arrows, spears, tree-trunks, boulders, beams, jagged rocks, monolithic slabs, raw sewage. And if that didn't dampen your ardour, boiling hot pitch – annihilation in a fucking bucket. One time they even threw down a lion, and the bastard beast ripped the shit out of the nearest tower-tossers before it could be speared. The Scaean Gate was the gate of fucking hell. And that's exactly where every soldier went who tried to storm it. Troy could not be taken by force. We settled down to a long war of occupation.

Which suited us just about as sweetly as a snake up the arse when you've just sat down on the old desert lily. We were used to being on the go. We were movers and shakers, sea-strikers. We made love to our hulls, and the old wine-dark sea was our element. We had the barbarian spirit and were short on patience. The plains of Troy were not for us, even when they were windy and raged like the ocean. For much of the year, they were just soggy, and there's not much the soldier enjoys more than a war against mud and malaria. If we'd really spent as many years in the Troad as Penelope heroically totted up for us, subject to its sweltering summers and its freezing fucking winters, we'd have been decimated by disease and the blackheads would have picked us off like fish in a pool.

The reality? The reality on the ground was this. There never was a siege of Troy. It was a war of occupation and raids, and the number of pitched battles could be counted on your two hands, even allowing for loss and for however few fingers the frostbite had left you with.

The so-called war in Troy was a low-key affair, consisting mainly of attacks with incidental civilian casualties and of attacks on civilians directly and deliberately — killing them, robbing them, raping them, abducting them, doing burnjobs on their houses and making their women do blowjobs on the conquerors.

We did all this at our leisure. Within spitting distance of Troy there were nearly thirty towns which had no special protection. Not that they had anything special to offer. But they had plenty of everyday materials, including women. And Anatolian women were inexhaustibly sweet in every conceivable way — literally. In fucking and conceiving, those women easily outmatched ours.

And yes, added to that, there was a hinterland to die for, as many did: grain-fields, pastures, cattle, rivers and streams, sheep and goats, woods thick with deer, seas leaping with fish. Worth occupying? Fuck yes, worth a war. Only not forever, for fuck's sake. Not for years and years. No war's worth that.

Years. A year is a long time when you can expect to be dead at thirty. And when any woman would have dropped her sprogs at twelve and be grandmothering their rug rats in her twenties. You can't trifle with the years. There were ten of them on the web. And that was only the actual duration of Penelope's war. Add to that ten years' military preparation, and it's impressive and epic. It's also preposterous. Twenty years on, and Helen herself would have been long dead. And if not dead, then she'd have been a fucking gronk and not worth fighting for. Picture it: crow's feet, claw hands, toad skin, ash hair. A gronk. And if she'd bared her breasts to Menelaus after that stretch of time, god only knows what sagging ruins would have flopped out in his face to make him wonder why he'd bothered. He'd have told her to keep them. He'd have told the blackheads to keep her too, and turned his back on Troy. But he'd have been dead himself by then in any case. We all would. Penelope built the war large and long about us and undoubtedly did us proud. But if Troy had been true, it wouldn't have been our epic, it would have been our tomb.

War's a weird thing, though. There's a lot of talk about the realities of war, but there are times, especially in the hottest heart of a battle, when you're really under fire, that the unreality hits you, as if you weren't really there, somebody else is, some other fucker has climbed inside your skin and is slugging it out, using your carcass as an agency of attack and defence. You're there, but you're not there. And that's freakish. It's surreal. Sometimes Penelope gets it whole. Sometimes it's the actual unreality of the web that makes it so real.

There are certain things you'll never get from it. Two things in particular – there's no sound, and there's no smell. Nothing can recreate the hell that went on in your ears when the fighting got really feral – the screaming of orders barely understood, the shrieking of wounded and dying men, the whoops and war-cries, the high strident clash of arms that scarred the sky with splinters.

And the stench. Even the cunningest hand of a woman at the loom can't convey the whiff of war. You don't even need a battle for that. The camp stank. After you've been slaughtering beasts for a year in the same place, that place will never smell the same again, not if Poseidon himself hurls the whole ocean over it. The tide recedes and still the ground is greasy with death. You wash away the animal shit but the stink stays. It stays because it's not just the stink of faeces, it's the stink of fear, dumb beasts crapping themselves when they smell what's coming. Soldiers shit themselves too, but the excrement of men has a different smell. And off the field, away from the smell of death and terror, there's still the other stench, the inexorable eternal stench, wicked, mature, overripe, blowing over you all day from the open latrines.

'Hey, fill in those fucking crappers, will you? We're breathing in gas fucking gangrene over here!'

'No fucking point, lads, you'll have to stomach it – it's just the Big Motherfucker farting again!'

'Up his arse, Thersites!'

'Hooah, shitmate! Go on, give us your fucking number!'

Thersites again, speaking for the poor sodding squaddie who ate beans and barley, not cuts of roast, and who drank piss for wine. Probably his own. They were scum and they stayed scum, washing their blackened carcasses in the scurf of the sea, not in bronze baths. No handmaidenly caresses for them, no white aristocratic fingers lathering their balls and lingering on the job. These poor sods wouldn't have known what to do with a chair other than burn it and keep warm. They sat their arses on the cold ground and got piles, and in the brass monkeys weather, all through the freezing fucking nights, they slept beneath their shields, if they were lucky enough to have any, while we hunched up snug under our rugs and fleeces. Their horny feet were black and bare; if any of them wore sandals, they were made of dried shit and fell apart in the first rains. And for sex they wanked – if they were choosy. If they weren't so choosy, they went to Camp Syphilis and took their chances with the whores and gronks. They dug the shitters, shat them up, and filled them in. They hewed wood and drew water.

Then they went out into the field without armour and got shot to pieces. They had no life. A horse had a better life in the Greek army. And these were the poor bastards Thersites spoke for, the old contemptibles.

Sometimes they looked up at the sun. Helios, clothed in gold, rolled over them day after day, month by month, season after season. He had nothing to do but draw time behind him at his unvarying pace, serene in the pure blue, the emptiness, above and beyond the black agonies of camp and field.

'Lucky fucking cunt!'

'Who?'

'The fucking sun.'

Helios heard it and burst into golden laughter, rolled slowly on. He was in no hurry.

Down below, rats ran among us, attracting the flies and the fleas. Some seasons dysentery paid us a visit. Soldiers lay down with it and never got up again. They shat their way straight to Hades. When the wind blew towards the town, the citizens shut their shutters and burned fragrant firewood. They were all right, they were snug. We lay low and exposed in the bog and suffered it.

The dog days were hell too, and every cunt wanted to be cold and wet again. Shivering's better than itching, they said. At least you can keep warm in the field. You can always go out and fight. And that's about your only option. That's the useless thing about long wars, the shortage of options.

And then right on top of all that came just what we needed. Just what every army needs to cap the crap – the fucking plague.

FIFTEEN

The gods were to blame for it. Of course they were. In times of catastrophe on a vast scale, people always blame the gods. It gives them a reason to believe in them. On this occasion, though, they gave the old story a popular twist. Why were the gods pissed off? Aga-fucking-memnon. Rumour had it Apollo was angered by the Chief Motherfucker's scandalous handling of the Chryses–Chryseis affair.

Here's how it happened. After her abduction, Chryseis became Agamemnon's bed-slave, and after a while her father Chryses came to the camp to request her release. She was part of the spoils of war, and in normal circumstances he could have expected rightly to be told to sod off. Except that in this case the father just happened to be the priest of Apollo, and he arrived with all the paraphernalia of office, the sacred garland and golden staff, together with a whacking great ransom and in all reasonableness of spirit. Armed with all this, he begged Agamemnon to let his daughter go. In return, he said he'd put a special word in Apollo's ear for Troy to fall to the Greeks – this made him a Trojan traitor, useful to us – and for Agamemnon himself to get back safe to Argos. And soon.

Old Chryses' request generated spontaneous applause. Approved by all. Here was a priest who had the ear of Apollo and could turn the divine tide in our favour. By this time, we'd been dug in for fuck knows how long, but it had been long enough, a long and bloody war of occupation with nothing achieved except a heavy loss of life on both sides – not our sort of war. The men were sick of it. They wanted to go home. Chryses' offer gave them a chance. It was a dazzling ransom, and the old boy was, after all, a priest as well as a father and deserved respect.

He got fuck all from that motherfucking cunt masquerading as our leader. The moron told him to sod off and die, and if he ever came back he'd personally strangle him with his god's garland and stuff his holy staff up his arse.

That was just for starters. It went on from there.

'Don't let me catch you fucking skulking about the ships again, cringing for support, attempting to demoralise the men, undermining me, I know what you're at! You can just get back to your holy mumbo fucking jumbo, where you belong. A stupid stick and a few fucking ribbons won't help you. This is a war, not a religious debate!'

Enough? You'd think so. But no, not enough for Agamemnon.

'As for your daughter, you can forget her. You've seen the last of her, old man. The loom and my lust are her future, a slave to both, got it? She'll grow old in Argos, a long way from here. That's after she's done satisfying me in bed. And that'll take a while, believe me. By the time I'm done with her there's nothing she won't know. I'll educate the bitch. And she'll never see her native land again, not you, not any of her loved ones. Clear? It fucking better be, because that's it. So you can sling your hook, you old cunt, and you'll be dogmeat if you don't!'

Verbatim. Difficult to credit, and a disgraceful way to speak to a priest and a suppliant. But that's exactly what you expected from Agamemnon and it's what you got. Not a brain in his fucking head.

Look at him now, the poor old man.

After leaving the Greek camp, he slides silently away, terrified for his life at first, picturing his beloved daughter brutalised in the bed of a boor, washing his household's clothes, lugging water from the well, a slave to the shuttle and the loom to the end of her days, far from her native land. When he is clear of the camp, his tears and fears turn to fury and he wanders along the long thundering shore, where the sea's harsh breathing strikes his ears, the crash of breakers and the suck and drag of shingle on the long lonely unlovely beach. The sea, as always, seems to render all human speech irrelevant, but being a priest he lifts his wet face to the clouds and prays loud, long and hard for vengeance.

'Apollo, son of Leto of the lovely locks, I beg you now, let those Greeks pay for my tears. And for my daughter's shame let them indemnify with your arrows!'

Apollo hears him and speeds down from Olympus with anger in his heart and arrows on his back. In the Greek camp, some of the soldiers swear they can hear the deadly arrows clang and rattle in the god's quiver, and his coming is like the coming of the dark, because what he brings is exactly what Chryses has asked for, what men fear the most, and what his arrows represent: death by plague.

Apollo stands above the Greek camp and lets fly, loosing the lethal hail of poisoned darts. He starts with the mules and the dogs, then he turns on the men themselves. He cuts them to pieces, his arrows raking the ships. For nine days and nights the missiles rain down on the camp, and the stench of dead Greeks goes up to high heaven. A second camp rises up along the beaches, a camp of dead men on their pyres, the flames aspiring to the stars, and each night they blaze over the sea, turning it to liquid fire.

By the tenth day Achilles had had enough – we all had – and called a meeting of the generals. At the meeting, he asked Calchas to explain what was happening. As our resident seer, Calchas saw to the squaddies' spiritual needs. It's sometimes helpful for soldiers to know they've got gods on their side. It's certainly useful to generals to be assured of approval for their wars, approval on the highest level. Or to be advised instead that something has fucked up. In this instance, it didn't take a prophet to announce that. Calchas announced it all the same.

Under protection from Achilles, he let Agamemnon have it. He, Agamemnon, was the cause of the plague, he was the reason our army was dying. As our leader, he had shown himself to be incompetent and insensitive to say the least, and that was putting it mildly. He had grossly insulted the priest of Apollo, and the long and the short of it was that the lovely Chryseis would have to be given back to her father. Without question, without delay, and without ransom either. The chance for that had long passed. That was the deal.

Agamemnon erupted. 'You cunt! Always you, Calchas, always fucking you, you fucking godfreak! You've never had a good word for me, always undermining my authority. At Aulis it was Iphigenia who had to die, on your testimony. And my name is fucking mud now with my wife after that affair. You've never seen anything ahead but bad. Mostly you've seen fuck all – for a so-called seer!'

'It's got nothing to do with it,' said Calchas. 'As usual you're trying to twist the argument away from what's in front of us. In the first place you've refused a perfectly reasonable ransom –'

'I was well within my rights and I still am. I refused the ransom because I didn't want to give the girl up. I still don't. Why should I? She's mine. I fucking won her. And I intend to take her back home with me to Argos.'

'Where, as you say, you have a wife waiting for you.' Achilles was on his feet.

Agamemnon rounded on him, spitting fury. 'If you want to know, she's ten times better in bed than Clytemnestra!'

'Even as an unwilling partner?'

'All the better! I don't mind admitting it, a hundred fucking times better. And I'm not the first soldier to prefer a bed-slave to a wife, am I? But if that's the way the wind's blowing, so be it, the girl can go back to her father. It's agreed. Except for one thing. I won't give her up without compensation, I'm making that clear right here and now.'

Achilles spoke quietly, coldly. 'What compensation do you have in mind?'

'A replacement, perfectly simple. Chryseis is my property, my prize. You've all got your whores here and your hetairas back home. I see no shortage of sluts bouncing about your bivouacs each night, and you bastards all look sleepy-eyed in the mornings. Some of you can barely stand up, let alone fucking fight. Do you really imagine I'm going to stand and dangle my balls and let myself be robbed while you lot carry on having your fun? No fucking way. I'm telling you, I'm going to be reimbursed.'

'But you've already been offered a good ransom, brother.'

Menelaus was thick and slow as fog, though you could tell from the look on Achilles' face that he had some idea of what was coming. Agamemnon leered.

'Thank you, brother, but I've made it clear I don't want paid in precious metal. It's a girl for a girl. Get it?'

'We've no such fund,' said Achilles, 'to compensate incompetent leaders for their incompetence. So where exactly do you propose to find a replacement to satisfy your lust? The men have their prizes – all the girls have been allotted and shared out long since. You can't ask us to pool everything and start again.'

'No? Maybe you're right, maybe I can't ask it. I can fucking order it, though. As your leader. What do you think of that?'

Everybody looked at Achilles.

He kept his cool. 'Look, leader – if that's how you want to be addressed you'd better start by earning the right to it. It's perfectly simple: you have to give up the girl. I'm sure in spite of what Calchas has said we can renegotiate the ransom.'

Agamemnon waved a big arm.

'Still not getting it, are you? Let me spell it out for you then. I *am* giving up the girl. But I'm not accepting any ransom. I piss on the fucking ransom. I wouldn't take it in a tart's arse. I'll help myself to your prize first, or some other fucker's, but your bit Briseis will suit me nicely, now that I think about it. One way or the other I'll not be left empty-bedded.'

There was a stunned silence, broken by Achilles, who whipped out his sword and stood ready to swing at Agamemnon.

'You bastard! You barefaced fucking cheat! Always grabbing at the fucking truffles! And always grudging the next man what's his by rights! My prize was hard won. I won it as I always do – in the front line, where you're never fucking seen! You wouldn't know what the front line looked like. You couldn't even find your way to it. And my prize came from the men, by the way, out of the ranks – it was a tribute from the force. You can't take away what's been given by the army, not even as leader. How would you expect the troops to follow you after that? Mine won't, that's for sure. A common fucking grifter!'

'Now hold it there, Achilles –'

Nestor was trying to rise.

'No, I'm on my feet, Nestor, I'm having my say. I'm going to give it to the bastard straight. It's high time somebody did – long past it!'

He turned to face Agamemnon full on.

'Listen, bastard-face. I had no quarrel with Troy when I followed you out here. No Trojan ever called me Greek dog. No Trojan ever killed a friend of mine, or milked a cow, or as much as trod on a blade of grass. I came here for your sake, you ungrateful cunt, for your own ends and for your brother's, to bring back his Spartan whore and help you loot everything you can lay your thieving hands on, you common thief. And coward to boot, while we're about it. You've never had the balls to go out on a raid. You leave that to better men, and when the fighting's hardest you always fall back and let me take the brunt of it. Don't think the men don't see it for themselves – always the middle of the deployment for you, safety in numbers and well away from the front, though you're first at the trough every time after the heat's over, your snout's always quickest in at the snatch and grab, front of the fucking queue for you then, the pig who wants the lion's share. Well have it, pig-face. But I've not come all these miles to burn and murder other people just to be treated like shit to suit your avarice. Or to die in a conflict that for me has neither meaning nor fucking morality. So you can stuff your war. I'm fucking off. I'm withdrawing the Myrmidons. I'm taking my ships back to Phthia.'

'Take them!' Agamemnon waved him a mock salute. 'Deserter!'

Howls of protest from Achilles' followers, but Agamemnon had been stung.

'It's what you are, you and your fucking Myrmidons! Cock-suckers, every one of them, taking their turns with Patroclus! Well you can fuck off, all of you, yes, you can take your fucking ships. And I'm taking your woman. And you know why? Because I can, that's why, because I'm Chief Motherfucker, which means I have the power, it's as simple as that. I might have relented if you hadn't been so bastard arrogant just now. But you always think you're number one, don't you? Well then, this will fucking teach you, and any others like you –'

Agamemnon glared across the ranks.

'– to learn your fucking place. And to be loyal for once.'

'Loyal!'

Achilles should have left it at that but rose to the bait.

'Loyal to you? A fucking buffoon! A dog-eyed, doe-hearted drunkard! I've been everything including loyal in spite of your awesome fucking inadequacies. But now you've exposed yourself for what you really are – a mean little bully, like most cowards. And you'll regret it. You'll regret it on the day the Trojans' best man cuts your troops to pieces and you'll wish my Myrmidons were there to defend you, you spineless cunt! But on that day, we'll stand back and watch you die and we won't lift a fucking finger!'

Agamemnon spread his arms wide, acting out his offended innocence. 'You see? What did I tell you? Disloyalty, desertion – and a monstrous fucking pride. As if we needed him for a victory. And he's actually revelling in the prospect of our defeat. I could have him executed right now for treason!'

Shouts from all quarters. The Myrmidons drew their swords. Nestor had heard enough. This time he rose and put up his hand for silence. He spoke slowly and quietly as usual, shaping his phrases like a draughtsman in his dry, dispassionate voice.

'Agamemnon, I ask you, forget your rank for now, and step aside from the path you've adopted. Don't stoop to robbery, I beg you, because that is precisely what it would be. Achilles is quite correct, you can't take back what has been given by the army. The girl was gifted not to you but to Achilles. Do the decent thing and let him keep her. And you, Achilles, learn to sweeten your words when you address your leader. Agamemnon is also correct. Your tone is entirely arrogant and excessive, leaving aside the treason. A little modesty might become you better.'

Old Nestor of Pylos, sand and surf, polish and politics. He'd seen two generations fly up and vanish with the smoke, and he knew how to cool the tempers of the third generation, using the choicest phrases culled from his sweet-tongued oratory. His portrait graces the web. His tongue drips diplomatic honey. His cloak is embroidered with bees, emblems of his industry and craft, always attuned to the overview, the ultimate aim. On this occasion, however, even his famous rhetoric had no effect. Achilles was already walking out of the Assembly and Agamemnon was bawling after him.

'Insubordination! You all see it! Treason and desertion! Dead man walking! Come back, you bastard, and obey orders!'

Achilles paused in his exit for one last blast.

'Fuck your orders! And fuck you! And fuck all of you for letting him get away with it! Take the girl. I'll not stoop to fight you for her, though everybody knows I could flatten you with a single blow. I won't, because I don't fight with cowards, especially cowards who pull rank. But just try to take anything else that's mine, you filthy bastard, and I'll spill your fucking blood for you, it'll run hot off my blade, and my spear will blacken with your bowels for everybody to see and cheer. Just give me the excuse for it and you're out of action, friend, you're a fucking dead man!'

That was it. Achilles and Patroclus swept back to their tent, Achilles swearing he'd fight no more under Agamemnon. He didn't set sail as he'd threatened, but he might as well have done. He withdrew the Myrmidons and announced that the Trojans could come and set fire to the Greek fleet for all he cared; he'd only defend his own ships if he were attacked.

Agamemnon was a lot more worried than he made out. To save the army he agreed to launch a ship to take Chryseis home to her father. But he also carried out his threat to take Briseis from Achilles in exchange, and he sent his two heralds to bring her, by force if necessary.

It wasn't necessary, and the two men were embarrassed, but Achilles broke the ice for them.

'It's all right, I've nothing against you men, you're obeying orders, that's all. I know what you think of them — and of the turd who issued them. Do what you have to do. But you can bear witness for me: that man Agamemnon has lost the plot, he's stark raving mad and ought to be relieved of his command. If the men don't know it now they'll know it when they need me most. And by then it will be too late.'

He said his goodbye to Briseis. The poor bitch went unwillingly. Who'd want to leave Achilles to be teamed up with Agamemnon, who by every account made love with all the sophistication of an ox? But neither of them had a choice. The girl went with the heralds, and Achilles went to his tent, turned his back on Troy and broke down in the arms of his chum.

Achilles leaves his tent, strides from the camp, wanders along the desolate beach, scanning the barren waves, and weeps into the water. And his goddess mother comes to him in the form of a mist arising out of the infinite ocean, up from the depths of the endless heaving water, where she sits with Nereus, her father, the Old Man of the Sea. The cool mist comforts Achilles, enfolds him, and he tells his troubles to it, whispers his sorrows into its white encircling arms, which soon become the arms of Thetis. Her face and figure appear too, and her long golden locks, drenched and glistening with brine, and suddenly there is the complete form of his mother, kneeling beside her son, asking him the reason for his tears, though she knows already. And so Achilles explains everything to her and asks her to go to Zeus and beg for revenge against Agamemnon. He wants a revenge that will involve the whole army. He wants the Greeks to be driven back to their ships with huge loss of life.

'Hurl them back on their hulls,' he urges. 'Let them feel the barnacles on their backs. Drive them into the sea itself, and make the sea turn red. Then we'll see how they like their commander. Maybe this will teach them the lesson they need to learn. They could have spoken up for me. But they let a thief and swindler have his way.'

Tears stain the sea-nymph's cheeks and blur the divine eyes. But it is not only her son's grief that moves her – she has her own sorrow, knowing all too well what fate has in store for him and that he is doomed to an early death on the plains of Troy. But she strokes his head and leaves him with her kisses, assuring him she will do her utmost to move Zeus against the Greeks while her son stays by his ships and takes no part in the fighting.

On his face, he feels the last touch of his mother's fingers, arms and hands dematerialising as white mist. Half goddess, half vapour, she trails away from him, then turns again into Thetis of the Silver Feet and speeds upwards to snow-capped Olympus, to clasp the knees of Zeus.

I was given the job of taking Chryseis home and giving the priest back his daughter. In return, he'd pray to his god to take away the plague. We sailed there with a quick wind chasing us all the way, making love to our sail there and back, keeping it big-bellied, with the dark-blue waves hissing and singing round our prow.

The old boy was overjoyed. Blood and wine were spilled and we gorged ourselves on roast meat well washed down, and sang sweet songs to Apollo. As you do. The god must have been pleased. He gave us a good night's sleep and a breezy morning to blow away the thick heads and cobwebs and waft us back to Troy. Aurora's rosy fingers brushed the east, the sail filled and billowed, the archer Apollo himself appeared at the stern, sped us forward with a following wind, and the wave round the stem spat like a snake all through the dark choppy waters to the Greek camp, now free from plague.

High above the camp, on snow-clad Olympus, Zeus listens to Thetis's earnest entreaty, bows his sable brows. The ambrosial locks roll forward, all Olympus shakes, and, in spite of Apollo, fates are sealed. Achilles' wish is granted. He hears the soft whisper in his ear, his mother's voice, coming at him out of the breathing sea.

'He's fucked himself!'

Achilles came striding back along the shore, back to his ships and his waiting Myrmidons.

'The Chief Motherfucker has fucked up! He won't know what fucking hit him! And serve him right, the obnoxious arrogant bastard! Fire away, you blackheads, burn the fucker alive!'

At the camp, we found Achilles eating his heart out for his lost girl. In his solitude and bitter anger, he longed for the din of battle to tell him that the Greeks were in deep trouble. We were his friends and comrades, but he'd have been glad to see half of us butchered in an afternoon just to teach Agamemnon his lesson.

SIXTEEN

Something is speeding through the starry night. Down from Olympus it streaks like a meteor, silent and bright, following the pointing finger of almighty Zeus, headed for the Greek ships, for Agamemnon's tent. It's a false dream, an evil dream, the first part of Zeus's plan to grant Achilles' wish and his mother's petition by luring the Greeks into a battle with false expectations of success. The god has instructed it to enter Agamemnon's dreamless head and fill it with fantasies.

Wake up, it tells him, prepare the army for action. The Greek hour has come. Strike the Trojans now, and you'll take the city in a day.

And so the king lies and dreams of what is not to be . . .

What exactly put it into his head we never knew. Maybe the poor fool did dream something. Maybe there are such things as lethal dreams, sent by the gods. Maybe there are gods. Maybe evil exists. All I know is that on the morning after we got back from delivering Chryseis, Agamemnon gave the order.

'The whole army will immediately stand to its arms!'

It had come to him during the night, he said. Troy's time was up and the city was there for the taking. Call it a commander's instinct. Today's the day. We launch a full-scale attack on Troy and we sweep through its streets, leaving not a man alive. Then we go home.

He didn't advance a single military reason for the plan, but it didn't matter. He'd inspired the army, not so much with a vision of victory as with the hope of every individual soldier, the hope all soldiers feed on: to end the war, stay alive, and go home to wives, children, old folks, soft beds, sweet sleeps and all the happy tedium of peace.

But he didn't inspire Thersites.

'So you scented victory during the night, did you? Maybe you farted in your sleep. That's about all the victory you'll ever smell from that old arsehole, believe me, lads! He's fucking honking!'

Roars of laughter from the men. Fury from Agamemnon.

'Shut the fuck up, you gobshite! You're the only arsehole around here, with Achilles gone, and an obnoxious one at that, you bandy-legged buffoon!'

The bandy legs were the least of Thersites' defects. He was short and club-footed. His shoulders were so misshapen they almost met over his sunken chest and they were topped by a pointy egg-head, bald but for a few short sproutings of hair. His tongue was too big for the ugly gash of a practically toothless mouth, and whenever he opened it a stream of invective was released at somebody, invariably one of the top commanders, with Achilles and Agamemnon his preferred targets, along with myself. I always accepted his insults with a shrug and a grin because the comic routine provided the troops with a necessary therapy, so I reckoned. The filthy quips never failed to make them laugh. You only had to look at the ugly bugger and you started laughing, and when he played to the gallery the obscene entertainment always made a demoralised man feel better. Nobody else could have got away with the things he said, but Thersites was licensed to jest and not get killed for it.

'So the Chief Motherfucking Farter hasn't had enough yet, eh?'

To get an idea of Thersites' voice you had to imagine a turnip talking. The raw, saw-edged, strident whining started up and the men grinned and cocked their ears.

'What's biting your big fat arse now, mule breath? What more can you possibly want, you insatiable fucking thief? Treasures and trollops, you just can't get enough of either, can you? Your huts are so full of fucking spoils you've nowhere left to stuff them, have you? Except up that monstrous arse! Is there room to ram another fistful of gold up there – gold some poor Trojan sod has paid for ransom? It's ten to one the capture was made by one of the lads and you've scooped up the takings as usual, right up your jammy arse! Which is where he hides his fucking nuggets, boys – he shits them out and stuffs them back up there when no one's looking, after he's done his business. That's why he won't shit with the rest of us, that's why he hogs his own private crapper, so he can stash his ill-gotten fucking gains where neither man nor beast would care to look. Fuck me, he's so fucking mean he grudges even his turds an exit!'

The men were helpless by now, but Thersites was just getting into his stride. He knew that if Agamemnon laid a finger on him they'd revolt.

'Laugh away, lads, you may think I jest, but I'm telling you right here and now you're looking at the worst unprincipled swindler that ever led an army into the field. Led – that's a joke, by the way. And you poor bloody infantry, you'll sail for home right now if you've any sense.

What, line up behind that arsehole? You can't. Because he won't be in the front, will he, where he can fart on you, he'll be well behind you, in his fucking tent, rear support command, while you get shot to pieces. And he'll be well behind Briseis too, mounting the new piece of arse he filched from Achilles, showing her how the fucking bull does it! That's the only rear support you'll ever see from that pair – a non-useful bitch and a complete fucking turd-chaser!'

Agamemnon caught my eye with a desperate look and I knew what he meant. Moments ago, the men's blood had been up and they'd been ready to dig out blind. As usual, Thersites had swung them against their leader and against the war. He had to be stopped. There was only one thing for it. I grabbed the bastard and threw him to the ground in front of the whole army. Then I ripped off his clothes, exposing every inch of his deformities. Softer hearts would have been shocked, but the rank and file had no hearts to soften. They were hard bastards and they laughed, this time at Thersites' expense.

'What a fucking freak!'

'A cunt of a chimera!'

'A fucking abortion!'

'The ugliest fucker on earth!'

'And he'll look even uglier,' I said, 'after this.'

I laid about his back and shoulders with my staff, the ceremonious one with the big golden studs all the way down. They brought out a huge bloody great chain of weals on the bastard's back, like a line of hills, as big as the studs themselves, all the way along the spine. He screamed and doubled up, hiding his scraggy tackle with one hand and fisting away tears with the other, blinking like an imbecile. I raised the rod again and he yelled for mercy.

'All right,' I said, 'but one more fucking cheep out of you and I'll give you a proper thrashing that'll make you more than fucking blubber. You won't recover. And you'll be on shit patrol for the rest of the war, rank or no rank. That's if I don't take you out personally into the desert and throw you to the camel-shaggers! Leadership? Who are you to be lecturing us on leadership? Good god almighty, you're not even a man yourself by definition! What's that old horse-cock hanging between your legs? You couldn't even get it up a cunt-cap, could you? Look at you!'

Thersites clutched at his clothes and scuttled off, whimpering. I wasn't proud of hurting the poor bastard, but even by his standards he'd gone too far, and Agamemnon now owed me one. All the same some of the men grumbled and looked sullen. I wasn't sure I'd got off with spoiling their fun, but Nestor seized the moment to bring them back on side.

'What a waste of time this has been! Words are not weapons, lads; you know that well enough. And windbags are not far off being traitors – like that scatological idiot Odysseus has just rightly dealt with. Go home indeed! Why be in such a hurry to go home? Eager to see your women? Who wouldn't be? But haven't you forgotten something? There are Trojan women here that need seeing to first – and I mean seeing to! Hundreds of them up there within those walls, maybe even a couple of thousand young virgins who've never tasted a man. And wives who've had it often enough, but never from a Greek. And they'll be needing it all right when their husbands are delighting the dogs instead. Yes?'

An enormous yes.

'And you wouldn't deny their women that pleasure, would you? No?'

An enormous no.

'Look then, here's the plan. We can topple Troy's towers in an hour, raze the whole city in a day, just as Agamemnon says. I say no soldier goes home to his woman till he's taken a Trojan woman. Or two. And made them pay for everything this war has cost us. Cost you. Take ten women if you feel like it, there'll be plenty of pussy to go round. Spear your enemies first, lads, and then start spearing their wives and daughters, night after night, till you've spilt enough white stuff to float us back to Argos! What do you think, then? To war?'

To war.

🖾

Picture the base of a beetling cliff, thrashed by the crashing waves, flung at it by every gale that blows.

Picture the early bees falling thickly on the quick spring flowers when the sun with Taurus rides.

Picture a forest fire, a furious blinding glare, gathering speed, and raging faster than a massed chariot charge, when the war-horse nostrils flare and the muzzle's flecked with foam . . .

Picture the long-necked swans, flock upon flock, like the floods that foregather in Asian meadows by the streams of Cayster, flying upwards and settling and rising again until you can hear the entire plain ringing, clangorous with their cries.

Picture the swarms of flies that buzz about the April cowsheds when the buckets brim and spill with milk and the milkmaids' breasts are splashed and Taurus rides again.

Picture those scenes, charged with so much natural energy, innocent life, idyllic beauty, and you have some idea of how Penelope pictured the Greek army on the move. The thunderous applause that followed Nestor's speech was like the crashing of the sea at the base of that steep cliff. The swarms of bees poured out from the black ships, stitched in thickly, and with such loving patience and skill. As ever, there was a curious paradoxical aptness to Penelope's imagery. No soldier going into action has his mind on milk-pails or bees or the buds of spring, and yet these are the innocent things he's missing at that moment, the very scenes that might inspire him to survive, to animate the instinct to fight and win and so return to the innocent idyll, the old life, far away from war and the frenzied cries of the commanders.

'Move out, you motherfuckers, move out!'
   'Red on red, lads — and watch your arses!'
   'Up to the front, dogfucks, up to the fucking front!'
   'Shift and scuttle, you turtlefuckers, let's hear your balls clang!'

The illustrious Agamemnon had assembled an amazing army, the wonder of the web. The Boeotians alone were a sight to behold, culled from the uplands of Eteonus to the spreading meadows of Mycalessus. They came from dove-cotted Thisbe, thick with wings and murmuring moans, and from Coronea, from grassy Haliartus and the impregnable city of Lower Thebes. There were soldiers from holy Onshestus, from the deeps of Poseidon's sacred wood, from Arne where the black grapes hang thick, and from furthest Anthedon, bordering the back of beyond. They sailed in fifty ships and there were a hundred and twenty young Boeotian men in every ship.

That was just one of a myriad of companies. Others came from Aspledon and Phocis, from Salamis and Ormenion and Pherae and Argissa and scores of other places. Penelope showed all the homelands, the whole majestic fleet of ships thrusting from their scattered harbours and converging on Troy, and the soldiers pouring forth.

There's Elphenor, leading the fiery Abantes, so fleet of foot, with their cropped forelocks and their long flowing manes walloping the air behind them. They're lunging as they march, practising on the move with their ashen spears, and it's obvious they're lethal spearmen, they're so eager for the real thing.

Nestor may have been old, but he commanded ninety ships. He'd brought them from sandy Pylos, from the lovely land of Arene, from Helos and from Dorion. Achilles commanded the troops from Pelasgian Argos, Alus and Alope, from Trachis, his own Phthia, and from Hellas, land of lovely ladies and spellbound men. These were the Hellenes, the Achaeans and his beloved Myrmidons. But now they lay in disarray and the ships were waste and idle, not even drawn up in battle order. Their glorious commander hung about the hulls like a ghost, still eating his heart out for Briseis, for whom he'd sacked Lyrnessus and stormed the walls of Thebe. Or so he had made himself believe. It was grief for the lovely girl and anger against Agamemnon that kept fifty shiploads of sailors and a crack regiment stranded on the beach while the rest went into the field.

Gouneus brought twenty-two ships from Cyphus, leading out the Enienes and the intrepid winter-bitten Peraebians, battle-hardened men who made their homes round wintry Dodona and farmed the fields by the delightful streams of Titeresius, pouring into the Peneus.

There was a powerful-looking pair leading the men from Minyaean Orchomenus: Ascalaphus and Ialmenus. As a girl, their lovely mother had ascended secretly to an upper room in the palace of Actor and had lain naked there for the war-god himself. Ares laid by his lance and made love to her instead, tamed by her charms. There she lies in the web – naked, young and lovely, years before Helen and Troy. But her sons inherited their father's bellicosity, and their thirty ships were foremost in fight.

Medon led the men who'd come with Philoctetes from Methone, Thaumacie, Meliboea and rocky Olizon. But the great archer himself still lay in agony on lovely Lemnos, the snake that had bitten him lying at his side, woven coiled and glittering into the web.

And Podarces took over from his brother Protesilaus, whose blood had been first to stain the beach and whose men had followed him from Phylace and flowery Pyrasus, from sheep-strewn Iton and sea-swept Autron and Pteleus, deep green and lush with grass. Back in Phylace, his young wife Laodamia lies with lacerated face in a half-built house, ash on her hair and emptiness between her thighs where her husband should have lain, King of Thessaly, his coral bones now strewn deep in the whelming sea.

Every hero in Greece was there that day, the greater of the two Ajaxes more prominent in Achilles' absence, and the finest horses therefore the matching mares of Admetus, with Achilles' peerless steeds withdrawn. Their great master lay with his bosom friend Patroclus, heartsore by his ships, seething and grieving, and the splendid steeds stood idle beside their empty chariots, champing the clover and the marsh parsley, their long ears twitching as they heard the familiar sounds of thousands of men and horses on the move, going gladly into battle, every one of them ready to die.

Sighting this majestic spectacle from high up on snowy Olympus, Zeus turns to wind-footed Iris and orders her to alert the Trojans and prepare them for action. And so the Greek army, its armour ablaze, its heart on fire, will march straight into Zeus's trap. They will engage bravely, fight well and inflict heavy casualties, but ultimately they will suffer colossal losses.

Iris speeds like an arrow down to Troy, disguising herself as Polites, one of Priam's sons and a lookout atop old Aesyetes' tomb. Polites was still there, spotting the danger, when Iris ran before him to the palace, where Priam was conferring with Hector and the other generals.

'The time for talk is over,' gasps the goddess. 'Arm yourselves and get out there! The Greeks are on the move. The entire army has left the ships! It's a full-scale attack!'

The response was immediate. Hector led, followed by Aeneas, Pandarus and the two sons of Merops, Adrestus and Amphius, whose seer father had divined their deaths in battle and had pleaded with them to stay at home. But they went to war, laughing at their father and ruffling his white hair, and so died the deaths he had predicted for them.

They were followed in turn by Asius, Hippothous and Pylaeus, and by Acamas and Peiros, leading the Thracians, hot from the Hellespont. Pyraechmes led the Paeonians, bearing huge curving bows, Pylaemenes led the Paphlagonians, and Odius and Epistrophus brought the Alizones from faraway Alybe. Commanding the Mysians were Chromis and Ennomus, an augur who failed to foresee that soon the birds would be picking his white bones clean, after the river fishes had tasted him first.

After that came the Phrygians, eager for action, then the Maeonians. The barbarous-tongued Carians followed their captains Nastes and

Amphimachus, the charmer, all decked in gold and dressed to kill. He was another of the unfortunates who would encounter Achilles in the riverbed on the day the Scamander ran blood, and Achilles would help himself to the dead man's gold, dead men having no need of decoration. And lastly came Glaucus and Sarpedon, who would not see the end of the war, leading the men from Lycia and the swirling streams of Xanthus.

And so the two armies approached each other with destinies already woven and the outcome known only to the gods. If you could have stood and looked at this amazing array of men, all glittering and greedy for action, you might even have believed, in some forbidden part of your heart, that war was nobler than peace, and the field sweeter than home.

SEVENTEEN

With Hector leading them, the Trojans go out with loud shouts, like the cries of cranes flying south over the seas before the cold days come. And there the cranes go, taking off, winging away from the wintry glooms, their wing tips almost touching the Trojan helmets, brushing the purple plumes as they leave them to their war and take their clamour higher into the skies, over the crash of waves.

The Greeks, by contrast, march in silence, shoulder to shoulder, quietly breathing out their courage. Nestor's finger touches his old lips. No need to sing and shout – better the dignitas of the slow silent march. There's a sinister chill about it that can paralyse an enemy with terror. Everybody shouts and swears when they're afraid.

Stamping across the plains of Troy, the Greek feet soon kick up a dust cloud as thick as the mist the south wind sends swirling across the summits of the hills, making the shepherd grumble and the robber rub his thieving hands, both watchful for their trade, far from the trade of war.

And so it continues – the heart-stopping spectacle of two great armies about to clash. And the world around them goes about its business, the clouds unconcerned, the birds with worries of their own, intent on life.

But before we could engage, something happened. A soldier stepped out from the Trojan ranks and signalled to both sides to halt. He put out an open challenge: he'd take on anybody in the Greek army who was willing to meet him in single combat, bumboy or slag, even a man if we had any. He'd face up to him right here and now and spill his brains for him, and the rest of us could just fuck off home, if we had any sense, and learn not to mess with Troy in future.

'Who the fuck's that?' asked Agamemnon. 'Who's the fucking time-waster?'

I knew him by the panther skin on his back.

'It's Paris,' I said. 'He thinks he's Heracles today.'

But Paris got the shock of his little life when none other than

Menelaus came charging out of the ranks in his chariot, screeched to a stop in a cloud of dust, jumped down and ran out into no-man's-land, baying for his blood. He couldn't believe his luck.

'I'll kill the cunt! I'll cut him to fucking pieces! He's dogmeat!'

Paris had intended to impress, as usual, but lost his nerve when he saw who was taking up the challenge. He slunk back into the ranks as quickly as he'd left them and Hector gave it to him.

'You fucking wall-boy! Stick you on a mural with the painted soldiers – that's all the fighting you'll ever do, you pretty fuck!'

That was just the start of the tirade. Hector let both armies know what he thought of his little prick of a brother, the curse of Priam's house and the shame of the city. He'd sneaked off with the wife of a better man when he was away from home and now he was shitting himself at the thought of having to confront him. We all applauded and asked for more. Hector obliged.

'You and your lyre and your good looks! They'll be fuck-all use to you when you're stretched out face down in the dust with a Greek spear up your arse! By rights you should be in your tomb already, stoned to fucking death for what you've done!'

Hector had changed his tune a bit since the first embassy and Paris winced under the withering criticism. But he took the shit and dug deep.

'All right, I admit it, I bottled out. But I'm calling you out again, Menelaus, and this time there'll be no retreat, you've got my word on it.'

Menelaus shouted back. 'The word of a wife-stealer and a funk! A backstairs fucking skulker!'

But it was too good an opportunity to miss, and so it was agreed that the two top leaders, Priam and Agamemnon, should meet to discuss the necessary arrangements, the truce and the duel.

'I want that old cunt out here,' said Agamemnon.

'And he'll come,' I said, 'but for fuck's sake try to keep the tone diplomatic.'

'I don't want any of his arrogant bastard sons present. They're unscrupulous fuckers and they'd wreck a treaty for the hell of it, just as soon as they'd fart in your face.'

'Bravely spoken,' I said, 'but let's put it this way instead, shall we? We'll say that young men are exceedingly impetuous and unpredictable, and that if an oath has to be taken, it should be taken by older and wiser heads.'

'Whatever,' said Agamemnon. 'Just get the old cunt out here.'

So we slit the lambs' throats and dropped them gasping to the ground, where the dark red life ran from them. We poured out the wine, mixing it with the blood, and agreed on a set of rules for the duel and a form of words for the oath.

It was simple enough: Paris and Menelaus to meet in single combat with no backup on either side, the winner to keep Helen and all her wealth, and all the rest to make a treaty of peace between them. If Menelaus lost, the Greeks would leave. If Paris lost, the Trojans would pay us a substantial recompense and hand Helen over to us.

Antenor spoke the final words that sealed the oath.

'Whoever breaks this treaty, may his brains stain the ground, just like this blood and this wine. And may foreign invaders hurl their infants from the highest cliffs and topmost towers. May they ravish their wives and rape their daughters and take them home to their own beds, wives and girls to the loom and the well, old and sick to the sword and the flame. And all males to have their throats cut.'

'Too fucking right,' said Agamemnon.

Priam bowed gravely. After which Antenor led him back to the city. The poor old bugger couldn't bring himself to stay and watch the fight. He said the stress would be too much for him to bear. He knew that if his son fell down Menelaus would start by cutting his balls off. By the time he'd finished with him Priam might get back a body for burial but it wouldn't be a joined-up one.

Under truce the two armies sat down in opposite rows and watched as the combatants, armed to the teeth, stepped out into no-man's-land. They both looked impressive in silver and bronze and tin, protected by helmet and cuirass and shield and greaves and carrying sword and spears. But everybody knew that underneath all that flash was an arsehole and a prick. Which was which?

It didn't matter. All that mattered to each soldier was that it was somebody else's life and not his own now on the line. Everybody was happy and relaxed. Big Ajax was grinning all over his ugly mug.

'I love a good fight! I wonder who'll win? Mind you, I could wipe out the two of them together with one arm tied behind my back and only one leg to stand on.'

Nobody gave a fuck about that. We didn't care how well they fought. We didn't even care who won, just as long as it brought the war to an end. And if they killed each other, the two sides would give the bastards a combined round of applause and we'd all go home.

Both men's helmets had huge horsehair crests and the plumes nodded ominously as they advanced. They stopped. Everybody shut up.

A moment of sudden and complete silence. There were only twenty paces left between them . . .

5.

Penelope shifts the action far from the plain to an upper chamber in the palace complex, high up inside the city walls, an inner sanctuary removed from the world of dust and blood and men. Here at her loom sits Helen, the prize fought for by two civilisations, two armies and their many allies, and now by two men, who prize the world's desire more than their own lives, or the lives of thousands of soldiers. In this quiet chamber she sits spinning her story, the story of her life and of the war – a web within a web. And this domestic scene in Troy stands at an almost surreal remove from everything that exists on the plain outside and down below. The remoteness of this soundless, inner world of spinning and weaving from the terrible rending and tearing that is the work of war is also a symptom of its helplessness. The two armies know the terms of Helen's fate long before she does. And when the walls of Troy come down, that remote and soundless bubble-world will suddenly burst, and the quietly weaving women will find themselves widowed, childless, abducted, raped, enslaved.

Into her web Helen is weaving all the sorrows and sufferings that both Greeks and Trojans have undergone for her over the years. It is the ninth year of the war. And although it is a huge purple web of double width, even the weave within the weave cannot contain all the miseries she has caused.

At that point, one of Priam's daughters, Laodica, came running in, nimble-footed as Iris, to tell her what was happening: her husband and lover were about to fight for her, and Helen was seized – so she later said – by an uncontrollable yearning for her husband and her home and her own people. It came to her all at once, the enormity of what she'd done, and in a sudden blur and flurry of tears she got up and left the room and ran up onto the battlements by the Scaean Gate.

Up there, talking to Priam, sat the very old men of Troy, the city elders, bald and toothless, withered white-headed survivors of forgotten wars. Extreme old age had put an end to their useful days, and now they sat like cicadas, chirping bitterly, sweetly, of days gone by, and regretting the present too, because of the war. Yet even these shrivelled old men of Troy, the cicadas with voices so piping and shrill, whispered when she came into their midst that she was strangely like a goddess to look at, and they had to admit it was small wonder that men were ready to suffer so much for such a creature.

Was it? Take an even deeper look at her, and see if you dare to disagree.

She appeared on the battlements with the wind in her hair, swept sweetly across her mouth and blowing her dress against her breasts and legs, half hinting at what had made Paris so ravenous for her and Menelaus so mad to bring her back. She shone, she glittered, she glowed. She wore clothes that had been saturated with the best olive oils before being washed out again. And she was fragrant – scented with hyssop, sweet sage and cypress, anise and rose. Beneath the celebrated tresses, her smoky eyes were dark with galena, charred almond shells, soot and frankincense. Penelope is strong on those particular details.

And if you care to look closer still, the detail draws you further in.

Her dresses were dyed with saffron and indigo and madder red. Eggs and onion skins, salt and vinegar and human urine – there was no end to the concoctions that had gone into her garments. Gold discs glittered on her, sewn into the clothes. Her breasts were tightly bodiced to keep them high and pouting. Sometimes she wore them bare. And Paris kept wax casts of them, so the whisper went among the cicadas, though he could cup the real thing any night of the week and bury his head between them.

Go on, feed deep, deeper still on the detail – the bodice insistent, the long hair flaming past the waist and running in rivulets across the forehead. Look again into the kohl-blackened eyes, wide and inviting, how they pull you in like the forest pools of woody Ida.

So the old men on the walls mused on Helen. They gorged themselves on the gossip of her slightest move. Love, they murmured, runs after her like puppies.

'And men,' muttered the Trojan women, 'sniff after her like dogs after bitch-cunt, their balls hard with lust.'

They eyed her up and down as they said it, assessing the charms, calculating the lives she'd cost them, the misery, with her slinky ankles and follow-me-fuck-me sandals, and those breasts held so high. She was the one to die for all right: home-wrecker, marriage-breaker, man-maddening, enticing, libidinous bitch-whore, the gorgeous grave of so many soldiers. One bitch, so many battles.

And even the cicadas conceded, even the chirping, shrivelled kings of politics, who'd bathed in moon-browed Helen, even they conceded, in spite of the faint far-off tingling in their dry old balls. A goddess, yes. All the same, we can let this goddess go, we can do without her. Let her go away in the ships, and let the Greeks leave us to see out our old age in peace, our last failing decrepit days. Old age is hell enough without the hell of war.

But Penelope won't, can't, still can't let her go, won't leave her alone. Obsessive jealousy? hatred? fascination? reluctant worship? Fixated, she lets Helen take control of the web, filling it with images of other women – not the statues or murals, or the beauties you see on vases and drinking bowls, firm-fleshed females with plump bums, luscious lips, perfect breasts and pearly teeth – no, none of these. Instead you have the parade of life as it really is. Look at the gaps in the teeth, the moustaches on upper lips. Observe the squints and scabs and warts, the sagging mammaries, the bulging buttocks, the white wobbly atrocious thighs. That's other women, Penelope rages. That's how men are made to see us, when Helen's in the room.

And here she comes again, looking even more than half divine among these sad wrecks of womanhood. She's back on the walls to launch her counter-attack on Priam's grave advisers, the old men who worship her but would let her go. Along the battlements she sways and paces, the swing of her hips intoxicates. The wise cicadas perched above the Scaean Gates – they muse again on those ankles, breasts and thighs, and once again they lose their wisdom momentarily. Her beauty muddles their statesmanship. Maybe she should stay after all. Under the silver hairs and bald scalps the brains go soft as she fills them with regret for all they've lost, all the errors and wrong decisions they've made in their time. And though it's too late now to bring back their past failures and rectify them, put right the old muddle of their lives, somehow she seems to offer them that very possibility, for one illusory moment, whose effect lingers like sorrow, like joy.

On she goes, making love to the air as she walks. The wind kisses her and comes away unsatisfied. Even gentle Zephyrus abandons Flora and follows Helen, wanting more. You follow him as he follows her, you follow those swaying hips, and the air in her wake is not only scented by her but quickened by her movement, and the invisible tremor you're left with is the only measure of her beauty. You can't quantify it, can't put it into music, words or even pictures. Only Penelope comes close, though even she can't capture the complete Helen effect. The web can't catch her movement, her scent, her palpable aura. You can't find it in a nipple, an eyelash, a toenail. You weave the entire face and figure and it's still not there, though it's reaching for the unreachable. Only music perhaps might succeed in expressing the things for which we quite simply cannot find words. But there is no known music, no melodies yet composed that have translated her into sound.

What was it about her? Somehow her very presence seemed to summon up some glorious past. She poured scorn on the trivial babble and bubble of the present, just by being there, just by existing. She unsettled people, and what was so unsettling was that they couldn't say what exactly she made them want, or why. She pointed the way to something else, apart from herself, beyond herself, something all men ache for, as a soldier aches for home, the desert for water, as the drowning man craves air, the exile a breath of native land, and yet that something remained undefinable. She inspired an ultimate longing, a pain that had no herb to heal it, a sadness that had no object of satisfaction. It was an objectless anxiety, an absence, an emptiness, a longing that was an end in itself and so could never end, like the futile human quest for happiness, perfection. It was a longing for a longing, if you like. What more is there to be said? Helen was Elysium. She was the only possible paradise that remained impossible, the one that was lost and would always be lost. That's why she caused such pain.

And on top of all that you just wanted to fuck her. Every man did. If he didn't, he wasn't a man. Even the old men on the walls, even though they knew they couldn't, even if she'd lain with them one and all. She was the full-fleshed ghost of their old desires, their vanished lives.

'Wouldn't it be nice,' said one to another, 'just to take her clothes off? That's all – just take them off. Nothing else.'

But Priam, always courteous, silenced the licentious twittering. He spoke gently to her, seeing her distress, and asked her to point out by name the various Greek heroes. That was Penelope's device, her means of putting us on parade for the web. Naturally, in nine years of war – in web-time at least – Priam would have known all the illustrious Greeks by sight long since, and by name. Looking at the two armies drawn up on the plains below, and the two contenders facing one another in between, he assured her that any blame lay not with her but, along with the outcome, in the lap of the gods. Some of the wives standing by sniggered that the cause and the blame lay not in the lap of the gods but in her own lap – right between her legs, to be precise. She was used to such sneers, but Priam silenced them too.

So Helen leant over the battlements and pointed out the brightest stars in the Greek firmament, blurred here and there by the wisps of mist that had begun blowing in from the sea.

Pride of place went to Agamemnon, king of men. He had a head like Zeus, an eye like Ares to threaten and command, a waist like the war-god's waist when Aphrodite lay with him, and a breast like Poseidon's on a day when the white horses ride the waves. All idealised to the sky, the principal omissions being shaft of satyr and brain of bull.

But all this was private propaganda and truth the common soldier, lowest on the list. Ajax, Idomeneus – Helen went through all of us, special mention being made of myself, son of Laertes and king of rocky Ithaca. Not that my infamous stature was enhanced. I stood shorter than Menelaus by a head, though I was broader-shouldered, as in life, and looked more imposing, the statelier of the two. When I spoke, men listened, though at first glance you wouldn't have thought I'd be a man of any address at all. But this is where the real Penelope touch came in, the image I liked best of all. Out of my mouth floated a few white flakes, scarcely noticeable at first, but then the flakes came bigger and faster as I spoke, getting into my rhetorical stride, the imagined words falling as thick and crisp and cruel as the flakes in a winter blizzard, and you knew, although you couldn't hear the speech from the soundless web, that you were privileged to be listening to a matchless speaker, the master of debate. Words were always my best weapons.

But where, Helen was asking, were her two brothers, Castor the horseman and Polydeuces the boxer? Hadn't they too come from lovely Lacedaemon? Or couldn't they bring themselves to enter the field for the sheer shame of it, knowing that their sister was up there on the walls, the bane of the Trojan women and the lust of the old men's loins, her reproach wide in the world? Little did she know, even as she asked, that they were lying long dead in earth, in the lap of lovely Lacedaemon, their native land.

That imaginary ignorance of hers was a false twist in the web, a touch of pathos, a touch of Penelope's cunning hand, twisting history, nothing more. But now Helen stiffened and caught her breath. Down on the plain the duel for her was about to begin.

Paris threw first and the spear was dead on target. You could see it from the second it left his hand and went whistling and singing down the wind, intended to split his opponent's skull. But Menelaus thrust up his shield to meet the missile and it bent to hell on the bronze.

'Shit!'

'That's right, pretty boy! Now try mine, you useless fucker!'

Menelaus hurled – with equal accuracy and a combined strength and speed that made the spear go like an arrow. Both sides shouted in anticipation.

'Fucking hell!'

'What a fuck-surge!'

'Check three!'

'No, bronze to balls, man! Cover your fucking tackle!'

'Too fucking late!'

'He's dogshit!'

'The war's fucking over!'

If only. It was far from that. Paris traced the trajectory, and, instead of using his shield, did his show-off bit by swerving. He almost bought it on account of that act of vanity, but he got away with it. A close one, though. His tunic was ripped at the side, but that was all. He whooped and punched the air – then shagged it for good measure.

'Fuck you, Menelaus! And fuck your wife too – only I'll be doing it again tonight, old man! And you can chew your snot!'

Menelaus went red-eyed and berserk. He dropped his shield and came charging up to the little bastard, chancing the second spear. Paris didn't even have time to use it. Menelaus was on him and the sword flashed down like lightning, a real skull-splitter. But the blade shattered on the crest of the helmet and the jagged splinters flew everywhere.

'Fuck!'

Menelaus gawped at the stump in his hand and Paris gave him a sort of glazed grin. The luck of the gods, that bastard.

Not for long, though. Menelaus grabbed the plume and pulled him to the ground. Then he started dragging him back to our ranks, where he'd have torn him to pieces for sure. Even now, he was half-throttled by the chinstrap and still dazed from the blow on the head. It looked like he was dead meat and the expedition was over. Our men were cheering already and there was even applause from sections of the Trojan side. But then the wind that had blown his tart's breasts into prominence did him a huge and unexpected favour. It brought the sea-mists gusting suddenly inland in thick swirling white shrouds and the duellists disappeared. Nobody could see his own hand in front of his face, it was so dense. Then the veils parted, and there stood Menelaus looking like a complete idiot with an empty helmet in his hand and no sign of Paris. The little prick had given him the slip.

'Fuck! Fuck! Fuck!'

He smashed the helmet to the ground and came stomping back to the ranks. He was furious but was greeted with loud applause.

'It doesn't matter – you've won!'

'He left the field, the cowardly bastard!'

'The cunt scarpered! He ran away!'

'Terms of the oath. He's fucked up. Helen's ours!'

'It's over, lads – we're going home!'

Agamemnon sent heralds to the walls to proclaim his brother the winner, given Paris's abandonment of the duel, which amounted to surrender and defeat. Code of combat. They demanded that the oath be honoured, with the immediate return of Helen and all her goods, plus the promised recompense and a cessation of hostilities forthwith.

There was no immediate answer to that. Paris had turned up in the city unhurt, apart from the red weals on his worthless neck, and instead of hiding his face in shame the cynical bastard sent out a message that he hadn't run away, he'd been spirited off in the mist by Aphrodite, his protectress – which was his way of telling us to go and fuck ourselves. He'd lost consciousness and found himself back in Troy, simple as that. No one had lost or won. The duel was a draw. There would be no surrender of Helen, no recompense, nothing.

Menelaus stood and screamed at the walls.

'Treacherous fucking bastard!'

Silence. And a few stones.

If the citizens could have had their way, they'd have flung the cunt over the walls and lobbed his trollop after him. They loathed him to a man and her to a woman. But he was the king's offspring and could do as he pleased. Which is exactly what he did. Take a look and see.

Lapped by warm water, Paris lies back in the bronze bath and lets the maidens pour balm on his bruises. Daintily hidden underwater is one maidenly hand. Paris has a faraway, contented look on his face. He is happy to rise up and stand naked before the girls to be dried and admired. Then he puts on soft-scented clothes and makes for Helen's bedchamber.

She isn't there. She is still up on the walls, sighing her soul towards the Grecian tents, longing for her husband – at least that is how she makes it appear. She is surrounded by the Trojan women. One of them plucks at her dress and murmurs in her ear.

'Come down from the walls. Paris is back home from the field and he's waiting for you in bed. You wouldn't believe how dashing he looks, though he's just been in a duel. Fought for you. He wants you to make love to him. He's gagging for you.'

Helen turns to her. She looks quite like the old wool-worker who used to make the most beautiful yarns for her back in Sparta, and the voice is the very same. But as she looks closer, she sees through the disguise and flashes back at her.

'Make love to a coward? Never. He's not back from the duel – he ran from it! And I'm not running to his bed. Why don't you get in instead? Or will it give you a bigger thrill to watch the two of us doing it?'

Aphrodite reveals herself in a gorgeous explosion of anger and beauty.

'You stubborn wretch! Don't dare provoke me. If I desert you, you'll find out what it's like to be friendless on Olympus. Now get down there and do your duty – to me and to your husband!'

Helen leaves, suitably subdued but whispering under her breath.

'He's not my husband.'

And when she enters the room and sees him lying expectantly on the bed, she lets him have it.

'Back from the battlefield, are you, dear? I thought you were fighting my husband. But I saw you run from the better man – the man I was mad enough to abandon to follow you here and be the mockery of the world. It was the fog that saved you. Why don't you be a man and get back out there and face him?'

'I will,' said Paris, 'on another occasion. And I'll be luckier next time.'

'Lucky? You escaped with your life – by running away!'

'Aphrodite looked after me. I was born in her ascendancy, and I offered up a golden apple on her altar. She won't let me down.'

'Golden apple! Not that old story again. She didn't give me to you – you took me. From my husband. You took me when I was alone and vulnerable.'

Paris rises swiftly from the bed.

'I took you because you were the most beautiful woman I'd ever seen, and you still are. I wanted you then and I want you now. I've never wanted you so much, not even on that first night – do you remember it? – the first time we were really free, when I brought you aboard and we sailed off from Sparta and spent the whole night in each other's arms on the high seas, and later made love on Kranai.'

She flushes suddenly. He seizes the moment and her, clutching her flanks and crushing her to him.

'Helen, I've just escaped death. Do you know how that makes a man feel when he's with the woman he loves? I've never before felt such a wish to live, such a desire to lose myself in your sweet body. I love it! I love life! I love you!'

He takes her by the hand and leads her towards the bed. She follows him without another word, responding to his urgency with her own sudden urge. She follows her own nature as the creature of the moment. Soon she is panting under him, her legs in the air.

Such is the warp and the woof — a weave of truth and lies. Aphrodite? There was no Aphrodite. The goddess was a mere metaphor for what lay between Helen's legs, simple as that — an open, insatiable cunt.

EIGHTEEN

Down in the field, a truce was still technically operational, and up on Olympus Hera was busy urging Athene to use her powers to make the Trojans break it. Three scenes then, a triptych: Helen under Paris, fucking like a rabbit; her husband foaming at the mouth as he rampages through the ranks, shouting for Paris to show his cowardly carcass and fight again. And now Athene, shooting like a star from high Olympus, leaving behind her a sparkling track, a wake of sheer radiance to dazzle the army. Landing in the ranks, she turns herself into a Trojan and whispers something in Pandarus's ear. With one hand she's pointing to his bow, with the other to Menelaus. It's easy to guess what she's saying.

'Look at him, the fool, prowling up and down looking for Paris. He's completely exposed because of the truce. Why not pick him off with an arrow? Shoot him down right now, the idiot! There isn't a soldier wouldn't thank you. No husband, no Helen, don't you see? No need to return a woman to a dead man, is there? What's a corpse going to do with a live woman? Can a corpse fuck? Go on, get him – now! To hell with the ceasefire!'

It didn't take a god to put any of that into Pandarus's head. Sheer fucking perfidy, that's all it took. He looked at his bow. A beauty it was, made from the horns of an ibex that he'd shot in the chest. Pandarus smiled to himself as he remembered how he'd lain in wait for it then brought down the beast as stealthily as he now aimed at Menelaus.

Not that we saw any of that. But Penelope did, close up and in slow motion. He drew back the ox-gut till he felt the notch touch his chest and saw the fearful bronze point come all the way back to the bow. The ibex horns were now a circle. He let go, the string sang its terrible song, and the arrow went whistling down the wind, its feathers fraught with agony for Menelaus.

'Fuck!'

'What's the matter, brother?'

'Some cunt has conned us! I'm hit!'

'Shit!'

But Menelaus's day hadn't come. The arrow had struck him on the belt, but the wound was shallow. It looked bad enough, though. All we saw was the dark flood running down his legs and thighs, as if he was pissing blood.

'Those fucking truce-breakers! They've fucking done for you!'

Agamemnon saw it all in a flash – Helen unreturned, the expedition futile, the war abandoned, a retreat in empty ships, his brother's bones left mouldering in enemy earth and his own name a mockery among boasting Trojans.

'So much for the sons of Atreus, they will say, kicking up the dust over your grave and pointing out to sea. One a corpse on the plains of Troy, under the starry sky, and the other gone home empty-handed after a dead venture. All a waste of life – and time.'

But Menelaus was laughing as Machaon the leech quickly exposed the wound and examined the gash.

'A scratch. Look, it's hardly gone in any depth at all. Right, Machaon?'

'Right. But another inch and it would have done enough, you lucky cunt!'

Machaon eased out the point, sucked the blood and slapped on a handful of herbs. Woundwort, birthwort, old wine and garlic to fight the infection, willow bark, poppies by the dozen, dozy with sedative, to send Menelaus to Morpheus while the blood-clotting yarrow did its work. He dressed the wound with sheep-grease and honey. Helen wasn't going to be a widow after all, at least not today. And the war was still on.

You don't see much of a battle except what's in front of you and what you can catch out of the corner of your eye. For the big picture and the exclusive scenes, for the mass and individual slaughter outside your range, you have to go to the web. All put together from debriefing and intelligence, all a construct, a blend of fact and fascination with a bright dash of fantasy.

The two Ajaxes led the biggest combined force: Little Ajax the Locrians and Big Ajax the soldiers from Salamis. They were joined by the Cretans, led by Idomeneus. The massed men at their backs glowered menacingly, like the cloud a goatherd spots from his weather-tower in the hills, bearing down on him from the sea, driven by the west wind and turning pitch-black as it speeds his way, making him shudder and drive his goats quickly into the nearest cave. And there wasn't a Trojan soldier alive looking at that cloud of men who didn't wish he was a goat safe in a cave with the flock rather than facing the Ajaxes and Idomeneus on the open plains of Troy.

Fantastic detail? Not out of a field report, for sure, but no less true for all that. Not untrue either that the Greek battalions rose like the waves gathering on an echoing beach to crash on the shingle or smash into the base of a cliff, sending the bright spume flying upwards and the white fire licking the crags. Not untrue that the Greeks and Trojans picked up speed and sounded like two massive mountain rivers on the move, tumbling to meet in some deep ravine with a clash and a roar, the shuddering shock of sudden contact, bronze on bronze, the bosses of the shields slamming and ringing together as the first screams rent the air. Nothing imaginary about those brutal screams.

Simoisius screamed when Big Ajax killed him, hitting him in the chest with his spear. Until he ran into Ajax, he'd been a fine young soldier, born by the banks of the river Simois amid a flock of sheep. Tickled and nuzzled, Simoisius had been his mother's little nipper. He'd grown tall and slim-built, and when Ajax's spear plunged in by his right nipple, he went down slowly like a stately poplar in a riverside meadow, felled and left to season by the wainwright to make felloes for fine chariot wheels. Except that a tree has some use when it falls, whereas a man when he falls has no use at all. So now Simoisius lay useless in the dust, unable to repay his mother's tenderness. But the tears she shed for him were caught in the web and held there trembling, like drops of dew, and not untrue.

I made a good kill myself – one of Priam's bastard sons, Demokoön. He never saw my spear coming and never even knew he'd been hit. The bronze thudded in at one temple, drove right through the brain and came out at the other: the perfect hit, the perfect way to die. Wiping the brains from the bronze, I glanced up and caught the Thracian captain, Peiros, hurling a jagged lump of rock. I dodged it, and it hit Diores, the Epeian captain, on the right leg, close to the ankle. The rock broke the leg-bones brutally. He toppled over on his back, screaming and helpless and stretching out both hands. But Peiros was too quick; he sprang out and jabbed his spear into the fallen man's belly, close to the navel. When he wrenched it free, the intestines poured into the dust in a neat pile just beside him.

But Peiros took too long about it, admiring his handiwork and even stopping to remove the helmet and kick Diores savagely in the head before turning to make his dash back to his place in the ranks. He was stopped by Thoas. The spear sank deep into a lung. It would probably have been enough to kill him, but Thoas made sure of his man by kicking him over and stabbing him deep in the groin and again in the chest.

'There you go,' said Thoas, 'that ought to do it.'

He fancied the armour, but the top-knotted Thracians quickly moved in to defend their chief's corpse, and Thoas got out just before the knotheads surrounded him.

And so the two captains, Thracian and Epeian, lay stretched out side by side, two kings united by death, and by a cause that concerned neither but had brought them together briefly to die together in the dust – almost as if they were not enemies at all, but fallen friends. That was far from true, although it had a kind of truth, a truth of its own, known only to soldiers. All Penelope's images have a truth of their own, even if the web can't convey the feel of the thing, the sheer thrill of the kill, the euphoria and insanity of survival.

And yet the web provides something that's missing from the hell and high kicks of action. All that comes out of a battle is a win or a loss, and a long casualty list. A cold roll-call of names, nothing more. The honoured dead. Nothing frostier than honour, nothing so impersonal, nothing so aloof. But Penelope, however briefly, looks at each man as he dies. She looks at how he dies, takes note of his name, his kin, those who survive him and mourn him. Hers is a remembering web, a funeral tribute, a means of grieving. It is an endless cortège, allowing space and face to those who fought and died, saying something, however minimal, however ephemeral, about their moment in history, and so transcending the terrible abstraction that is death. History can so quickly trash our missing persons, overwhelm our dead in the dust of fallen towers. Penelope freezes the moment, makes a picture, bears witness. Remember that. Remember it as you contemplate all that follows, the bloodshed, the butchery, the human loss.

SCENES FROM THE WEB: FOR THE FALLEN

PHEGEUS and IDAIUS, the two sons of Dares. They came at Diomedes in their chariot and Diomedes tried to take them both out. He caught Phegeus in the chest. He crashed out of the chariot and his brother jumped after him – not to help, but to escape the second spear. Their father was a priest of Hephaestus; maybe the lame god decided his venerable old priest shouldn't be crippled by a double loss and so spared the second son. Or perhaps Idaius was just lucky that day: he got back to the ranks, brotherless but with his life.

ODIUS, leader of the Alizones. Agamemnon aimed at him as he turned his chariot. The spear slammed between the shoulder blades. Odius looked down in disbelief and saw the point sticking out of his chest. He fell from the chariot without a sound, under the stamping hooves of his own horses, and his skull was quickly crushed inside his helmet.

PHAESTUS, son of Borus, who'd come from the lush lands of Tarne and never returned to them. Idomeneus saw to that. The force of the javelin toppled Phaestus right out of his chariot. He crashed, gasping, to the ground and the dust swirled up and the loathsome dark engulfed him.

SCAMANDRIUS, son of Strophius. He was a great hunter, trained by Artemis herself, so they said. He could bring down anything from the skies above the mountain forests. But the long shots he was famous for were of no use to him now. Nor did Artemis appear on the scene to offer any assistance when Menelaus's long lance went clean through his back between the shoulders and cut through the chest. He'd discovered all too briefly, all too bitterly, what it was like to be the hunted rather than the hunter. He fell face down, the force of the fall driving the spear back out again, thick with his blood. His armour clanged and night descended on him.

PHEREKLOS, son of Tecton, Harmon's son. He was an expert carpenter. Nobody had nimbler fingers. A great favourite of Pallas Athene too, so it was said. He'd built all those trim ships for Paris when he'd sailed to Sparta on that fateful trip. But he was a better shipwright than a runner. Meriones ran after him and stabbed him hard from behind. The spear drove all the way through the right buttock, and the bronze, missing the pelvic bone, bit into the bladder and pierced it through. Phereklos dropped to his knees, screaming, and fell on his face, the nimble fingers clawing the dust. He left behind him the trim ships, his pride and joy. Also a trim young wife, the love of his life. She was very badly raped when the city fell and did not survive.

PEDAEUS. He was one of Antenor's illegitimates, but to please her husband the lovely Theano had brought him up as if she'd borne him herself. She even suckled him when she was nursing one of her own. But she wasn't there to nurse him when he received his death-blow. Meges caught up with him as he ran for his life and thrust the spear two-handed into the nape of the neck. The spearhead sliced between the jaws, splitting the tongue at the root. He could still scream, though, and did so as he struck the dust face first, biting with clenched teeth onto cold bronze, the hateful taste of death.

HYPSENOR, son of Dolopion, priest to the river-god Scamander, killed by Eurypylus, who ran after him and slashed at his shoulder with his sword as if he were reaping. The entire arm dropped in the dust, useless. Hypsenor stopped running and stood and looked at the arm, feeling the bleeding stump in grief and disbelief. Then he stopped looking as Eurypylus slashed next at the neck. The head hit the dust too, its lips still saying something about the arm. There was no need to complete the sentence. Eurypylus had saved him from that and from a much slower death.

ASTYNOUS and HYPEIRON, both killed by Diomedes in spite of an arrow wound he took in the shoulder from Pandarus. The spear struck Astynous above the nipple. Then Diomedes swung at Hypeiron with a huge sword. It hacked through the collarbone and split the shoulder from neck and back. He left both men lying there, bleeding to death.

ABAS and POLYEIDUS, the sons of a very old man, Eurydamas, the dreamer. He saw visions and believed in them. But he was short on visions when they went to the front. He never dreamed that they'd be stretched out headless in the dust after Diomedes had caught up with them.

XANTHUS and THOÖN, also slain by Diomedes and also sons of an old and ailing father, Phaenops. These fine young striplings were the fruits of his winter loins. But they dropped long before their time, far from ripeness, leaving the old man lonely and broken-hearted and with nobody left to whom he could bequeath his considerable wealth; it all went to distant cousins. He never saw his handsome lads again, except in the bitter dreams of age.

PANDARUS, another victim of Diomedes. Pandarus watched the missile all the way and positioned his shield correctly. But there was a spin on the spear, and the sun was in his face. Skimming the top rim of the shield, the spear split open his nose, close to the eye. It cracked the jaw, sliced away the tongue, shattered the white teeth and came tearing out under the chin, ripping the dear life out of him on its way. Pandarus had

had plenty to say up to that point, but though he was still alive when he hit the ground, he spoke no more words. The armour clattered on him, making the dust fly up around his last agonies. Night came down and closed his eyes.

AENEAS, wounded by Diomedes, but not killed. He'd leapt from his chariot to protect Pandarus, and Diomedes caught him on the leg with a jagged boulder — a massive and accurate throw. It tore the flesh and broke the sinews, completely crushing the cup-bone, where the thigh turns in the hip. He crumpled up in the dust. And would have died there if Aphrodite hadn't saved him. Even then he'd never have fought again. But the white arms of a goddess can work wonders. They wound round him and whisked him off to another section of the web, where she magically healed her son's hurts. A good story. How else could a Trojan escape a Greek, except by divine intervention?

DEICOÖN, killed by Agamemnon. No magic for him, no divine help. The javelin pierced both shield and belt and sank deep into the abdomen. He thudded to the ground with a clattering of armour. Agamemnon ran up and wrenched out his spear, twisting it savagely. The bowels came spilling out of him and he lay wriggling in a spreading pool of blood that darkened the white dust around him.

MYDON, killed by Antilochus. He smashed him on the elbow, excruciatingly, with a heavy lump of rock. Mydon cried out as the reins, with their lovely ivory trappings, slipped from his limp hands and trailed on the ground. Antilochus followed up the throw with the quick dash, tumbled Mydon out of his chariot and leapt on him like a beast. He drove his sword through the man's head by the temple. Mydon fell for the second time, this time with a great sigh, and was trampled by his terrified horses. He was crumpled up with both head and shoulders buried in the dust, but the horses' hooves soon flattened him out.

AMPHIUS, killed by Ajax. He was the son of Selagus, an extremely rich landowner in Paesus who would have given all his lands to get his son back safely from the war. But that was impossible once Ajax's javelin found its mark. It penetrated Amphius's belt and drove in deep. Amphius crashed on his back screaming, the spear swaying in his belly. He'd never inherit all that wealth, never take an old man's walk through those expansive cornfields stretched out glittering in the evening sunlight. Instead, young Amphius lay stretched out on the plains of Troy, a rich and powerful man, but powerless to change his destiny.

Ajax ran up to retrieve the spear. He wanted the armour too, but a hail of javelins came down on him like a skein of long-necked geese flying south in the fall of leaves, filling the skies with their cries. As the hissing geese shrieked down on Ajax, he tried to fend them off with his shield, but they kept on coming, so thickly that eventually he retreated.

COERANUS, ALASTOR, CHROMIUS, ALCANDER, HALIUS, NOEMAN, PRYTANIS. All killed by me, Odysseus, no details necessary, for modesty's sake, and their names on the roll of honour. For what that's worth.

And the hero of the hour in the web?

Only one hero – Death. Beautiful death, glorious death, *kalos thanatos*, descending like sunset on doomed men, the darkness wrapping them up fast, as though they were sleepy children. Penelope didn't show Death as he really was, strolling among the wounded at his leisure, allowing ample hours of suffering. Death was in no hurry on the plains of Troy, when the blood turned slowly black from the bronze bite of the poisoned arrows and soldiers puked and shat their way to Hades, and the dogs' long tongues sucked out their marrow when their sharp teeth had finished crunching on their bones. You won't find that on the web.

And glory? Staying alive is glorious. War is stripping the enemy and not getting stripped yourself. War is acquisition. You grab what you can under the hail of spears and then you get out. You don't leave a man with a cap on his skull or a rag to cover his balls or his arse. Take life, take property, take all. That's how it goes.

For us, Diomedes was the hero of the hour, brighter than the brightest star of summer. His crest and shield flamed like Sirius and his spears rained down on the Trojans like meteors, like the Pleiads shooting through the midnight skies in August when the air is clear, like one of those winter torrents, swollen by the rains, that tears down trees and flattens dykes, destroying the landscape. Nothing that stood in his way survived.

It was while he was watching this onslaught that Aeneas urged Pandarus – soon to be a dead man – to bring down Diomedes if he could.

'I've shot the cunt already!' yelled Pandarus. 'And Menelaus! Both the bastards should be dead meat by now. Why the fuck didn't I listen to my father? He told me before I left for the front to fight from my chariot. And I paid no attention to him, did I? I thought I'd get the glory with this fucking thing!'

He threw down his bow in disgust and kicked it away from him.

'It's let me down. I wish I'd left it on its peg by the door. When I get home again the first thing I'll do is chuck it into the fucking fire!'

So said Pandarus, little knowing that he wouldn't be going home again, not today. Not ever. Aeneas took him on a different course, in his own chariot, pulled by the horses of Tros. Their mission: to take out Diomedes.

'Now's your chance,' shouted Aeneas, 'to follow your father's advice!'

Sthenelus saw them coming and shouted to Diomedes to retreat.

'From that pair of testicles? Never!'

'They may be testicles but they're no fucking dunces! And you're wasted!'

'Am I? We'll see about that!' Diomedes stroked his javelin and pointed with it. 'See these horses? They're the best ever.'

And they were. The son of Cronos, the great god Zeus, gave their sires to Tros in exchange for Ganymede. Anchises put the mares to them, bred without permission. The mares foaled. He got six horses, kept four, and gave Aeneas the other two.

'They're only fucking horses!' said Sthenelus.

'No matter. They'd be a cracker of a prize. A match for Achilles, I'd say — any fucking day!'

Seconds later Pandarus and Aeneas had charged up to within range, and Pandarus let fly his javelin. It pierced Diomedes' shield and Pandarus whooped.

'A hit! A fucking hit! You're a dead man!'

'Think so, do you?'

The spear hadn't penetrated the armour.

'Fuck!'

'If I were you I'd try sword practice. You're not much of an archer, and your spear's no good. But you won't have time to rectify that. You're the dead man, you loser!'

Diomedes hurled.

And that was the encounter in which Aeneas lost his horses and Pandarus his life. Along with many a fellow Trojan. The Greeks cheered.

'We're drubbing the cunts — keep at them, lads! They're on the fucking run!'

Even allowing for Penelope's prejudice and her fondness for Greek bronze in Trojan teeth, the web is right: the Trojans were taking a bad thrashing, and Sarpedon, King of Lycia, lashed out at Hector bitterly.

'You Trojans are doing next to nothing – your allies are standing between you and annihilation. I've come a long way from Lycia, leaving behind a lovely wife and a beloved son, far from here by the rushing Xanthus. And I've left lands and property that my neighbours are eager to get their greedy hands on. Have I brought my men all this way only to watch you cower like beaten dogs before a few thugs got up in bronze? What sort of men are you? Make a stand at least!'

Hector rallied his men. 'Make a stand there! No giving ground! Stand and advance!'

'We can't! It's a three-sixty fucking attack!'

'Make a fucking circle then, you motherfuckers!'

'It's a fucking rout – they're cutting men's heads off here!'

'Then fucking stick them back on again! Show some fucking balls!'

Aeneas killed the two sons of Diocles, Crethon and Orsilochus from Phere. Their father himself had trained them up in arms and he saw them off proudly to Troy. It was a great adventure for them. But the adventure ended for Crethon with a spear in the forehead which split his skull in two, and for his brother, who tried to save him, with a sword-thrust to the throat as he bent over him, grief-stricken. The two brothers' blood mingled as they died in each other's arms.

Menelaus and Antilochus came running up with their spears, and Aeneas, who'd hoped for double spoils, retreated when he saw the double opposition. The dead brothers were dragged back behind their own lines.

When Hector saw Mydon go under his horses' hooves he made for Antilochus. The first spear struck Menesthes in the eye and sank deep into the brain. Antilochus tried to wheel his horses round but Mydon's terrified mounts got in the way. The second spear went through one side of his neck and out the other. He made a frantic effort to pull it out but fell forwards and soon gave up the attempt – and his life.

Then Tlepolemus and Sarpedon contested – the long javelins left each man's hand in the same split second. But Sarpedon's spear was swifter. It hit his opponent in the neck and the blade went right through the middle and came out. The darkness came down on Tlepolemus. He never saw his own spear strike Sarpedon in the thigh, shaving the bone. His friends rushed in to carry him off – well out of the war, the long heavy javelin still dangling from the leg. It would be a surgery job to get it out. Sarpedon limped like Hephaestus for the rest of his life – which meant he didn't have to limp too long. But Tlepolemus was past all pain.

That was one of our bloodiest encounters.

But it wasn't over. Ajax hit Acamas, the Thracians' best fighter. Then Diomedes' terrible bronze sliced through Axylus's cheekbone and entered the lower part of the brain. His charioteer stood petrified as the Greek charged up, freed the spear with a wrench and plunged the point, thick with his master's brains, into his eye.

Euryalus killed Dresus and Opheltius with two easy spear-casts and then went like an arrow after Aesepus and Pedasus. Born of the water-nymph Abarbarea among beds of violets on the same riverbank where they were conceived, these two lads were stripped of their lives and their armour. Their father, Bucolion, mourned their loss with scalding tears and went softly all his days thereafter in the bitterness of his heart. He couldn't forget them, or the day of their conception, coming across the lovely goddess by the river when he was out shepherding his flocks. And Abarbarea wept too, her tears dropping over them and turning to pearls, shrouding her sons from the slavering dogs of Troy.

The tears glitter in the web as the killings continue.

Polypoetes killed Astyalus; Teucer killed Anetaon; Antilochus killed Ablerus; Agamemnon killed Elatus; Leitus killed Phylaeus; Eurypylus killed Melanthus; and I, Odysseus, killed Pidytes. I chopped off the wrong arm — he fought on briefly with the remaining arm, the one holding the sword. Then I stabbed him hard in the thigh and the sword jammed in the bone, the blade splintering as I tried to wrench it free. I finished him off with two spear-thrusts, one to the groin and the other through the throat. I'd aimed at the eye but botched it. That put Pidytes in some pain before he died.

Now it was Adrestus's turn. His horses, careering across the plain, had stumbled on a tamarisk root, snapping the shaft of his chariot and pitching him on his face in the dust, completely exposed, the wheel still spinning wildly next to him. He looked up half blinded to find Menelaus standing over him, javelin in hand. Adrestus wrapped both arms round his enemy's knees.

'Take me alive and my father will pay you a fat ransom.'

Menelaus hesitated.

'He's fantastically rich. He'll pay anything – you name it. He'll stump up a fortune if he hears that you spared me and that I'm alive and well on your ship, a prisoner of war.'

Menelaus lowered his lance and looked ready to soften and accept. But Agamemnon came running up.

'No captives, brother! No mercy, no ransoms – not today, nobody to be taken alive, no matter how much is offered. All die, even the baby in the belly. And they die unpitied – especially the baby in the belly. We're going to cleanse the earth of this race, wipe them from the planet, every last rat. We don't need their ransoms – we're going to take them anyway. Understood?'

So Menelaus thrust the knee-clutching suppliant from him. He landed on all fours and Agamemnon hacked him flat and down to darkness, unransomed and unpitied.

'Get to the front, you motherfuckers!'

It was a band of horse soldiers from Nestor's contingent. His youth had long gone but he still rode with the chariots and issued orders and advice. He was a crafty one too: he put his charioteers in front and his best infantry in the rear, so that the second-raters and the poorest fighters stationed between them couldn't escape the heat. They had to stand and fight with the rest of us. Or die. But Nestor always kept a small cavalry detachment to keep an eye on the other contingents and catch out the slackers and the funks.

'No fucking looting, do you check?'

'What the fuck do you think you're doing, soldier?'

'None of you funks skulking back to the ships with your fucking plunder, do you hear? There's a fucking war on here, you cunts!'

'Touch that fucking armour and I'll cut off your head and shit down your fucking neck!'

'Move up, move up, at the fucking double, you motherfucking slack-arses! Intensify the attack!'

So we did. And the unstoppable Diomedes now faced Glaucus the Lycian, son of Hippolochus, mid field. Diomedes went on the verbal offensive.

'Ready to die, Trojan-lover?'

Glaucus stood his ground. 'Ready if you are, Greek-beak!'

Diomedes grinned. He hated cowardice. 'Who the fuck are you, first? I like to know who I'm taking out.'

Glaucus came closer, his shield carelessly slung to one side. Diomedes gripped his spear tighter, eyeing his opponent's unprotected throat . . .

'I'm not about to die.'

The mighty Glaucus speaks loftily.

'And why do you ask me who I am? Do you want to know my race?

You've already guessed I'm not a Trojan. What does that matter? Aren't the races of men just like the forest leaves? They drop and are scattered by the wind. And spring brings in another generation. Nevertheless, I'll tell you who I am, if it means anything to you.'

And he identifies himself as the grandson of Bellerophon of Argos, who slew the Chimera and the notorious Solymi, who defeated the man-slaughtering Amazons and the elite soldiers sent to ambush him by the King of Lycia – the king who later offered him his daughter and half his kingdom.

Bellerophon lost the favour of the gods in the end, though, and went out alone over the Aleian Plain, far from the paths of men, eating his heart out in solitude. All the same, both Argos and Lycia are the lineage of Glaucus and the blood he boasts of.

Diomedes is more than merely impressed. He reminisces about how his own grandfather, Oineus, entertained Bellerophon in the old days of their youth. They became firm friends and exchanged gifts. This is a hint. And when Glaucus doesn't take it up, Diomedes decides to be more direct.

'Let's do the same,' he says, 'for old time's sake. Let's exchange our armour, for instance, like heroes on the field.'

So, for old time's sake, Glaucus exchanges his golden armour for the bronze that Diomedes is wearing. The gods must have addled the Lycian's brains, or his eyes are blinded by the magic of the moment and his heart by the yarns of yesteryear. Certainly he doesn't use his head, because that trade costs him the value of a hundred good oxen for the worth of nine.

Some will say that the grandfathers' exchange of gifts provided the pattern. Oineus offered a bright purple belt, and Bellerophon handed over a large two-handled gold cup. As sorry a bargain for Glaucus as for his grandfather – so his wife will sneer at him when he returns home and proudly shows her Diomedes' armour, only to be called a fool. She will little realise the extent of the bargain. Glaucus leaves with far more than his opponent's armour, and she will have her husband safely home. If they had fought, she would never have seen him again.

A good story. A woman's story. One for the web. And not a word of truth in it, except the inexorable truth of myth. It did sometimes happen at Troy that enemies met and parted without loss of life on either side, even after they'd just beaten hell out of one another. But as for parting as friends — never. The fighting was just too bitter for that. And fraternisation was next to impossible on the dusty plains of Troy.

Hector, on the other hand, appears in the web at that point, exactly as I'd seen him when the blackheads rallied and counter-attacked and we lost ground. I could make out the rim of his shield tapping him above and below, on his ankles and the back of his neck, as he marched calmly away. He was making for the city. Menesthius was standing next to me.

'What the fuck's he up to? Can't the cunt take any more?'

Iphinous was on my other side. 'He's calling it a day, it seems.'

'Don't fucking believe it,' I said. 'He's gone to get that dog-fuck of a brother — to bring the bitch back to the battle. Just you watch.'

It didn't take a poet to picture Priam's palace with its colonnades and its chambers of polished stone, where the king's fifty sons slept with their wives in fifty private apartments, Paris in one of them right now, his cock rammed hard up Helen's cunt, ready to come, her arse high in the air, and the sweet Spartan hand giving him the reach-around, cupping his balls for encouragement.

Hector came storming in and was stopped by his mother. She tried to offer him a bowl of wine, but he brushed it aside, spilling it over the floor.

'Where is the little whoremaster? Fucking murder out there and he's nowhere to be seen. Men down all over the field — and all on account of a shitbagging little cunt who can't keep his cock under control! Where is the bastard? I wish he was dead at my feet right now!'

Hecuba shut her eyes and clapped her hands over her ears. Her women surrounded her and whisked her off out of earshot of Hector's obscenities, telling him they'd go and arrange an apt gift for Athene's altar right away.

'You do that,' said Hector. 'And then guess what? We'll all just bend over and the Greeks will beg leave to kiss our arses and all will be forgiven. Just don't wipe them first — and they'll suck up all the more! And if you stage all that with a lyre and dancers I might even fucking believe it — if I'm drunk enough!'

So the best and brightest robe was chosen from among the broidered garments, worked by the Sidonian women. Theano the priestess laid it on the knees of the goddess's statue and the women's wailing prayer went up, a prayer to shatter the spear of Diomedes and bring him down in the dust, to die at the gates of Troy.

Hector heard it and swore to himself. 'And that'll keep Diomedes off our fucking backs for the rest of the day, will it?'

He reached Paris's quarters and threw open the door . . .

Helen regretted everything, naturally, and wished the thundering waves had swept over her long ago.

'Or if I weren't dead beneath the sea, that I were at least the wife of a better man, as I was once, instead of being what I know now I'll always be – a song in men's mouths. A song of scorn and scandal. And eternal reproach.'

Hector then went to see his own wife, Andromache. She was the daughter of the Cilician king, who once lived below the lovely wooded hill of Plakos in Thebe of the High Gates, before it was sacked by Achilles. She held out their infant son to his father and begged him to stay home, crying that if he returned to the front when it was so dangerous and didn't come back, she'd rather be in her grave. Already she'd lost her father and her seven brothers, all slaughtered by Achilles, though he'd burned the father's body and buried him honourably, and the mountain nymphs had planted elm trees by his barrow. But the brothers he'd killed all in one hour as they stood among their white sheep and shambling cattle, and the ransomed mother died later in Priam's halls, struck by the arrow of Artemis.

All of which Hector knew and had heard many times before, but never before so pleadingly in the terms in which Andromache now spoke.

'And so, my love, you're husband and father and mother and brother to me now. You're all I have in this world, other than my son that's soon to be fatherless. Don't go back today, I'm begging you. Stay at home.'

Soldiers returning to the front know these speeches well. They can say them by heart. And Hector was equally emotional in his answer. He told her he knew the day would come when she'd be dragged off into slavery, the wife of some soldier prince, or as his concubine, to toil at the loom for another woman and fetch water from the wells in far-off Argos, to end her days as a downtrodden mumbling old drudge with no will of her own and nothing left to live for. And he hoped he'd be dead in earth long before it happened.

'That's all I hope for now, dearest wife. I hope they've thrown the dirt over my head long before that day. I hope they've piled it deep enough over my corpse so that even in death I don't hear your screams as they murder our son and haul you out of your home. I hope I'm deep enough in Hades not to hear any of that.'

A good speech, yes?

In fact, he told her not to be a snivelling bitch. She'd undermine morale with her woman's wailing. And interfere with his aim. Soldiers returning to the front don't give way. They can't give way. If they did, they wouldn't go back. But everything was there in Penelope's rendering, all that ought to be there, crafted from the heart: Andromache's tears, Hector's breast-beating, the fall of Thebe-under-Plakos, the mountain nymphs, the elm trees, the dead parents, the father's tomb, the slaughtered siblings, the snow-white sheep, the shambling cattle – and the arrow of Artemis, shown for a second time in the web, repeating the pathos, heading for the heart of the already heartbroken mother, tipped with mercy, fraught with her death.

Hector took his son briefly in his arms. The infant was terrified by the hard armour, the helmet, the high nodding plume, and he bawled. The bloodied father stank of dust and death. He kissed him roughly and handed him back to the scented breast of his mother. Then he collected his brother and went back to the war. As soldiers do.

NINETEEN

Imagine you're an old water-rat, your arms and arse aching after hours of ploughing the brine with your polished pine. Hours have turned into days, weeks. The oar-blade has rubbed fuck out of your fingers, blistered your palms. You're chinstrapped, sick of it, can't hack it a fraction longer.

Then a sudden breeze gets up . . . Sweet!

That's how the blackheads must have felt when Hector appeared with Paris at his side, both of them good to go and armed to the teeth. A loud cheer greeted the bastards. And they went straight into the kill-zone.

Paris was first. Menesthius bought it with a single throw of the Trojan's javelin and fell back in the chariot with no time even for a grunt. Goodnight, Menesthius. The reins slipped from his fingers and the horses went on the loose in the thick of the fighting.

Hector downed Eioneus, also with a single throw. The blade went into the neck just under the brain-bucket and he crashed sideways out of the chariot. Some brave cunt tried to help the horses, gone wild among the missiles, and he took an arrow in the throat and another in the back.

Iphinous was on my right, shouting fuck knows what. He got one in the shoulder from Glaucus. I yelled out to him to hold on – it wasn't lethal – but he lost control of the horses and tumbled in the dust, screaming. It must have gone deeper than I'd thought. He was still fumbling with the long shaft when Glaucus ran up and lopped his head off, right under the chin, a neat job. The blackheads were on a roll.

Then fuck knows why, but priestly fucking Helenus put an end to it and gave us a breather. He went to Hector with a plan, a challenge. A single-combat duel, Hector against any comer. He said it would please the gods. The gods! When you're already on the offensive and knocking fuck out of the enemy? Well, that was his area of expertise, and any cunt who knows the mind of the gods, well, you don't want to ruffle him, one of the god squad, no, you'd better fucking listen. And we Greeks were the last to be putting up any objections. So Hector signalled for a cessation of hostilities and both sides sat down and were glad to.

The rules were simple: the winner to strip the loser of his armour but to release his body for a decent burial.

'And I'm fucking sure,' gloated Hector, 'that I'll be the one sending you back over a piece of dead Greek meat. But don't worry, the corpse won't be the loser either, not altogether. You can build your dead man a mound so fucking huge . . .'

Here he ran out of words.

A mound so high, so imposing under the clouds, the slow sunsets, that some seaman of the future, sailing the Hellespont, will easily descry it, looming up across the wine-dark sea, like a fist thrust up at Olympus, and he will tell his crew, 'See, brave lads, there is the monument of so-and-so, struck down in a duel by Hector in the ninth year of war in Troy. He must have died gloriously, don't you think? A beautiful death.'

A beautiful fucking death.

'The only thing left to decide now,' said Hector, 'is, who's the lucky fucker? Which of you Greeks wants to go for it, the big black mound? And the big fucking sleep?'

Silence in the ranks. Not a spear clinked, not a single piece of armour rattled. Every cunt sat tight and shat himself, terrified of being singled out. Volunteer and die. Sit still and shit again. Operation certain death. Who the fuck could blame them?

Menelaus could.

'You fucking NUBS! You're like a pile of frozen turds on a frosty fucking morning! Call yourselves men? Your bed-bitches have got more spunk in them. They sucked every last drop out of you last night and you've got fuck-all left for the fight. Well you can sit there and jerk off, every one of you – I'll go out and fight the motherfucker myself!'

And that would have been goodnight Menelaus if it had been serious, and if his brother and all his cronies hadn't jumped up to stop him, as the little shit knew perfectly well they were expected to do, and would. The gutless turd was only putting on a show.

'You're a brave man, brother,' said Agamemnon, affecting to go along with the histrionics, 'but you're no match for Hector. He'd chew you up and spit you out in seconds. There'd be fuck-all left of you to bury. Better leave this to a more equal fighter, somebody better matched – somebody like myself, for example, since that deserter rat Achilles is safe in his funk-hole and there are no men left in the field. It looks like it's down to me. It's no job for a leader, but if no other bugger has got the balls . . .'

Groans from the men, who could see precisely what the prick was up to, playing the same game as his arsehole of a brother. And to avoid further embarrassment Nestor stood up.

'Leaders, please, sit down. And listen to me, everyone. All of Greece would weep to hear of this. Ye gods, if only I had my youth again, instead of all these useless years on my back, I'd have been out there myself by now, long ago. I remember when the Arcadian spearmen fought the Pylian levies beneath the walls of Pheia. It was at the river Celadon, by the swift streams of Iardanus . . .'

The men relaxed their stiff limbs and lay at ease. They knew we were in for one of Nestor's long recalls, a mixture of diplomacy and nostalgia.

'It was exactly the same situation – we were challenged by their best fighter, a man called Ereuthalion, and he was some sight in his armour, let me tell you. That armour had once belonged to King Areithous. Everybody called him the Mad Maceman because he never fought from any distance at all, with a bow or even a spear. He always used a mace instead. He'd swing it about with amazing strength and skill – he could break whole ranks with it, and front lines just crumbled in front of him. Huge man, handsome too. Women went wet between the legs as soon as they saw him, so they said. He was some man.

'And when he finally met his end it wasn't because he was bettered in the field, not him. Lycurgus killed him by trickery – lured him into a narrow pass, where he was not only completely cornered but couldn't do his thing with his mace, and Lycurgus struck him right through the belly and back with his spear, easy as target practice, and stripped him of his armour. Whoever wore that armour looked like the war-god and nobody was ever beaten in it. He was Ares' man.

'Then Lycurgus grew too old to fight, as happens to the best of us, and he passed the armour on to Ereuthalion, his squire, another gigantic man, and it was the Maceman's armour he was wearing when he challenged us that day. The whole army was scared, each man too intimidated to take him on. But I was a spirited lad in those days. I had youth on my side and cupfuls of confidence. So I stepped out and stood up to him, and I killed him.

'It wasn't easy – don't misunderstand me. But if you tell yourself you can do a thing, that's half the battle. The funny thing was, after I'd killed him, I don't mind telling you, I was more scared of him dead than alive, he cut such a figure even sprawled out in the dust, all his length and breadth. He looked bigger lying down than standing up. A colossus. I recall asking myself, ye gods, did I really take on this titan, and kill him too? I must have been mad. But even big men must fall one day. They all have their day. And when they do, they hit the ground with a harder crash. That's how it will be with Hector too – who, by the way, is nothing like the size of the man I killed that day, big as he is. Hector will fall in his turn – to the better man. The only question is, which of you is the better man?'

Old Nestor had done it again, the cunning old cunt. He may have been the veteran stuck in his own heroic past, but his piece got nine men up on their hind legs, myself included. I thought I'd better show face, though I knew I'd be no match for Hector in a straight fight. I hoped Nestor would just pick somebody, but he said lots would have to be drawn. It was a one-in-nine chance, and it fell to Ajax. I'd survived another day.

Hector looked a bit pissed off when he saw who his opponent was going to be – the big ugly fat fucker himself. You had to admit he looked formidable behind his shield. It had been made from the hides of seven ferocious bulls. The eighth layer was bronze, and man and shield together stood like some tower that could never be taken. Fucking impenetrable. But Hector came out to meet him, and the two approached one another without flinching, not a blink.

They went through their war of words. Ready to die, cunt-head? Your job, arsehole! And after honour had been satisfied in the time-honoured way, they dropped the shit and engaged.

Hector threw first, and his cast pierced six layers, no less – Ajax displayed the damage later – but not the seventh. And there was still the bronze.

Then Ajax took his turn, and you could hear the spear go all the way through. He was a formidable thrower. But Hector swerved expertly and averted certain death. They each threw again after that, and the pattern repeated itself, non-penetration and missing the target – like a bad night in the brothels, quipped Menelaus, enjoying the spectacle. The cunt knew he was safe.

Insults, spears, and now the rocks. Hector picked up a big black jagged bastard and it bounced off the boss with a clang that could have been heard halfway across the Hellespont. Bull's-eye. The blackheads cheered. Ajax staggered back two lengths and tottered, but he wasn't going down. He flung down his shield, picked up a rock twice the size of Hector's, and charged him with it. Hector turned to run for it – then stopped, turned again and braced himself. So did both armies. When Ajax threw, you knew about it. There was a motherfucking crash.

Everybody rose. The shield was already weakened from Ajax's two spear-hits. Now it crumpled, jamming Hector under it as he went down, his arms and legs waving like some fucking beetle. Ajax charged up on him, ready to crush him. Hector was dead.

But the bastard was only briefly on his back. He rolled over, wriggled free of the shield and was on his feet in a flash, his sword drawn. Ajax was no dunce with the sword, but everybody knew Hector was ten times faster and he had a lot more skill. Now Ajax was fucked.

He was saved by Agamemnon, who yelled to the heralds for intervention. The light was failing and it was no great idea to continue the contest in the dark. Each man had acquitted himself well in the field. Enough was enough. Call it equal.

Boos from the blackheads. It was a cop-out, and they knew it. But the two combatants exchanged gifts of honour, Agamemnon killed a bull in recognition of Ajax's good stand, and we agreed to a cessation of hostilities for the day. Total relief all round, both sides. Nestor proposed a truce for the recovery of bodies and the building of a funeral pyre, with more time allowed for the erection of a barrow over it. The blackheads agreed.

What they didn't know was that Nestor's plan included using the mound as a base for building high walls with gates to protect the ships. A deep trench lined with stakes parallel to the walls would obstruct any attack.

But Priam used the opportunity to apologise for the Trojan perjury in breaking the first truce and surprised everybody by now offering a surrender of all the Spartan property. Paris even said he'd offer some of his own goods if it brought about the end of the war, but that he'd never surrender Helen. Agamemnon replied that Helen was the whole fucking point of the war, lying through his arse as usual.

So the war would continue. But it would be interrupted for as long as it took to find and bury our recent dead. An honourable business and one that shouldn't be rushed. The dead deserve decency, dignity, respect – and time. So we knew we'd get our walls and ditch under way while the mourning ceremonies were properly conducted and no one was looking.

We met at dawn, not to kill each other but to collect the killed and save what we could from the dogs and vultures. No easy task to distinguish friend from foe, even after we washed away the clotted blood and made out the facial features, if any were left to identify. Priam had forbidden outward mourning – no loud cries or wails, no cursing or abuse, and we tried to observe the same decorum as we milled about among one another, Greeks and Trojans rubbing shoulders in a solemn silence, stifling the curses, though the hot scalding tears dropped quietly on many a dead face.

Some ships happened to put in from Lemnos with a consignment of wine, one thousand gallons, a gift from Jason's son Euneus to the Atreidae. The rest of the cargo was traded for bronze, iron, hides, live beasts, women, slaves. That night we drank deep.

We ate well too, dining on the bull, and on slaughtered oxen that knew nothing of war but died anyway, as all living creatures must die, men or beasts. No distance away we could hear the enemy also wining and dining themselves in great style, drinking to their glorious dead. And for that space of time they sounded not like enemies at all but just like men, like us, men mourning their friends and kin, lamenting the curse of war, bloody war, the scourge of humankind. But our slaves were already building the fortifications on the bones of the dead, and there was ominous thunder all night long, disguising their labours, and telling the tremblers, those who listened to thunder and pondered its meaning, that the long list of the dead was far from complete, and that there were many more casualties yet to come in this long and bitter conflict.

TWENTY

Nestor nearly bought it after the truce. We'd only just got back into action when I spotted his third horse in difficulty. The worst kind. An arrow had struck the beast in the brain, and I could see it sticking out just at the place where the mane starts growing – a lethal spot for a steed. But it hadn't killed him outright, and he was rearing about in his death throes, throwing his companions into a complete balls-up. Nestor was still slashing at the reins when Hector came charging up at him, and the old bugger's life was suddenly in the scales.

I heard Diomedes yelling to Nestor to get his shield up, which he did, just as Hector's spear thudded into it. A breath between the old man and the pyre.

Diomedes shouted again. 'Leave the fucking horses! Get in here!'

Nestor didn't wait for the order to be repeated. He clambered up into the chariot beside Diomedes and the offensive swung suddenly against Hector. Diomedes hurled, Hector did his swerve, and the missile missed but killed the charioteer, Eniopeus, hitting him in the nipple and sinking deep into the chest. He let go of the reins with a shriek and keeled over out of the chariot, on a straight course to Hades.

'Fuck!'

Hector's grief was brief. He left Eniopeus dying in the dust and galloped off to find another driver, Archeptolemus, and got him in fast behind the team.

The thunder that had rumbled during the night erupted now into a sudden motherfucker of a storm, and a lightning bolt scorched the earth right in front of Diomedes' pair. Hector whooped.

'Thank you, god! Who says Zeus isn't a fucking Trojan?'

The horses reared and backed and nearly tumbled the two out of the chariot. Nestor dropped the reins but grabbed at them again, wheeled about and drove back to the ships, full gallop, with Diomedes screaming in his ear all the time to stop and turn around and face Hector. No fucking way. I joined them PDQ with the whole blackhead army and a hailstorm of spears at our backs. We were lucky to escape unscathed.

Hector's taunts harried us all the way, the bastard. 'Well run, pussies! You too, Odysseus! Home safely now, boys, back to your funk-holes, you splitters!'

Diomedes turned in the chariot, but it was trundling like fuck, almost airborne, and there was no way he could aim a spear at his pursuer.

Hector jeered. 'And you – you fuck, you were the one who was going to be first to scale our walls and rape our women! I'll see you in hell before then!'

Diomedes' face was black under this harangue. That bastard really knew how to wind him up. But when I glanced back, I could see Hector's grinning white teeth and the mad whites of the eyes underneath the helmet, and I knew he'd shortly be flinging more than insults. I shouted to Diomedes to protect himself, just as he was screaming at Nestor to stop and turn and let Hector have it.

'No you fucking won't!' I roared across at him. 'He'll be on you before you even take aim! Get your fucking shield up, man! And keep on going!'

Nestor kept on going and didn't stop till we reached the ships. That didn't mean we were safe. With the whole army behind him, Hector maintained the charge.

'On them, lads! Their walls won't hold – they're not even half up yet! And our horses will clear that idiotic ditch! Built during a truce! Never trust a fucking Greek, eh? Not even a dead one. Not unless he's on his pyre! So let's do some real damage here, lads, what do you say? Let's set the fuckers on fire!'

'Fire, fire, fire!' The last word was picked up by the infantry running behind the chariots. They roared their fucking heads off and the sound went over our heads like a wind. We could smell the torches now, see the flames, hear Hector's incendiary orders.

'I want to see those big black ones burning, one and all, and every fucking Greek go up with them! They'll have no place left to go! Let the sea dowse the bastards! Leave the old man for me. And that cunt Diomedes – he's mine!'

It was no secret that Hector fancied Nestor's shield. Made from solid gold, it was the talk of the gods, famous to the skies. He also wanted Diomedes' breastplate, so sweetly fashioned it could have come only from the fires of Hephaestus, forged on Olympus, and with the crippled smith's mark on it, so they said. So Hector, tamer of horses, spurred on Tawny and Whitefoot, Dusky and Dapple, calling to his driver to whip them harder, and relentlessly they sped towards the ships. It was payback time now for all Andromache's epicurean feeding, all that honey-sweet grain soaked in wine, and for all their fancy names they came at us like death. Hell followed them, and their hooves struck sparks out of Hades.

Worth a stand then? What else? When you see the end coming at you like that and the ocean is at your back, what else is there to do but make a stand? Agamemnon reminded us of how we'd lain in Lemnos, gorging our bellies on beef and bragging that one of us was worth a hundred Trojans, two hundred.

'You stuffed your fat arses that day, didn't you? Stuck your faces into the brimming wine-bowls till you were fucking legless. Each one of you was going to thrash a regiment, remember? Of course you don't, you drunken bums, strutting your stuff with not a fucking enemy soldier in sight, you pissheads! And now Hector shows up and you're shitting yourselves, even Diomedes! Shame on the lot of you, you nancy boys!'

That did it. Diomedes swung into action. He'd had an earful of insults already. He spotted Agelaos on the charge and made for him – a straight collision course. Agelaos lost his nerve and wheeled round his horses for an immediate retreat. Too late. Diomedes struck him beautifully between the shoulders and drove the spear all the way through and out the chest. He jerked it out again savagely, opening up the man's back, and parts of the heart came out, still twitching, attached to the bronze barbs. Agelaos crashed backwards out of the chariot and the dust swirled up around him.

Agamemnon whooped. 'And now the rest of you!'

The Ajaxes came out, leading their men in a counter-charge. So did Eurypylus and Idomeneus, with Meriones and Menelaus, and Agamemnon bringing up the rear, for all his tough talk. Teucer tucked himself well in, as ever, behind the shield of Big Ajax. They operated a well-tried system. Ajax would slowly shift his shield to one side to let Teucer select a target. He'd shoot a man stone dead in the crowd – he was a deadly accurate archer – and as soon as he saw the man fall he'd take cover again with Ajax, like a kid cowering behind its mother's skirts and peering out at danger. Quite right too. It was a dangerous world. And Ajax had seen him through it, coaching the little cunt how to be a clever sniper. And a snake in the grass.

'First find your target. Then wait till he's looking good. Hit your target before your target even knows you're fucking born. After that you're invisible again, right? Then it's eyes on again and it's goodnight number two. And so on. That way you'll do damage. You'll be hot shit and famous in the ranks and the enemy won't even fucking know who you are.'

And that's how Teucer now proceeded to massacre a careful selection of men. Under cover of Ajax, he took out Orsilochus, Ormenus, Ophelestes, Daetor, Chromius, Lycophontes, Amopaon and

Melanippus. One by one, they dropped into the bountiful lap of earth that both gives and receives. On this occasion, Teucer gave, and the insatiable earth received.

Agamemnon was ecstatic. 'Eight arrows and eight men down. Don't you ever fucking miss?'

Teucer fitted another arrow.

'If I do, I usually hit the target next to him. What does it matter? A dead man's a dead man. His name doesn't count.'

'Not unless it happens to be Hector,' said Agamemnon. 'That mad dog is still on the rampage. Can't you take him out for me?'

'I'll have a go,' said Teucer.

And he let fly, but Hector saw it coming and bent low beneath his shield. The arrow hit Gorgythion instead.

'What did I tell you?' said Teucer.

Gorgythion, son of Priam. His mother, the gorgeous bride Castianeira, shaped like a goddess. She came all the way from Aesyme to be wedded to Priam, and she blossomed in the belly at once, warming the old king's winter seeds. Thus she grew Gorgythion in her secret garden and brought him into the world. But now her grown-up flower droops beneath his own helmet's weight, his head sinks down, dropping to one side like a crimson poppy heavy with its own seed, bowing even more under the refreshing spring showers.

Agamemnon laughed.

'Well, it's Persephone's lap for that bastard.'

'Yes,' said Teucer, 'but I missed the main target. Let's try again.'

He took a second shot at Hector, who ducked once more, this time exposing Archeptolemus, who'd hardly been behind the horses any time at all. The arrow whanged into his shoulder.

'No problem,' said the charioteer. He grinned at Hector. 'It's only a flesh wound. I can live with it.'

Then he doubled up, screaming. Teucer's next arrow had bitten deep into his pubic bone.

'I'd like to see you live with that one,' laughed Teucer. 'At least you've got a good Greek arrow between your legs now – better than a Trojan pizzle!'

Archeptolemus fell from the chariot and went down in the dust, clutching at his groin.

Ah, how his girlfriend, the beautiful and seductive Euphronteia, had liked to play Cupid's arrow games with him as they lay together, shutting her eyes while her wandering hand wondered on which part of his body the little love-god's dart would land next. It was always the same part. But Teucer's arrow as his only erection would be no fun for either Archeptolemus or his girl.

'Fuck!' Hector's grief was brief again. 'My drivers keep fucking dying on me!'

And he left his comrade writhing in the dust, yelling to his brother, Cebriones, to jump up and take over the horses.

Cebriones did it with a grimace. 'A bad day for your charioteers, brother!'

But Hector had had enough of the incoming fire. He vaulted out of the chariot and charged straight at Teucer with a great lump of rock in his fists. Teucer had felt cocky enough to come out from Ajax's cover, and he was loosing off arrows thick and fast. He'd just selected the next arrow from his quiver, bitter with bronze for some poor fucker, when he saw Hector closing. He pulled back the string and took a quick aim. Too late. Hector was on him before he could fire. He smashed the rock down on Teucer's shoulder just where the collarbone connects to the neck and chest. The string snapped and he dropped his weapon. His right arm was now useless. He'd have died in the next second but for Ajax, who was up in a flash to cover him. Two comrades carried him back to the ships, and he howled all the way. Hector had buggered him. And that was the end of Teucer's archery. For the time being.

After that, Hector was unstoppable, and Agamemnon had no emergency defence plan. Sunset – that was our only EDP, as it so happened. And not a moment too soon. Hector withdrew his forces with the failing light. We breathed again and crashed out. We were fucking exhausted.

The blackheads didn't go far off, though. Some sort of field meeting went on and we saw some parties trooping into the town and coming back with firewood and supplies. Soon we caught the scents of roasting meat as hundreds of little fires bejewelled the darkness, reflecting the stars. Hector clearly hadn't abandoned his plan to burn the ships. He was going to camp out on the plain through till dawn, just in case we decided to make a dash for the open sea and home. Then we'd get some sharp arrows up our arses on the way out, just to give us second thoughts about ever coming back again. Either that or, with a good supper inside them, they planned on attacking again before sunrise as we slept.

No fucking way. We lit up too.

And so, all night long, the plains and beaches of Troy burned with a thousand campfires between Xanthus and the Grecian tents. They sparkled like the uncountable constellations on those magical nights when the upper air is quiet and windless and every mountain-top and headland stands out clear. The Milky Way up above was mirrored by the fires below, star for star reflected, as if the land were sea, and an image of the mighty heavens displayed beneath. And, for once, the magic was real – the warmth of the campfires, the smell of the roast meat, the taste of wine on the tongue, the muted laughter and chatter of men in the darkness, men divided by war but united by the common need to feed and sleep, by the majesty of the universe and the peace of nature, the night in its silence, the stars in their calm. It did seem silly that such a lovely night should be followed by such slaughter, that men who wondered at the stars should get up and kill each other and cough up their lives in the glaring light of another senseless day. And all the while the horses stood quietly by their chariots, happily champing the rye and white barley, mindlessly awaiting the dawn.

TWENTY-ONE

The night passed, as all nights do, and the dark sky rusted. Aurora stood naked in the cold ocean, stroking the east with rosy fingers. The tumbling waves went red, then gold. We were set for heavenly weather. It did seem a shame to have a war on such a day.

Apart from that, and although I'd been in more shit-holes than I could remember, this one made even shit smell sweet. An emergency meeting was called at first light. One big obvious question: what the fuck should we do next? And in the absence of any big obvious answers, our glorious commander actually came up with one himself. Perhaps, after all, we should call it a day and go home? Clearly we were as low as we could go on fortune's wheel. We'd lost the favour of the gods.

That much was a grasp of the fucking obvious and the way out was a shit suggestion, though naturally it produced loud rumblings of approval till Diomedes pitched in.

'What? You mean just fuck off? And eat the shit of defeat out of Trojan arses? Not me. I'd rather die. I don't know about the rest of you spineless shites but I'm staying here. Embrace the fucking suck. What about you, Odysseus?'

'I'll stay,' I said.

Nestor stood up.

'Well said, Odysseus. And Diomedes. As for you, Agamemnon, I will now discharge my mind concerning you and your leadership.'

He waited for the ripple of excitement to die down before resuming – with his slowest and most emphatic of deliveries.

'It's very simple. You've degraded a man of consequence, a man of honour. Our best man – certainly our best fighter. You've treated him shamefully, humiliated him in public, and all to satisfy your vanity and greed. You pulled rank to get what you wanted, what you weren't even entitled to. That much is incontrovertible. Now as to the present position: we're in a mess, and we need the Myrmidons to help us out of it. What you need to do – and you need to do it urgently – is this. You need to swallow your pride and apologise to Achilles. Admit you were out of order, say you're sorry, and do what you can to win him over before it's too late. What do you say? Am I getting through to you?'

Silence in the ranks for a few seconds. Then Agamemnon drew a deep one and spoke.

'Loud and clear, Nestor. CFB. I accept everything that you say. I was a shithead, I admit it. I'll try to put it right. I'll send Achilles an apology, a full one. And I'll accompany it with gifts.'

'You'll kiss Achilles' arse!'

A voice from the ranks.

'That goes without saying,' said Nestor, 'but they will have to be gifts of some substance.'

'They will be.'

'Of considerable consequence.'

'I hear you. They will be. Here's what I'll offer him — and this is just off the top of my head, you understand. Seven brand new tripods, ten talents of gold . . .'

'Stop!'

Nestor spoke in his sternest voice.

'You're not getting the feel of this, my boy!'

Agamemnon nodded impatiently. 'Let me get there. That's just the small fry. I'll also offer twenty copper cauldrons, not one of which has felt a lick of flame; ten — no, twelve prize racehorses; seven women, every one of them absolute beauties, and skilled craftswomen — they came from the sack of Lesbos.'

'Which was taken by Achilles, by the way.'

Nestor was keeping up the pressure.

'And you pocketed the spoils!'

The voice from the ranks again, this time drawing a loud clattering of swords.

'Yes, and now I'm giving back. And while we're about it, he can have Briseis back as well.'

'Now that you've fucked her from backside to breakfast time!'

Agamemnon wasn't having it easy. But he didn't lose his cool. He held up both hands as if in prayer.

'My oath on it, right here and now, I swear to the gods: I never laid a finger on her!'

'No — only your lawless fucking leg!'

'His godless fucking knob!'

'Up her arse twenty times a night!'

Agamemnon didn't rise to it. 'Ignoring all that filthy rabble backchatter, I'm not done yet. To the Lesbians I'll add twenty — yes, twenty — Trojan women, the paragons and apples of their race. And he can take his pick of all the other spoils from Troy, if only he'll help us take it, after he's got us out of the shit we're in now. He can load up his ships, all fifty of them, with all the gold and bronze they can carry.'

'Enough to sink his fucking fleet, eh?'

Nestor waved away the jibe and gestured with both palms upraised that more than enough had been offered. But Agamemnon had just got into his stride and was getting carried away with his new-found generosity. He was also basking in the atmosphere of general approval, a rarity for him, in spite of the cat-calls.

'You've heard fuck all yet, you ignoramuses at the back. Now for the jewel in the crown. Listen to this. He can also have his pick of my three daughters, Chrysothemis, Iphianassa and Laodice.'

'Why not make it four? Call Iphigenia back from the dead, why don't you?'

'When the war's over he can be my son-in-law, with a handsome dowry chucked in. What do you think of that, then? Any scoffers got anything left to say?'

'Yes. Are you fucking done showing off?'

'As a matter of fact I'm not. Did I say jewel in the crown? Make that jewels. I've got something else to offer.'

You had to hand it to the bastard. Most of the time he was a first-class cunt, but when he climbed down, he climbed down in style.

'After the choice of daughters, to top it all off, I'll offer him seven fine towns. Not his pick of the seven — do you hear what I'm saying? — I mean all seven. And they're none of them shit-holes either. I'll offer him Cardamyle, Enope, Hire, Pherae, Antheia and Aepeia.'

'That's only six!'

'And Pedasus. And fuck you. All seven.'

Seven seaside towns, kissed by the blue ocean, deep-meadowed, purple with vines, shambling with cattle, snowy with sheep . . .

'All in the farthest part of Pylos and all to die for. Their citizens are no shit-kickers, I've told you, and they're no fucking insurgents either, they're prosperous and peaceful, and they'll accept him as their overlord without question, on my say-so, and pay him tribute, no quibbling. I'll give him all of the above if he comes back on side right now. He doesn't even have to win the fucking war, just help us fight it. Clear? And after it's over, the cunt will be like a king. What do you think?'

The whole Assembly rose to its feet, cheering and stamping and waving swords. Nestor lost no time in nominating who should take this truly sumptuous offer to Achilles. Old Phoenix to go first, he said, followed by myself and Big Ajax, with Odius and Eurybates as duty heralds. We were to do everything we could to placate the sulking bastard and get him back to the front line.

Achilles was thrilled to see us. He may have liked to lounge about with the lyre, or with Patroclus's hand in his crotch, but he missed the sweat of fighting, the blood. He was born to kill. As soon as he saw us he jumped up and asked Patroclus to bring in a bigger mixing-bowl and go easy on the water. Nothing but the best for his old friends. And he saw to the fodder with his own fair hands – the backs of a sheep, a fat goat and the chine of a huge hog, laden with lard. He jointed the lot himself, carved the joints and spitted the slices. I admired his expertise. Then we tucked in for a good hour till we were all well stuffed.

'Right then,' he said, 'it's clearly a deputation. You didn't come here to drink to old times. What's on your mind, lads?'

They all looked at me. I took a slow swig.

'Achilles, I'll give it to you straight. We're fucked. Unless you come in with us. The enemy is practically on the ships. They're all set to fucking burn us. We need backup fast. We need your regiment. Either you bring them into the field or it's goodbye Troy and goodbye Argos. We'll never see home again.'

I went through Agamemnon's impressive catalogue of offers, building up from the tripods and the talents to the bigger stuff, the horses, the Lesbians, the twenty Trojan charmers, the pick of the dowried daughters, the seven seaside cities. And Briseis back untouched. Agamemnon would even take the oath he'd never been up her, back or front. I laid it on thick. If I'd listened to myself, I'd have been so convinced I'd have gone to bed with Agamemnon. I'd have bent over for the fucker.

'Quarrels are deadly, Achilles. They defeat armies, split nations. And pride can be lethal. Time to climb down now. He's done it. What about you? What do you say?'

Say? At first the bastard son of Thetis said fuck all. Stony silence. Not a fucking word. We waited.

'Achilles –'

'I heard you, Odysseus, and I'm considering my answer.'

Silence again. Then he stood up.

'Well, here it is.'

And the cunt let rip.

He hated Agamemnon worse than hell gates. Hated him for his hypocrisy as much as for his greed. And for his total lack of respect for his men, not to mention better men than himself, the big ugly fat fucker with his fistful of bribes.

We were getting the general picture but Achilles was clearly going to round it out to the last detail.

'Seven seaside towns does he say? The slippery bastard. I took those fucking towns, twelve of them if he wants to count, heaps of spoil, and all handed over to a leader who led from behind and *on* his behind, while I stuck my neck out in the front line every single time. And for what? Dribs and fucking drabs. He kept the lion's share for himself. That's how it works. You risk your skin and he does the raking in. Every single time. You get the bronze, he gets the gold, the sweat of the gods, every time.'

A little throat-clearing from Phoenix – but nobody could deny the truth of what Achilles was saying. We waited. He hadn't finished.

'Then he went on to rob me of my woman. And now he wants to give her back, does he, the grovelling bastard, still smelling his own fucking musk, even when he's arse-licking. Well he can stick his sorry sweeteners up his arse. He's a swindler and a trickster and a cheat. And always will be. As for his seaside towns, they're less to me than a pot to piss in, you can tell him that. You can tell him he can offer me the sun and the moon and it won't win me over. They'd be tarnished by association. I have no interest in any of his offers, or in helping him out of the crap-pit he's got us into. I don't give a flying fuck for him and his war of greed. I've had it up to here. And I don't give a fuck for his daughters, either. I don't care if they come with silver tits and golden arses. I don't care if they come with cunts like Aphrodite's. They're not worth the sea-dust on your horse-cock. Marry a daughter of Agamemnon's? I wouldn't even piss on the bitches. Have I made myself clear?'

As a fucking bell.

'If not, let me spell it out for you once and for all. I am not going to accept anything from that greedy thieving arsehole, and I'm not going to help the cunt out either. What I will do, however, is this. I'll load up my ships tomorrow and clear out. In three days from now, if I get a good crossing, I'll be back where I should have stayed in the first place, with my feet set firmly on good old Phthia and the deep soil of home. And I'll never leave my country again to serve in a fiasco like this. Never, never, never.'

A long pause. The others looked at me round-eyed.

'Is that it, then?' I asked. 'Are you done?'

A grim smile.

'Nothing more to say?'

What more could he have said?

Quite a lot, in fact, if he'd wanted to. Or had been capable of it. He could have expanded on his last point and said that here in Troy he was sick for home as a man in a desert is thirsty for water, he craved it that much. He could have said that at home he'd have some hope of living, because war is not living, it's existing, surviving, nothing more, from hour to hour, day to day. He could have asked what life is, after all. Could have said that it is not something that can be compared with the legendary wealth of Troy, even though it may be there for the taking. Could have pointed to horses and cattle and asked what they are but beasts, nothing in the mould of a man. Could have said that cauldrons and tripods can be lost or won, bought and sold, forged and stolen, damaged, discarded, but that you can't buy back a man's breath once it's left his body, once the life has left the lips and the spirit has flown, you can't steal back his soul from the dark.

He could have said that Agamemnon didn't even speak the same language, didn't understand the difference between daughters and tripods and Lesbian women, and didn't understand another man's hurt pride because pride is an abstraction. You can't weigh pride. Or eat it, or fuck it. That Agamemnon was too steeped in his own meticulous and blind brute mania for power even to begin to understand the language of Achilles. That kind of learning was just too steep a curve for him. He was fucking clueless.

He could have said all that. He could have made the speech of a lifetime, the one Penelope gave him in the web, the one he never made, with lovely Phthia looking idyllic in the background, and his old father standing in the doorway waiting for him far from the hell of Troy. He could have said that we were all on our way to the grave, with no choice in the matter, but that his particular journey could go one of two ways: remaining in Troy and resuming hostilities, in which case he knew for sure he'd earn the immortality of the hero – 'I'll end up dead, in other words,' he could have continued, 'the oblivious recipient of posthumous fame, the worst kind. I can feel it, Odysseus, I can feel it in my bones, an early exit and no homecoming. Or I do go home, to obscurity and long life. An anonymous old man, a one-eyed veteran if I'm lucky, with nothing to do but stare at the sky. Or a dead hero. It can't be both. I've got to choose. And I've chosen. So you can go right back and tell your leader which it's going to be. You can tell him where to shove his towns and his daughters and his war of aggression. I can do without any of them. So there's no point in him sending you or anybody else again. He can send Hermes himself and it will make no difference. I won't even be there to listen. I'll be long gone.'

That's what he could have said, if he'd had any sliver of philosophy in him. Or a drop of poetry. But Achilles was no man of fine speeches; he was a killer. Agamemnon had made his offers and Achilles had rammed them right back up his arse. And that was that.

Phoenix did have a go, as Nestor had asked him to, and we refilled our wine cups. Sure enough, we got the old man's life story, how he'd dandled Achilles on his knee, fed him with his own hand, held the cup to the clumsy little lips and mopped up the slobberings and spillages from both their clothes, stained by Achilles' infant dribblings . . .

'You were the son I never had,' concluded Phoenix. 'Come over to us now, while the gifts are still on offer and before you feel the flames eating up the ships, yours included. By then it will be too late. Or if it isn't, and you are forced to act on your own impulses instead of heeding Agamemnon's entreaties, you could still save the army, being the great soldier that you are, but he may withdraw the gifts. And you may yet be forced to fight, for reasons that are hidden still in the clenched fist of destiny, but you'll fight for no reward. Not unless you come out and fight now.'

Phoenix let his words sink in.

And with what result?

None whatso-fucking-ever. Achilles was happy to think of the old man as a second father, but he didn't give a toss for Agamemnon's inducements, whether they came with a moral entitlement or didn't come at all. As for the sentimental stories about his childhood and his infantile eating habits, these were an embarrassment and he begged not to be reminded of them.

'In conclusion, Phoenix, an old man's breath is limited and therefore precious. Don't waste any more of it. I piss on your leader's greasers and I piss on him. And I piss on the Greek army that let him get away with it. Fuck them one and all!'

Phoenix put his head in his hands, but Ajax erupted.

'Well fuck me! What a fucking display! Rancour and arrogance and fucking obstinacy all the way! You're full of fucking malice, you are! And what gets me is that it's all over a girl, one solitary fucking girl. A piece of arse. And you've been offered seven – twenty fucking seven. And all the rest! Are you fucking mad? The big fuck has climbed down. Why can't you? Why can't you fucking unbend, just a little? I'm telling you, your fucking stubbornness will kill you in the end!'

Waste of air. He wasn't even offended. He even agreed with much of what Ajax said, but it altered nothing. He just couldn't forgive what had been done to him. He did ask Phoenix to stay the night and ordered the women to make him up a bed. Achilles turned in with a girl he'd abducted from Lesbos. Patroclus took a slave from the sack of Enyeus, a girl called Iphis. Phoenix slept in the corner.

We left them to it.

Back in Agamemnon's quarters, everybody crowded in, eager to hear the outcome of the embassy. I didn't embellish it, didn't spin it out.

'This is my report,' I said, 'and Ajax can back it up. He pisses on you and on all your offers. At dawn tomorrow he'll be launching his ships for Argos. And he advises the rest of us to do the same. The war's over.'

Agamemnon was stunned. And speechless. He went black with rage.

Diomedes found his voice.

'He was always a conceited cunt,' he said, 'a hard proud bastard. Fuck him. Shit floats, but I hope the fucker sinks before he reaches home. As for me, I'm staying. And those without balls can piss off with the Phthian cunt. The rest of us — let's get a good night in the sack. Tomorrow we may have the fight of our fucking lives on our hands. What do you say?'

Unanimous applause.

But it was a muted applause, a ripple. We were all thinking about what tomorrow might bring.

TWENTY-TWO

A lone god stands high on Olympus, the stars scattered around him like seeds in spring flung from the swinging hand of the sower, a chaos of light in the immense darkness. The god can't sleep. He looks out across the constellation of campfires down below, burning before Troy. And he listens to the sounds of the flutes and the reed pipes, the low drone of the soldiers, their mutterings and grumblings muted by distance and sharpened by darkness, the crude comfortable noises of humanity. He bends his ear to the Trojan side. They sound relaxed, as if they are going next day not to war but to a dance or a party. Now he inclines his ear to the Greeks and detects Agamemnon's tossings and turnings. The enemy exudes confidence, and he feels the opposite. His own leadership is in tatters. He gets up and dressed.

Menelaus is doing the same. He appears in his brother's tent and, after a brief word, goes to rouse the other leaders, including Nestor. The old man's advice is simple. What is needed now, and needed desperately, is intelligence, up-to-date information about the enemy's strategy and battle-plan. And the best way to obtain that intelligence is to find a Trojan straggler, cut him off and bring him back to the camp, or at least bring back the necessary information. What is needed now is a raid.

Everybody goes quickly quiet. But the inclining god hears the muttered curses.

'Hell! A fucking raid! Somebody's balls are in the scales . . . who'll be the lucky cunt?'

The god grins briefly. Such words, thinks the god, are like shields and spears, part of the soldier's battle-pack. It was ever thus. He sighs. And waits to see who and what will emerge, far down below.

It was Diomedes who stepped up.

'Nestor, I'll be brief. The idea of a raid actually appeals to me. I think you're right. But we all know what it means to be caught between enemy lines and given the spy treatment. I'll go, but only if I have the right man to go with me. It's easy to kill a man when you're out there on your own in the dark, but a hundred times harder to bring the fucker in alive or make him sing. You know what they say — a corpse sings no songs. A dead man doesn't even fart. Give me a good partner and I'm your man.'

Nestor looked around.

'Anyone?'

'I wouldn't mind paying the Trojans a visit,' I said, breaking the silence. After that, dozens of brave cunts volunteered, knowing full well they were safe and that Diomedes would choose me.

Which he did.

'Right,' I said, 'the less breath wasted the better. Zero dark thirty — that ought to have been the time for this caper. Look at the stars. The night's two-thirds gone already — we're into the last watch. Let's move.'

We went out into the black starry night, sticking to the shadows and picking our way through the strewn corpses of the field.

⑀

And the lone god went into action. He should have stayed on Mount Olympus. But if truth is the first casualty in war, the impartiality of the gods comes next. The lone god was a devotee of Hera, that hater of Trojans, and, to win favour with her, he sped down to the Trojan camp and selected a man called Dolon, who was listening to Hector address the leaders in the Assembly.

'What do you think — are these Greek bastards up for it? I mean, are they actually ready for combat? Or are they considering a retreat, possibly complete withdrawal? We've got the bastards on the back foot, yes. The question is, are they completely fucked? They may be so fucked up they haven't even set a proper watch. Who'd like to find out?'

Silence.

'I thought as much. Whoever does it will be risking his neck, that's for sure. But not for nothing. I'll give the top team of horses in the Greek army to the man who carries out this mission — even if it doesn't produce a result.'

Dolon was suddenly standing up and speaking, taking himself by surprise. He felt possessed. He was a rich man, well stocked with gold and bronze. Not much to look at — the only son in a family of six children — but he was quick, a nippy runner, and the perfect man to cover the ground. He was also acquisitive. The lone god had chosen well.

'I'll do it, Hector,' he said. 'On one condition — that the horses and chariot you give me from the spoils are the ones driven by Achilles.'

Hector frowned.

'Fuck you, Dolon. I meant apart from those – I've earmarked them for myself.'

Dolon grinned.

'I'm sure you have. But you said the best in the Greek army, and these are the best. Everyone knows that. Let me have them and I'll do the job for you all right. I'm not sticking my neck out for second best.'

Hector spat.

'Double-fuck you, Dolon – but done. They're yours. You'll be driving them for the rest of your days.'

Neither knew that Dolon's days were numbered.

The lone god knew, though. He watched as Dolon picked up his bow and javelin, slung the pelt of a grey wolf over his shoulders, fitted a weaselskin cap on his head and set off in the dark for the Greek ships that he'd never reach. The god took the wings of the approaching dawn and sped off again up to high Olympus to report to Hera.

We weren't far into the field when I felt Diomedes' hand over my mouth.

'BMO!' he hissed.

Diomedes was like a cat in the dark – fantastic eyesight. He'd seen the black moving object slinking among the dwindling lights of the campfires and stars. I nodded, took his hand from my mouth and whispered back.

'Some fucker's got exactly the same idea as us. How should we play it?'

Diomedes brought his lips close up to my ear. His beard tickled.

'Lie low and let the cunt go by. It's a blackhead spy. We'll double back and snatch the bastard once he's past. They've probably volunteered a good runner, so you're the man, Odysseus. If he's too fast for you, threaten him with your spear. But don't kill him, whatever you do. Keep heading him off in the direction of the ships. Away from his own lines.'

We lay down among the many dead that lay rotting and unburned. Some skulls were packed tight with earth. They were the long lost ones, skeletons unclaimed by either side. Among them were the fresher corpses that still smelled of flesh and blood. The BMO flitted past us, deftly threading its way among the stiffs. We waited a minute or two, and then we ran after him.

He heard us and hesitated. The poor bugger probably thought it was friends sent to call him back. Why else would anyone be running at him from the Trojan side? Perhaps Hector wanted the mission called off.

'He's thought better about it, the greedy bastard! He wants to keep those fucking horses for himself!'

But when it got through to him that we were Greeks, the bastard panicked and put on a spurt. He was a good runner. He was also a stupid fucker, legging it in the wrong direction and making straight for our lines.

'He'll be at the outposts in less than a minute!'

'He will at that rate,' I said.

'Fuck it! The sentries are going to kill the stupid bastard unless we stop him. Then some other cunt will get the glory and we'll have nothing to report!'

He let fly with his spear but threw to miss. The weapon whistled over Dolon's right shoulder and thudded into the dust. It stuck there, swaying and vibrating, and a plume of dust particles flew up, weirdly lit by the embering camp fires. Dolon stopped and stiffened.

'That's right,' Diomedes hissed at him, 'Freeze or you're dead! Stand still and you live!'

The man's face was chalk-white in the paling darkness. He was scared shitless.

'Don't kill me, please!' he wailed.

'Keep your fucking voice down!' Diomedes hissed at him again.

'Yes, yes, just don't kill me, please! I'm rich. So's my father. Take me back to the ships and he'll make it well worth your while. Just take me alive, I'm begging you.'

I put my finger on his lips. He was trembling all over.

'Get a grip on yourself, man! And quieten down, or the fucking sentries will hear you and we'll all be under fire, do you hear? Don't be so scared – that's the last thing we want. Now calm down and tell us just what you're up to. Are you out to spy – or are you just a filthy looter?'

'A looter, me? Never, no, I told you, I'm stinking rich. No, Hector sent me.'

'Why?'

'He wanted to find out if the ships are guarded. Or if you've given up and are ready to retreat.'

'I see. And were you sent or did you volunteer? Tell me the truth and be quick about it, because I'll tell you something for nothing. I can always tell when a shifty little bastard is lying, and I react badly to being lied to. I lose control. I do terrible things to a man. I can't help myself. I kill him so slow he's screaming at me to get a move on. And that upsets my concentration and I go even slower. So I think you'd better tell me now.'

'All right, all right – I volunteered.'

'Why?'

Dolon tried a nervous smile. 'Bravery?'

'Or bribery?'

Panic filled his eyes.

'Yes, I can see it in your face. You were bribed. The truth again now – quick, you little cunt! What were you offered?'

I pointed my spear at one of his eyeballs.

'All right, OK, OK – I was offered Achilles' horses and chariot.'

'Achilles' team? Really? But I don't understand – the horses are with Achilles, and Achilles isn't even in the game right now, as I'm sure you're aware. So how could Hector hope to lay his filthy fingers on those horses and just give them to you?'

Dolon swallowed. 'What he meant was, he'd give them to me once we'd – once he'd defeated you.'

'Ah, I see, once you'd defeated us. So it wasn't bravery that motivated you. Or loyalty. Or patriotism. It was greed.'

'And fucking presumption!' Diomedes broke in. 'I ought to cut your balls off for that! What makes you think you're going to beat us, eh?'

Dolon flinched.

'Never mind that,' I said. 'You'll have to forgive my comrade. Have you met Diomedes, by the way? Now *he* is patriotic, a true fucking patriot. He'd kill anyone who isn't a Greek. Any fucker at all. You, for example. But the point is – returning to the subject of your little visit across the lines – you were just itching to get your thieving hands on those horses. A fantastic prize, I grant you. And I have to congratulate you on your taste. No, no, I admire it, I really do. But can I just tell you – spirit of helpfulness and all that – Achilles' horses, well, they're hard to handle, a nightmare actually, for anybody except Achilles. They're high-spirited, you see, and I suspect they're made of sterner stuff than you, my friend. Frankly, I don't think you're strong enough for them. Because, if you don't mind my saying so, you're no hero, just a common thief. A snooper and a sneak. A little fucking land-rat. Do you mind my plain speaking? You don't mind if I humiliate you a little, do you? Maybe that's all I'll do. Rather than kill you, I mean.'

Dolon dropped like a shot and clasped my knees.

'No, no, humiliate me, please! I want you to. Only don't kill me. You haven't heard the details of the ransom yet. This could be your lucky day. I'll make you rich. And I'll tell you anything you want to know.'

'I think you'd better,' I said, 'and I appreciate your offer, I really am interested, and it's very kind of you. I do actually have a few questions for you, and I'd like you to be quick with the answers now – none of your fibs and fudges. Got it? Don't take time to think about it. Instant replies. Are you ready?'

'I'm ready.'

'Right then. And in the following order. One: where was Hector when you left him just now? Two: where was his gear? Three: where were his horses? Four: how are your sentries arranged and where are the other men sleeping? And five: what's the next move? Are they planning on returning to the city, or do they intend to take advantage of their advanced position? Don't let me confuse you – I'm simply asking if they intend an immediate all-out attack, or not. Which is it? The truth now, in all cases, and don't make a meal of it. Be succinct.'

Dolon kept nodding furiously throughout the questionnaire. He couldn't wait to complete it.

'I've no problem with these questions, on the whole. Right now, Hector is in a meeting with his advisers. They're holding a night conference by King Ilus's tomb. Do you know it? Very quiet.'

'Naturally. And you're right, a tomb's a nice quiet place for a conference. No fear of being disturbed, eh? No input from the dead, no barracking, no time-wasting opinions. Good, that's a good answer, a good start. I like your style. Maybe I won't kill you after all. Carry on.'

'Well, I'm not entirely sure about questions two and three, I swear to you, but I can tell you that Hector wasn't armed when I left him, and I imagine that he left his gear in his tent, and his horses will be close by. As for question four, regarding the sentries, nothing special was arranged. Every unit's got a fire, as you can probably see. The sentries keep signalling to each other to stop themselves from nodding off, that's all. The allies aren't even on guard – they don't have their women and children to worry about, not like us. They leave it to us to keep watch.'

'Makes sense.'

'Yes. Now question five –'

'Hang on, I want more detail on that last point. Where exactly are your allies tonight? How are they deployed? Spell it out for me. You really are doing very well so far.'

'Well, the Carians and the Paeonians are closest to the sea; so are the Leleges, the Caucones and the Pelasgi. There are also those units that have been allocated to the area near Thymbria – that's the Lycians, the Mysians, the Phrygians and the Maeonians.'

'Fucking hell, soldier, I think I'll make you a general – in the Greek army! You're a military genius. How'd you like that, eh?'

Dolon laughed and started to relax. 'It's a good offer. Frankly, I don't mind which side I'm on, so long as I'm paid. Actually, I'm wondering if I can offer you a good piece of advice – unsolicited?'

'Go ahead.'

'Why worry about all that lot – the allies, I mean – when you can much more easily attack those Thracian bastards at the end of the line? I don't like them much. They're new arrivals and cocky little cunts, so fucking sure of themselves, strutting around already, thinking they're going to win the war for us. And their leader, Rhesus, he has the best horses I've ever seen.'

'Apart from Achilles' you mean.'

'Yes, well, that goes without saying.'

'You've got something of an eye for a fine horse, haven't you?' I winked at him. And at Diomedes.

'I don't mind admitting it,' Dolon grinned. 'I wasn't serious about Achilles' horses, by the way.'

'Not serious? Why the fuck not? They're unparalleled. Nothing on four legs can touch them. I could let you see them at close quarters. I could introduce you to Achilles. He might even consider giving them to you – as a gift, you know?'

That made Dolon laugh a lot more than was necessary. 'Now you're teasing me. No, I told you, it was all a bit of a joke, a misunderstanding. I was never really serious.'

'Of course you weren't. I wasn't serious about introducing him to you either. Not safe. He's a killer. Always on the lookout for a fight. And you wouldn't want to fight the great Achilles now, would you?'

'Not if I could avoid it!' Dolon couldn't stop laughing now. 'But let me answer question five.'

'Question five? Do you know, I've forgotten the question myself, what with all this chinwagging. You're away ahead of me again. Remind me, will you?'

'Our tactics. Our next move, remember?'

'Ah yes, that's right. Of course. But you know something? I think I can deduce your next move from everything you've said already. Let me save you the trouble of going over that one. Instead, I'll tell you what, why don't you tell me more about those fabulous horses that belong to Rhesus? I like the sound of them.'

'Do you want a full description?'

'General will do. I'd like to be able to recognise them, that's all.'

'That's easy. They're whiter than snow. And swifter than the wind.

That's how you can tell them.'

'An absolutely original description. You should have been a poet. Do you play the lyre?'

'Well, I –'

'Never mind. And the chariot?'

'Chariot?'

'I'm willing to wager such horses pull no ordinary chariot.'

'Ah, right you are. Magnificently made, yes, a masterpiece of art, all tricked out in silver and gold. That bastard Rhesus denies himself nothing. And he's got golden armour too and wears it off the field just to show off, the swaggering little fart. Just one piece of it would make your mouth water. It's fit for Ares.'

'You don't say.'

'In fact, if I were you, I'd pay Rhesus a visit before morning. He's had plenty to drink – they all have, a good skinful, the whole regiment, drunk as cunts, ever since they arrived. I can take you to his position if you like, point him out.'

'No, no, that won't be necessary. Thanks anyway, but I think I'll pick him out from your description. You really are a mine of information – absolutely priceless!'

'Yes, and what with the way they're positioned, that armour is yours for the taking. And the horses. And the chariot. But tell me, what's the plan? Are you going to take me straight back to the ships? Or take me with you across our lines? I could be useful there. Or do you want to tie me up and leave me here till you've checked out all my information? I promise I won't try to escape.'

I clapped a hand on his shoulder and gave it a squeeze.

'Well, Diomedes, what do you think? Back to the ships? Take him with us? Tie him up? He's certainly played fair by us – more than fair. He's given us a lot more than we asked for. What's the verdict?'

Diomedes peered at me in the dimness, trying to read my expression. He wasn't a good reader of tone either. He looked down at Dolon, who was still kneeling.

'He's played fair by us all right. But he's played fucking foul by his own side. He's a treacherous little shit. And do you know what? I have the feeling that he'd change sides like the weather, and be a thorn in everybody's fucking flesh. Whereas if I just cut the cunt's throat right here and now, he won't be bothering anybody. Or betraying them.'

Dolon looked up at me desperately.

'He's got a point,' I sighed. 'You can't deny it. But let's try it to one more time. Diomedes, don't you think, though, that he could be useful?'

Diomedes shrugged. 'Useful, how? He's told us all he knows. What more do we need from him? His own lot don't need him either, do they? He's not exactly the bravest soldier in Troy, is he? Or the truest. Better at running than fighting, if you ask me. And not even a champion at that. No, I think if you want my opinion, this little cunt's better out of the war.'

Dolon lifted up his hand, meaning to touch Diomedes' bearded chin. At the same time he started to speak, to plead for his life.

He didn't have time. Diomedes unsheathed his sword and swung it at Dolon's neck all in one go. It was expertly done. He slashed through both tendons, and the blood gushed from the trunk, its arm upraised for clemency. Dolon was still speaking when his head hit the dust, and the last sentence was never completed, though the mouth kept on twitching curiously, as if the dying brain was frustrated at not being able to convey the words, his lips, teeth and tongue still busy trying to articulate the thought.

Not for too long, though.

'Nice hat,' I said.

I picked up the head, which had stopped speaking, and removed the weaselskin.

'Pity about the blood.'

'Fucking blood – gets everywhere. Nice wolfskin too,' said Diomedes, stripping it from the bleeding trunk.

The pelt was more badly bloodstained. Weirdly, the trunk hadn't fallen but was still upright, on its knees, and the blood had fountained all over the fur.

'Fuck,' said Diomedes. He held the garment up. 'Finders keepers?'

'It's a deal,' I said. 'Wolf to you, weasel to me. Maybe they're made to match us.'

'I'll tell you what, let's leave these items here – they'll be safe enough – and collect them on our way back.'

'From the Thracians?'

'You, Odysseus, are a fucking mindreader.'

'And you are the fountain of commonsense. This head has told us all it had in it, and all we needed to know. There's bugger all to be gained from calling on the Trojans tonight. But the Thracians now . . .'

We ditched Dolon's things in a nearby tamarisk bush and marked the spot with an armful of twigs and a fistful of reeds.

'Wait a minute,' said Diomedes, 'what about this fucker?'

'What about him?'

'I don't know. He looks stupid, just kneeling there, and without even a fucking head.'

'Stick it back on then,' I said.

I tried it out. Diomedes squinted at it, frowned, then rearranged it, back to front.

'Looks wrong every which way.'

'Stupid cunt. Better lying down, don't you think?'

Diomedes placed his foot in the middle of Dolon's chest and kicked. The trunk fell and the head rolled off a few paces.

'A slight improvement,' I said. 'He had a stupid face anyway. Better without it. Let's go.'

We quickly picked a path through the corpses till we reached the Thracian camp.

Dolon's information had been impeccable. There they all were, drunk asleep, just as he'd said, their gear all stacked up close by. Rhesus was in the middle, his horses tethered to the end of the chariot rail. The golden armour gleamed in the approaching dawn.

'There's our target,' I whispered. 'You do the men, the nearest ones. I'll get the horses.'

Diomedes leapt into the camp roaring like a lion, spreading terror, stabbing left and right, killing with lightning speed. The infernal noise he made was hardly necessary, I thought, though I knew he was fond of screaming – he thought it paralysed the enemy with fear just long enough to kill him. I followed him like a gleaner, hauling each corpse clear by the foot to make way for the chariot and mounts. Twelve men got the chop in as many seconds, and Rhesus was number thirteen. He was still fast asleep when Diomedes came up and stole the life from him. His heavy breathing came to a stop.

'Dolon was right,' said Diomedes. 'That bastard's breath stank of booze. And he was farting in his sleep. The world's a sweeter place without him.'

I unfastened the stamping horses and tied them together. There were shouts and clatterings from further up the line. Diomedes' war-cries had wakened the entire Trojan army.

'Let's get the fuck out of here!'

We didn't forget the tamarisk bush near where Dolon and his head were lying. As soon as we'd collected his things we made for the ships. Everybody crowded round. Nestor was ecstatic.

'Odysseus, you never return from an adventure empty-handed.'

'Excuse me,' said Diomedes, 'I was there too.'

'First among equals, you two,' laughed Nestor. 'But where did you get these horses? I've never seen the like. Surely some god met you on the way!'

'We ran into a god, all right,' I said. 'A god of information. But the Olympians don't drive these beasts – Rhesus does. Or rather did. They were his.'

'Are the Thracians here?'

'New arrivals. Thirteen fewer than they were. We killed fourteen altogether tonight.'

'Who was the fourteenth?'

'A spy called Dolon. We spied the fucker before he spied us. He did plenty of talking. An insane talker. He completely lost his head!'

'Sounds like the Diomedes touch.'

'The very same.'

Laughing together, we all went over the trench. I stored Dolon's bloody pelts in my ship. Diomedes decided against the wolfskin but kept the weapons we'd taken from him. Then we went into the sea to wash the sweat from ourselves. We were filthy. After that, we freshened up in the polished baths, got the oil on, dressed and sat down to a very late supper, well earned. It was a lot closer to breakfast, as a matter of fact. But we ate well and supped some stuff. Made Dionysus – or indeed any other god who happened to be up at that hour – look sober.

TWENTY-THREE

Agamemnon arms at dawn and Penelope arms in style. This is his day of glory.

His cuirass fairly sparkles – of its parallel strips, ten are of dark-blue enamel, twelve of gold, twenty of tin. On either side, three snakes rise in coils to the neck. You can almost hear them hissing at the jugular. But they are beautiful, works of art. Made of iridian enamel, they shimmer like rainbows.

The shield is otherworldly: ten concentric bronze rings and twenty studs of glittering tin round a dark-blue enamel boss. Its centrepiece is the grim Gorgon's head with awesome eyes, flanked by Panic and Rout. More a weapon than a piece of armour. You could crush a skull with it, or a man's chest.

The helmet has four plates and is double-crested with a purple horsehair plume. The greaves glitter with silver clips, and as well as his sword he carries a brace of spears of exceptional length. He looks the part of a leader, outshining even Achilles and Hector, though the latter looks the more ominous, if less glorious, like a malignant star that sallies out from a cloud and plunges suddenly into the mist, filling the sky with portent.

And now the two armies approach each other.

Picture the long row of reapers who start their day from opposite ends of a wealthy landowner's field, advancing inexorably on each other, scything down the swathes of barley until at last they meet in the middle with laughter and handshakes and relief, throw down their implements and sit and drink together in the sudden stubble, strewn with lopped poppies, among the freshly scented sheaves.

So Greeks and Trojans advance, except that they meet not for fellowship and refreshment and ease but for the bloody struggle, the conflict with only one outcome for many. For few will part where many meet . . .

They clash. And men fall and sway in swathes like the corn, the killers and the killed. The gods sit high on Olympus, exulting in the spectacle, glorying in the jar and jangle, the flash and clatter of bronze, the heaps of dead.

'Forward, you motherfuckers!'

We fought under a cloudless sky. Olympus stood bare and empty, no gods to be seen. Or heard.

'Murder the cunts, come on! Let's do some fucking damage here!'

We broke the front line first time. Agamemnon wiped out Bienor and Oileus, his driver, using up both spears. The driver got it first. The spear impacted so hard it pierced the helmet and sank deep into the bone of the forehead. Bienor got the same treatment, bone and brain giving way to bronze. Agamemnon stripped the pair of them and left them lying naked, their limbs ghostly white.

Then he wasted Antiphus and Isus, legitimate and bastard sons of Priam, both in the same chariot. The two spears again. The first one hit Isus in the chest. Antiphus ducked the second and briefly saw it bounce off a chariot.

'Bloody hell!'

He gasped with relief and breathed again. The bastard couldn't believe his luck. But just as he stood back up and glanced over his shoulder Agamemnon split open his head at the ear and stuff came out.

'Fucking beauty!'

He stripped that pair too and left them lying bare. Then he killed Peisander and Hippolochus – next of kin Antimachus, their father. He was the one who'd stood up in the Trojan Assembly when I went with Menelaus on the peace mission and he'd said we should be butchered on the spot. Agamemnon remembered that when he saw the pair of them in a spot of bother. They'd lost control of their horses and their chariot was all over the place. Agamemnon charged up.

'Let me help you out!'

He struck Peisander in the chest with his long spear and knocked him off the chariot.

'There you go!'

Hippolochus didn't wait. He jumped out, scared shitless, and stood with both arms held up, begging for mercy.

Agamemnon bent down and slashed each arm off at the shoulder. Hippolochus hardly had time to change expression before his head was slashed off too.

Agamemnon didn't let it go at that, though. He jumped down and gave each of them a pussy wound, a post-mortem cut in each head, a terrible one, even in the case of the disembodied head. It was a lesson to their father, he said, to treat ambassadors with some respect.

'Now you'll know, you old fuck, how to behave!'

He stripped their corpses too. His arms were steeped to the elbows by this time, red as a butcher's, and his face was spattered with brains. He'd done enough. But he wouldn't stop – he carried on charging after Trojans in retreat, hacking madly from behind. He was high on something, that was for sure.

And so many an empty chariot rattles along the battleline as the charioteers lie dead and dying in the dust, far more enticing now to the vultures than to their lovely young wives. In spite of their recent advantage and the amount of ground gained, Hector's men are in full retreat, driven back to the tomb of old King Ilus in the middle of the plain, and even beyond that point to the old oak tree and the Scaean Gate. There, however, the Trojans make a stand.

Agamemnon's next meeting was with Iphidamas, Antenor's son, from the meadow lands of Thrace, fleecy with sheep. His grandfather, father of the sweet-cheeked Theano, had tried to keep him at home with the offer of a delightful daughter of Aphrodite, lovely to look on, but he cut short his married bliss, enticed from the sweetly parted thighs of his new bride by the news of the Agamemnon expedition to Troy with all its promise of plunder and exciting action in the field. A night with Aphrodite, an eternity with Ares. Alas, the young man had little idea exactly what he was getting into.

It became clearer to him when he met Agamemnon, though Agamemnon missed with his throw. Iphidamas seized his chance and ran in, thrusting with his own spear. He caught his opponent below the corslet and felt the contact.

'Got you, man! It's a strike!'

He tried to drive the spear home, putting his whole weight behind it. But the point bent and Agamemnon wrenched at it. As Iphidamas fell against him, Agamemnon quickly whipped out his sword and drove it into his throat.

'That's a strike, boy, right in the fucking windpipe! Now let's hear you gurgle!'

Iphidamas falls to his knees, his strength ebbing from him, the sorrowful spirit flitting quickly from the bones. In no time at all he has entered the big bronze slumber, leaving his lovely young wife to the widow's lonely sleep. He'll never see her again, or the pleasant meadows of Thrace, where they first made love among shy violets blue and on beds of buttercups. Now he rests his weary limbs on beds of asphodel, while she . . . Ah, see her now, see how she lies, dreaming of his return. But he'll never part those dreaming thighs again.

And he paid a fortune for her too – a hundred head of cattle at the time, with the prospect of a thousand more to follow, sheep and goats from his flocks, filling her father's fields. Others will tend them now. And, in time, another man will attend to that unmanned bride, desolate in Thrace, dreaming of the return that is not to be.

🄻

Penelope knew a thing or two about celibate beds and lonely couches. She lingered on such scenes with a knowing hand.

'I'll fucking kill you, man!'

Iphidamas had an older brother, Koön. He saw his little brother die, and his eyes blurred and burned. He made for Agamemnon and managed to hit him.

The blade of the spear passed clean through the forearm and Agamemnon shuddered when he saw the blood. Koön saw the shudder and stooped to rescue his brother's body – which was the last mistake he ever made. If he'd had his wits about him he'd have pressed home his advantage and finished his opponent off. But Agamemnon jumped on him, caught him under his shield and floored him. Then he hacked off his head. Koön hadn't thought it through – he'd buggered up Agamemnon's left arm, not his fighting arm.

'Stupid cunt!'

So the two sons of Antenor lay together in the dust, their destiny fulfilled. But almost at once the pain of the wound began to bite and Agamemnon ordered his driver to get him back to the ships.

'At the fucking gallop! Before I bleed to death!'

The horses flew before the whip, their breasts flecked white with foam, their bellies white with dust.

The tide was turning yet again. As soon as Hector saw the horses' heads turn for the ships, he scented victory and urged his men on. He himself cut down a whole run of men, felling them like tender saplings, though they were all experienced soldiers and commanders: Asaeus, Autonous, Opites, Dolops, Opheltius, Agelaus, Aesymnus, Orus and the stalwart Hipponous – nine Greek leaders going down in as many minutes, one after another, part of the web now, their names threaded into posterity.

Then Hector swooped on the rabble.

He hit them like the west wind when it blows a full gale at sea and scatters the south wind's massed snow-clouds, and the big seas lunge and plunge as the whistling wind flicks the spindrift in the sailors' faces and the foam flies high.

A nice picture. And an apt one too. We were about to be overwhelmed.

I yelled to Diomedes. He couldn't hear me above the din, so I signalled to him for support. He came and stood with me and threw. The spear hit Thymbraeus in the chest and brought him down. I took out his squire Molion. Then we got the two sons of Merops, and Diomedes made an easy hit on Agastrophus, who was horseless and trapped after insisting on leaving his chariot behind and going into the front line on foot.

Now Hector loomed up, and Diomedes hurled at him and struck the crest of the helmet. Hector staggered. Diomedes whooped.

'Got the bastard!'

The triple plates had stopped the bronze just short of the skull. But the impact knocked him nearly senseless. Hector fell, clutching at the ground. You could see from his glazed eyes that the world had gone black for him. And if Diomedes had got to him in time, he'd never have seen the light of day again. But he managed to stagger to his feet and lurch back into the lines.

'I'll fucking get you yet, you cunt!' shouted Diomedes and started to strip the man he'd just killed.

But Paris was watching, like the little snake he was, from the tomb of Ilus. He leaned against the gravestone, took aim, and coolly loosed an arrow. It looked like it was falling short, but it got there, just. Maybe some god cheered it on. Diomedes never even saw it coming. It pierced his right foot. The point went right through the sole and pinned him to the ground where he stood. He was so shocked he was speechless, just stood there staring in a daze at the stricken foot, literally riveted. Paris saw it and ran out from his ambush. The little prick knew he was safe. He taunted his target.

'Fucking nailed you! O fucking joy! Where would you like the next one? Other foot suit you? Or would you like it in the belly? Or the eye?'

'A scratch!' yelled Diomedes. 'You haven't even hurt me! And how the fuck could you? You fucking bow-boy! A skulking fucking archer! Too scared to see the whites of the eyes, eh? Shoot from a distance instead, you gutless sniper! You sad little lady-killer! It's all you'll ever fucking kill!'

Paris laughed.

'I wouldn't be too sure of that, cripple!'

He selected another arrow and fitted it to his bow. But Diomedes saw it coming this time and, pinned down as he was, managed to deflect the missile with his shield.

'You'll have to do better than that, pretty boy — that's poorer than piss!'

Paris cursed and reached for the next arrow. Diomedes kept at it, intent on upsetting his enemy's aim.

'When I shoot back you'd better fucking watch out! One hit from me and your kids are fatherless and your bitch is a widow with lacerations to improve her looks! Except you don't have any kids, do you? Haven't even got it up yet by the looks of things! As for you, you'll be rotting soon, and it won't be the girls circling round you then, dancing boy, it'll be the fucking vultures!'

Paris's next arrow went wide.

All the same, Diomedes was feeling the pain. He sat down and wrenched the arrow out of the foot, unpinning himself from the ground. The effort and the agony were written all over his face. I helped him retreat before Paris could fire again. Then I came back to the line to look for the little cunt, but found myself hemmed in. I took out a few, but a spear from a fucker whose comrade I'd just killed ripped right through my shield and tore the flesh from my side — I felt it bite. Then the stupid cunt turned and ran. I gave it to him right between the shoulders, and he reached the earth, dead on arrival. I knew I had to call it a day and shouted for support. Big Ajax came up and covered me with his shield. Menelaus helped me to his chariot, and Ajax left us to it. When I looked over my shoulder, I could see him back on the attack.

A mountain torrent sweeps down to the plains, tearing away the tall trees as it goes and scattering them in all directions as if they are straw – hundreds of tons of oaks and pines flung like driftwood into the sea. That's how Ajax flings himself on the Trojans, inflicting unmendable wounds, demolishing many a horse and man as he storms the plain.

Hector saw none of this. He was heavily engaged on the far left, on Scamander banks, where a furious battle was being fought out round Nestor and Idomeneus. We were taking heavy casualties. Even so, our lads would have stood their ground but for that cunt Paris, who fired another arrow, a three-barbed bastard that hit Machaon in the right shoulder. Machaon was by far our best physician, and a physician is pure gold, worth a hundred squaddies. Idomeneus yelled to Nestor to pick him up and head back for the ships on the double. Nestor went like the wind, with Machaon hanging on to the sides of the chariot for dear life and the arrow sticking out of his shoulder. It was going to be a bugger to get out.

Meanwhile, Hector's driver, Kebriones, saw the situation on their right and he brought the two of them up fast. Hector's best men were right behind them, galloping over wounded men and corpses and shields. The axles and rails were bright with blood. Ajax fell back. He was reluctant to go but he'd no choice.

Was he a lion or an ass? The lion retreats from the herdsmen and the ass from a band of boys. The lion is unwilling to leave the fold and the ass the cornfield. Even though the boys break heavy sticks across the donkey's back, he keeps on eating until he has taken his stubborn fill, and only then does he consent to go. The lion shrinks from the hail of missiles and blazing torches but still tries a charge or two. Only at dawn does he finally slink off, growling and disgruntled and still hungry for blood.

Peacetime, life back home. Ordinary life has its hardships too, and its difficulties, but eventually the cornfield and the sheepfold are left in peace. The corn grows high as the tides of the sea, the fleecy sheep cover the plain and are left in peace.

Peace again – and the dream of home, the dream all soldiers dream.

Back at the ships myself now, I could see Achilles and Patroclus standing high on the stern of Achilles' ship, watching the conflict. Patroclus was pointing to Nestor's chariot as it charged up and the wounded Machaon was helped into Nestor's tent. Patroclus jumped down and started running. Achilles was sending him over to find out the situation – he was good friends with Machaon. I got there just before him. Machaon was hurt but would live. I wanted him to have a look at my own wound. A sick doctor can still heal, and the wound was fucking sore.

There was a girl in Nestor's tent, Hecamede of Tenedos. She'd been given to Nestor by Achilles after he'd sacked the place, and she was the kind of girl whose beautiful hair you longed to see spread out unbraided on your pillow. She went on her knees in front of me to offer me a drink, and the next thing I knew I was picturing her kneeling there, holding not a wine cup but my cock, stuck hard in her mouth, her head bobbing like a bird's with real relish, then her lips pulling away, flecked with semen. A nice thought. One not to be found in the web, though. There's only so much a man will tell his wife. Instead, Hecamede gave me an onion to flavour my drink, with yellow honey and barley mixed in. I made do with it. And I let my imagination see to the rest. Could you blame me? Fucking hell, even when he's wounded, a soldier's still a man. And his life but a span. All the more reason to indulge a pleasant dream, when death has flirted with you in the field. And you give way to the longings of the flesh, the only antidote to war. Why then, let a soldier drink. And dream.

We were supping up when Patroclus came in. He looked a bit sheepish, as well he might. He'd never picked up anything more lethal than a fucking quoit while the rest of us had been getting shot to pieces in some of the worst fighting we'd encountered since we came to Troy.

'Achilles asked me to find out . . .'

He waved vaguely at Machaon.

'That's right,' said Nestor. 'But he's not the only one.'

He indicated me.

'Stay, and we'll let you have a full account for Achilles, if he's so suddenly interested in our casualties.'

'I was ordered to report on Machaon, that's all, you'll have to excuse me.'

Nestor spread his arms.

'The entire army is taking a hammering,' I interrupted.

Nestor nodded.

'And as well as Odysseus here, Diomedes has been hit. And Eurypylus, I've just heard. And Agamemnon.'

'Agamemnon?'

'Yes. Do you want the full list? God, if only I were young and strong again like I was all those years ago when I killed the Epeans and took so many cattle and sheep and horses, I'd fight to the death. To the fucking death!'

Nestor never swore. Everybody looked up.

'Patroclus, I beg you, can't you persuade Achilles to relent? Or won't he at least let you put on his armour and lead the Myrmidons into the field? Maybe you could trick the Trojans into thinking he's back in the war? You know, demoralise the enemy? It's worth a try.'

Patroclus left at once to report to Achilles. On the way, he ran into Eurypylus. He'd taken one of Paris's arrows in the thigh and was losing blood faster than a horse can piss. Patroclus stopped. He knew what to do. He'd been taught by Chiron, the good centaur – if you care to believe in centaurs – and by Achilles.

'Yarrow for the arrow,' he said.

Eurypylus knew what was coming and bit on the bronze.

'Better clench your fists too,' Patroclus said, putting a spear-shaft into his hands.

Then he cut out the arrow from the flesh, bathed the wound and crumbled the bitter healing root over it, which both staunched the blood and acted as a sedative, taking away the pain.

Meanwhile, Hector had reached the wall again. But the Trojan mounts refused the fosse with its sharpened stakes, fucking suicide, and even Hector could see that there was just no point at which a horse could risk the ditch, not trundling a chariot behind it. This was a job for the infantry.

There's always one heroic fucker, though. One of their leaders, a crazy cunt called Asius, spotted the narrow causeway we used for our own retreat, and he led his company across it, making straight for the open gate. They ran right into Polypoetes and Leonteus, our Lapith champions, and the next thing they knew it was raining fucking boulders. Damasus was the first casualty. He took a massive one on the top of the head, dropped from the full height of the wall. It splintered the bone and scattered the brains. He struck the ground, where he was quickly joined by other casualties of the rain of rocks. But it was the wind-drinking spear of Idomeneus that stopped Asius in his tracks and put paid to his bid to be a hero. The spear struck him in the chest with such force that it spun him round. He started to stagger back to the line but didn't get far. The second spear pierced him right between his retreating buttocks, coming out at the navel, so that he was speared both ways now, front and back. Not much fun. He died screaming unheroically.

That ought to have been omen enough. And it was. But Penelope added another to the web. High above the ditch, a soaring eagle, clutching in his talons a writhing snake. The reptile reared and struck the bird, which dropped its prey and flew screaming down the wind. Polydamas was a brave fighter but also a believer in augury. He urged Hector to heed the portent and not to dispute the ships further. His leader rounded on him angrily.

'I'll kill any man who retreats or who encourages others to retreat. Birds are nothing to me, whether they fly east or west or wherever, with or without their supper. We have only one aim, to fight for our city and for our wives and children. Today that means taking the war to the Greeks. Reptiles and birds must fight for their survival, and so must we.'

And his men followed him, cheering.

It was as if a god had heard Hector. A moment later, a wind awoke in Ida and blew a thundering great dust cloud straight at the Greek ships.

'There's another omen for you!' shouted Hector.

And the Trojans rushed the wall and started dragging at the ramparts, tearing down everything they could from the recent construction. They would have passed through the gap, but the Greek soldiers rushed up and closed them off with their shields. Ajax strode up and down the line like a perambulating tower, ordering the army to stand fast, and the rocks and boulders flew thick and fast across the wall like snowflakes on a winter's day when the newly tilled fields and the hills and harbours and jutting headlands all are blanketed and only the rolling breakers on the beach remain uncovered.

Hector would never have got inside the gate that day without an inspired assault.

It came from Sarpedon, King of Lycia.

But all inspiration comes from the gods, and Zeus reached down from

Olympus and set Sarpedon on fire. The king stepped up to Glaucus, brandishing two spears, and addressed him quietly.

'Glaucus, we have the best of everything in Lycia by the banks of Xanthus, its wheatfields and orchards, and the people look up to us as if we were gods. Let us see to it today that they respect us all the more, and always honour us even after we are dead. Imagine if they can only say, "No, our kings are no cowards, and it's not fat cattle and bursting vineyards that make great kings, nor their succulent roasts and sweet wines and flowing cups and their high seats at the feasts – it's their brave hearts and dauntless spirits that take them foremost into the front line, flinging themselves into the flame of battle, always first in fight." Imagine.

'And imagine if we could not only live through this war but afterwards be sure of enjoying immortality. If I thought that were possible I'd neither go out into the front line myself, nor send you into the field to cover yourself in glory. But things aren't like that, are they? There are a thousand fates round about us, as many ways to die, and there is no escaping all of them. One is all it takes, and that one will get you in the end. So whoever wins the day, us or our enemies, let us go forward and do or die.'

And the two of them pressed on ahead, shoulder to shoulder, with the Lycians at their backs, bounding like mountain lions on the flocks, heedless of the shepherd's desperate defence.

'The fucking Lycians! They're fucking headed our way!'

Menestheus the Athenian saw them coming and shouted to his herald Thoas.

'Get both the Ajaxes down here at the gallop! Or get Big Ajax to bring Teucer! You know what these savages are like when they get to close quarters!'

Thoas knew. He ran along the inside of the wall with the message and came back with Big Ajax and Teucer, leaving Ajax the Runner to hold the line. When they reached the sector defended by Menestheus, the Lycians were already storming the wall. Ajax arrived just in time to greet Epicles with a boulder to his skull. Epicles dropped like a diver headfirst from the tower, almost in slow motion. But he hit the ground at speed all right, already dead.

There in the web, there goes the spirit, if you care to see it, flitting sorrowfully from the bones. I didn't see it myself. I saw the body, though, saw the blood and brains spill from it as it fell, saw the limbs splayed at strange angles after the thud.

Teucer got Glaucus in the arm and he clambered back down the wall, lucky cunt – Teucer had aimed for the eye. But Sarpedon pressed on, struck upwards, and speared Alcmaon. Sweet for you, if you can spear a man who's above you. But he was a hard bastard. He tugged at the spear just enough, and Alcmaon came with it. Sarpedon swerved as the body fell past him, spear and all. Sarpedon now had both hands free. He pulled hard at the undefended section of the rampart, and the battlement gave way. A motherfucker of a breach it was, wide enough for a company to get through.

'Fuck!'

That was Ajax.

He and Teucer let fly at Sarpedon together. He caught both spear and arrow on his shield and reeled back under the double impact, shouting for support. The Lycians roared their bloodcurdling battle-cry and came on us all the harder, but still our lads defended all the more, and soon the wall ran with the blood of both sides. The Lycians couldn't break the wall, and we couldn't shift the bastards off it. They were like limpets. So we just stood our ground and hacked each other to pieces.

It was a cruel hour, as the poets say, when the bitter bronze bit into human flesh, sending many a fine young man not home to his next of kin but to the long home of an early grave, and from there into anonymity and endless night.

But it had to go one way or the other eventually. And at last Zeus gave the glory to Hector. How else could it have happened? How else could Hector have hoisted up a massive rock the size of himself, a rock that even Achilles and Ajax together could never have lifted, not even an inch from the ground? There he stands – with the rock held aloft, high above his head, like Atlas holding the globe, though you can also see the hand of Zeus, clear as day, doing the actual work. He – Zeus, Hector – hurled it at the double doors, the hinges burst, the timber shrieked and tore, the bar gave way, the rock crashed through – and in leapt Hector, unstoppable except by gods, a man on fire, but with a look like nightfall on his face. Only a god indeed could have faced him at that hour, and the greatest god of all was on his side. The Trojans poured through, we fled to the ships, and the terrifying din filled the sky.

TWENTY-FOUR

Anyone with a god's-eye view of the earth could turn his gaze from Troy that day and survey the tranquillity that exists beyond the unending conflict of war.

That is exactly what Zeus does, turns his shining eyes north, well away from the two armies, leaving them to carry on the futile and bloody struggle free from Olympian intervention. He gazes across to the Thracians, the Mysians and the Hippemolgi, the drinkers of mares' milk. His bright eyes rest on the Abii, the most peaceful of the peoples of the earth, who never disturb his serene detachment or cause him for one moment even to contemplate any involvement in human affairs. His eyelids droop. A benign and lordly smile spreads over his august features. And he doesn't give Troy a second glance.

But the web of the sea is stirring, and an ancient shape rises out of the waves. Poseidon, protector of the Greeks, is far from impartial. He soars up out of the ocean, up to the highest ridge of wooded Samos, and there he sits, enthralled by the spectacle of war. Perturbed, though, by the Trojan advantage, he leaves Samos and plunges back down again, deep down into the golden chambers, into the glimmering green depths, surfacing again, this time with the face, shape and voice of Calchas. He is about to defy Zeus and intervene, inspire the Greek army to make a stand, even in their hour of defeat, and save the fleet.

He materialises in the Greek ranks, and this is what he says.

'Oh, if only some god could speak to you, instead of me, he'd tell you that the time has come to make your greatest stand ever. You must keep Hector from the ships. If you fail in this, there will not only be no ships, there will be no army. You will have nowhere to go. Instead, you will be slaughtered in this country, not in one battle but gradually and systematically. You will be picked off in tens and hundreds as you flee and hide and wander. You will be scavengers. You will be decimated down to the last man, and there won't even be a memory left of you or why you came to Troy. You will be less than the spittle that is left in men's mouths. Not even the Trojans will care to remember you in song. Not the clang of a single string. You see then? The ships are your survival, they are your life. You must fight for them now, fight for your lives.'

Inspired by this speech, the Ajaxes add to it at once, rallying the troops for battle.

'You call yourselves Greeks! Are you raw recruits or what? Your mothers would prefer to see you dead than lying down like this to an inferior enemy. Never mind that we've been let down by our leaders; good soldiers can quickly recover. Good soldiers wish to go home victorious and with all the spoils of war, not with their tails between their legs. Are you forgetting what's on offer? Let's take lives, lads, lives and wives! And sail home to Argos with bursting hulls and with not a ship surrendered. What do you say? Will you form up behind us and fight?'

A tremendous roar follows this speech and the lines are quickly formed, an impenetrable hedge of men, standing helmet to helmet, shield to shield, and with spears bristling so close together, so densely packed, the army resembles one gigantic porcupine, ready to inflict injuries and death on any enemy that comes within range.

But the Trojans are not intimidated. Hector himself comes bouncing up on the Greeks like a huge mountain boulder tossed into the air by a rain-swollen winter river. And his men mass behind him like a great barrage of rocks, following the leader, thundering support.

'Let's finish the bastards! Go for it, you Lycian lads! Do you want to fuck your wives again? And you Dardanian boys, you know you love it! A good old hand-to-hand scrap! Nothing to beat it! Go for the brains now! Forget the fucking balls! They have none! Come on, let's do some damage! Spill some blood!'

Deiphobus was first out, first to respond to the rallying cry, eager to make his brother proud of him. Meriones marked him and threw, hitting the shield. The lance snapped at the socket, and Deiphobus lived.

Imbrius did not. Teucer switched to his spear and hit the target first time. The target toppled like a tree to the woodman's axe, blood spreading from his head to form a widening dark circle in the dust. Shacked up in Pedaeum with Medesicaste, one of Priam's illegitimate daughters and something of a shrew, Imbrius had often quipped to his friends, 'Life's a bitch and then you marry one', his jesting laced with rue. But there's no bitch like destiny, whether the life be long or short. And Imbrius would hear Medesicaste's scolding no more.

Teucer came for the armour, but Hector hurled at him, warning him off. The spear missed by a whisker and hit Amphimachus in the chest, killing him quickly. He died in the arms of his friend, Ajax the Runner. Ajax swore and hurled back at Hector – a glorious throw. But Hector was too well protected. Even so the impact sent him staggering backwards. We dashed in and grabbed Imbrius, dragging him off behind our line. Ajax was still black in the face with rage over the loss of his friend and he hacked off Imbrius's dead head, picked it up and spun it high in the air, hurling it to the other side. It dropped like a ball at Hector's feet.

'Present for you, cunt-head! An even uglier mug than your own!'

Hector snarled, snatched it up again and lobbed it back hard at Ajax, who didn't even bother to hold up his shield, but spread wide both arms, grinning.

'Trojan bonces? I'm fucking terrified!'

The head was still helmeted, and the flying metal, weighted by the skull, broke the bridge of Ajax's nose. He yelped and clapped a hand to his face.

Hector yelled back.

'There you go! That'll improve your mug! And you'll have to throw a lot more than that, you cunt! Even the fucking Gorgon won't stop us!'

Behind him, the blackheads just kept on coming. And we knew if we didn't hold the line we'd never get back to Argos, never see home again.

So all day long the noise of battle rolled. It was deadlock. A tug-of-war with not an inch or an ounce either fucking way, the two sides heaving and sweating at a rope knotted by the gods. That's how it was at the battle of the ships. And no one could undo that knot, though it undid many a soldier.

Then our excellent old Idomeneus flung himself into the fray with a roar. He may have been a grizzled veteran, and he was amiable enough off the field, the soul of courtesy, but in battle he became a terror. And he lost all his decency. Within seconds he'd caused panic among the blackheads by killing Othryoneus. This young man had just come from Cabesus, attracted by the war – or rather by Cassandra, easily the most stunning of Priam's daughters. But when he was asked to cough up for her he reckoned he couldn't afford it and promised to pay Priam in war service instead, saying he'd perform wonders and making it known he'd soon drive the Greeks into the sea and pack us back to Argos in no time at all.

And he still believed this – the little prick from Cabesus was busy parading about in the front line, doing fuck all except look pleased with himself, when Idomeneus confronted him.

'Best get your sad arse into the rear, grandfather – this is no country for old men!' jeered Othryoneus.

Idomeneus didn't waste any energy on words, not yet. He hurled with all the strength and skill of the seasoned soldier. The javelin struck the man full in the belly, splitting the bowels, and stuck there swaying and vibrating, till Idomeneus wrenched it out and the entrails along with it, scattering them at his side. The eyes were already glazing over, but Idomeneus bent down and spoke softly in his ear.

'So much for your wedding plans, eh? You'll never taste Cassandra's cunt, you loser! But I will, old as I am, and fuck her for free too! And you've paid the bride price – with your fucking life, double loser!'

The dying man's hand reached out and fluttered slightly, as if he were trying to seize his killer by the throat. Or maybe he was meaning to plead for his life, which already lay spilled at his side. Either way, it didn't matter. Idomeneus swept the arm aside and slashed off the hand with his sword. He picked it out of the dust and held it over the glazed face, dripping blood.

'No, you won't be groping Cassandra with this tonight, will you? And what about your prick?'

He threw away the hand and sliced off the genitals, holding them up.

'Want me to take this to her? Wedding present?'

By now he was speaking to a dead man.

'Shame. She'll have to make do with mine. Well, let's get you back to the ships, dogmeat!'

And yet away from the theatre of war this actor of evil was the personification of kindness. He just couldn't do enough for you. Back home, his grandchildren simply adored him. And other women envied his wife such a considerate and courteous husband. They couldn't understand how he could be a soldier. That's war.

But Asius saw Idomeneus dragging off the body. Asius had elected to advance on foot with his chariot following, the driver keeping the horses immediately behind him.

'I want to feel that horse-breath hot on my fucking neck! Keep up! Keep up!'

He tried to close with his target, but Idomeneus saw him coming and got in first – got him in the gullet just under the chin, and the bronze ripped out his throat, coming out at the nape of the neck. Asius crashed backwards, the horses reared and stamped, and before the driver had a chance to wheel them round he took a spear in the belly from Antilochus. He joined Asius in the dust and Antilochus took charge of the horses and chariot. Idomeneus got the corpse safely away.

He shouted to his men.

'Back to the ships with the armour! And give my apologies to the dogs – a one-handed corpse with neither cock nor balls. A disappointing dish, but what the fuck!'

Idomeneus turned round and got eyes on his next target, a royal one, Alcathous, son of King Aesyetes and married to old Anchises' eldest daughter, Hippodameia. She was the light of her old folks' lives, bursting with brains and beauty, and they had scoured the broad acres of windy Troy for a good match for her, turning down many a rich and gifted suitor. Alcathous was the man, and a handsome stripling too. But what brains and beauty he had of his own were destined to be spilled in the dust. Alas. And a completely unnecessary waste, as it turned out, because he saw Idomeneus coming and saw the spear cast from a fair distance and had plenty of time to swerve or get his shield up. But the silly cunt did neither. He just stood there, frozen with fear, like a petrified rabbit, and took the spear deep in the chest, where it vibrated to the last frantic heartbeats. Idomeneus scowled. You can't taunt a man whose heart has ceased to beat. So instead he wrenched out the spear and stabbed and stabbed again at the senseless head. And this was the man who'd sit his granddaughter on his knee as gently as if she were a kitten.

Next he challenged Deiphobus, who wisely reckoned that the luck of the gods was with Idomeneus today and it made more sense to call for backup. He spotted Aeneas on his way up and shouted.

'It's your brother-in-law, Alcathous – he's down. Can you help me?'

'Down? Wounded?'

'No, he's bought it! Let's get the body.'

Aeneas came running up, saw Idomeneus, weighed up the situation and threw. Idomeneus dodged, and the spear quivered in the ground behind him. He returned the throw, missing both Aeneas and Deiphobus, but the spear struck Oenomaus in the belly, breaking the plate armour and releasing the innards.

Idomeneus bent to strip his man, but a hail of missiles came at him, including one from Deiphobus, who missed his target but hit Ascalaphus, so fine a fighter they called him son of the war-god. The stray spear struck him deep in the heart, plunging in up to the butt, and he crashed back and lay quiet in the dust, the spear twanging like mad.

Doesn't matter whose son you are – the war-god's or a latrine queen's. When you take a hit like that, for you the war is over.

The battle began for Ascalaphus, whose body belonged to Deiphobus. Or so he thought. He'd just ripped off the helmet when he took a spear in the shoulder from Meriones. Polites saw the strike and ran up to help. He half carried his brother to his horses, which got the bastard back to town in time. He was losing a lot of blood.

It was hotting up. Aeneas came charging up fast on Aphareus, aiming for the throat. You could see his eyes, like chips of ice, fixed on it. Right on target.

And as in spring-time the showers assault the young flowers and render them wet and heavy, so Aphareus's head lolls slowly sideways, a tender bloom laden with rain, and he crumples up in crimson sleep, at rest under his shield.

Fucking sure he did.

Then Antilochus took out Thoön, stabbing him hard from behind and severing the vein to the neck. Thoön collapsed backwards, clawing the empty air. The blackheads all rushed up to save him from being stripped and Antilochus was forced to withdraw.

Adamas came after him and was about to make his stab when Antilochus suddenly turned with his shield up. The spear drove into the centre of it and stuck.

'Rammed and jammed!' Antilochus grinned. 'Ready for your punishment, loser?'

Adamas turned and ran.

Meriones ran faster.

'Say goodnight, soldier.'

He struck the poor bastard horribly, first spinning him round then driving the javelin in hard between the genitals and the navel, the worst of wounds inflicted by man or war-god and the last place a soldier wants to be hit. But there it stuck. Meriones kept the weapon in and watched until the writhing stopped.

Helenus saw red and came up screaming. Meriones got out of the way sharp and Helenus hit Deipyrus instead. It was a savage slash and a fabulous one. The big Thracian blade sheared off the helmet and along with it half the man's head, exposing the brain. Deipyrus too went into the dark.

Now Menelaus lost it. He lunged at Helenus. But he was half blind with rage and only just managed to slice his man's hand. Which was just as well, as Helenus was fitting an arrow to his bow at the time. The arrow went off harmlessly and the blackheads dragged him off to safety, Menelaus's spear still trailing from his hand.

'My spear!'

'Never mind your spear!' I yelled. 'Enemy eyes on you!'

Peisander already had him lined up and threw. Menelaus whipped up his shield and the spear snapped. Menelaus charged him with his sword out, and Peisander whipped out an axe. I took a second to admire it. A lovely piece of bronze with a long polished olive-wood haft. But Menelaus didn't have time for the aesthetics. The heavy blade came crashing down on him and must have made his head ring like hell. His helmet held, though, and Menelaus swung back with his sword, striking Peisander low on the forehead, just above the base of the nose, a fucking skull-cruncher of a blow. The bones cracked and splintered, the blood sprayed out, and Peisander's eyes spilled out of his face. He reeled for a second or two before dropping dead.

Menelaus spat on the corpse. 'Better smell your way to hell then, you eyeless arsehole!'

He stood there for a few seconds, staring down at the body. Next thing we knew he'd sunk down beside it, his head in his hands.

'What the fuck's he doing?' shouted Meriones. 'He's a sitting duck!'

What was he doing? What was he thinking? Or what was Penelope thinking for him as she wove his expression into the web? She captured him so precisely, you could almost hear the words . . .

Will it never end? Why can't we finish them, or they us? Men tire of everything in the end – of music and dancing and eating and drinking, of sleeping and making love. Even of love itself, of all those things that endure so much longer even than conflict. But these Trojans and their allies, they're bloodthirsty beyond belief, gluttons for war and all its miseries. And so are we. It's inhuman. And yet it's what we humans do, and what we are. And I'm sick of it, weary under the sun, tired, tired of being a man.

Menelaus was having a breather before going back to the butcher's yard. He ripped Peisander's armour from him, handed it to his men and returned to the front line, where he came under instant attack from Harpalion, the Paphlagonian.

Big mistake. Harpalion must have thought Menelaus was feeling weak or dizzy and decided to go for glory cheaply. A big thing to go back to Paphlagonia and say you'd killed the Greek leader, second in command. Except he never saw fucking Paphlagonia. His spear stuck so deeply in Menelaus's shield he couldn't pull it out. So he turned and ran back to the lines, where his father was waiting for him. That was his second error of judgement. Meriones lined him up, calmly fitted an arrow to his bow and fired. The arrow drove deep into the right buttock, passed clean through the bladder and came out under the pelvic bone. Harpalion collapsed, screaming his head off and wriggling like a worm, the arrow still in him and the blood pouring out of him, a dark gush in the dust. The Paphlagonians lifted him into a chariot and raced him back to the city.

The speed was unnecessary. Death was never going to come quickly, not with a wound like that. But it would come all right, no matter how fast they drove, or how slow. His father went with him in the chariot, bent over him, sobbing all the way. He was Pylaemenes, King of Paphlagonia, and he'd brought the youngster proudly to the war at Troy, laughing off a seer's prediction that he'd die there. That was the initial mistake. But you don't need a seer to tell you not to go to war. Not if you can fucking avoid it.

Harpalion, as it happened, had spent a lot of time with Paris. They were great chums, even lovers, so it was rumoured. He'd certainly drunk plenty of Paris's wine in their long nights together. A friendship ended by Ares. Paris swore and loosed off an arrow into the crowd, not caring where it struck. Euchenor took the hit.

He was another one with a seer for a father – Polyidus of Corinth, whose sad duty it had been to inform his son that if he stayed on at home he would contract a painful and lingering disease. The years would waste him and prostrate him and he'd die in bed. If he sailed with the Greek fleet he'd be killed in action. So his fate was forked; there was no third way. He turned his back on prostration, indignity and pain, and went off instead to the end he expected every day in Troy, to be so suddenly engulfed by the unlovely and eternal night.

So it was no accidental arrow after all. Paris shot at random but the gods guided the missile. It came whistling at his head, giving him no time either to blink or think. Target, contact, whack! His destiny hit him near the ear, just under the jaw, slicing upwards through his head, so that he escaped the prolonged agony he'd elected to avoid. A quick death, then. An arrow through your head. It has to be.

A good shot for the blackheads, with fate on their side. All the same, the bastards were being punished. Both Ajaxes stood in the field like two immoveable oxen, giving them sheer hell. The Runner didn't have his Locrian troops with him – they were well in the rear. But they were firing effectively enough from back there. They weren't the close-combat sort, much preferring the bow and the sling, and their rain of missiles was beginning to grind down the enemy spirit. Hector galloped up and down the line, calling in the best men, but he could hardly find one that was both alive and unwounded. The battle for the ships was proving costly to both sides. He collected a bunch of blackheads and held some sort of emergency field meet, Hector's horse rearing and stamping and pawing the air the whole time. They must have been debating whether to withdraw, regroup and attack later or go for the charge. Paris joined them, and a minute later they came at us. We answered them, dug our heels in. Men down on both sides, fresh bodies all over the field, with heaps of wounded, and the noise of battle rang on and out across the windy plains and all the way up to Olympus.

TWENTY-FIVE

Something had to give. And it did. Hector led one more charge, an all-out fucking attack, and it broke us. Nestor was still with Machaon, but when he heard the commotion he came riding up to find us in full retreat and the blackheads pouring over the wall. A complete rout. We were all wounded. Nestor looked at Agamemnon.

'Well?'

'Well what?'

Agamemnon looked finished, totally shagged out. Nestor was bone-weary too – he had a right to be at his age – but he still had that glitter in his eye.

'What's the plan?'

'Plan?'

'We need a new action plan, and we need it now.'

We waited. Agamemnon leaned on his spear, breathing heavily.

'I'll give you a new action plan, Nestor, and it's the best one yet. Withdrawal. End the war. We're fucked and we know it. We just need to admit it. I move we get out now while we still can. Otherwise we'll die here and never see our homes again. There's no shame in saving our skins and getting back to our families, is there?'

Nestor grew gaunter. 'I don't believe I'm hearing this.'

'Don't you? Well, I'm telling you all the same, you're fuck-all use to your families if you're a corpse on a foreign field. Tonight you'll all be dogmeat, and tomorrow dogshit, crapped out on the plains of Troy. Then they'll roll your bones into the ocean and the rest of you will be fish turds. There won't be a scrap of you left to fucking bury. No hero's grave for any motherfucker – just a drift of shit in the sea. How does that suit you?'

Silence and black looks all round. Anger and dismay. A few of the leaders looked at me. They were expecting an eloquent answer to the pathetic defeatism they'd just heard. It didn't need eloquence. I asked the cunt if this was his idea of leadership – to run away?

'After so long a struggle? And all those good men gone? For nothing? Fuck you, man, no! That would suit us fine if you were commanding a crowd of cowards but you're in charge of soldiers. We've been through

183

wars before – some of us have known nothing else, since we were young men. It's what we do. So for fuck's sake ask us to act like soldiers if you want to act like a leader. If not, step aside.'

Sufficiently withering. He winced under it. I gave him some more.

'And how do you propose that the men manoeuvre the ships into the sea and hold the lines at the same time? Have you thought it through? The blackheads will be all over us and we'll be wiped out. Call that a leadership decision? There's precious little behind it – except the brain of a sparrow and the teeth of a fucking hen!'

Agamemnon ground his teeth.

'Nobody ever accused you of holding back, Odysseus. But as you're so superior to me in all departments, can I ask you – any of you – does anybody have a better idea? Some brilliant strategy – other than the heroic fucking death? Or the fucking unheroic, as it will turn out. Anybody? I'm all ears. Let's have it. The floor is yours.'

The bastard had got out of it. And he was right. Nobody had a clue what to do. There was some mumbling and throat-clearing and then Diomedes said something about visiting the field and pressing the men to fight harder. It was hardly Greek strategy's finest hour. Field? What field? There was no fucking field. Our backs were to the water and the blackheads were all over the place. We were the crutch brigade, FUBAR, sheep to the fucking slaughter.

It was the one point in the war I felt so desperate I could almost have prayed for divine intervention. I didn't. But we could certainly have used some special help at that juncture. And so Penelope decided to send us some.

Here she is, in all her glory – the goddess Hera, setting out for Lemnos, dropping to the Pierian range and to idyllic Emathia, sweeping the snow-crests, the white hills of the horse-breeding Thracians, skimming the highest peaks but never deigning to descend too close to the ground. From Athos she soars over the foaming ocean, scanning the heaving sea, gliding like a gull, unwetted above the white horses, their manes blown back by the wind. And in that majestic way she comes down to Lemnos, where she finds the object of her quest, Death's brother, the god of Sleep, and at last touches down.

She has already visited Aphrodite, artfully masking her true motives, and so has at her disposal all the armoury of female charms and the whole panoply of words, the sweet bewitching words that turn a wise man into a fool. And there is no fool like an old fool, even if he be a god, as well she knows, and as Zeus is soon to find out. But to be sure of her success, she asks Sleep to seal the bright eyes of Zeus for her as soon as he has lain between her thighs and drunk deep at her secret well. Armed then with these charms and escorted by Sleep – she bribes him easily by promising him one of the delectable young Graces – Hera speeds back across the sea, leaving Lemnos and Imbros behind her. Sleep then hides himself in a pine tree while Hera alights on Gargarus, Ida's highest crest, where Zeus is resting.

He doesn't have a chance. The pendants hang from her earlobes like clusters of mulberries, the colour of her nipples as she bares her white breasts . . .

The grass springs up beneath them, the dew-wetted hyacinth and lotus, the clover and crocuses crowding round, lifting them from the ground, making them up the tenderest of beds for their hour of love.

Alone. And yet not alone. An audience accompanies the coupling gods, diaphanous, divine, looking on, all those females, mortal and immortal, whom Zeus has loved already. Zeus's memories of all those previous women stand there, each one personified, as if present and seeing unseen. Ixion's wife is there, who bore him Peirithous; Acrisius's daughter, Danaë, whose slim ankles linked themselves round his ribs and gave him Perseus; Phoenix's daughter, who gave him Minos and Rhadamanthus; Alcmene of Thebes, mother of lion-hearted Heracles; Semele, whose son Dionysus brought purple pleasure to men; Demeter, Queen of the Lovely Locks; the incomparable Leto . . . The pleasurable memories are endless, and the thrilling contrasts and resemblances. Even Hera herself is present! But the younger Hera, who had first ravished him. The great god now surrenders all reason to her again and is reduced to oblivion in her arms, while Sleep slides down now from his pine tree and plays his part.

This leaves Poseidon, protector of the Greeks, free to intervene.

A god-almighty storm got up – no warning – and came screaming over the sea, over our ships, hitting the Trojans at the wall. It was the motherfucker of all hurricanes, and it was at our backs. It did us some damage, but it did a lot worse to the other lot. It was like being given extra arms and legs and horses and chariots. We were hurled at the bastards. The sea swept us up the beach and all over them. They were swamped. It was a decisive moment.

Hector didn't buckle. Give the bastard credit: he led a fresh assault, screaming at his men to snatch victory out of the jaws of defeat. He threw at Big Ajax, but the spear failed to penetrate. Ajax ran in and hurled a huge rock at Hector, hitting him in the upper chest just below the neck. The impact twirled him round like a kid's top, and he crumpled up, gasping. He looked fucked for sure. And Ajax was already whipping out his sword. But the spears came at him, and a hedge of men surrounded Hector and got him into his chariot. They hurried off out of harm's way, with our lads snapping at their heels and the Ajaxes right out in front.

When they reached the Xanthus, they stopped to lay him out on the ground and splash water over him while their spearmen kept the Ajax boys at bay. They were close enough to see the bastard apparently revive and sit up. But then he threw up a mass of black blood and fell down again.

'He's fucking had it!' shouted Big Ajax. 'Let them take the cunt! He's dogmeat!'

After that sudden boost to morale we attacked as though we'd gone mad – as we very likely had. Hooah for the rush of fucking battle! The Runner loosed off a fantastic shot and struck Satnius, a famously beautiful lad – the son of a water-nymph and a handsome mortal, if you believe Penelope, conceived among the reeds of the river Satniois to the sounds of lapping water and slurping cattle. You could say he was just too young to meet the early death Ajax gave him – except you could say that about every soldier, even the ugly ones. We were all too fucking young to die. But even Penelope, no friend to the blackheads, deplored his demise and wept it into the web. The tears were Naiads' tears, purer than pearls, more lasting than bronze.

Polydamas was intent on recovering the body. He was a shit-hot spearman and hit Prothoenor just below the shoulder. The blade drove deep into the upper chest, close to the throat. Close enough to do the business. Prothoenor fell, clawing up fistfuls of dust. And he kept on clawing too.

Deep night descended on his eyes?

In your dreams, soldier. Death on the web is swift as the shuttle, soothing as the loom. Death on the field is hard and slow.

Polydamas hooted and cut the air, recreating the shot.

'How d'you like that one? Fucking plum job, don't you think? Tell you what, motherfucker, you can keep the spear. Use it as a walking stick – to help you down to hell, you fucking fragment!'

Big Ajax heard the boast and answered it.

'Try one of mine, loudmouth!'

But Polydamas leapt to one side and avoided certain death – spelling death for Archelochus. The lance, not intended for him, struck him as beautifully as if he'd been the target, right on the uppermost segment of the spine, where the head met the neck.

'Oh fuck!'

It was his farewell speech, the last two words he ever said. Both sinews were severed and he came crashing down face first. Ajax whooped and ran to retrieve his spear. But Acamas was already over the body. He was Archelochus's brother, and grief and rage made him reckless. He brandished his spear and screamed at Ajax.

'Bring it on, arsehole! You don't scare me – and neither do you!'

A Boeotian called Promachus had just darted in on the sly to try to snatch the corpse from between Acamas's legs. He thought he was covered by Ajax. He thought wrong. Acamas rammed the bronze blade deep into the man's bent neck and forced him into the dust, gurgling and choking.

'Who's next? You want some?'

He'd spotted Peneleos coming at him. But then Peneleos thought better of it and went instead for Ilioneus, the only child of Phorbas, the famous sheep-owner. Peneleos hit out one-handed, and the spear plunged into the target's left eye-socket, just beneath the eyebrow. It went straight through the brain and came out at the nape of the neck. The eyeball shot out along with it.

Deep night's descent?

In this case, yes. Instant death. There was no need for Peneleos to follow it up; the man was no more. But he whipped out his sword and slashed down at the drooping head, hitting at the neck.

'Just making sure!'

Chopped head and helmet together tumbled in the dust.

Like a summer poppy fallen to the scythe . . .

Or like a chopped-off head still wearing its helmet. What else does a chopped head look like? This one still had the spear jammed through the eye and sticking out of the neck. Poppies didn't come into the picture by any stretch of the imagination. Peneleos held up the spear with its spitted head and jeered.

'See what I've cropped? A blackhead! That's how a Greek can reap, you worthless cunts!'

He planted his foot on the face, wrenched out the spear and ripped off the helmet. Then he picked up the head by the bloodstained hair and lobbed it high over the lines.

'Have it back! For the family! I'll keep the armour! And the dogs can dine on what's left – bollocks and all!'

The eyeball was still stuck to the spear-point. Peneleos flicked it off. The fight raged on. And once again it was the hour of the Greeks.

TWENTY-SIX

Zeus wakes to merry hell. What he sees wipes the love-smile from his lips and the post-coital tenderness from his dewy eyes. The Trojans are fleeing the Greeks like small fry from dolphins, Poseidon pursuing like a killer whale, and Hector stretched out helpless on the ground, gulping up black blood.

The great god rises in fury and all hell breaks loose on Olympus. Poseidon is called off and Hera threatened with the punishment she fears most: to be dangled cosmic high, with her hands lashed together above her head and anvils hanging from her ankles. She's suffered it once before and shudders at the thought. So she is brought back at once into line, submitting to the wrath of her lord, and the tide of battle suddenly turns.

So much for the web.

Fortunes change in war, that's for sure, whatever directs them — accident, anger, the blind hammer. All we saw was the sea-change. Literally. The storm that had assisted us died a sudden death, and we couldn't believe what we were now seeing: fucking Hector not only fully recovered and back in action but marshalling his troops again and looking lethal. As if the gods really had come down to fight on the Trojan side, give Hector the eternal antidote and fuck us all to Hades.

Our immediate strategy was the only possible one, to mass troops by the ships and put the crack regiment in the vanguard. This worked, and for a time the two front lines never wavered. For a time. Till the blackheads made another huge fucking push and broke our ranks.

Oh for the Myrmidons!

A faint fucking hope. We suffered a flurry of casualties and gave ground. We could hear Hector screaming at his men to advance on the ships.

'Any shirkers and I'll chop your fucking heads off on the spot! Come on girls, get your arses into action and shit all over those ships! Never mind the fucking spears — torches, torches, torches! Charge, you fucking ladies, charge!'

It was like a tidal wave rolling the wrong way. They surged over us and kicked in the trench, destroying the banks and using the collapsed soil and rubble to fill up the ditch. Then they poured through the breaches, chariots and all, and in no fucking time at all they were at the hulls.

Ajax and Hector contested the first ship. His men hurled hundreds of torches, flaming with pitch, and many of the bastards found their mark. But a man hurling a torch instead of a spear provides a perfect target, and Ajax took out whole ranks of the fuckers as they threw, his men passing him spears and grabbing the torches wherever they landed, lobbing them backwards onto the wet shining sands and into the surf. Men and torches went out together one after another. Goodbye, bright spark of life! Salutations to the shadows!

Then Hector ran up close to the ship, risking his life. He hurled at Ajax, a perfect shot. But Ajax swerved and the spear struck his old squire Lycophron in the head just above the ear and drove through the bone, deep into the brain. Lycophron fell soundlessly onto the sounding sands.

'Bastard!'

Ajax yelled for Teucer to come up and return fire in their time-honoured fashion. He stood by Ajax and aimed at Cleitus, who was busy with the reins of his horses and wasn't even looking when the arrow plunged into the back of his neck.

'Nice one!' shouted Teucer.

'A fucking beauty!'

Ajax clapped him on the back. Cleitus toppled from the chariot, clawing at his throat with both hands.

Teucer's next shot was intended for Hector. But the bow-string snapped and the shaft went wide, falling harmlessly to ground. Hector's time had not yet come.

Instead, he smelled victory.

'They've just lost their prize bow! On them, lads! They've fuck-all left now! Let's finish it!'

'Do you hear that?' shouted Ajax. 'He says we're fucked. And do you know what? He's right. But do you know something else? That's what makes it so easy! Don't you see? We've no fucking choice! We're out of options! It's save the ships and live, or lose them and die. Unless you plan on swimming back to Argos — and that's one long haul! So it's shields and spears now, and keep your arses to the sea! We can do this, lads! We can hold them! We can hold the fucking line!'

And we did hold it too. And so the stand-off continued, with lopped limbs and chopped heads on either side, spilled brains and strewn bowels and arrows that would never come out again without taking all that mattered with them, and none too soon. Life lingered bitterly, loath to leave. And few died fast on the field.

You want euphemism? euphony? poetry? sweet lies? Study the web.

Hector's eyes flash fire and his mouth foams. You can see the white stuff blown from his beard like the spume from a wave-beaten rock, like the hot froth from the nostrils of the war-horse, charging madly into battle, terror in his eyes. That was Hector — a wave of the sea, a steed in the fray. See the cliff-wall of the Greek army assaulted by the battering-rams of the Trojan breakers, their screaming the sound of the shrieking ocean winds, the voices of the storm. The breakers won't stop, and neither will the cliff-face give way. Until, at last Hector, insane in his assault, bursts through the line, a lion in the fold, a man on fire from head to foot, his long hair flaming like a mane as he plunges into the herd and the herdsmen scatter and the beasts are terrified.

That's vivid, vital, beautiful. Is it enough? If not, there's more. See the Trojans follow their leader, falling on the Greek lines like the great swollen waves that sweep unstoppably over a ship. They crash across the gunwales, pounding stem and stern. The decks disappear, hull and masts are lost in the welter of water, the wind shrieks in the shrouds and the seamen's hearts freeze as they hear it yelling in their ears, and they wade up to their armpits now, feeling the cold ocean in their mouths and death in their bowels, and they catch from afar the wailing of women within palace walls and a sore sobbing in Argos.

We didn't see it quite like that. But we knew we were facing the end. Only Nestor refused to buy it, old as he was. Old and indomitable. You'd have thought he'd have been the readiest to go. Well, fuck that, he said. His white hair flying, he brandished his spear and gave us the old heroic stuff. For our glorious dead, for our beloved country, for our wives and children.

'Hold the line or you'll never see them again!'

Ajax sprang into action. Inspired, he leapt from ship to ship, swinging a gigantic pole, whirling it among the torchmen as they swarmed up the hulls and over the gunwales. He brained the bastards dead by the dozen and they fell back off the ships like fireflies, dropping their torches. Fucking heroic. That was how Ajax snuffed them out. That was the battle of the ships.

But it was far from over.

TWENTY-SEVEN

The Myrmidons were sat on their arses, and Patroclus was still in his tent applying ointment to his hurt friend when his bed-slave shouted to him to come out and take a look. He left the wounded Eurypylus and stuck his head out.

'Hades in a fucking bucket!'

He ran to Achilles, who was sleeping off one more session of sweet fuck all. He dragged him from the sack and hauled him outside.

'Go on, rub your fucking eyes – and tell me what you see!'

Men down everywhere, the best men stretcher cases, the ships about to be fired and the blackheads crawling all over them like fucking ants. Ajax's last stand was in ruins.

'Achilles, is this enough for you? Are you satisfied now? Or are you so full of malice that you'll see us all go down, including me? And you!'

Eyes of green iron. The muddy-blond locks waved in the wind. No, he didn't fucking relent. Not even then.

'It's got nothing to do with me. It's that arsehole that's to blame, as you well know, that so-called leader. I told the bastard, I gave him his chance, he wouldn't take it. Hell mend him then, the cunt! He's fucked the entire army, he's shat on the lot of you, and now they can all wallow in it, his mess of fucking turds!'

Patroclus looked hard at his friend. Hurt pride and hatred had turned him into what he was now, a cruel, pitiless man. No point in pleading with him then.

Except perhaps for one brilliant possible solution. A way out.

'Achilles, I understand you, I do. And I fucking love you. And respect you. So I won't try to change your mind. But here's what I propose. If you won't provide backup, then let me do it. Let me do as Nestor suggested and lead the Myrmidons into the field. Let me wear your armour. If I'm taken for you it may just break the Trojan spirit. But in the end all of Greece will know the real truth – that you refused to budge, that you held on to your honour. And I'll be covered in glory! What do you say?'

What could he say? It was an exit strategy, just as Patroclus had said. And one of the oldest tricks of the trade, among the stratagems of war. But the oldest tricks work best. And it was definitely an opportunity for

Patroclus to prove that he was more than just Achilles' eternal friend.

Achilles gave it one second's thought.

'Right,' he said. 'Save the ships if you can. But if you succeed, for fuck's sake don't get carried away and run yourself into a trap, all right? Turn the tide and leave it at that. Above all, don't go chasing after fucking Hector. Don't mess with that cunt, do you check? Once you've got him on the run, turn around and report back here to me. We'll take it from there. But for now, no unnecessary heroics. Have you got that?'

Patroclus nodded, little knowing that he'd begged for his own death. And Achilles gave him the armour, not knowing that he was giving him that death.

A fateful moment then. And a glorious one. And one worthy of a speech. Of quality.

Achilles delivered it.

'Great god, if only they'd wipe each other out, to the last man, Greeks and Trojans, and you and I would be the only ones left – how contented I'd be then, to pull down Troy's proud towers, all by ourselves, just the two of us!'

And then sail happily into the fucking sunset. Yes, the green-eyed golden god of the web gave the speech all right. But Patroclus didn't hear it. He listened to Achilles' last instructions and waited for the glorious armour to be strapped on.

Back at the ships, Ajax was in all kinds of shit. Missiles were pelting him from all angles. They were bouncing off his helmet, making his head ring, and his left arm and shoulder were aching from the constant effort of swinging that monstrous fucking shield of his from left to right and over his head to keep off the terrible iron rain.

Hector saw that Ajax was exhausted. Braving the friendly fire, he shot out without warning and advanced on him. He hacked at Ajax's spear just below the socket, slicing the blade clean off. Ajax stared into Hector's eyes for less than a second and looked at the spear-shaft in his hand. He shot his shield right up in front of him and fell back, unable to take him on. The blackheads cheered and made another surge. They threw in all their torches and fire flamed up from the first ship. The rest of them would be torched in a matter of minutes. The fleet was fucking tinder.

Achilles and Patroclus heard the cheer, looked across and saw the glare. Patroclus let fall the breastplate with a clang.

'Too late. The ships are ablaze. We're fucked.'

Now Achilles acted.

'No, it's only one ship, look! Arm yourself, as fast as you can! I'll assemble the men! Move it!'

Patroclus armed himself to the eyeballs and looked every inch Achilles, formidable in the shimmering bronze, like the sun on the sea in the early morning light. He chose Automedon as charioteer, who yoked for him Achilles' famous wind-drinking horses, the rapid stallions Xanthus and Balius. They looked legendary in life and scarcely needed the fabulous pedigree – foaled for their sire, the Western Gale, by the storm-wind filly Lightfoot when she was out grazing in the fields by the far-off Ocean Stream. And into the traces went the superlative Pedasus, Bold Dancer, not an immortal horse, but the best of the thoroughbreds, who could easily keep pace with the fabled pair.

The Myrmidons were eager for action: fighting is better than boredom for the dogs of war. And as there was no time for a load of bullshit, Achilles cut short the harangue.

'Men, I know some of you may think I'm an absolute cunt and that I've let you down. But if I am, and if I have, it's all down to a bigger cunt, and you all know the one I mean. I won't help him, not now, not ever. But I'm letting Patroclus go in my place, to save the ships if he can, and save the expedition. You take your orders from him. Clear? CFB, boys – it fucking better be! This is what you've been waiting for, so go for it, go for fucking glory! Come back on your shields if you have to, but don't come back without them!'

To loud cheers he turned and went into his tent, where he poured himself a long drink, a bitter grin twisting his lips as he thought about Agamemnon. He spoke softly into the cup.

'His hour of need. And I never lifted a fucking finger for him. Patroclus will be the one to save the cunt's miserable skin. Fuck him!'

⑤

Achilles opens the lid of a beautiful inlaid chest, presented to him by his goddess mother, the silver-footed sea-nymph Thetis. Among glittering tunics, thick rugs and cloaks, he keeps a golden goblet untouched by any lips but his and from which he pours out libations to no other god but Zeus. This he fumigates with sulphur, rinses in a rill of fresh water and fills to the brim with the best of the sparkling wine.

Then he throws up his eyes to the sky, pours out the libation and prays to Zeus, to whom the Pelasgians pray, the lord of wintry Dodona, to crush the helmets of the enemy, to splinter their shields and break their spears, to let Patroclus spill their brains, save the ships and cover himself in glory. And then return unscathed in his armour with not a hair of his head harmed.

And thunder-loving Zeus hears every word but only half bends his head and shakes his ambrosial locks ever so slightly. It means that he'll grant only part of the prayer and withhold part. He intends to give the glory to Patroclus in saving the ships – but he denies his safe return. Such is war. Some soldiers go on to glory and never come back to bask in it or to wear the laurels they have earned. Their immortality exists in the listening ears of their proud, broken families and friends. And in their remembering mouths and their brimming eyes. That's how it is with Patroclus. He will never see Achilles again.

And now, like wasps that fizz out from a nest sliced in two by tormenting boys, the Myrmidons pour out from behind the ships with a bloodcurdling din, through which the voice of brave Patroclus can be heard, urging them to slaughter. And as soon as the Trojans catch sight of what they take to be Achilles in his armour, leading the flower of the armies of Argos, their hearts sink, the lines weaken and waver and break, and each man, sensing death, glances frantically around for an avenue of escape.

Leading from the front, as is Achilles' wont, and imitating the great hero's war-cry to perfection, Patroclus is the first to throw himself into the throng by the burning ship. He hurls his javelin into the seething mass of men and at once strikes dead the Paeonian leader Pyraechmes, who led his men so proudly in their purple-plumed helmets all the way from Amydon and the banks of the ample Axius. He receives the lance in the right breast between the shoulder and the nipple and falls on his back with a crash, clutching at the shaft now cruelly rammed through flesh and jammed behind bone.

The Paeonians panic when they see their proud captain and their best fighter fall. They disperse like the chaff at threshing time on a warm and windy day when the winnowers and the winnowing wind work together and the husks fly up and apart and are scattered harmlessly upon the early autumnal air. So the proud Paeonians are dispersed and strewn by the threshing Myrmidons, leaving their king and captain humbled in the dust.

This allows the Greeks to breathe. Patroclus swiftly extinguishes the fire on the half-burned ship and sweeps it clear of Trojans, who begin to fall back at once when they see their allies crumbling.

Patroclus's second target is Areilycus. He takes a spear in the thigh, a bone-breaking thrust that cripples him instantly. No time to limp, though, for his life is quickly cut short by the chariot wheels, the charging hooves and the rain of spears.

Thoas dies at once. Menelaus strikes him over the upper rim of the shield and runs him exactly through the heart – happiest of deaths in the field.

Amphiclus makes a rush at Meges, his spear aloft, aiming for the head, but Meges ducks low under it and forestalls him with a thrust right on the root of the thigh, where the muscles are bunched thickest and toughest. Meges twists his weapon savagely, tearing apart the sinews, and leaves Amphiclus to share the fate of Areilycus, fast mangled among the plunging hooves and flying wheels. The Greeks are picking off the Trojan leaders.

Nestor's two sons, Antilochus and Thrasymedes, eager to please their heroic father, kill two brothers between them, Atymnius and Maris. Atymnius is struck in the side and falls, fatally wounded. Maris charges up for a revenge thrust, but Thrasymedes strikes him on the right shoulder, severing the ligaments. The bone comes out completely, and he falls over his dying brother, cradling him with his one good arm and waiting for death's black cloud to descend. The pair do not have long to wait and are quickly crushed in the dust.

Ajax the Runner springs at Cleoboulus, sweeps aside his spear with his huge sword and runs it into the neckbone all the way up to the hilt and out at the throat, the blade coming out steaming. Then he hews off the head and sends it rolling in the dust, the eyes still twisting and twitching in the helmet, as if trying to locate the bleeding trunk to which they belong. Or as if the brain behind those frantic eyes is trying to piece together what has gone amiss that can never now be mended. They stay open but stop seeing.

Peneleos and Lycon clash with their swords. Lycon hits Peneleos on the helmet, and the blade shatters into fragments. Peneleos slashes at his neck behind the ear. A single string of skin still holds the head attached to the trunk as he falls.

Idomeneus hurls at Erymas, who is shouting something at the time, and the spear goes straight in at the mouth. The relentless bronze tears all the way through, drives through the bone and tissue just beneath the brain, splitting the brain pan and shattering the teeth. The eyes fill up with blood and scarlet streams spray from the nostrils. The lower part of the skull is a black bloody hole. Erymas falls on his back, both hands pressed blindly to the missing mouth, as if attempting to find it and stem the terrible flood of blood. To spare his efforts, Death comes down and clouds his corpse.

As wolves pick off lambs, choosing at leisure, so the Greeks pursue the fleeing Trojans back across the ditch, Hector included. He abandons those men who find themselves trapped in the trench when their chariot shafts snap. They are surrounded and butchered where they lie, struck full of spears.

Many steeds are riderless. They flee, their hooves pounding like the rumbles of a fearsome storm when the earth is drenched on a wild November day, when Zeus hurls down the rain and sends the black clouds hurtling across the hills in scudding gusts. And Patroclus hounds the riders as they make for the city, the thundering hooves sending up the white dust clouds from the plain to meet the flying white clouds in the echoing skies. He cuts off some companies, blocking their retreat and wheeling them round from the city and back again towards the ships, where they run into the soldiers at the rear, waiting to butcher them.

Patroclus is eager to participate in the butchery. He throws at Pronous and hits him in the heart, ending its business. Then he notices Thestor, who has dropped the reins in his panic. He spears him through the right jawbone, shattering the white teeth. The spear comes out on the other side of the jaw, and Patroclus levers him clean out of the chariot and over the rails, like a fisherman who has hooked a monster of a fish and lands him quivering on deck. So quivers Thestor, open-mouthed and stunned to be hooked so suddenly out of life, out of the element of existence. Patroclus swings his catch high and drops him on his head. He is a doomed man before he hits the ground, but the hammering hooves of his own horses quickly kick the rest of him into the dark.

Erylaus sees that Patroclus has thrown all his spears and takes a chance, rushing at him with drawn sword, hoping to close and become the hero of the hour. But he is out of hours. The spearless Patroclus is ready for him with a jagged rock. He smashes it straight into his opponent's face. Few go near Patroclus after that, and he carries on his rampage among the terrified Trojans, a wild wolf slavering, lacerating the lambs.

But Sarpedon swears at all this shrinking and slaughter and calls back his own fleeing Lycians as he leaps from his chariot to face Patroclus, who jumps down too, determined to kill the Lycian king.

Zeus, glancing down, knows the fates and is distressed for the hero, who is his own son. He is in two minds. Thought and action are the same to him – he could make either one out of the other and could easily snatch up his darling and set him down unharmed, back on the rich soil of Lycia, far from the battle, safe from war and all its sorrows. But he knows that to do so would be to open the floodgates to all the other gods to do the same, to save their favourites and break their enemies and thereby wreck the dictates of destiny. And the ox-eyed Queen of Heaven, so recently condemned for her own interference, is not slow to remind him of this. So, with a deep sigh, Zeus sends down a shower of bloody raindrops on the earth as a tribute to his beloved son.

It is doom-hour for Sarpedon.

First Patroclus kills the king's squire, Thrasymelus. He hits him deep in the belly and brings him tumbling down out of the chariot, groaning his life out on the thundering ground. Sarpedon hurls back and misses but strikes the horse Pedasus. This causes chaos until Automedon cuts loose the screaming steed and clears the other two. Sarpedon hurls again and misses again. Patroclus grins as he feels the whistling wind of it and takes his time with his own throw.

It is well aimed. The spear thuds home just below the beating heart.

Sarpedon falls forward on his face, driving the spear right through and out at the back. He turns over on one side, weakly using his last breath to beg Glaucus to save his corpse. Patroclus leaps down and sets his foot on Sarpedon's chest.

'Your corpse is dogmeat,' he gloats.

He wrenches free the spear, which is followed by the diaphragm, and by the sad soul of Sarpedon, lamenting his lost youth.

Glaucus gives way to grief only for a moment before turning his grief to anger. He rallies both Lycians and Trojans – Sarpedon has been the bulwark of their city, next to Hector – and both sides now clash over Sarpedon's corpse, which lies so covered with dust and gore that nobody will be able to identify him. The fighters swarm around him like the big flies buzzing round the milk-pails in the spring when the sun rides with Taurus and the milk splashes over the rim and forms white puddles on the kindly soil. There the flies land at leisure and drink greedily, creatures of instinct. So Myrmidons and Achaeans on one side, Trojans and Lycians on the other, also impelled by instinct, fight over Sarpedon, the one to desecrate the enemy, the other to save his body from the flies. And Sarpedon is the centre of a struggle he knows nothing of. For him the war is over.

And for Epeigeus, once ruler of Budeion, a fine old town. But he killed a kinsman there, a man of consequence, and, facing the death penalty, went on the run and was taken in by Peleus and silver-footed Thetis. So he went with Achilles to the war in Troy and meets his death there, instead of in Budeion. A man must die somewhere, no matter how hard he seeks to alter the time, the place. He is just bending down to strip a corpse when Hector comes up and smashes him on the head with a huge boulder. It opens his skull, and he sinks to his knees, clutching at his head, his fingers dark with blood. He falls on the corpse he was trying to desecrate.

Patroclus curses when he sees Achilles' friend die like this, and he responds by picking up the same boulder and smashing Sthenelaus with it on the side of the neck. Sthenelaus chokes soundlessly for several seconds and falls into the dust. The Trojan line draws back a spear-cast after that.

Then Glaucus kills Bathycles, stabbing him in the chest with his spear, held in both hands and driven in with great force. With the bronze point now sticking far out of his back between the shoulders, it is clear Bathycles will have to say a fast farewell to all his wealth. He is one of the wealthiest of the Myrmidons, with a lovely house in Hellas he'll never see again.

Maddened by his death, Meriones strikes at Laogonus. He strikes mercifully in spite of his anger, driving his spear deep into the man's neck, just under the jaw and ear, and following it up with a quick stab through the right eye, far into the brain. No lingering death for him.

Aeneas, equally infuriated, hurls at Meriones and misses. The spear sticks in the earth behind him as he ducks, and it throbs there till Ares reaches down and stops it with his heavy hand. The two then stand and taunt one another till Patroclus comes up shouting at them to desist.

'Words are for the council, weapons for war. When you want to kill a man, fire! Don't talk!'

And he kills the nearest Trojan. Then he leads the assault again with such ferocity that both Trojans and Lycians buckle for the second time and fall back, letting the enemy do what they would with Sarpedon's already battered corpse. Patroclus rips off the armour, which he sends back to the ships under his name. And he stoops low now, ready to do outrage to the dead hero.

Only now does Zeus intervene, only after Sarpedon is dead. He orders Apollo to whisk the body far away from the blood and dust and din of the battlefield to save it from desecration and the devouring dogs. Apollo swoops down like lightning. With his own healing hands, the god washes off the clotted gore, bathes Sarpedon in a fast-flowing crystal river, anoints him with ambrosia, clothes him in immortal robes spun of Olympian light and sends the twin brothers Death and Sleep to carry him quick as the invisible wind, sweet and fleet, all the way back to Lycia, to a column and a tomb, and all the honours of the dead, so that his parents can mourn their son and translate their grief into the proper terms, with the sounds of sacred songs pouring balm in their ears, sung by his stricken sisters.

And so the soldiers' music and the rites of war spoke nobly for him, deep in the beauty of the web, where art prevails and war is always glorious. No mention there of the unspeakable actions performed by Patroclus on Sarpedon's corpse. No head hacked off, lacking its ears and nose, no genitals stuffed in the gaping mouth.

'There you go, cunt-head – try your own cock for size! Ask Hector for a fucking blowjob, why don't you? You'll be seeing him in hell soon enough!'

That's how it was for Sarpedon: just another mother's son left in pieces on the field, fragmented by war – like his parents' lives. They never saw their son again and lived with grief, their only companion, to the end of their lives.

And that was the point at which Patroclus, having committed his atrocities, should have stopped and turned about and ridden back to Achilles to report, as ordered. Instead, steeped in blood and still breathing hatred, he called to Automedon and drove on to his destiny, to meet Hector. He was a fool.

But he didn't panic when Hector came at him, snarling and shaking his long hair like a lion. He lined up Hector's charioteer, Kebriones, who was holding the reins in both hands as he charged down on him at full gallop. Patroclus aimed at the whites of his eyes with a massive lump of rock, jagged and sparkling. Kebriones was so close and coming up so fast he didn't even have a second to duck or change direction. The piece of rock smashed in his forehead, completely crushing the bones, so that both his eyes dropped from their sockets and struck the dust. Kebriones fell headfirst like a diver and the life left his bones.

Patroclus jeered.

'What an acrobat! I didn't know Troy was such a town for tumblers!'

He rushed up to the body and grabbed it by the feet to drag it away. Hector leapt out of the careering chariot and seized the helmeted head. A tussle began as the two front lines drove into one another like the east wind and the south wind stripping the deep woods in the forest glade, cornel and ash and beech boughs lying broken together in a jumble. So lay the soldiers, friend and enemy together. So lay Kebriones, broken and bloodied in the dust, stripped of his dignity, oblivious now to the lost joys of the charioteer, champion of the throng, and to all the spears and rocks and arrows raining down around him. Little he cared who won the struggle for his corpse. In the end it was taken by the Myrmidons and given to Patroclus, who in the fury of the hour fell into greater savagery still.

He stabbed and sliced at the torso of the eyeless charioteer until he had exposed the freshly dead heart. Then he plunged one arm in deep, almost up to the elbow, and ripped it out, still twitching, to the surprise of all who witnessed it. The blow to the brain had not yet stilled its beating. He thrust it into his mouth and ripped it to bits, raging like a mad dog. Hector stared, speechless. Even he couldn't withstand him, he decided, in the terrible ferocity of his rampage. He was unstoppable. But as only the gods are invincible, it had to be Phoebus Apollo in all his terrible strength who came between them and put an end to Patroclus, giving the glory to the enemy. Who or what else could have struck Patroclus so suddenly on the back and knocked the breath from his lungs? What could have happened to the helmet that was so quickly ripped from his head as if by an invisible hand, and went rolling off under the stamping hooves, the helmet of Achilles that had never before been fouled by as much as a speck of dust or a drop of blood? And how else did the spear shatter in his hands, the shield and baldric fall from his shoulders and the corslet come away unclasped, unable to protect him any longer?

Only Apollo.

And Patroclus knew it, knew that what happens to all men in the end was happening to him now. His time had come. So he stood there stunned and squandered by his own savagery, godstruck, and vulnerable to the first man to come on him at the breathless end of his killing spree.

That was young Euphorbus, as it happened. He came up behind him unseen and struck him between the shoulders, as simple as that. It didn't take the hand of a god after all to wipe him out. Who needs Apollo in the end? You stick a spear in a man, stick it in deep enough and hard enough, damaging flesh and bone, and the man dies.

Except that Patroclus didn't die. Not at first. He didn't even fall. And Euphorbus stood there and shat himself, wondering what the fuck to do next. Supposing the bastard turned around and started fighting. Then he'd be the fucking dead man.

'Fuck!'

Euphorbus hauled the spear from the wound and ran back to the lines as fast as his little legs could carry him. He was just too terrified to face Patroclus, wounded and weaponless as he was, and without even a scrap of armour, totally exposed.

But Patroclus had no time to turn and Euphorbus needn't have worried. Hector himself came up from the front, seeing that Patroclus had been hit, and ran at him, spear in hand.

'Yes! Fucking yes, yes, yes!'

He drove the spear deep into the belly. That made Patroclus fall all right. And Hector triumphed over him.

'You sad fucker! You're buggered now all right, you bumboy! You boasted you'd sack our city and rape our women, you cunt! You and your fucking freak! And now see what rotten luck he's brought you! You should have stayed in fucking Phthia, you fucking loser!'

Patroclus's eyes were glazing over already, but a few words bubbled on his lips, indistinct and crimson. 'Brag away, you bastard, but you didn't kill me. I was hit from behind by a nobody. And fate came first before him. You came in a poor third. But you'll be first for the pay-off when Achilles comes after you. Then you'll see what's what. Then you'll see who's who . . .'

So Patroclus fell silent and Hector scoffed.

'Do I care? For all that doom-talk? Female fucking chatter! Achilles can come whenever he likes. And when we part, we'll see which one of us is left standing!'

He thrust the corpse with his foot, kicking it off the spear. And seeing that he was now speaking to the dead, he stopped speaking and turned his attention to the matter of the armour, the glorious armour of Achilles. Which Patroclus was still wearing. It hadn't fallen from him after all. Of course it hadn't. Armour doesn't simply fall off in the field for no reason. The Apollo story was a myth.

TWENTY-EIGHT

Menelaus saw Patroclus go down and ran up hotfoot to retrieve the body. He had to make his way through the crossfire. Hector was already handing the armour to his soldiers to be taken back to the city. Meanwhile Euphorbus had crept back out of the lines and was skulking around the corpse, claiming his hit to all and fucking sundry.

'Hector finished him off, but the bastard was as good as dead after I'd hit him. Fair and square.'

'Fair and square,' echoed Menelaus, advancing. 'And right in the fucking back!'

Euphorbus nearly lost his nerve again when he saw Menelaus but tried a bit of bravado.

'What the fuck does it matter how you fall down?'

Menelaus answered quietly. 'When the fall is all that there is, it fucking matters.'

A luminous moment for Menelaus. But Euphorbus snorted and got ready for the throw. He wasn't into philosophy. Menelaus stopped him.

'Before we do this, can I just say – I've killed your brother. Did you know? He got it from behind too. But only because he was running at the time. A skulker, just like you. Brothers in fucking arms!'

The black news sinks in, drawing forth a loud lament from Euphorbus.

'Alas, if my brother is already in the dark, then I will do what I can to lighten it for him. And what better light in the dark than to see your sad soul descending there, departing your dead bones. Not that this will dry the tears of our sorrowing parents. Nor will it comfort his desolate young wife Phrontis, a new bride left alone on the bridal bed, with lacerated cheeks and empty belly. But if I succeed in sending you down to Hades it will be the better for all, including your own worthless wife.'

A good speech – if he'd made it.

What he actually said was, 'Go and fuck yourself!'

It was all he had time for before he hurled. But bronze held against bronze – the shield turned the point. Menelaus jeered and sprang at his man.

'No, fuck you, you fucking back-stabber!'

He drove the spear into the soft throat and right through the tender flesh of the neck. Euphorbus dropped, guttering, to the ground, clutching at the long shaft, and at the blade sticking out behind him. This made Menelaus laugh.

'An awkward arrangement, isn't it? Here, let me help you.'

And he wrenched the barbed blade back out again, bringing with it the windpipe and all the soft tissues, and putting an end to life. Euphorbus had lovely soft curls, like the golden Graces, you had to admit. He spent hours braiding them, tying them up with gold clasps and twisting them lovingly, one with silver twine. Menelaus unpicked them equally lovingly, one by one, before starting to strip away the armour. Blood was the only embellishment he left on that lovely head – before he cut it off. A soldier shouldn't waste time on his hair. It's a distraction. A good helmet might have helped.

Hector was back up double-quick, making for Patroclus, stretched out naked in the dust. Now that he'd seen to the armour, he wanted the corpse. Menelaus yelled for help and Big Ajax came up to support him. Hector fell back again. There was no way he was going to take on the two of them. Menelaus he could have done in his sleep, but with Ajax on the scene – that would be for another time. Glaucus went mental when he saw the retreat. He raced after Hector.

'What the fuck are you doing, man? Are you seriously going to just fuck off and let them have that cunt's corpse, as easy as that?'

Hector glared.

'What's it to you? I've got the armour – the rest is dogmeat!'

He turned on his heel, but Glaucus wrenched him round by the shield.

'Dogmeat nothing! That corpse is fucking gold! You're forgetting Sarpedon. An exchange of bodies. What it is to me, since you ask, is that not one of the Lycians will fight for you again if you don't even try to save Sarpedon. We'll all go home tomorrow. And you can say goodbye to your town. You'll never survive without us.'

Hector threw a glance at the retreating soldiers who were taking Achilles' armour back to Troy.

'Wait there, Glaucus!'

And he leapt into his chariot and chased after them. He was quickly back with the armour.

'Right you fucking are! I'll put it on here and now – and we'll see if we can get hold of that corpse for you!'

He stripped on the spot, exchanging his armour for Achilles'. He didn't know it, but he was dressing for death.

Zeus knows it and makes a speech about it, a threnody of regret.

'Ah, proud hero and unhappy man, how little you know how close you are to death! You have donned the war-gear of the greatest of the Greeks, and in it you will hold sway, but only for a time. The hour of reckoning must come, when even that glorious armour will fail to protect you. Andromache will never unclasp it and take it from you. For there will be no homecoming for you from the battle, doomed star!'

Hector never heard that speech. Men can be as deaf to the gods as the gods are to men. Shit happens – and both sides close their ears.

Now Hector led a ferocious charge, which we met with a fence of shields and a rain of spears. He came through the rain with Hippothous at his side, Hector covering while Hippothous got his baldric fastened to one of the dead man's ankles and started dragging him backwards through the stramash. We were starting to fall back. But then Big Ajax swung his men round again and went charging in himself like a deranged bear. He struck Hippothous on the head as he bent over the corpse. It was a killer blow. The huge spear splintered the helmet and the skull and scattered the brains. Hippothous dropped the corpse and became one himself.

Remembering deep-soiled Larissa, perchance? Remembering, as he died, his home in fertile Thessaly? Remembering the scented vines, the purple noons and flushed sunsets, and the parents who loved him, and whom he'd never see again?

Perchance. More likely he didn't have the time – not with his brains out and spread over a wide area, his thoughts hardly together. But who knows what last thoughts slip from the split skull of a dead soldier? For anybody who cares for such thoughts, there they are in the web. A far cry from the field. And each thought a lyric stitch.

Hector targeted Ajax, but he bent sideways and Schedius got it instead, just under the collarbone. The point came out the back, below the shoulder, and down he went, with the usual loud clatter of armour and the cloud of dust.

Ajax hurled back and hit Phorcys. As always, the Ajax bronze inflicted maximum damage. It shattered the corslet and Phorcys fell, clutching at the dust, his bowels passing out under him as he sank on all fours. Goodnight, Phorcys.

Then Lycomedes hit one of the Paeonian allies, Apisaon, who happened to be their best fighter. The spear hit the liver, his legs buckled under him, and his soldiering days were over, gone with his life into the barren ground. He'd seen the last of fertile Paeonia. We were prevailing.

Aeneas tried a charge, Apollo-inspired, if you like. Or just inspired. And we took plenty of casualties. But Ajax made us form a shield-wall round Patroclus, a ring of defence without a single chink, not a fucking eyehole.

'Any cunt breaks the circle and I'll break him in two!'

It worked.

And so the two sides fight on and on over their oblivious hero, the fallen Patroclus, and the iron clamour of iron men rises up to the coppery sky, through the barren empty air, through the great uncaring waste spaces, up to Olympus, accompanied by the shrieks of dying men, while down below their ghosts gibber and weep as they flit into the deep House of the Dead, saying their long goodbyes to life, sweet life, and all its pain. Some say the dead know nothing, and some say they feel the separation from life and that this in itself is hell enough, so that in the end all men go to hell.

The horses of Achilles, meanwhile, are filled with pain. They have seen their great charioteer slain by Hector and now they refuse to move, no matter how much Automedon coaxes and chides, and even lashes. But these are no ordinary horses. So they stand apart from the battle and weep, stand like the statues of steeds, as if they have been sculpted above a hero's tomb, their bent heads drooping earthwards, their long manes trailing in the dust, and the huge hot tears rolling down off their muzzles and wetting the dust like rain, till even Zeus himself can endure it no longer and takes pity on them.

'Poor noble beasts, sharing the miseries of men in their futile, wasteful wars, why? Why did we give you immortals to a mere king on earth? A man like any other man, doomed to die? Why should I let you suffer like this sorry specimen, man, of all earth's inhabitants the unhappiest and the most wretched?'

And Zeus gives them heart, so they shake the tear-stained dust from their manes and gallop into the throng while the great god clouds over Ida, hurls his bolts, and thunders deep and loud and long, bringing victory now to the Trojans and terror to the Greeks.

That at least is how it could have looked, to a lady at the loom, to anybody with one iota of imagination. One thing was for sure. Even Automedon didn't have the skill to handle these horses and bring a spear into play at the same time. He yelled out to Alcimedon to change places with him, and he dismounted to fight. Hector and Aeneas saw this and advanced.

'No fucking contest!' jeered Hector. 'As feeble a pair of charioteers as I ever clapped eyes on!'

Chromius and Aretus tagged behind, thinking they'd easily demolish the Greeks and get their thieving hands on the horses. They were deluding themselves. Automedon had Alcimedon right behind him. He could feel the horses' breath on his neck. And he shouted to Menelaus for support.

'We're in deep shit here! We could use some help!'

Menelaus came up fast, and he brought both Ajaxes with him.

'Fuck! Look at the fucking opposition now!'

Aretus hardly got the words out. Next thing he knew he had a spear sticking through him, a present from Automedon. He sprang forward, a bit like an ox on the farm when the farmer sneaks up behind it with the biggest and sharpest axe tucked well behind his back. The ox knows him, and idly wonders what the two-legged idiot is up to because he looks so gormless. Then two-legs whips out the axe and swings it high, hacking four-legs behind the horns, shearing through the sinews and laying open the neck, an unmendable red cleft. The beast's legs buckle and it falls backwards now. That's exactly how Aretus went down – first the spring forward, then the backwards collapse, just like the ox under the axe.

Hector hurled at Automedon and missed. Then the Ajaxes loomed up and the Trojan pair retreated, leaving Aretus to be stripped. Like the ox, he wasn't dead yet. But the Ajaxes soon saw to that, cutting his throat only after he was naked, so as not to spoil the armour more than was necessary.

Now the struggle hotted up. Dead as he was, Patroclus was still taking lives. Menelaus hit Eëtion's son, Podes, one of Hector's best chums. They'd grown pally over the wine cups, and Hector was filled with grief to see him fall, especially as the spear struck him in the back as he ran from the Ajaxes. But it was a Menelaus hit. The bronze brought him crashing down as he ran, and his forehead hit a rock and split right open.

'Nothing going your way today,' gloated Menelaus. 'Some you win, some you fucking lose!'

The spear was still swaying in the dead man's back. Like a tall poplar, bending to the gale.

Not the way Hector saw it. He screamed as if he'd been hit himself. We thought he fucking had at first. But it was just the rallying cry for yet another assault. The cunt could fight all right, you couldn't deny that. And on top of that, it was like he had the fucking gods behind him. Thunder had been rolling away during the whole battle and now a sudden crash deafened us. Hephaestus was providing reinforcements, and even the sound effects were intimidating. Our boys turned and ran.

The blackheads picked them off in quick succession. Hector took a hit from Idomeneus but the spear snapped and the bastard lived. Idomeneus would have died for sure then, but Coeranus came charging up with Meriones in his chariot, and Idomeneus jumped up with them for protection. Hector threw at him and missed, but he hit the driver who'd saved Idomeneus's life. Hector's spear struck him under the jaw and ear, shattering all his teeth and tearing them out by the roots. Brutal dentistry. But the bronze blade didn't stop there – it split his tongue in two. He dropped the reins, and Meriones picked them up. Coeranus toppled out of the chariot, toothless and fork-tongued, like a snake. He'd come with Meriones all the way from the city of Lyctus, only to lose his life to Hector. Meriones handed the reins to Idomeneus.

'Get going! And don't fucking stop till you've got us to the ships!'

Idomeneus hesitated.

'And Coeranus? What about him?'

'Leave him. He's had it. And so have we if we don't get away!'

Idomeneus lashed the horses, leaving the man who'd saved him lying dying in the dust. Meanwhile, Menelaus checked that Antilochus the runner had survived the latest attack and ordered him to race to Achilles with the news.

'Tell him that Patroclus is dead and that we've lost the war! Go like fuck! Go, go, go!'

Antilochus sprinted off, but Menelaus shouted him back.

'No, wait! Just tell him Patroclus is dead and leave it at that. The rest will sound like begging.'

Antilochus turned again and went like an arrow. Menelaus hurried back to the Ajaxes and to the struggle for Patroclus. The shield ring was still holding there, though the front line was in tatters. They hoisted the remains shoulder high and managed to move them to safer ground, only just holding off the swarms of blackheads biting at our heels all the way, still trying to win back the corpse.

⌐

TWENTY-NINE

When Achilles heard that Patroclus was dead, he threw the dust over his head and shoulders, tore his clothes and howled out long and loud, a bitter cry.

'I told him not to do it, not to try to be a hero, and now he's lost his life for me, the only man I ever truly loved!'

He reached for his sword, and Antilochus seized his wrist with both hands and held him hard, afraid that he intended to end his life with a sudden cut to the throat. Meanwhile the maidservants fell around him, beating their breasts as he grieved.

'I loved him more than life itself, and I let him down. I let the army down, let down the people!'

His crying was terrible. Nobody had ever heard it before, not like this. Thetis heard it and returned it, wailing from the salty depths of the sea, and the Nereids gathered round her, and they too beat their breasts. Then the whole immortal company rose out of the waves and came to Troy's coast, to the ships of the Myrmidons, and Thetis inquired of him – though she already knew the answer – what could be troubling him so deeply now that his prayer had been granted. The Greek army had been driven back to the ships just as he'd asked, and disaster was staring Agamemnon in the face.

He gave his stark answer.

'The price was too great. It was the life of Patroclus. And I cannot pay it. I cannot bear to live a moment longer without him. I am ready to die and eager for death.'

Thetis smiled sadly and stroked his long hair.

'A bitter death, my son. Have you forgotten the tempering taste of retribution, the sweet relish of revenge?'

Achilles blinked up at her through his tears. He was like a baby.

'It's what you have to do,' the goddess said, still stroking him. 'It is the true course of action and it is the only one that will recall you to life.'

'Hector has my armour,' Achilles said simply.

'Ah! As for the armour, forget it. I will bring you glorious new armour, and I will bring it from the gods.'

Another sound, a very different sound was now heard, carried across the trench, across the Trojan lines, across the plain and into the city. It rang through all of Troy. It was Achilles' terrible war-cry. It was heard by the deep-breasted women of Troy, who knew all too well what it meant for them, and for their husbands, sons and daughters.

That was when the struggle for Patroclus ended. The Trojans gave up the contest, and the Myrmidons brought the corpse back to the camp. Polydamas then advised Hector that the army should withdraw to the safety of the city, where even Achilles would be unable to hurt them. They would never take the town, and the Greeks would continue to wear themselves out in a war of attrition they could never win.

'Fuck that!'

Hector spat and looked towards Troy.

'I'm fucking sick of it,' he said, 'sick of being cooped up in there. What is it anyway? It's not a home, it's a fucking prison.'

Too stark? Too banal? Try it another way then. The Penelope way. The way Hector could never have said it.

'Ah, there was a time when our city was the talk of the world! But now all the great houses are emptied of their artworks. All our treasures have been sold — they have gone to Phrygia and Maeonia, all in the cause of this futile war. And for what? Home after all is a barren enough place unless you feel free there, free and unconstrained, serene under the skies. But freedom is what we lack, what we have never felt for so long now, and I fear we will never be free again, not until we can crush the Greeks once and for all and beat them backwards home. That is my one hope. For the luck of war is for every man, they say, and the killer is killed one day in his turn, even Achilles.'

A fine speech — if not exactly Hector.

'As for that lover boy, he doesn't frighten me for all his hallooing. He'll only succeed in losing his voice. And that'll be a good rehearsal for when I shut the cunt up for good. No, we'll face the bastards on the plain at dawn. And bring the war to an end.'

Whatever was said, the fatal decision was taken. And the Trojans stayed out all night on the plain.

Darkness fell. And all night long Achilles wept for his friend.

'He and I will lie together in Trojan earth,' he said. 'For I know now that I will never go home. But I will have Hector's head before I die. And I will take twelve Trojan youths to kindle Patroclus's funeral pyre. I'll take them alive and keep them for the flames. Until I've done as much, I will touch neither meat nor wine. Nor will I wash or change my clothes. And, lacking my armour, I'll put on no armour at all, rather than wear another man's. Unless Hector brings it back to me, every piece. Which means I'll fight him naked, since I expect there will be as much chance of Hector's returning the armour as there is of armour falling from the sky, forged on high Olympus and sent down by the gods.'

Certainly Achilles made some such speech. And what followed in the web was inevitable.

Thetis rises from the depths of the sea, soars up to snowy Olympus and enters the house of Hephaestus. He has remained ever grateful to her, and to Eurynome, the daughter of Ocean, for keeping him nine years safe in the deep sea-caves when he lived in fear of his life, hiding from his mother – who hated him because he was a cripple. Now Hephaestus will do anything the sea-nymph asks of him.

She goes over all the most recent events: Agamemnon's greed, Achilles' anger, the retreat to the ships, the counter-attack, the killing of Patroclus and the loss of the immortal armour.

'And now,' says Thetis, 'my son will fight Hector naked if his armour is not returned and will surely therefore die – unless armour is forged for him now, right here and now, on Olympus, and sent down by the gods.'

'And men must never imagine,' says Hephaestus, 'that the gods never send them gifts, especially in such an hour of need.'

So Hephaestus sets to work.

He makes a magnificent corslet that blazes like a furnace and greaves of glittering tin. Then a huge helmet with a crest of gold, far outshining anything in the lost armour. But the real fire from the forge of Hephaestus is kept for the making of the shield. It is five layers thick with a gleaming golden rim and a silver baldric, and with many pictures and devices wrought on it in gold.

First he depicts the earth and sky and sea, with the sun, the stars, the full moon, the Pleiades, the rainy Hyades and the Bear that watches Orion the Hunter with a wary eye.

Second, an image of two fine cities. In one there is a marriage feast taking place. There are lovely youths with flutes and lyres and dancing. The other city is besieged by two armies. On the city walls the women and children are keeping watch with the old men, condemned by the years. Ares and Pallas Athene are shown in gold, and there's an intricate scene of an ambush by a riverbed where cattle are drinking and Strife and Panic are shown going about their work. The Spirit of Death can be seen dragging off a wounded man and a corpse through the crowd. She wears a crimson cloak, soaked red with the generations of shed blood, spilled by war.

Third, a wide fallow field, with the ploughmen and their teams being given a goblet of wine at the end of each furrow, and the golden field turning black under the plough – a miracle of craftsmanship.

Fourth, a field of ripe corn, with reapers swinging their sharp scythes, and gathering binders and an evening meal. It is a king's field, and the king looks on as a great ox is slaughtered for the reapers' repast, for he is a generous king and a good leader of men, and the meat is sprinkled with the white barley.

Fifth, a vineyard heavy with dark grapes, laughing boys, one with a lyre, and girls carrying the grapes. Round the vineyard is a ditch of blue enamel, and round that a fence of tin. The boy singing to the lyre is singing the lovely song of Linus, a song of longing, plangent and pure, a sad summer dirge.

Sixth, a herd of cattle with two lions attacking the bull and the dogs barking and snapping but afraid to close. The oblivious cows, fashioned of gold and tin, are emerging from the byre and shambling down to a brook to drink. The brook is beaten gold, reflecting the gleaming sunlight, and the herdsmen too are made of gold.

Seventh, a pasture in a glen, with a great flock of white sheep, all made of pale gold.

Eighth, a dancing place, like the dancefloor Daedalus designed in Cnossos in Crete for fair-haired Ariadne. Young men and newly nubile girls with pouting breasts and bellies are spinning on it and running in lines to meet each other and touch hands.

Ninth and last, the great River of Ocean runs all along the outer rim of the shield, glittering liquid all the way, metal mirroring water, a magical exchange of elements.

If you had seen this shield, even without having heard the story behind it, you would have known at once that no armourer on earth could have made it. You would have sworn that it was indeed a creation of Hephaestus himself, and that a falcon whistling down the wind was the flight path of a goddess swooping down with it all the way from snow-clad Olympus.

And yet all this glorious workmanship, this golden tribute to the sweetness of life, was fashioned not for the arts of peace but for the place of burst brains and strewn bowels and bloodied dust, the field of conflict and the theatre of war. And the shield, which Penelope, not Hephaestus, made for the doomed hero, depicted with bitter sweetness the enormity of what Achilles stood to lose when he lost his life. The dancing and drinking, the cities and the sea, the elders and young lovers, the stars and the gods up above, the feasting and singing, the pipes playing over the fertile fields, the whole parade of human existence – this is what you lose when you go to war and the shield of life suddenly fails.

🖵

THIRTY

Down along the beach alone went Achilles, and he wandered between sand and foam, following the curving tide, finding no place to go. He was rent by grief and anger and his very soul was torn in two. Sometimes the scalding tears blinded his footsteps, and he walked into the waves and threw the cold surge over his head and face, salt upon salt. Then he stood up and uttered again the terrible war-cry that cracked the sky and announced the fearful summons.

The whole army will immediately stand to its arms!

He repeated his vow that he would touch neither food nor drink until Hector was dead. Nor would he put on battle-dress, not until he'd stripped his own from Hector's corpse. He'd fight him naked under the sky.

But Thetis appeared out of the waves, holding the immortal armour, golden and dripping, the work of Hephaestus. She handed it to him and told him to go to war.

'As for Patroclus, let him be for now. No amount of tears can sow sweet life back into the flesh of a corpse. Or wash death from the white face of a breathless man. Think instead of what must now be done. Put aside your anger, be reconciled to Agamemnon, and join the lines again.'

So the Assembly was called. Everybody waited nervously, wondering what would be said, what could be said, after so much bloodshed and bitterness. Achilles went straight to the point.

'I can't believe it. I can't believe I've acted in this way. Over a mere girl. I can't think what made me do it. Except my own stupid pride. I could have wished that she'd been killed instead by an arrow of Artemis the very day I took her on board my ship, the day I sacked Lyrnessus. All those Greeks that have died in the dust of Troy – they'd have been alive now. Their deaths are on account of my anger. I wish I could obliterate that anger, unsay all the harsh words and bring those soldiers back to life. But I can't. The best I can say is that I'm sorry and that I regret it bitterly. For my part, the quarrel is ended, it's over. Now let's go to war.'

A noble speech, rewarded by thunderous applause, and a polite nod from Agamemnon, who took the floor, unlike Achilles, who had spoken from where he stood.

'Yes, it's been a hard time for all of us, and it's been laid at my door. But I have to say I wasn't to blame. My judgement was blinded, certainly. But by whom? By what? A man doesn't deliberately blind himself. By the gods then, what else? They blinded me for their own inscrutable purposes. I had to submit to their will. But now I'm ready to make amends, just as if the fault were really mine. Which it is not. I'll pay compensation exactly as I proposed, all the splendid gifts the excellent Odysseus has already offered you.'

The excellent Odysseus did not appreciate his name being dragged into this disgraceful demonstration of hypocrisy, stupidity and stubborn pride – as if the mention of him lent Agamemnon's response a degree of acceptability and decorum, which it certainly did not possess. As if he actually expected his men to swallow the speech as a true apology, which it certainly was not. To his credit, Achilles ignored the sham and shambles of an answer and replied calmly.

'Thank you, Agamemnon, but the gifts can wait. Offer them at your convenience. Or don't offer them at all. Keep them if you prefer. I don't even want them. All I want is to engage the enemy. And I mean now. This is no time for gifts. Let's take the field!'

Impatient as he was, he had to be restrained. The troops could not be sent into action without a meal, regardless of Achilles' fast. And while they were eating their rations, Agamemnon insisted Briseis be returned to Achilles' tent. He swore he had not touched her all the time she'd been with him, and he sacrificed a boar to seal the oath. Talbythius swung the still twitching carcass far out into the grey sea for the fish to nibble to the bone.

But when Briseis came in and saw Patroclus lying there so horribly mangled by the pitiless bronze, untouched by oils or unguents as yet, the clotted gore still sticking to him, she screamed and tore her clothes, slashing her bared breasts and lacerating her cheeks with her long nails until the blood ran down her neck. She threw herself on the corpse.

'Alas, why should I stay beautiful? And what is there to live for? What is my life after all? A chain of sorrows linked by wars, nothing but wars. My husband was killed in action defending his country and my brothers too, when Achilles came and sacked our city. I wanted to die. And you, Patroclus, you were the one who showed me compassion at that time and refused to let me weep. Even when Achilles was sometimes harsh, you took my part, you never failed to soften him, you were always so gentle to me. And now even you have been taken from me. How can I ever be happy again?'

And Briseis's bitter words, and the hot scalding tears dropping on the cold corpse set off all the others, so that the tents were loud with the wailing of inconsolable women. But it wasn't Patroclus they were crying for. Deep in her heart each woman was lamenting her own unhappy lot, reflected in Briseis. The moment had exposed in each of them a private bitterness and a secret sorrow. All of them were victims of war, cruel war. And the sound of lost lonely unhappy women left the tents and filled the unlistening air, rising up through the blue spaces, all the way to the blithe, deaf gods.

This in turn set off Achilles again.

'Poor women – they have suffered loss. And I myself could have suffered no crueller a blow, not even if they'd come to me with news of my father's death in Phthia. Or my own son's in Skyros. Maybe they're both dead anyway, who knows, dead in earth long since, while I've been fighting this sickening war, so far from home.

And all for what? For nothing, absolutely nothing that matters to me, not personally. For what then? For deadly Helen, Helen whose very name turns men's blood to ice. And for my leaders. What do I care about my leaders? Or about serving my country? It's got nothing to do with my country, or with serving it. It never did. And I lost hope of home long ago. All I could hope for, all I was left with, was that you, Patroclus, you at least would have got back safe to Argos, leaving me dead in Troyland. At least you might have spoken to my son in Skyros, told him stories of his father, and comforted my own poor father in Phthia, crushed by anxiety and old age, and by daily expectation of my death and the shock announcement that every parent of a soldier dreads.'

And Achilles broke down and gave way to grief, great shuddering sobs that shook his whole body.

So the sound of human heartbreak filled the ear, like a shell that echoes with the long-lost, inconsolable ocean.

But now the Greek soldiers came pouring out of the ships, as thick as snowflakes swirling when the wind sweeps cold and icy out of the northern sky and the wintry snow-clouds go scudding over the earth.

And Achilles glittered above the entire army in the immortal armour, his helmet like a star, the spear as tall as the original ash on Pelion, the shield like the moon at its fullest, like the beacon gleam of a farmland fire, seen by seamen high on the uplands when the stormwinds drive them down the highways of the fish and their hearts are sick for home.

Automedon took the reins, and Achilles leapt in beside him, bright as Hyperion in all his glory, calling to the four-footed sons of Lightfoot to bring him safely home again and not leave him behind as they did Patroclus, abandoning the friend on the field.

The twitching ears of the stallions picked up the unaccustomed unkindness in the voice, and had they been ordinary horses they would have galloped all the faster, imagining that the master was dissatisfied with their speed. But Xanthus was far from ordinary and was endowed with the power of speech. So the horse spoke, and told Achilles that they were not to blame, that no wind could outstrip them, not even the west wind, swiftest of all, nor was it their sloth that had caused Patroclus's death, nor yet uncaring animal hearts, but destiny, unshunnable, and Apollo, most sudden of the gods, and the bitterest critic of Achilles.

'And destiny awaits you too,' said the horse, rearing his head and flicking the barbed words back to Achilles with a shake of the mane, 'a destiny equally unshunnable, and death at the hands of a hero and a god.'

'I know my fate,' said Achilles. 'I have known it of old. But before I meet it I intend to kill Hector, the murderer of my friend. And I will make all of Troy finally sick of blood.'

THIRTY-ONE

A god gazing down from the snow-peaks of Olympus would have seen the Greek lines drawn up for battle by the black-beaked ships, massed around the maddened Achilles, and the Trojans facing them on the higher ground of the plain, all ready to clash again. But the sky's imagined auditorium stayed empty for the spectacle. War has no audience other than the uncaring air, the vacuous clouds.

In Penelope's web it was otherwise, naturally. A great gathering of the gods that day, summoned by Zeus, who saw that Achilles' embitterment was sufficient to inspire him to acts of superhuman slaughter and even storm the walls of Troy itself, thereby cheating fate. This was no ordinary day in the war: this was a day of destiny.

Zeus wisely split the supporters into their two camps and kept them apart, as even on Olympus fights could break out during an important contest, and a god hurled from heaven could fall headlong for a day before landing flat on his back – on Lemnos or Lesbos, for example, unable to speak or move, or even breathe for another entire day.

On the Greek side, Zeus placed Pallas Athene, Poseidon the World-girdler, called from the sea, fiery Hephaestus, luck-bringing Hermes and all their followers. And on the Trojan side, among their supporters, sat Ares of the Flashing Helmet, Phoebus Apollo of the Flaming Hair, Xanthus, Leto of the Lovely Locks, Artemis the Archeress, chaste as ice, and laughter-loving Aphrodite.

The slight preponderance favoured the Trojans, but Zeus ruled that the influence of the inspired spirit of Achilles required a counterbalance, even among the spectators. Olympian evenhandedness should prevail. But after a brief speech he gave the gods permission to descend and invade the field, assisting either side as their sympathies and antipathies dictated, always within reason.

'As for me, I remain neutral and above all that unseemly squabbling and interference. I intend to stay exactly where I am.'

And he selected a shady Olympian glen, took his seat, and prepared to enjoy the spectacle.

Enjoy. A barbarian, then? Ah, but this is art, Penelope's art. And in art objectivity towards human suffering is not sadism but neutrality, dispassion. A god does not strictly enjoy the spectacle of pain, he merely permits it. War is a part of the eternal scene, like poverty or plague. Nobody wants war, but nobody, it seems, can do without it.

What is it, after all? It's theatre. The actors love it – it's their profession, their trade – and the spectators need it. To fill up the hours of boredom, perhaps? People in the end get tired of peace. And who says that war is a curse? It's water in the desert of dullness.

Be seated then, if you please, before the endless human pageant. Welcome to the theatre of war.

It started formally, with a duel between Achilles and Aeneas, who couldn't believe his eyes when he saw Achilles charging at him weaponed to the teeth but totally without armour.

Of course he was.

Immortal armour? Forged by Hephaestus? Achilles had meant what he said. He'd wear fuck all until he'd got his own armour back on his back and avenged his friend. Aeneas hurled at him, but Achilles moved with extra speed, unencumbered by armour, and the spear whistled overhead. Aeneas lifted a big boulder and made for Achilles.

'I'm going to crush the cunt!'

They ran at each other, Aeneas reckoning that their combined speeds from opposite angles would produce extra impact and cause maximum damage to his unprotected opponent. If it was an accurate hit he'd shatter every organ in the upper body.

'And burst his fucking heart!'

End of the war.

But the two never even closed. The Myrmidons, anxious for their unarmoured captain, charged up so close behind him and in such a mass that they kicked up a huge fucking dust cloud and both fighters vanished in the choking white swirls. When it cleared, Achilles was left standing on his own, coughing and cursing and rubbing his streaming eyes. The rock that had been meant for his chest was lying on the ground close by. Aeneas hadn't fancied a fight with a crowd of Myrmidons as spectators, liable to become participants. He'd fucked off. Been spirited away, if you will. However it happened, the first encounter was a bloodless one.

It didn't continue like that. Iphition came at Achilles like a fucking maniac at full tilt. But the silly bastard forgot to stop. Achilles stabbed at him with his spear as he came at him, aiming high and hitting him in the forehead. The whole head came apart, split neatly in two, such was the force of the impact.

Iphition was born from the belly of a Naiad – a good cue for a fine speech from his killer. So Achilles addressed him thus.

'Ah, my friend, you began life, I believe, cradled in the smooth white belly of a water-nymph, by the swirling fish-filled rivers of Hermus and Hyllus, at the Gygaean Lake, a beautiful place for your father's estate. But this is where your cycle ends, on the dusty plains of Troy, far from these rushing waters. And the estate will seem less lovely to your father now, since you will not be returning to inherit it, and he'll never see his only son again.'

A speech worthy of an equally fine scene. And there it is: the swirling rivers, rich with fish, streaming far below snowy Tmolus in the fecund Hyde country, where his father Otrynteus, sacker of cities, had lain with the Naiad, unlocking her cold knees and warming her white belly with the hot sperm that became Iphition.

Beautiful.

Nothing beautiful about his brains, though, oozing out from the skull, split sweetly as a nut, or the blood clotting the darkening dust. Achilles left him where he lay, to be ripped to bits by the chariot wheels where the two front lines met, and to be crushed by the pounding hooves. There was time really for only the briefest of speeches.

'Goodnight, loser. Incompetent fucking cunt.'

Demoleon was Achilles' second kill. He came up on his flank and hit him on the side of the head. The helmet he was wearing was useless. The driven spear pierced bronze and bone, going in at one ear and out at the other.

Hippodamas was next. He was a tough young lad but didn't like the look of Achilles coming at him in the killing zone and tried to get out of it as fast as he could go. Not fast enough. The flying spear struck him in the lower back and emerged at the abdomen. He roared like a young bull about to die at the altar with a cut to his throat. A nice quick kill.

There it goes, like a butterfly, Hippodamas's spirit flitting from the bones. Sometimes the bones are in no hurry to say goodbye. But even this strong young lad thrashed about for less than a minute before he died.

Achilles was already lining up his next target, Polydorus. He was Priam's youngest and his favourite, a fantastic runner, proud of his speed. But he was also a smart-arsed young cunt, shit-spoiled, and allowed to think that he always knew best. He didn't. He didn't know that Achilles, though a lot older, was also a lot faster. And so this windy little shrimp flew along the front line showing off and doing fuck-all else – till Achilles spotted him and sprinted after him in hot pursuit.

The javelin caught him just where the buckles of the belt fastened and the corslet overlapped. It came out below the navel. He stopped running and looked down at it in surprise, stopped in his stride. The second spear hit him slightly to the right of the first, and he sank to his knees, holding on to his bowels with both hands, fiddling with fretful fingers, as if he could somehow get them back in place. He needn't have worried. Achilles came up and sliced off his head with one slash of the sword, and Polydorus fell dead and headless on his back, the hands still clasping, the intestines seeping through the blind twitching fingers.

When Hector saw his youngest brother die like this, he saw red and ran at Achilles, roaring and shaking his spear. He made the perfect throw. He'd have speared him like a fish, but like greased lightning Achilles bent and scooped up a nearby shield and whipped it in front of himself – just in time to stop the hurtling bronze. Its song of death ended with a sudden thud, and Achilles wrenched it out of the shield and took aim.

'Try it out from this end, cunt-face!'

But Hector had already retreated into the lines. He didn't fancy facing Achilles with two spears of his own as well as the weapon he'd just lost. Achilles yelled after him.

'That's right, run, you cur! Dodging down the corridors of war as fucking usual, fucking evading me, that's your game! But it's only a matter of time now! I'll nail you soon, you cunt!'

And he went on to kill Dryops and Demuchus.

Dryops didn't even know it was coming. He woke up to find Achilles' spear suddenly sticking through his neck, sending him gurgling into the dust. Demuchus, a big handsome bastard, got it in the knee first of all – a well-aimed boulder, shattering the kneecap. He fell clutching the ruins of his leg and screaming in agony. Not for too long, though. Achilles ran up and stabbed him in the belly with his long sword, then in the neck and eye, rendering him well and truly extinct. And not so handsome now.

Achilles looked around calmly for his next targets. He picked out Laogonus and Dradanus, the sons of Bias, tumbling them from their chariot, the first with a short spear-cast, quick and simple, the other closer up with a fast savage slash of the sword, reaping the head like another poppy under the scythe.

Young Tros was next. He saw it coming and saw how he'd fucked up — wrong place, wrong time. He could easily have been elsewhere. And he did the wrong thing too. When you see Achilles advancing on you, you can either fight if you feel lucky, or you can run away. What you don't do is stand and beg. Which is what Tros did. He came right up and clasped him by the legs, behind the knees, begging for mercy. Achilles could take him prisoner. Or just spare the poor cunt instead, on account of his age. He was only a slip of a lad, after all, hardly worth killing. But as the slip of a lad spoke, Achilles bent slightly, and without a word slit open his belly. The liver ran loose, drenching the boy's legs and darkening his lap. Achilles kicked him away with a snarl.

'You blackheads want your kids to grow up? Don't dress them up as fucking soldiers. It's a man's game. I'm not in the mercy vein today.'

And he left the youngster to die where he lay, and selected his next kill.

That was Mulius. Achilles drove in hard through one ear and out the other. The javelin jammed briefly in the brain. The eyes widened for a split second as if in disbelief. Achilles laughed.

'Yes, a bit sudden, wasn't it? Sorry about that. Better check out the damage.'

He threw him to the ground, wrenched out the spear, and stabbed him again twice, this time in the back of the skull. The whole head came apart.

Achilles whipped round and saw Echelus behind him.

'You want some?'

Echelus had been aiming at Achilles' naked back but wasn't fast enough. He still had his javelin arm bent back when Achilles ran up and chopped at his head. The long blade sliced it open.

'Too fucking slow.'

Out of the corner of his eye he caught Deucalion driving at him. He stopped the thrust with his own spear, piercing his opponent's fighting arm and destroying the elbow tendons. Deucalion looked at his arm, suddenly weighed down by the heavy spear and dangling uselessly at his side.

'Fuck!'

Then he looked up again and stood there stupidly, waiting for the death he knew was coming. One second, one sword-chop — and the wait was over. Achilles' reaping cut sent the head flying, and it went rolling away under the chariot wheels. The trunk still stood there stupidly, spouting blood and marrow from the neckbone.

'Take a rest!'

Achilles kicked it flat. The juice continued welling up from the vertebrae and spilled glistening on the ground.

Rhigmus, son of Peiros, was next. Driven by his squire, Areithous, he came up on Achilles at a mad gallop just as he was killing Deucalion, obviously reckoning that the distraction made him an easy and unsuspecting target. He should have thought harder. Achilles turned and hurled, tumbling Rhigmus from the chariot with a spear in the chest. The driver was terrified and wheeled the horses round, trying to escape. Then he gave a gasp, looked down in surprise and saw the bronze blade sticking out of his chest. Achilles had driven right through between the shoulder blades. He joined Rhigmus in the dust, and the horses bolted. Achilles clenched both fists, threw back his head, shook his long bloodstained hair, and screamed at the sky. The bastard had gone stark raving mad.

THIRTY-TWO

The blackheads were on the run, a mass retreat. When they came up as far as Xanthus, Achilles split them in two. One lot he sent scurrying back to the city. The rest he cornered in a bend of the river where the waters ran deep. He left his spear standing propped up against a tamarisk tree and leapt into the water with one long loud murderous fucking yell.

He was nobody's fool. Being naked, he moved easily among the enemy, all of them heavily armed and armoured and many of whom drowned in the depths even without his assistance. They scattered like small fry while he thrashed the waves and committed unchecked butchery. A great spectacle. It would have taken only six men to surround him and cut the courageous cunt down. But each of those six would have had to be a man ready to lose his life for the others and for the cause. And not one fucker fancied that prospect. So they died retreating instead. Screams filled the air. Lopped limbs and heads bobbed briefly, brightly, on the surface. The river ran red.

Some he didn't kill. Just as he said he would, he took twelve alive, a selection of the youngest. With his Myrmidons, he tied their hands behind them and ordered them to be taken back to the ships. Then he returned to the slaughter.

He could hardly believe his eyes when he saw Lycaon, one of Priam's sons, struggling out of the water. They'd met before, on a night raid, and Achilles had taken him alive and put him on a ship bound for Lemnos. He was ransomed by a friend from Imbros, who got him safely away to Arisbe. But the silly cunt ran away from his protectors, fuck knows why, and made his way back to Troy. No place like home, I suppose, even when home's a fucking battlefield. Anyway, bad decision. He'd been back in the war just eleven days. This was the twelfth, the day on which he found himself staring into those terrible green eyes for the second time in his life. For a moment, though, he relaxed and grinned happily. Achilles was smiling, the green eyes actually crinkling with laughter and recognition. And Achilles even extended his hand, helping the poor bastard out of the water and onto the bank.

An irresistible scene? For Penelope — of course.

Achilles laughed out loud.

'Will you look at this? Wonders will never cease, will they? It's you again – a dead man dodging destiny, taking on the whole heaving sea to die a second time. Is every Trojan I've captured and ransomed going to turn up again? As if the high seas were no obstacle at all to determined homecomers.'

It was true that this had happened before to Achilles – ransomed prisoners reappearing, gluttons for punishment.

'But I'll tell you what. As the sea clearly gives up its dead, let's give it another go, make it a little harder for you next time, increase the challenge. You'll win a medal if you can meet it. Let's see. Let's see if an earth-grave can finally hold down this plucky little fighter of fate.'.

Lycaon stopped smiling.

'What I'm going to do is this. I'm going to try sending you not to Lemnos this time but to Hades. And we'll see if you come back so easily as you did from sacred Arisbe. Or will the good old promiscuous earth, who hugs and cuddles so many brave young soldier lads in her lap, manage to hold you down at last, I wonder, in her long loving embrace?'

Achilles lost his grin and made his thrust. But Lycaon ducked the spear and ran in under it, grabbing Achilles by the knees.

'Wait!'

'They all say that,' laughed Achilles. 'Funny, isn't it? So predictable.'

'No, wait, before you strike, listen to me, please! You took me alive once, kept me alive, fed me, ransomed me, broke bread with me, enriched yourself. We sat together at your table. And now I'm back in your hands after only eleven days with my family.'

'Ironic, isn't it. So?'

'It's almost as if it's meant – you know, in a funny sort of way, as if fate intended us to be together.'

Achilles made an impatient gesture.

'No, but listen. My mother Laothoe's father is old King Altes, leader of the Leleges. Right now he's high up in the old fortress of Pedasus by the banks of the river Satniois. You've already butchered my brother, Polydorus. Leave my mother one son, I beg you!'

Achilles frowned. 'What makes you think I find your family history so interesting? Why do you think it will make any difference? For let me tell you right here and now, it won't.'

Lycaon reached up and touched Achilles' chin. 'Yes, but what I really want to say, what I should have stressed in the first place – Priam's my father, yes, agreed, but my mother is not Hecuba. You see?'

'Um . . . no.'

'What I mean is, what I'm trying to say is that the belly and the breasts that nourished me and fed me never fed Hector. We're not really brothers. As a matter of fact, I don't even like him all that much. He's an arrogant bastard if you want to know the truth. And an obnoxious bugger.'

'Really?'

'Really.'

Achilles shook his head. 'Really. Well, well. So you'd deny both Hector and Hecuba then. What sort of a son and brother are you?'

'That's the very point I'm trying to make, you see – I'm not a son or brother. I'm neither. I'm not from the same womb as the one that bore Patroclus's killer. We're practically unrelated.'

'Enough!' roared Achilles, his anger rising. 'You're only making it worse for yourself. And if you think I'm going to stand around here all day listening to the story of your life and lineage, you can think again. I don't need it, and it changes nothing. You're a child of Priam, a Trojan, and that'll do for me. I tell you, if you were a beetle crawled out from Troy, crept out from under the Scaean Gate, I'd crush you underfoot without compunction, though in general I've nothing against beetles. But Trojan beetles – that's another thing. It's enough that you're tarred with the Trojan brush. And for that black mark, I'm going to kill you.'

Lycaon still didn't give up. He clutched him all the tighter around the knees.

'I'm pleading with you, Achilles.'

'I know. But why? Why?'

For a moment Achilles looked almost wistful and Lycaon's heart leapt. Achilles reached out and stroked him softly on the cheek with one finger.

'Why, dear boy, why? Why make such a meal out of it? It's common fare, the cup we all sup from. We've all got to die, every one of us, me too. Look at me. What do you see? All you see is your killer. But you're looking at a doomed man. For all my strength and stature and physical beauty – forgive my immodesty – I too have a date with destiny. And it will be soon. Yours is just a little sooner, that's all. But it's fate, my friend, it's unavoidable. So be a man and accept what must be, and what was always going to happen.'

Lycaon knew it was useless, but he stretched out his arms anyway, spreading them wide, as if awaiting the cut while still making a last appeal. Achilles ignored it. He thrust at the collarbone near the neck. The blade disappeared deep into the tender flesh. Lycaon sank slowly forwards, his forehead touching the dust, as if in prayer, as if in further useless entreaty, as the dark blood poured out of him, discolouring the dust.

Lycaon went into the long dark.

Achilles picked him up easily by one leg – he'd been a light-footed lad – and swung him into the river.

'You should have stayed in Lemnos, lad. But you couldn't, could you? Your fate lay here, long awaited. You had an appointment to keep at Xanthus. Well, you can bed down with the fishes now – they'll kiss your wounds all right. And the Scamander can send you out to sea to rock you in her bosom tonight. Your mother won't, that's for sure. And the deep-sea finned ones will nibble your kidneys and finish you off.'

Lycaon's last farewell.

And that was pretty much how he ended his life – though with a lot less talk, certainly on Achilles' side. Not that Achilles wasn't a great gabbler. He could talk. But when he needed to kill a man he didn't have much to say. Doubtless Lycaon must have died wishing in his last moments that he'd stayed in Lemnos, drunk wine in Arisbe and lived to tell his grandsons the story of how he'd been captured by the great Achilles, no less. But he'd tempted fate. And on the second occasion fate was less than kind to him. Goodnight then, Lycaon. Your war is over.

Coming out of the water now, further down the bank but in full armour, Achilles saw Pelegon's son, Asteropaeus. Another perfect scene for the loom, since Pelegon was a lovechild of Periboea, the first and loveliest daughter of Acessamenus and the river-god Axius, the spirit of the wide Swirling Stream. When Periboea let fall her robe and stepped naked into the river to refresh her delicate white limbs, the river-god gasped at her loveliness. He couldn't contain himself and caressed her intimately where she stood among the reeds, licking her between the legs with liquid tongue, and so arousing her until she lay with him willingly and conceived Pelegon.

He turned out to be such a strong swimmer that everybody in that region said his father had to be the river-god, it was so obvious. He had only to leap into the water and the waves parted for him. It was clear too that his son Asteropaeus had inherited this divine power. And he had not floundered in Scamander when Achilles turned it red but had swum to safety. Now, however, he left the water where he had felt secure and decided to try his luck against Achilles on dry land. First error of judgement.

Achilles looked at him in disbelief.

'Who the fuck are you, wet boy? You look as if you've just been fucking born! You can't be serious. And what's with the two spears?'

Asteropaeus was holding a spear poised in each hand, ready to throw simultaneously. It was a favourite trick of his. He was also encouraged by Achilles' apparent defencelessness. Another error of judgement.

He spat out his defiance bravely enough.

'You ask me who I am? I'm the lucky cunt who's going to stick you – twice! And you seem to be the newborn one, by the way.' He laughed, gesturing at Achilles' genitals with one of the spears. 'Apart from that, I'm a son of Pelegon.'

'Never heard of him.'

'Well you're hearing from his son. He could eat your fucking spears, Argos-arse! And a top swimmer he was too. Those who saw him swim said he was fathered by Axius.'

'People will say anything,' snorted Achilles. 'And I don't give a fuck who fathered you. Or who fathered your father. But what's it going to be, river-boy? Are you going to show me your breaststroke? Or stand there and jabber? Or are you going to fight at last?'

Asteropaeus threw both spears at once.

'Ambidextrous too? Multi-talented. Guess what? I'm unimpressed.'

The spearman's strength was divided, and neither spear had the power or speed to inflict a fatal injury. The flashy trick had failed to pay off. Not only was Achilles unharmed, he even responded with a trick of his own by catching one of the two spears in flight. The other nicked his right elbow. Neither had flown accurately enough. He held up the arm.

'A graze, I'm afraid. Time for you to join your ancestors now – right in the fucking river!'

Asteropaeus managed to swerve and avoid the cast, and the spear hit the riverbank with such force and at such a speed that it sank in up to half the length of the shaft. There was still time for Asteropaeus to make one last error of judgement. And he did. He turned and tried to pull the thing out. Impossible. He turned back again, this time in sheer terror, to find Achilles already over him with his sword, which he thrust into the belly, twisting it savagely from side to side. He pulled it out and stabbed hard again, this time to the right, and then again to the left, twisting it so that the entire entrails uncoiled and slithered out into the dust.

'Bowels out. You should have stuck to swimming, river-boy.'

Achilles laughed and kicked the screaming Asteropaeus away from him into the river, where the screaming changed to a muffled gurgle. The body stained the water red and brought all the little eels crowding round in eager attendance. The bigger fish were quickly there too, joining the eels, ripping into him, nibbling the organs, gorging on the fat.

After that, the mad bugger killed seven men in quick succession, shearing and slashing, wasting no words, hurling them into the river, dealing out death and dismemberment like some insane engine, some terrible killing machine.

It was at that point that a colossal storm broke loose — thunder and lightning, rain, howling winds, the whole fucking catastrophe. Easy to interpret. Easy to depict.

And so there he is, the river-god himself, fearful Scamander, rising in protest over the amount of slaughter and ordering Achilles to desist — his channels were so choked with corpses and his clear streams so fetid and greasy with the slithering innards of men. Achilles heard the order but refused to stop the bloodbath. Mad and brash enough even to take on the gods, he threw himself on more Trojans, polluting the god's proud habitat. Scamander decided he would take no more.

The river had been close to flood level already, and in no time it burst its banks. The wind increased to hurricane force and Scamander raged and roared like the high seas. Trojans who'd been cut off took advantage of the chaos to try to escape — those who reckoned that the odds against drowning were better than those against surviving an attack by Achilles.

When he saw this, he plunged in after them. But now the swirling waters rose high around him, dark with divine anger, almost drowning him. In his sudden terror, he reached out as he was swept along and clutched at a nearby tree, a full-grown elm bending over the bank. It held him for several seconds, but then the bank collapsed and the entire tree, roots and all, came away. Still holding on to it, he managed to reach the other bank where the course narrowed. Here he scrambled ashore and started running.

The river came after him.

Achilles was a swift runner, famous for it, but an angry river-god in full spate runs faster than the fastest horse in the course. The plains of

Troy were quickly flooded and afloat with the bodies and body parts of butchered soldiers.

And soon Achilles was swimming again, or rather being dragged like a rat through the river at terrifying speed. The mountain streams of Simois joined in the general inundation, bringing rocks and tall trees tumbling down in tons. Achilles, with logs and corpses whirling dizzyingly round him, was convinced he was about to die. And even in these hectic moments, with no time to think, he pictured himself lying afterwards deep in the mucky sludge, under the flood.

I'll be rolled beneath the sands, he thought, deep in silt and slime. And the shingle will be piled high above me. That will be my barrow, and the Greeks will never find my bones beneath it, and my Myrmidons will go home without me. And there will be no tomb in Phthia.

Even as he gave way to fleeting self-pity, the lightning struck again, and everything that grew along Scamander banks caught fire: elms, willows, tamarisks, rushes, lotuses, irises, galingale – all went up in flames. The river itself appeared to be on fire. And now the reason for it materialised.

There it is. There he is – red-hot Hephaestus and his scorching breath, attacking Scamander, taking the part of Achilles, siding with the Greeks. Scamander roared in anger and agony. The elements of fire and water, mortal enemies, mingled excruciatingly. The gods themselves were at war.

And there was another god at war with Achilles that day. It was the one he'd fought with so long, the god of his own anger. It pursued him wherever he went. It made him blind and deaf to all reason, ignorant of himself. Instead of accepting that enough was enough, and that he'd been lucky to escape with his life, after the river's retreat from the fire, he went straight back to where he'd left off, back to the butchery, determined to destroy, still pursuing his course of slaughter, still pursuing the fleeing Trojans back to the city, still harried by his own anger.

Old Priam climbed up to a bastion and saw him coming, like a killer whale driving the dolphins to the shallows, where the massacre would happen. Agenor was the last of the shoal – and Achilles was closing on him fast.

Priam screeched out his order.

'Open the gates! Our army is in retreat. Our men are being picked off like flies from behind. Open the gates and let them in quick! Before that madman reaches the town!'

All the same, Achilles might have made it through the open gates and caused havoc in the city if Agenor hadn't decided to be a hero.

Not an easy decision, even though he had to think it through fast. It must have gone something like this:

If I keep on running, the cunt is going to catch me and I'll die a coward's death. Or I could slip away in the confusion, reach the foothills of Ida, bathe in the river, refresh myself, regroup, sneak back home in the evening, under cover of night. Sounds good. But what if the bastard sees me skulking off and comes after me, gets me on my own. Safer to stick with the crowd, nearer the town.

What's it to be? Stand and fight? Run and be caught? Go like a sheep? Sneak the other way and still get caught? Fuck! What do I do?

Stand my ground? Yes, stand my ground. No shame in that at least, though I'm a fucking dead man.

And as Achilles came charging up, still picking off stragglers, Agenor suddenly stepped out and faced him, blocking his path.

He stopped, surprised, and Agenor took quick advantage of the moment of shock to launch an attack without a verbal preamble. But he was tired with running, the spear had fuck-all force behind it, and it came down low. Achilles grabbed it and raised his own spear arm.

And Agenor would have died on the spot. But something made Achilles hesitate. After the flood and storm the sun had come out again, scorching the recently inundated plain, and the steam was rising from the ground. Achilles felt the sudden heat on his face and blinked, rubbing his eyes. Agenor looked around him. The whole town was shrouded, and the retreating Trojans, including himself, were enveloped in thick white swirls of mist.

'Fuck!'

Achilles ran about every which fucking way, searching for his missing man, his drawn sword thrust out in front of him. Sometimes he thought he saw him, a dark shadow in the wet sweltering veils. But he was following a phantom.

Who is the sun-god, after all? Phoebus Apollo. Some say so. Some say that's who spirited away Agenor in the film of heat. That's who ran ahead of Achilles, making himself look like the ghost of Agenor, fooling Achilles by letting him chase him all the way across the wheatfields, heading him off again in the direction of deep-pooled Scamander. Who else, they say, could have done it but a god? And all the time Agenor was elsewhere. He'd joined the last of the stragglers, the wearied remnants of that last battle. They'd long since entered the town and had shut the gates.

THIRTY-THREE

ᓚ.

Penelope could never give the Trojans credit for anything – and who could blame her? It was Troy that took Odysseus from home. What wife takes an impartial view of the enemy? So when a Greek spear missed a Trojan target, it had been deflected by the war-god, who sided with the Trojans. Or when an arrow fell short or failed to fly true, it had been breathed on by Artemis, or blown by Aphrodite, who enjoyed such pranks. That's why the steam that followed the storm had to be the work of Phoebus Apollo. That's why it was Apollo who saved Agenor, took on his likeness, and lured Achilles away until the Trojans were safe inside their walls. It would never have done for Agenor alone to have saved the day for Troy, but he may have done just that – saved the city by facing up to Achilles for that brief encounter. The Myrmidons had dutifully halted to watch the outcome and cheer on their leader, and Agenor and the last of the straggling Trojans got through the gates in the nick of time. Clang! A close-run thing.

But now it was Hector's turn to stand alone outside the Scaean Gate, ready for his destiny. He couldn't bring himself to cower inside the city listening to the taunts that Achilles lobbed over the walls, worse than rocks or blazing pitch-balls. So he ordered the gate to be unbarred and stepped out. The gates slammed shut after him. Through the clearing mist Achilles saw the lone figure standing at the great gate, dwarfed by it. He grinned, his teeth and weapons glittering as he advanced. But the eyes were green ice. He was still naked.

Old King Priam saw him approach, his spear-point blazing bright as Orion's dog in autumn when Sirius rises, glaring through the gloom and bringing plagues and fevers on mankind. The old king groaned and cried down from his bastion to Hector, urging him not to face up to Achilles alone.

'He's too strong for you, even for you, my son, and he's a cruel and pitiless killer, a complete savage, already the butcher of so many of my fine sons. All dead and rotten.'

And he entreated Hector to spare him the crushing sorrow of seeing him killed too, with all the woes that would follow.

'My daughters mauled and dragged off in tears, their rooms plundered, our women raped, our children hurled from the highest towers, our infants dashed against the walls, their brains spilled out on the ground. And I myself slaughtered at my gates, ripped to bits by my own dogs, the dogs I've fed with my own hand, maddened by the taste of their master's blood.'

Hector howled and covered his ears. 'Achilles is at least more merciful than you, father – he doesn't use torture!'

Priam was relentless in his grief.

'No, listen to me, my son. When a young soldier lies dead, killed in action, disfigured by wounds, even death can open up nothing in him that isn't lovely and honourable. His gashes are noble and beautiful to behold. But when an old man's genitals are torn off by the dogs, he sinks into the pits of degradation. There is no sadder sight among all the sufferings of men than that of the dogs devouring the grey hairs of age. And this will surely happen if you stay outside the gates and face that madman, who hates you worse than hell.'

But Hector wouldn't listen, not even when his mother arrived and stood with Priam on the battlements, baring her breasts. Not even when she flew madly down to the gates, ordered the sentries to open them and let her out to stand by her son – so that even Achilles was shocked, and halted his advance out of respect.

The old woman took one of her breasts in her hand and thrust the withered thing at her son, pulling down his helmeted head and begging him to take pity on the pap that had suckled him.

'If that savage kills you, as he surely will, we'll never see you again to give you an honourable burial. He'll throw you to the dogs, whatever's left of you that he hasn't eaten raw himself. Even your bones will be shredded to powder out there, and your white dust blown over the Hellespont. There will be no resting place on which I can drop my tears and water your tomb!'

Hector tried to tear himself away, but the frantic old woman clung to his armour with amazing strength, still insisting with that single finished nipple.

'Look at it! Take your fill of it, as you did when you were an infant. Feast your eyes on it again, the breast I unbound for you night after night to stop your sobs. And now I'm the one who's sobbing, and you won't take pity on this breast, to quieten me!'

Achilles watched and waited. Yet even the sight of his mother's hot tears raining down on her ruined bitter breast was not enough to deflect Hector's heart. So the distraught old queen ordered the sentries to shut the gates against her, and she screamed to the skies that she'd stay there and be slaughtered with her son if the contest went Achilles' way. Hector was compelled to command the guards to drag her back inside the city, where she was restrained by her women. And now Hector turned again, the gates shut behind him, and stood with his back to the tower, ready for Achilles.

And suddenly the unthinkable happened: his nerve failed him. At the sight of Achilles advancing on him, fast and furious, he turned and fled, flew as the dove flies from the mountain hawk, swiftest on wings; ran fast along the cart-tracks, past the watch-tower and the wild fig tree where he'd played as a boy, much taller now, both tree and man; and on to where the two springs of Scamander rise, the hot spring and the ice-cold one, where the Trojan women used to wash their clothes and laugh and chatter and sing songs in the time of peace, long before the Greeks came on the scene . . .

Steam hung in veils over the hot spring, while the other gushed up water clear as crystal, cold as snow. See them now, see them always, repeated eternally. Nearby stood the lovely wide stone troughs, where wives and daughters laundered the shining linen, laying it out on the smooth-laid stones as they do even now, giggling and singing and waving to Hector as he ran past, blowing sweet kisses to him as he fled from Achilles.

So Penelope wove the washing day and the day of Hector's death into one, the two that never were, except in Hector's mind. Peace was a dream, and Hector remembered only in a flash as he flew past the now desolate springs how beautiful life used to be, before Helen came.

Faster now the two men ran like the wind, the one pursuing, the other fleeing, swift as racehorses when the course is marked and the prize is set. But the prize for which they raced today was Hector's life. And horse-taming Hector was doomed to die.

Three times round the city walls they went, with Hector each time attempting to make a dash for the gates, all the while trusting to the archers on the walls to choose their target, take careful aim and take out the pursuer, ending the chase, and perhaps the war.

But Achilles was a fast-moving target and much too dangerously close now for a comfortable shot without endangering their own man, their fleeing hero. And Achilles kept cutting Hector off and edging him out to the plain, also signalling to his own men not to shoot at his quarry, he was so eager to bring him down himself – not for glory, not for kudos, but for sweet revenge, to slake his hot thirst in Hector's blood.

It couldn't go on. Hector was an innocent man, a soldier. He was not Paris. All he had ever done was defend his people, their homes and families. He had slain Patroclus as part of the chance of war. Patroclus could easily have been the killer, Hector the fallen. But it had to end. Even with the odds high in favour of the naked Achilles, unencumbered by armour, the distressing spectacle of a rabbit running from a wild dog could not be allowed to continue. And so on came the gods to bring it to a conclusion, this time deserting Hector. Such are the ways of the inscrutable Immortals.

Zeus raised the balance high, hung out the beam, held it steady, and Hector's scale dropped dead. Phoebus Apollo left him then, a man on his own, and Pallas Athene came to Achilles' side.

'Hector's time is up,' was all she said.

And she took on the likeness of Deiphobus and prepared for the moment of massive deceit.

Hector's head was whirling. It was like one of those nightmares in which the dreamer appears to be flying fast to get away, but isn't actually moving a muscle. He is rooted to the spot and the pursuer's breath is hot on his neck and yet he too is somehow frozen in time. Achilles leaned on his spear for a moment, and Hector, glad of the breather, stopped too. Because his head was in such a whirl he imagined he saw his brother Deiphobus standing by the wall. He blinked in disbelief. Then he closed his eyes in gratitude and relief and turned his face up to the sky.

'Thank you, gods! He's come out to help me in my hour of need! I'm not alone!'

What to Hector was a mirage, a trick of the tired and desperate brain as death drew near, was destiny in the web, the treachery of the gods stitched into human life, the art of the universe, absolute, unknowable. And believing Deiphobus was behind him, armed and dangerous and backing him up, Hector turned and faced Achilles.

'I lost my courage, I admit it. But I've found it again. We'll settle the issue now. But first let's make a pact, that the winner will not desecrate the loser's corpse but will return it for honourable burial. For my part I give you my word on that score.'

Achilles approached, stood a spear's throw away, and glared at Hector.

'A pact? You must be mad. Do wolves make pacts with lambs? Lions with men? You and I, we're enemies to the end. And in the end. And after the end. And it will be a bitter end for you. First I'm going to kill you. Then I'm going to throw your carcass to the dogs and share in the meal. Meanwhile try this for size in your Trojan heart!'

Achilles hurled and Hector dropped quickly to his knees, sensing the trajectory, and crouching low so that the spear sang its bronze song over his head and stuck quivering in the ground. Hector uttered his war-whoop, a loud ululation. He brandished the bronze with relish.

'Now try mine, Greek nude!'

The spear was dead on target, speeding straight for Achilles' unprotected heart. He assessed it accurately, but instead of swerving, he snatched up a lump of rock, which he held against his chest. Bronze struck boulder and both broke, the useless spear bouncing harmlessly backwards. Anyone could see, though, that it was Pallas Athene who not only returned Achilles' own spear to him but placed herself in front of her favourite, acting as his shield. Anyone who saw that could also see that Achilles was not naked after all but rather impregnable in the immortal armour. He was doubly defended. Perhaps Hector saw it too. He at once turned to his brother for help.

There was no brother, and there never had been. Deiphobus was a dream, a desire, an imposture of the deceiving gods. And yet death is never inevitable, thought Hector, at least not to a moving target. Realising he was on his own after all, he decided to make one last stand, a brave one, as it had to be, and he charged full tilt at Achilles with his drawn sword thrust before him.

Achilles eyed up his opponent's armour as he came at him and fixed on the one unprotected place, at the gullet, where the collarbone joins the neck, a choice spot to kill a man. And before Hector could close, he drove his long lance with perfect precision straight at this spot. The blade passed straight through and far out the other side. Hector had practically run onto the spear, and combined with Achilles' strong sudden thrust, the force of the strike was tremendous. But it didn't slice the windpipe, and Hector could still speak. Not that speech could do him any good now.

Achilles stood over him and crowed.

'So you played safe, you cunt! Killing Patroclus when I was out of action! And you took my fucking armour from his body, you bastard! Didn't you stop to think I'd never rest till I got it back and made you pay with your miserable life, you sorry piece of shit?'

Hector's eyes were already glazing over, but he spoke clearly and quietly. 'Achilles, I'll ask you one more time, for honour's sake, for the fellowship of soldiers, accept the ransom, the gold and bronze –'

Achilles cut him off. 'Don't talk to me about the fellowship of soldiers, you cunt! I'll cut your fucking flesh from your bones myself and eat it raw! Ransom? Not your own weight in gold, big as you are, not all the gold in Troy will save you from the dogs. They'll rip out your liver and the vultures will dine on your tripes. End of fucking story. Say goodbye.'

He stamped his foot on the dying man's chest and tensed himself to wrench out the spear.

'I see you what you are,' whispered Hector, his voice barely audible now. 'A heartless dog yourself. Very well, you can join your own kind in savaging my corpse. But every dog has its day, and yours is coming soon, I can see it. You will die at the walls of Troy when the hand of Paris, with Apollo's aid, brave warrior as you are, will smite you down.'

'Fuck you!'

Achilles yanked hard and the gush of blood followed. Hector was a corpse. His killer ripped off the armour and invited the Myrmidons to step up.

'Go on, every man – have a fucking stab!'

Most of them wouldn't have had the balls to face Hector alive and man to man, but a number of them accepted Achilles' invitation, stabbing him in one place or another and cracking jokes.

'Remember when he set the ships on fire?'

'He's not so fucking hot now, is he?'

'The cunt's gone cold.'

🔲

Then Achilles dishonoured Hector's body, and dishonoured himself in the process. He slit the tendons of the dead man's feet from ankle to heel, passed thongs through the slits and tied them to his chariot, letting the head drag behind, then lashed the horses, which galloped across the plain, dragging the body of Hector behind them, the head that was once so beautiful tumbling and trundling and trailing in the dust, furrowing all the plain, with the long black hair flowing out behind, tangled and whitened and torn. And the clouds of hot dust rose thickly behind the chariot in a lengthening white train, like the train that follows the plough in the drought when the farmer paces fast behind the oxen over the dry clods, lashing and laughing and anxious to sow.

That's how Hector's head tumbled in the dust.

Hecuba saw it all from the walls and tore her face and hair, while old Priam had to be held back from rushing out of the city gates to entreat Achilles to cease his savagery. The king sank to his knees among his servants and grovelled on the ground.

'Leave me alone, all of you! He has a father too, Achilles, even Achilles has a father, old Peleus. Perhaps he'll remember him and relent, for the sake of all grieving fathers, whose sons are soldiers. He's killed nearly all my sons, and I'd give them all to have Hector back, dead as he is, to have his body to hold. Oh, if only he'd died in my arms! Or if he'd died in infancy, and I'd never known him grown up in all his strength and beauty. How happy I would be now!'

Hecuba led the mourning, wailing that her days were done. And Andromache heard the sounds of lamentation from the upper room where she sat at her loom. She was working on a lovely purple tapestry, a floral design, and she had just asked the maids to prepare a hot bath for her husband, when the sounds of shrieking and sobbing tore the air. She dropped the shuttle, flew from the chamber and saw the crowds gathered up on the walls. Her heart began to hammer, she felt she was choking, and found she couldn't breathe. Her mouth went so dry that her tongue clove to her palate and she lost the power of speech. Lifting her skirts and clutching her breast, she ran up to the battlements, pushed through the throng of people to look out across the plain – and saw it, her husband's body being dragged in triumph and disgrace, backwards and forwards in front of the city. She screamed and reeled back unconscious into the arms of her women. And when she came to she wept bitterly.

THIRTY-FOUR

When he got back to the ships, Achilles flung Hector's body down in the dust beside the corpse of his comrade on its bier. The Myrmidons, exhausted and battle-scarred, ate and drank eagerly, but Achilles extended his vow, and swore he wouldn't even wash himself until Patroclus was laid on the pyre. Then his friends went to their tents, leaving their leader to lie down on the beach beneath the stars by the sounding sea, and, as the waves washed up at his feet, his senses gradually lost their hold on the scent and sound and spume of breakers, sleep wrapped its dark blanket round him, and the sorrow slid from his heart.

As he slept, he dreamed of Patroclus, who came and took his hand, regretting that they would never sit down together to laugh and chatter, telling each other their innermost thoughts – as they'd done ever since Patroclus's father had first brought him to Peleus after he'd accidentally killed a playmate in a quarrel over a child's game of knucklebones. And Achilles asked now, all these years of special friendship later – though he was asking the strengthless dead in the dead of sleep – that their two ashes be buried together in one urn, just as one heart had contained the two men and one soul the two spirits. For they had loved one another with a love that could never be surpassed, not by the love of women.

So Achilles murmured as he struggled in the troubled web of dreams. 'Let me get through the gates of Hades, past this army of souls fending me off, the shades of the unhappy incapable dead, and let me reach you and stay with you. Don't let them separate us, friend, don't let my bones be buried apart from yours. Death will unite us eternally. Oh, when I think of it all now, the hopes we had in our hearts, the plans we laid, in spite of time, the dreams we dreamed when we were young . . .'

And he reached out, stretching from his bed on the beach, to take Patroclus in his arms again. But the dream-shadow couldn't be clasped, and it vanished away like smoke, like sandmarks under water, leaving him with a faint wail.

Dawn's pink fingertips gripped the skyline now, and her rosy hands quietly stroked the sea-lanes of the east. The wood-gathering began. Agamemnon had sent out many men and mules to the spurs of Ida to cut and bring back timber for the pyre. The Myrmidons made a procession, chariots in front, infantry in the rear, to accompany Patroclus to the place on the shore that Achilles had chosen for him. Here they would build the barrow that would eventually contain both himself and the friend of his heart.

Achilles had long vowed to give his long yellow hair to Spercheus, the river of his homeland on his return to Phthia, but now he cut it off, staring bitterly across the wine-dark sea and saying that his father's wish had not been granted and never would – he'd never come home, would never see his own country again, and so he'd give his long hair not to Spercheus but to Patroclus to take with him to the House of the Dead. For Spercheus had been deaf to his father's prayers. So he laid the long lovely locks, shorn from his bent head, into his friend's dead hands, and he wept. Then the company went off to the ships. But the dead man's closest comrades stayed behind to do what now had to be done.

They built the pyre a hundred feet long and wide, and in the centre they placed Patroclus. The pale corpse, wrapped in the flame-coloured shroud, prefigured the fire that would consume it. Slaughtered sheep and cattle were heaped on the fire, together with jars of oil and honey. Achilles slew four fine horses and cut the throats of two of the nine dogs that Patroclus used to feed with scraps and crumbs from his own hand. These animals too he hurled into the flames.

Then – and this was the hardest thing – the twelve Trojan youths Achilles had taken were cruelly butchered and, while still seeing and alive, were pitched into the roaring flames to augment their last agonies.

The Myrmidons asked about Hector.

'No,' said Achilles, 'the flames are too quick for him. He'll be flung to the dogs. They'll chew his bones, and the vultures will gouge out his eyes.'

That was still his intended revenge, and his anger burned brighter at the thought of Hector's corpse rotting slowly under the sky. Except that Penelope would not have it that way. Not that she cared for Hector – she hated him – but she was uneasy about Achilles' ugliness of soul that reflected so badly on the Greeks. So she told a different version of the story of the unburied body.

And so Aphrodite kept the dogs from Hector and poured oil of roses on him, while over the corpse Phoebus Apollo drew a cloud as protection from the scorching sun and a glittering veil to keep away the wriggling worms. An exquisite arrangement. Art is long, existence short, as they say, though dogs and decomposition are facts of life, and death's door is always ajar.

Achilles now prayed to the winds. Iris delivered his message and veered off, setting a speedy course for Olympus. The pyre burned slowly at first, until the north wind and the rushing west wind came roaring over the sea, answering Achilles' call, and the sea surged and sang in response as the two winds tossed and whirled the flames together. So all night long in the howling winds Achilles paced heavily round and round the pyre like a man of lead, pouring out wine on the earth as he went, drenching it blood-red from a golden bowl for the burning bones of his friend. The tears fell from him.

Night and silence, broken only by the crackling flames. The Plough rusts slowly against the sky, turning in the field of stars. Dawn glimmers, the sea wrinkles, the pyre dwindles, and the flames drop down to embers and ash. And so Achilles drops, unconscious, exhausted, on the sand.

When he woke he gave his orders.

'Collect the bones carefully. It will be easy to identify Patroclus, because his bones will be at the centre. I want them placed in this golden urn and sealed with a double fold of fat, two good layers to protect them until the time my own bones come to join them, which will not be long now. Then the seal can be broken to let me be with my friend again.'

So they quenched the pyre with wine. The ashes fell. They gathered the white bones, weeping over them, and placed them in the golden urn, covered with a linen cloth, and put this in Achilles' tent. Next they marked out the circle for the mound, laid the foundations where the fire had been and heaped up the earth for the barrow.

No need for an imposing tomb yet, Achilles said. A simple one would suffice, until his own time came. Then, finally, those of the Myrmidons who'd be left after Achilles had gone would place the two together and build the barrow broad and huge and high.

And so it was done. But still Achilles wouldn't let them turn and go, not until they'd held games in honour of the dead. And all this was done too, except that Achilles would not race his own horses. They were the horses that Poseidon gave to Peleus, and Peleus to Achilles, and that could never be bested. Clearly unfair then, and unsporting, to enter them for the games. It is not every day you race horses that were the gift of a sea-god. And it is not every day you see horses in mourning. Yes, still they wept, those fabulous horses, wept on the web of devotion for their lost glorious charioteer, their tears trickling slowly down their long drooping manes, as only the tears of mythical horses do.

THIRTY-FIVE

Achilles threw himself to the wolves of sorrow. The many images of his friendship with Patroclus crowded round him like stars, peering through the windows of his eyes, open or shut, staring at him with white cold faces, like the white face of his friend before it flaked and vanished in the flames. He lay on his back and on his front and on his side, unable to find sleep. At last he'd rise and wander aimlessly along the beach, watching the dawn as it painted the salt-waste – pink at first, glimmering and glowing like a rose in the slow summer, then liquid gold as the sun came up.

But yet another dawn and sunrise brought him no hope; Aurora and Apollo were false to him. He could view the world only through the dim flickering of the torches he'd lit for the dead, the sombre flames of the funeral pyre on which he'd burned those precious bones, and not in the light of a false dawn or a garish day.

So he'd return from wandering the shore, yoke up his horses and drag Hector's body round and round Patroclus's tomb. Afterwards, he would fling it aside in the filth so that the desecration could continue.

The Olympians grew uneasy. Although, unknown to Achilles, the golden aegis of Apollo hung over the body as it lay in the dirt, although it fended off the dogs and maggots, even so the gods disapproved of this prolonged and pitiless savagery. They wanted to send Hermes, the slayer of Argus, to steal the corpse away and so end Achilles' shameful acts of anger, which disfigured his reputation as a hero. But three of the gods wouldn't hear of it: Poseidon, Pallas Athene and Hera – all powerful players on Olympus.

Behind the cold grey eyes of Athene especially there burned still a hot hate for Troy because of Paris's crime. Not the crime of wife-stealing in particular – there was nothing unusual there – but the greater sin of slighting the goddess when he had chosen Aphrodite for her beauty and had been awarded in return the madness of his heart's desire, the madness that had caused so much suffering and destroyed so many young lives.

After eleven days, however, Phoebus Apollo stood up on Olympus and spoke his piece. Achilles had lost all honour. All men must mourn for those they have loved and lost, but within reason. They must also learn to let their dead go and not allow the heart to be eaten up by anger. The human heart is made for suffering and endurance; bitterness does not become it. Achilles had lost his humanity as well as his honour. In desecrating senseless flesh, not in the heat of battle but in the deliberate vein of avenging anger, he had murdered compassion and made ugliness his objective. He was flouting the gods.

So Zeus sent Iris to Thetis, ordering her to go to her son and bring him to his senses again. Thetis obeyed, telling him that the gods now frowned on him and that he should return Hector to his family and accept the ransom for the dead. Achilles agreed. In truth, his revenge-thirst had been slaked at last, and he could drink no more from that cold and bittersweet cup.

Then Zeus sent Iris to Priam's palace, which was a scene of terrible grief, with daughters and daughters-in-law sorrowing for the newly dead, and Priam himself prostrate on the ground, his old bones all muffled up in his cloak and the white dust piled over his already white head. The old king seemed cut in stone, an abject figure, his face and shoulders defiled by the dung and dirt he'd gathered from the ash-pit and the midden where he'd grovelled, scooping up and throwing over himself the leavings of the table and of bodies, human and animal. Now he sat inert in his filth.

Picture it – a king sitting among excrement and cinders, and bright-coloured Iris appearing like a rainbow to deliver the Olympian order: Priam should go now to the Greek camp unprotected, with only one old man to drive the gift-laden mules, and he should ask the grief-weary Achilles to accept the ransom for his son.

The stricken king, still sitting among the ashes and slops, informed his wife of his intention. Hecuba was horrified.

'What, go to that inhuman brute? He'll tear your head off and slaughter you without a shred of sentiment. He butchered my son, and he'll smash you like a fly. He's a monster, not a man, and if I could only fasten my remaining teeth on his wolf's heart I'd eat it raw and gnaw the flesh from his bones.'

'Enough, woman!' roared Priam. 'Cease squawking at me like some bird of doom! Nothing but songs of death. I've had enough of death! But if he kills me, I'll be glad to go. I can't live another day like this – and my son unburied. So you can give over your wailing. I'm going.'

He collected together the best of the remaining treasures, sparing nothing, including twelve robes and cloaks, many sheets and mantles and tunics, ten talents of gold, two tripods, four cauldrons and a magnificent gold cup which the Thracians had presented him with once on embassy. It meant nothing to him in his loss, not now that the thing closest to him had been ripped from his heart. And, exactly as he had been ordered, he set out with just the one old man to drive the mules. Hecuba screamed at the guards not to let him out of the city, but they had to obey their king.

At the gates, the sight of the mourners drove him mad.

'About your business, you dismal lilters, you useless weepers, you lugubrious louts! Have you no sorrows of your own, no griefs in your homes that you have to hang about here mourning on my behalf, dinning my ears with your whimpering and snivelling, and drowning me in your rain of tears? I don't need it.'

He laid about them with his staff, and they scattered and ran from the crazed old king. After that, he turned on his remaining sons, Helenus, Agathon, Pammon, Antiphonus, Deiphobus, Hippothous, Dius, Polites – and Paris. And he cursed them one and all.

'You – look at you! I had the finest sons once, and not one of them is left alive. I've lost all. You're not my sons. The war has cropped the flower of my family, and see what I'm left with! Only the sons of shame remain to me, the wasters and revellers, the heroes of the dance and the drinking tables. You earn your laurels with the ladies and the soft-livers – when you're not otherwise busy fleecing your own people of their sheep, you scum! Oh yes, I know you all. Can't one of you at least yoke up these mules and set me on my way to bring back your brother's body if I can? That's if the Greek dogs have left anything of him to bury.'

They were not all idlers. Their main fault was not to have been killed. They had survived their illustrious brother, and now his shadow would always be over them and his shade haunt them. But they felt ashamed after this outburst from their demented father, and they did as he asked. Hecuba had abandoned her attempts to prevent him and she begged him to pray to Zeus for a good omen.

The skies stayed empty after sunset.

But Penelope felt a fellowship with the woman of sorrows, and she wove into the web the dark rider of the air, the great eagle with wings outspread. He was one of those dusky hunters, the colour of a grape as it ripens and takes on the succulent dust of a vintage bloom. And though no such eagle appeared, or any eagle for that matter, to lift the old king's hopes on his splendid wings, Penelope's bird was an accurate enough image of the old man's emotion, spanning the huge extent of the hope that must have filled his heart, wing-tip to wing-tip, soaring to the gods.

Hermes came in too, hot from Olympus by order of Zeus, to guide Priam through the Greek camp and render him invisible until he'd arrived at Achilles' quarters. Otherwise he'd have been butchered long before he reached him, or seized for ransom. And how else could he have done it unless by divine aid? A cool and courageous spy with a streak of daring or with a clever comrade can make his way through enemy lines. But two old fossils and a train of mules, clanking with treasure? Easier to make way for the gods – if there's room in your universe for gods and you are not the prisoner of a closed mind.

Enter therefore Hermes. The Argus-slayer bound to his immortal feet the famous golden sandals that bore him up on the pathways of the wind over land and sea. Disguising himself as a young man, he intercepted Priam just as he and his ancient retainer had passed the tomb of Ilus, stopping at the river to let their beasts drink. Hermes approached and pointed out the danger Priam was putting himself in. Passing himself off as a squire of Achilles, he offered to befriend the king and lead him safely to his son's killer and to the body of his beloved son.

'But what about his condition? Isn't he by now less than butcher meat? Isn't he mere offal and gnawed bones?'

Hermes smiled radiantly.

'No, that's just the wonder of it. He's exactly as he was twelve days ago when he died. Even though Achilles has dragged the corpse around the tomb every morning without mercy, the body doesn't suffer, doesn't decompose. That's what the gods can do for those they love. And it is obvious the gods loved Hector like no other.'

So Hermes acted as their guide to the Greek camp and conducted them to Achilles' quarters. He moved the massive beam that secured the gate, the one it took three strong men even to lift. That's when Priam understood that his kind helper was no human being after all. Having fulfilled his orders, Hermes revealed his identity and left, telling Priam not to be afraid but to go right in, walk straight up to Achilles and tell him who he was. He'd already laid sleep on the eyelids of the sentinels in their bivouac at the rampart gates.

You could say, of course, that Hermes was unnecessary. You could say that sheer exhaustion was sufficient to make the sentries sleep. You could say that soldiers who have been engaged in a long conflict and have recently routed the enemy in an all-important battle for survival have every right to sleep. You could say that they felt safe in supposing that the enemy would not attack again that night, not so soon after such a hard battle. You could say that the Greek army had grown relaxed and confident following Hector's death. You could say that the Myrmidons in particular, much as they respected their leader, were sick of mourning and long faces and restraint and had been partying for some time now in the long nights, drinking and singing and sleeping it off. You could say that there were a great many men out and about on those nights, men less interested in revelry than in looting, stripping the many corpses that strewed the plain between the Greek ships and the city, and that it was not unusual to see carts trundling back to camp in the dark, clinking with bronze, carts that nobody troubled to intercept or even ask who they were and what they were about, as if they didn't know.

Or you could simply smile and say you believed in gods.

Whatever the truth of the matter, Achilles was certainly shocked. He was sitting a little apart from the main company, at a table with two friends, and he'd just taken some food and drink when this unkempt old man entered the hall, came right up to him, knelt down and kissed his hands. Achilles instinctively reached for a weapon, then stopped. Everybody looked up and stared in amazement.

Priam spoke first.

'Yes, it's me. I am who I am. Think of your father tonight, Achilles, as I'm sure you think of him often – an old man, just like me, perhaps beset by his enemies and no son at home to defend him. But even he has the happiness of hoping for his son's eventual return, however improbable it may seem to him now. I don't have that happiness, and I never will. I have only my grief. The war has taken the only sons that mattered to me, all of them killed in action by Ares in his anger. I am begging you now, for your own father's sake, to reverence the gods and honour the dead. Give me back the body of my son for ransom. And remember that I have had to endure what no man should – I have lifted to my lips the hands that slaughtered my son. I have kissed in entreaty the hands of the killer.'

As Priam spoke, Achilles did remember his own father, the father he knew he would never see again, and his heart filled up with grief. He took the old king by the hand and put him gently away from him so that he could sit on his own for a moment and control the spasms of sadness, the shaking, shuddering sobs that suddenly took hold of him. And the combined sorrows of the two men, young and old, filled the quarters and brought lumps to the throats of the hardened soldiers who sat around.

At last Achilles stood up and lifted the old man from the ground, pitying his white hairs. He sat him down beside him and begged him to let his grief be silent for a while.

'I know you are a man of many sorrows. But I too, old man, must give up this grief at last, by the order of the gods. Of what use is it in the end? Trouble and suffering are our lot, and we must endure it; there is no other way. The gods, it seems, have woven sorrow into the very fabric of our fated lives. If it were not so, we too would be gods. And even the hottest tears in the end go cold on the face.'

Priam raised a trembling hand, but Achilles touched it softly, asking him courteously to hear him out.

'The gods have two pitchers, one brimming with sorrows and one with joy. From these is poured out our destined portion. Most men are given a mingled vessel. But to certain other men the gods give nothing but sorrow. Madness comes over them, and they wander lonely and desolate over the bright earth, unhonoured either by gods or men. It is a tragic portion and a terrible one. My own father had blessings, fabulous wealth, good fortune and a goddess for a wife. But he will have no sons in his age and will never see me again – this I can tell you here and now because it is known to the gods. I have been far removed from this father of mine for so long. And to what purpose? What have I been doing all this time? Causing misery both for you and for him, in this awful bloody war.

'No, listen to me –' as Priam tried again to interrupt –'I'm almost done. You too were happy once. From Lesbos to the Hellespont, they say there was none happier. Or greater. And now the gods have brought you bitterness out of the sea, out of the sky. You have been brought low. But you have to bear it and put away your sorrow, the years of siege and suffering. You must stop grieving. Tears won't bring your son back to you. Though waterdrops will one day wear down the walls of Troy, no amount of salt you can shed will ever make him stand up again. Your own day will come before that happens. And all your sorrows will be over.'

Priam listened. But he persisted in his mission, asking Achilles not to delay any longer but to take the ransom and release his son's body. He wanted no philosophy: he wanted his son. 'And may you yet come home at last in peace because you took pity on me and showed me mercy.'

Achilles looked at him, and for a moment the old insane anger flickered in his eyes. 'Don't drive me mad, old man, I beg you. I can tell you that I have already decided to give you back your son. But leave me a little. The truth is, I hardly know myself any more. It's this miserable grief. It's made me mad. And I don't want to lose control again and do you harm, a supplicant under my own roof, such as it is. That would be dishonourable, adding to the dishonour I've done you already. Just let me be, please, for a few moments.'

The old man understood and held his peace, and Achilles stumbled from the room and out of the lodging, under the stars. Automedon and Alcimus went after him and brought in the ransom. Achilles ordered the women to wash the corpse and anoint it as best they could and to dress it well away from Priam, in case the spectacle of what had been done to his son should cause him to lash out in his grieving anger and make Achilles also act in a way he would later regret. And when the wounds had been disguised, he took Hector in his own strong arms and laid him on a stretcher, calling on the ghost of Patroclus not to be angry with him because of the rich ransom – though it was not the ransom that had touched his heart. Then he went back to Priam.

'Now let us eat and drink together.'

Priam was reluctant, but Achilles was patient with him and asked if he knew the story of Niobe. Priam knew it; everybody in the world knew it. But he let Achilles tell him the legend, as he appeared to take some comfort in the telling.

And so Achilles reminded the king of how Niobe had lost all her twelve children, six daughters and six sons, because she'd boasted about the number of her offspring, setting herself above Leto of the Lovely Cheeks, the mother of Artemis and Apollo, who had only those two children to show for herself, lovely though she was, whereas Niobe had twelve. And in their anger against her stupid pride, Leto's children quickly saw to it that very shortly she had none – not a single child left. With their arrows, Artemis the Archeress and Apollo of the Silver Bow bereaved her utterly and without exception. And her offspring lay for nine days unburied in their own blood, exactly where they'd fallen, not unlike Hector. Only on the tenth day did the gods grant them burial.

And even Niobe took food at last, when she'd wept her heart away. As do all of us. As indeed we must. And now they say Niobe herself is turned to stone and still broods on her grief, far away on the lonely mountains among the cliffs, the untrodden hills of Sipylus, where they say the wood-nymphs come to sleep after dancing on the banks of

Achelous. There stands she still, poor marble Niobe, in her lapidary grief, brooding on the desolation she caused and which the gods gave her. Yet even Niobe ate and drank when the time came.

'And so must you, old man. I have been turned to stone,' said Achilles, 'but now I'm flesh again, and you've made my heart beat once more.'

So they ate and drank together, the killer and the man he had bereaved. War had divided them and grief united them, and, despite himself, Priam admired Achilles, the strength and beauty that made him like a god. The king asked for a couch for the night; he was so exhausted, having not slept since Hector's death, and now the food and wine had made him give way at last. Achilles had handmaidens pile couches in the portico, afraid that if some of the chiefs came to talk they'd spy Priam and inform Agamemnon, who'd be sure to say Achilles had gone soft and ought to be overruled.

Achilles asked the old king how long he'd need for mourning. Nine days, said Priam, with the burial on the tenth and the barrow built over the burned bones on the eleventh. And on the twelfth day there would be a return to war. Achilles readily agreed to a truce for these eleven days, and Priam lay down in the porch and gladly slept, though with many thoughts still running like troubled streams through his head and heart as he dreamed. Achilles slept with Briseis by his side, beautiful Briseis, whose beauty was scarred now by her own nails.

But Hermes did not sleep. He returned in the middle of the night, entered invisibly, and whispered in the king's ear to get up and go, afraid that if Agamemnon accidentally discovered him in the camp, Troy would have to pay a ransom three times heavier than he'd already paid for Hector. Or worse. There was not enough left in the coffers of the shattered city to meet such a ransom, and the price might instead be Priam's life.

Priam sat up suddenly, alarmed in the darkness. Had it been a dream? He roused the herald and they left unseen as the golden dawn broadened over land and sea.

Cassandra saw them coming as she stood on a tower of Troy, tall as pale-gold Aphrodite and every bit as alluring. She climbed to the summit of Pergamos and cried to all the people to come and greet dead Hector. Her shrieks brought out the whole town from their sleep, and they thronged the gates, waiting for their king's return with his load of grief. He shouted for them to make way for him, and they crowded after him and watched as Hector was laid on a stately bed.

Andromache comes first.

She draws down his dead head on her breast and weeps for him.

'And for my fatherless son, and for our city that will surely be toppled now, and for the women and children that will be carried off in the murmuring hulls, and our own boy along with them, unless the Greeks choose to kill him right here and now, in revenge perhaps for some friend, some comrade that Hector killed – he brought down so many hundreds and filled their mouths with dust – and for which the little mite will be hurled from the highest tower to spill out his brains in front of the city.'

Hecuba is next.

Baring her ancient breast again, she draws down the dead head to it and puts the nipple to the still lips, screaming to the gods to bring the life-giving milk back again into the glands, to flow once more into the mouth, to bring her child alive again and make her boy grow strong.

'Even though Achilles took so many of you in the field or sent them overseas, sold them into slavery in Samos or in Imbros or in smoke-capped Lemnos, bring me one, just this one, I beg you, back to life, O ye gods, to suck my breast and live again.'

The breast lies withered on the face, the nipple dry, the mouth without motion, the lips without language.

Last comes Helen.

She laments that she never heard a single bitter word from Hector in all the years of blood she has caused. Even when everyone else reproached her – brothers, sisters, the brothers' wealthy wives, who stood to lose their husbands, their fortunes and their freedom, even their lives – even then, the kind and courteous Hector never failed to take her side. Now he is gone, and there is no one left in the whole wide windy city to befriend her. 'So I weep for you, Hector, and for my wretched self.'

Even as she speaks, they turn away from her with a shudder, she the cause of all their grief.

Finally, they go up to the mountains to bring down timber for the pyre, sure of Achilles' truce. Nine days they mourn. And on the tenth, as the sun rises, they carry Hector out of the gates, lay him on his pyre and set fire to it. And the next morning, when Aurora makes the sky rosy with another dawn, they gather round it again and quench the dying embers with blood-red wine. And his remaining brothers and friends gather up his white bones and put them in a golden urn wrapped with a purple cloth. Then they lay the chest in a grave under broad slabs of stone, and over it they heap up the barrow, looking high over the Hellespont. They troop home, back inside the city walls, and prepare for the solemn feast in the palace hall.

And thus hold they funeral rites for Hector, tamer of horses.

PART THREE
THE HOMECOMINGS

After Hector was wiped out, things hotted up again, and the conflict that had dragged on so long reached its end at last. Inevitably bloody. You expect nothing else after a long war.

With his best son now a handful of heroic ashes, Priam looked about him for extra backup. He got it from an unexpected quarter, a woman soldier and an interesting ally, Penthesilea, leader of the Amazons. She was a Thracian and a queen, a daughter of Ares. A glory girl. The Thracian bit was true, at least, and she had had her day of glory in the field, even if Ares didn't show his face. Nor did Apollo, though she was just up his street, an archeress of incomparable ability. She took out scores of us all in one day, until Achilles killed her. Unknowingly, as it happened. It was only when he wrenched out his spear after a shit-hot throw and took off the helmet that his mouth fell open.

'Fuck!'

He removed the upper-body armour and exposed a pair of tits. Aureoles like Aphrodite's. Chestnuts.

'Double-fuck!'

She could have been his captive, his queen.

'He's falling in love!' laughed Thersites. 'And with a woman too! Wonders will never cease!'

Achilles didn't answer. He was staring into the dead face. Thersites jeered again.

'Look at you, you pathetic cunt, bubbling over a slut! And an Amazon slut at that, you sloppy old darling!'

'Shut the fuck up!'

Thersites kept on gnawing the bone. Never could know when to stop. Blind and deaf to the signals. Not dumb, though. The yapping carried on.

'It's her fuck-hole you'd like, isn't it? Come on, admit it!'

'Enough!'

'You fucking heroes. Can't keep your dicks under control!'

'I'm warning you!'

Thersites ignored it. He jabbed the pale corpse in the eye and spat on it. 'She was picking off our lads — and you're still fucking drooling over her!'

Achilles went white with rage. 'Get away from her, you bastard!'

Thersites grinned. 'In a minute.'

He kicked open the legs, revealing everything that made Penthesilea a woman.

'Well, I'd say that settles it — she's female all right. Quite a crack on her, eh? There you go, whore! Try a few inches of Greek bronze up your Amazon cunt!'

He inserted his spear and thrust up hard, grinning round at the gathering of faces, waiting for the applause.

'And that's the only hard-on you'll get up you now, fair Thracian — this arsehole Achilles hasn't got the balls for it anyway, not since his little bumboy went belly up, eh?'

Achilles reared up to his full height and smashed Thersites on the side of the head. He used his bare fist, no weapon, but it was so powerful a blow you could see the shattered teeth spraying out and scattering on the ground. Not that he had many but he'd fewer now, not one left in his head. It didn't matter to him. He was killed instantly.

Everybody went quiet.

Thersites was a piece of shite — or had been. But even a piece of shite is worth something, socially speaking, if he's an aristocratic piece of shite, and Thersites was every ugly inch the noble shite. He'd crawled out of an elegant arsehole, the working part thereof, uppercrust. It was blue blood that had just been stopped in those shitty veins. And Achilles had stopped it. Some of us were happy enough with that, but there were plenty who'd fed on his venom, and they were the ones who now did the muttering.

It had to be cleaned up, however you looked at it. Achilles knew that, even as Diomedes came up and shook hands with him over the corpse, assuring him of no bad blood. But the blood was there, still trickling from the ruined head — strange to see Thersites lying so quiet and peaceable — and that blood was going nowhere, not until Achilles did.

'It'll only take a few days,' said Agamemnon, coming up and clapping him on the shoulder. 'A couple of weeks at most.'

Thersites had been no friend to Agamemnon.

'Lesbos?' Achilles asked quietly.

'Lesbos.'

And that's how Achilles came to leave for his cleansing.

He should have stayed in Lesbos. There was a saying, live in Lesbos — and live! While he was away, one of Priam's last remaining allies,

Memnon, came into the field. He was the son of Eos and Tithonus. Eos, Titaness of the dawn, loved Tithonus so badly she couldn't bear the thought that one day he'd die. So, as Penelope told it, she begged Zeus that he'd live forever, just like the gods, and stay with her always, always by her side. Zeus agreed but must have forgotten to stem the ageing process while he was arranging the immortality, with the unfortunate result that while Eos stayed as young as the dawn, naturally, and never an hour older, Tithonus shrivelled up into a grasshopper of a man. Shrunken with age in time's fullness, but still chirping and gibbering away uselessly to himself, he became a burbling idiot, a desiccated wisp, his tunic stained and mouldy with old food, his shrill twittering getting on everybody's tits, especially Eos's, and her tits were still in the dawn of womanhood, needing a young man's handling. So Tithonus had to be locked up in a remote corner of the palace, out of all sight and hearing. And probably smell.

That much was true — he lost his marbles well before his time and became a pest, with confinement the only answer, short of chucking him off a cliff. The Zeus story was invented, naturally. And a Titaness of the dawn sounds like a fabulous mother for Memnon. Fabulous is the word. A winter's tale. A myth. But whatever his parentage, Memnon came in at the end with his contingent of black soldiers, for which Priam had paid through the nose.

He paid for nothing. The mercenaries were useless. On the very same day, Achilles and his Myrmidons came back from Lesbos — just in time to knock hell out of them and crush Priam's last remaining hope.

But Achilles died that same day at the Scaean Gate, just as Hector had prophesied. Not that Hector had the gift. Leaders are always coming out with that one — you will fall outside our walls, you will die at our city gates . . . One of those times it has to be true, and this was one of those times.

After Memnon was routed — with shameful ease — Achilles chased the blackheads back inside the city. But Paris was watching from the main tower over the gate and shot him from a height, from a safe distance, and from inside the walls, a triple chicken. It didn't take Apollo either to bring Achilles down, though the web shows the god pointing to the famous heel, showing Paris where to aim. An old story, that one. Truth's simpler than myth. Getting the angle right was next to impossible, and sure enough the arrow fell short. The nick on the heel was a pure fluke, but the nick was enough. The arrow was tipped with poison.

Stories do the rounds, stories that dress death up nicely and make it meaningful. Penelope liked the one about the heel best of all. Thetis had dipped the infant in the Styx, to make him immortal. But she had forgotten about the point where she'd held him between finger and thumb, the heel. O the almighty gods — as fallible as the rest of us! And that's where Paris's arrow struck him, in the only place where he was vulnerable, the exclusively mortal heel. And the arrow was assisted on its way by the iron arm of Apollo.

It's a breathless moment — the Scaean Gate swings wide open on its hinges to let the retreating army through, Achilles plunges through the gap like a dolphin after fry, and slinky Paris up there watches and waits. Apollo is at his side, bending the bow, lowering it slowly, the god's hands on mortal hands, guiding, finding the angle of elevation, assessing the correct trajectory with the cold blue geometry of his eyes, whispering all the time in Paris's ear, telling him when to let loose . . .

Fancy an even truer version? It's simpler than ever. Paris shot Achilles not in the heel, with Apollo's aid, but in the back, and all by himself. Face him in the field? The little prick never yet saw the whites of enemy eyes. Not when he could fire an arrow instead, the serpent's weapon, and tip it with venom like the slippery shit he was. Which was exactly what he did. If he'd really aimed for the heel and had hit him there, fuck me, it would have been an amazing shot, given the distance, the angle, the fast-moving target. Only a god could have set it up.

But what does it matter in the end? Same difference to Achilles. A dead man's a dead man, and for Achilles the war was over. That was as close as he ever got to Phthia. That was his long homecoming. Dead heroes never stop returning home, lacerating their loved ones with each new day. And his old father didn't have too many days left. He died of a broken heart.

At least we got the body out. Achilles had gone well through the gates and died inside Troy. Ajax made the dash with me, and we went in together and battled for the corpse. Sheer fucking hell it was in there, but we got out before they shut the gates and minced us. Achilles was assured of his burning, and his reunion with the ashes of his friend, silly sentimental old bastard — Thersites had been right about that. Still, that's what he wanted.

The sea-nymphs rise, robed in foam, following Thetis to the shore. Out of the waves she comes, accompanied by the Muses and her immortal sea-girls wreathed with seaweed red and brown, combing the white blown hair of the waves, wafting out of the ocean wastes to bewail her son. The unforgettable crying ascends to the skies, spreading out over the wide waters, and Zeus sends down a great rain of tears.

We held the usual games for the dead hero. They lasted seventeen days, and the blackheads were thrilled with the breather and kept the ceasefire as we'd done for them when they were burning Hector. There were great prizes up for grabs. I wrestled Ajax for Achilles' arms and thrashed the bastard. He thought they were his for the taking – and true, he should've won, with his height and bulk and all, but it's easy to outwit an oaf. Use an idiot's own strength against him and suddenly he's on your side.

Another story went round that, unknown to us, Nestor had sent spies into Troy to find out whom they took to be our top soldier now that Achilles was ashes. The spies eavesdropped on a couple of gabbling girls. One said Ajax was top notch because he was the one who'd dragged Achilles outside the gates and got the body to safety. The other said anybody could haul a corpse, even a girl could do it, and Achilles was slender built, whereas Ajax was a mountain. That was the easy bit. Keeping the Trojans at bay had made the rescue possible, and that took more effort and a braver man, she said – and that was down to Odysseus. Nestor went with that view, one with which I fully agreed, and the weapons came to me.

Well, spies were always in and out of Troy, and girls gossip, but I know I beat Ajax fair and square and left the bastard breathless on the ground. After which, he went AWOL, and subsequently stark raving mad. He slaughtered all our cattle, undoing months of work that had gone into the raids. He even whipped two rams to death, mistaking them for Agamemnon and Menelaus, so bonkers had he gone. In the end, he topped himself, the stupid cunt, so we buried him in a stone coffin, no pyre for him, and he's there in the web, still sulking in hell – which was all the homecoming he got.

But all that happened after the sack. In the meantime, we were planning revenge for Achilles. Our hero had been killed, unheroically, and we weren't going to let Paris get away with it. Nestor called a meeting to discuss the question of how to kill a non-combatant, a fight-funker. A bow-boy. Answer: with another bowman, but an even better one. And who was our best archer? Philoctetes, who was on Tenedos, where he'd settled some time after we'd left him on nearby Lemnos paralysed by a snakebite. He could easily have been demobbed, but the poor bugger couldn't bring himself to go home in that condition – fucked up not by action but by a snake. So he had opted to stay on instead and perfected his art from a sitting position, till he was the best archer in the known world. Even before that, there was probably no one standing who could have beaten him. And now he was the bee's knees – a crippled killer, but still a killer.

We sent Diomedes over to Tenedos to being him back, knowing it would be no easy mission. It wasn't. Diomedes told him his contribution could win the war. He said he didn't give a flying fuck for the war – after all, it was the war that had fucked him. We'd foreseen that answer and we'd sent Machaon along with Diomedes to work on him, medically. Machaon was hot shit when it came to drugs. He didn't cure him completely, but the treatment worked wonders, and in a matter of days he was firing his arrows standing up. Back on his feet, he stepped on board with Diomedes, a little gingerly but with an expectant grin cracking his ugly mug. His mission was to kill Paris.

I planned it all myself. The first stage was to wind down our attacks to a minimum and make it look as if morale was low. Then I asked for volunteers to expose themselves as easy targets and draw the bastard's fire. Big rewards were on offer. Even so, there were only two volunteers and they never got their rewards. They both bought it on the first day. After that, no more volunteers. So I volunteered myself for the job, bringing up a siege-engine, right up to the walls, but making sure I stood out. I needed men for this job, but they'd fuck-all else to do but shove under cover and just stand there watching me out in the open, apparently giving orders. I'd be a sitting duck, the only target in Troy. They were happy with that. Bastards.

Sure enough, Paris went for it, thinking he was in for another easy kill. I saw him out of the corner of my eye, up on his killing tower, his balls (if he had any) tucked well out of harm's way. What the cunt didn't know was that Philoctetes, hidden inside the siege-engine, was peering out through the slit and lining up his own kill. He saw Paris and slid his bow slowly out, just a fraction. Meanwhile I could see Paris getting me in his sights, the sniping little shit. My bowels trembled. I knew it would be a poisoned arrow, and a flesh wound would be all it would take. Philoctetes had the same set-up, but that would be fuck-all use if Paris got in first, and my man was in no hurry.

'Get a move on!' I hissed at him between my teeth. 'I can see the cunt's knuckles now, white as fucking snow!'

Still Philoctetes hung fire. 'I only get the one shot, remember? Wait till he shows more of himself.'

'Wait till he fucking does for me, you mean!'

Twang!

I watched Paris's arrow leave the bow, saw him crane his neck, eager to follow the shot. I had one second. I hit the deck. Philoctetes fired. We heard the scream. The arrow hit the ground just behind me, and the tower above us thickened with figures. The wailing started up.

He'd taken it in the side and had nearly fallen off the tower, he'd been leaning out so far. Philoctetes had gone for the neck, so it was a long way from his best shot. But then Apollo wasn't directing it. Maybe he was even diverting it. Neck or side, it didn't matter. The Hydra's burning blood was in the bastard's veins, and nothing would shift it. The cunt was buggered, and he knew it. All of Troy knew it, by the sound of it. He'd only one hope left in the world now – Oenone, the wife he'd deserted for Helen. She could work miracles with herbs, concocting antidotes even for the deadliest toxins. They said her potions could bring dead men back to life. Once she'd revived a man who'd been stone-cold for three days.

What were his chances? Oenone was still living on Ida with the children he'd left her with. You'd think he'd feel shame even to ask an abandoned partner, but he couldn't tell shame from self-regard, and the narcissistic little shit was in extremis, and in extreme agony. Next day, before dawn, the cunt was carried on a litter all the way to Oenone. Her frightened kids hung onto her skirts – they'd forgotten who their father was and had no idea that this gasping bastard staring up at them had once sired them on Ida. She looked down at him with stone-cold eyes.

'Get back to your Spartan, you pathetic piece of shit! You heartless little whoremaster! Back you go to her, and let her cunt cure you!'

They carried him back down the mountainside, and he was dead before they reached the edge of the forest. His last request was to be burned and buried right there and then, on Ida, where he belonged, the little shit-kicker, where if he'd stayed and shagged his sheep, countless lives would have been saved.

They built the pyre and set fire to it, the wailing flying up with the flames. Oenone heard the howls, saw the sparks, like swarms of bees, red-hot, buzzing over the treetops – and guess what? She relented. Can you believe it? Came running after them down the mountain, too late, screaming that she still loved the bastard in spite of everything that he'd done, the selfishness, the humiliation. After all this time she still cared for him. A last embrace, then, not too late for that? No, never too late. She leapt up onto the pyre in her grief, clasping the burning body in her arms. The sparks went mad and the flames flew up as man and ex-wife mingled, man and wife again, one flesh, feeding the flames. The poor kids had run after her and flew to the pyre screaming for their mother and had to be restrained, orphans as they were now. And that's how Paris went back to his first wife and came home again to Ida.

THIRTY-SEVEN

With Paris dead, the fair Helen was free to return, or be returned, to her first husband – or so you would have thought. But her history was never going to be so simple. She'd escaped a seducer, cheated on a spouse, been widowed and was now so eminently available again that her late husband's brothers, Helenus and Deiphobus, fought for her hand. Priam should have let the pair of them slug it out. Instead, he gave her away to Deiphobus, and a mightily pissed-off Helenus stormed out of Troy and defected – to us! He came over to the Greek side. That's the effect that whore had on men.

Agamemnon rubbed his grubby fists, and Helenus was debriefed immediately. The treacherous cunt couldn't do enough to help us. He squeaked his fucking head off, crap mostly, but he did come out with one interesting idea – he advised us to get into the city under cover and steal the Palladium from the temple of Athene. This, he said, would seriously undermine Trojan morale, or what was left of it, at this stage of the war.

And who was volunteered for the job? The master of dissembling – old Odysseus. Of course he fucking was. Talent doesn't always pay. In this case, so goes the tale, I had to be beaten up till I was badly bruised and blackened and bloodied, swollen out of all recognition. Then I exchanged clothes with one of the latriners so that I smelled to hell. And in my rags, reeking of turds, I limped into the city as a beggar.

That was the easy bit. Getting into the temple and back out again with the Palladium – that was something else. Penelope made it easier for me. In her web, I found a way to Helen – as if – and said I'd protect her when we took the city if only she'd help me now. She played along, spun me the story that she'd always detested Paris and hated Deiphobus even more. She wanted to get back to Menelaus and Sparta. Of course she fucking did. The war could only go one way now.

'Ever considered escape?' I asked her.

Old Odysseus – still full of cunning. But she wasn't fazed.

'Many times,' she sighed. 'And tried it often enough. I've lost count of the number of times. Only the guards up on the ramparts there could put a figure to it, the times I've been caught up there, all roped up and ready to go over the wall.'

Once, she was nearly hanged, she said, when they hauled her back up again. She had only been feet from the ground.

'Liberation is all I thought of. But I'll make another attempt tonight and create a diversion for you while you get out on the other side with the Palladium.'

She was betting heavily on the Greek side now.

'Fickle bitch!' spat Penelope, warming to her own woven account. 'Perfidious whore and a half! And treacherous to the last thrust of her cunt!'

On the subject of Helen, Penelope's language deteriorated. On the web, she was more tasteful and restrained. Theano, Antenor's wife, can be seen helping me. She was priestess of the temple, and apart from being married to a pro-Greek man, had been worked on by Helen. So there she stands, Theano, arms outstretched, handing me the Palladium.

Nice idea – and one I'd have tried if I'd thought it could have worked. A sweeter story for sure than the one that's true.

One good moonless night I crept into the city with Diomedes. We got in through a drain so stinking wicked it must have been the main sewer running right out of hell. Piss and shit are bad enough on their own, but put them together and you have a sickening concoction. We emptied our insides on that journey, puked our fucking rings up. Even temples require an egress for shit, and holy shit smells the same as any other. But where there's an egress there's an ingress, and we made it into the holy of holies, snatched the Palladium and got out fast, back through hell's large intestine and out under the walls. We were just about dead with the stench by the time we made it back to base, but the Palladium was ours. They'd lost their talisman, their divine trinket. Troy's hour had come.

And so had Sinon's.

Sinon. A good name for a trickster and a spy. A name for bane and bad luck, vexation, plague. A scourge, a curse. He was the chink through which we finally infiltrated the city.

I didn't like the cunt, and I'd put up his name to be sacrificed when we left Troy. You can't end a major war without a sacrifice. Some poor fucker has always got to pay that price, the one for the good of the many, and even if you don't believe in gods, or do but don't put much faith in them, you make out you do, just in case. What have you got to lose?

Sinon didn't much fancy the honour of being the sacrificial goat, so he fucked off and hid in the marshes. He was found and given the choice to bleat his blood out on a stone, as planned, or to go undercover and trick the Trojans into believing that we'd all finally just got up and fucked off. It was a dangerous game to play, but it gave him the chance to stay alive.

Beaten and bruised, caked in filth and dried blood, fettered up to his balls and smeared with faeces, he was left behind on the shore when we sailed away – no further off than Tenedos, a couple of hours' sailing time on a good night. With the fleet tucked well into the creeks and coves and out of sight, Sinon's mission was to convince the blackheads that he was a deserter and had escaped execution.

They didn't take too much convincing – we'd done a good job on him. He was found by some shepherds, who swallowed his story and took him into Troy to be cleaned up and questioned. Priam drank it all in, every word. It was obvious anyway, wasn't it? We'd burned our camp, and why the fuck would we fire the huts if we'd be needing them again? And we didn't. Any idiot could see that. We'd left Troy – and without Helen. We'd had enough. We'd thrown in the sponge. The war would become a byword for a classic shambles, Greece's greatest catastrophe and cock-up of all time. Sinon was simply confirming what their eyes told them was true, and, instead of slitting his throat, they crowned him with laurels – after they'd scraped the shit off him. The partying got under way, much jubilation. There would be a bunch of sore heads come dawn. And some poor cunts with no heads at all. What cures a Trojan headache? A Greek axe.

But let Penelope tell it her way. Truth can be too trite, too simple a trick for legend to accept: a fake withdrawal and a spy covered in shit, followed by a surprise attack when the enemy was off his guard, not to say blind fucking drunk. Banal? That's what made it work, the simplicity, the unoriginality, the traitor within the gates, the stuff of annals, old in story. But not the stuff of myth. And after such a long and bloody struggle, mass slaughter and men turned into smoke, maybe you do need something else, something other than just a cheap swindle, without a drop of drama, or glamour. What you want is something big and unusual and memorable. What you want is the Trojan Horse.

There it stands in the web for all time, towering before the Scaean Gate, a lofty stallion, all in polished pine, purple, gilded, glorious, its amber eyes installed in emerald, sea-green, incorruptible, its white ivory teeth twinkling in the dawn. Behold the golden bit and bejewelled bridle, the flaming reins, the flowing tail twisted with gold, with bright silk ribbons richly hung, and the hooves all mounted with polished tortoise shell. All this the astonished eye can see.

What no eye can see is the secret trapdoor, the belly than can open like a woman's and bear men. What you see is what the Trojans themselves saw, a splendid steed and a magnificently crafted tribute to the horse-taming tribe, the people of Troy, traders in horses, an acknowledgement of their special mastery and eulogy to the equestrian art, even an apology, if you like, for the death of Hector, tamer of horses – and for the long war of occupation. A parting gift.

A deadly gift. Into the belly of the horse, hidden in the hollow body, crept nine Greek soldiers along with myself: Anticlus, followed by Epeius, the shipwright and builder of the horse, Thrasymedes, son of Nestor, Eumelus, Demophon and Aeamas, sons of Theseus, Little Ajax, Teucer, brother of Big Ajax, dead over the arms matter – and of course Menelaus, eager to be first on the scene, ready to slit his wife's white throat.

This is the litter of nine to be delivered by old Odysseus, Odysseus of the many wiles, master of stratagems. The horse will give birth, Sinon will kindle a fire on the grave of Achilles, the fleet will return, the traitor's hand will slide the bolt, and the city will fall. This is the litter of nine that will suck the dear life of Troy away.

Impossible, surely impossible. Look, the plains of Troy lie empty and deserted. Except for the horse, they haven't left a straw. And on the wide sea not a sail in sight. It's over, the long siege is over, the war is ended. Troy held out after all. The sacrifices were not in vain.

And yet. And yet . . .

When you run out of reasons that explain human stupidity, you can always blame the gods. But shifting the scene to Olympus doesn't change the truth. The horse wasn't fated to be taken into Troy. It didn't have to be. Men are masters of their fates. There's always a choice. And there's always a right choice and a wrong choice. The Trojans made the wrong choice. Why?

Why? You could call it collective suicide. Nations do that all the time, committing suicide, pursuing policies contrary to self-interest. It's written into a national psyche. Given time the nation will destroy itself. It will wage a futile war. It will show weakness when attacked. It will lose its borders, let them grow soft and porous. It will be taken over by foreigners. Its administrators will sink into gross incompetence, betraying the nation. That is the Trojan Horse. And bringing the horse inside the walls was the first step to self-slaughter. The leaders opted to pursue the policy that was contrary to the welfare of the country.

Was there an alternative? No, there was not an alternative; there were many alternatives, all sorts of options. Burn it, dismantle it, drag it out to sea, leave it to stand there on its four legs and rot in the rain, blister in the sun, a memorial to war, a monument to folly.

All of which they debate before bringing the horse within the gates, rolled in on its magnificent wheels. The Greeks have thought of everything, made it easy for them. Yet even now, now that it's inside, even now there are choices left to them. Consecrate it to Athene? Hurl it back down from the walls? Chop it into kindling? Raze it to the ground? Yes, raze it, torch it! The hidden contingent starts to sweat, the smell of fear fills the darkened space, swells the horse's belly. Suddenly the wooden womb is no longer safe. The men whisper about whether to reveal themselves, throw themselves on the mercy of the enemy. Mercy? What mercy? They know well enough there will be no mercy, not for men whose mission was to infiltrate and kill. But death by sword or spear is better than being burned alive. Better to die like a soldier, then. Crisis inside the horse . . . Until the bonfire idea is discounted and the men breathe again.

But the crisis isn't over. Helen now appears on the scene. She wheedled out the truth about the wooden-horse scheme at the time of my Palladium mission, and now she plays her double game, her old favourite. Round and round the horse she walks, imitating the voices of the soldiers' various wives, urging the men to show themselves.

But there's nobody in there, the people say, laughing at her antics.

It doesn't matter. If there are men in there and she teases them out and gets them killed, she won't have to face the wrath of Menelaus, who'll be dead. And if the horse is empty, so far so good, she survives another day. But the Greeks inside are suffering now, anguished, overcome by the familiar sounds of their wives' accents. The impersonation stabs them to the heart. They are sick for home.

Three times she completes her circuit of the stallion, stroking its flanks, grasping the great phallus Penelope put on it for the purpose, rubbing it slowly up and down, bringing her lips to it, putting it into her mouth, sliding her tongue along its length, making the mob cackle and roar, getting them on her side, cooing all the while to the spellbound men that if only they come out they'll get the same treatment. The wives have waited so long for this moment. The people laugh all the harder. Helen is human after all, if over-fond of cock. She is a fun princess. And it's good to be still alive and laughing in the good old city of Troy, with the Greeks gone and Helen forgiven.

Euphoria.

Too much for Anticlus, though. He is about to call out when I clap one hand over his mouth and chin and the other over his throat. He struggles briefly. I crack the neck and he goes limp in my lap. The small sounds he makes are soaked up by the laughter. We sit it out. And eventually Helen ceases her cooing.

Relief.

Short-lived. Enter Cassandra, priestess of catastrophe. She strikes the horse with her staff, demonstrating its hollowness. She utters auguries about the hollowness of Greek gifts and the Trojan triumph. An untrue offering, a hollow victory. But Cassandra is fated never to be believed, and the citizens of Troy have had more than enough of doom and gloom. It sits ill with their present mood. They want cheer and good hearing, not Cassandra's spectral wailing. She is shouted down.

But it's not over yet. Enter now, on Cassandra's side, Laocoön. As the priest of Apollo, he supports her prophecies. The horse, he declares, is hollow in all senses and should be destroyed for the false thing that it is. The crowd is less inclined to laugh at the venerable priest.

'This horse,' he says, 'has a bad pedigree. Let me tell you why.'

The people are quiet now. His story is an intriguing one. His talk is authoritative, enthralling. Minos, King of Crete, had a wife, Pasiphaë, who wanted more than he could give her sexually. She craved satisfaction, and in the end she wanted it from a bull, excited one day by the sight of its member, a red gleaming poker sticking from its belly. This poker was adapted to the fires of her hot lust. So to get close to the bull, she hid herself inside a wooden cow, and the bull entered her and she uttered a deep long sigh, her lust at last slaked. But the hybrid offspring of that unnatural coupling was the half-man half-bull creature that fed on human flesh, none other than the terrible Minotaur. A forbidden union, a monstrous outcome, concealment, deception, a wooden replica, bringing death and terror.

'And this horse is made in the same mould and must be destroyed before it destroys Troy.'

One more time we sweat, thinking that surely now the game is up. And it surely would be, except for one final entry: the sea-snakes.

These marine monsters would have some distance to travel overland, but Penelope shows them coming straight out of the salt sea, with the spume shaken from them like flakes of white fire. They seize the old priest and both his sons who have run to his side to defend him. The terrified people run back, turning to stand and watch from a safe distance as all three, caught in the deadly coils, are slowly strangled. The bones crack, the muscles burst, sinews snap, the life is brutally crushed out of them, and the breathless bodies lie mangled in front of the horse, the gods' displeasure made obvious to all. The horse is no deception; it was Laocoön who spoke false. Apollo sits powerless on the clouds, Athene triumphs, and the monsters slither back into the sea, back to Poseidon who sent them. The horse is hung with garlands. The city is doomed.

Another good story and, as always, with a speck of truth. There were snakes all right; there are always snakes. But the snakes that killed the Trojan priest were Greek ones, the snakes I'd slipped through the gates already, snakes in disguise. They were the usual suspects, speakers of northern Anatolian, agitators and spies. They roused up the rabble against Laocoön and had him removed under so-called official escort, to a place where he would be persuaded to see the error of his ways and let the people have their way. When your head is filled with political error, an axe is the best persuader. Or a good strong pair of hands in the case of this troublesome priest. He was strangled, certainly. Only the stranglers didn't come out of the sea, they were much closer to hand. After that the agents whipped up the celebrations, kept the mood buoyant, the drink flowing.

That was the point at which Aeneas left town. Nothing left to keep him, nothing to stay on for, not in a city that mocks its priestesses and murders its priests. The spies reported that he'd led a small unit of soldiers south of the city to his own territory in the Dardanian valley, under Mount Ida, and so avoided the onslaught that he knew was to come.

A rat from a sinking ship? A realist rat. And Penelope gave him glory. She made him stay on and fight his way out from where the action was hottest, carrying his father, old Anchises, on his back, leading his family to safety, away from the flames of burning Troy that licked the stars.

Night holds its breath. The city lies drunk asleep under the sky, oblivious to the sea's huge hush. Sinon lights his beacon on Achilles' tomb. Helen, who has gone home with Deiphobus, waits until he is asleep then lights a lamp and sets it in her window to guide Menelaus to her side if and when the time comes.

The lookouts on Tenedos see the lights in the sky, more lovely than moonlight. The Greek fleet steals back across the dark waters, aiming to reach the beaches well before moonrise.

As soon as the moon rises, visible through a chink, Epeius slides back the bolt in the belly; the trapdoor opens, and the horse litters the deadly offspring, the lethal few, chosen to slit the throats of the snoring sentinels and open the gates to the Greeks.

Night and negligence – great allies, especially after the enemy's drunken day-long celebrations. It doesn't take long to dispatch the guards, unseam the city. The beacon dowses the stars, the torches flare over the dead sentries, their gashed throats glittering, flickering, the pale face of Artemis turning the dark face of ocean to gold, the waiting sails etched black on the beaches against the serene backdrop of sea and sky – a scene of infinite beauty and calm.

All so easy, really, once the horse is inside the gates, simply to lie and wait for night and for Sinon's signal. Two hours from Tenedos, another two for the five-mile march overland to the city walls. Then they slip from the belly, slit the throats, slide the bolts and the troops pour in. Down goes Troy. The broad straits of Sigeum reflect the flames. The Greeks sack the city and win the war, beating the enemy with their own best weapon, the horse.

Except of course that there was no fucking horse – unless you call an abandoned siege-tower a horse, the one we left outside the walls the day we took out Paris. A wooden horse? That's a fucking laugh. If there had been a horse, you wouldn't have caught me inside it. The chances of being rumbled – too high by half. A grand stratagem for the web. But not for war. No, we did it the old way, the tried way. Get your man inside, get him to spin his yarn, and if they buy it, they're fucked. No glamour in that. The blackheads bought it, and it was all over: nothing left to do but the sack – and all the usual slaughter.

THIRTY-EIGHT

Odysseus, sacker of cities, tell it as you saw it, old man, but tell it quickly. All sackings are much the same, Troy like any other, except for the easy entry. The fleet stole back beneath the blanket of the dark, the first soldiers arrived at the open gates and stormed through, making for the citadel, killing as they went. Black night was ripped open, silvery with the screams of women and their children.

Children falling from the walls, tumbled onto spears, crushed underfoot like rotten apples, women's thighs parted savagely, wives and daughters raped in their rooms, in the streets, in open doorways, wherever they were found, and the old and bedridden slaughtered where they lay, waiting for the swords. Down from the citadel came the prizes, the princesses, dragged off to the hell of their new lives, the loom, the bed, the well, sexual slavery, to be spat on by foreign women and tormented by their brats, to eke out a miserable old age in an alien place. For them, only suicide could end the only end to war.

Some of the Trojan women did kill themselves first, as some women always do, preferring to escape the humiliation. But they were still raped. When soldiers are on the rampage after a long war, no woman is too old to be raped. Or too young. Or too pregnant. Or too ugly. Or too dead. Some were raped repeatedly, squad-raped, and some were buggered till they bled and sometimes died.

What else to expect? Many soldiers had never seen their own children, born to them in their long absence. They had watched their comrades die, one after another, with no wives' tender hands to give them their obsequies. In hundreds of Greek homes, widows died unhusbanded and old men were left childless, sitting in the shadows. Or their sons came home too late from the war to see their fathers buried. Soldiers who have suffered want their enemies to suffer, and rape is a better revenge than killing because it's extended. You kill your man and it's over, the gore goes cold, congeals. But you part the legs of his widow, his daughters, as often as you are inclined, taking your revenge slowly, over and over, slaking a double lust, desire and anger. Rape outlasts war. It can go on for the rest of your life.

After all, they raped your queen, took her from her home – and now you rape their women, a fair exchange for fair Helen. Anything wrong with that? And just for good measure you fuck them up the arse, because they fucked up your life, and your family's lives. All's fair in love and war, and rape is always there, the eternal weapon, wherever there are wars, wherever there are men. All is excused, all are culpable.

Raping their way through the city, the soldiers reached the citadel. One of the contingents was led by Achilles' son, Neoptolemus, eager to get revenge for his famous father, though for my money he was an opportunist. We burst into the inner citadel with him, along with Little Ajax and Menelaus and their men. Priam and Hecuba were clutching the altar of Zeus with their son Polites. Other than Aeneas, who'd already exited the theatre of war, he was about the only son left to them now. Their arms were wrapped around Andromache and Astynax, their grandson, who was also with his nurse. Cassandra was apart from them at the altar of Athene. Helen was nowhere to be seen.

Neoptolemus went straight into action, hurling his javelin at the Zeus-altar group. Polites took the spear in the chest. Neoptolemus grabbed him by the hair and hacked off his head, throwing it over his shoulder. It rolled all the way to the palace doors. Hecuba screamed and ran at him.

'You savage bastard! You're a disgrace to your father! At least Achilles gave us Hector's body back because he remembered his own father!'

'Shut your mouth, you old hag!'

'You'll have to shut it! Achilles? You don't even belong to him, you young cunt! Some fuckpig lay with your mother!'

'I'll fucking shut you up myself!'

He made for Hecuba. Priam put himself in front of her and threw his spear. But it wouldn't have bothered a blue-arsed fly; he'd no throwing strength left in him. Neoptolemus kicked the weapon aside with a laugh.

'You useless old cunt!'

He took Priam by his white hair and dragged him, howling, well away from the altar. Both men slipped in the son's blood. At the palace doors, he hacked off Priam's head and threw it down beside his son's. Hecuba ran up and down shrieking hysterically. Neoptolemus strode back to the altar and tore Astynax away from his nurse. He threw him at the nearest soldier.

'You! Keep the brat safe for me. It's off the highest tower for this lad. Lose him and I'll fucking kill you.'

Thus the tender infant was wrenched from the bosom of his lovely-haired young nurse. And taking him by the foot, as Thetis had held his father, Achilles' wrathful son flung the child from the battlements so that his bones were broken, and crimson death and stern fate took him at his fall.

So they say. I wasn't there. Another of these fairytales went round that I'd murdered the kid myself, using him as a weapon with which I clubbed his grandfather to death. That would have been a first for me, if true. But I know that Neoptolemus killed Priam, and he very likely did the grandson himself. Astynax certainly went off the wall. He had to — laws of war. You can't let them live, the sprogs of dead heroes, not if you've had a hand in their father's demise. They grow up with hate in their hearts, and hate brings them after you, even if it takes years.

By this time Andromache was screeching and kneeling in front of the altar, her arms spread wide.

'Kill me! Kill me!'

'No fucking chance!'

Neoptolemus picked her up and threw her at another soldier.

'Back to the ships with her! You're destined for my bed, girl. While Hector rots in hell, I'll be sweetly fucking his wife.'

And so Andromache is enslaved by the son of the man who had slaughtered her husband.

'I've heard it said,' she weeps, 'that a single night takes care of any woman's aversion to a conqueror's bed, and that time soon cools the bedsheets of the first husband. Yet even the draughthorse, severed from his faithful friend and partner in the yoke, feels the sudden absence, grudges, and will not pull unless compelled to by the whip. And is not man higher than the poor beasts? And is not woman ever mindful of her first love?'

Well, she said something when the time came, and it might well have been words to that effect. Right now, all she did was scream. And she had a lot more to scream about — Neoptolemus hadn't finished bathing his hands in her family's blood. Polyxena was next on his list. Achilles had seen her fling her bracelet from the city walls to land in the scales and make up the weight in gold that would ransom her brother's body.

At that point, the hero had gone weak-kneed, the chump, and now even after he was dead and gone, he still wanted her. Only now she'd have to be his bride in the Elysian Fields.

Or so Neoptolemus had dreamed. Apparently. True? Apparently. How do you explain dreams? So she was picked out now to die later, as a sacrifice, to appease Achilles' angry ghost and slake his limbo lust.

Cassandra was next. Little Ajax had his lecherous eye on her, and Athene's altar didn't even make him blink. He grabbed the girl and wrenched her away. She spat at him and tore herself free, running back to the altar. Everybody laughed.

'Better watch that one's claws, man, she might bite your balls off!'

Ajax flushed. 'Not before I've shagged the bitch! Right in front of her fucking goddess too! I'll enter her holy of holies all right, don't you fucking worry!'

And he threw her to the ground.

She screamed at him that she was a virgin sworn to the gods, but he smashed his fist into the side of her face.

'That shut you up? I don't give a tinker's toss for virgins. And I don't give a fart of my arse for the gods!'

She was unconscious and bleeding when he raped her.

'There you go, girl – some good Greek seed up your holy Trojan cunt! Do you the world of fucking good!'

Nobody applauded. Nobody even spoke. He stood up and frowned. 'What?'

Agamemnon told him what. Later he kicked him out of the camp for blasphemy. He'd crossed the line. He'd violated a priestess on her own altar, and Agamemnon was now covering his big fat arse just in case. Added to which, he fancied Cassandra himself, ever the old Agamemnon, and as the crime had already been committed by another party, he argued, he was entitled not to let the spoils go to waste. He could claim Cassandra as his own with no guilt attached. She was no ordinary booty either, easily the most ravishing of all Priam's daughters. A princess to die for – literally, as he later discovered when he took her back to Mycenae, not knowing what was to follow.

As for Little Ajax, his days were numbered. Very shortly he was to join Big Ajax out in the long dark – he would drown on the way home. Athene saw to that.

'He won't get away with it!' she hissed all over the web. 'Nor will the Greeks for letting him off and letting him go. Banished from the camp, indeed. Some punishment that! It was light enough to make a mockery of me. No, I'll hit their ships. Zeus will give me the fire-power. And you, Poseidon, you will fill the sheltered straits of Euboea with drowned corpses, litter the white sands with stranded shoals of the dead.'

Poseidon went off in a gleeful rage to stir up the Aegean – nothing he liked better – and to deliver the drowned men to the shores of Myconus, the tearing reefs of Delos, Skyros, Lemnos, the headlands and ragged edges of Caphareium. And from all those barbarous-toothed edges they came together for the last time, those scattered corpses, all going down together in a ragged line to Hades, with the sea in their mouths.

Ajax had sailed off in his anger, cursing Agamemnon and all the Immortals. Had they heard him? Certainly. Poseidon had wrecked his ship, after all, and Ajax had only saved himself by clinging to a rock. And even from his rock he raged and swore, till Zeus grew tired of it and thunderbolted him where he clung and ranted. Man and rock disappeared down the sea's white throat, never to be seen again. And that was that. This is how his war ended, and it was as close as Ajax ever got to home.

Neoptolemus didn't wait for us. He left early with his prize, Andromache, and landed in northern Greece, conquering Molossia. He kept Andromache as his queen for seven years, then got the itch and travelled to Sparta in quest of Hermione. First he had to consult the oracle. Delphi gave him a bad answer, and instead of accepting it he demanded another. When the same answer came back, he did an Ajax – burned the shrine then marched off to Sparta and took Hermione by force. He returned via Delphi where he ran into Orestes, who killed him on the spot. They buried him under the temple he had destroyed. Like his father, he never saw Phthia again. And Hermione returned to Sparta, where she married Orestes – after he'd been punished for the murder of his mother. Confused? Confusion is an entitlement . . . and I'll be coming to all of that. Only one thing is clear here: the killing of Neoptolemus required no act of purification. Delphi decreed that this had been no murder but an execution.

Diomedes was one of those who got back to a disloyal wife and to a kingdom that had disowned him. She'd grown tired of waiting and had taken a lover whom the people had accepted as their king – they'd grown tired too. Women and nations – they both need a leader. So Diomedes left them to themselves and sailed off with a shrug, westward to Italy, where he went on to enjoy a ripe old age and one filled with honour.

Nestor returned safely to sandy Pylos, and he too grew sleek in his old age, though so many of the younger men he'd led to Troy were quiet dust now, sleeping on its plains and shores.

Few Trojans got out alive. Antenor did – with my help, if you want to believe it. He and his wife Theano were spared during the sacking because they hung a leopard skin from their window – an emblem of my personal protection, and I saw to it that the pair of them escaped with their family and their best possessions, all because they'd helped me steal the Palladium. In spite of the insane slaughter surrounding them, they calmly walked free.

Another good one – the likely story that Agamemnon was so touched when he saw Aeneas carrying old Anchises on his back, out of flaming Troy, and leading his little son by the hand, that he let them all go – Aeneas, Anchises, Ascanius and Creusa, Aeneas's faithful wife, before he ditched her for Dido. The perfect family procession. And Agamemnon after all was the perfect family man. Or perhaps Creusa disappeared in the confusion and never made it to Mount Ida along with the others? This would leave Aeneas free to sow his illicit oats on Carthage.

Or did the perfect protector of families, having agreed to let them all pass, pick off Creusa from behind and keep her for his bed? That would be much more like the Agamemnon we all knew. But what do I know? I know what's on the web, and I also know that the sack of Troy saw many casualties, including truth.

What really happened to Hecuba, for example? One thing's sure, the old bird didn't go quietly. When Agamemnon was snatching the raped Cassandra from Ajax with the holiest of motives in mind, Hecuba fairly spat her poison at him.

'Fine – take her! And take your fill of her! But when you fuck my daughter, you fuck Apollo in the mouth! Do you think your nights will be spent so sweetly with a sacred receptacle for your stinking Greek sperm? Not that you'll have many nights left after what you've done! You're a fucking dead man!'

Or words to that effect.

Did Agamemnon waste her on the spot? According to Penelope, no – she gave her instead to Helenus (now one of us) to pacify the old crone. And he took her away, still raining down her hell-and-devastation curses on all of us. He got her as far as the Hellespont and then she dropped down dead. She'd had enough.

Enough? No, enough's never enough, and, like the sea, storytellers will never let the dead rest, will they? Always returning to us in one form or another, like the sea giving up its dead. So the web went on from there, weaving Hecuba into a black dog baying nightly among the graves and following Hecate on witching nights. Hear how she howls, that female hound! And her mound is marked on the web, a sailor's landmark, Cynossema, the bitch's tomb. Maybe the dog's a metaphor, an image of her abasement by loss and enslavement, multiple sorrows. Or maybe the soldiers stoned her to death like a dog. Maybe she cried like a dog in her grief. All I know is I heard her swearing blue murder at Agamemnon, and, if words could kill, he was dead before his time.

It all ended in quarrels. What else do you expect from war? What else would you expect from Agamemnon? He and Menelaus fell out about Ajax's crime. Menelaus couldn't wait to get back with his whore to Sparta, but Agamemnon wanted to stay on and allay Athene's anger – so he said – with prolonged sacrifices and all due ceremony. In other words: as we're here, let's fucking plunder the entire fucking hinterland of Troy. As we're here. We've sacked the city – why stop there?

Same old greed. Menelaus said they'd already made amends by stoning Ajax. That, said Agamemnon, was a fucking laugh and a half. A couple of stones had been thrown, yes, but as a formality, nothing lethal. Ajax got away with a few bruises. Most of the stones had been deliberately wide of the mark. Nobody knew that the bastard was about to be drowned anyway on his way home.

In the end, the two leaders and brothers, friends in sunshine and in shadow, agreed to leave separately, and Agamemnon eventually reached Mycenae, where a good hot bath was waiting for him – a bloodbath. Clytemnestra carried a long memory of her murdered daughter and had plotted with her lover Aegisthus to whack the murdering cunt the minute he got back. Hecuba had been right when she prophesied. He was dead already – only sooner even than any of us might have imagined.

It was all too easy. Home he came at last in conquest, home to Mycenae, soldier from the war returning, striding in victorious, his vessels laden with spoils, his concubine Cassandra by his side, his triumphant feet treading the purple cloth specially laid out for him on this day of days, the king's causeway, the cock of the midden. Clytemnestra spread her lips in a grin. She opened her arms, and he swept into them unsuspecting, crushing the breasts that had suckled his dead daughter long since and filled her lover's fists only minutes earlier – Aegisthus's semen was still fresh and hot inside her. O Agamemnon, stormer of Troy, king of men, trample the deep-sea purples now and enter your palace halls . . .

The great feast was ready for him, prepared in style, juicy chines of goat, chopped and cooked just the way she knew he liked them. She'd posted a watchman on the palace roof at Argos, his duty to warn her of the exact moment the beacon flashed – the last in the chain of fires that would signal Troy's fall and the imminent return of the Greek fleet. Countless times she'd gone out and shouted up to this lookout, 'Watchman, watchman, what of the night?' And this night the cry came back to her, the newsflash from the fire, thrilling her down to her pubic bone. The sea was on fire, Troy town had fallen, the walls were down. Her husband, the father and killer of their lovely girl Iphigenia, was coming home . . .

She couldn't wait to pour the bath. But she had things to see to first. Her son Orestes was sent away to his uncle Strophius, and she kept her other two daughters, Chrysothemis and Electra, well hidden. Agamemnon had a bad track record with daughters. Clytemnestra never forgot, never forgave. She kept Aegisthus hidden too.

She had to wait, as it turned out. He was held up by a storm. But she sent out ships to scour the sea-routes and report on his schedule. By the time he finally returned, it was a hot hate that awaited him in Argos, and a huge hot dinner – after which he was so bloated he could barely stand.

His wife's supporting arm saw to that. She did the business herself, led him to the bath, did the honours too, cupping his balls and sucking his drunken member as he wallowed and rolled . . .

'Oh, I've been dreaming of that, all through the war!'

'Really, my dear? And were you dreaming of this, I wonder?'

Stories about how he fell grow like flowers around a man's corpse. He was bathed first and feasted afterwards, he was cut down at table, suitably stuffed. Penelope showed it the way she preferred it, with him stepping heavily out of the bath and Clytemnestra slipping over his wet head the splendid new robe she'd made for him, gorgeously embroidered with her own white hands. She'd sewn up the neck and sleeves. He struggled for a few seconds, giggling. Was it a joke, some sort of mistake?

No, no mistake. No joke either. The concealed axe comes down on his fumbling skull with a splintering crash. In the same second, Aegisthus comes in from behind, sliding through the door, sword in hand like a lethal penis, penetrating back and belly, behind and through, coming out hot and smoking, and sticking there, stopping just short of stabbing Clytemnestra, who is holding him from the front.

She lifts the axe again . . .

And again and again.

Penelope couldn't let it go either, varying the scenes according to the stories. Aegisthus holding him down in the bath, gurgling, while Clytemnestra gives him three stab-wounds, each on account of his crimes, each calculated to disable but not to kill, not outright. The wounded man has time to drink in her words along with the crimson bubbling bathwater.

'If you'd killed her to save our city, I could have understood – or to help our house, or even to save our other children, the one sacrificed for the sake of the many – yes, I could have understood, even forgiven, but you killed our girl to save a slut – a slut who couldn't keep her legs closed! You killed her for a cuckold brother and for your own vanity and greed. Glutton, slut, cuckold, cunt! So then, you murdering thug, this is for Iphigenia! And this is for Helen! And here's one for Cassandra, your holy whore!'

The bath runs red as he bleeds. Agamemnon burbles, gurgles.

'And when you ran the slut to earth, when she spread her desperate legs for Menelaus, did you all take turns? How many of you fuckpigs fucked her first? She was well raped, they say. But she always did like a ring of stiff pricks around her, the filthy bitch! And I'll bet you fucked with the best of them, you disloyal bastard!'

Agamemnon makes a dying effort, rising weakly from the reddened water as his strength ebbs, his belly bubbling and sounding like a whale. She seizes the cock and slices it off, stuffing it in his mouth.

'There you go! That's as much as your Trojan whore will get from you tonight. And she's next for the chop.'

She leaves the room, axe in hand.

Enough then?

No, still no, still it goes on, the endless weaving, the versions of what is true and untrue and just possibly true. Let him stand up unharmed, go out and arrive all over again, entering his hall for a third time, not in history, but in art – Penelope's triptych. Here he comes once more. Clytemnestra watches his fatal entrance under her battlements.

'Look! Look at the bastard! See how he struts!'

Behind him stretches the sea, infinitely gentle, infinitely cruel. He has put it behind him now, that vast factory of purple. Or so he thinks. Clytemnestra stares at it through eyes that flash and flood.

'I'd have traded all of it, the whole ocean with all its purple dyes, the wine-dark sea and all its hidden riches, for the life of my daughter. But he wouldn't give her to me. And now I'll make him remember. How I begged . . .'

He is naked, ready for the bath. Three times she strikes him: the first time with the axe they use to butcher the bull or the boar in his prime. The blade sinks deep into the soft fat flesh between the shoulders and the neck, opening him up, a startling gash, gaping, like a red mouth. This is followed by two strokes of the sword – first in the belly to make him bellow in his agony and anger, surprised like the beast by the sudden betrayal, and then the thanksgiving stroke to the heart in the name of Hades. She sends her husband to hell with the life pumping out of him in three places, frightening, fast.

It isn't over. Aegisthus appears now and kicks him into the bath.

'In you go, boy!'

He plunges and gutters, sputtering lumps of blood.

Farewell, Agamemnon, butcher meat, king of men. Remember Iphigenia.

Why did she do it? We know why. Except that Iphigenia alone wouldn't have put him under the axe – if only he hadn't come home with Cassandra. He'd followed the murder of their daughter with the murder of their marriage. Some said so. Ah, but she'd already taken Aegisthus as her lover and lord. The axe had been sharpened, the banquet prepared, the bath poured.

So she'd murdered him for all that his Trojan venture had cost her. But Clytemnestra saw no problem surrounding herself with the spoils of that hard-won war: the golden chariots, the bronze weapons inlaid with ivory, the silver necklaces, gold-studded dresses, drinking bowls of solid gold – and Asiatic women, captured, captivating, women wearing Idaean robes clasped with gold brooches. All the while, Agamemnon's blood was turning black and rotten on the dungheap, where they'd emptied the bathtub, swilling his lifeblood away, the now cold gore. With genitals still stuffed in the mouth, the naked, memberless corpse was thrown to the dogs.

Enough now? Surely enough.

Not quite. When the dogs had eaten their fill, the bones were scraped together and given a quick burial. Drink-sodden afterwards, Aegisthus went out and danced drunkenly on the shallow grave. She came out and joined in. She was drunk too. Then the pair of them pissed on the grave, openly and together, the two pools of urine mingling, indissoluble, intimate. They were united in crime, inseparable. Even after the poor crude monument was put up, Aegisthus went out and pelted it with fistfuls of rock, yelling like a lunatic.

'Where's your sprog now, then? Not showing up to defend his father's honoured bones? He knows what lies in store.'

King now, he'd have murdered Orestes, he was so ruthless, but the mother refused to reveal his whereabouts. He'd have killed Electra too, but for her mother. Hardening his grip on power, but paranoid with it, he wanted both children dead and offered a reward to anyone who killed Orestes, contenting himself, according to the less bloody version, with marrying off Electra, still a virgin, to an old obscure peasant, burying her not in the ground but in the social wilderness. As good as dead.

Yet one more variant on this. It's Clytemnestra who gives away Electra to the peasant – a sham marriage and a means of concealment. But Electra manages to get messages to her brother and they plot their revenge, a web of lies and disguise. Orestes returns from hiding with a false identity and the news that Orestes is in fact dead. Aegisthus breathes a sigh of satisfaction and relief, little knowing that the dead man is standing right beside him.

The dead man strikes Aegisthus on the joint of the neck, shattering the spine, chopping it so savagely that his whole body writhes, and he jerks in huge convulsions, shuddering horribly before he dies. Orestes throws off his disguise and is hailed by the people. A neat ending.

And it could have ended there. Except that Electra was not quite done with him. She triumphed over his corpse.

'You – you destroyed my life and my brother's, though we'd done you no harm. You took my mother, though my father was still alive. Then the pair of you murdered him foully. You killed the commander of the great Greek army, though you yourself never went to Troy. Now you're punished.'

Clytemnestra stood and screamed and tore her hair.

'Silence her!' said Electra.

And Orestes thrust the sword that had killed Aegisthus into his mother's soft white neck. Electra seized the hilts along with him, helping him with his thrust as hard as she could, eager for complicity. And so Agamemnon's bloody homecoming had been avenged.

THIRTY-NINE

A bloody end awaits Helen too — so thinks Menelaus as hot he breaks through Troy's destroyed defences, eager to avenge a ten-year hate and sullied honour on one adulterous whore. Through streets of smoke and crimson gore he strides, and hence by quieter ways, till now the innermost chamber fronts him, and so he swings his sword, and with exultant words crashes into the dim luxurious bower, flaming like a god.

High sits white Helen, enthroned, lonely, mournful and serene, awaiting her fate . . .

Did she? Was she? Truth is, after marrying her brother-in-law Deiphobus, the tricky bitch did the dirty on him when we took the town, filching his sword and spear after sex and leaving the bastard weaponless when we broke in. Menelaus was on a mission, and I came in with him. Deiphobus didn't even beg, I'll say that much for the cunt. He knew it was useless. He spread his arms wide, like a bride on her wedding night, waiting for the first stab. Hoping it would kill him.

No fucking chance. Menelaus gave him a quick jab in the belly. This was going to be a slow death. He ripped off the bastard's ears, then his nose, then his cock and balls. After that he chopped off both arms and legs. The lower limbs took more effort. By now the torso couldn't move about much, but what Deiphobus lacked in mobility he more than made up for in the vocal department. The mouth did plenty of screaming. Menelaus did other things to the face and stood back to view his handiwork.

'I'm sorry you're getting the heavy end of it,' he apologised. 'If Paris had been here he'd have been getting the lion's share. But as he's in absentia I don't have that satisfaction, and, well, you see my position.'

Deiphobus made terrifying sounds.

'What, not dead yet, you cunt? Good — try this for size then!'

The old genitals-into-the-gob trick. Or in this case, into the ragged chasm where the mouth used to be.

'Helen suck your cock too, did she? You'll have to suck your own now! Not for too long, though. That's enough!'

He hacked off the head.

That's when she came running in, a widow again, holding out her late husband's weapons, eager to show her first husband that she was back to being a dutiful wife — not to the third husband but to the first, now her husband for the second time. If he wanted her, that is. Did he want her? Did she want him? She saw what was left of Deiphobus and screamed and froze. Couldn't help herself. Menelaus went berserk.

'What, blub for your Trojan cunt-licker, you whore? Snivel to my fucking face, would you?'

He ran at her but slipped in the gore and slithered all the way to the wall. Helen unfroze, turned and ran. Menelaus got up, cursing, and slipped and slid again, crashing into one of Deiphobus's still bleeding legs. What a fucking farce! He picked it up and hurled it after her, then charged.

She tore through the streets — a lot quicker than Menelaus in all his battle-garb. He ripped it off as he ran. The people saw her, saw the chase, and the cries went up.

'It's the whore! Stone her! Stone the whore!'

Mostly they were women, picking up stones as they ran. But Menelaus and his men reached her first. She'd sought sanctuary. Different versions deposit her in various temples — Athene, Apollo, fuck knows — I wasn't on that little run myself. Penelope opted for Aphrodite, whose little slut cowered in a corner of her temple in bad need of some protection at that point. Aphrodite was nowhere to be seen. Menelaus dragged Helen to the altar and threw her on it. She struggled to her knees, and he raised his sword . . .

But he never used it. She knew all she had to do was let her dress fall. It was worth a try, and if that was the extent of Aphrodite's intervention, who knows, maybe it was enough. And that's what Helen did: she stood up and let her robe fall to her waist. The famous breasts bobbed out. He hesitated — fatal error — and swore. Fuck.

The rest is history.

He had not remembered that she is so fair. And that her neck curves down in such a way. And he feels tired. He flings the sword away and kisses her golden-sandalled feet and kneels before her there, kneels before the altar, Aphrodite's acolyte, the perfect knight before the perfect queen.

Was that how it was? Something like that. Probably. When he paused, she knew she had him by the balls. She let fall the rest of the robe, all the way to the floor. He stared into her gorgeous fucking face, down to her breasts and belly, to the dark triangle where her hand was reaching. A gesture of modesty? Hilarious. Or a signal. As if to say to him, what a waste, eh? What a fucking waste.

What a fucking waste of men. Of lives lost for this. A pair of tits and a cunt.

His sheep's eyes lost their anger, liquid with lust. He hadn't been with her for so long. And a little ageing had added to her charms. She was the dream-fuck of all time and she was ripe for him, the perfect wet whore. Slowly he lowered his arm. She smiled.

'Sheathe your sword here,' she said, taking the empty hand and thrusting it between her legs.

The other hand opened, the great blade clattered to the ground, the beacons were lit on Ida, on Tenedos, all the way over the ocean and across to Aulis and Mycenae and Lacedaemon, where it all began. The war was over, the boys were coming home. The Spartan whore was coming home. She was going to be queen again.

Why? Why the stopped blade, stuck in time? Was lust stronger than hate? Did the oldest of flames rekindle in heart, or groin, or in both? See how Zeus looms, hovering protectively over the cowering woman, not strictly intervening, not even speaking, but putting the silent question to Menelaus nonetheless, the question woven into his lips and eyes and brow. Are you sure about this? Is it what you really want, to murder my only mortal daughter, my one girl, the Queen of Sparta, who made you, a thing of nothing, into a king? Go home without her and you will die old and alone, a forgotten corpse in the stallion lands of Argos, a fistful of dust, whirled by its winds into oblivion. But spare her, and the deathless ones will whisk you off to the world's end, sweep you to the Elysian Fields, where life glides on in immortal ease, all because you are Helen's husband, the rightful one, all her former lovers dead, and the gods will count themselves glad to count you the son-in-law of almighty Zeus. All that. Or you can kill her right now – and you cut the cord between you and the rewarding gods.

If that's how it was, then did the poor bastard ever really have a choice?

I keep on saying it, but truth isn't simply the first single casualty of war, it's a multiple one. Everybody sees everything differently, tells it differently. Some of the versions are packed with dialogue and some with mostly monologue – Helen's. She has a lot to say, and she blames everybody except herself.

'First there was that odious old bitch Hecuba, out of whose ugly cunt crept Paris, the snake. Then that ancient doting dimwit Priam, who ought to have ordered the infant cut to pieces in front of him the minute he dreamed about that firebrand, the old fucker.'

Helen could swear like a trooper when it suited her, and right now it suited her mood, suited her most. Her life depended on it.

'He put him out to Ida instead, to take his chances. And look what happened – he grew up to be a handsome bastard, a philandering bastard, and was made sole judge of a beauty contest. And not any old beauty contest, no, just the most important contest in history, that's all. The rest is the history of the Trojan War.'

'Got anyone else to throw your own shit at?' asked Menelaus.

Oh, yes, plenty. That wasn't even the half of it, as Menelaus well knew. She was merely the excuse for war, his gold-grubbing big brother's excuse. She was bought and sold for her looks, a plaything of men. After which, he buggered off to Crete and left her unprotected with that back-stabbing womaniser who had Aphrodite on his side. Aphrodite was to blame. How could Helen compete – or withstand her?

'Aphrodite saw to it that I wasn't in my right mind, I tell you, when I ran away with him. She got into my brain.'

'And he got into your cunt!'

'I was a slave of love. I was made irresistible to him, and he to me.'

'Are you done?'

'No. After Paris was dead, don't you think I tried to get back to you? Even before he was killed, I tried. Time and again I was caught on the battlements with ropes for a descent. I told Odysseus. Ask him. Once I was nearly hanged in the attempt. They pulled me up half strangled. Ask the sentries.'

'I can't. They're all dead by now. Or better be. Are you done?'

'No – that brother of his, I didn't choose to marry him. When did I ever have a choice with you men? He forced me into it with his talk of raising up seed to his dead brother, the unnatural barbarian, and all the while you arsed around outside the walls and couldn't bring them down, though I was longing for it. Call yourself a soldier? You weren't even a king till you married me. You can take your full share of the blame, along with the gods.'

Ah, the gods. As if the gods would have bartered Argos to the barbarians. People who've run out of reasons always blame the gods when they can't confront reality. And if not the gods, then the stars, their parents, their lineage, their children, their country, their leaders, the latrine-lickers — anybody but themselves. Even the fucking cat would catch the blame if he didn't catch the mouse. Aphrodite? There was no Aphrodite. She wasn't even in the fucking room. Aphrodite was Helen's wetness, the lust between her legs — or so argued the impartial Penelope. The Spartan whore saw Paris and her cunt itched. She saw Troy too in his retinue, and she turned her back on Argos, the treacherous tart, dazzled by the east. A Spartan palace was a hut to her now. No soldier dragged her by the hair. She couldn't wait to get on board, to hitch up her dress and present the purple crack.

Look, there she is, doing just that. There on the web is the cunt that caused the Trojan War. Abducted? Abducted my arse! She went like a fucking arrow from Sparta. And as for being caught on the battlements of Troy — any decent woman would have thrown herself off the very first day. Hecuba said she'd begged her a thousand times to get her fancy arse out of the city. And would she? But then Priam had a soft spot for her, didn't he? So did Hector. So did the old sober buffers up on the walls that day. Fact is, once they'd seen her they never saw straight again.

There was even a story that the famous breasts weren't real, that at crucial moments, when her destiny depended on it, Aphrodite intervened and lent her her own. False tits. So what? Men don't much care whether tits are tits or something else, so long as they can get a good eyeful of them. Or, better still, a couple of fistfuls. Stick a pair of tits in front of most men and their brains are in their balls. Truth doesn't much matter any more. Nothing fucking matters.

'Anyway,' said Penelope, 'she was a whore. How could she be anything else? Look at how these Spartan girls are reared – prancing about with boys and scarcely a stitch to cover their snatches, as good as naked. It's in the blood.'

Menelaus was eloquent in her defence by the time he got her home – it had been a long journey. They met a big contingent of his people who'd have marched her straight off to a stoning party to pay for all those Spartan lives, young men cut down cold for a hot whore. And here was the worst cuckold in history standing up to defend his own disgrace.

'She has proved invaluable to Greece and Sparta in the end, quite apart from all the rich pickings we've brought home. Think of the bigger benefits of the war, the sharpening of nautical knowledge, the increased military skills, better weapons, a better army, experience, a gathering of fleets from all over Greece, a more united set of peoples. War can be an effective educator, worth its price. Pain can be a better teacher than beauty or joy. Yet the beauty she was born with, though it brought about the mother of all wars, that very beauty has made it all somehow worthwhile, hasn't it?'

Hadn't it?

Yes, of course she was worth it.

'Right,' said Menelaus, 'let's put all this behind us, shut it down, deep down inside, enjoy oblivion together, all the rest of our blind lives.'

Sometimes amnesia can be a blessing. That's how it was for the pair of them.

However it was, they left Troy together as man and wife, cuckold and whore no more. At Cape Malea they were hit by a storm and their ship was driven off course – Crete, Cyprus, Phoenicia, Ethiopia, Libya; they did the rounds. In Egypt they were held up again by contrary winds – so they say. And did an Agamemnon. Menelaus got hold of two Egyptian kids – and I don't mean goats – and slit their throats to blow the winds back to Argos. Which worked – so they say. It must have worked, mustn't it? Because back they came. The Egyptians chased after them but they got away. That's what they say.

They also say that in Egypt Helen was presented with a golden spindle. But some women think the spindle was a euphemism – it was a prick, a golden one, absolutely erect, balls and all. Some people will say anything. Especially Penelope. She put the prick up on the web.

Back in Sparta, Helen soon settled down, ran the palace, renewed her relationship with the daughter, held parties, mixed drinks, gossiped about Paris and Troy, and all of that almost as if none of it had ever really happened, as if it had been just a good story, nothing more. As maybe it was. An old story of old time. A myth.

*

Old stories long to be retold. And when they are, they reopen old wounds that start to bleed again. An awful lot of lads bled to death at Troy – that was no myth. Helen didn't bleed, though, and that was no myth either. That's the strange thing, strange but true. She died in her bed, the place she knew best. But that's another story.

There are dozens of them. Menelaus actually found her in bed when we took Troy. She was shagging Deiphobus for the last time. Menelaus killed him and forced her on the bloodied sheets. We all crowded round and waited our turn, a gang of rapists round the bed. Everybody wanted a piece of her. Every man wanted to say he'd fucked the most expensive whore in history. So she never made it back to Sparta. She was gang-raped to death. In other stories, she did make it back and did live idyllically but was driven out of Sparta after Menelaus died and swung from a tree on Rhodes, hanged by an angry and embittered war-widow, Polyxo.

Bitch-whore, killer, filthy slut, destroyer of ships, cities, men, she was civilisation's worst enemy, the inspiration for the gang that came to take her. But she made the sword fall where it should have struck home. She made the spearman's fingers itch to touch her. The archer's arm shook, the arrow missed its mark and he lay dead. She brought down buildings stone by stone.

She was even on the ocean. On my nineteen-night journey by the stars, after Troy, I watched her brothers, Castor and Pollux, bestriding the black seas on their white horses, as Helen's star set fire to the ship, leaping from mast to keel and crackling the sheets. She wouldn't leave us alone, even when we were struggling in the deeps. She was always there, striking with her lightning. Even where she left her footprints, it was said, priests stirred in their graves, hurled away their tombstones and stood erect and lusting.

But she shed tears. Penelope took trouble with them. They were tears not of remorse but of regret, lamenting her lost beauty and the pains of love. The tear-pools produced a bitter herb, and women came quietly crowding round these dark forest pools — as we'd crowded round her bed, drawn by the pools of her eyes — to gather the helenium, withered matrons and green girls all together, old women's worries or menstrual troubles, they all shared a common aim, to taste what had sprung from the eyes of the world's loveliest lethal female, hoping to possess a drop of her lustre, just one little hint of her terrible beauty. And they all went away with a new look on their faces. So her legacy lived on. She was the shining one, the sun, abducted by winter and repossessed by summer. She would never die, not until time stopped.

FORTY

My own homecoming took longer than the others'. An epic homecoming it was. And all the time, I dreamed of it, as only soldiers do. Home. In my case a windswept mountain, Neritos, trembly with leaves, on an island – rugged, sunny Ithaca, my island, close by Doulichion and Same, woody Zacynthus, and from all of them the slow smoke spiralling upwards from the home fires, white columns rising quietly into the sky. And with something hurting in the chest, where the heart once was. Soldiers know this something like no one else. But it was to be a long time till I saw that smoke feathering the air. I was sick for it. There were times I thought I'd never see it again.

That, at least, is what I told Penelope. And it wasn't untrue. What I didn't tell her about was the other me, the second self, the one that wasn't ready to come home, not yet, maybe not ever, the one that was shit-scared to. Scared of what? Scared of closing the book of war. Scared of peace. An old campaigner gets split down the middle. He can't just barge back in through the open door; he's got a companion now – no concubine, but one that shares the bed, shares everything. The marriage is now a threesome. An old sea-dog on the way home, however, has one advantage over an old soldier – he trusts to the winds to do the work, to make the decision: when, where to, what next? Is it homeward bound? Or is the long trick not yet over?

The sea-winds that took us from Troy brought my twelve crimson-beaked ships to Ismarus, the city of the Cicones. They were not prepared for hostilities, and it was obvious they were no fighters. Ready or not, they were sacked, and we wiped out most of their men. The rest ran for it, leaving their wives behind on the retreat. No balls – what would the women want with them anyway? We took the good-lookers on board to sail them back to Ithaca. A fair amount of raping went on. But I made sure the whole thing was done correctly and that the women were fairly shared out. There was no way I'd act like Agamemnon, always after the pick of the pussy and the plunder.

I did spare one man in Ismarus. He was called Maron and he was the priest of Apollo, Apollo being high up on the Cicones' god-list.

We ripped into this man's house – it was in a very pleasant location, a grove sacred to the god – and three of my men were already hauling his wife's robe up to her waist when he dodged the blade that was intended to kill him and threw himself in front of me with a nippiness surprising in an old-timer. The wife was young enough to be his daughter, if not granddaughter, and she looked like quite a bedful. The splayed thighs and wine-dark gash flashed at me from the floor. That distracted me for a second, long enough for him to grab me round the knees.

He was going to go through the usual speech, and I wasn't going to listen to it, but he pleaded his priesthood and I thought about that. I'd never seen Apollo in my life and didn't expect to, but where gods go you'd best tread softly, just in case – play it safe. Better an old worn-out myth on your side than a god-driven fucking hurricane heading your way out of a sky you thought was empty. Storms at sea have a habit of making you believe in gods.

'Let her go,' I said. 'And you, old man, you'd better thank Apollo.'

He did more than that. The old priest was so grateful he said he'd pray to the god right away for my health, prosperity and safe return. Not a bad offer considering I'd just sacked his city. He saw to the prosperity himself by loading me up with gold and silver, never mind the bronze. He saw to my health too, pledging it with a dozen jars of wine – not any old vintage, either, but something really special he'd kept hidden away, he said, and to prove it he broached a jar on the spot and filled the cups to the brim.

Nectar? The word does not exist that could convey the taste; nectar will have to do. As for the kick, he said you could mix just one cup of this drench to twenty of water and still go woozy. I believed him. That wine hit the god-spot and took you straight to Elysium. The fumes could almost knock you out, and when you were sleeping it off, he said, the wine had properties that worked wonders for the blood. I didn't know it at the time, but that brew was more than just salubrious. It turned out to be a life-saver.

After the spoils, the men wanted to cut and run. The wind was good for Ithaca and they were eager to get under way. I said we'd stick around; they belly-ached, and I bullshitted them – just for the night.

'Besides, there's plenty of fresh pussy around here,' I said. 'Do any of you have a problem with that?'

They did what soldiers do, obeyed orders. Maron prepared cuts of meat and plied me with wine. I was careful to water it. I wondered whether he was a slippery old shit who planned to slit my throat the minute I was legless, but he was knocking back more cups than anybody, and I gave him the benefit of the doubt and collapsed in the portico.

I woke up in the dark, wrapped in the long white arms of his wife. I thought at first I was having a wet one, but dreams don't come with scent, and this one smelled good. She was just a girl. Her tongue probed my mouth.

'And your husband?' I whispered.

'No need to worry on his account, Odysseus. Or about the code of honour, if that bothers you. I'm part of the hospitality – a gift. If you want me.'

I wanted her. She climbed aboard and swept her breasts slowly from side to side over my face, letting her nipples stroke my lips. Then her long black hair was brushing my belly and she began the blowjob, a long slow one, a tantaliser, taking just the right time. She knew what she was doing.

'Do you like that?'

I couldn't speak. I was breathless. On Olympus.

'And now it's my turn.'

She rammed herself hard onto me and guided my hands to her breasts. The nipples stood out like bursting chestnuts. Then she brought my hands round to her haunches. I gripped them while she did the thrusting. A beauty of a bum, rounded, big and firm. I inserted one finger into her arsehole. She shuddered suddenly and howled and I flowered inside her. The howl modulated into a girl's giggle and she sank slowly onto me with a long soft sigh.

We stayed in Ismarus for another twenty-one days.

'And some fucking blunder that turned out to be, Odysseus!' as the crew wasted no words in telling me. 'And all on account of an arousing arse!'

'It was not an arousing arse,' I said, 'it was an arse to die for.'

'And some of us did die for it too!'

So they did. Not on the web, of course, where you can see the hapless captain, Odysseus, urging his crews on, eager to be away from Ismarus, longing to plough the watery waste that lies between him and his hearth, where his faithful wife, the soul of patience, waits with outstretched arms, a far cry from Clytemnestra.

Plough the barren waste? Odysseus wouldn't prefer to plough a firm and fertile belly, would he? Why would he want to be fucked each night by a broad-rumped nymph when he could be slogging at the oars,

hauling home to Ithaca, to farming and fidelity? Perish the thought —
and piss on the real villains of the piece, the crews, the drunken cunts,
knocking back Maron's wine, slaughtering the sheep and cattle, and
shagging the arses off all the women in sight.

Not so far off the mark, in fact. Some of the free women, the ones
we hadn't taken on board, took to approaching the ships and bringing
wineskins and baskets of bread. They also lay on their backs for any
sailor who cared to slip them a trinket from Troy, a bead, a bangle,
anything no longer worn by the Trojan women, who now wore only
shackles. War doesn't put a stop to the world's oldest trade, it promotes
it. We took these women to be the local whores.

Wrong. Approximately one hundred percent fucking wrong. They
were the wives of the Ismarus quitters, and a fucking good job they
made of keeping my men horizontal while their husbands went up-
country getting backup from the neighbours. And the neighbours, as it
turned out, were neighbours from hell, nothing like the peaceable breed
we'd overrun without a man down. This lot were fighters, just like us.
This is for the record — not all Cicones are spineless.

One dim dawn we heard it, a drunken rumbling, distant, like a dream
of Troy, thunder in the mountains. The priest had risen early to pray in
the grove. The goddess of the grove was praying under me — with her
legs in the air. Nothing to worry about. Next thing, the fucking chariots
were among us. Sometimes you don't know it's happening till the door
gets kicked in. This was one of those times. We had to arm in the dark,
and not all of the men could find their arms. Some of them couldn't
find their cocks either — afterwards, we found them lying there with
their throats cut and as cockless as can be, courtesy of the last shag in
Ismarus. Easy to slit the scrotum of a man who's just shot his spunk
into you and is now snoring his drunken bonce off.

Too easy. I lost more than seventy men. We didn't surrender a single
ship, but still they broke us, the bastards, the line we formed couldn't
hold, there were too many of them, and by the time we made the ships,
there wasn't a single woman left on board, not even the women we'd
brought from Troy. All gone. The Cicones had whacked us, and it was
down to me. I had to admit I'd shot an arrow through my foot.

'Your foot? You've shot one up each man's arse! And all for a bit of
fucking skirt!'

Tell it not on the web, Penelope, spin it my way, the way I told you,
only don't give the girl a name. If I knew it, I've forgotten it. She was
Maron's wife, that's all I know. Not quite all, if you want to know. She

was a fuck from the gods, a priest's pussy, an altar gift. Apollo was on my side after all.

We weren't far off Ismarus when that hellish daytime darkness came down, the deadly calm kind that tells a sailor in his bowels what's coming next. The gale struck us out of the north and quickly turned into a hurricane. It hit us broadside. The sails were ripped to shit in seconds.

'Lower the masts!' I yelled.

We lowered – and rowed. And rowed and rowed. For two days and nights we rowed for dear life, nothing to eat or drink, no time to weaken, to unbend, not a second, till the third morning cracked open with a gorgeous dawn and we reached the Cape of Malea.

Malea. Fucking Malea. The old-timers had a saying: when you round Cape Malea, forget the folks at home. Forget farms, fires, sunsets, children, your wife's breasts. Forget the dreams of age. We'd almost rounded it when the north wind hit us again, this time combined with a bugger of a swell and a current that shoved us right off course for Ithaca and forced us past Cythera. That's what happens when you hit the blue hump of Malea. You can come down sweetly with a northerly at your arse all the way, alter course through three hundred degrees in a jumble of whitecaps and find you've turned into a headwind that can wreck you on Crete or cuff you out onto the open sea, where you can be anybody's – gods', monsters', the sea's breakfast. We avoided the Cytherean reefs, but the oarsmen could do fuck all. One second there was a sea coming over the side Olympus high, next second it was sucked so far down there was nowhere to bury the blade. The oarsmen were ploughing empty air. We were whipped downwind towards Libya. Nine stinking days on end, a cunt of a storm that threatened to make corpses of us all. And there wasn't a day on which one ship or another didn't lose a man. By the time we struck land, we didn't know where we were. We could have been in Africa. And the ships were battered to buggery. But they were still good to go. It was the men that were wrecks. Never mind, they said, we'd come to the right country.

Or so it seemed. As close as you get in this life to paradise. We'd reached the land of the lotus-eaters.

That's what Penelope called them. They were dope-heads – but let them be lotus-eaters and lend addiction an enhancement. None of us much cared what the fuck they were on that first landing. When you've been climbing walls of water for nights on end and every second expecting the big one, the one that sends you down the sea's white gullet to greet Poseidon, the first thing you do when you hit land in the dark and feel the old earth under your feet, solid and unshifting, is to stagger up the beach a few steps, just out of reach of the sucking tide, and drop down in a dead heap into a long fucking slumber. That's what we did.

*

We woke with singing in our ears. Dreaming again? Always the dreams. Then I thought I was dead and that the next life hadn't started off so badly – till I realised the trilling lilting figures bending over us were real, and human, and I sat up and took stock.

They were unarmed – that was the first thing that checked out. They were also bare buff, starkers, not a stitch other than the strings of beads; the men all hung out and the females bristling with pubes and boobs. Essence. They had the longest hair I'd ever seen, both sexes, and with flowers twisted in, the same flower, the clear favourite around here. The lotus flower.

And the language? Couldn't understand a fucking word. Not that it mattered. Most of the time they didn't speak at all, they sang, went around singing like they were in some sort of trance. It didn't take long to get the picture; they were stoned out of their minds. And whatever they were on turned them on, especially the women. They didn't waste any time – they came right onto us, literally, and started rubbing their nipples and stroking their pussies and letting us see by gestures what they wanted, just in case we were too dumb to work it out. Their men just stood around grinning and singing and giving obvious approval. If we hadn't hit the Isles of the Blessed, this was the next best thing.

Ask a sweaty, hairy sailor for a shag and you won't have to ask twice. The only thing that had bucked under me since Maron's wife was the sea, and this was altogether pleasanter than being shagged by Poseidon. It got even weirder. My piece of pussy had just changed position and come on top when one of the girls tapped her on the shoulder. She got off without a word and strolled over to another couple while the new arrival took over. The same thing was going on all over the beach – free love in an open-air commune, one in which you knew you could very willingly waste your time. For a time. Which is what we did. For a time. The nights reeled like drunkards and we drowned in the deep stench of flesh, armpits thick with musk, lips groggy with lust. And by day, sun, sea and still more sex, and all in a glorious narcotic stupor. What more could you ask for?

So Odysseus beached his ships on the island of the lotus-eaters, where it was always afternoon, and whose inhabitants spoke to the crew in a strange tranquil language that needed no translation. Benignly mindless, the words dropped softer than petals from blown roses, night-dews in dry stone troughs, tired eyelids on tired eyes.

They looked about them. Forests, mountains, mountain streams. But the streams were silent as dreams, each descending slowly like downward plumes of smoke, muted by distance. There were waterfalls too, clifftop-spilling cataracts that seemed to pause rather than fall, and from far below the wet haze rose in an unheard slow cloud. In the farthest distance were three more mountains, higher still, impossibly lofty pinnacles, capped with snow, in the blue swoon of the sky, up among the gods.

And out of the green gates of the forest they trooped, the strange race, bearing baskets laden with flowers and fruit. Unafraid and uncurious, they stroked the mariners' salt-stiff hair, smiling and singing and encouraging them with gestures to eat. Some strolled over to the ships and put their faces briefly to the black hulls. A sea-girt people, yet they had no knowledge of ships, nor any understanding of the weapons that lay scattered on the sands, emblems of war.

The crews accepted the fistfuls of fruit which the islanders crammed into their mouths, and instantly they lost their cares, lost all desire even for home, or for struggling ever again against the grey wastes of water that lay between them and their almost forgotten families. The eternal bench, the eternal oar, the roll to starboard, roll to larboard, the plunging prow, the soaring stern, the salt in the throat, the eyes gone mad with studying the sun and staring out the stars – all that and the life of never-ending hardship, never-ending toil: how easy it seemed now to embrace the sweetly offered alternative.

And this is what the lotus-eaters seemed to sing.

> *Stay, sailors, stay for the songs*
> *that bring sweet sleep softly*
> *down from the yellow skies,*
> *stay here with us, on deep cool mosses,*
> *sleep by the streams where the long-leafed*
> *flower weeps, the sun-drenched poppy hangs*
> *in summer stupor from the scented crags,*

and wake to hear this song, and fall
asleep again, and dream eternally.

Sailors, all things invite you: stay
away forever from the weary sea,
the drift of change, accept instead
the hour of ease, the purple noon,
the lotus fruit that leads you idly
to Elysium. Why feel the weight of sorrow,
why work an hour longer, why work
at all? Stay here with us in our yellow
lotus fields, our isle of dreams.

Seduced thus by the lotus and the lilting voices, the mariners urged their captain to let them stay. Odysseus alone was adamant against it and alone refused to eat the lotus and succumb to the power of the drug. But one of his own crew, a man called Eurylochus, spoke eloquently and at length in favour of the alternative life.

'Let there be an end to it, Odysseus,' he said. 'We've all had enough of it, the sea, the sky, the toil and trouble. What is life but war and work and words, and in a little while our deeds are ash and our lips are dumb. Why go back to it, to any of it, the diurnal drudge, the shifting sea, the armed struggle, the cruel world, our hearts war-weary and our eyes gone dim with staring at the pilot-stars? Let's stay on here and live for peace, not war, ringed not by enemies but by friends, the mild-eyed melancholy lotus-eaters, mindless with ecstasy, a lifetime's ripening easing us into death, dropping like apples sweetly into our graves.

'What better life could be? What better than these yellow dreams? With half-shut eyes and ears of stone to hear the distant rivers, the gurgling streams, to watch the crisping ripples come and go, the curving lines of tide advance, recede, futile as strife, absurd as time. Where are those we knew? Faces of infancy, friends in the firelight, where are they now? They lie beneath the land they tilled, sleepers in earth, no weary limbs resting at last on beds of asphodel, each one we loved shut up forever in an urn of brass, far from the Elysian Fields, two fistfuls of white dust, a sigh in the grass, no more.

'And nothing endures. Why strive to keep what dies? Let's live instead this never-ending hour, banish the memory of our wedded lives, the hot tears grown cold on chimney-stones. Our sons are in our places, our wives warm-bedded now with other men, thinking us all long dead.

We'd come like ghosts on smokeless hearths to trouble them – a tale of Troy, no more, a song, a story, stopped in men's mouths. No, lads, we'll not go home where home's no more, we'll stay and rest and sleep and swoon, and see the long bright rivers stitched on the yellow fields, the purple hills, and never change our sky, and we'll study war no more.'

Odysseus heard out this speech in gracious silence and even applauded the speaker at the end. 'Well delivered, Eurylochus. I never knew you were such a poet. You should have accompanied yourself on the lyre. Not that it would have made any difference. You could have said all that in two sentences. I appreciate your point of view, but it's secondhand and it's lotus lingo. I still speak the language of the real world, and in that language, we're leaving. That's a reality; that's a fact. More to the point, it's an order.'

Even so, it proved hard for Odysseus to assemble the crews and ensure that all twelve ships were ready to cast off. In the end he used what force was necessary in the face of mutinous indolence. He made fires, burning the lotus baskets on the beach, forbidding the natives with drawn sword to bring more, and hurling the sailors into the sobering cold white breakers. Some he even had to tie up under the benches, releasing them only when they were well clear of the island. Many had sworn they would jump ship the moment they were loosened and swim straight back to the land of the lotus to live like gods again, they said, careless of mankind, untroubled in the mind, free from the cares and sorrows of their kind. But Odysseus had given orders that not a man was to be untied until the effects of the drug had worn off and the lotus had left them – with their minds restored. And so the resourceful Odysseus succeeded in taming his rebellious men. And leaving the land of the lotus-eaters, they once more put to sea, heading north in the direction of Crete.

FORTY-ONE

We whitened the wine-dark sea with our oars and headed north. But we'd sailed for less than half a day when a bastard of a gale got up, a northwester, and kicked us south again, and east. Down it came, the starless blackness, and it was one of those nights when nothing exists except the inkiness overhead and the roaring white sea beneath, and the whole time the hurricane howling in your ears and tearing your hair. The sails were shredded again, the oars impossible. The dope-heads I'd brought by force screamed at me that I'd dragged them out of the good life to plunge them into hell with the sea in their skulls and the quick glinting fish nibbling their ribs — that's not quite the language they used, but however it's put, it was true enough at the time and I couldn't deny it.

Then the sea shifted under us, as it does, and we could feel ourselves being ushered in somewhere by long white rollers, and suddenly we were safely aground. We tumbled over the gunwales — here we go again — and slumped down and slept, curtained off by a clinging night mist.

Dawn slit open the east. Rubbing our eyes, we glimpsed hills in the distance, shimmering in the pink morning mist. Closer to shore the land was level and looked to be deep-soiled and fertile, except that there wasn't a sign of cultivation, only wild wheat and barley, and wild vines growing thickly but untended, ripened by rains. Then we saw the thin, slow columns of smoke starting up from the mountains. Hill tribes? Always bad news, barbarians, the savage sort who can't be arsed to till their own fields. Thunder seemed to be coming out of the mountains, which was weird with good weather on the go. And now we heard the bleatings of sheep and goats. Shepherds, then? The men cheered up, picturing cuts of mutton roasting on the spits.

'I wouldn't count on any wine to wash it down,' I said, 'looking at the state of those vines. Whoever lives here does fuck all. They rely on earth and sky to do the work.'

When the mist burned off we saw that we were on a small wooded island at the mouth of a mainland bay, and with a natural harbour, a beauty of a nook where you could lie a ship without rope or anchor. The strange thing was, there wasn't a ship in sight, not as much as a small boat, not even a coracle. Who were these bastards? Not a trace of trade, and no buildings either, not a civilising finger pointed anywhere. But the wild goats were plentiful, and we were famished, so I said we'd stay here for the day and eat and then scout out the mainland the next morning. We brought down over a hundred goats for our twelve ships. We'd drawn off as many jars of wine as we could carry when we sacked the Cicones, so we ate our fill of roast goat and washed it all down with the red stuff till sunset.

Another dawn. I ordered the fleet to wait by the island while I took my own crew over to the mainland to reconnoitre: this was a place that could be worth colonising one day. As usual, the crews bitched about wanting to get home, but I told them I would see if there were any rich pickings to be had before we moved out.

We soon found a sizeable cave close to the shore. It was overhung with laurels and fronted by a sort of courtyard fenced in with boulders and timber, pretty basic. I took my twelve best men inside, leaving the rest to guard the ship. As an afterthought I took along a goatskin of Maron's wine, the special one, as a possible gift for anyone showing us hospitality. We weren't holding our breaths for it.

But there were encouraging signs – folds of lambs and kids which the absent owner had kept penned inside the cave, and there were brimming milk-pails and baskets crammed with big cheeses. No sign of bread or wine, though. What was the matter with these people?

'Let's grab as many of these cheeses as we can carry and fuck off while we can.'

Eurynomous was always the first to beat a retreat. I told him that since we'd come this far we were going to find out who lived here. My curiosity was aroused.

'Your curiosity will fucking kill us all!'

But he got stuck into the cheeses like the rest of us. Later we killed a couple of the kids and made up a fire for roasting. By evening we were stuffed.

'I don't suppose he'll mind,' I said. 'Hospitality to hungry strangers is the first law of life.'

And the second law of life is that you don't nod off in a strange place with your weapons stacked by the door. We woke to find our fire gone out, light fading fast, and a big black shape filling the mouth of the cave. We shrank back into the shadows. He hadn't seen us yet – if it was a 'he'. The shambling manner suggested some sort of beast. But he was human all right, a mountain of a man, and a shaggy bastard too.

He crashed a bundle of faggots to the floor, ready to make a fire for supper, then he stopped the doorway with a rock so fucking big it would have taken two Ajaxes to shift it. Next thing, there were sparks, and then the tongues of flame shot up and showed us more of our host.

God almighty, he was ugly! A complete fucking abortion. One of his eyes was missing – either a malformation or some accident or act of aggression had left him with just the one. There was scarring over the socket, the skin like a lizard's. This cunt was going to give us grief, I knew it. My brain was racing. An opponent with half his eyes – that gives you half a chance. It gives you an edge. The fire roared into life, and he saw us.

'Who the fuck are you?'

We stared. The freak spoke Greek.

'I asked you who the fuck you are. Cattle thieves? Pirates? You're thugs on the make, aren't you? Out on a spree. Well, you've come to the wrong fucking place, you cunts!'

He spotted the remnants of our meal.

'Fucking hell, and you've been making free with my food and all, you fucking plunderers, I'm going to fucking kill you!'

'Wait!' I said. 'We're Greeks, like you. We're what's left of Agamemnon's army, on our way back home from Troy. We're not raiders, we're just simple soldiers and sailors, driven off course, and we've come to you as guests.'

He grinned, exposing a row of jagged yellow teeth.

'And we ask you to honour the gods, bearing in mind that all suppliants who are dishonoured by their hosts are avenged by Zeus.'

The host snorted. Mucus shot from his nostrils and ran down his chin.

'Nice speech, but it won't wash here. Listen you, I'll tell you right here and now, I've never heard of Troy and I've never heard of this cunt Agamemnon. I don't give a fuck about Zeus either. Zeus means fuck all to me and neither do you, arsehole! You're well out of touch with the way things work in these parts. Permit me to demonstrate.'

He lurched across the cave and grabbed the nearest man by the neck. The poor bugger didn't even have time to scream. In the same second, the freak smashed his head against the side of the cave. The skull shattered, and the brains splashed out across the wall and slid to the floor. I started up, but he blocked my way.

'You want some of that, bastard-face? Just try it and see!'

The men looked at me, shit-scared. We could have tried to rush him and make for the weapons, but we'd somehow frozen. I reckoned I had to keep him talking. I pointed to the still twitching corpse.

'What good did that do you?'

'What good? What the fuck do you mean, what good? That's fucking food down there!'

We stared at each other. He read what we were thinking.

'That's right, you've got it. Greeks, did you say? Well, Greeks will do me fine – it's all the same to me.'

He laughed and farted. 'One at a time, though. I'm not a glutton!'

More gut laughter and more farts.

'Only one question – which fucker's next?'

He reached out for me. I had to think fast. 'Wait!'

'They all say that.'

'No – listen!' I put on a whining voice and cringed, wringing my hands. 'Not me, please, I'm begging you! Take any one of my men instead of me and I'll make it well worth your while.'

More snorts, more snot.

'No you won't, I've got no fucking interest in your gold, it's fuck-all use to me!'

'It's not gold, it's better than that.' I picked up the Maron goatskin.

'It's the best drink ever made, believe me. Drink this and you'll feel like a god!'

'I don't want to feel like a fucking god! And I've tasted wine before. What do you think I am, you stupid cunt?'

I poured a good slap into one of his wooden bowls. 'Just taste it.'

He lifted it and sniffed, hesitating. 'I'm not a wine drinker. Anyway, how do I know it's not drugged or poisoned or something? Do you think I'm completely fucking stupid?'

'You're right,' I said. 'But look, to prove it's not been spiked, I'll take the first swig.'

I gulped enough to convince him but not enough to befuddle me.

'And I'll ask each of my men to do the same in turn. If it's poisoned, we all die.'

I passed the bowl to Eurynomous with a wink, and he swigged and handed it to the next man.

'All right, all right, you've made your fucking point. Now give it here!' He grabbed hold of the bowl and slurped greedily. As soon as it hit the spot his expression changed.

'Hey, that's fucking good stuff. Got any more of it?'

'Right now just the one skin, sir, but there's plenty more where that came from. I can go and get it for you right now if you want me to.'

'You'll stay right where you are! And you'll go nowhere except under my supervision. Now let's have the rest of that!'

I poured him out three more draughts in succession, each of which he threw down his neck the way a dog bolts its food. The wine didn't even touch the sides of his gob. And still no effect. This was worrying. I weighed what was left in my palm. He saw my expression, misinterpreted it, and grinned.

'Don't worry, I'll leave you some. And you'll be well rewarded for it.'

He chuckled as I charged his bowl from the now nearly empty skin, wishing I'd brought another. The cunt had the constitution of an ox. At last, though, I saw the tell-tale look come into his eye, and his speech started to slow.

'Another . . . another . . .'

'Your wish is my command. Not to finish it off would be an insult to the wine. A nice nightcap, don't you think?'

'Insult to the wine . . . nightcap.'

The swigs were shallower now, and each one brought him closer to the oblivion he was about to enter. When I saw he was ready to take the plunge I decided to taunt him a little.

'And now, you drunken fuck, what about my reward?'

The men panicked and gestured frantically at me. The bastard wasn't completely unconscious.

'Reward?'

'Yes, you said you'd make it worth my while giving you this wine, so what's the prize, cunt-face?'

'The prize is' – drunken burping and laughter – 'that you'll be the last to die. I'll leave you till the end. How's that suit you, eh? I'll roast your Greek heart and liver and dine in style!'

One hand slumped heavily onto his naked gut. The bowl slipped from the filthy fingers of the other hand and clattered on the floor.

'But tomorrow will do for that. And the next day, I'll shit you into little pieces.'

Snigger, slobber, fart. Blind drunk the bastard lay, his head sagged to one side, burping up blood-red wine. We rushed to the entrance and collected our weapons. Then we put our combined weight against the rock and shoved like fuck.

'Right, now to cut the cunt's throat!'

'No – wait, lads,' I said, 'I've something else in mind for this one-eyed arsehole. I'm going to make the bastard suffer.'

I shoved my sword-point into the hot embers and waited till the blade was glowing a good old red. Then I aimed carefully at the one good eye ...

The screaming followed us all the way to the ship. I'd blinded him, but not killed him. I wanted him to have plenty of time left to reflect on the virtues of offering hospitality to strangers.

'And who knows,' I said later to Penelope, 'maybe he's seeing better now. They say blind men develop an inner light. Maybe he's even grateful!'

But at the time I couldn't resist the urge to run back a little way closer to the cave to let him have a parting shaft.

'Enjoy the rest of your life, loser! By tonight you'll be wishing I'd killed you!'

The men came running back to drag me away. 'For fuck's sake, listen to the racket he's making! The bastard could have friends. He could bring down the whole country round our fucking ears!'

And that's how it happened, though I don't mind admitting that over the years I grew fonder of Penelope's version of events, as she wove it, and as you would expect. The mind's more cradled when the grave is near, and you acquire a taste for fables, stories to sweeten death's bitterness. In the web, the friends were the Cyclops, a race of one-eyed giants, of which he was one, and the thunder we heard on our first approach was the sound of their voices, bellowing to one another from their mountain caves, where each lived out his solitary life without a thought for society. The one we met stood as tall as a tree, and not twenty men could have shifted the rock with which he sealed the mouth of his cave, trapping us inside with him. If we'd killed him in his drunken stupor, our bones would have mouldered there along with his. A plan altogether more cunning had to be contrived.

The monster lunged at us as soon as he saw us and snatched up two of the crew. They were like puppies in his huge fists. He bashed their brains out on the cave walls and ripped their limbs apart with his bare fingers. Then he spitted the best body parts and roasted them quickly over the fire. The stench of burning human flesh filled the cave and made us vomit. The feed was too awful to describe.

'Now I'm going to sleep,' he said, 'and if any of you try anything during the night you'll never get out alive. You'll never shift that rock, not if you chipped at it with your swords for a hundred years. But before I rest I want to know a few things, now that I have a good full belly and I'm feeling talkative. You, the captain – what do they call you?'

'An easy name to remember.' It came to me in a flash from the gods. 'They call me Noman.'

'And you say you've come all the way from Troy, wherever that is. I didn't see your ship. Where have you beached her? Or is she at anchor?'

I saw through the ruse at once.

'That's just the problem,' I said, 'we have no ship, god help us. Poseidon wrecked it on the rocks.'

The giant roared with laughter. 'Poseidon, you say?'

'Yes, and the rest of the crew perished. We're the only survivors, with no means of reaching home again, unless you help us.'

The ogre was helpless with laughter now.

'Of course I'll help you. But as we're no shipwrights, I'll have to help you in some other way. So I'll help you by reducing the number of your crew. Then, if any of you are left by the time I'm done with you, you can get home on a couple of logs — if Poseidon will let you!'

And he took two more men for breakfast the next morning, ripping and snapping, rending flesh and bone, and this time gobbling them down raw. Then he left the cave with his flock of rams to take them to pasture, stopping the mouth of the cave again and promising to be back for supper, when the crew would be cut by another two men.

He kept his promise. It was obvious he'd carry on in this way until he'd eaten us all. That's when I hatched the escape plan and gave him the goatskin. He plunged into his drunken sleep, burping up chunks of half-digested human flesh in a flood of wine — a gruesome, stomach-heaving spectacle. But we breathed deeply and prepared ourselves for what we had to do next.

There was a slender tree-trunk lying at the back of the cave, as tall as a ship's mast. I needed to cut off a fathom of it to be sure of penetrating the eye, and the cutting had to be done with our swords, each man cutting in turn. When the fathom was cut, I sharpened it to a fearsome point and held it in the glowing embers until it was a lethal weapon, hardened and white-hot.

'Right, you savage bastard, I'm the man with no name, and you're just about to become the man with no eyes. Or should I say eye? Say goodbye to seeing.'

I dragged the terrible thing out of the embers, and four of the crew gripped it with me, getting ready for the turning and the thrust.

'Ready, lads? Now!'

We drove the great glowing poker deep through the eyelid, and the eyeball burst.

'Not too deep!' I didn't want to penetrate the brain.

As we plunged, we twisted and turned, like shipwrights drilling a ship's timbers, and the blood boiled and bubbled up around our scorching torch. Everything was burned to a cinder in seconds, including the very roots of the eye. I could hear them crackling and popping in the intense heat, the hiss and steam louder than when the smith suddenly plunges a new-forged axe or adze into ice-cold water to temper it.

For a heart-stopping second I thought I'd killed him – until we heard a shriek, the like of which I never heard before, not in nine years on the killing fields of Troy. The cliff around us reverberated till we thought the roof and walls of the cave would collapse and entomb us with the beast in his lair. But he sat up and tore the stake from the still sizzling socket, and, as it came out, the socket spouted more hot blood, splashing and scalding me and the crewmen who stood closest. The beast's skin was singed all round the wound, the single eyebrow burned away, and the coarse hair above it on fire.

The monster staggered to his feet and barged about the cave in agony, blundering into the walls and gashing himself, half searching for us with blind fingers, half maddened by pain and groping for the milk-pails to pour on cool relief. I kicked them over, dodging under his huge legs, and he cursed and clawed and shrieked all the louder.

The screams were heard far off on the windy mountain-tops by his fellow Cyclops. They came striding across the distant peaks in no time at all and along the valleys to the shore. We heard them gathering outside the stoppered cave-mouth.

'What ails you?' they called. 'Is somebody robbing you in there? Or trying to murder you?'

'Noman!' he bellowed back at them. 'Noman is here! Noman has hurt me!'

And so they went away again, the dimwits, calling back to him sagely that if no man was harming him, then he was probably mad, and his sickness had been sent by the gods. And there was nothing they could do about that, given that the Cyclops and the gods did not see eye to eye, so to speak. The best thing he could do would be to seek the help of Poseidon . . .

Meanwhile, we still had to get out of the cave, and the mutilated monster still had to attend to his beasts. Next morning the ewes would bleat to be milked and the rams to be pastured. So while the ogre moaned, unable to sleep, I bound the rams together in threes, and under each middle beast I fastened a man, so that he was protected from detection on either side and could pass out of the cave unharmed. I fastened myself to only one ram, but he was the biggest and strongest and fleeciest of the flock. And in this way we waited for morning.

The merest crack of sky glowed through the blocked entrance, but at last the stars rusted away, the east was flecked with red, and the eyeless ogre groped his way to the door, opened it, and hunkered down with outstretched arms and hands that fumbled in all directions, thinking to catch us on our way out, as if we were complete idiots. Still whimpering with pain, he called out to the beasts, feeling along their backs as they filed out and probing between their shaggy flanks. He never though to check their bellies.

So the men got out, by stratagem. My ram came last, slowed by my weight. He addressed it affectionately and stroked its back, wondering why it was last in line today when it was wont to lead the way, first in line, proudly to pasture: first at the stream, first at the flowers, first to crop the fresh young grass, first back home again to rest and shelter.

'Are you grieving for me, dear lad? Is that it? Are you sorrowing for your master, blinded by the hand of Noman? Oh, if only you had understanding and a voice, you would tell me where he is skulking right now. Then I'd smash his skull and scatter his brains across these walls and breakfast on him, flesh and blood and bones. That at least would be of some comfort to me in this torment. But on you go now, out to pasture, and I'll stay behind and search every corner until I have found him.'

By that time, I was out of the cave. As soon as we were at a safe distance, I untied myself and my men. We grabbed the fattest of the rams and took them with us to the ships – along with the king of the flock to shatter the savage's heart of stone. Our comrades were horrified to hear what had happened to six out of the twelve, but there was no time for tears. We took our places on the benches and struck the white surf with our oars.

Once offshore, I couldn't resist a parting shot.

'Hey, Cyclops! It's Noman calling you – remember me? I'm the one who frizzled your eye out and left you the blind blundering dunce that you are now. Our ships weren't wrecked, by the way. The only thing that's wrecked is the rest of your life! But if your manners should improve with suffering, especially your table manners, you can thank me for it. Right now, you're a blight on all the codes of honour and an affront to men and gods. At least I've taught you something about hospitality – and how a guest repays a bad host!'

There was no answer. But the monster reached round and tore off the top of a mountain, rocks and roots and towering trees and all, and, aiming for my voice, hurled it at us with a thunderous roar. We watched it form its arc and shuddered as it hovered overhead before falling into the sea just beyond us.

Relief was short-lived. The enormous splash created a backwash that engulfed our prow, almost swamping us, and drove us all the way back to shore. The monster heard the shouting and heaving as we pushed off a second time, and he reached for another missile. This time it struck the sea astern of us and gave us a huge push, beyond even the ogre's range.

Again the men tried to stop me, and I heartily wish some god had struck me dumb, but my blood was up, and I stood in the stern of the vessel and shouted across the dancing sea.

'If anyone inquires about your missing eye, tell them you were unwise enough to cross Odysseus. No man crosses Odysseus and gets away unscathed. Noman — and Odysseus. Got it? Remember both names — if you can!'

A great groan emanated from the shore. 'You devil! You got the better of me when I was asleep. You're no Greek hero! You're a puny trickster. But I'll remember your real name now, and you'll have reason to remember mine — Polyphemus, son of Poseidon, to whom I now pray that you never see home again. Or that if you do, you'll be the sole survivor of all your ships and find no friendly welcome — just suffering and spears and certain death!'

The blue-haired sea-god heard his son's prayer — and granted it. The sea was to become my worst enemy and strike me at every opportunity. For now, however, we were safe. We reached the little island where our comrades awaited us, and we told them all that had happened. We lit fires on the beach and dined on Polyphemus's fattest rams, well washed down with good red wine; we also washed down all fears of Poseidon and the monster's promised revenge. Only afterwards, when our bellies were full, did we sit down on the sands, the sea in our ears, and weep bitterly for our dead friends.

We wept and slept on the beach that night, the ocean whispering through our heads. And when dawn drew the curtains, fingering the east, we rowed out once more, onto the grey waters, stained pink by yet another sunrise.

FORTY-TWO

For nine days we sailed without a hitch and with a gentle west wind at our sterns, nudging us slowly home, and on the tenth day we saw Ithaca on the skyline and the spires of smoke going up. We came so close we could hear the bleatings of sheep and the bells tinkling from the fields. I could even distinguish from those tinklings which sheep were mine. The sounds of home — so sad, so fresh, so terrifying. A dreadful depression came over me, a sudden crushing weight on the cranium. I couldn't shift it, couldn't understand it. Everything was the same, nothing changed. The war we'd fought, all those men dead; it meant nothing here, it had nothing to do with home. The adventure was over. My legs buckled. Home is so sad. I wanted to cry.

I didn't have time.

Mediterranean storms come out of nowhere and go back to the nowhere they came from in a matter of minutes. Or they can last for hours. Or days. It was a storm like that, a nowhere storm. It sucked us from the shoreline and out again onto the open sea for so many sunless days and black nights we didn't know where we were.

Do you believe that? You'd better. Isn't it easier to believe it than to try to understand why a soldier could be just too fucking frightened to go home? Why a sailor who could smell the seaweed and hear the gulls would actually give the order to turn back? How to translate that sound, that smell, the slow old smoke of home? What to equate it to? The sorrow after sex, spiralling into emptiness, the dread of all endings, the emptiness of all emotions after the comradeship of battle, the fear of peace, the fear of life itself, that sort of thing.

And that's the truth of it. There really was a storm that sucked me away from Ithaca, but it was an inner storm, one that had fuck all to do with the sea or any of the elements. The truth isn't always useful, especially if there's an alternative, a better explanation of why things happen as they do. A myth, if you like. This one is called the Aeolus adventure, and it's a way out for a wandering hero and a husband who won't come home. So let the web do its work, let Penelope spin her yarn.

The storm drove the crew demented, the shrieking in their ears elemental and inhuman, like Polyphemus screeching in his pain, and they raged against Odysseus's insatiable curiosity which had led them into the Cyclops' lair, and the arrogance which had brought the vengeance of Poseidon down on their heads. They were certain now to be gulped down by the deeps and their bones rolled about the ocean eternally, their spirits wailing their demise in the shape of the eternal gulls that circle the skies, the souls of lost mariners, unburied and unwept. It was only when they struck the happy land of Aeolus that the crews ceased to curse their commander.

Aeolus was the god-empowered wind-keeper of the deeps. He lived on his island home, surrounded by a barrier of bronze, its cliffs falling sheer to the sea. With his six daughters and six sons combined in incest, he sat banqueting on his island home, and life at his court was one eternal feast. When Odysseus arrived, Aeolus insisted that the crews partake of his table and their captain tell all that had happened at Troy and after the end of the war. There were adventures enough to satisfy a hundred hearers for a year's feasting, and Aeolus was so taken with Odysseus by the end of the narrative that he gave him an unusual parting present to help him on his way. It was an oxhide sack in which he had imprisoned the winds, leaving only the west wind free to chase them home. The mouth of this sack had to be kept secure, and it was tied tightly round with a lovely silver cord.

And so all went well with the fleet until Odysseus sighted Ithaca, whereupon, exhausted by his adventures and overcome with relief and joy, he fell into a deep sleep. Until then he'd been managing the sheet single-handed night and day, eager for the quick run home and unwilling to entrust the task to anyone but himself, so anxious was he to see Penelope again. The sheer strain of this finished him off, and he gave way, knowing that the crew could easily handle the ship and bring her safely into port.

It was a fatal error. No sooner did his men see him asleep than they put their treacherous heads together and concluded that the mysterious sack presented to their captain had so many bulges and was secured so tightly that it must have been crammed with gold and silver. It was obvious Odysseus was planning on keeping the loot for himself and sending them home empty-handed. So they slipped the sack from his sleeping fingers, undid the cord . . . and let loose all the howling winds of heaven.

Odysseus awoke with Ithaca fading like a dream into day as the entire fleet was swept back out onto the open ocean. Penelope stood on the shore, tearing her long hair to no avail. The crimson beaks jabbed the other way, away from home, eating the ocean. The winds did the work of nine days in three, and by dawn on the fourth day the fleet had been buffeted all the way back to Acolia.

The wind-keeper couldn't believe it. All his family crowded round the harbour and stared in amazement, asking what had gone wrong. To have been given complete control of the winds and then to have lost that control completely – how? Odysseus denounced his own crew, and they hung their heads in shame to support him, but it failed to impress Aeolus.

'A man who returns after all these years and allows himself to fall asleep within reach of his homeland deserves a bungling crew and is not worth helping. In fact, it would be unwise and unsafe to assist such a man. There is surely something in your soul that must be worked out between you and the gods. No, I'll not succour you a step further. Find your own way home.'

And so Odysseus was expelled from Aeolia without a breath of wind in the sails. Nothing left to do but row.

And we did row – after hitting a three-day storm. We rowed for another seven bastarding days on a windless sea, with arms of ash and hands of rope and backs and shoulders to match, and we were dropping at the oars from sleeplessness and sheer fatigue when we saw buildings looming up on the skyline, a city built on high cliffs that fell steeply into the sea for hundreds of feet. Impregnable. Only the gulls could have got into that city, and when we drew closer we could see the snowstorm thronging the rocks and hear the screeching through the white thunder of the surf beating the cliffs. But even the seagulls rose no higher than midway to the city, shuttling endlessly in the spray, their cries as wild and relentless as the surge.

The crew were in no doubt.

'This is an arsehole of a place! Let's turn about.'

But I wanted a closer look. 'Whoever lives up there doesn't fly in on wings,' I said. 'There's got to be a way in.'

Sure enough, we skirted the cliffs and soon found it, a natural harbour, small but inviting, a quiet little haven for sailors weary of the sea and the endless rowing. The men perked up.

'Well done, captain, let's get in there and rest up.'

But at the last minute I held back. I didn't like it, the narrow mouth with the cliffs towering up on both sides, no manoeuvrability in an emergency.

'Emergency? What fucking emergency?'

I moored my own ship to a rock just outside the entrance on the seaward side and ordered the other captains to do the same. The bastards ignored me.

'Look, you've found us a harbour. Good for you. Now we need to rest – that's the only emergency!'

Against my orders they went in, and what they found was worse than any emergency. They rowed into a slaughter-hole. The last ship had just gone in when all hell broke loose. Suddenly, the cliffs bristled with figures all along the summits and the upper air went dark with missiles, a hail of rocks hurtling down on the fleet. They were bigger than anything that could have been lifted, let alone thrown, and must have been balanced up there on the clifftop edges, all ready to be levered off. The nice quiet haven was a death-trap.

Whoever was up there didn't like us, that was for sure, and the bastards didn't even have to take aim. The fleet was so tightly packed the ships filled up the harbour, and every rock that came crashing down found a target. The ships were splintered into driftwood. Some sank in minutes. The harbour was filled with swimmers thrashing about among the tangle of oars, most of them bleeding and badly injured, trying to find a way out.

But there was no way out, no shore to swim for, and the retreat to the open sea was blocked.

And now the natives showed face, emerging out of a circle of caves lower down the cliffs. They were stark-naked, barbarian bastards armed with long harpoons. There was no way they could have built that city up in the air. They must have been some kind of hunter army, kept as slaves by the citizens to procure them meat from the sea. And they were lethal. The crews were speared like fish to the last man, and the waters of that hell-harbour went red with their blood.

Laestrygonians. That's the name Penelope gave them, turning them into giants and cannibals for good measure, as if we hadn't had enough of both. They spitted their human catches and grilled them over slow fires, dead or alive, the wounded still quivering in the flames. All I could do was to cut the hawsers of my own ship and order the crew to row for their lives – which they did, with spears whistling after us and falling short, thank fuck, otherwise we'd have been roasted along with the rest of the fleet. There were no survivors.

And now we were one ship at the mercy of the sea. We sailed on with heavy hearts, bitterly regretting our dead friends and the gruesome manner in which they'd died.

The sea, the sea. Who would cross it? Who in his right mind would want to travel that grey waste of water, the unspeakable vastness of the ocean? What is it? There aren't even any cities in it. It's an element that exists to hurt, to entrap, to corrupt, to seduce, to make you lose your way and ultimately kill you, if it can. But what is the right mind, and what man is ever in it? What sailor can resist a harbour, or an island, even when every island he encounters is an island of death and deception? Even when the island is home?

We were a long way from Ithaca, and other islands lay between us, strewn across the sea. The next was a small one, attractive enough on the face of it, with a good harbour and no hint of danger, a tranquil atmosphere, welcoming. A clifftop crenellated with cypress trees, scents of cyclamen, wild mint, sound of birdsong and bees. The works. All the same, we ran the ship ashore in silence before slumping bone-weary on the beach to sleep off our struggles and our grief, still heartsore for our perished friends. We lay there like statues for two whole days and nights.

Before dawn on the third day I woke up ravenous. I left the men still sleeping and made for the summit of the nearest hill. I was hoping to spot some sign of habitation or food – the crew would wake up famished. The entire island was covered with thick forest, in which anything could have lurked, but nothing was visible. And then I saw it right in the centre: a needle of smoke rising calmly into the sky. Somewhere in there, somebody had a home. And where there's a home, there's food. The only odd thing was the sudden quietness. For all the expanse of forest, there wasn't a twitter, just this huge and birdless silence. Why no dawn chorus? Maybe it was too early. Yet already the heat was intense. It was weird.

I thought about striking out in the direction of the house, but decided I'd best get back to the crew. And then, like a prayer answered, an antlered stag stepped smartly out of the woods. Drawn by the sun, no doubt, he was on his way to drink at a small stream, and he crossed my path without even being aware of me. I hurled my spear and struck him on the spine. He fell in the dust with a sob. It sounded almost human.

The men were still bleary-eyed when I got back, bent double beneath the dead weight of this magnificent beast, but when they saw him they jumped to their feet, wide awake at the prospect of food. We built a big fire and roasted meat all day long till sunset, washing it down with the last of the sweet wine from the ship and the cool clear water from the stag's drinking place. He provided quite a banquet. And when darkness fell we slept soundly again beside the sounding sea.

When the sun came up, the crew wanted to get going, but I said I'd seen smoke in the centre of the trees and was off to investigate.

'Are you quite sure about that?'

Eurylochus. I asked him what he meant.

'You don't get it, do you? You never fucking get it. Last time you decided to investigate we lost six men to that cunt with the one eye.'

'Well, he's a no-eyed cunt now. I paid him back, didn't I?'

'It didn't bring our friends back, though, did it? Not to mention getting the rest of the fucking fleet wiped out.'

'They disobeyed orders.'

'It's true,' piped up Antichus. 'Odysseus can't be blamed for that disaster. But right now it's different. You say you want to investigate. But what exactly do you need to investigate? So somebody has a fire going on the island. So what? Let them get on with their meal. What's it to us? That's what I'd like to know.'

'So would I!' Eurylochus had had his say but he couldn't keep his mouth shut. 'Yes, what is it to us? The weather's fine, the wind's fair, we're good to go. So why not fucking go? Don't you ever want to get home?'

Home again. The word stirred up strong emotions in the men. I could feel the wall of resentment and accusation building against me, as if it had been all my fault, as if Troy had been my idea. As if there had never been a Helen, a Paris, an Agamemnon.

I dug my heels in.

'For your sins, Eurylochus, I'm putting you in charge of twenty-two men, half the crew. I want you to locate that house I spotted and report back. But when you find it, don't take any chances, do you hear? You stay outside till you've weighed up the situation, no matter what happens. That's an order. Then you get back here with your report. That's all.'

Whatever happened, I didn't want them blaming everything on me. Eurylochus now shared the responsibility. While he was away, I filled a pitcher with the dregs of the strong stuff and passed it round undiluted. As they were quaffing, I casually mentioned some of the tight corners we'd been in at Troy, the things we'd been through together. The jug passed from lip to lip, and the remembering mouths murmured about our exploits with slurred nostalgia —we'd likely all go down in history, and even be sung as heroes hundreds — maybe thousands — of years from now. This was the mood I wanted, and it was helped along by the growing heat of the morning sun. Soon the whole company was at ease and in no mood to go anywhere. I was careful not to drink more than a sip myself; I wanted to stay sober until Eurylochus returned.

I got a shock when he did appear, running out of the wood on his own, not a man behind him. I jumped to my feet.

'What the fuck's going on? Where are the men?'

He told me the story.

They had found the house all right. It was in an open glade, with cats sidling in and out of the wild flowers. So far so good. There were dogs too, but not ferocious ones, suggesting a civilised household. It was a world away from that cannibal cunt in his cave, especially when they heard a woman's voice singing sweetly from inside the house. Even so, Eurylochus obeyed orders, miraculously, and said he'd stay outside and spy through the big open window, which was overhung with foliage. The rest of the men went inside.

The lady was a beauty. She was working away at an old loom as she sang. There were maidservants flitting about, four of them, all shapely young girls and good-lookers. There wasn't a man in sight.

A safe house then. And in spite of being alone and unprotected, the woman didn't act afraid when the men entered, even though they came in with drawn swords, just in case. She introduced herself as Circe and asked to be introduced to each man individually, clasping and kissing the whole company as tenderly as if each man were her long lost lover. Then she sat them down on couches and ordered the girls to bring them sweet Pramnian wine mixed with amber honey and barley meal and sprinkled with cheese. When the trays were brought in, she produced a jug and poured a small quantity of liquor into each man's draught.

'It's a relaxing drink,' she said, 'to free up your minds and bodies from the hard times you have been through. You'll soon feel the effects.'

She passed her hands lightly, absentmindedly, over her breasts.

'It's also an aphrodisiac, by the way. And should you feel so inclined, well . . .'

She waved at the four serving-girls. They stood in a row holding hands and giggling.

'So drink up, lads!'

Eurylochus admitted he was on the point of forgetting his orders and going inside to join in.

Except for what happened next.

One after another, very quickly, the men slipped from the couches and hit the floor. They lay there helpless – not unconscious, but giggling and grunting utter gibberish.

'Drugged!'

'Drugged? And the rest! Just wait till I finish my report.'

They were out of it, completely. The girls stripped them naked. Then they got naked themselves. Some of the crew they tied up, others they got onto all fours and sat astride them, ordering them to lick the arses of the other girls in turn and snuff out the truffles. The men appeared to enjoy it, Eurylochus said. They were in Elysium.

'I'll give them fucking Elysium,' I said. 'You stay here with the rest of the company. I'm going to get them out of that fucking brothel!'

I took up my bow and my sword with the silver studs and made my way through the woodlands. I soon got lost and wished I'd brought Eurylochus along to show me the way. After an hour of cutting a path through a dense patch, I stumbled into a small clearing and felt so buggered I flung myself down on a bed of flowers and fell asleep in the sun.

I dreamed briefly. In the dream Eurylochus appeared, to my relief, and pointed the way. He picked one of the flowers I was lying on and said I could crush its juice as an antidote to the drug I'd be given when I met the witch-woman. I woke up with a start. I wasn't going to take any fucking drug, that much was for sure. As for the flower, I must have scrabbled about in my sleep, because one of the blossoms was clutched in my right hand, root and all. The flower was milk-white, but the root was long and hard and black. The purplish bulbous tip looked like an Ethiopian's erection, and tendrils hung from it like hairs. All it lacked was balls.

I wondered vaguely about the dream. Antidote? Witch-woman? Bitch-woman more like. Yes, this root looked like the right treatment for her. I considered it for a second then threw it away.

'Fuck it, I'll use my own.'

I took the route of the dream and reached Circe's place in no time at all. I'd been very close. No sign of any of the crew, but I heard female laughter from somewhere inside the house. I called out, the door opened, and I was looking into the green eyes of Circe.

She was a stunner. True, I hadn't been close to a woman for a while, not since Maron's wife, but this was no ordinary female. Tall, trim, a draped column, her hair was tied up and held with a gold clasp. She looked like fucking aristocracy, so piss elegant I felt like a pig in her presence. I pictured the robe falling from those sculpted shoulders, all the way to her feet, revealing the clefts and curves, the comely hair loosened and wild, cascading past her hips in a bright blonde waterfall, her cunt uncurtained and aroused. Easy to imagine myself submitting to her will. As if reading my mind, she gave me a long slow bow, allowing me to see down between her breasts to the dark flash below the belly. I looked back up into those green eyes.

'So you're the captain of the crew?'

'That's right. And where are the crew?'

'They're being looked after. You can join them shortly. But first some refreshment.'

She led the way in and went straight to a niche, waving me to a chair. I stayed on my feet. When she turned round she was holding a large golden cup. I played along.

'Only one cup? I never drink alone.'

I put the cup to my lips and tipped my head back, turning my back on her at the same time and making my way over to the niche. By the time I'd poured her a cup, the unswallowed draught was back in mine. I returned, holding the two cups. She tilted her head and laughed.

'Too late for that, you fool, you've quaffed already!' And she flung the contents of her own cup in my face. 'Now, down on your knees, boy, and lick my feet! You'll lick a lot more by the time I'm done with you.'

One second later, she was standing shocked and stark-naked in front of me, the ripped robe torn open in one go by my hands. I crumpled it up, wiped my streaming face with it and flung it away. I pulled out my sword and stuck it straight out, pointing at her belly.

'Yes, I might get round to licking your pussy, lady. If I feel like it. But right now I'm not the one that's going to do the licking!'

Fear filled the green eyes. She dropped to her knees, clutching at mine. Her tits were crushed against my thighs. She reached out for the erection and brought it to her lips.

'That'll do you fuck-all good either,' I said. 'Now, in a little while you are going to call off your bitches and get my men unhooked. Or I'll drag you backwards through the forest, naked as you are, all the way back to the ship, and then I'll loose you to my crew. They haven't tasted a woman in a long while and they'll be very glad to see you, believe me. After that, I'll cut your throat and fling you to the fishes. But not before I've fucked you up the arse. Alternatively, you can take your chances with me right here and now and see if you can satisfy me. If you can, good for you. If you can't, you're fish-shit. What do you think?'

Relief flooded the green eyes. She let go of me and lay back on the floor, her thighs splayed wide.

'No,' I said, 'that's not it, not quite. Since you like to treat men like pigs, you should find out what it feels like. Assume the position.'

She hesitated, afraid again, uncertain what to expect.

'Like this.'

I grabbed her by the haunches and turned her over on her knees, arse in the air. The gates of life glared at me again, daring me to come through. I parted the crack and let her have it. One deep gasp from the fair Circe. I don't mind admitting it, I was fully aroused by this woman, and not just sexually. This wasn't rape. I wanted her, all of her, to the core, to the soul. I reached up from her belly to her breasts, dangled apples, their nipples hard as leather. And that arse — so innocent and unprotected, stuck out there in space like a newborn planet, and already starting to thrust back at me. I came out for a second to take in the view.

It never fails to thrill me, the sheer incongruity, the smooth white buttocks, blank as alabaster, and that black barbaric fracture, ancient with hair. It was like a rape in itself, a self-rape, a split in nature, primitive, fissured, foreign, shockingly savage. I came back in slowly this time, relishing the imprisonment, the pressure on the prick, the incarceration by the cunt, its monstrous mystery, the heavy whirlpool suction, the juice.

I could feel the spunk running, and I came out again, wanting to prolong the pleasure, but this time she gave me the reach-around, pulling me back in by the balls, and twisted onto her back again, still keeping me inside her, wrapping her long legs around my neck.

'Now!'

At the last thrust she bucked up hard, dug her heels in and cried out — one long lingering cry wrung out of the abyss of ages. Then she shuddered under me, and I collapsed on her and we lay heavy and fulfilled together in an unbroken silence.

It had to end.

'Do you love me?' The clear green eyes drenched me like the sea, soaked my heart through.

'I've only just met you.'

'And?'

It didn't take any consideration. Of course I loved her. 'Of course I love you.'

Whatever it meant, it was true.

'And you'll stay with me?'

'I'll stay.'

What was it exactly, this feeling? It was the ship's hunger, not for the horizon but for the harbour, that charmed circle between her legs, the safe haven, home. How had it happened, the dominatrix dominated? What was the drug? And who was in control? Whose spell was it? I knew I was under it, whatever it was, and that I had to stay, oh yes.

'I'll stay with you, Circe.'

She smiled. 'And the crew?'

'Leave them to me.'

They didn't need too much persuading, not when I told them what was waiting for them: baths of warm water, baskets crammed with meats, an endless supply of wine. Circe lived in style. And to crown it all, four willing girls, happy to do bad things nicely, with all the chastity of cats. Who wouldn't want to stay awhile? Who in his right mind would want to cross that treacherous sea? Much better to turn your back on the ocean and try to forget, forget.

And forgetting is what we did on that island. That's what it was for. So I forgot — forgot to tell Penelope about Circe, about what really happened. A soldier has a lot of forgetting to do when he comes back home after a long war, and there are some things he can't be expected to remember. Or doesn't want to remember. In any case, Penelope did the remembering for me. She even gave the island of forgetting a name.

Aeaea, island of the enchanting enchantress, the lovely Circe, a goddess, sister of a wizard and one of the children of the sun, borne by Perse, the daughter of Ocean. Circe, the encircler, who enmeshed Odysseus on her island and willed him with her wiles to lie with her, preventing his longed-for return to Ithaca and to the Penelope for whom he pined nightly.

Circe's house in the centre of the forest was patrolled by wolves and lions, but they were drugged and friendly and fawned on the advance party. Even so, the crew were terrified by these beasts and glad to get inside the house, where Circe showed them great hospitality. But into the Pramnian wine she introduced the drug which robbed them of all memory of their country and the homes and families awaiting their return. She then struck them with her wand and turned them into swine, but still with the minds of men, so that they dropped tears in the sties into which she ushered them, flinging pig-fodder at their feet and ordering them to eat. Thus she left them to wallow in filth.

Eurylochus sped back to tell his captain what had happened, and Odysseus immediately struck inland through the forest to find the house of the sorceress and free his men from her spell. He would never have succeeded in this venture had he not been met in the forest by Hermes, god of the golden wand.

'Look,' said Hermes, 'I know your mission, and it is a commendable one, but it is doomed to failure. You will not get the better of this witch unless you take this antidote to the potion she will put into whatever food or drink she offers you.'

And Hermes the Giant-Slayer gave Odysseus the herb with the black root and the milk-white flower which the gods called moly, difficult for a mere mortal to dig up out of the ground but easy for a god. He then instructed Odysseus exactly how to subdue the sorceress, whereupon he left him for lofty Olympus.

Everything unfolded as Hermes had predicted. Circe gave him the poisoned drink and struck him with her wand, ordering him off to the sties to wallow in the mud with his friends and eat pig-fodder. She was terrified when the hero remained unchanged and threatened her with his sword. That's when she invited him to her beautiful bed, where in love and in the sleep that followed they might learn to trust each other. And this was an invitation which Odysseus could hardly refuse, being at the behest of a goddess, though first he made her swear, according to Hermes' instructions, that she harboured no evil intentions and would do him no harm when she had him naked and vulnerable between her sheets. And so she swore, and so they went to bed.

The green eyes encompassed me again like the ocean. Night after night, she let fall the robe and loosened her hair. Night after night, she led me to her couch, lay down and extended those long white arms, like swans' necks. I fell into those arms gladly, gratefully, and she reached out and took hold of me. I never wanted to leave. She read my body language, the tiredness of limbs and mind.

'Anchor here, Odysseus, ride at anchor, always. Never leave me.'

I burst into tears.

'I know,' she said, 'I know what it is. It's the war, isn't it? It won't let you go. It will never let you go — not even years after it's over and you've been too long from home.'

Home. It was here, on her belly, in her cunt. And more, more than home. Truth lay between her legs, and so did I, night after night. The harbour crooked its arm around me, excluding the ocean, eclipsing Ithaca. She drew me deeper down, down into the gentle swell of her breath. I heard the sigh of another sea. Night after night. And I wept. For all the friends I'd left at Troy, for my lost childhood, for my mother and father, and yes, for my Penelope, who would never know the truth. I told Circe I would never go home.

And so it might have been, so it might have gone on forever, until the wheeling constellations brought round the long hot days and the dreams of summer, when time stands still. And under the curse of time my men began to tire of Circe's girls circling among them, sharing them, sharing themselves, never their own.

The four maidens were the nymphs of the springs and groves, born under boughs in crystal fountains, born of the ocean-flowing rivers. They spread chairs with purple rugs and brought silver tables, which they laid with golden baskets of bread and meat and bowls of sweet red wine, mixed in golden cups. They made baths of warm water and bathed all the men as Circe washed their captain's memories out of him and clothed him in a new tunic, threaded without sorrow, into which not a hint of nostalgia had been woven. Only the present existed.

The men kept longing for their homes and for the sweet girls of Ithaca, who were innocent of all that Circe's experts understood about the arts of love. I assured them they were imagining a past that existed now only in their heads.

'The girls of Ithaca,' I said, 'are girls no more. They're matrons with low-slung tits and sagging bellies. They've been ploughed and cropped, they're worn-out fields. And the matrons are now old maids, all wrinkles and no teeth. The old maids are ash.'

They didn't like that, and I had to tell them that the young girls of Ithaca, just in bud, were not waiting for a rag-tag straggle of veterans, scarred by war, to warm their beds. Their sheets were far from cool.

'Ithaca's a dream,' I told them, 'Circe's girls are real. You have everything you could ask for here. Why change it?'

But they kept on coming at me, in ones and twos and sullen clusters, sometimes the whole crew – deputations, day after day. And in the end, I ran out of answers.

'It's been a year,' Eurylochus said one day.

'No it fucking hasn't – it only feels that long.'

'It's been a fucking year.'

I was sad in Circe's arms that night, and it wasn't post-coital sadness. She felt it too.

'I know you're leaving me,' she said. 'And I know why. There's no need to explain.'

'It's the crew,' I said.

'I know. But I know it's more than that, it's more than the men. What are they, after all? They're the voices in your head, that's all, telling you to be away again. I know you, Odysseus. This island can't contain you, can it? You want to feel the flinty globe underfoot again, you want to feel your feet washed again by the cold ocean.'

'Very poetic.'

'And very true, don't you think?'

It was true. And why? Why do we need it, the toil and trouble, the stress of battle, the blood and thunder, the uncertain sea? It's something to do with not being static, not being bored, it's something to do with pitting the wits instead, pitting the wits and surviving, staying alive. It's something to do with death. And with hell.

'That's right, Odysseus, you'll have to go to hell and back. And as soon as you leave me you'll be in hell. For a time.'

And thus Odysseus lay supine and sad for a whole year while the lovely goddess lay with him, on him, and pleasured herself constantly, and all that time he longed for Penelope. And when the year was up, she agreed to let him go but assured him there was no going home until he undertook the next stage in his long journey – to find the Halls of Hades and Persephone the Dread, and there to seek out the spirit of the blind Theban prophet, Tiresias, who had seen Athene naked and had his eyes blasted out – though in compensation for this punishment she had given him the gift of prophecy. Tiresias knew things about people. Only Tiresias could help him come home.

'But how to find the House of the Dead, Circe? Who can sail a ship into that darkness?'

And the goddess gave him the way.

'Darkness is the only door. First, the north wind will waft you on your way, over the River of Ocean to a wild coast and to Persephone's dusky groves, where the tall black poplars grow and the willows shed their seeds. Beach your boat there, on the edge of the eddying ocean, and proceed on foot into the House of Decay, the mouldering home for the dead. There the Styx breaks into the Wailing River and the River of Flaming Fire, which swirl around a rock to pour their thunder into Acheron, Water of Sorrow. At this spot dig a trench a forearm's length and make it square, and around it pour your offering to all the dead, honey and milk mingled, sweet wine and water, sprinkled with white barley. The perished dead will hear your prayer. Promise them a sacrifice when you are back in Ithaca, and now sacrifice a young ram and a black ewe, turning their heads towards Erebus, with your own head turned away, facing the River of Ocean. Then all the souls of the glorious fellowship of the dead and departed will come up to you in their hundreds, and your crew must quickly skin and burn the beasts, killed by the pitiless bronze for pale Persephone, while you sit still, your sharp sword in your hand, and let not one stray spirit from the swarming phantoms of the dead approach the blood until you have had speech with Tiresias. He will appear and will direct you home again across the cold fish-glittering seas.'

These were Circe's instructions. And when Odysseus informed his crew that they were bound for Ithaca that very day, they were overcome with joy, but when he told them about the journey they must make first to the House of the Dead and Persephone the Dread, they wept hot salt tears and bitterly tore their hair.

We suffered a casualty just before we left. Elpenor was the youngest of our bunch – not much of a soldier, or a sailor either, for that matter. He'd got himself as drunk as a lord the previous night and had gone up to the roof for fresh air and fallen asleep. He was wakened at dawn by the racket we made as we got ready to move out and, completely forgetting where he was, poor bugger, toppled from the roof and broke his neck, killed outright.

'Well, that's another silly cunt waiting for us in hell,' said Eurylochus. 'The more the merrier when we get there.'

Hell. What is it? A story to chill a child by the fire on a winter's night? An extension to mere extinction? A life of a kind beyond the grave, however horrifying, however awful? Some say hell's nothing, and therefore nothing to be afraid of. Who'd be afraid of nothing at all?

But that's the very thing that frightens, isn't it? Nothing is precisely what hell is, because hell is loss — loss of what you want and can never have, loss of what you had once, knew once and can never have again, never know again. That's the cause of all unhappiness. And the ultimate loss is the loss of life, the eternal exile, the expulsion from light into darkness. That's hell.

In the end, all men go to hell, good and bad. It makes no odds how you've lived; hell is the end of life, the land of nothings. And for the bereaved, until they too die and lose even their loss, hell is the nothing they're left with, the loss of the loved ones that will never return.

Soldiers sometimes say that the battlefield is hell. But when you've played your part on that stage for long enough, far worse is the hell of leaving the theatre and wondering what to do now the show's over. This is the hell of coming home, where you think you'll be somebody, but where you discover that you're nobody, you're no man, not like in the field, where the next soldier relied on you. Home is hell. Soldiers' dreams are hell. For a sailor, the unharvestable sea is hell.

I dreamed of hell once, not long after leaving Circe. Though I didn't have to dream it to be in hell; I was in hell already after leaving her, just as she'd said I'd be. It wasn't a bad dream, just weird, as dreams always are, though this one was weirder than weird.

I dreamed I'd gone to hell — I'd made the actual journey. There I ran into Tiresias, the blind Theban, who knew things. In the dream, he told me to take an oar once I reached Ithaca and make a last journey with it — but not a sea journey. I had to set out on foot carrying this oar till I reached a people who'd never seen the sea, never even heard of it, a people who had no salt to sprinkle on their meat. And I was suddenly in this foreign country, trying to tell them what a ship was. Some of them thought the oar I was carrying was some sort of winnowing fan. I picked up a sharp stone and drew a ship in the dust, with all the oars out. They thought it was a bird and the oars were wings.

After we left Aeaea, we were swept north – and north and north and further fucking north, relentlessly, till we were shrouded in cloud and mist and didn't glimpse the sun or stars for nearly a week. We couldn't even tell the difference between night and day; there was just this darkness hanging over us, as heavy as the thick black cloth over a friend's urn.

One day, we struck land. Or one night, or night-day, or day-night. As desolate a place as I'd ever seen, barren crags, clinging mists. The crew refused to go ashore – they were fucking sick of my exploits, they said, and how I'd dropped them in one shit-hole after another. I couldn't blame them, but I told them I'd go ashore solo this time and see what I could find out. Without sun or stars, we hadn't a clue where we were, so I struck out, desperate for some clarity. I found nothing but an unexplained heartbreak inside myself and fields of asphodel stretching away from me, millions of white spikes rising up out of the bloated bulbs on which, so the old stories went, buried corpses gorged.

Soldiers fallen on the field with the life pouring out of them often cry out for their mothers. There's a small boy with a hurt knee or cut finger in every grown man. And when the man is about to die, that small boy cries, wanting his mother to patch him up and hold him. At that low point in my journey, it was my mother I wanted more than anything, my dear old mother Anticleia. That's when I knew I was in hell, just wanting to see her face again, to hear her voice and knowing, long before I reached Ithaca, that I never would.

There were moments in that dead land, on that dead shore, when I thought I saw her right in front of me. I reached out into the mist for her, and my arms embraced emptiness.

'Where are you, mother? What are you?'

'Wind,' came the answer. 'Air. All bones and flesh and sinews gone, burned away by the flames. But what's left can still suffer. Even air can suffer, even a breath can feel sorrow. Even the wind can be sad.'

The tears ran from me. Was I still dreaming?

And then I felt it – drying the tears, literally, a breeze on my face, ruffling my beard. Wind. And a blue bore of sky overhead. I could see the ship sitting quietly in the tide, her sails fluttering. I started to run.

The crew were relieved. They crowded round me. 'Where have you been?'

'In hell,' I said.

'Is that all? We thought you were in trouble!'

'I am in fucking trouble, and so are you. I need to see Circe again.

One last time. Set a course if you can, for Aeaea.'

They stared at me. 'What the fuck are you talking about? We want to go home!'

'And home you'll go, lads. But right now we have a reverse wind, and it'll blast us back to meat and wine and warmth, to the sun and the stars.'

'And to that woman! That fucking woman – who you want more than your wife!'

'I'll ignore that,' I said. 'Circe has the sea in her head. I need to speak to her again. I need her knowledge to bring us home, that's all. I want what's in her head.'

'Between her legs, you mean!'

We found her again in less than three days, bustled back by the quick bright wind, steady as she goes. The men stayed on the ship. They'd had their fill of Circe's girls. I registered their protest, but all the same I was back in her bed and glad to be there, though I knew this really was the last time. I poured myself into her.

'Well,' she said, 'and where did you go to after you left me?'

'To hell.'

'I told you. You'll be back there again, long before you reach home. And even after.'

We were blasted by the north wind out to the deeps, to the far-off frontiers of the globe, cuffed all the way to the fog-clung country of the Cimmerians, the people of perpetual darkness. We crossed the deeps and came to a savage shore and then to Persephone's Grove, just as Circe had said. We saw the big black poplars and the seed-shedding willows, and we beached the boat by the churning strand and marched on to the place where the two rivers converged, spilling their thunder into Acheron. There I dug the trench and made my offerings, promising in Ithaca to slit the throats of a barren heifer and a jet-black sheep and to pile the pyre high with treasure.

Meanwhile, the sudden gush of blood brought the ghosts of the gone ones surging up from Erebus, the pale shoals of the dead, eager to drink the spilt blood and to taste departed life again. The numbers were unimaginable, as were the dark depths from which they swam: fresh young brides who'd known only an hour of love, untouched virgins, innocent and green, unmarried boys, old men with all of life's sufferings falling like long shadows behind them, young lasses feeling the first thrusts of love and the stabs of sorrow in their hearts. And then came the mass of men who'd died like cattle in the field, some still wearing their bloodstained armour, some stripped and naked, just as they'd been left, unburied in the dust, hundreds of battle-dead, their stab-wounds still showing where the bitter bronze had let sweet life go and sent it wailing to this terrible place. The battlefield was nothing compared to this, so many gaping mouths, crimson lips on pale carcasses. And the screams of the field were just a fraction of the anguish of those lost souls, the combined howling of that horrible host.

But there was to be no pity for them, not until Tiresias had drunk the dark blood and outlined the next stages of my voyage and the extent of all my travels across the fish-gladdening waves, until gods and oceans finally let me go. Even then, the shoals of ghosts still had to form themselves into an orderly line so as to drink the blood in turn, one by one . . .

Elpenor, as the most recent of entrants to the horrors of Hades, came up first in the jostling throng, and it pained me to point my sword at him, barring the way to the blood, while he poured out his sorrow. How do you cheer up a soul in hell?

'Hey, Elpenor!' I exclaimed. 'How did you manage to get here before me? You've been faster on foot than I've been by boat, though the black ship sped like a seabird!'

Souls in hell lose more than bones and muscles and blood; they lose all laughter. And Elpenor reminded me gloomily that in my haste to get away I'd left his body unburied and unwept on Circe's island, where it still lay rotting. Perhaps Circe counted on my returning for it, and he begged me to pick it up for him, to put in again at Aeaea and burn him with all his arms, and to put up a mound for him there against the grey uncaring sea, a memorial to a luckless drunkard, and a sea-mark for sailors to steer by in time to come, charting a course far from the House of the Dead.

'And Odysseus, will you take my oar to Aeaea and crown my mound with it, the oar I ploughed the sea with when I sat on the benches with my mates? All that ploughing, though to the wave-blooms on the broad sea-plains there comes no autumn, no reaping of the unharvestable ocean.'

I promised Elpenor I'd see to all of that, and still we stood there facing one another across the blood, as if he were an enemy, knowing that nothing but death could unite us again, and that was a union which I longed to postpone.

After Elpenor, there appeared Anticleia, my heart-cracked mother, but I could not allow her to approach me, stricken as I was with grief, until I had spoken to Tiresias.

Up he came out of the dark and ordered me to put up my sword and back away from the trench so that he could drink the blood and tell me my future. And so he found the voice he'd had in life, the very same. As always with Tiresias, it was no short speech.

'So, Odysseus, you have left the sun to visit this joyless place where laughter and light are excluded and sweet life a bitter memory. But you are not yet ready for the House of the Dead, your time has not yet come. Only a man of many troubles would come here, and although I know how you long for home, I have to tell you that the gods have more trouble in store for you, and they will make your homeward voyage harder still. Poseidon hates you for what you did to Polyphemus. To you he was the dreaded anthropophagite, a man-eater you blinded for your revenge, but he was also the Earthshaker's beloved son, and the father will shake you up on the seas before he's done with you. He will open wide his white throat, and the sea-bed will stare you in the face. Even so, you may yet reach Ithaca with all your crew intact, but you must run a tight ship. Just be sure to take extra care when you arrive at the Island of the Oxen of the Sun. The cattle on Thrinacia belong to the sun-god, who sees everything under the blue sky. Touch them at your peril, and if your friends do so, they will perish, every one. You will lose your ship and you will come home broken and alone, with no crew to help you, on a foreign vessel, only to find a pack of wolves eating up your estate – ruthless, worthless beings, contemptible scroungers and seducers aiming to lure your wife into a marriage that will make a king of the winner and rob you of everything, kingship, country, the companion of your former years. One way or another – and it will not be easy – you will have to kill these suitors, destroy them to the last man, and the conclusion will be brutal, bloodier than any slaughter-house.

And even then, your travels will not be over. For if you clear your land of locusts, you must then shoulder your oar of polished pine and take it to the people who have never seen the sea, or tasted salt, or sailed the crimson-cheeked ships, and you must plant the oar in the soil of that country, making proper sacrifices to Poseidon. Only then will he allow you to come back home at last, where you will enter into an easy old age, exhausted but encompassed by calm, your people happy and prosperous around you. Your own death will steal up on you almost unaware, a sweet and gentle death, come to you out of the swing of the sea, to take you down, loaded with years, into the ebb. That is all.'

'Wait,' I said, 'tell me more. These last words – how to interpret them? Will I die on land or at sea? Is it literal? Will I die at the ebbing of the tide? Is it the ebb tide of old age?'

The seer's shade flickered. 'Other spirits are anxious to speak to you. Allow any ghost access to the blood and it will converse with you as if alive and rational. Deny access and the rejected spirit will fall away and leave you in peace. Your mother sits in silence, wordless without blood. I have had my say and must retire.'

'But your last words – what do they mean?'

The blind Theban was sucked away, back into the dark, his last words broken whispers, echoes.

'The life will ebb out of you . . . death . . . the sea.'

Old Anticleia now approached, dipped her lips into the dark cloud, drank the black draught, and looked at Odysseus with the hollow eyes of death, sparked with recognition. Her lifeless lips trembled, blood-bedashed, pale, impassioned.

'My son, I thought it was you, and now that I've drunk, I know you for my child. But why and how are you here, since you are still a living being? This is a dreadful place, worse than the western gloom, the Rivers of Fear, and the dead, cold ocean and all its wastes. It's unthinkable. How long since you left Troy? Have you been to Ithaca? Have you seen Penelope and your son Telemachus? Or are you still voyaging? And why did you break your journey to look on bitter death before your time?'

'Dearest mother,' he cried, 'I am under orders. I needed to speak to the soul of Tiresias to seek his advice and hear his prophecy for me. No, I've not yet seen Achaea, let alone Ithaca. I've been doomed to wander, to struggle and fight, from the very day I left Penelope for Troy. The war is over but not the struggle, and the Theban's prophecy is that my sufferings are far from done. And you, dearest mother? I have dreamed about you. How did you come to die? Did you linger long? Or did the arrows of Artemis fly gently into your heart? And what of my father, and my wife and son? Do you know anything of them, other than what Tiresias has told me?'

'All are alive,' came the reply, 'and you know already that Penelope is so. But she sheds many tears as the slow nights pass without you, and patience is her only companion in the dark. You son is of age and protects your rights as best he can against the detestable suitors, but he is one against many. As for your poor father, he lives the life of a recluse, and has long since left off sleeping in a real bed with sheets or rugs. In summer he lies out on leaves, high in the vineyard, and in winter sleeps in the ashes along with the labourers, stretched out by the fire, grief-stricken, clothed in rags, pining for your return, as old age dogs his heels and death draws near. That is what killed me in the end; not Artemis the Archeress, unerring with her dove-like darts, but sheer despair of ever seeing you again, home from the war – my son, who once brought such sweetness into my life. I gave up hoping for your return and died of a broken heart.'

The cruellest scene in the web. Even dread Persephone would have shown more mercy than Penelope. I broke down and wept as my mother spoke to me, and I reached out to her with outstretched arms, only to embrace air, a shadow, a dream. It was the pain I'd felt in Cimmeria, the harrowing hell of eternal separation.

'O god, mother, why can't I reach you? Why won't you let me come to you even for a moment? Can't we clasp our arms around each other even in hell and drink each other's tears? Can't we draw some cold consolation, like poor wine, from that bitter mingling? Or has sullen Persephone sent me not my mother but some surly shade to torture me even more in my torment?'

Odysseus wept like a little boy.

'My son, O thou, my lovely boy, your sufferings have been greater than any man should have to bear. But this is no trick of Hades, this is merely the law we all obey, and the last measure of our mortality. The sinews that bind bones and flesh together melt like snow in the blaze of the flames. Life leaves the charred bones, flies from them like a dream, the bright soul from the formless ash, soundless, impalpable, and all that was you becomes less than a butterfly, fragile for an hour in air. You can never capture it again, never have it back. It flutters down to here – here where we have become nothing but a dream in the dark. That's why I cannot clasp you in your pain and bring you comfort as I used to do. But you, my son, you are no dream, you are not for the dark, not yet, and you must hurry now back to the sun and to life, which is still sweeter than death, in spite of all its sorrows.'

So his mother flickered and faded, her sad countenance sinking from view, like the face of one drowning and descending into the depths for the last time, never to be seen again.

She was followed by a host of women, the illustrious wives and daughters of princes, all thronging in their thirst to the life-giving blood, a thirst for that one moment of human contact with the world they'd left behind. Like some ghostly host on the attack, they would have stormed the trench, but Odysseus used the sword to compel order, and so, one after another, they approached and drank and told their stories, which is all that was left of them.

First came Tyro, who married Cretheus, son of Aeolus, but fell for the river-god Enipeus and kept wandering along his beautiful banks, until one afternoon Poseidon appeared, disguised as the god, and embraced her at the mouth of the river, where its water rushed out into the salt sea. He undid her virgin girdle, and as she drew him downward gladly onto her white belly, he caused a dark wave to come over them, tall as a mountain, and it hid the intercourse that took place between them. The two bodies rolled together, following the wave, fresh and salt, girl and god, one flesh in the sudden surge. But Poseidon also sealed up her eyes in sleep, and when she woke, as if from an exciting dream, he revealed his identity and assured her she'd conceive, since a woman's belly never fails to swell beneath a god's fruitful thrust. In due course, she bore Pelias and Neleus, and then three more sons to Cretheus. And so she told the story of a sweet life. But nothing, not even a god's seed in her belly, could save her from the common lot that draws all mortals down to death. Bewailing that mortality, she too vanished from view.

Next came Antiope, whose two sons founded Thebes; then Alcmene, Amphitryon's wife, who lay with Zeus and bore Heracles; then proud Creon's daughter, Megare. After them came the anguished Epicaste, still hanging, exposed even in Hades, her naked body dangling from the long rope that stretched up out of the House of the Dead all the way to the roof-beam high in her own house, where she had taken her life. She had committed incest with her son Oedipus, who had murdered his father and married his own mother. Her ignorance did not excuse the act, and a mother's curses were all that Oedipus was left with as he eked out the tortures of a remorseful life.

After Epicaste came Chloris, loveliest of ladies, wedded to Neleus, who had been so struck by her beauty that he paid a huge price for her. She became his queen in sandy Pylos and was the mother of a glorious brood, including Nestor and Pero, whom all men wanted to wed and bed.

Leda was next, mother of Castor and Polydeuces the boxer, both held now by the green earth, but each alternately alive and dead on different days. And Iphimedeia, who swore she'd slept with Poseidon and bore the tallest sons ever known, Otus and Ephialtes. They were the famous pair who dared to try to reach and overreach the gods, attempting to pile Ossa on Olympus and Pelion on Ossa, those lofty, leaf-trembling peaks, and so build a staircase beyond the blue gods. But the famous Apollo from the belly of Leto of the lovely tresses, the son of Zeus, ended their ambitions, and instead of mounting to heaven they descended to Hades before they had even grown beards.

On they came in an endless procession: Phaedre; Procris; lovely Ariadne, snatched by Theseus from Crete, though he never reached Athens with her because Artemis slew her in sea-girdled Dia.

More, yet more – Maera, Clymene and the execrable Eriphylae, who betrayed her husband for blood-money. What a line it was – women who'd lain with gods, who'd borne and been born of heroes, women who were the wonder of men and made them mad, miserable and even happy. It made no difference: lovely, dreadful, doomed, they'd all slipped and fallen into the earth's fruitful lap, where they lay levelled and lifeless, their shades in Hades now almost indistinguishable, the tenuous wailing wafers of once-women, each of them now a ghost without glory, lamenting the lost intimacy, the honey of life.

And now Penelope . . .

Penelope? Penelope in hell? No, not in hell. Penelope: patient, solitary, sedentary, pictured not in Hades but on her web, presiding wisely over the luckless line of the female fallen, Penelope the dependable prize for me, the hero who spurned goddesses and sorceresses and fought monsters and crossed cold oceans and came back to her warm bed in the end.

Persephone held out her hand to me approvingly, while with the other impatient hand she arrested the endless line, loomed up out of her dark house and scattered it in all directions.

Suddenly Odysseus found himself staring into the dead face of Agamemnon, whose fate at that time was still unknown to him.

'What's this?' Odysseus asked.

Agamemnon drank the blood, sobbed, stretched out his arms. But strong and supple as they'd been at Troy, they were hollow when they tried to clasp Odysseus.

'Why? How? What happened after Troy? Were you shipwrecked? Did you never reach home?'

The king gave a great sigh, like a wailing wind. 'If only I'd been wrecked as you say, on some friendly reef! It would have been better for me never to have reached home.'

And he told his story, lamenting bitterly a death by betrayal and domestic malice – not a hero's fall on the field.

'They didn't even have the decency to shut my eyelids or close my gaping mouth and give me grace for Hades, but they left me lying for long enough like a beast in the shambles, stripped of the last shred of respect, tricked and killed by the worst bitch ever to spread her legs for a lover when her husband is away from home. I tell you, Odysseus, never trust a woman. And when you reach Ithaca, I advise you not to advertise your arrival as I did, but slip into port on the sly and take your household by surprise.'

He finished talking and the tears rolled down their faces as they shared their memories and sorrows.

Tears for Agamemnon? His hell was of his own making, and the day he drove a dagger into his daughter was the day he sealed his doom: he was not murdered but executed by the unforgiving Clytemnestra. But Penelope put the bright tears on my face, more than I'd have shed even in hell if I'd met that ox-brain there. True, though, that what happened to him was shocking – after a successful expedition and surviving the long war to come home to treachery and a bloody death. Whatever I felt for him as a man, the soldier in me pitied him.

There were tears too for Achilles. My first impulse was to congratulate him on his everlasting fame. At Troy he'd been a killing machine when he wasn't a sulker, and his courage never failed him. He'd covered himself in glory and was now a great prince among the dead.

He stared at me when I said this. A dull angry glare.

'Prince? Immortality? Glory? What are you talking about, Odysseus? Look at me, look long and hard, and look around you too. What do you see? I'm no different from your poor old mother, no better off than a wretched weakling or the most abject coward that ever fled a fight. What sort of immortality is this? What sort of glory? If you think this is rank and fame, you can have it. I'd gladly give you all my glory, every iota of my immortality, for just one drop of your blood in my veins. Wretched though you may think life is, let me tell you, to be able to speak and feel again with those you've loved, I'd quit all kudos to have that back, just for a moment. I valued it too lightly when I had the chance, sacrificed too much of it. That's what heroism does for you. Heroes don't fit in. You end up on your own. I'd rather be a slave now above ground in the land of the living than a king among corpses. A corpse has no glory, a shadow has no pride. The kingdom of the dead is the largest of all kingdoms, an infinite empire, but all its citizens are done with life. All that mattered is no more. Who would rule them? Who'd be one of them? Not I. There's no glory in a fistful of grains. There's nothing honourable about ash.'

But when I told him all about the glorious exploits of his son at Troy, the dead eyes gleamed briefly, and the great runner turned without another word to me and went off with his long light strides, so familiar, across the fields of asphodel.

Makes you think, doesn't it? Death addressing life across the impossible gulf and telling the impossible truth – that nothing matters. Achilles had known it already. He knew it when Agamemnon tried to buy him off with ownership, with bribes, and he said even then that all the wealth of Troy wasn't worth what his life was worth, what life is worth. Death puts an end to all that dross. And all the time we thought we had substance and meaning, we had nothing, our lives were nothing, we didn't even have a place to live, because the earth isn't even ours, we're wanderers, nothing more. No man is anybody.

Yes, that does make you think. It made me think. About the war. About Troy and everything we did there. What were we but a gang of thugs brawling over a whore? A cuckold and a cunt. And a pile of scrap metal – gold. And where were we then but in hell, when we didn't even have a home to go to beyond the beach. War was our home. And that was hell on earth. The other hell was just a matter of time. But some men never see that far. Even that thug Ajax stood aloof from me in the hell-web, still bitter about the defeat I'd inflicted on him back at the ships over the arms of Achilles, the prize I'd won fairly and which had put him to his grave.

'So, Ajax, it's come to this, has it? Still sulking over a pile of rust?

Even in hell you've learned nothing. Not like Achilles. He's got it whole at last, he's seen through all of it, the shams and facades of heroism and war. I thought death would have matured you by now.'

Not a sound from him. Not a single fucking word. He turned his back on me and walked back into Erebus, back into the dark. Some men never grow up; they stay stupid. And this was one oaf whose ignorance was his own special hell. Maybe he was even happy in it, in his own way.

Enough then? Enough of hell? Never. Hell is endless. I saw Orion still hunting the beasts he'd slaughtered on the lonely hills; Tityos still stretched helpless on the ground, his liver ripped by vultures, his penance for assailing the lovely Leto as she crossed the meadows of Penopeus on her way to Pytho; Sisyphus still wrestling with his rock; Tantalus still tormented by the fruits he could never reach, the water he could never drink; and Heracles still with his bow, looking ready to loose off arrows in every direction. Hell was in his face as he glared around at targets, and even the invulnerable dead shrieked and gibbered and ran from him, scattering far and wide. He recognised me and came up.

'So you're just like me, Odysseus? Your many exploits have landed you in hell, have they? Have you nothing better to do with your life? Mine was nothing but struggle, but I was sent to hell when I ran out of things to do, and I was ordered to come here and bring out the terrible Hound of Hell. I did it too, with help from Hermes and bright-eyed Athene. And I dare say you too have gods on your side. But they won't save you when your time really comes.'

Hell crowded in on me after that, and the dead swam at me again in their pale shoals, swarming around me and wailing their eerie cries. I felt sudden panic, suffocation, and the green fear of that dreadful darkness in which some gorgonising terror could have lurked, sent by Persephone to strike me dead as stone. I got out as fast as I could, and when I reached the ship I ordered the crew to board and loose the hawsers and to row without delay. The oars were aided by a good current which swept us down the River of Ocean, and a sudden fresh and friendly breeze on my face persuaded me that I had left that terrible place behind me, that I'd been to hell and back and had learned something about its awfulness. It's a place without a breeze, without a ray of warmth, without a drop of blood, without a flicker of life. For some it's an extension of the errors of life, of a life not lived when the chance was there, and lost too late to make it right in time.

FORTY-FOUR

We did burn and bury the dead Elpenor, for decency's sake, high on a headland, and built him a mound with a monumental stone on top, surmounted by his oar, almost as if he'd asked for it and we'd followed his instructions. Except that dead men don't ask anything. So they don't ask to be taken home.

Which doesn't mean that you won't be brought back home dead from a war like Troy. Or at least more dead than alive, and still fighting the war inside you. Men talk about the end of the war, but the war doesn't end: it comes home with you. The battlezone shifts, that's all. Different weapons, different defences.

On the way back, I kept asking myself about home. And about hell. What my dream of hell had meant. And what Circe had told me about the post-war trials I'd have to face, the monsters of the mind, the sirens of seduction, the arms of oblivion, in which all women turn into goddesses.

'Home is sweet when you're away from it, Odysseus, when you dream of logs on the fire and wine in the cup and a woman's belly in your bed. A firm breast is filling up your fist and the nipple tingles on your tongue. A good dream of home. Not so sweet, though, when you wonder who's fucking your wife while you're in the field. Not so sweet when you get there and find the milk's gone sour. Or when you ask yourself what you're going to do next.'

Next. What next? The hell of home, burying my oar in the earth, never to feel the liquid thrust of the sea against it, never again the push against ocean, the magic moment, the fluency of escape from the earth-bound life. A life without salt. A winnowing fan. Seafarer become farmer, back to tilling the thistles, the sweaty soil under which he'll lie soon enough, unthanked, anonymous. Goodbye to the watch-fires, the comradeship, the plumed troops, the glorious charge, the horses, the thrill of survival, breasting waves, wars, coming through, coming home – goodbye to all of that.

Women are mind-readers. No matter what you keep back from them, they'll get behind your eyes, they'll suck it out of you, your deepest need, your darkest dream, the private hurts. What I didn't or couldn't tell

Penelope she reached in and probed for, like a field surgeon. The hell-dreams went up on the web, just as she saw them, or chose to see them. There was no stopping the glorious story. Her husband was a hero, and heroes have to overcome the enemy, the obstacles, the hells that open up between husband and wife to make the hero's love stronger and his return the more heroic: monsters, gods, women, wine, songs, the sea and all its islands, and its dead, the perished dead. And the singers of the dead.

The Sirens were the singers of the dead, and Circe's chart started with them.

Sail south for Levkas. Your first next encounter will be with half-women who bewitch with their beautiful voices every passing ship that sails within earshot. For once heard, however fleetingly, their songs cannot be resisted. They suck in the sailor to certain death and sing his soul away. No homecoming for him, no sailor safe home from sea, with wife waiting and children waving, not for the mariner who hears their music and its imperative allure. Sail too close and you will join the ranks of dead men.

On your approach to the Sirens' Isle, you will see them, Odysseus, their mouldering bones rolling in the tide, littering the meadows where the women sit and sing, sometimes frolicking in the foam. These are the skeletons of the seamen who stopped to listen and were compelled to stay. If you wish to live and avoid that boneyard, speed on past the sweetly lethal fields. The winds will drop, your crew will take to the oars, and you will have to plug their ears with soft beeswax, so that they sit stalwartly on the benches and pull stoutly on the oars, heedless of what they cannot hear. If you yourself wish to listen to the irresistible, leave your own ears unplugged, but order your men to lash you, body, hand and foot, to the mast, and to pay no attention to your mad mouthing. Tell them to tie you all the tighter and refuse to free you, and so sail on regardless through the thrilling songs of death.

Should you survive this hazard, you will only sail straight into another, which will be one of two, depending on the route you choose to follow. One route will bring you to the Drifters, also known as the Wandering Rocks, at whose beetling base blue-eyed Amphitrite drives in her breakers in rollings of white thunder, a boiling cauldron, and a surge so high and wild that the seabirds never fly by unscathed, not even the ambrosial doves that veer off to Olympus. Not even Zeus can cut the casualties — he must replace them every one, for Amphitrite is Poseidon's spouse and the capricious Queen of the Sea.

Take that route, and, be assured, you'll see how all the other seamen who ever tried it ended up. They're sea-drift now, flotsam, white bones whirled by waves, tossed with the timbers of their ships, and their dead heads loll, listless as seaweed, aimless, empty as dreams, blind and uncaring in the joyless surge. If you do see that much, it will be the last thing you'll see, and your own heads will join that jostling throng and all that wreckage, you and all your crew. There's no escape.

Not unless the gods help you, as Hera once helped Jason. The glorious *Argo* was the only ship ever to make that passage and come through, homeward bound from Colchis. And it took the love of a powerful goddess to stop that ship from splintering on the crags with all its crew, lost in the waves' white flames, as will surely happen to you, Odysseus, and to the last man on board, should you choose that route. For no goddess loves you as Hera loved Jason, and the mortal woman who loves you with all her heart sits at the loom in faraway Ithaca, powerless to save. Even I, Circe, cannot save you, not unless you elect instead to stay with me on this enchanted isle and end your struggles here. Are my breasts not sweeter than the Wandering Rocks, with the storms of white fire sweeping their feet and the sea heaving with broken spars and drowned corpses?

The ideal hero brought home again, the dream soldier back to his dream wife through the worst journey in the world. I was enmeshed in Penelope's web — and deader there than I'd have been at the hands of the Sirens or of Amphitrite.

Or of Scylla and Charybdis, the next dreadful venture on Circe's sea-map, two more female monsters to block the route to Ithaca. Circe, watching over her wanderer, was joined in thought by the fair Penelope, wearing her years like the bloom of dust on a golden bowl, long unused but still glorious to behold.

So if you avoid the Drifters, you'll face two more dangers, and here too you will have a choice. Or you will appear to. But study the chart carefully and you will see that this choice has already been made for you.

The higher of the two rocks is unscaleable, even if the most nimble climber had twenty hands and feet to help him on his ascent, or descent. For the rock is polished marble. Not only that, but halfway up the peak, facing west, and running down to darkened Erebus, sits a mist-hung cave, so high that not even an expert archer's arrow fired from the deck beneath could ever succeed in reaching it. All the arrows that were fired at Troy could not help you here. And in that cave lurks Scylla, the worst monster ever created. Her bark is a ludicrous yelp, and when sailors hear it they laugh. But the first sight of her quickly wipes the smiles from their faces. Twelve legs with clawed feet, dangling like tentacles, and six swaying necks, scarily long, each head furnished with a triple row of terrible teeth. With these, she sweeps the roaring seas beneath without ever having to leave the cave: swordfish, dolphins and dogfish are dragged from the deeps by that grisliest of fisherwomen. Even the ocean monsters are taken from their lairs. And if a ship steers past her, it's never without the loss of six members of her crew. This happens with unfailing accuracy – one man picked off at leisure for each of those six heads. It's an inevitability you have to accept – go there and you are six men down, even if you get through, which is by no means certain.

Now you'll be thinking about the alternative, but this is scarcely tempting either. The other crag has a huge fig tree growing out of it, lush and shaggy, better than Scylla's polished tombstone of a rock, or so you might think. But beneath it sits the dreaded Charybdis, sucking hard at the dark waters. Three times a day she draws them down, exposing the very sea-bed, the black sands of the bottom. It's a sight to freeze the bowels of the most salt-bitten sea-dog. And three times a day she spews them up again, raging like a cauldron on a blaze, and the flung spray soars upwards higher than the peaks on either side, raining down again like white fire. Go there when she gulps and not even Poseidon could save you, though that is the last thing on his mind. Ships and sailors are simply sucked to the bottom of the world and never seen again.

Is there a safe middle way through the strait? The distance between the two terrors is no more than a bowshot, and if you avoid the one you face the other. No, there's no middle way – you steer closer either to Scylla or Charybdis, and from these directions you must already have decided which to choose.

The green eyes of Circe gleam at me from the web. Will it be possible, I wonder, to steer clear of Charybdis and be ready to take on Scylla myself when she attacks the ship?

The green eyes blaze.

You always were a stubborn fool, always swimming against the stream instead of going with the flow. There is no taking on Scylla, as you put it. Do you think it will be like facing six Trojan soldiers at once, or even twelve? Listen hard. Scylla was not born to die. There is neither defence nor attack against her. She'll be trapping men till time stops. Put off one second by attempting to fight her and she'll simply take six more men at the next snatch. How many sailors do you think you can spare? How few can work the ship? Charybdis means certain death for all of you, but if you are quick past Scylla, you lose the six men and sail on. Accept this – she's unshunnable but not inescapable. Speed on therefore, drive the ship like the wind.

'Homeward bound?'

Alas, no. If you survive these hazards, your next landfall will not be Ithaca. On the way south from Levkas, you'll see a trident sticking out of the sea. That's what it looks like, at least. It's three hilltops, three headlands, and you know you'll be approaching the island of Thrinacia, which is home to seven large herds of sheep and the same of cattle, fifty head each herd. They're prize beasts, so beautiful your famished mariners will at once wish to begin slaughtering and feasting and living like kings. But be advised, the man who touches them will not live long, for they are sacred animals. The cattle are the oxen of the sun, and the sheep also belong to the sun-god. All the herds that pasture there are his, and they are immortal; they neither lamb nor calve, never a birth or death. Even their shepherdesses are divine – the lovely nymphs Phaethusa and Lampetia of the glinting locks, the sun-god's own children, whom glowing Neaera to Hyperion bore, and brought them up, and later took them to Thrinacia to be the protectors of their father's fatted cattle and his magnificent white sheep. Leave them be, therefore, and there's a chance that all of you may yet arrive at Ithaca. Harm them and you die, the entire crew. And even if you yourself should escape death, Odysseus, you'll come home later rather than sooner, much later, condemned by the years, friendless, alone, and in a very bad way.

What a journey! What madness mapped out! What madman would attempt it? And in rejecting Circe's safe embrace and setting out instead to meet gods and monsters of the deep, what could I be other than a madman? Lover, husband, father, soldier, son, veteran adventurer, wanderer by circumstance and not by choice, hero from the wars come home, home-bird on the wing, hell-bent for Ithaca, all against the odds, Poseidon, Persephone, all that heaven and earth and hell itself could possibly throw at me.

*

We left Aeaea, scudding along with a fair breeze behind us, and approached the Sirens' Isle. Sure enough, the wind went out of the sails and a flat calm fell on the water. So we stowed the sails, and the men took their places on the benches and began to row, whitening the level water. I took a wheel of wax, cut off a good lump and kneaded it to a softness under the sun. With wedges of this, I stopped the ears of the crew and ordered two of the rowers to lash me to the mast before returning to the benches – just in time, as it happened, because the Sirens had seen our ship and sent their songs our way.

Songs? They were no songs; they were liquid honey, dripping in the air, filling ears and mouth and mind with longing, such a longing . . . for what?

> *Glorious Odysseus, stop your ship*
> *and linger, listen to our singing*
> *and voyage on with greater wisdom,*
> *for we know all things, all you did,*
> *all you suffered in the long struggle*
> *on the sea-sounding beaches*
> *and on Troy's resounding plains*
> *where the men of Argos went to war.*

The songs went on. The things they were singing about, the beauty of the dead, the heroic dead, the epic past, the glories of war – yes, god help me, I missed all that, I loved it all, the thrill and stress of combat, the sheer simplicity of it all, of simply staying alive, I wanted back to it, back to the great Achilles whom we knew, to Agamemnon's war, to the mighty dead. It didn't matter that they were strengthless now, that it was over, that Achilles was a wailing wafer, sadder, wiser, mordant in Hades, it didn't matter, the songs persuaded, corrupted. I cursed and swore at the crew to stop and let me drink it in, the wine of war to the very lees, but they only rowed the harder, past the rolling, mouldering bones and the ravishing singers, with homecoming hot in their hauling, every muscle, every pull on every oar, and no returning, no going back to the war that killed Achilles.

And so we passed the Sirens' Isle according to plan. But casualties were assured when we came to the straits, Scylla to starboard, to port Charybdis, and the ship in a bowshot's compass, steering for sweet life. The sea was spinning downwards on the port side, and we could see all the way down its whirling, tunnelled sides, all the way to the black sands of the sea-bed in which the skeletons of seamen lay embedded, till Charybdis churned and hurled them to the sun. The crew screamed, terrified, and we steered for Scylla.

If I'd told them that six of them were destined to perish, and in what manner, they'd have refused to go on, and the only alternative would have been to turn about and return to Circe. But their gallant captain, the home-driven husband, kept quiet on that point, and the six were snatched, just as Circe had predicted. We skimmed out of the straits with the shrieks of the taken men tearing us apart. There they are – their arms outstretched to me, calling for help, calling my name, Odysseus, Odysseus, my captain, my captain! Their captain had sacrificed them, and a great captain he was too, who'd barter boatmen for his home and the heroine of his hearth. What were six ordinary able-bodied seamen to the pleasures of Ithaca?

So the captain came through. The hero had survived the terrible females who eat a man whole and swallow him up. He had survived encirclement, sucking and grubbing, total consumption, and now the intrepid hero arrived at the lovely Island of the Oxen of the Sun, where the sacred sheep and the broad-browed cattle of the sun-god grazed in bliss, shepherded by the nymphs that were his own offspring. The eyes of all the crew were gladdened by paradise, but their captain issued the strict order to avoid this island and put it astern, as advised by Circe of Aeaea and Tiresias in Hades. Their bitterness and disbelief were hard for Odysseus to hear, for they had been through so much together that they were a fellowship like no other.

'Odysseus, you're an iron man, a survivor, bitter as bronze. Your body never lets you down; you don't let it. But we're ordinary men, no heroes, soldiers at the end of their tether, mariners tired by the sea. We are burned under the sun. And now night is falling and you want us to be sailing blindly on into fogs and storms and the sea-god's anger, when we could be harbouring safely here and cooking ourselves a hot supper on this idyllic isle. You wish to slake your wanderlust, but we need to fill our empty bellies and drink wine, and above all rest and sleep. What can be wrong with that, for one night? In the morning we can rise refreshed and be on our way, set sail for Ithaca. What do you say?'

Against his better judgement and against the iron orders he'd been given by both living and dead, goddess and prophet, Odysseus gave in, only after the crew had promised to a man to leave the sacred cattle well alone and to content themselves with subsisting on the ship's rations until they reached Ithaca. Then they beached and prepared a good supper, for Circe had stocked the boat and there was plenty of fresh spring water on the island, and after they had eaten they remembered the comrades they had lost in the straits, and with full bellies they wept for the dead again according to nature.

But next morning the stormy weather struck the island and blotted out the world. Black skies and raging gales day after day, there was no let-up and no leaving. The south wind howled for a month, at the end of which every last scrap in the ship had been eaten and the men were ravenous. The mutinous mutterings started up. Why starve in the midst of plenty? What sort of captain refuses to feed his crew based on the babblings of a lecherous witch and a dead prophet? Odysseus had probably dreamed it all anyway, or dreamed it up, another excuse for delay, another obstacle in the long journey home. It was all he could do to keep discipline and face them down. And so, gnawed by hunger and quarrelling bitterly, they waited for the weather to change.

It didn't. And Odysseus went inland a little to be out of their whispering and grumbling, which was building up now to outright revolt. He came across a quiet spot and prayed to the gods for help. In answer, they sent him to sleep, and while he slept Eurylochus worked on the crew.

'Listen, mates, our clever captain says we'll be shipwrecked or something if we touch these cattle. Well, I'd rather gulp down a few mouthfuls of cold seawater than die a lingering death, tormented by hunger. Starvation is a horrible way to go. I'm ready to take the risk and avoid the worst of deaths. Are you with me?'

The sweet scents of roasting meat awoke Odysseus from his deep sleep. He stood up, horrified, and ran back to the ship. Too late. They'd slaughtered the fattest of the cattle and had fallen to at their feast.

The sun-god's anger blazed, obliterating Odysseus's puny human fury, and he called on Zeus to punish them.

'Otherwise I'll descend into Hades and bring daylight to the dead.'

Zeus answered him. 'Calm yourself, and shine as you always do for living men on earth, to whom you bring light and life. As for those cattle-killers, they're dead men. I'll hit their ship and smash it to kindling. One strike and it will be splinters, litter on the wine-dark sea, and they'll all be fishfood on the deep sea-bed – all except Odysseus, who did not sanction their sacrilege but forbade it, and who must be permitted to fight his way home and confront the suitors who beset his patient and devoted wife. But he will not go unpunished, I assure you, for many troubles lie yet between him and his Ithaca.'

Then the skins of the slaughtered cattle stirred eerily and crept along the earth, and the roasting flesh groaned and moaned on the spits as if the joints were still alive and felt the flames, and the entire island echoed uncannily with the sounds of ghostly lowing. Even so, the crew continued to kill and consume for six more days, slaughtering Hyperion's paragons. What's done is done, they said, and cannot be undone. If there were consequences to be faced, they would be faced on full stomachs.

The consequences were dire. No sooner had Odysseus put the island astern than the crew saw a blue-black cloud loom up out of the west and descend on the ship. The frown of Zeus glared out of the cloud, and it came so low that any sailor could have climbed to the top of the mast and touched the god's beard and begged for mercy.

Their fates were sealed. The hurricane hit the ship with such force that both forestays broke, the rigging plunged into the bilge, and the mast toppled aft and split open the helmsman's head, crunching every bone in his skull. He tumbled from the poop, his brains flying, and plummeted straight down the long dark passageways of the waves. His fluttering spirit joined the seabirds as he wailed his descent into hell.

Zeus was only warming up. Now he thundered and struck, and the already stricken ship reeled under the force of his bolt, and sulphur filled the air. Odysseus clung to different parts of the disintegrating ship, shifting for safety. He could only watch as his crew were pitched from the deck and flung overboard one after another, every man. There was to be no homecoming for any one of them.

Now Zeus turned his attention to Odysseus. Larboard and starboard, he saw two terrifying seas charging up on him like herds of stampeding cattle, snorting and foaming, and he crouched down deep between them, waiting to be slammed and pounded to pieces.

The big-browed waves butted the gunwales, kicking up the sea–dust, the white flying foam. They struck together and ripped the ship's sides clean away from her keel, which was swept away, far along the seas, a naked spine without its ribs, and, clinging to it like a little limpet, the apparently doomed Odysseus.

Never say doomed. The backstay was a leather rope, and Odysseus used it to lash the mast to the keel and so give himself a chance to ride astride the two timbers. Made fast to their fate, he was hurtled along by the howling winds and found himself staring into the roaring ocean, inches from his eyes. He thought he was looking into his grave.

Not yet. And not here. The hurricane went back into the west and was followed at once by gales from the south. Odysseus understood that he was headed back to that awful strait and that the gods now made sport of him for their pleasure before the end of his life. Sure enough, after being propelled all night long he saw Scylla and Charybdis looming up again out of the dawn, still at their baleful trade. Scylla would hook him up in a second, indiscriminate among dogfish and dolphins, while for Charybdis it was her downward hour, and the last for the hero if he remained on the raft, to be whistled down to death, down the long corridors of the sea. So he prepared himself, made a mighty leap from the keel, and clutched wildly at the branches of the fig tree . . .

Impossible even for an Olympian athlete, but easy for a woman at her loom to pluck up a man up out of the spiralling staircases of the ocean and weave him instead to a tree, from whose branches he would hang like a bat until mast and keel, still lashed together, came spinning up again out of the death-hole. Only then did Odysseus let himself go — and drop.

Like a stone . . .

I went so deep down into the water I thought I'd never come back up again, but with bursting lungs and blacksmith's heart I broke the surface and saw the beautiful blue sky. I got astride the timbers again and rowed with my arms as best I could till I was clear of the strait. And then I drifted — for nine days and nights if you can believe that, if you want to believe it — till I was almost dead of hunger and thirst and exhaustion and cold. It wasn't until the night of the tenth day that the gods ended my suffering and I was washed up at last on a friendly shore.

FORTY-FIVE

I was delirious when she found me. I'd almost drowned. And that old story about drowning, the one about the story of your life flashing past you – it's fucking true, I can vouch for it. Reliving the war in Troy took less than a second, a conflict lost in impossible time, then setting sail, a burping cannibal, a vulnerable slut, fuck her into loveliness, never let her go, leave her for home, for hell, the strait and narrow – no, no, come back to her, back to the war, the glorious dead, the deadly dream, the songs the Sirens sang, the thousand ships, Achilles, Agamemnon dead, the ox-meat dribbling down beards, burned by the sun, eating the gods, eaten by the sea, all my men, all those men . . .

The tumbling thunder in my skull assured me I was drowning, and what struck me in my last moments of quarter-consciousness was the sheer fucking banality of it, the whole pointless process of collapsing, capitulating to the common lot. But now the sting and hiss of the tide told me no – I was ashore among the rollers, I'd made it, I wasn't going to drown, wherever I was, whoever I was. I was lashed to the keel of the wreck – the shipwreck, oh fuck! All those sailors, all those men at Troy, eaten by the earth, eaten by the sea: did I say it or think it? No, sea in my throat, speech impossible, sunlight, blinding brine, wet sand, don't try to talk yet, yes, you've just about had it, haven't you? Have I? Had I? Fresh water in a shell, held to my lips, water, fresh, not salt, fresh as Helicon, oh, nectar! Oh, fucking nectar! Her unbraided hair fell over me, a river, a waterfall, black gold, hanging round her eyes, more water, drink the river, drink her hair, nectar . . .

'Are you a goddess?'

'If you want me to be.'

'Where the fuck am I?'

'Thapsos.'

'Where?'

'Thapsos island. You're safe, sailor man. Who are you? Where did you come from?'

'Hell. Out of fucking hell.'

'Well, you'd better come home with me.'

'Home. Husband?'

'Drowned.'

'Drowned?'

Drowned, drowned.

It was a simple house, with a simple bed – if a bed with her in it could ever have been called simple. That first night it was. I must have slept for sixteen hours straight. Maybe it was sixteen days. I don't know where she slept. But when I woke up I was warm, for the first time in what felt like years. There was a fire in the hearth. I smelled cedar-wood, gorgeous guff, aroma of Aphrodite. She bathed me in front of it, just like a slave-girl, washed away the sea-scum, applied old wine to the most recent scars and gashes, of which I'd become quite a collector, courtesy of Troy, and other wars. I was starkers, but that didn't bother me, or her. She was no fancy lady. She trimmed my hair and gave me a good oiling all over.

'You have a nice thick prick.'

Rest of me's sea-shrivelled – too long in the water. Check the balls for barnacles.'

'These aren't balls – they *are* barnacles.'

'Well, you've seen everything now.'

'Yes, better put some clothes on, and we'll eat. These are some of my husband's. He was taller than you.'

'Was he also older than you?'

'Younger.'

'Too bad.'

'Fisherman. Lost in a storm, never came home. Known only to the gods.'

He would have been missing her cooking, if he could still eat. She was a great cook, the best since Circe – grilled goat and great grog. You can't beat it, coming back from the dead. And that cedar-smoke again.

'Aroma of Aphrodite.'

This time I said it out loud.

'Aphrodite, eh? And what about Morpheus?'

I asked her where my couch would be.

She stepped out of her robe – it took one incredible second – and lay back on the one bed, back in the cedar-scented darkness. There was another scent. The shadows danced around her, round that other darkness, between her legs.

'Couch? I'll be your couch tonight.'

She drew me down onto her smooth Olympian belly.

'And you'll never need another. You'll never want another either, I can promise you that.'

She kept that promise. For quite some time.

'And you never re-married. No other young men on Thapsos?'

'Some.'

'And suitors?'

'Plenty.'

'And?'

'None that suited. None that suited *me*.'

'But me – why? For fuck's sake, I'm old as the sea – with barnacles for balls.'

'Now, Odysseus, old lad, I already had a fisherman. I don't need another.'

'What do you mean?'

'You're fishing for compliments, I fear.'

She gave me that side-long smile, the one I came to recognise, the irresistible one, the one that always spoke the unspoken – fuck me. I'm too shy to say it, even my eyes are shy. Fuck me.

I fucked her.

I fucked her, she fucked me, we fucked each other. Nightly. We fucked the stars round the sky. We fucked the steadfast constellations round the year. The Great Bear growled at us. Can't you two do something else? Anything? Arcturus winked. Aldebaran understood. There was something beyond bronze and pillage and raping women. Something? Can stars speak?

Calypso was that something.

That's her name on the web, the one Penelope gave her, the hidden one, the concealer, the one that explains her hero husband's long concealment, the long sojourn on ... what was the island again? Ogygia? Let it be. Let it be Ogygia. Let Calypso be her name. Let her clothes hanging out to dry be sails in the fury of my heart, in the longings of my soul, billowing me back to Ithaca. Why not? Nothing is what it seems to be, nothing is but what is not, and the sea is littered with islands that make the impossible possible, even probable, even Ogygia. Then yes, so be it, Ogygia was the home of yet another goddess, the one with the voice of a mortal woman but the wiles of a witch. None other than the daughter of Atlas – who else but the fair Calypso?

And yes, she had to be a goddess, like all the rest. She was the goddess of oblivion. No woman could have kept old Odysseus against his will, Odysseus of the many wiles. It was the old story, the story of the web, the story of my life. And as island goddesses live in caves, Penelope made her up an enticing one, a lofty cavern surrounded by a grove of elegant alders and poplars and sweet-smelling cypresses where the birds roosted during the murmuring nights, falcons and seabirds and owls. A great vine hung over the mouth of the cave, thick with clustering grapes, purplish-pink, fit for a goddess. Inside the cave itself there was ample room – its walls expanded as you entered, but the entrance was little more than a fissure, a shaggy slit. It was the cave of making, the cavern of eternal male desire. And what went on inside it was a love-making divinely imposed on her poor shipwrecked spouse, the long-suffering Odysseus.

The meadows round about were thick with parsley and sprinkled with violets, and fresh crystal streams gurgled through the long lush grasses. Stonecrop ran along the limestones, a wine-dark topping, a haze of campions, marigolds, chrysanthemums, spires of viper's bugloss, orange and yellow and pink, and wild sweetpeas and madness-curing alyssum – all accurate, including the cedars and the cedar-smoke, woodsmoke wafted across the island like an aphrodisiac, hanging in the air.

Accurate? It had to be fucking accurate. I'd become quite the floral scholar on Ogygia, with nothing else to do but pine for home, and so I spun the story and Penelope spun the web. Flowers are innocent, unlike actions, and as for our thoughts, supposing they're unhealthy, unwelcome, even ugly? Better to be slippery than to tell the truth, at least not the whole truth.

And yet . . .

And yet islands are not innocent. Even plants are not as innocent as they seem. Zeus bewitched Europa as she plucked flowers in a field, with a crocus he breathed from his mouth. Creusa was raped by Apollo as she picked crocuses. Hylas was pulled down and drowned by nymphs as he drew water from a spring in a hollow surrounded by herbs. Helen herself was the heart-eating flower of love. And the god Pan – stop to refresh your feet in his pristine springs and he'd bugger you in a second, or crush your skull with his club. Calypso's island paradise, with its meadows of parsley and crocuses, violets, irises, hyacinths, narcissi and roses, was the scene of Persephone's rape by Hades. King of the dead. The island was a trap, and the surrounding sea was Calypso's loom. She was an abstraction. She was unreal.

And yet Penelope got every detail of Calypso absolutely correct, the upturned tits, the full-moon aureoles, the curtaining hair, everything down to her smallest toenail, as if she'd been watching us fucking. How did she do it? Her mind-reading again, or else I talk in my sleep, telling all to Morpheus. Or she sees my dreams.

When Calypso stood up, her long black hair hung to her ankles. In bed, that hair was spread across the sheets like spiked black lightning. And after sex she'd cover me with it, no other covers, and go to sleep. I never moved from her. Leave her couch? Only death could have made up another couch for me, on which I'd have stretched out longer. I'd lost all my friends. I was alone and far from home. The sea was strewn with snares, its islands illusions, enchantments. Leave her? Leave her couch? I didn't even want to leave her side. I must have felt like that for all of those seven months.

So for seven years, Odysseus was Calypso's cold reluctant lover, a bed-slave on Ogygia, and not one night passed when he was not required to make love to her, she being free from all courses of blood, being a nymph and also a love-nymph, satisfied during each act of love by her captive's enforced thrustings, and always lulled into a sweet sleep in his arms, but ever exacting his amorous embraces again in the morning, and the next night, and all night too, till Aurora's pink slit opened up the east on another morning and Aphrodite rested. The bewitching nymph had saved him from the sea but had saved him for herself. Out of Poseidon's white cauldron and into the wet fire . . .

   . . . *of her unquenchable cunt.*

Who would not weep to see it on a web? An exhausted Odysseus, supine and confined, in bondage, and Calypso coming down on him . . .

   . . . *like a nympho.*

And with sweet mouth and extracting tongue consuming him, erect on Ogygia, till her lips . . .

   . . . *suck out my essence.*

Her lips suck forth his soul. See, where it flies . . .

   . . . *my butterfly soul. See where it goes, over the ocean, back to my bonny, leaving me lifeless every time, the spirit flying free, homeward to Ithaca, every time.*

And so you see, it sickened and died. Everything wearies and grows tired: empires, affairs, sex with the same lover, night after night. It cloyed and then it jaded. The sword grows tired of the sheath. My body wearied of her. It makes no difference how you phrase it, the truth is simple and has to be confronted. But whenever I talked about going home and seeing my wife again, her answer was always the same. She stepped straight out of her robe and stood clothed only by her hair.

'Did your wife ever look like this, Odysseus?'

I had to admit I'd never seen a woman like her.

'And she'll look even less like me now, now that time has taken its toll. The crow's feet will be stepping out from her eyes and strutting all over her wrinkled face. The frost will have settled on her hair. The hips will be wider, the belly broader, the buttocks bulging, the breasts blue-veined, sagging, hanging loose . . .'

'Oh, for fuck's sake, come off it! The war didn't last that long – you make it sound like ten years!'

'Doesn't it feel like it?'

I had to admit it did.

'And for her too – even longer for a woman at home. Age occurs on the inside, you know, working outwards. You'll see.'

She smiled her goddess smile.

'But when can I go home, Calypso?'

The smile froze.

'Home to what? To her? She'll grow old and die, as women do. This is your journey's end, Odysseus, here on Ogygia. This is the sea-mark of your utmost hopes, Calypso your prize and only desire. Stay here with me and you will never grow old. I offer you an eternal present, an erasure of all awareness of past or future. I offer you immortality. There are plenty of precedents. I'll make you a god.'

This was going nowhere. I was going nowhere. It was time to bring on the Immortals.

Athene complained to Zeus, who in turn employed Hermes to go to Calypso with the Olympian decision, that enough was enough. It was time to release Odysseus from bondage and send him on his way. The Ogygian sojourn was over. Ithaca awaited him. And so did the suitors – although they didn't know it yet – who were plaguing his patient wife and attempting to seduce her, murder her son and seize her husband's estate. A terrible revenge must be taken, and only Odysseus could exact it. Calypso's ardour came second to the divine dictates. Destiny is unshunnable.

And so the giant-killer himself, golden-sandalled Hermes, with wand in hand, plummets down like a stone down from Olympus, all the way from the upper air to the Pierian range. From there, he swoops over the sea and skims it like a gull, hunting the finny prey, now down the desolate gulfs of the dreadful deep, now across the infinite blue ploughlands and the crumpling graveyards of the waves, its wing tips wetted with spray as it speeds, taking the troughs and crests in its flight and never slowing its course. So Hermes rides the ocean, tirelessly to Ogygia, where the nymph of the braided tresses still holds Odysseus against his will and nightly seeks to wean his heart from Ithaca.

Calypso is seated weaving in her cave, fragrant with cedar-smoke and thyme. She sings sweetly as she works the loom – golden shuttle, golden voice. The cave brims with her lilting and her labour. Odysseus sits apart, disconsolate on the shore, torturing himself as always with tears, studying the skylines with streaming eyes and sobbing out his soul across the barren wastes that lie between him and Ithaca, where Penelope also sits weaving, keeping the suitors from her chamber door and pining for the husband who pines for her.

ⴄ

The scene made the gods weep too. See, they said, this hero of Troy, a cold lover compelled to gratify the desires of a hot goddess who has long since ceased to please but who plots to marry him against his will. The sweetness of life has ebbed from him, and the years wheel round him like the gulls. And that was the scene Hermes, messenger of the gods, found when he dropped suddenly on Ogygia.

Calypso was surprised to see her visitor.

'A rare one indeed,' she said, looking up from the loom.

'Rare? That goes without saying,' said Hermes. 'Not even a winged god would choose to go scudding across the vast tract of salt water I have just covered. I thought I'd never get here. But as you can see, I did. And I'd better tell you right away, this is no courtesy visit. I'm under orders from Zeus. So are you. And you must obey.'

The nymph's eyes clouded, but Hermes did not soften the message.

'Here it is. You have Odysseus here with you, a prisoner to your passion, and you've had him for seven years. It's been long enough. As a matter of fact it's been too long. It's time to give him up. You have to let him go. It's as simple as that.'

Calypso's lovely lip trembled and the clouded eyes rained tears, the dewy tears that only a goddess can drop. The quivering lips tried to form a word. Hermes said it for her.

'Why? You want to know why? I'll tell you. Athene went to Zeus and Zeus appointed me as envoy and here I am. There's really nothing more to add – except the obvious, which is that a man who spent ten years away from home fighting and who has since been dogged by disasters at sea and one misfortune after another on land, followed by a further seven years' captivity on this island – nearly twenty years all told – is long overdue his reward. He has the right to return at last to his wife, not to mention his estate, which is presently being eaten away by lice. You've made him satisfy you every night in your bed – I can see how well used it is, if you don't mind my pointing it out – and you've had your fun. It's over. Zeus has decreed that Odysseus is not destined to end his days with you, nor to enter into immortality on this flowery isle, lovely and pleasant though it is. Be ready to say goodbye.'

The grief of the goddess quickly turned to rage.

'You Olympians, you're all the same, loose livers yourselves. It's perfectly in order for you to sleep with whomever you please, using concealment and force when it suits you, but you can't bear to let a nymph have a mortal man for her bed companion even when she has chosen him openly.'

Hermes smiled.

'Bed companion? More of a bed-slave, wouldn't you say?'

'I'll ignore that attempt to avoid the issue. I can sit here all day and enumerate examples of what I've just said. I can weave them into my web, if you like, and it will be a long one!'

She reeled them off.

Rose-lipped Aurora fell for Orion, offending the other gods, and in the end Artemis, in all her chastity, got up from her golden throne and attacked him with her arrows, gentle but lethal, leaving him dead in Ortygia.

And when the lovely Demeter felt the deep need in her, she lay back in the thrice-ploughed fallow field and enjoyed impetuous intercourse with her beloved Iasion. The goddess's love struck him like thunder and he was raised to ecstasy, but Zeus hurled his own thunder at him as soon as he heard of it and struck him dead.

Odysseus was as good as dead when he was beached on Ogygia. But for a certain nymph, he would not have survived.

'And if you want him to stay alive, Calypso, you'd better let him go. Otherwise he may share the same fate as Orion and Iasion, and you yourself may not go unpunished. You don't want any thunderbolts aimed at Ogygia, do you? Or even the arrows of Artemis.'

So Calypso came down to the edge of the sounding sea and told Odysseus to cease his sighing and end his long scrutiny of the skyline. The Ogygian sojourn was over.

'And yet.'

She couldn't refrain from saying it.

'And yet, if you only knew the further miseries and dangers that lie in store for you before you reach Ithaca — and Ithaca itself will be a bloody affair — you wouldn't lift a foot from this island to risk your life on the barren sea encircled by ruthless enemies. No, you'd stay if you only knew. You'd embrace immortality — and me.'

Encirclement again, the greatest fear, the greatest desire, the wrath of Poseidon, the arms of Aphrodite. No man is made of stone, and it takes an iron man to resist a thrusting belly, bared for him nightly. Odysseus was such a man and the gods gave him the best words with which to answer and appease the nymph.

'Calypso, you are lovely beyond compare, and my wife is a mere mortal. In that respect you are queen of my heart. But I can't deny that I long to see my home again, and the wife of my youth, and whatever awaits me out on the wine-dark sea. Shipwreck, suffering, death itself — I am willing to hazard all, as the sailor does, for home, where my heart is, and for the son of my loins. One more adventure is nothing to a man who has endured as I have endured, for I have lost everything. Let it come on then, and let me go.'

One last night of love in the shaggy cave. Calypso took her fill of him. Penelope stands patiently by the bedside, in spirit, on the web, filled with understanding and with deep admiration for her husband's stoicism. A man must harden himself when a goddess insists on intercourse, especially when it is to be for the last time.

'Don't be in too much of a hurry, Odysseus.'

'All right,' I said, 'take your time.'

'The last time.'

The last time on Thapsos. The last time on Ogygia.

Calypso saw him off in style. The goddess herself was not powerful enough to produce a ship, but she provided all the tools; a big bronze axe with a sharpened double blade and a handsome olive-wood handle was put into one hand, and a shining polished adze into the other. Then she took him to a part of the island forest where the alders and poplars and firs shot up tallest into the far blue sky, all long seasoned timbers which had lost their sap and which would make a buoyant boat to course the waves. Odysseus felled twenty of these, cut the keel, fixed the flooring, fitted the deck, shaped the gunwales, stepped the mast, saw to the yard, the steering oar, the sails, lashed the braces, halyards and sheets on board, and dragged her down on rollers into the shining sea – all in four days and all on his own, a single-handed hero, while the goddess stacked the vessel well with wine and water, and with corn and delectable meats. It was a glorious departure.

I rolled over from her and lay propped on one elbow in the thinning dark. Night had almost rusted away; dawn bled through the open door. Aurora was at it again. She stayed as she was, sullen, legs still splayed, spilling the trickling seeds, like thistle-milk, froth of the fields, summery but sad, an expense of the self, a waste. A shame.

'Shame on you, Odysseus.'

'You say?'

'You can pump your spunk into me just as if it were the same as any night, just as you've done all these months – and then walk away from me, just like that, as if it hadn't happened. As if I'd never happened to you. As if we hadn't happened to each other. That's a fucking shame. Wouldn't you say it was a shame?'

'It's a shame.'

'And a waste.'

'And a waste.'

'Then why?'

'Things happen. They do happen. And they unhappen. Like people. Like life. And death.'

'Well, this is death for me. I just don't understand why you've got to go.'

I went to the door and looked out, confronted the east.

'Not another fucking beautiful day! It's that skyline, you see. You see? It drives me fucking mad. Can't you close your legs?'

'You mean where you wounded me? And there's always a skyline, by the way, wherever you are. You'll see it in Ithaca just the same as you see it here. Our lives are skylines. What else is there?'

'Another skyline. Only not the same one. I have to change my sky.'

'It's boredom then, isn't it? As simple as that? You're bored with me. I'm not enough for you. No woman will ever be enough for you. Am I right?'

Was she right?

'Listen,' I said. 'Once I heard of a city where the people lived in constant fear of a barbarian invasion. They were a civilised people, and they were terrified. The invasion was imminent, so their spies informed them — any day now. So they prepared for it. They prepared themselves so well they were almost looking forward to it. And do you know what? It didn't happen. The attack didn't come. The barbarians just fucked off and attacked some other city. And guess what? The citizens were disappointed, frustrated. They didn't know it, but actually they wanted war. They wanted war because they'd grown tired of peace. They were sick of it. In the end, the horrors of boredom are a lot worse than the horrors of war. I don't know if the story's true, but it rings true to me. There's a truth in there somewhere. Maybe that's why I don't really want to go home, if you can believe that. But it's also why I have to leave here. This has been home for me, it's become home, it is home, and I have to get away from it — not from you.'

'Take me with you then.'

'You know I can't.'

'I know you can't.'

'Forgive me?'

She closed her legs.

'Unforgiven.'

'I'll come back one day.'

'No you won't.'

I had to build myself a raft in the end. There were able-bodied shipbuilders on the island but none that would help me. She was well liked and had talked to every cunt under the sun. I was abandoning her.

I'd used her. I was the betrayer. I was the biggest bastard on Thapsos. Cold looks were the best I got. I got into a few fights as well, collected a few more bruises. She didn't patch me up this time. I was out of her house by then, sleeping on the beach. It was like old times.

When the day came, it was one awful exit. A really sad ending, you could say. Even a bad ending. The raft did have a steering oar and a makeshift mast, and a rag of a sail. Apart from that it was a joke. If there had been a sea-god he'd have shaken his white hair and the ocean would have roared with laughter. It fucking roared all right. But no one was laughing.

Sometimes I feel I could blend into the web, into Penelope's image of me, even into the events and scenes she wove around me. What's life, after all, but fact and fiction truly blent? Images of ourselves we accept as accurate, stories we stack up in our heads to barricade reality, combat death, block truth. Why not have it then? A fusion of the two, truth and lies, neither false, neither true. The web exists in space and time. It inhabits its own autonomous world, like a poem or a song. It can free the spirit and lift the heart.

So the island astern of me – Thapsos, Ogygia, what you will – was lost to sight, and yet once more, O ye laurels of adventure, it was just me and the open sea. A fantastic fucking feeling. The heart-heaviness lightens, blue water all around you, and nowhere, everywhere to go, the universe your compass, your old friends the stars. You can't explain it to anybody who's never been a sailor – that enormous sense of being on your own on the ocean, and nothing, absolutely nothing between you and those cold sparklers, the calm constellations, nothing to come between you and the journey, no wars, women, monsters, gods, no complaining crew, while you navigate niftily by those cosmic candles, your night-lights, putting your whole trust in them alone, and the only sound the hiss of the deep giving way to you beneath your probing keel, your pregnant sail, making love to the slinky sea, insatiate, steady under the stars.

That's how it was. And there I stood, night after night, an old man alone on the ocean, with only a few planks of poplar poised between me and its upward thrust, its unutterable emptiness and depth. I never once closed my eyes in sleep. I kept them open, unblinking, on the eyes that winked back at me, all night long, always watching the Pleiades and Boötes setting slowly, and always keeping the Great Bear on my left, watching him too as he wheeled about with a wary eye, always observing Orion from a distance, the hunted keeping track of the hunter, and telling me I was headed east, which was all I knew.

After only a few hours of that, you're absurdly elevated, as if on drugs, your soul spread out across the skies, like the Milky Way, spermy in space, and you suddenly get it whole again, the night in its silence, the stars in their calm. Hours, days. After seventeen nights of it, you're more than ready for the next island, you've shed the Calypso part of yourself, like a snakeskin, and a new man steps ashore – into the arms of one more woman. Ye gods! But the new man has to be re-born, he has to be washed up, pushed up, fucked up at her feet, kicking and spluttering and coughing up brine, out of the womb, the swinging chains of the sea, after an epic oceanic struggle, reaching land again against the odds.

The land, sighted on the eighteenth day, was Scheria, the land of the Phaeacians, the supernatural sea-kings, who, if not quite gods, were at least the special friends of the gods. I saw their hills rise up out of the mist, and the coast that jutted out to meet me was like a shield laid out on the sea. Landfall. At last. Thank fuck.

But Poseidon had other ideas.

'So he thinks it's going to be that simple, does he?'

The sea shook with laughter. A great big belly-laugh.

'But his bowels will be full of brine before he boards the next woman. Let him try riding me for the next hour – I'll show him how I can romp!'

Trident in hand, he called up the clouds, summoned the winds and struck the sea. A white squall came blasting out of the north, spearheaded by a sea that bore down on me like the toppling towers of Troy. Darkness swooped on the waves. It was the old story, and I was so close to the coast it broke my heart.

The wall hit me – one puny man against the whole fucking front line. I was swept straight from the raft and rammed hard and fast down the sea's gullet, so deep I thought I'd never come up again alive. I heard the whole ocean in my head, rumbling, an army dreadful with drums. It seemed a Troy ago till I broke the surface and saw the sky – still raging at me but offering me air, my element. The raft was close by, nearly capsizing; I struggled back on board and clung on as the waves tossed me, a tuft of thistledown blown on the wind at harvest-time.

And now the lightning ripped the skies. Zeus was joining in, hurling at me like a hundred Hectors. I cursed the day I'd left Calypso. No proud burial-mound for me now, no headland barrow. The fish will feast on me, and then I'll be fish-shit drifting on the tide, to be chewed at all over again by the tiny life-forms that nibble on the dead detritus of some desolate beach.

It took a nymph, naturally, to rescue me.

She was Leucothea, once a woman named Ino, daughter of Cadmus, and now a divinity of the salty depths. The sea is not all heartless and empty of hope. She took pity on me and declared that if Poseidon was determined to throw all the elements at me every time I set sail, it was only right to even things up a little and give me a fighting chance.

She surfaced and raised herself up a little out of the water, holding on to the raft. Even so close to drowning, I couldn't help admiring her pert breasts, dripping brine.

'Pay attention. Take this veil, take off all the clothes Calypso gave you, wrap the veil round your waist and swim with it. With this lifebelt, I promise you won't drown. As soon as you feel the land under your hands and knees, unwrap the veil and throw it away from you, far out into the wine-dark sea. As you do so, avert your eyes, and I'll be there to catch the veil and take it back with me into the deeps.'

'Why do I have to look away?' I asked.

The nymph smiled, her lovely breasts bobbing in the water. There was a small circle of calm round the raft.

'You need to concentrate on survival, not on me. I know you, Odysseus.'

She handed me the veil, and just in time. Poseidon sucked up a wave like a mountain and sent it curling and hurtling down on me. It smashed the raft to pieces, leaving me with no option but to do as the nymph had said. And, at that point, assistance arrived from no other than Athene. She checked the winds, put them to sleep, and brought up a good strong breeze out of the north to flatten the waves in my path, enabling me to avoid sudden death and swim again for Scheria, this time with the help of the veil. The intervention of nymph and goddess had made it possible.

But it wasn't over. Two nights and two more days I struggled in heavy seas, sometimes thinking that in spite of the veil it was all over for me after all. And at the bright-haired dawn on the third day, with the wind falling away and Poseidon tiring of his sport, I finally sighted again the sea-kings' coast and heard the thunder of surf on its rocks.

But there was no harbour, only sheer cliffs and sharp ragged reefs like teeth. I couldn't believe it — how could there be seafarers without a port? Not only that, but I was being swept right at these reefs with the speed of a ship all set to ram another. I cursed and screamed — where were my helpers? — and braced to be flayed alive, broken bones and drowning only seconds away.

It didn't happen. Athene was still there. The grey-eyed goddess appeared alongside and showed me a small rock ahead. I managed to stop the onward hurtling by grabbing at it wildly as I passed and clinging hard to it while the monster wave rolled on and smashed against the reef in smithereens and salt. But I only managed to hold on for a few seconds. The colossal back-rush of the wave ripped me right off the rock again, stripping the skin from my hands and fingers. I saw it for a second — the skin left sticking there, like the suckers of a squid torn from its hole; and then the surge was over my head once more.

And yet once more Athene came to my rescue. She pulled me to the surface, guided me clear of the rollers and found a natural harbour for me, a sheltered little river-mouth free from rocks. I drifted gently to shore, still clinging incredibly to the big timber-knot which was all that was left of the raft. I let it go, not forgetting to unwind Leucothea's veil and hurl it into the sea-rushing river.

Downstream it hurried, back into the hands of the lovely-breasted nymph. Athene also faded from the scene, and I knelt on all fours and kissed the wet ground. Then I dropped like a log among the reeds, salt water gushing from my mouth and nostrils, my body battered and swollen from nineteen days and nights in the sea. My lacerated hands streamed blood and stung with salt. I had to find shelter for the night, away from the hard frosts and chill winds and drenching dews that would follow. I forced myself to my feet, staggered to the nearest copse, found a likely thicket, crept in between two bushes and heaped myself up a quick couch and coverlet of dead leaves, thick enough to keep three workers warm in the worst of winters. Even then, sleep came hard at first. I was stark-naked and shivering. But Athene had still not deserted me. She hovered over me briefly in the darkness, laid a charm of Morpheus on my burning eyelids, and gave me rest.

FORTY-SIX

Nausicaa lies sleeping. The bed is sumptuous, because her father is Alcinous, King of the Phaeacians, on the island of Scheria. Once they'd been neighbours to the plundering Cyclops on the broad acres of Hypereia, but now they are settled here. They are a rarefied breed, close to the gods, and the king divinely led. Nausicaa is guarded by the two ladies of the bedchamber, stretched out at either doorpost of her room, both women gifted with great beauty by the Graces. Nausicaa herself is even more beautiful, in build and looks as bright and glorious as a deathless goddess.

It is early morning, before dawn. The doors to the girl's bedroom are solid and firmly shut, and the beautiful chambermaids bar the way. This means nothing to Athene, fresh from the sea, where she has been assisting Odysseus. Passing through the polished oak, easy as air, the goddess glides across the room to the bed and breathes into Nausicaa's ear, the slightest sea-whisper in a beached shell asleep on the sands. Athene has not forgotten to disguise herself or her voice. Any young girl, should she happen to stir, would be blinded by the sight of a goddess turning up at her bed-head, especially unannounced, so she has taken the precaution of assuming the form and likeness of Dymas, the daughter of a sea-captain, a girl of Nausicaa's own age and one of her best friends. It is the voice of Dymas, apparently, that is now whispering into the girl's dreaming ear.

'Nausicaa,' says the voice in the shell, 'shame on you, lazybones. Here you are, sleeping your young life away, while all around you lie all those lovely clothes, neglected and unwashed, and not only here but all over the palace. It's littered with laundry. And you on the threshold of marriage, I should think, with every noble young man for miles around sighing out his soul for you. And why not? Who wouldn't want a Phaeacian princess to be his wife, especially one with your looks? But not if all the guests turn up tricked out in dirty old duds that haven't seen water for weeks. Unthinkable. You'd best avoid the shame of it and prepare for the wedding that's just around the corner. Who knows, you may meet the man of your dreams any moment now. Say goodbye to your virginity – and start planning things this very morning; don't leave it any later. I'll tell you what, ask your father to set you up with a wagon and a couple of mules immediately after breakfast. In fact, with all those spreads and dresses and the many rugs and sashes lying about, why wait for breakfast? It's a long way, don't you think, from the town to the washing-pools? Better hurry.'

After delivering this speech, the bright-eyes goddess speeds back up to Olympus, where the blithe gods spend their unending lives in the white radiance of eternity, undrenched by rains, unshaken by gales, untroubled by frosts or snows, untouched by the mortality that brings bitterness into the lives of men.

Meanwhile the east grows roses. Nausicaa sits up, rubbing her eyes, still filled with her dream, and runs to find her mother. She is already sitting with her women, spinning the yarn that is stained with sea-purple, the rich dye of the deeps. Her mother listens and smiles.

'It's a good dream,' she says.

She tells her daughter to speak to the king. Being close to the gods, he at once understands what is afoot and arranges everything, including picnic provisions, so that his daughter and her entourage can breakfast at the washing-pools. He also orders olive oil to be taken along in a golden flask.

'You'll need to bathe after the washing, all of you, and after bathing you will want to anoint yourselves with a good soft oil.'

And so it is contrived. Driving the mules with their cartloads of washing, Nausicaa and her maids come down to the clear pools so freshly fed by the swirling river that even the most stubborn of stains can be scoured clean of grime. They drop their bundles into the troughs, tread them hard, rinse them free of all dirt and spread them out cleanly in a line on the sparkling wave-washed shingle of the beach. Then they strip off their sweaty clothes and bathe naked in the giggling sea, rubbing themselves all over with olive oil, those sturdy-hipped, thick-haired girls with shaggy armpits, surrounding their cool nude princess and the honey-gold locks piled on her freshly washed head. Afterwards, they picnic and dance and sing and play ball while they wait for the clothes to dry in the hot noon-bright sun.

Little do the light-hearted girls imagine Athene herself taking part in their game, but just as Nausicaa throws the ball to one of her maids, Athene's invisible arm intervenes, deflecting the plaything so that it drops not into the girl's outstretched hands but into the deep eddies of the current, causing all of them to shriek with laughter and exaggerated alarm. This wakes Odysseus from his long sleep in the leafy lair, where he still lies hidden.

The screams were tearing my sleep apart. I was awake enough to imagine the worst from that shrieking. Rape? Murder? A raid? Where had I landed now? Not fucking savages again!

Or perchance the cries of the mountain nymphs who haunt the rugged hills, the rivers, springs and fields, and had tripped light-footed down to the sounding sea so early in the morning to frolic in the tide?

Only one way to find out.

So it was that Odysseus emerged from his thicket, holding a verdant branch before him to hide his manhood. This caused the startled maids to shriek all the more, as if he were a mountain lion advancing on the herd, compelled by sheer hunger to attack the pens.

And a mountain lion with flaming eyes might have proved a sight less frightening than the one the unprotected women now beheld: a naked male, long-haired, tangle-bearded and begrimed with brine, bearing down on them with a rustling branch for genitals. A wild man. Still screaming, they went scuttling off in all directions along the jutting sandy spits of the shore. All except Nausicaa, whose stillness made her stand out.

As did her stature – taller by a head than the tallest of her maids, this unwedded girl. As for her looks, it was not unlike the scene in which Leto looks on as her daughter Artemis the Archeress comes down the mountain-tops along the high ridges of Taygetus or Erymanthus to hunt wild boar and follow the shy fleet-footed deer, with all the nymphs crowding round her, joining in the sport. All are lovely, all are divine, and yet Artemis surpasses each one of them and proves the paragon both in stature and in beauty. So it was with the Phaeacian maids and the radiant Nausicaa, loveliest of them all. She stood her ground and held her gaze, waiting calmly to see how Odysseus would act and what he would say.

What the fuck do you say when you're standing bare buff in front of a gorgeous grey-eyed girl with only a fistful of forest covering your cock? Not to mention the inevitable effect she's having on you that even sea and circumstance combined haven't quite suppressed.

Penelope said it for me – as ever – and turned a plain-speaking peasant wench into a princess, an island tribe into a race of nautical aristocrats, a clay house into a bronze palace, the entire island into a Poseidon protectorate, and me into the most polite of orators, if one suitably embarrassed by his exposed and scruffy condition.

'When I first saw you, I took you for Artemis among the Immortals, but now that I stand so close, I have to confess, the comparison fades. In fact it's worthless – there's no comparison at all. Not with any girl I've ever seen. Or goddess either, for that matter. Your parents and brothers must be bursting with pride and pleasure, not to mention that luckiest of men who has the good fortune to win your hand in marriage, if such a man lives and breathes, for I cannot even imagine one worthy enough in the worlds of men or gods.'

Nausicaa blushed under the shower of compliments.

'And I can tell you, only once have I seen anything even approaching your elegance, only once in my life, but it's that one beauty that remains with me, now I'm reminded of it.'

'Oh? And who was she, eloquent stranger, who made such an impression on you?'

Odysseus shook his head. 'No, it was no woman, for no woman could compare with you. It was not even a she. It was long ago, in Delos.'

'In Delos. How lovely that sounds. In Delos. It sounds so far away.'

'Far enough. I saw a young sapling there once, a palm tree, standing straight and tall and lovely as you – nearly. It was growing by the temple of Apollo, and it was an attendant fit only for a god. In fact, it was against this tree that Leto leaned when she gave birth to the twins, Artemis and Apollo. Perhaps that is why they call Delos the shining isle.'

'Well, you're a long way from Delos now.'

'And a long way from home.'

'And you seem to have lost your clothes along the way.'

'That's right. Beaten up by the sea, stripped and robbed of all I had. That's Poseidon for you.'

The grey eyes glanced down and up again, a fraction.

'Not quite all. Poseidon left you with the main equipment, I see. Better hold on to it. Don't lose it, whatever you do.'

Shrieks from the girlfriends who'd come back up from along the beach, aware that I wasn't a danger to them. I waved my branch at them.

'Put it back!'

'Don't threaten us!'

'Who's threatening you?'

'Don't tempt us then!'

Yes, these were peasant girls all right. They'd seen a thing or two.

'So what happened to you, then?'

Odysseus dropped to his knees and told his story, but only the most recent events – how he'd steered for seventeen days and nights on the wine-dark sea, alone under the stars. On the eighteenth day he'd seen the coast, had been struck by a storm and rescued by a sea-nymph, with the help of a goddess. Then he had swum for two more nights and a day before making it to shore.

'In the sorry condition in which you see me now.'

'It's amazing.'

'Nineteen days from Ogygia – and this is the twentieth – and I'm still alive.'

'It's epic.'

And Odysseus begged her for some of the linen that was lying out to dry, first inquiring of her if he might know her name.

'Nausicaa is my name, and my father rules here – Alcinous. My mother's name is Arete. They are the king and queen of Scheria. You have reached the country of the sea-kings. I notice, though, that you have not yet given your own name.'

Odysseus cleared his throat. The princess saw his hesitation and stopped him.

'Forgive me, sir, I was forgetting my manners. It's enough that you are a shipwrecked sailor, swept upon our coast, a man battered by gales and gods. Names are nothing to us. You are a soul in distress. You need help.'

She directed her maids to conduct Odysseus to a sheltered place and bathe him in the river, but being too gallant a man, he begged for privacy.

'I'd be reluctant to bathe in the presence of you braided-haired ladies of breeding. Be kind enough to stand apart while I, with fresh river-water, sluice the brine from my skin and scrub the sea-scurf from my hair.'

And the scum from my arsehole — the last of Poseidon's parting presents, along with the stabs and gashes, and the skin from my fingers left sticking on some godforsaken rock, somewhere out in that godforsaken sea. How I hated that fucking sea! How to get it out of me?

How? Apply the usual old wine, a flask of olive oil, and a comb to tease out the beard and order the long thorny locks, now bushy as a hyacinth in bloom. Add a cloak and doublet, freshly laundered and a touch of Athene's invisible fingers, and once again it's a new man that steps out from the bushes, magically transformed. Nausicaa was impressed.

'I think the gods have sent him here,' she told her white-armed women, 'to be my husband. Strangers so seldom light on us here, so far out are we across the surging sea, and now that he has come, I pray that he stays.'

She advised Odysseus to let her reach home ahead of him with her maids and to conceal himself meantime in a grove of poplars sacred to Athene, so as not to attract attention to himself among the islanders, who were friendly enough in general, but who were Poseidon's people, wedded to the sea, and didn't take too kindly to foreigners, especially if it looked as if one of them was interested in their princess, she having already turned down so many good men of her own race.

'If you don't mind my mentioning that fact,' she said with a smile.

Odysseus said he didn't mind and that it didn't surprise him.

'Good. After that, you should head straight for the high-battlemented city, passing the temple of Poseidon until you reach the palace. You can't miss it. Enter and walk straight up to my mother, who will be sitting spinning the sea-purple in the firelight with her back to a pillar, her usual place, and all her maids about her.'

Odysseus said it sounded idyllic.

'My father's throne will be nearby, and he'll be sitting drinking his wine like one of the gods, as if Hebe had just filled his cup. But you must ignore him and slip past and clasp the queen's knees. That's if you value your wish to get back home safely and in good time.'

Odysseus did exactly as the girl had dictated. And to make certain he didn't miss his way, a tellingly bright-eyed girl carrying a pitcher just happened to cross his path and offered to direct him. Athene was taking no chances. She even poured out around him an invisible mist to protect him from the local seamen who give cold looks to strangers, and she repeated Nausicaa's instructions that he should go straight up to Arete.

'She is a goddess in Scheria, for she is of the same blood as Alcinous, who married her after her father Rhexenor fell to silver-bowed Apollo. Both were the sons of Nausithous whom Periboea bore to Poseidon. And among the sea-god's great gifts to Alcinous is an orchard of pears and pomegranates, sweet figs, grapes and olives, fruiting all the year, as does the vineyard where the west wind always blows, and everything is laid out in a four-acre garden outside the courtyard – so you can't possibly miss the palace.'

Indeed, it was hard not to spot it. Even without the silver lintels and the doors of beaten gold guarded on either side by two dogs doomed never to doze or die, or even to grow old, sentinels forged in gold and silver by Hephaestus – even without all this, the building, with its bronze walls and blue-glazed lapis tiles, stood out.

Within the palace entrance, fifty maids were busy, some cleaning and polishing the gleaming bronze and gold artefacts, others grinding the apple-golden corn, and others again sitting at the loom or twisting the yarn, their quick fingers flitting like aspen leaves. Soft olive oil dripped from the thickly-woven fabrics they had just finished making, for the Phaeacian women weave as skilfully as their menfolk navigate, and handle a loom as lovingly as their seamen do a tiller or a sail.

Further in, the sea-kings sat round the walls on seats spread with lush purple coverlets. Others were seated at tables, eating and drinking. Odysseus ignored them and walked straight up to Arete and placed his hands on her knees, begging her to take pity on an unhappy wanderer, to show him some hospitality and send him on his way. Then he went and sat like a suppliant among the ashes.

His entry had been concealed by the mysterious mist, but this now dissolved and everyone stared at him in astonishment. The venerable lord Echeneus, the elder statesman of the palace, spoke to the king.

'Alcinous, it's up to you of course, but in my opinion it's unseemly that a guest should be sitting there among the ashes like a beggar. In the name of all-thundering Zeus who watches over strangers, will you offer him a seat and some food and drink?'

The king got up at once and took Odysseus by the hand, placing him personally in his favourite son's seat right by his side. A maid brought clear fresh water in a golden ewer and poured it into a silver basin so that he could rinse his fingers. Another brought fresh bread and meat from the larder, and a young man served him the heady-honeyed wine. Odysseus was struck by the extent of the hospitality as the sea-kings were not famed in legend for their love of strangers but were a world unto themselves and a breed apart. But only after wining and dining the stranger and courteously refraining from inquiring as to his identity did they now wait with obvious curiosity to see if he would tell them his story, as was only natural.

Odysseus told them only so much at first, starting well through his travels from the time of his sojourn with Calypso.

'Night after night she insisted I make love to her.'

'And did you?' inquired Arete.

'Every night for seven years.'

At that point Nausicaa got up, flushed, and went out into the night.

'I had no choice. There is no saying no to a goddess and there was no satisfying her.'

'You poor man, you must be exhausted after the labours of Sisyphus.' The king grinned. 'Though not perhaps so unpleasant a labour as rolling a rock up a hill without the satisfaction of ever reaching the peak!'

The hall rippled with laughter.

Odysseus winked back at the king. 'I reached the peak, but instead of resting had to start all over again.'

That night, after so many sufferings, Odysseus slept the deepest of sleeps, and next morning Alcinous took him down to the ships where the Phaeacians held their assemblies, and the king told his people that the gods had sent a stranger whom he liked so much that he would like him to stay and be his son-in-law.

'By the sound of him, he's a man who could people this entire country with my grandchildren!'

He also had reason to believe, he said, that his daughter Nausicaa would approve of this arrangement, except that the stranger, who had not yet given his name, had already asked for guides to take him home – wherever that might be – and that a ship should therefore be made ready and manned by the best mariners in the land, to transport the stranger wheresoever he should direct.

While the ship was being made ready, Alcinous led Odysseus back to the palace hall, where a blind minstrel and the Phaeacians' favourite poet, Demodocus, sang sweetly and soulfully about the Greek heroes at Troy, and in particular about a quarrel between Odysseus and Achilles.

It was too much for Odysseus. When he heard the songs of Troy, the tears sprang to his eyes and rolled down his cheeks unchecked, glistening like dew on his beard, and he quickly had to hide his head in his cloak. The king was close enough to see this and leaned across.

'What man, never bury your face in the sea-blue fabric, not here. You needn't be ashamed of a few tears, friend. After all, he really is a superb singer, isn't he? Beloved by the Muse, who mingled good and ill in the drink she gave him, depriving him of his eyes but letting him seduce with the sweetness of his song, so persuasive he could pull tears down Persephone's cheek, who has seen so many dead, and even draw the iron drops from Dis.'

'Tears?'

She felt the wetness on her neck. I couldn't stop the sobs. She hugged me tight.

'And from such an iron man.'

Iron tears. Some fucking iron. Some hero.

'It's all right,'   I said, 'I'm all right, I was just remembering, that's all.'

'A woman?'

'No, not a woman.'

'A man, then.'

'No, not a man either. Many men, so many. Thousands of them. Where are they now?'

'Ah, so it's the war. It's always the war.'

The war that never ends.

'Where are they now?'

Gone to grave-mounds, every one.

'Don't cry,' she said.

She took my hand and pressed it into the soft wetness between her legs.

'The war ends here.'

She'd taken me to her parents' house. We'll do it a favour and call it a house. Not exactly a bronze palace, but it was a step up from a mud hut. At least it wasn't another fucking cave. And I was made welcome enough — food, drink, clothes, chatter. It was a home. There was a scruffy dog by the blistered wooden door. Who needs doors of beaten gold? And what else does a man need? What else does a woman need?

The old folks went to bed, and she took me outside behind the wall of the pigsty, with the swine grunting encouragement on the other side. I started to say something, but she put her hand over my mouth and her fingers to her lips. She dropped down and lay back in the straw, pulling her dress over her head and pulling me down on her. She fumbled quickly for my prick and gasped when she found it. I was ready to be gentle so as not to wake up the parents through the thin walls, but she thrust herself up onto me with a little cry. Then she fucked with the sort of innocent earnestness that made me wonder if it was her first time. I scented blood. It was her first time. She made tiny squeaking noises like a little mouse or piglet. Then she flooded me with her orgasm.

At first I thought she'd peed on me in her excitement, but then I remembered the drunken talk in the camps at Troy, the gabbling about the bed-girls, comparing notes. I kept hearing about the women who wetted you when they came, and I had asked silly, stupid questions, exposing my ignorance. Diomedes had teased me about it.

'What, never been drenched, Odysseus? You haven't lived! You get back a lot more than you put in – it warms your balls like a hot bath!'

I thought about it as I lay looking at her and stroking her upturned rump. She was short and plump-bummed, which suited me fine. This time there had been something else, though, a weird reciprocity, two tides meeting, a conflux, a melting into one another, a mingling, a precious libation, mutually poured out of the ocean of love – fuck me, I'm no singer, but she was making a poet out of me. She'd made me stop and think. She'd given me something, something different. What was it she'd given me?

Peace? Was that the word? I think that was it. I was at peace with her. It felt simple. Sometimes we'd lie for hours afterwards, still in the coital position, me still inside her, still melting and resolving into that vaguely sad post-coital calm. If not pure peace, then at least a suspension of judgement, or decisions, or worries about anything at all, and we'd murmur to each other. She'd ask me about the stars as she lay on her back behind the pigsty, her short legs still tucked round me. She had a great view of the heavens. I couldn't see them; my view was of her left earlobe, but I could picture them, of course, and tell her what was up there and what planets were on the wander. She was no star-gazer – the whole thing was absolute fucking chaos to her – and she never could piece together a hunter or a wagon or a bear, even though I was teaching her with eyes in the back of my head, as it were. That intrigued her for some reason, and I liked her fascination. I suppose I liked being admired too, though I admitted there was nothing clever or unusual about it. I'd done a lot of travelling in my time, and I'd got to know the stars, that's all, as travellers do, even better than I'd got to know people. The stars were a lot more reliable, that was for sure.

'But you're a traveller no more,' she whispered, squeezing me with certain muscles and giggling when she felt the hardness suddenly return, quickly filling up her little cunt.

'Your wanderings are over.'

We fucked again. Under hunters and wagons and bears. And she told me she loved me. And why not? Nausicaa – the ship. That's what her name meant, she said, roughly speaking. A ship without a sailor. And the sea had brought her a sailor. And together we made her go. Of course she loved me.

Did I love her? I'd say I loved her. Who wouldn't? She was funny, sunny, wanting, giving, uncomplicated, compact. A sweet little fuck. Her folks took to me as well, even said to come inside, there was no need to do it behind the pigsty anymore, they'd turn their backs. And they wanted grandchildren. They'd run the farm in time, after I'd grown old, older. After I'd gone. So why not? Why the fuck not indeed?

I could have told them it had something to do with those very words – grown old, gone, and that I didn't like the sound of them, they sounded too much like an ending, like sheathing your sword and letting it rust, letting your life rust. I could have told them I had my own farms to see to, in whatever state they were now, and if they were still mine. I could have said I had a wife I hadn't seen since before the war and a son who'd be a young man. I could have said I might even have grandchildren by now that I'd never seen and never would unless I got back home. I could have said that although I'd been washed up here a naked vagrant, I was actually no beggar but a king. I was not a fucking nobody.

A somebody then? A king without clothes? A king without a crown? Lost it in the ocean, had I? Poseidon had pilfered it, ripped it off, tossed it away on the waves. He'd made a pauper out of a prince; he'd made a man into no man, Noman. And I could have said that I was missing all that I'd had, all that I'd been, that I was pining for the hearth, the hills of home, pining for my Penelope, for my Ithaca.

Would it have been true? Yes, we all long for Ithaca, it's true. Except that we all know Ithaca isn't really there: it's a mirage, a deception, a lie, as illusory as the horizon, that long hard clipped line drawn across the world, the boundary that beckons you and hems you in, because you can never get there. But still you can't resist it, the pull and counter-pull, the old smoke of home, the need to blow it away, to break the bolts and shackles of the ocean, shutting you in, the desire to touch the intangible, to break the line, just like at Troy — break the fucking line!

Yes, I could have said all that, or something else. But in the end I didn't. In the end I said nothing. I just slipped away, like a deserter, slipped away on a quiet night-tide as she lay sleeping on the straw, a slight smile on her half-open lips, her white teeth glinting a little in the stars, of which she still remembered next to nothing. Somehow I loved her for that innocence of hers, and I don't mind admitting it — that night cost me a few fucking tears.

'No need to be ashamed of them,' repeated Alcinous. 'Perhaps the song reminded you of something, or of someone?'

'Both,' replied Odysseus.

He was weeping like a woman who has just seen her husband fall in the field while fighting for his country and his family. She screams in her grief and clings to his corpse for dear life, but the enemy soldiers behind her smash their spear-butts into her back and drag her away from him, bruised and weeping bitterly into bondage. She will never see her children again. That's how Odysseus wept when he heard the songs of Troy.

The king immediately announced that there had been quite enough song for now and that it was time for a change of mood, and for games. Odysseus at first declined to take part, but was stung into action by a taunt from a man called Euryalus.

'Let's face it, you're a bit on the short side for a contender, and you look more like a broken-down merchant skipper from some derelict old tub. From what I hear, you didn't even manage to handle that so well either. Washed up without a paddle, weren't you?'

Odysseus kept his temper and answered him quietly. 'You're a nice-looking boy, though I suspect the gods have bestowed on you more beauty than brains.'

'Or balls!' called a voice from the crowd, provoking laughter.

This maddened Euryalus and might have led to a challenge, but he was contained by the elders. 'You want to prove you're the better man?' was all he said.

Odysseus took the field and calmly picked up the biggest quoit of all.

'There's only one way to prove a fool a fool,' he said.

He hesitated, just for effect, then swung the disc. It sang its path well beyond all the other throws, and all the champion oarsmen shrank from the stone as it hurtled over their heads and thudded into the ground, where Athene was waiting in yet another disguise, pretending to be one of the crowd.

'Right out in front!' she cheered. 'Well beyond the rest of the bunch! We Phaeacians have met our match today, we'd better admit it. The sea can break the strongest back, but you're far from broken, my friend. As I see it, Euryalus had better eat his words.'

Silence in Scheria. Alcinous broke it.

'Well, stranger, it seems we can't compete with you – and why should we try? We're not the best of boxers or wrestlers or runners. I have to admit we like the lute and the dance as an accompaniment to our eating and drinking, and we love our warm baths and our sleep. We are a civilised people. But that doesn't make us softies. On the ocean we are unsurpassed – not as raiders and colonisers, carrying terror in our hulls, but as traders and geniuses of the sea. What's more, we have the power and goodwill of Poseidon behind us, unlike your good self, sir, and our ships travel faster than thought. One of them, at your own request, will see you shortly home. Which is just as well for you, I think, since all your ships appear to have perished, and you came here, as Euryalus rightly remarked, on what was left of the last of them, a naked keel. Or were you simply naked?'

It was the speech of a superb diplomat, one that Agamemnon could have learned from, Odysseus thought, and one that had put both men in their places while remaining gracious. At the same time, the king called upon Euryalus to apologise, which he did both readily and nobly, giving Odysseus a great bronze sword with a scabbard of carved ivory. A great many more gifts followed from each of the princes in turn.

The king then commanded Demodocus to play again, this time with dancers to accompany him. They were all in the first flush of youth, all beautiful. Odysseus was struck dumb with admiration for the art of these Phaeacians.

Alcinous now asked Odysseus for the rest of his story, and wondered why he had wept earlier over the tales of the Greeks at Troy. Clearly, it was time for the hero to tell all, including the secret of his identity, and when he had finished the long account of his sufferings, both in the theatre of war and in the broad and barren arena of ocean, there was not a dry eye among the oar-loving audience.

The king rose to his feet.

'Odysseus,' he said, 'for now we know your name, your wanderings and your struggles are a greater story than any man's. I believe it to be the greatest story of all time, and I think it will never end. Yet you have come here asking us to do just that – to put an end to your great story by sending you home. A strange position to put me in. Part of me wishes your wanderings would end here, with my daughter. But I see now that this cannot be. Another part of me wishes your wanderings would never end, they are so heroic. But end them I shall. It would be inhuman not to. The time has come for you to go forth and endure the destiny that the heavy spinners spun for you at your birth. You will return at last to Ithaca, starting at dawn, for I noticed tonight that you kept turning your face to the setting sun, as if spurring him on in his descent and urging him to rise again.'

Back in the palace more gifts were bestowed, a copper heated over the fire, and Odysseus was bathed and anointed in a style he had not known since his time with Calypso.

Nausicaa stood by one of the pillars, tall and slender and stately, watching him quietly with her sad grey eyes.

'So you are married already,' she said. 'Well, may the gods guide you and go with you. And when you are safely back home in your own country and in your wife's bosom, perhaps you will remember the girl who found you on a foreign shore. Or perhaps you will forget.'

'How can I forget,' answered Odysseus, 'the girl whose gift to me was life itself?'

Next morning her parents and all their court conducted Odysseus to the ship they had generously provided for him, and he boarded, waved farewell, and shouted loudly to them as the rowers bent to their oars, wishing them a prosperous old age, and Princess Nausicaa a joyful marriage, and all happiness to be theirs until death took them out of this world forever.

And I could have said that my heart was fucking breaking as the little trader took me away from that sweet girl, its oars dripping moonlight and pearl, putting more and more ocean between me and a love I'd known. As ever. I could even have said that I was coming to the end of the line, and that the travels were almost over, that old Odysseus, though still unslaked, still hungry for skylines, suckling his blood, homed yet for Ithaca, his roots and hearth-ease.

So the splendid ship leapt into the swell, plunging like a chariot team under the whip. No falcon could have kept up with her as, with soaring stern and plunging prow, she ploughed the blue acres of the sounding sea, her wake always whitening the wine-dark waves. No hulking tramp then, no derelict tub after all, but a sea-going miracle such as could be constructed only by the sea-kings, Poseidon's special friends. It was laden with the gifts they had heaped on the hero. The dark waves roared around the stern, where Odysseus lay at peace, freed from the long years of bloody war and anxious wanderings, the countless curses and catastrophes that had followed him on the cruel seas and prevented his sorely wished return to home. Sick at heart for many things, but safe now in the hands of the master mariners, his sea-troubles over after twenty long years, gratefully he gave way and entered oblivion, lulled by the sea-music into a deep sweet sleep, like the sleep of death.

PART FOUR
ITHACA

The return to Ithaca. An epic event after so long an absence, don't you think? And you can hardly have our local hero slinking back surreptitiously on some beaten-up tub, dumped like an old dog on the shore to find his own way home and work out what to do next. Unthinkable. And it didn't happen that way – at least not on the web. Penelope saw to that. She gave the homecoming an entirely different spin.

Here's how it goes.

I was still sleeping when we reached Ithaca. Not that I was needed – the sea-kings knew all the creeks and coves, and they spotted the haven between the two headlands, named after the sea-god Phorcys, with the long-leaved olive tree at the harbour head and the shady cave nearby, sacred to the Naiads – the cave with two mouths, the north one for humans, and the south one through which only the gods could come and go. The old wives of Ithaca used to gabble about these water-sprites, the nymphs who came there to see to their hallowed work, weaving their wonderful sea-blue webs on the great stone looms while the never-failing springs gurgled all about them at their labours and the bees buzzed in and out of the stone basins and the two-handled jars they used as hives.

But I was oblivious to all that as my escorts lifted me out of the stern, still sleeping, and laid me on the sands, out of reach of the sucking tide, the tricky liquid fingers of Poseidon. They stacked all the Phaeacian gifts against the olive tree and sailed off again without waking me, though dawn had broken. The Phaeacians soon put blue furrows on the ploughlands of the sea, and they were quickly back within sight of their native Scheria.

I found out later that they didn't make it. Poseidon's anger never left him, and though I was now safely back on Ithacan soil, he continued to hound me in the only way he could, by attacking my friends. He was waiting for them not far from the home port.

'So you think you can offer safe passage to an enemy of mine and get away with it, do you? Think again!'

They braced themselves for a squall, but the salty old sea-shaker had something much worse in mind. One smack from his crashing hand –

and ship and crew were frozen, turned to stone in a twinkling together, anchored to the sea-bed, the ship and her petrified sailors now nothing more than a rock off Scheria, a rock whose shape bore witness to the crime of their convoy and Poseidon's eternal anger.

Safe? I'd woken up alone and unprotected on a home soil that was crawling with dangers. I wasn't even sure at first that I really was in Ithaca. The entire landscape was veiled in a mist, and I couldn't recognise a thing. I looked about me for the old familiar hill-tracks, the sleepy bays, the steep crags, the green trees of home. Where were they? What I couldn't see, being a mere mortal, was the goddess standing on the edge of the web, working her wonders. Pallas Athene had sent the mist to hide me. Sitting there beside a pile of treasure, I could easily have been robbed and murdered by the first bandits to happen along. And there was also the need to disguise me from the murderous suitors, and from my own wife and son, servants and subjects. Athene needed to allow me time to form a plan of action, to take the suitors by surprise and make them pay for their crimes. So she appeared before me as a handsome young shepherd, cloaked and sandalled and carrying a javelin, a likely looking lad. And when I asked where I was, the bright eyes mocked me gently. Only an idiot wouldn't know he was in Ithaca.

I could have cried on the shepherd's shoulder. But disguising my relief and explaining my ignorance, I spun a tangled yarn. I'd killed a man in Crete and had had to flee. This was after I'd fought at Troy. It had been a long campaign and I'd come back with all the spoils that were stacked now against that tree. The man I'd killed had tried to rob me of what I'd won, and one tar-black night I'd ambushed him and given him a breastful of bronze to remember me by in Hades. He never knew what hit him. After that I had boarded the first ship I could find – a Phoenician – and paid the captain to take me to Pylos or Elis, but they were driven off course and landed in Ithaca. They ditched me and my booty on shore and set sail for Sidon, leaving me to my treasures and my troubles.

'Old Odysseus still!'

I was studying the sand as I spun the yarn, as if deep in thought, and when I looked up the shepherd had turned into a tall beautiful woman, dazzling and accomplished, obviously a goddess. She was laughing at my story and congratulated me on it.

'But you're quite right to be so wary. This place may be home, but it's a death-trap for you if you reveal yourself, so listen to what I have to say.'

First she hid the gifts at the back of the cave, stashed well away in the gloom. Then she sat me down under the olive tree and brought me up to date with all that had happened in Ithaca over the past nineteen years, and what was going on now. Penelope had of course proved herself to be the soul of patience and piety, faithful to her long-absent husband, even though most folk openly pronounced him dead or at least unlikely to return.

This admirable stance of hers came at a price. She had suffered and was still suffering the agonies of not knowing for sure if she'd ever see me again, and not a dreary day nor slow night passed when she didn't wash her worries with her tears or bury her sorrowful head in her hands. Worse than that, for the last three years she'd been under intense pressure from her father to declare me dead, or missing presumed dead, and to re-marry. During these last years, she'd been hounded by a pack of wasters, idle young aristocrats, each of whom entertained high hopes of marrying her with tempting offers and becoming king in my place. Penelope was a beautiful woman on whom age had bestowed depth and desirability, but it was the potential power and not Penelope that spurred on these unprincipled profligates. Whoever controlled Penelope would control Ithaca. Technically, she was still married, but to a husband who was a war statistic or an accident at sea, either way long forgotten. And, either way, throne and bed were empty. Both needed to be filled.

For a long time, she'd kept this gang of wastrels at bay with a smart ruse, assuring them she'd marry, but only after she'd completed the weaving of a shroud for her husband's poor old father, Laertes, who was failing badly now and wasting away. The shroud had to be ready for his eventual demise, and though this was expected any day, still his body clung to life, though his spirit was long gone, a spirit extinguished by grief for his lost son.

Every day, Penelope wove this shroud – and each night she unravelled it again in secret, so that it was never finished. When one of her maids, a slut who was sleeping with a suitor, betrayed her, they confronted her with her trickery and insisted she make her choice. Again, she continued to procrastinate by giving encouraging signals to all of them while sending out secret messages to selected individuals – thus playing them off against each other. But they had grown wise to this stratagem too and were now demanding her decision. Time had almost run out for her.

It would have run out far earlier but for the fact that the spongers were having a high old time at my expense – slaughtering my beasts and lording it in my house and grounds, stuffing their fat paunches and swilling the best wines down the soft white necks that I now dreamed of slitting. They were out of control, living it up like locusts on the rampage, living on the fat of the land. My land. I burned with sudden blood-lust but also felt helpless and uncertain.

'What should I do?' I asked Athene.

'You don't have to do anything, not right now. I'll do it for you.'

She explained the first stages of the plan.

'First I'm going to wither your skin and snow white hairs on your head and in your beard, which I will tangle with knots and thorns. Then I'll drain the shine from your eyes till they're weak and watery and running with rheum. I'll give you a stoop and a stumbling step. I'll clothe you in the vilest rags, blackened by smoke and rotten to the nose. I'll crack your vocal chords so that your voice will be unrecognisable. I'll even alter your accent. Your own mother wouldn't be able to identify you, not even if you were to go back down to Hades and confront her. Nobody will know you.

'And now for the next part of the plan. Cutting this disreputable figure, beggar and vagabond, you'll go to the hut of your old swineherd – yes, that's right, Eumaeus, he's still alive, and about the only loyal servant you have left, for he's still attached to your memory and serves Penelope as best he can, though the suitors give the orders now, decimating your herds and running riot in the palace.

'You'll find Eumaeus pasturing the pigs out at the Raven's Crag and by the Springs of Arethusa. There they eat the acorns they love and drink deeply from the pools, fattening their carcasses for the gullets of the suitors. Go there now and introduce yourself, tramp as you are. He won't spurn you, and even as a stranger you'll get all the details from him, I promise you. He hates the mob that's now running the house and would do anything to see them ousted. Just don't give him any inkling of who you really are, that's all.'

'And you? What will you do? Are you going to leave me now? Where will you go?'

'I'm going to Sparta to bring back your son.'

'Telemachus – in Sparta? With Menelaus?'

'He hasn't given up hope, not altogether. You have to remember how long you've been away. That infant Palamedes put in front of the plough is now a young man trying to assert himself. And now that he's of age he's trying to take on the suitors and he's gone to Lacedaemon by way of Pylos to see if Nestor or Menelaus have any news of you, and to find out if there's any chance that you're still alive.'

'But it's a wasted journey. Menelaus won't have a clue what's happened to me since Troy. But you do. Why didn't you just tell the boy, instead of letting him go off chasing seabirds?'

'Because this trip will be good for him. Trust a goddess. Telemachus is a young man flexing his muscles and finding his feet. And he'll need to keep his wits about him. The suitors have sent out a ship of their own to intercept him. That's their plan – to ambush him on the return trip. They want him out of the way. That way it will be easier for one of them to marry Penelope and seize power. But don't look so worried! They won't get far with their plan. And if *our* plan succeeds, it won't be too long till their families are throwing the dirt over their dead heads.'

Take out the preternatural arrival, the petrification by Poseidon, the nymphs and shepherds, the cosy chat with Pallas Athene and the miraculous metamorphosis, goddess-provided, and that's roughly how things fell out. Which leaves very little in the way of truth. If Athene had really shown up to help me out, it would have been a first. As it was, I had to see to the disguise myself.

That wasn't so hard, being an old master of the art, added to which the freebooters that took me to Ithaca were in no hurry, and by the time they put me ashore I'd grown my hair and beard and smeared myself with ship's pitch and a lot more. I took on the bouquet of the bilge, the stench and speech of sea-dogs. I was revolting. Even the tars themselves gave me a wide berth. By the time my feet touched terra firma, a dog wouldn't have given me the time of day.

Or so I thought.

In any case, I didn't need a goddess to tell me to check out the lie of the land. There was no question of turning up and throwing open the door on Penelope. Greetings, I'm home from hell. Home from hell? I'd fucked all and sundry – so why wouldn't she have too? Time cools your bedsheets, and what woman doesn't want a man who can feel and see? Not a cold ghost or a pile of bones on some lonely shore. And look what happened to Agamemnon. Home from the wars to a good hot bath of his own blood, murdered by a bitch and a bastard. One hell of a homecoming, that bloodbath, comeuppance or not. I'd heard various versions of it on the long route home, but they all ended the same way – bloodily. Not wanting Agamemnon's reception, I was coming in by the back door.

I climbed up the old stony mountain path through the forest, feeling more of a revenant than a returner. A soldier's ghost. I was making for the hut of my old steward, Eumaeus, the pigman, not even knowing whether or not he was still alive.

He was. He was sitting on his own in the porch, cutting himself a pair of sandals from an oxhide. Everything looked pretty much the same, except for the courtyard he'd constructed around the homestead, built of solid quarried stone and hedged all along the top of the wall with wild pear, with a stockade running all the way round outside, forming an extra protection. It was a good sign. He was a tough old bugger, and he'd been busy in my absence. He had twelve sties safe inside the yard, a good fifty sows and their litters to a sty, with the boars outside, and four watch-dogs on guard, savage looking bastards. I had to suppress my instinct to go right in and congratulate him on his work. I hung back, thinking that if I could recognise him so easily, maybe he'd see straight through my disguise.

I didn't have the time to debate it. The four brutes twitched and sprang up and flew at me, all teeth and slavers. I dropped my staff and sat down fast on my arse to appease the bastards. It didn't stop their charge, and I'd have been shredded if Eumaeus hadn't dashed out and checked them.

'That was a close call, old man,' he panted. 'Are you all right?'

I said I was in one piece, and I was glad that all he saw was a broken-down old beggar. So far the camouflage was working.

'They'd have ripped your throat out in two seconds – they're bad buggers. But that's what they're for; they earn their keep. You'd better come in.'

He took me in and sat me down on a brushwood seat, which he covered with a thick goatskin. I reckoned it was his mattress. He brought out bread and wine.

'Now then, sup up. And once you've seen off your hunger and thirst, we'll eat properly and you can tell me all your troubles. You look as if you've been through a few.'

I'd not come short on sorrows in my time, I had to agree. 'But it's great to be given good hospitality. Your employer's a lucky man to own you.'

He shook his head and spat. 'Lucky? And I'd be fucking lucky too, if I had an employer. He'd have pensioned me off by now with something better than this. A nice bit of land – and a beddable wife to go with it, know what I mean? That's what he'd have done, if he'd stayed in Ithaca.'

'And why didn't he?'

'Because he went to fucking Troy, that's why, like the rest of his generation that got sucked into that pointless fucking war.'

I ventured the suggestion that bringing back Helen was maybe not so pointless. I wanted to hear what he would say. He got up and stamped around the little hut.

'I'm amazed you'd even consider that point of view, my friend. They got sucked in by lies, I'm telling you, leaders' fucking crap. Odysseus knew it well enough, but there was fuck all he could do to avoid it. Every cunt knew what that war was about. What's any war about? Expansion, envy, avarice, prejudice, power. Helen? Helen my arse. She needed her crack filled, and she filled the young men's mouths with dust. She was a good excuse, that's all. What's a tart worth to the towers of Troy? No fucking comparison. You'll have to excuse me, old chum, I get steamed up when I think of my master lying dead out there – and all for the sake of the glory boys and the greed. And yet why should I care if kings rot or return? I should care if it rains, that's all. Kings are clouds blown by the winds, well over my head.'

I started to mutter an apology, but he stopped me.

'No – my job, apologies. Here you were about to tell me your troubles, and what do I do? I start spitting out mine like a madman and an arse. Pardon me, and let's make up with a fucking good feed.'

He took two young porkers and killed them and singed them in no time, then he chopped and skewered and soon had the joints roasted on the spits then served up piping hot with a good sprinkling of white barley. He put a crude olive-wood bowl in front of me and mixed in the water and wine. He handed me a cup.

'I'd give you better, friend, but the best around here gets eaten up by that pack of lazy, lickerish dogs who call themselves suitors. That's a fucking pretext for idleness and ambition, even leaving the lechery out of it. Suitors? Cunt-sniffers and upper-crusters, every single one of them. They won't leave my mistress alone.'

'Can you blame them for that?'

'She's a fine-looking woman, it's true – but they're shits to a man.'

I kept my face hidden in the bowl.

'Are any of them in bed with her?'

Eumaeus shrugged.

'How would I know? She seems to keep them at bay right enough, the bastards, but who knows what goes on in the dark between the sheets. Some nights they say there's at least one of them doesn't go home.'

'Any one in particular?'

'Well, there's Amphinomous; she's supposed to be fond of him. And Eurymachus, the richest of the bastards. Then there's Antinous, but he's a complete cunt. I don't know. Sometimes there's more than one at a time, if you know what I mean. That's just fucking tongue-wagging, of course. But some of her maids are having it off with them, that I know for a fact. And a woman has needs like a man, doesn't she? And if her husband's dead, what does it matter?'

'Does she think he's dead?'

'How do I know what she thinks? Does she know what she thinks? Half the time I don't know what I fucking think myself. Do you know what you think?'

I said I thought Odysseus was still alive.

'They all say that.'

'Who's they?'

'All the tramps and roadsters.'

'But what would you say if I told you I had reason to believe it? I mean hard evidence.'

Eumaeus spoke quietly.

'Beggar as you are, I'm going to beg *you* – don't, please, come out with that one. It's got a beard by now. Every wanderer who pitches up here turns out to have seen Odysseus. Or they've heard he's still alive or he's about to reappear. But not one of them has ever come up with the hard evidence you say you have, at least not hard enough to convince his widow. She'll listen to what you have to say all right, and she'll get upset, as women do when they hear their loved ones may have survived the war, when they know in their hearts they're just as dead as they can be. This one is a story without an ending, and somebody is always keeping it going, and all for the sake of a square meal and some wine to wash it down. Give enough detail and you'll even get a tunic with a nugget sewn in, and a cloak to keep out the next winter. You wouldn't believe how many Odysseuses have been sighted in different countries at the same time – a dozen true stories and every one a lie. So don't even think about adding another, don't stoop to it, there's no need. I'm telling you for sure, Odysseus is a corpse, a dismembered one. Dogs will have eaten him long ago and the birds will have pecked his bones nice and clean. They're out there on some shore and his ribs are letting in the rain. Or they're deep beneath the sands of some barren beach. Or they're rolling in the ocean. What difference does it make? If he'd been given a proper burial, we'd have been sent word about the barrow long ago. But we never heard a thing about it, and that's because there's nothing to hear. He's got no mound. He's a lost soul. He went out to fight and never came back and never will. It's as simple as that. I can't make it any clearer, can I? I'll never see him again.'

A long speech. A short silence.

'And if you did?'

'Won't you give up? If I did see him again I'd die happy, that's all. Sometimes I do see him, you know.'

'You do?'

'Yes, and then I wake up. Every fucking time.'

'Listen,' I said, 'you're not dreaming now, are you? And nor was I when I heard news of him. I totally agree with you about the tramps and their tales, but I'm not like that, and I hate the guts of those lying bastards who'd wring a widow's heart to earn a crust. I may be poor, but I've got more self-respect than that. All the same, I'll claim a reward from you if I may – call it a bet – when Odysseus returns. As return he will. A new rig-out would suit me best, as you can see. What do you think? Is there any chance of it?'

Eumaeus laughed out loud.

'You're a persistent bugger, aren't you? More bugger than beggar if you ask me. But let's hear you out. I'm sure it'll make for good listening. As to the rig-out, if I had the means, I'd see to it right now, though it's one reward I know I'll never have to pay.'

So I spun the swineherd a long and tangled tale of my adventures. They included a seven-year sojourn in Egypt, and they were so detailed I almost believed all of it myself. That wasn't so difficult. Like all good lies, they had a basis in truth. I said I was a Cretan (false) who'd fought at Troy (true) and that after various other exploits I'd been shipwrecked on the coast of Thesprotia (true and false), where I'd learned that Odysseus was still alive (false and true). The Thesprotian king had assured me on his own authority that Odysseus, whom he'd met, had gone to Dodona and was thinking about how to approach Ithaca, possibly in some sort of disguise. In the end I was betrayed by some sailor scum who'd been ordered to take me to Dulichium but fleeced me instead, the bastards, and would have done for me if I hadn't escaped. I swam to safety, hid in a thicket and finally made my way to the hut of an extremely decent swineherd. Now what was it they called him?'

Eumaeus laughed even louder.

'I think you're destined to be a survivor, my friend.'

'Then so is Odysseus, I would say.'

'And so you reached Ithaca just before him, eh? Well, it's quite a story, and I believe it too. Not every word, mind you – it's the bits about Odysseus that don't ring true, but I don't think you're doing it to curry favour with me. On the contrary I think you genuinely want to please me out of the goodness of your heart, and that's why you embroider your exploits so attractively. You'd like to give me hope. It's not necessary, though, believe me. I learned to live without hope a long time ago. Same with lady luck – we got a divorce. I told you already, if Odysseus had been killed in action, the whole nation would have built him a mound by now, and a splendid one too, for all the world to see. No, he's an unknown soldier in an unmarked grave. Or he's beach debris, sea-drift. The storm-fiends have spirited him away. Wherever he is, he's not on Ithaca.'

I decided to persist a little longer.

'You've been bloody good to me, sir, and if it turns out that I'm lying, I want you to have me thrown from the cliffs as a warning to other cheats and liars. In fact, I insist on it.'

That made the swineherd chuckle.

'No way to treat a guest, especially one who tells such sweet lies, and so well meant. But come on, let's eat up again. The men are coming back with the beasts.'

The air was soon full of the cursing of herdsmen and the grunting of swine. Eumaeus shouted to them to quieten down and bring in the fattest boar in my honour.

'We don't usually allow ourselves such luxuries. The choicest cuts go down the gullets of those fucking gallivanters at the palace. But tonight is different, you're my guest. And I reckon we'll do the scumbags out of one fine meal at least.'

At the dinner he did the carving himself and personally saw to it that I was awarded a special slice from the whole length of the chine. It was a great spread and a good mood settled over the hut, the workers tired but well fed, a little sleepy with wine and pleasantly relaxed in the crackling firelight. The night closed in black and stormy and a wet west wind sprang up. I heard ghosts in the rain – it was that sort of weather. They were the ghosts of old friends, all those comrades who'd fallen at the gates of Troy, on her beaches, and on the windy ringing plains. And those others who'd vanished into the ocean's endless belly.

That was the point at which the depressing emptiness opens up, the moment when whatever you're holding slips from your hand and you ask yourself the oldest question in the world: what's the fucking point? Nothing matters. It never has mattered, never will. And all those friends you knew died out there for nothing in a war without a cause, their lives as weary and meaningless as the wind. The night rain is filled with their aimless ghosts.

Luckily, one of the workers, a nice young lad, changed the atmosphere for me.

'You fought at Troy, they say. I wonder, could you give us some idea of what it was like? Any story at all. It would be great to get an eyewitness view, a first-hand account.'

Murmurs of appreciation. It gave me an idea, and I decided to give the lad his story, a good one with a touch of mischief in it. Old soldiers never die.

'Troy, you say? Old Troy town. Fucking hell, that takes me back. I wish I were as young and fit as I was that night.'

'What night was that?'

'Oh, it was the night we led the surprise offensive on the city. That was some night, I don't mind telling you. Odysseus and Menelaus were leading the attack and I was third in command. You wouldn't think it to look at me now, would you? But war is like time — it has a way of making you look and feel like shit.

'Anyway, it was winter, and when we came up to those walls in the dark — fuck me! The way they towered above and frowned down on you, so fucking solid and massive, making you feel so small. You felt Troy could never be taken, would never be taken, not ever. We fell back a bit and lay down in our armour among the marshland reeds. These plains were like soup in winter, and this was some fucking winter. There was a north wind blowing, but it dropped all of a sudden and one of those quiet frosts came down — you know the sort I mean; it's cruel because it's so fucking quiet, you know what I'm talking about, I mean a wind you can understand, like a sword coming at you, something you can duck, get out of the way of, but that soundless frost — it's like a fucking ghost.

'After that the snow fell. Another soundless attack, the silent fucking enemy again, thick white flakes in their millions, bitterly cold, blizzards of the stuff. An enemy makes himself heard, for fuck's sake; you get used to the noise of combat. It's the fucking silence, I tell you, that's what I can't stand. Then the ice piled up, thick on our shields. We were using them as shelters, extra protection, except I didn't even have a cloak, did I? I'd left it back at base, not thinking it would get so cold. That's what kills you in the field too often.'

'The cold?'

'No, not thinking. Anyway, by the third watch I was desperate. The stars had wheeled well round. The Great Bear was arse over tit. Odysseus was stretched out next to me. I gave him a dig in the ribs, and he sat up at once. That's what I liked about old Odysseus. Ask him about something, anything, any time of the day or night, and he was all ears. He always had his wits about him.

'"Hey, Odysseus," I said, "I could use your help. My arse is a slab and my prick's an icicle. My balls are about to drop off. It's a stiff you'll have next to you soon, and a fat lot of use I'll be to you when we attack."

'"And what exactly do you want me to do?"

'"Anything, only make it quick!"

'To be honest, I thought he might have lent me his cloak, but not him, not Odysseus. Instead — and this was typical of the old schemer — he turned and whispered to the rest of the company.

'"Wake up, lads. It's occurred to me that we've come too far from the ships. We're vulnerable, too small a contingent. I need somebody to take a message to the commander and request reinforcements, right away. But he's got to be a good runner. Any volunteers?"

'There was a young fellow called Thoas lying close to us. He was one of those death-or-glory types and one hell of a runner, a real action man. He hated doing nothing, and he was probably freezing his balls off like the rest of us and glad of the chance to warm up. Anyway, he accepted the commission and shot off, leaving his cloak behind, of course, for ease and speed.

'"Will you look at that," said Odysseus. "Somebody's left a cloak lying about. As it seems to be going a-begging, you might as well have it and keep warm, don't you think?"

'That was Odysseus for you. He would have missed his own cloak so he got somebody else's for me. He never missed a trick. I was never so glad to get a cloak.'

Every man was snoring by the time I finished – except Eumaeus.

'A great yarn, friend, and I nearly believed it. I bet you nearly believed it yourself.'

I spread my arms wide.

'A great bid for a cloak too. I'll tell you what, we don't have any spares here, and nobody's got the wits of Odysseus either, but if you can manage in your rags for the rest of the night, we'll see what happens in the morning. Odysseus's son might be back from Sparta.'

'Telemachus?'

'Yes, he went off in search of his father, for news of him. His ship's due back in port any day now, and he'll see that you're properly kitted out before he sends you on your way. In the meantime, you won't go cold.'

He rose and made me a bed of fleeces right next to the fire, and he gave me an especially thick cover which he kept for cold snaps. But he left the fire himself after a while and went out well wrapped up to sleep in the cold night air, close to the herd, javelin in hand.

'I'll just keep an eye on them,' he said. 'I can sleep with the other eye.'

I smiled to myself to see how attentive he was to his duties, just as if his old master were watching him.

Which he was.

And yet this decent old man thought I was far away and never coming back, a handful of white dust in the black earth or scattered bones at the bottom of the world, under the deep sea.

🗗.

FORTY-NINE

Telemachus's trip to Pylos and Sparta had been arranged on high, long before the return to Ithaca. Penelope gave her son the highest profile on the web, paving the way for his dramatic meeting with his father. It started with a conversation among the gods, up on the blue heights. After Pallas Athene had spoken to Zeus, the goddess decreed that the youth was old enough to imitate his father by putting out to sea in search of him, or at least some news of him, and she sped down from Olympus to offer inspiration.

He needed it. She found both him and Ithaca in a bad way, with the suitors swaggering about giving orders, openly groping the maids and stuffing themselves like pigs. The palace tables were awash with wine, and the music and dancing went on non-stop – they were forcing Phemius, the court bard, to play for them. Telemachus was sitting apart from them, a spiritless specimen, and he unburdened himself to the new arrival, Mentes, the Taphian chieftain. At least he thought he did. Mentes was none other than Pallas Athene in disguise.

'Just look at them, stranger, with their draughts and their dancing and the obscene amount they're wolfing down and putting away, slaughtering my father's fatted cattle and swilling it back with the best wine. What on earth do you think of this place? I'd be interested in your opinion, as a newcomer.'

Mentes agreed that it was distasteful.

'And immoral,' said Telemachus. 'And cowardly – living it up on the back of a man who can do nothing about it because his bones are festering in the rain under the godless skies. Or they're tumbling in the cold ocean. And if by any remote chance he's alive and unable to get home, there isn't a man for miles around who isn't trying to take his place. From Dulichium they come, from Same, from leafy Zacynthus, and from every crevice in rocky Ithaca, yes, the lice are crawling out of the woodwork. They're courting my mother and ripping through the finances, and there's nothing I can do about it. I'd go to the people but I'd get no help from them. The rich families among them are actually encouraging their brats to try their luck here, and they control the peasants, who can't be arsed anyway. Some of them don't remember

Odysseus, and most of them care even less. If he came back now they wouldn't blink an eye. But he won't.'

The goddess erupted in indignation, with such a bright blaze of anger she nearly gave the game away.

'Shame on you! Can't you confront this gang of thieves? How can you be so sure that your father isn't coming back either? Have you seen these white bones of his? Have you rolled with them in the ocean? Have you lain with them on the sea-bed? Have you held his ashes in your fist? Have you stood on his grave and planted his oar in the earthen mound? If not, then how can you say for certain that he's dead? And if he does come back suddenly and gets among that lot, I wouldn't give much for their chances, whatever their numbers. It would be a quick death and a grim wedding for the whole gang of them. He'd marry them all right, but it's Persephone they'd be wedded to, not Penelope.'

There was a flicker of a smile from Telemachus. And Athene fanned the little flame.

'Of course, all that lies in the lap of the gods, who could be closer to you than you think. But meanwhile, listen to my advice, as a man of experience. Starting tomorrow, when they're all sobered up, take matters into your own hands. Tell them to quit the palace and tell your mother to go back to her father – remove the temptation from the scene. Very likely she will refuse to go, but it will show everybody you mean business. As for you, take a twenty-oared ship and sail to Pylos to see old Nestor, and then go on to Sparta to red-haired Menelaus. He was the last of the Greeks to make it home, and he may know something. Nestor always knows things. If you discover that your father's dead, then that's it – your mother is free to re-marry, and you can rid the place of this scum. In any case, you're a man now and it's up to you to seize the day. Be like Orestes, why can't you? Man, what a name he made for himself when he killed that adulterous traitor who murdered his father. You could be the new Orestes, the Ithacan Avenger, the Suitors' Nemesis. You'll be a song of the centuries. Think about it.'

And the goddess left him to do so, flitting like a bird through a slit in the roof, back to Olympus. The young man now knew he'd been with a god and felt the change. He was inspired.

So was Phemius the bard. He was singing about the Greeks coming back from the war and about all their sufferings under the gods. The lyrics drifted up to Penelope in her lofty chamber, and the lyre strings plucked at the old wounds. Down she came, down the steep staircase, flanked by two loyal maids and masking her face from the suitors. But then the sobs shook her and the company witnessed her tear-stained cheeks.

'Phemius,' she cried, 'no more of that! You know it kills my heart when I hear it, for it comes too close to home and cuts me to the bone for my absent husband whose name sounds through the land from Hellas to the heart of Argos.'

Much to everybody's surprise, Telemachus cut in.

'A poet, mother, must sing as the spirit moves him, and not at the behest of a bunch of thugs who care more for their bellies than for the arts. You have to accept that a sad song will sear the heart but also open the mind. And it is a shut mind that is the enemy of art. Be brave and keep your mind open, including the possibility that my father may yet return and loosen the bowels of that lot over there. And if he doesn't — well, he wasn't the only one to be destroyed by Troy. That war was the end of thousands of men. But if he does come back, you'd better shut your ears and eyes to what will happen. Best go to bed then — it could even happen tonight.'

Surprise shaded into astonishment and anger among the suitors.

'Who's lit a fire under this impudent young pup all of a sudden?'

But Penelope went back up to bed as advised and lay weeping for her husband till Pallas Athene closed her weary eyes in sleep. Meanwhile, down among the shadows, the suitors muttered about the change in Telemachus and showed their bravado by boasting that no offspring from Penelope's belly would keep them out of her bed for much longer.

'Who's going to be the one to share it, eh?'

'Maybe more than one.'

'Maybe two at a time? Or even three?'

'Why stop at three?'

'Who's for going up there right now and giving her a good seeing to? We'd soon hear her sing to a different tune, and it wouldn't be Troy!'

The coarse talk continued into the small hours. But eventually the last of the bunch staggered drunkenly home and Telemachus went up to bed, escorted by the torch-bearing Eurycleia, whom his grandfather Laertes had brought home long ago when she was a girl for the price of twenty oxen. He had never slept with her for fear of displeasing his wife, and she had been nurse to Telemachus — and before that Odysseus as a child. Now she secured Telemachus's door and left him planning out in his mind all night long the journey Pallas Athene had devised for him.

Early next morning he called an Assembly of the Ithacan leaders, in which he was supported by the venerable Aegyptius. The elder statesman didn't know it yet, but his soldier son, Antiphus, who had sailed with Odysseus, was the last crew member to be eaten by the savage Cyclops in his cave. But he did know already in his heart that his son was dead, and it was with tears in his eyes for that lost son that he now begged from the leaders a hearing for the son of his king.

Telemachus went straight to the point.

'You all know what's been going on here in the palace with that mob of lazy wasters practically hanging round my mother's neck and using their so-called courting as an excuse to justify their sponging and their lust for power. They could have approached her father formally and correctly, but instead they've elected to fleece me of my inheritance, eat us out of house and home and drink us dry. Suitors? They're scum, filthy parasites. Yes, my masters, it's your sons I'm talking about — many of them here among us. In the name of shame, and for decency's sake, I ask you to call them off and let them go back to frittering away their own inheritances instead of mine, and to squandering their own estates — your estates — if that's the way you're happy for them to behave. And if you won't do it, then I will. I'm giving them formal notice to quit my house — now!'

Telemachus finished speaking, flung his staff on the ground, and burst into tears.

Silence.

The leaders had never heard a word from him in public, let alone an outburst like this. Nobody knew quite what to say. At last Antinous, the chief parasite, replied on behalf of the suitors. His face was dark with rage.

'That was some speech, Telemachus, ugly and spiteful as it was! And I'm telling you right here and now we won't accept it. Everybody knows it's not us to blame, it's your mother. You know very well what I'm referring to, don't you?'

Of course, the old story, Penelope's shroud for Laertes, the winding-sheet that got wound down by night, spun up again by day and wound down again in the dark, night after night until the ruse was discovered.

'Well now we're calling her bluff. And yours, Telemachus. The years of nocturnal unravelling are over, my boy, and she's been made to finish the web. Now you can send her back to her father, if that's what you want, and let the pair of them make the choice and reach a decision, instead of this endless shilly-shallying. That's what's eating up your estate, young fellow, not our greed, or lust, or politics, but your mother's devious and infernal procrastination.'

Applause, loud and prolonged — which did not perturb Telemachus in the least.

'So, Antinous, you ask me to push my mother out into the street, do you? A fine thing for a man to do to the mother who bore him. Would you do it? Yes, very likely you would. But I'm not tarred with your brush. Carry on as you are, then, do as you are doing, fatten yourselves up for the kill. You'll be so soft and fat you won't be able to lift a finger — wait till I cut you down in the house you're trying your best to ruin with your profligacy and riot!'

'What the —?'

There would indeed have been a riot if Zeus hadn't capped that stirring speech by sending down a couple of eagles to wheel about the meeting place right above everybody's heads. Down the wind they swooped and screamed, wing to wing, feathertips touching, and with terror in their eyes. Then they started ripping into each other with beaks and talons as they swung off eastward over the rooftops of the town, over the sounding sea. The whole Assembly stood stunned into silence, till one of the elders, Haliserthes, made a pronouncement. He was a scholarly soothsayer and a respected birdlorist.

'Friends, you've seen the portent with your own eyes, and it is a portent. Now I shall interpret it, and advise these suitors accordingly. A day of doom is approaching for them and for us all. Odysseus is close. And if these young men wish to avoid disaster, they should go back to their homes while they can and never set foot in the palace again. Indeed, we ought to compel them to this course of action. Even then they may not escape what's coming to them.'

Some of the suitors went green about the gills, but their other spokesman, Eurymachus, stood up to the prophet and saved the day for them. So they thought.

'Off you totter, old man. Your grandchildren are waiting for a story. You can give them the one you've just told us, the one about the birds — which, by the way, go about their business in the clear skies without a thought in their feathered heads for us. What they do has absolutely no bearing on human affairs, except in your superstitious old skull. We don't buy your divinations and your pathetic mumblings. Odysseus? Pity you didn't go to Troy and perish alongside him. Why didn't you warn him not to go if you're so clever? A goose could have told him! But now you'll be expecting a backhander from Telemachus for sucking up to him against us. Let me tell you something: your speech just now was an incitement to violence, and if that happens you'll face the consequence — a hefty fine, one that will break your heart besides your back. Have you got that? Now get out of here before you come to harm!'

There was applause from the cronies. Haliserthes turned away, subdued. Eurymachus carried on.

'As for you, Telemachus, here's my advice. We're supporting Antinous's perfectly reasonable proposal to you to send your mother back to her father and let them sort out a wedding between them. Until that happens, we're staying in the palace, and we don't care what you think about it. Do you see us shaking in our sandals? A milksop and a greybeard? No, you don't scare us with your rhetoric, or with your daft prophecies, for that matter. Here we are, and here we stay. And unless Penelope stops giving us the runaround and acts honestly and responsibly, we're going nowhere, and neither are you, pipsqueak, because there will be no inheritance for you, my lad. We'll eat you all up!'

Roars of approval from the youngsters and applause from the elders. And an end to Telemachus's little rebellion, crushed in its infancy, or so they imagined, little knowing that a goddess was giving him speech.

'Going nowhere, am I? That's where you're wrong, Eurymachus. The fact is, I'm going to Pylos, and to Sparta. And I'm going tomorrow. I want a speedy vessel and twenty good men to crew her, and I'm going to find out once and for all about my father. Somebody must know something. If I find Odysseus is dead, I'll build him a mound and my mother can re-marry. If he's still alive somewhere, then I might just resign myself to your daylight robbery for a little longer – until he returns to rip out your livers and throw your noses to the dogs! That's it. The people have heard my case. I've no more to say.'

'But I have!' shouted old Mentor above the uproar. 'I want to say that I don't give much thought to these suitors – it's their own necks they're sticking out, and if they're for the chop, fair enough, that's their affair. They've been asking for it. Why should we care if they come to a bad end? No, I reserve my rage for you spineless individuals who've been letting them get away with it. Even now, you've kept your mouths shut, with never a word of reproval or restraint, not a syllable. In my mind, you're even guiltier than them. They're in the minority, and you have the numbers and the authority to control them, yet you let the abuse continue. How can you call yourselves leaders?'

Up sprang Leiocritus. 'I've heard enough of this inflammatory talk against us. It's just as Eurymachus has said – here we are, and here we remain, until Penelope puts an end to this procrastination.'

'And if Odysseus does appear?' asked Mentor.

'And what if he does? Are we going to run from a broken-down old veteran? Maybe with one eye by now, an arm missing, or a leg, or whatever's left of him? A bunch of young bloods like us? I think we'd see him off soon enough, if he even had the nerve to take us on. Penelope may have missed him in bed, but she'll get little action between the sheets from a corpse – which is what he'll be in the very first minute if he really thinks he can take on all of us at once. He can't. It doesn't matter what he did at Troy, or what he says he did, or what he thinks he did. We're just too many for him here, so let's relax. And by all means, let Telemachus go stravaiging off to Sparta if that's what he wants. He's got the time to waste, and the cruise might bring him to his senses. Maybe the sea air will do him good, clear his mind. I know exactly what we're going to do. We're going back to the palace right now and we're going to order up the biggest banquet ever for tonight. We're going to feed like fighting cocks!'

The meeting dispersed, leaving Telemachus to seek the solace of the shore, where the sounding sea pounded the sands and ground the shingle. He looked out helplessly over the grey waste. He'd tried his best, but he'd been bullied and thwarted at every turn. He wetted his hands in the bubbling surf and held them high over his head, lifted in prayer.

Athene heard him and came at once. She appeared in the person of Mentor, but he knew who it really was.

'Telemachus, take heart. You've spoken well today and you're no milksop. Most sons are pale shadows of their fathers, but you're a credit to yours. The suitors? They're fools and dead men. Forget them, their days are numbered. Go back home, ignore them, let them tie the noose tighter round their miserable necks. Their end will be bloody, believe me. And tomorrow, set sail. Don't worry, I'll pick a crew for you and rig out the ship. You see to the provisions. By sunrise I want you well away, out on the open sea.'

The words of the goddess struck fire from Telemachus. When he reached home, he found the suitors skinning and singeing goats and fatted hogs, preparing for yet another riotous night at the palace's expense. Antinous, who'd had a few drinks already, tried to offer him one to calm him down and charm him into a spirit of camaraderie, but Telemachus cut him dead.

'No, Antinous, I gave you your chance, and you threw it back in my teeth. Now I'm going to let loose all hell on you, either from here or from Pylos or Sparta. You've been warned.'

Hoots, curses, howls of derision.

'We're trembling.'

'My hair's turning white.'

'He's up to no good, that lad.'

'Bollocks. He's all bluff.'

'He's asking for it.'

'You heard him say it: he wants our blood.'

'We should have his – before he gets Nestor's men to come and cut our throats.'

'Or sets the Spartans on us.'

'Maybe he's off to the faraway islands, on the lookout for charms and drugs to spike our drinks.'

'And rub us out while we're sleeping it off.'

'Or perhaps he'll pay a visit to the poison people in Ephyre, then slip us something really deadly that'll do for us in one go, lay us all out cold, ready for our shrouds.'

'We'd better do for him first, then.'

'Yes, it's a bad business when your host won't drink with you because he's thirsty for your blood instead.'

'Self-confessed. A would-be murderer. It's the motive that counts.'

'It's in his heart.'

'It's in his blood.'

'Just like his old man.'

'But just like him, he might get lost at sea and never come back.'

'Another useless sailor.'

'A chip off the old block. Couldn't even find his way back home.'

'Back to Ithaca.'

'And that's what'll happen to the sprog.'

'You can count on it.'

'Especially if we were to make it happen.'

'If we went after him, for instance.'

'Or lay in wait for him.'

'We'd soon cut short his sudden taste for sea travel.'

'Then we'd have to go to the trouble of sharing out all his property among us.'

'What a nuisance, eh?'

'What a chore!'

'Some father.'

'Some son.'

A voice whispered in Telemachus's ear.

'Let them gibber – it's what they do; it's all they're good for. Soon they'll be gibbering for mercy. And there'll be none given. Then they'll just be gibbering ghosts. It's all over for them.'

So Telemachus left them to get drunker still and to brag in their cups. He called on Eurycleia and told her his plan, asking her to help him prepare the provisions for the next day's voyage, the jars of oil, the amphoras of old rich wine, the copper keg of honey, the wheat, the barley and bronze.

The faithful old crone burst into tears. 'My poor little mite, what madness is this? Who put this scheme into your noodle? It will never work, this voyage of yours. Your father never came home from the sea. Do you want to imitate a dead man? You won't last five minutes, I tell you. The minute they see the back of you, these louts will be plotting your downfall. They'll stab you in the back first chance they get. Don't give it to them. Stay where you are and keep an eye on them. My god, they could follow you in a ship of their own, launch a surprise attack and sink you like a stone, with only the seagulls as witnesses – and the fishes, who have no tongues. Don't do it, I beg you.'

Telemachus put his arms around his old nurse and wiped away her tears. 'Listen, old mother, you've no call to worry about me. I'm not worried about myself. Do you know why? A goddess watches over me. A bright-eyed goddess with golden hair.'

And indeed Athene was always either at his elbow, or she was bustling about town disguised as Telemachus himself, appearing with such a blaze of authority that there was no lack of volunteers, and each one of the twenty crewmen felt honoured to be sailing with the king's son, young as he was. Everything was arranged before nightfall. The goddess ran the ship into the black water, stowed all the gear, moored her, assembled the crew and issued their orders. After that, she returned to the palace and lulled the suitors into a state of sleepiness and drunken stupor that had them keeling over the benches, the wine cups slipping from their fingers. Asleep on their unsteady feet, they staggered off home.

Eurycleia was sworn to secrecy. Penelope was not to know what her son was up to, not for a dozen days at least, unless she found out on the palace grapevine. And Telemachus now left the palace and made his way down to the shore, where the long-haired crew manned the vessel and awaited his orders. They cast off the hawsers, sat down on the benches and prepared to pull on the oars of polished pine.

They didn't have to. Out of the west came a sudden wind, called up by the bright-haired goddess of the flashing eyes. The wind thumped the stern of the ship and sent it bobbing out onto deep water, singing across the wine-dark sea, plunging and coursing through the waves, hissing like a snake. All hands on deck. They hauled up the mast and hoisted the sail, pulling on the plaited ropes of dark oxhide. And now, hit by the wind, the sail swelled like a pregnant woman in the marketplace, proudly presenting her big belly as she strides steady-footed among all the round-eyed virgins who have never been struck by the seed. So the wind now struck the ship, speeding her through the choppy waters all night long and into the pink streamers of the dawn as she ploughed her way to Pylos.

🔲

FIFTY

In Pylos, the citadel was sending up its early morning smoke, and the appetising aroma of roast meat scented the air. Nestor's people were assembled on the beach, offering up jet-black bulls to Poseidon. Nine companies, five hundred men to a company, and each offering nine bulls. Nestor was doing Poseidon proud. The old charioteer of Gerenian fame was a busy man this morning, but his etiquette never left him. As soon as he saw the trim ship and the strangers disembarking, he had them brought to the feast, seating them on fleeces on the sands and putting into their tired hands refreshing wine cups, sparkling gold and brimming with the best wine.

When he understood that his guests were from Ithaca and that he was looking at the grown-up son of his old comrade, Odysseus, the old man lapsed into nostalgia, not unmingled with bitterness. Telemachus urged him to tell him all he knew.

'Troy. My god, what scenes that name evokes! What memories! What men! But I'd be lying if I didn't admit to the miseries we Greeks suffered there on the misty seas, on the windy plains, under the wheels of the Trojan charioteers and the rain of their archers – though I fancy we were superior spearmen and better at the hand-to-hand. Even so, we couldn't bring them down. Our best men fell before those walls, or were wounded – Ajax, Achilles, Patroclus, my own lovely boy Antilochus, who was so dear to me and was the swiftest of them all, so fleet of foot and such a brave fighter. And now the light-footed lad lies out there all alone and far from home. Oh yes, it was a costly war, and it broke our hearts. And after nine years the city still stood. But in the tenth year, your father came up with the stratagem of the wooden horse and brought the proud towers tumbling down. We sacked the city and sailed for home. And that was nine years ago, nearly ten.'

The old soldier fell into a pensive silence and wiped away a tear. Telemachus cleared his throat and gently suggested that as the story was so stirring, he might be good enough to take it up again, possibly with some news of his father. Nestor said he would get to that part.

He took his time over it, telling the whole story of how Athene had sparked the bitter quarrel between the sons of Atreus, so that

Agamemnon stayed on at Troy, while the rest of the fleet, laden with spoils and captive women, their girdles round their hips, sailed for home, Nestor himself along with Diomedes – with Menelaus, now split from his brother, following in their wake.

'He caught us up at Lesbos. We were wavering there, unsure about our best route. Should we opt for the long passage along the rugged coast of Chios and so on by the isle of Psyrie, keeping it to port, or should we cut inside Chios instead, past the windy heights of Mimas? We prayed for guidance, and the gods gave us the answer: sail straight across the open sea to Euboea and escape danger. It was a good answer. Menelaus joined us and we all whistled down the freeways of the fish and made Geraestus in the dark.

'On the fourth day, Diomedes anchored in Argos. I kept my own course for Pylos. The Myrmidons reached Phthia, Idomeneus arrived in Crete without a casualty, and the sea took nothing either from Philoctetes, not a man lost, except all those who had not survived the war.'

'And Odysseus?'

Telemachus nudged the remembering veteran as politely as possible, at the same time hoping to coax the precious words out of the remembering mouth.

'Ah, Odysseus, yes – no, he'd left us by that time. We were all at loggerheads, you see, and he turned his twelve ships round at Tenedos.'

'Why did he do that?'

'He decided to renew his allegiance to Agamemnon, so he swung the curved prows round and sailed back to Troy. Then I was split up from Menelaus. We never quarrelled, but we were just off the Cape of Sunium, where Attica impends on the sea, when Phoebus Apollo aimed an arrow at Phrontis.'

'Phrontis?'

'Menelaus's helmsman. He was holding the steering oar at the time, and the ship was driving hard, but he just dropped down dead, struck by the gentle dart, and although Menelaus needed to press on, he wasn't prepared to drop the body overboard. He'd been the best of steersmen and had guided the ship through many a gale, so Menelaus held on at Sunium in order to allow the man a proper burial.

'That was bad timing, as it turned out, because when he was under way again a gale got up. He'd reached the steep frowning brow of Malea when the seas lifted like mountains and the fleet was divided. One lot were dashed to Crete and the Cydonians, along the Iardanus. Do you know where Gortyn ends? There's a sheer rock out there, and the south-westerlies whip in the big rollers against a headland to the left, in the direction of Phaestus, with nothing but the reef for protection. It's a notorious trouble spot, and the crews were lucky to survive. They made it ashore, but all their ships were splintered on the rocks. Every last vessel. That's what happens when a god-gale hits you. Zeus doesn't mess around. And when Poseidon takes prisoners, they don't live to tell the tale. Yes, they were lucky.'

'And Menelaus?'

'Was driven on to Egypt with his five ships, all that was left of the blue-prowed fleet. So he was far from home when his brother was murdered. If he'd been around it would have been Aegisthus who'd died, not Agamemnon. He'd have been flung out on the plains for dogmeat and carrion, and not a Greek tear would have been sprung for him. Do you know that while we were fighting that bloody war, that coward was taking it easy in Argos? His war effort consisted of seducing his own cousin's wife while the kinsman was besieging Troy. The only siege that skulker carried out was to her bed.

'At first Clytemnestra turned a deaf ear to his proposals. But he tried the other ear, and she was soon on her back with her legs in the air. Afterwards, Aegisthus seized power in golden Mycenae. To the people he was just a murderer and a usurper, but he crushed them and kept them under his thumb for seven years, till Orestes returned from Athens to avenge his father. And a red end it was for his mother and her lover. After that, Orestes called all his friends to a funeral feast for the mother he had hated. And Menelaus joined him that same day.'

'So you have no more on Odysseus?'

'The truth is, I came home without a clue about the ones we'd left behind, or the ones like your father who went their own way. News has filtered through to sandy Pylos over the years, but you know what news is, especially when the years have gnawed away at it. And there was nothing really definite concerning Odysseus, other than tall tales and the tittle-tattle of tramps.'

Clearly there was nothing to be picked up in Pylos, and Telemachus suggested he would try his luck in Sparta, leaving right away.

'God forbid, young man!' exclaimed Nestor. 'Send the son of Odysseus on his way, as if this were a house of paupers? No, you'll sleep here tonight and leave in the morning, on the condition you call in again on your way back and tell me what you've learned. You can either sail on to Sparta, or, if you prefer, take the land route. I can give you a chariot and fast horses, and my son Peisistratus to guide you. He's the last of my sons, the only one who hasn't married, and he'll go with you gladly. I gather Menelaus has just returned from abroad, quite a long journey, and he may well have picked up some fresh news of your father, more than an old object like myself could possibly provide. Even the information I've given you is well out of date by now.'

Telemachus thanked the old leader and stooped to kiss him, but Nestor stood up, took his hand in his, and looked sternly and steadily into his eyes.

'One last thing – don't spend too long on this visit. Learn what you can, then leave. Don't be too far from home. Remember Agamemnon, Clytemnestra, Aegisthus. And remember Orestes, who came back and killed his father's killers. Ithaca is not without its usurpers, so it seems. At least that is their intent. But you can stop them in their tracks, if you act quickly.'

They all retired for the night. But as soon as Aurora brushed the east with pink fingers, Gerenian Nestor rose and ordered everything to be made ready. A heifer fell under the axe, gushing her life's blood, and was soon roasting on the fire, with the sparkling wine sprinkled over the flames. They ate and drank their fill, but only after Telemachus had been bathed by Nestor's youngest daughter, the lovely Polycaste. Then the horses were harnessed to the chariot, Peisistratus took the reins, Telemachus jumped up beside him, the whip flicked, and the swift and willing steeds sped off to the plains, eight hooves kicking up the white dust and quickly putting the high citadel of sandy Pylos well behind them.

Another dawn and two more sunsets stained east and west, and still the yoke swayed up and down on the sweating necks as the two princes thundered on under the big skies.

FIFTY-ONE

When they reached the rolling lands of Lacedaemon, deep in the Spartan hills, they found Menelaus busy celebrating a double wedding. He had chosen a Spartan beauty for his beloved son Megapenthes, and his daughter was being married to Neoptolemus, son of the great Achilles. The two travellers were taken through the courtyard and into the palace, under the high roof. They looked up and all around, open-mouthed at the sheer splendour. Everything shone as if it were lit by sunlight or moonlight – gold and silver, amber and ivory, copper and bronze. Polished baths, golden ewers, silver basins, glittering wine cups, baskets of bread, platters of meat – the princes were served in style after the girls had bathed them and rubbed them down with oil, taking away their dust-shrouded tunics and dressing them again in good clean clothes. Menelaus sighed with satisfaction, pleased by their expressions of admiration and awe.

'Yes, it's quite a sight for strangers, and I'm glad you make no effort to conceal your appreciation. Why should you? And I make no attempt to conceal how well I did out of the war. Why should I? It cost me ten years of fighting and the lives of many good men. But there's more than a touch of Troy here.'

'It's like heaven,' said Telemachus, his arms spread wide.

A slight frown from Menelaus.

'Heaven, eh? Maybe so. But I'd go to hell to have all my old friends back with me instead, all those who fell at Troy so long ago, and my brother especially. He didn't die at Troy, but it was Troy that killed him, indirectly. No amount of Trojan wealth will ever bring him back to me.'

'Even so,' said Telemachus, 'this is unrivalled. Now I know what it must be like on Olympus.'

That made Menelaus laugh. 'Well, that is a very great compliment, my boy. But there everything is immortal, whereas even these gold goblets you're drinking out of will perish eventually, even if it takes centuries, millennia. Having said that, I don't mind admitting that few can rival me, as you say, in terms of wealth. I brought all this back in my ships from Ilium, from Cyprus and Phoenicia and from Egypt. I visited the Ethiopians and the Sidonians and the Erembi. I saw Libya too. All that is quite apart from Troy. And there I had to fight for what I won. But I did fight and I did win, in spite of the hardships, and all I can say is that I'd give up — well, let's see, two-thirds at least of my entire estate if that could make my old comrades come back to me again. Yes, I'd go that far. I'd be content to live with a third of what I own just to have them back with me right now in this hall, all those heroes who died at the gates of Troy, before we captured it, and others who died at sea, so far from their native Argos, where the splendid steeds graze. Yes, I'd be happy with that, a mere third of everything I have just to bring back those heroes from the dead, even for one hour. I miss them so. I miss them one and all.'

'Anyone in particular?'

Menelaus hesitated.

'Without hesitation . . .'

He hesitated again.

'Without hesitation, I should say that if there is one man I miss most of all, even more than my own brother, that man is Odysseus. Nobody worked harder to bring about the fall of Troy, and he got no reward for his efforts, for god alone knows where he is now, or where his white bones lie.'

When he heard this, Telemachus hid his face in his purple cloak, and Menelaus saw the young man's shoulders shake. He was embarrassed and wondered whether to ask his guest for his identity at that point or to carry on with his story. He was saved from his predicament by the sudden arrival of Helen.

Down she came, descending with her ladies from her lofty scented chamber and looking like Artemis with her distaff of gold. At once the accessories appeared for her, brought by the adoring maids: a luxurious chair with a stool for her feet, a soft woollen rug, a silver work basket, a gift from Alcandre of Thebes, and from the same Egyptian woman the famous golden spindle. The basket ran on castors and was trimmed with gold. The spindle lay across it with its purple wool, brought by her lady Phylo. It all added up to an image of perfection, everything a woman could have or want to have, everything she could want or want to be. If she acted like a goddess, it was because she had been made to feel like one, with the spoils of Troy all around her. She was back in Sparta, but she was more than Queen of Sparta. She was Helen of Troy. A legend in her time.

Being the daughter of Zeus, a legend, and the nearest thing to a goddess, she went straight to the point.

'I may be wrong, my lord, but don't I see a certain family resemblance in the younger of the two strangers who are our guests?'

Menelaus stared.

'You know, my dear, I've been asking myself where I've seen this young man before. Or rather not him, but –'

Helen spoke it for him.

'His father.'

'My father.'

Menelaus rose at once and threw his arms around the young man.

'I can barely believe it, but I see now that it's true. I don't know why I didn't see it before – here in my own house after all these years, the only son of my best friend of the war. My god, if only he'd come back, I'd have taken him out of rocky Ithaca and given him a city of his own, right here in Argos. We'd have been neighbours. We'd have met constantly to remember the old times, and it would have gone on like that to death's door and even the darkness beyond. Of all the men who followed me to Troy, he was the one. And the one who above all others earned his reward, the reward he never had. We went through hell together. And good times too. And we loved one another, none closer. And now the gods have sent his son to console me with this thought, that wherever Odysseus is now, he is not dead, not as long as this image of him is alive and above the earth. This surpasses the only other tributes we can pay to poor mortality – a tear on the cheek and a lock of hair from the beloved's head.'

This speech drew tears from Telemachus and from Peisistratus too, who remembered his beloved brother, Antilochus, one of the many who never returned from Troy, slain in his case by the splendid son of the dazzling Dawn. Even the child of Zeus broke down and wept with all the others, the incomparable Helen of Argos, terrible as the crocodile of the Nile, the lass unparalleled.

But she could not cry for long. And to ensure the transition to a happier mood, she now slipped into the mixing-bowl a powerful drug which she'd been given by another Egyptian woman, Polydama, wife of Thon, Egypt's fecund earth always affording ample examples of grief-stealing herbs. This particular drug was one of those sweet oblivious antidotes to sorrow, one of heartsease, free from gall. To take one sip was to forget your troubles and to be incapable of grief, not even if your mother had just died that very day or if you'd seen your son or your brother cut down before you. Not a single tear would trash your face. This was the anodyne that was drunk by all.

After it had taken effect, Helen told the story of how Odysseus had beaten himself black and blue and slunk into Troy undercover like a filthy old beggar, the first part of his plan to take the city by trickery and stealth.

'He was a master of disguise, and I was the only one who saw through it. A child of Zeus cannot be deceived, you know. But I didn't betray him, even though he killed a number of Trojans in tight corners and got back to base with a wealth of information. I was glad to help him, because even then I was sick for home and already regretting the infatuation imposed on me by Aphrodite when she put me under the spell of Paris, luring me from lovely Lacedaemon all the way across the wine-dark sea with a womaniser who turned my head for a time and made me abandon our innocent daughter, my bride-bed and a husband who had – has – all a woman could wish for by way of brains and manly beauty.'

The loud applause from Menelaus was echoed by the entire company. Afterwards, he regaled the gathering with the story of the wooden horse, assuring Telemachus that it was his father who had brought the war to an end.

'He had that streak of daring in him, apart from mere courage. But most of all he was a strategist, unrivalled in his craft. He used mind over matter; that was his strength.'

By the end of the story, the deep of night had crept upon the conversation and everyone retired sleepily to bed. But Telemachus lay awake under the stars, out in the forecourt, his mind filled with his father. Menelaus slept at the back of the palace. Helen lay at his side, breathing sweetly and evenly in her long robe. When Aurora's crimson fingers imbued the east, Menelaus rose and stirred his guests. He asked Telemachus directly if there was anything else behind his surprise visit to Sparta, anything he could help him with. So Telemachus told him about the difficult situation back in Ithaca, and how his best hope lay in finding fresh information concerning his father. Menelaus was indignant.

'So these cowards have crept into the lion's den while the lion is away from home. But when the lion returns to his lair, he'll tear them to pieces. Take my word for it, Odysseus will make short work of them.'

Telemachus asked him if he had any reason to suppose that the lion was still alive. Menelaus said that the last words he'd heard about Odysseus had come straight from the salty lips of the mighty and immortal seer, Proteus, the Old Man of the Sea, and it had been an epic undertaking, first to capture the Old Man and then to make him talk.

'But I did it,' said Menelaus, 'thanks to Eidothee, the Old Man's goddess daughter, who took pity on me when I was held up for twenty days off the island of Pharos, a day's sailing out of the mouth of the Nile, in the rolling seas out there. My men were starving and I needed to find a way home. No one knows the highways of the fish like the old seer, but first he has to be caught, and it was Eidothee who told me how to go about it. He eluded me for a long time and tried to evade my questions, but eventually I made him spill out directions, which, much to my dismay, involved returning to the Nile and resuming my voyage from there, after offering to the gods. I also made him disclose all the facts about my comrades and what had happened to them since we left Troy. I learned first about Ajax and how Poseidon had wrecked his long-oared ships on the great cliff of Gyrae and then split the rock in two, leaving one-half standing. The other half that Ajax stood on disappeared into the deeps and took him down with it, to gulp the sea and perish.

'After that, I got out of him the story of my poor brother, whose ship was spotted by a spy, high in a watch-tower. He'd been posted there by Aegisthus to look out for the rightful king's return, and this spy went straight to the palace and informed the usurper that the enemy to all his ambition was at hand. Aegisthus chose twenty men and ordered them to be ready to commit murder – and regicide. Then he ordered up a banquet and set out personally in a chariot to bring the king home, with an outward show of welcome but with ugly ideas hissing in his head. My brother landed and kissed the ground, the warm soil of home. The tears hung from his eyes and thronged his beard. He came up with his killer in the chariot, all the way from the coast, not guessing what was going to happen. And so Aegisthus feasted him and saw him into his bath, where he lay naked and vulnerable, his thoughts on his wife and the joys of bedding her again. He closed his eyes in anticipation . . .

And the room filled up with men, all twenty of them, with swords, Aegisthus and Clytemnestra among them. They were taking no chances. And they felled him as you would fell an ox in his stall, brutally and without warning. The king's men fought a last stand, but not one of them was left alive. Every one of Aegisthus's men was killed too; the whole twenty cut down in the palace to the last man. There are different versions of my brother's tragic death, but that is the version given to me straight from the Old Man of the Sea, and I have no reason to doubt it.'

Silence. Everybody was picturing the palace strewn with corpses, the big butchered body swamped in the bath, the water, dark with blood, spilling slowly over the sides, across the polished floor . . .

'And Odysseus?'

'Odysseus. Ah yes – Ajax, Agamemnon, and Odysseus. That's easy. Odysseus is in the home of the nymph Calypso, on the island of Ogygia. There he languishes, a captive with neither ship nor crew, a prisoner in her bed and a slave to her passion. His eyes devour the horizon and drop salt tears in the ocean, adding brine to brine, and all to no avail. That was the last glimpse of Odysseus caught by the Old Man of the Sea.'

'So there was no word of his coming home?'

'Not at that time, though that was a while ago. Let me finish my story, though. The seer ended by telling me about my own fate – which is not to experience the common lot and die in Argos where the horses graze, but to be sent by the gods to join red-haired Rhadamanthus in the Elysian Fields, which never feel a snowflake or a raindrop and hear only the tunes of the soft west wind blowing in from the ocean to refresh its folk. That is my destiny, and that is how the Immortals intend to treat me as the husband of Helen and the son-in-law of Zeus.

'So you see, I learned a lot off the isle of Pharos. The Old Man sank back into his native salt, and as night in its mystery fell over me, I lay down to sleep with the surf-beaten shore sounding in my dreams. Next morning I followed the Old Man's directions. I returned to the Nile, built a mound to the everlasting memory of Agamemnon and sailed back to my beloved Argos.'

While all this talk was going on, the suitors back in Ithaca were enjoying themselves as usual, unaware that Telemachus had carried out his plan. They learned about it only when Phronius's son, Noemon, approached Antinous and Eurymachus, asking for information about the ship Telemachus had borrowed for his expedition.

'Do you happen to know when he'll be back from Sparta?' he asked. 'Only I need my father's ship, you see. I want to use it right now to reach Elis, where I keep a dozen mares. Their mules haven't been weaned yet, and I need to break one in. Do you have any idea of when he's planning to return?'

Antinous raged.

'Sparta? Ship? Why didn't you tell us your father had lent him a vessel?'

'I assumed you knew.'

'Blast his eyes, I'll kill him! He's had the brass neck to bring the thing off. He's actually done it, the pipsqueak, and left us looking like fools! But I'll have him for this! Get me a nimble ship and twenty men, and I'll hide out in the straits between here and the bluffs of Samos. I'll waylay him on his way back, the insolent young pup, and I'll put a quick end to his travels.'

Antinous shot his mouth off so loudly that Medon the herald overheard every word, and he sped to Penelope with the news that Telemachus was in dire danger. She nearly fainted and for a time lost the power of speech. Eventually she asked, with tears in her eyes, 'But when did he go? I never even knew about it.'

'You weren't meant to,' said Medon. 'He put us under orders. He didn't want you worrying.'

'Worrying! I lost my husband, and now my only son goes off on the high seas in search of him and is about to be ambushed and slaughtered! O god, god save him! God help me!'

She uttered one loud long scream and collapsed in a heap. Down in the hall the suitors heard it and laughed.

'Do I hear wedding music?' one of them asked.

'Yes, you do. I do believe that's our tune she's singing. The crafty daughter of King Icarius will be getting married quite soon, I think. Little does she know her precious son is for the chop.'

'Shut your faces!' shouted Antinous. 'Pitchers have ears. If this gets out our plan may be scuppered. No blabbing. Let's just do what we have to do.'

Not knowing that Penelope already knew the truth, he strode off to the harbour, picked his twenty murderers, the same number as Aegisthus, and prepared to sail. Penelope lay in her room, surrounded by terrors. But at last she grew drowsy and the black thoughts receded as she lay down, entered the arms of Morpheus and succumbed to sleep.

But the flashing eyes of Pallas Athene were too watchful to close in sleep. She decided it was time to pay Penelope a dream-visit. King Icarius had another daughter called Iphthime, who had married Eumelus and lived in Pherae. Athene spun a phantom to look like this woman and sent it to Ithaca to save the sleeping queen from further distress. The phantom arrived at the door of her lofty chamber, reached for the strap that worked the bolt, stood by her sister's head and spoke softly.

'No need for tears, Penelope, when you wake. Know that the gods have no quarrel with your son and are on your side.'

Penelope heard Iphthime's voice in her sweet sleep at the Gate of Dreams and answered the dim figure from behind the gate.

'Surely you are a shadow sent by the gods? Or you have heard the voice of god? If so, and if you are immortal, you can tell me not only about my son but also about his father. Can my unhappy husband still see the sun? Or is he long dead in Hades?'

The dim figure retreated from her.

'Seek to know no more. This is not my mission. Of Odysseus, alive or dead, I can tell you nothing, and empty words are mere babbling in the dark.'

The phantom slipped out between the door and its post and melted outside like breath into the wind.

By this time, the suitors were out on the open seas with murder black in their hearts. Antinous arrived at the straits between Ithaca and the rugged bluffs of Samos. Here in the middle of the strait he found his hiding-place, the rocky little islet of Asteris, tiny, but with two mouths, and it was here that he moored, to lie up for his unwitting victim and murder him on the high seas.

But the victim was not unwitting. Little did the killers know that the goddess who watched over him had advised him of their plans. In fact, he'd known about them before he'd even set sail for Pylos, and he had no intention of returning to Ithaca by such an obvious route. He had his own instructions from the goddess about where to put in and whom to visit as soon as he landed. He fully intended to give the islands a good wide berth and sail on through the dark. He would land in Ithaca at the nearest point and disembark, sending the ship round to port. But he himself would proceed on foot to Eumaeus's hut and spend the night there. The swineherd would go to the city and give Penelope the news that her son was in from Pylos and safely home. That was the plan.

But to ensure that everything went smoothly, Athene now sped back to Lacedaemon and roused Telemachus early. Menelaus urged him to stay on for another dozen days, but there was no question of that. Nor could he afford to put off any time in Pylos on the return leg of the journey. Bigger things were taking shape, events that transcended the code of hospitality, and the gods had business on their hands, none more so than Pallas Athene.

'Besides which,' she said, 'you can't leave your mother alone with that rabble much longer. Eurymachus keeps raising the stakes for her hand, and her father and brothers are pressurising her to consent. Without your support, she may cave in at last. And in any case, you know what women are like. She might take all sorts of things out of the house with you being away and have them transported to her new husband's home. You know what they say – one hour between the second wedding sheets, and a whole lifetime is wiped out, the previous marriage forgotten. An hour, a lifetime. Think about it. And don't delay another second.'

So Telemachus presented his apologies, and Menelaus presented him with a two-handled cup and a glorious silver mixing-bowl, rimmed with gold, which had been crafted by Hephaestus and given to him by the King of Sidon. Helen went up to the chests where she kept her embroidered dresses and handed him a garment which glittered like a star.

'I made it with my own cunning hands,' she said, 'and it is for your bride to wear on the day of your wedding.'

The pair of princes mounted their chariot and red-haired Menelaus went up and raised the golden wine cup to drink their health.

'And whenever you drink from the bowl of Hephaestus and the two-handled cup, you will always, I hope, remember me.'

'I will never forget your kindness,' answered Telemachus. 'I only wish I could be sure of telling Odysseus of your warmth and generosity.'

At that moment, an eagle came swooping down the wind from the left, clutching in its claws a great white goose.

'It's an omen,' said Helen. 'Believe a child of Zeus. That goose was home-fed, a tame one from the yard. The eagle came down from the mountains and snatched it. So shall Odysseus swoop down on the suitors and rip them to shreds!'

Telemachus laughed and drained the cup. He threw it back into the hands of Menelaus. 'May your father, the Thunderer, bring his daughter's words true!'

They left Sparta and galloped back to Pylos, where Telemachus parted from Peisistratus, begging him to let him continue his journey home and not put off any more time revisiting Nestor '– who, indeed, would certainly see to it that you were detained for a dozen days, if not a dozen years by his reminiscences. But let me hear from you once you have reached Ithaca, now that we are friends.'

Just before Telemachus set sail, he was approached by a stranger called Theoclymenus. He had the reputation of being a prophet but was currently on the run after killing a kinsman, and he begged Telemachus for sanctuary and safe passage.

'If you're on the sea-road and dodging death and danger,' said Telemachus, 'then come aboard with us. My own father is a wanderer, if he's still alive, and I'm not going to forbid my ship to any good man in trouble.'

So they ran past Crouni and fair-watered Chalcis and, after sunset, pressed on for Pheae with the stiff wind behind them, sweeping them along past green and shining Elis, where the Epeians hold sway, after which Telemachus plotted a course for the spiky isles, wondering whether even with the good guidance of a goddess he would avoid the murder-ship and get through alive.

FIFTY-TWO

Back on Ithaca, I was supping up for the second night in the swineherd's hut. I put out a feeler to see if I could count on staying there or if I'd outlived my welcome and should go to town in the morning to beg my bread and bacon. The suitors would surely slip me a few crumbs from all that food they were consuming, I said, and in return I was ready to do some work about the place – splitting logs, firelighting, carving, cooking, wine-bearing, anything at all.

'I've been around – there's not a man to touch me in any of these departments. Old soldier, you know.'

Eumaeus snorted. 'Holy fuck, man, are you mad? These men are violent bastards, without a shred of respect for beggars, and so are their flunkeys and the hangers-on. They're nancy boys, slimy shits, all of them, the sort that don't get their mitts greasy, you follow me? The only grease you'll see on that lot will be on their fucking arses, or their snouts. But it doesn't mean they won't be handy enough to give you a good thrashing if they feel like it. They'd piss on you as soon as look at you. No, you stay here with me. You're no nuisance to anybody here, and when Telemachus drops by he'll see that you're properly looked after before sending you on your way.'

I thanked him and asked him about the youth's grandparents. Odysseus's folks must have been approaching old age already when their son was called up, surely? 'Are they still with you by any chance? Or are they no longer in the land of the living?'

A short pause. I could see that Eumaeus was emotional.

'One is, one isn't. Laertes is still with us, but he won't be for much longer, he's so crushed by the loss of his wife and son he just wants to die, that's all. He's had enough.'

'And the mother?'

'Anticleia. Sheer grief for her boy, that's what put her to her grave. There was no illness. She just died one day. As folk do. It's known in the trade as a broken heart. They said heart attack, but I reckon her heart just broke. Hang on, are you all right?'

'I'm sorry,' I said, 'I was thinking of my own old folks just now. Couldn't help being reminded of them, couldn't stop the tears. Carry on.'

'That's all right. Gets to you sometimes, doesn't it? There's not much more to be said. But I can tell you, Anticleia always had a soft spot for me, as I did for her. A lovely lady she was. I miss her. I miss her kindness, I can tell you.'

'Yes, but surely Penelope treats you just as well – or well enough?'

More snorts. 'I get on with work and I'm paid for it – meat and shelter, and that's as far as it goes.'

'What else is there?'

'What else? Fucking hell, there's more to life than food and a roof, isn't there? I miss the soft word, the personal touch, you know, the face-to-face chatter, a bite and a sup in the palace and a titbit to take home. There's none of that nowadays, fuck all. But it's not her fault altogether, it's the situation she's up against with these shitebags. They've changed everything. They rule the fucking roost.'

As we bunked down for the night, I pictured the brains of those bastards spattering the palace walls. This gave me sweet dreams.

Early next morning we were getting breakfast ready when I heard somebody approaching – a bush, a pebble, a twig. I got up from the fire. Eumaeus looked at me, surprised.

'Footsteps, you say? Fucking good ears you have at your age. I can't hear a fucking thing myself. But look, the dogs are wagging their tails and they're not barking. It must be somebody we know.'

He'd hardly got the words out when a young man showed up in the doorway and the dogs ran to him. He looked like any other youngster, but I knew it was my boy. He hadn't changed all that much. Still a bit of a weakling, I thought – a decent enough weakling, but a weakling all the same. Or at least not somebody you'd want on your right side – or your left – if you were facing the Trojan charioteers or breaking the battleline. No substitute for Achilles or Ajax or Diomedes. Yet there was something about the way he walked, the slight swing to that left leg . . .

He was well through the door of his teens when I left for Troy, but I couldn't help thinking much further back and remembering the little pink blob I'd seen at Penelope's milky tits, those blue-veined udders with streaming nipples. What were they like now, the breasts I'd lain between on my last night, before it all began? How far would they have sagged? Mother's milk had seen him off to a good start, and he'd grown tall, a good head above his father now. But he didn't have my build. I looked for the old block in the chip – the sturdy bulk, the broad shoulders and thighs and calves, the barrel chest, the wrestler, the runner who'd whopped Ajax in the foot race at Troy and taken the

Sidonian silver bowl – but I wasn't there. Well, it had only been a few years. How could I expect a metamorphosis in that short time? And yet he must be – what age now – twenty?

It wasn't just that I wasn't there. I couldn't find that other thing either, the thing that should have been inside me, the expected surge of joy, the flash of recognition. There was no lump in the throat or tear behind the eye, just this sudden depression. Why wasn't I glad to greet my own flesh and blood, my only son, for fuck's sake? Was time, that stubborn tricksy bastard, to blame? Or was it Troy? Or was it me? It was all happening so fast now after so long, and with such banality. A boy was coming through a gate. He was crossing the courtyard and entering the hut. There he stood in the doorway, with four dogs lolloping round him, their muzzles nuzzling his dangling fingers. So what? What did any of it mean?

But I lightened when I saw how Eumaeus rose to welcome him and how easily and pleasantly the young man greeted him.

'How are things, uncle?'

Uncle. I liked that touch. And I liked the way he greeted the pauper. He didn't flinch when he saw the thing in the corner that got up to offer him his place, a pile of filth in blackened rags.

'No, no, keep your seat, sir, this'll do well enough for me.'

He made for a stack of green brushwood, and the swineherd quickly threw a fleece over it before he could sit down. Some men think you're a prince if you plant your pampered arse on soft cushions, but Telemachus wasn't like that.

He was carrying a spear, too lightweight for my liking, which Eumaeus propped in a corner, and a bow and quiver. I could gauge the care he'd taken of the bow; it looked supple and strong, and the arrows were polished and sharp. These were all good signs. Maybe he wasn't my son for nothing. Eumaeus introduced me as a Cretan who'd tramped the world and fought at Troy and had known his father.

'Fought at his side, sir – and heard news of him since then. In Thesprotia.'

Eumaeus shrugged, and Telemachus threw a quick glance at me, nodded and smiled. This filthy scarecrow, steaming blackly by the fire, a hero of Troy and his father's comrade. Hardly. But his courtesy didn't fail him.

'Well, I'll bet you can tell us a tale or two then, old man. It's always good to hear news from abroad. But in the meantime, what can I be doing for you?'

Eumaeus cut in to say he'd already explained the unusual and difficult circumstances that would make it a bad idea for me to go to town on my own.

'Quite right, uncle. I'll certainly kit him out with everything he needs to see him back on the road — but not at the palace, where I can hardly call the house my own these days. And they'll have grown bolder in my absence, those bad lads. Could you keep him here with you at the farm? And I'll send stuff up to you. Now I know you need to get to work, but one last thing — please let my mother know I'm coming to see her. Could you do that for me?'

Eumaeus took his leave. Telemachus turned to me courteously.

'Apologies for this, but I fancy if I took you home with me as you are, you'd have to face the mockery of that mob in the palace right now. They treat the place as their own, and, as I'm sure Eumaeus will have told you, they piss on hospitality, but they help themselves to anything they want. They slaughter the beasts, the wine runs like water. Worse than that, they mock my mother with their loose talk about bedding her. They're screwing her maids — I might as well be blunt with you — not all of them, but there's a hard core of harlots that are working against my mother and giving these bastards the run of the place. They're a riotous lot, a rabble, and they'll be out of control as I've been away for a while, and I've no support.'

'That's where you're wrong,' I said.

He looked at me, his face a question — but a nice open one, not a frown.

'What's that you say?'

'I said you're wrong. You do have support.'

I said it quietly but firmly, so firmly he looked hard at me, finding my eyes, picking them out from among the matted hair, the blackened skin, the surrounding wreckage. He nodded at me, smiling slightly.

'Right, I see. And where is it, can I ask, this support?'

'You're looking at it, my boy, right here in front of you. I'm your support.'

He didn't lose the little smile.

'You're my support?'

'I am.'

A deep sigh.

'Look here, I know you've probably seen a bit of action, possibly even at Troy, if you say so — you look like you've lived hard. But I don't think I'm explaining this well enough. Let me put it to you this way, my old friend —'

'I'm not your friend.'

The smile began to fade. 'You're not?'

'No.'

He glanced at the spear in the corner.

'I'm not your enemy, either. I'm more than friend or foe to you. It's bigger than that. I'm your father.'

The smile went out.

Should I leave? Then come back in, and try it again? This is one for the web, isn't it? Easy on the web. On cue, Athene enters, an Immortal with flashing eyes, a goddess tall and stately, standing there in pigshit outside the swineherd's hovel, come at an awkward moment, come to break the ice, to sort it out.

Does she get her feet dirty? Goddesses don't get dirty feet – they don't even have feet, not in the fleshly sense of the word. A goddess is a presence, an immanence. And immanences don't need feet to sort things out. Pigshit doesn't worry them.

So Athene appeared outside the hut, visible to me but not, of course, to my son, since it's not to everybody that the gods reveal themselves, and they may materialise before one person in a room but not another in the same room as they so choose and see fit, or as circumstances dictate. There was a dictating circumstance right now in the swineherd's hut. A goddess needed to speak to me.

Believable? In a world where goddesses rub shoulders with men and even from time to time spread their legs for them, anything can happen. You'd better believe it. Such are the ways of gods. This one frowned at me through the doorway, and I asked my son to excuse me for a moment. Even heroes of Troy need to take a piss occasionally, and old soldiers certainly do. I said I'd be back in a flash.

'The hour has come,' said Athene. 'Royal son of Laertes, Odysseus of the many wiles, the time has come to confide in your son, reveal yourself for who you are, and bring him into the loop that will enmesh them all, these mutual enemies of yours. The two of you need to put your heads together and plan their destruction. And panic not – you are not alone. I'm here and I'm ready for the fray. They're dead men. I'll see to it that you drink their blood. But first, your son must know who you are. And he's got to believe in you.'

What the touch of a wand can do if it's wielded by a goddess! Shining clothes, increased stature, a bronze complexion, grey hairs removed, lantern jaws filled out, teeth whitened, stoop straightened, bruises healed, beard trimmed, hair styled, rheumy eyes turned to iron. The ultimate Olympian makeover. No wonder Telemachus got a shock when I stepped back inside, almost unrecognisable from the derelict who had gone out to pee.

Almost. But he could see I was somehow the same man. Or god.

'No, I'm not a god. But I am your father.'

'My father.'

'And you're my boy.'

His frown melted.

Time for tears? Dripping from the web, stitched there in silver, mine as I reached out and threw my arms around him – his eventually, unwilling at first as he struggled to accept it, afraid to believe but knowing it to be true, father and son resolved into one, one ultimate recognition of one another after twenty years.

'Be sure of one thing: you'll see no other Odysseus returning to you, no second coming. This is it. I'm it.'

He fell on my neck and we each gave ourselves up to the tears wholly – huge, scalding, sweet, bitter, desperate sobs, shaking us uncontrollably. We stood there for a very long time holding each other, both of us unable to speak a word.

Touching, don't you think?

'You're it?'

'That's right, I'm it. I'm your father, and I'm your support. And god knows you seem to fucking need it, right?'

Right.

Better draw the veil then, screen off the reality of the moment, that moment when the web is preferable – immeasurably so – to the awkwardness, the incredulity, the anti-climax, the acrimony and affront to expectation, the disappointment and head-shaking and hysterical fucking laughter. You're it?

I'm it. He's it. You're my father, he's my son. What kind of father? What kind of son?

'I don't believe it!'

Neither of us could.

'How could you take all this lying down? I mean, these fucking wasters! How could a son of mine . . . ?'

'Don't call me a son of yours! I don't know who the hell you are, you stinking tramp! I don't know that I even want to know!'

'Tramp? You were fucking courteous enough five minutes ago when you met me! When I was no man. When I was nobody!'

'You still are! You still are nobody! And I was nobody to you – till you came out with this father crap. Father? You broken-down old bum, look at you!'

'Yes, why don't you do that? Look at me. You don't know a hundredth of it, what I've been through, where I've been, what I am. Who I am.'

'Who you are. Who are you? And you don't know what I've been through either, while you were off strutting the world's stage.'

'Oh yes? Well I'm glad you call it that, because that's what war is, boy, it's the theatre. It's the part we have to play, and I fucking played mine.'

'And that makes you a hero, does it? The hero who buggered off and never came back, leaving his son in the shit.'

'I'm back now, and I'm going to do something about this shit. I'd have done it long ago if I'd been here.'

'You mean if you'd been me?'

'That's not what I meant. But while we're about it, are the people against you? Is your mother incapable? Are you really telling me that all of you put together can't handle a bunch of rakes? A handful of high-class hooligans? From what I hear, they're empty vessels, loud mouths. The biggest problem they're likely to cause is to their mothers, who probably sit up wondering why their bastard little brats aren't tucked up in their beds by suppertime!'

A moment's pause in the slanging match. And the little smile returned to his face. I liked that smile.

'A bunch of brats, you say? A handful of hooligans? Where did you get your information from, I wonder? From what I've heard of my father, I think his first move might have been to check out the size of the opposition. You don't know, do you? What's a handful, would you say – five men, maybe six? What's two handfuls – ten, a dozen at most? What would you say to two dozen? Would that suit you? Think you could take them on? Let me tell you then, there *are* two dozen, but that's from Same alone. Do you want to hear about the others? I haven't even started. Zacynthus sent twenty, Dulichium fifty-two, the pick of their best, with four – no, six – flunkeys in tow, and all with weapons. Add that to another dozen from Ithaca itself, plus the herald and the minstrel, and other servants, who may not be professional fighters but are handy enough at the carving, if you take my meaning, and well acquainted with the knife. Take Antinous and Eurymachus – neither is a dunce with the sword or the spear. How's your arithmetic, by the way? Are you counting? I'll do it for you. We could be looking at a hundred and twenty men, a hundred and twenty against us . . .'

'Wait! You said *we*. You said *us*.'

'I know. A hundred and twenty against us, against two.'

'But what a twosome, eh? Father and son.'

'Father and son.'

'Better get used to it.'

'Looks like I'll have to. But what about these odds? Enough for you? I know you like a challenge, but do you really think we'd come out of it alive? I mean, you don't happen to have come back with a hundred men, by any chance, who could fight on our side? You don't happen to have any allies standing by?'

'Ah, right. I was going to ask the same question.'

'Ah, right.'

Silence.

I could have said that I had two allies, each worth a million men – Athene and Zeus. But his question was a serious one and didn't concern the kind of allies who inhabit the clouds and are notoriously invisible when push comes to shove.

'But I have another question to ask you,' I said.

'Yes?'

'I saw you come in with a spear and a bow. The spear struck me as a little lightweight, but everything looked to be in good trim. I like a man who likes his weapons and takes good care of them. I'm assuming they're not just for show. So the question is, how good are you?'

'Follow me,' he said.

We went outside and he asked me to pick a target for him. A little old olive tree stood outside the wall, close to the gate. The sap had long gone out of it.

'Try that.'

'How many paces?'

'How many paces is the palace hall?' I asked.

He looked at me.

'If you see what I'm getting at.'

He looked at me again. No sign of fear.

'I know exactly how many paces,' he said. 'I played there when I was a boy, remember?'

'I remember too,' I said. 'I built it.'

'Thirty paces then.'

'Thirty-five.'

We paced out the length of the hall and turned.

'Now prove you're my son.'

The first javelin went straight to the mark and the old tree groaned.

'Well,' I said, 'I think I can feel safe enough standing next to the tree.'

'Not too close. We wouldn't want to halve our numbers.'

I retrieved the spear for him a dozen times. Not every one was a perfect hit and two whistled past. One nearly grazed me. But it would have given the Trojans something to think about.

'Not bad,' I said. 'Now the arrows.'

There were nine in the quiver. I marked the trunk of the tree. It was a generous target, but not a gift. Seven out of the nine whistled to the mark.

'You haven't wasted your youth,' I said. 'Who taught you?'

'Who d'you think? Grandfather.'

'Good man. I think we have a fighting force here.'

'Not quite. And not quite yet. Now you prove you're my father.'

'You know I am.'

'I know you are. But prove it.'

'Still not convinced, eh? That's my boy. Quite right. Why should you be? All right then, let me show you what a bundle of rags can do.'

I increased the distance by half as much again and started with the arrows. The bull's-eye was obliterated by the time I'd done. Then I doubled the distance and hurled the javelin. It was one of the best throws of my life. The spear struck the tree with a sharp splitting sound and a massive crack opened up in the trunk. I walked up to it and prised it open, using all my strength.

'Now I need a new target,' I said. 'Can you suggest one?'

'About a hundred and twenty.'

He made to clasp me.

'Not too close,' I said. 'Wait till I've cleaned off some of this shit. God knows what I'm harbouring.'

He ignored the health warning and hugged me tight, tears in his eyes.

'Father?' I said.

'Yes.'

Father and son stood in silence for a few moments in front of the riven tree. Telemachus broke the silence.

'What are you thinking?'

'I'm thinking there's a difference between a dead tree and men that aren't rooted to the earth. They can move and return fire, no matter how unfit the bastards may be. We need reinforcements.'

'And how!'

'No, I don't mean big numbers, but some sort of support. We do have one formidable ally – and it's not Pallas Athene.'

'I think we can discount her. Who is it then?'

'It's every soldier's best weapon, and his enemy's worst nightmare: surprise.'

The plan was hatched. First off, I'd spend a day with Telemachus to work on aspects of his archery and spearsmanship. An old salt could teach him a thing or two. At dawn the following day he was to go to the palace as if nothing had happened. Eumaeus would then bring me there, still in beggar mode, which would give me a chance to assess the enemy's strength and calibre. It would also let them get used to my being around the palace without arousing suspicion. Any abuse I suffered I'd put up with, and Telemachus was under orders not to defend me beyond the bounds of courtesy. We'd both swallow it. Some of these bastards would soon be swallowing bronze – a lot worse than insults – and we were to do nothing that might jeopardise our plan and save them from the fate that was now not far off.

'Two more things,' I said. 'One: when the time comes, I'll give you a nod. When you see that signal, I want you to collect all the weapons that are lying about and get them out, well away from the hall. Stick them all in the strongroom – every single one. These cunts are going to be left defenceless. If all goes well, you can even get the weapons out of there when they're not around to notice, and if anybody asks, just say you've seen how smoked up they've become over the years and you've taken them away for cleaning and polishing. In any case, weapons are always a temptation to men in their cups, and fun and games can quickly switch to quarrelling and scuffling, the sort of behaviour that might tarnish their chances as suitors and potential husbands – any shit like that will do, as long as you come out with it casually and don't make it sound too heavy. But remember to leave two lots of weapons close at hand, one lot for me and the other for you. All clear?'

'All clear. And the second thing?'

'The second thing, and the most important point of all, is to tell nobody that I'm back – none of the household staff, not Eumaeus, not even my father, and above all not your mother. Have you got that?'

'Got it.'

We took a breath for a second. A long second. We were each thinking about what was ahead of us. Then Telemachus spoke.

'Some of the women –'

'Are whores. I know, you already told me, remember? That's why we can trust nobody, especially your mother.'

'Are you saying –?'

'No. But these women are too close to her. They can easily winkle things out of her, blow all our plans to the moon. About your mother, by the way. Let me be blunt. Has she . . . ?'

He didn't help me, bit his lip.

'. . . slept with any of the bastards?'

He turned away, took deep breaths.

'I don't know. I can't say for sure. How do I know what goes on in my mother's bed? I know she doesn't respect any of them much. Except Amphinomous.'

'Amphinomous?'

'Well, she's under . . . a lot of pressure.'

'And so will they be. A lot of fucking pressure. And soon.'

'They'll be in for a shock right away,' said Telemachus, 'when they find out I'm back from Pylos – alive and kicking.'

They got a shock, all right. The Pylos ship made the port and sent a message to Penelope that Telemachus had disembarked and gone up-country and would see her shortly. As it happened, the messenger and the swineherd carrying the same message converged, but Eumaeus whispered his report into the queen's ear, whereas the sailor shouted his out as if he were bawling into a fucking hurricane. The suitors were stunned. And at that precise moment, the murder-ship arrived without its murdered man. Antinous came straight up to the palace, and Eurymachus laid into him in the courtyard, where the rest of the gang joined them.

'Where the fuck were you?'

'I still don't know how he did it! We kept our scouts posted, all along the windy heights. We kept replacing them. We never slept on shore. We were afloat all night, ready to trap the bastard. If we'd spotted him, he'd be dead by now, but somehow the little fucker got through and got back here. He's pulled it off and made us look like arseholes!'

'Yes, and like arseholes, we're about to be fucked!'

'How?'

'Because, you useless bastard, everybody knows we sent that ship out to get him, and you fucked it up! Now he'll call an Assembly and denounce us. They could take a hard line and deport us.'

Antinous shouted down the consternation. 'Then we'll have to act first, won't we? Where is he now, up-country? We need to trap him up there and get rid of him once and for all. He's a thorn in our fucking flesh. Then we can divide everything that's his among us — income, estate — and whichever one of us marries the mother gets her and the house. Everybody wins, except the sprog.'

Dead silence.

'Well, what's the matter?'

The matter was that murder at sea, where anything can happen, was one thing. Murder at home, Agamemnon's fate, was a different matter.

Amphinomous broke the silence. 'So we're going to murder him in his bath, then?'

The silence was heavier.

'We might do well to remember what happened to Aegisthus.'

Amphinomous was a decent sort, well descended, from the rippling grasslands of sea-green Dulichium. His father was King Nisus. The rest of the bunch respected him. And Penelope was fond of him.

'Anyway, I've heard enough of this,' he said. 'I never went along with the murder plan in the first place, and I don't now. Let's go to the oracles. If Zeus decrees a death, and if it's Telemachus to die, I'll not only approve it, I'll kill him myself. Will that suit you? But god's will has to be done, and until that's clear to us we should do nothing, and above all forget this bloody scheme. Our names are mud as it is. Let's try to clear them.'

⑤

Amphinomous's speech convinced the meeting, with the exception of the ringleaders, and they all streamed back into the palace and sat down. But Medon had eavesdropped again and heard every word of the courtyard debate. He hurried to warn the queen that Telemachus, though safely back, was far from safe.

'The vote was to leave Telemachus alone. But Antinous and Eurymachus still have it in for him. They're stubborn cunts — saving your presence.'

Penelope came down at once and accosted Antinous publicly.

'Now I know you for the murderer you are,' she spat. 'Or would be. You're all tarred with the same brush, in any case, with one or two exceptions. I know about your civilised intervention, Amphinomous, and I thank you for it. But I also know, Antinous, that you captained the ship that was meant to ambush my son. Do you honestly think you can get away with it, now that it's out in the open? Why don't you just go home now, while you have the chance, and leave us in peace?'

Eurymachus stood up to calm her down.

'Penelope, believe me, not one of us has any intention of harming your son. People come out with all sorts of rubbish at meetings, where they get carried away in the heat of the argument. They say things they don't really mean, just for the fun of it.'

'And do they also go to the trouble of sending ships into the straits between Ithaca and Samos and waiting there night after night to intercept a ship from Pylos – just for the fun of it?'

'That's another thing, and a bad thing, I agree. But I was never on that death-ship myself, and I'm not on any death-squad now, and never will be. Telemachus is my best friend. I'm proposing to marry his mother, for god's sake. He'll be my son. I'd kill the man who tried to harm him. My god, I can still remember how his father used to treat me as if I were his own son, as if Telemachus and I were brothers! No, when Telemachus dies it will be by the will of the gods and will have nothing to do with me, or with any of us. You have my word on that.'

So spoke Eurymachus to placate Penelope. But like the accomplished hypocrite he was, he spoke smoothly with murder in his heart.

Penelope was taken in by none of it. And with fears for her son weighing heavy on her heart, she retired to her own apartments on the upper floor, and lay in bed alone, as always, a statue of fidelity, carved out of patience. Only the moonbeam shafts slid coldly between her breasts. Only the shadow of the poplar stole slowly up the bed between her gently parted legs. Only the hot wet tears on her cold marble cheeks revealed that she was not an emblem but a real woman, a queen of flesh and blood. Otherwise she existed only in her art.

FIFTY-THREE

Sometimes I think it's fruitless to ask what's true and untrue in this existence of ours, where art and life, dreams and reality, jostle for the laurels and the memory plays tricks. It's one of those imponderables. How do you know what's going on in other people's heads? Half the time, you can't even trust your own head to tell you what's true, let alone whether truth exists. I look back on past events and ask myself if they really happened like that, the way I remember them. I ask myself if they ever happened at all. Troy itself seems unreal at times – except in the nightmares that tear the blanket of the dark and leave you bleeding out your fears, a helpless wreck on the bed. You know they'll never let you go, the monsters, not until you die. So every man's Troy lives on, sharing his life with him, while real life – whatever that may be – slips off into the shadows, a daily blur, and only the dreams are real.

I wasn't dreaming when I watched Telemachus leave the farm. He ordered Eumaeus to take me to the city and let me beg my bread at the palace, as we'd agreed. But what happened when he got there himself? Did Eurycleia weep tears of relief? Did Penelope emerge like Artemis, or like golden Aphrodite, and stun the suitors with her beauty? And did the spearman Peiraeus appear with Theoclymenus the fugitive in tow, his head buzzing with divination?

'Believe me, madam,' Theoclymenus said, 'I swear by almighty Zeus, Odysseus is in Ithaca even as we speak.'

They were still laughing about that when I arrived. I cut a contemptible figure, hobbling along after the swineherd, a bundle of black tatters with an arm protruding, clutching a stick.

We followed the rocky road down from the farmlands and stopped at the public watering-place to refresh ourselves with the clear spring water that tumbled down from the high rock and gurgled into a stone basin. An altar had been erected overhead, sacred to the nymphs, and alders encircled the place, enjoying the coolness, the moisture. It was a restorative spot for travellers. So it was into this lovely setting that there appeared the epitome of an arsehole – Melanthius. Though to say that he was the working part of one would be unkind to arseholes. He was driving down some goats – my goats – for the bellies of the greedy bastards he sucked up to, and I could see that the beasts he'd selected were the best of the herd. As soon as he spotted us, he let loose.

'Will you look at that, everybody? There's a sight for you now – one useless fucker leading another! A pig-licker with a pot-licker in tow! What the fuck do you think you're at, Eumaeus, bringing this pile of plague pus down to the palace? That's where you're headed, isn't it? He's on the scrounge, isn't he? Yes, it's you I'm referring to, shitebag! I know your sort. You're going to worm your way into the palace and polish the doorposts with your shoulders and your stinking arse. Am I right or am I right?'

'Shut your gob!'

Eumaeus squared up to him.

'He's with me, and that's all you need to know. In fact, you don't need to know anything. Nothing's any of your fucking business.'

'Yes, I can see he's with you. Shit sticks to shit, as they say, and this fellow shit of yours is going to be honking the place out begging for scraps, but isn't going to do a stroke for it, is he, the lazy fucker? You've no intention of scraping a pot or pan, have you? I know your sort. But you'd fucking well break sweat if you came to work for me, I can tell you. I'd build up your muscles for you, you old scarecrow. But that wouldn't interest you, would it? You'd rather stuff your gob, you fucking glutton, touting round the town for titbits. You'd steal the very shit from our arses, wouldn't you, you tosser? Well, turn up at the palace if you fucking dare – and this is what you'll get!'

He landed a hard kick on me, catching me right on the hip-bone. I'd never even looked in the bastard's direction – the insults and the kick were both unsolicited. I wondered whether to smash him dead with my staff or pick him up and spill out his brains on the ground, mouldy wine from a splintered pitcher. But I couldn't blow my cover, so I controlled myself and examined his nose instead, picturing throwing it to the dogs after I'd sliced it from his face.

He wouldn't let it go, though, and gave me a second one in the thigh with his heel.

I looked at him steadily. 'What would your old master think of your behaviour, I wonder, treating his guests like this?'

My question earned me another kick.

'That's what I think of my master, louse-head! And get this straight, will you? You're not his fucking guest and you're not mine either, you're persona non-fucking grata, you are! For your information, my master's not even a memory here. He's as dead as you'll be if I so much as smell you again. And good riddance, too. He took all our best men off to Troy and for fuck all. I hope his useless brat buggers off too, same as his father did. He's not in charge here either: the suitors run the show, and one of them will be my new master soon enough.'

Eumaeus had had enough. 'Who the fuck asked you for your input? You've no authority to open your fat trap. I'll fucking shut it for·you, though, one of these days. You're the quintessence of shite, that's all. An utter turd, what's left over. You're a bad smell.'

'Oh, you can yap all right,' snarled the goatherd. 'But I'll yap harder!'

I signalled to Eumaeus to be on our way, but he stood his ground.

'By god, if Odysseus were here you wouldn't yap at all. He'd put a quick end to it, and to you. You'd drop your dogshite right in the road if he appeared on the scene, the slack-arsed coward you are.'

'Except Odysseus won't be appearing, will he? Because he's the one who's dogshite. He's food for the fish. And his boy is going to go the same way very soon. Just you keep your little pig-eyes open and see if I'm not right. You don't have a fucking clue, do you? You and your scumbag pal — you'd better keep him out of the way, I'm telling you, or he's in for a broken head and smashed ribs if he comes near the palace. Do you hear that, dosser? I'll see to it myself once the footstools start flying.'

Pleased with himself, he turned and strutted off, gobbing on me as he passed.

'He'll go straight in and join them,' said Eumaeus. 'He usually sits opposite Eurymachus, his number one, where he knows he can stuff his gut.'

I pictured the gut too, sliding slowly along my spear while the dog chewed the nose. The nose would be the appetiser. The genitals would follow as a starter. And then the rest.

We reached the palace, and Eumaeus thought for a second.

'Listen, it's best if I go in first and check things out, then you can come in and join me. Don't wait too long, though. There are lots of slobs that suck up to the suitors. Some of them might take it into their heads to give you a thrashing and beat you away, just to curry favour. It often happens.'

'I'll not let it happen,' I said.

Eumaeus went in. I liked the way he'd stood up for me. He was no softie. I mulled over the idea of confiding in him when the time came and using him as an ally. Then I heard a faint whine.

Outside the palace, the dung-heaps were piled up — mounds of mule- and cow-shit, the fresher piles still steaming, waiting to be carted off to the farms for manure. An old dog lay stretched out on one of these mounds, crying softly. He was barely able to lift his head, he was so old and ill, but his ears were pricked up all right, and his tail fluttered. I went closer.

God almighty! I thought I'd seen everything at Troy. I never thought anything could make me weep, ever again. I'd seen too much. But I was wrong. I wasn't prepared for this. That old pooch wasn't just any dog — it was Argus, the hound, my own Argus, my once lovely dog and faithful companion, still alive after all this time, still waiting for me. He'd heard me talking to Eumaeus and had seen through the disguise and the accent. He'd heard his master's voice. He was the only one who'd recognised me.

I went closer still.

He was crawling with lice and half eaten away by flies, but he wagged his tail and dropped his ears. He was straining every nerve to lift himself to me but couldn't. The tears blinded me, and I had to brush them away quickly. They were spotted, though, by a trembly old beggar who was crouched nearby, watching me.

'Yes, it's a pitiful sight, isn't it?'

He got up and hobbled over, barefoot and bent.

'But I never expected to see somebody as broken down as myself spending a tear on an old dog. You've got some pity left in you, pal, and there's precious little of that around here. But you can't have known the dog, surely? You're not from round these parts. I've never seen you before.'

I cleared my throat.

'No, I'm a stranger round here, you're right. But why isn't this poor animal being looked after or else put out of his misery? If he were mine, I'd kill him at once as an act of mercy. Even a sick old dog deserves compassion. Whose is it, do you know? Surely his master can't still be alive?'

The old indigent shook his head. 'I'll tell you something. If his master came back, it wouldn't be the dog on the dungheap — it would be these bastards in there, and all their bitches.'

'Why do you say that?'

'Don't you know anything? Where have you been living? I'm talking about Odysseus. The dog was never the same from the day he left for the war. My god, you should have seen this hound when he was a young rascal. Odysseus raised him himself. No dog could come near him for stamina and speed. And he was a top notcher at picking up the scent and finding his way along the trail. I used to go out on the hunts myself. He was like black lightning, that dog, the king's pride and joy. He gave orders when he left for the dog to be taken care of. And now not one of those palace whores would think of bringing him a bite to eat, let alone clearing the lice. Look at him, he's eaten alive. Groom him? They'd kick him if they could be bothered. I throw him the odd crust myself when I can, but that's not often.'

'Do you? Then let me tell you something. You'll be dining with the king one day soon.'

Harsh laughter. 'Well, you've lost your looks along the way, but you've held onto one thing.'

'What's that?'

'Your sense of humour, pal. But look here, he thinks he knows you . . .'

'No, he's just glad of the attention, that's all.'

My hand shook. I wanted to reach out and stroke the dog's head, but I couldn't afford to attract attention. His eyes were still on me, almost blind, but seeing what he'd waited for so long. And having seen me, he wagged his tail one last time, laid down his head and died.

I hurried away, brimming with black anger. I thought my heart would come off the stalk.

'I'll murder the fuckers! Every single one! And their sluts.'

I went in and sat down on the threshold, just within the door, and I leaned back against the pillar that I'd watched a crafty old carpenter smooth from an old cypress decades ago, deftly trued and polished to perfection. Telemachus saw me come in and signalled to Eumaeus to bring me over some bread and meat from a basket.

'And tell him to feel free to go round the hall, Telemachus says, and beg scraps from each man in turn. A beggar can't be shy.'

I did as I was asked. I wasn't hungry, but I was curious to pick out the good from the bad among them. Or rather the bad from the worse. Not that this would save a single one of them. After Argus, every man was destined to die. Without exception. I hadn't gone far, and the food was piling up in my greasy old wallet when one of the suitors asked me where I'd come from. This gave the goatherd a chance to stick his nose up an arse.

'I saw that old bugger less than an hour ago, and I can tell you how he got here — he was wheeled in by the swineherd, brought here to scrounge from us, the free-loading old fucker!'

Antinous swore at Eumaeus. 'You ignorant old bastard, who gave you the right to bring him in here? Haven't we got enough scroungers in town without you dragging another one in tow, and right into the palace too, polluting the place and stinking us out? Look at him, for fuck's sake – what the fuck did you bring him here for?'

Eumaeus started to say something about the laws of hospitality but Telemachus cut him short.

'Don't get involved with him, Eumaeus, he's the worst troublemaker of the lot and he'd love the chance to have a go at you. As for you, Antinous, I appreciate your anxiety on behalf of the food – my food, as it happens – but I'd never order a hungry stranger out of the house – again, my house, may I remind you. So as long as you're in my house and eating my food, you can share it with those less fortunate than yourself. You can start by giving the old man something from your own plate – unless your greed has got the better of you.'

Antinous jumped up and grabbed the stool that his trim little feet were resting on.

'Give him something, do you say? Too fucking true I'll give him something – something about his fucking ears if he doesn't disappear!'

By this time I'd reached him, and I held out my wallet.

'Surely, sir, you're not going to grudge me a crust or a crumb, are you? You that look every inch a king yourself? Almost as if you own the place. All the more reason, I'd have thought, to award me the biggest share and put the others to shame. That's no more than what I used to do when I was one of the lucky ones, back in the old days. Yes, that takes me back – to Crete, actually, where I was once rich and powerful. I had it all, you could say – hundreds of servants, and I never once refused a beggar in the street, and certainly not in my own house. But that was before I was stupid enough to leave it all behind and sail for Egypt – with a pack of pirates. We made the Nile, and I anchored there and sent out scouts onto the heights to spy out the land. And what did they do? Went mad, they did, killed a lot of men and captured their women and children and brought them kicking and screaming back to the ship. I couldn't believe it, the sheer stupidity. Of course the alarm was raised, and the Egyptian infantry went on the move. It looked as though the entire Egyptian army had been called out. Their chariots came thundering across the plain, and we were cut off. Do you know what? Not a man stood up to them – they didn't have the balls for it. And it turned out to be a massacre, apart from the handful they spared for slavery. But they accepted I wasn't to blame, and they let me live and be taken on to Cyprus by one of their allies. I'll tell you about him in a minute. Let me see now, his name's on the tip of my tongue . . .'

'Shut your gob!'

Antinous was seething.

'You won't have a tongue much longer if you don't shut up! Spoiling our dinner like this with your interminable reminiscences, and every one a lie! Who cares? Nobody gives a flying fuck for who you were or what you were. Or what you are now, for that matter, which is an eyesore of a plague-boil!'

His eyes were blazing, and his hands were trembling with rage. I'd got under his skin. I could see he'd not stay cool in a tight corner.

'Dmetor – yes, that was his name, Dmetor. I'm trying to recall the name of his father. Iasus, that was it, he was the son of Iasus. He was king of the island, undisputed. And that's where I've come from. A long journey it was too. I'll tell you about it shortly, but I'm just in time, it seems, to beg a morsel from your plate. That's if you don't mind my asking again?'

'What the fuck? Is the old bastard deaf or something? Or is he just as thick as the shit he stinks of?'

Antinous was spitting by this time. He gave me a huge shove, and I let myself stagger backwards, scattering most of the food I'd collected.

'Get the fuck away from me! Just stand out there and don't fucking come near me again! Egypt? I'll Egypt you! I'll fucking Cyprus you! I'll give you Cyprus and Egypt up your old arse! You'll wish you were fucking back there by the time I'm done with you!'

I looked around, my now empty arms spread wide in appeal. There were a few sympathetic looks. I decided to get in one last dig.

'And here was I thinking your heart matched your looks, young man. How wrong I was. You're the sort who'd grudge a pinch of salt to a servant from your own larder, and yet you're helping yourself from another man's table and can't even pass me a bite of bread that doesn't belong to you anyway. What about that large loaf at your elbow, for example?'

'God almighty!'

He drew back his arm.

'If I can't make you, maybe this fucking will!'

I turned as he flung the heavy stool. It hit me hard on the right shoulder and bit into the bone. Melanthius clapped his hands and roared approval.

'Oh, well done, Antinous, you got the old bastard at last! Next throw's mine. And I'll crush his fucking skull if he still hasn't learned to shut up!'

Nobody else joined in, though, and I took advantage of the moment of silence.

'Well, in spite of your treatment of me, I wish you well, sir, especially with your marriage plans – though I have an idea you'll be dead before your wedding day.'

The goatherd gasped and picked up his own stool.

'The old bugger! Did you hear that, Antinous? Did everyone hear what he just said? Fucking impudence! Now he's for it!'

But Antinous sensed the ebbing of support and checked him.

'Never mind, Melanthius, don't let him get to you. I can see now he's half mad. But as for you, old man, you'd better grab what you can if it keeps your trap shut. I'm warning you, being crazy won't excuse you or allow you any more freedom of speech. You've stretched our patience enough as it is. One more word, and you'll be taken out and flayed from head to foot.'

'Flayed alive,' gloated Melanthius. 'I'll see to it personally. And I'll take my time over it. Slowly does it for you. The dogs will be licking your blood long before the life's gone out of you. That's before I rub the salt into your raw hide – a whole barrel. And I won't waste a drop. What doesn't salt your carcass I'll stuff down your gob. And if you need a drink before you die, I'll piss up your nostrils!'

This drew a couple of laughs, but everybody wanted to eat.

Telemachus brought me over some fresh food and asked in a whisper if I was all right.

'Never better. Enjoying the meal. And enjoying myself even more making a mental list. Antinous tops it, and the goatman comes a close second. There won't be long between them.'

Eumaeus came over and said that word of Antinous's assault on me had reached Penelope, and she sent her apologies. Clearly, she had lost all control.

Did she also request that I join her upstairs in her private apartments? She must have done, since there I am, a bundle of black rags sitting on a cushion, close to a scented queen – a cosy if unlikely twosome in her chamber, a good scene for the loom. On the other hand the word would have got to her by now that the stranger downstairs had tramped the world, Egypt and Crete, seen action at Troy, fought at her husband's side, heard news of him in Thesprotia. What wife wouldn't want to speak to such a man? Assuming she believed a single word of it, a syllable of hope spoken by a thing of shreds and tatters, begging for a crust. What wife indeed. So up on the web she went, and the stranger with her.

Downstairs, I sat on quietly, picking from my plate. I had plenty of food for thought. Telemachus left me with a secret wink, and Eumaeus finished his own meal and left for the farm. In the failing daylight, the drinking and singing and dancing carried on, and quickly turned into an orgy. The whores came down and lifted their skirts, bending their bare arses over the tables for the benefit of the young bloods. Proposing marriage to the woman upstairs and fucking her maids down below: they had turned the palace into a brothel. I saw the last rays of light splash the courtyard behind me, and I gloried for a moment in the sunset's red wreckage. I told myself the sun would only go down on their depravity one more time. But even as it set for the day, there was one more ugly scene to be played out in the palace hall.

FIFTY-FOUR

Enter Arnaeus, nicknamed Irus, a dogsbody to the palace suitors, also a vagrant of no fixed abode. He was a thug who didn't so much beg as bully his way through the streets of Ithaca. People paid up at the very sight of him, frightened to be accosted. There were plenty of broken noses to advise charity as the best course of action, even though it was obvious that he stood in no need of charity and could have worked for a living if he could have been arsed. He couldn't. He was a big bastard, built like an ox, so it seemed, and he had an appetite to match, both for eating and drinking.

Work? Why the fuck should I work? Why work when I can live on the handouts I get? If they won't give it to me, I'll kick it out of them. And if they still won't pay, I'll kick the shite out of them instead.

Can work, won't work was his motto. He relied on his appearance to earn him a living, the irony being that the appearance was deceptive. He was nowhere near as strong as he looked and lacked grit. He was a coward and a weakling in disguise, a typical bully. And this was the character who darkened the threshold where I still sat. He came swaggering in and went straight on the offensive.

'And who the fuck might you be? Get lost, old-timer, or you'll be heaved out by the ankle and you'll end up on your head. Go on, scram! Can't you see them tipping me the wink? This is my patch, and I don't want you pissing on it. Off you scoot now before I kick you up your bony arse and lay you out cold!'

I looked up, taking the measure of the cunt. All bone and no backbone. A gutless tough. I decided it would be fun to play along.

'That's not much of a greeting, friend, especially when I've neither said nor done anything to harm you. We're both beggars, I take it. Well then, I'm sure this threshold is big enough for both of us, wouldn't you say? If not, all I ask is that you think long and hard before you call me out. Because if you do, I'd better warn you, I'll give you a hair-colouring and a face-colouring too. You'll end up dyed in your own blood. How would that suit you?'

Irus gaped in disbelief.

'What? Fighting talk? From a beaten-up old bum like you? God above,

I'm going to fucking kill you! And I'll tell you how it will start off. A right from me, followed by a left – and you'll be spitting out whatever teeth you've got left in those mumbling old jaws of yours, you jabbering old idiot! After that, I'm going to mash you to a pulp for puppies to eat. Now tuck up your rags, grandfather, and I'll show you how a real man can fight. We're going to give these gentlemen some entertainment.'

'You mean you're going to earn your dinner for a change? I'd like to see you try!'

Everybody got up laughing and clapping and clearing away the tables, making a quick ring round us. Irus was already prancing around the circle, showing off his puny biceps and punching the air. Antinous was ecstatic.

'Hey, fellows, we really are in luck tonight! A boxing match laid on out of the blue. Irus versus the old idiot – what a hoot! It's hilarious. It's irresistible. Not only that, but now I don't have to get rid of the old bag of rags myself – Irus is going to do it for us! Still, let's be fair and offer a prize, make a night of it, what do you say?'

Huge cheering and applause.

'A prize! A prize!'

'What'll it be?'

'I'll tell you what,' said Antinous, 'you see these goats' paunches roasting over there? They're well stuffed with blood and fat for our supper. I say that the winner gets first pick of these. Seconded?'

Roars of approval.

'And what's more, he gets to join us for dinner every night from now on, and all other beggars are to be excluded. Seconded?'

'Seconded! Seconded!'

Antinous came over to me.

'Well, old relic, I reckon your long tongue has done for you at last. You've just about dug your own grave. Irus is going to kick the shit out of you.'

I nodded and spread my arms wide, looking rueful.

'I know. There's not much sense in a match like this. I don't know what came over me just now. I went too far, as usual. It's as you say, I seem to suffer from a long tongue. I don't suppose there's any getting out of it now, is there?'

'Too late! Too late!'

The loud negatives and headshakings were followed by uproarious applause as Irus tucked up his clothes and flurried the air with punches. The ring of men urged me on.

'Hurry up, hoary arse, don't keep us waiting! Show us what you're made of!'

'Old skin and bone!'

'It's only his rags that's holding him together! Take them off and he'll fucking fall apart!'

I tucked the rags around my middle and bared my chest and thighs, arms and shoulders. Gasps went round the hall.

'Fucking hell, will you look at that? The old bugger's built like a fucking champion beneath all that shit. We really are in luck, lads – we've got a fight on after all. Irus may have met his match!'

Irus was already looking white-faced.

'Fuck me, friends, let's forget it – how was I to know the old bastard was built like that?'

'Yes, but you're half his age, so it's an even fight.'

'Look, I'll tell you what, just for tonight I'll let the old fellow have the paunches, and I'll make do with what I can get.'

He tried to withdraw, but the suitors were having none of it. The ring of spectators forced him back into the centre.

'Back you go!' shouted Antinous. 'You started it, and by god you're going to give us a fight. And if you lose, by the way, I'm going to have you shipped off to Echetus. Heard of him? He's a maniac. He'll rip your cock off, balls and all, to give to his dogs. Nose and ears to boot, got it? Now get in there and fucking fight!'

Irus was shaking all over. He put his fists up and stood facing me, petrified. It was going to be like knocking over a statue. I considered killing him outright but decided that would be overdoing it. In any case, I didn't want to reveal my full strength and arouse any suspicion, so when he threw his first fist I landed a crushing punch on his neck, just below the ear. I felt the give beneath my fist – the bones being smashed in. The crunch was audible too as the jaw shattered. Everybody gasped. The blood gushed up into his mouth and came bubbling out as he opened wide, groaning and spitting, then he fell back grinding his teeth and drumming the dust with his heels. The rabble fell about laughing.

I wasn't done with him. I grabbed him by the ankle and yanked him out all the way across the courtyard to the gate. I propped him up against the wall, shoved his stick into his limp paw and warned him.

'Now sit there and fucking behave yourself! And that's not all. You're being given a job to do for the first time in your useless fucking life. I want you to keep the pigs and dogs away with that ugly mug of yours

– that's your employment from now on. See to it, and there might be a crust for you, if you can still swallow. Fail, and you starve. If I see one swine or canine get past you, I'll come back and give you a proper thrashing. And next time I'll finish you off. If you as much as move from that spot, I'll crush your skull, got it?'

His act was over, but he still had an audience. The suitors had followed us out to view the finale and they trooped back inside giving me loud cheers.

'Well done, old Atlas, you've just fucked up the worst glutton in town and the laziest scrounger in Ithaca. But he's off to Echetus now, eh, Antinous?'

Antinous had expected to see me murdered by this time, and he now had no option but to present me with the biggest paunch, hot and dripping from the fire. With better grace, Amphinomous selected a couple of whole loaves for me and raised his golden cup.

'Here's to better health, my friend, and better days ahead for you.'

He handed me the cup.

'And for you too,' I said. 'For you too – I hope to god!'

He looked at me curiously.

'Why do you say that?'

I hesitated.

'What do you mean?'

I decided to give him a chance.

'Amphinomous, I appreciate your decency. And if you can take an old man's advice, here it is. We human beings, we're a pathetic lot, aren't we? As long as things are going our way we never stop to think that there might be hard times ahead. But there always are – because that's our life, isn't it, sunlight and shadow? Right now, you're enjoying the good life along with these bloodsuckers who're living at the expense of an absent king. But what happens when the king comes back? Some say he's dead, but from what I've heard he's not only alive but is nearer to you than you know, and so is the day of reckoning. You strike me as not a bad man yourself, not at heart. So, for your sake, I hope you'll see fit to get out while you can. Go home, I'm begging you, before it's too late, before you have to face that man on the day he walks in here. As walk in he will, like a lion into his lair. That day will be a bloody day for that lot, and when the meeting's over, I don't imagine there'll be one of them left alive to wish they'd heard this warning of mine. You've heard it, sir. Take heed of it: that's all I ask, and take my advice – as easily as you take back this cup.'

I drank up and gave him back the cup. He looked sadly into the empty circle of gold.

'Who are you, old man?'

'I'm your conscience.'

'Right. And you pack a punch like a boxer, and you talk like an orator. But why should you be concerned for me? You don't know me.'

'I know you're not tarred with the same brush as that rabble. And I know there's going to be a bloodbath here – I can feel it in my waters. Odysseus is close, and there's no way he's going to part from these men without a terrible loss of life. For the last time, I'm begging you – leave, leave now, leave that lot to their fate, and don't share it. You don't have to.'

I looked as hard as I could into his eyes, willing him to get up and go. But he went back to join the others and sat down on his chair. He sat heavily, shaking his head and filled with the foreboding I'd deliberately instilled into him – but still he didn't listen. The moment he left me and walked back to the chair he'd settled his own destiny. It was the wrong end of a spear.

⌐

Destiny belongs on the web. Life itself, as they say, is a tapestry.

And so Pallas Athene now put it into the head of Penelope to leave her lofty apartment and descend like a goddess on the hall, with the dual effect of fanning the fever of the romantic rabble and enhancing her beauty in the eyes of the disguised husband, thus putting these two parties into increased opposition and bringing the conflict closer.

She turned to her housekeeper with a little laugh. 'You know, Euronyme, I don't know why, but I feel a sudden urge to go down and pay these lovers of mine a courtesy visit.'

'I thought you detested them?'

'I do. But still I want them to see me. Don't ask me why.'

'Well then, you'd better tidy yourself up. Just look at these tear-stained cheeks. Let's get you ready.'

'No, Euronyme! What, preen myself for those men? Absolutely not.'

But Pallas Athene thought differently.

And so Penelope feels now so suddenly drowsy that her body droops like a flower heavy with rain, and she sinks down onto her couch and falls into a divinely contrived sleep. The goddess gets busy. She is using a heavenly cosmetic like the one Cythereia applies when she puts on her crown and dances with the Graces, her skin whiter than ivory, her breasts voluptuous, her stature tall and imposing. And then the white-armed maids appear to conduct Penelope downstairs, and she awakes and rises like Aphrodite from the sea to stun the suitors into a heightened state of amazement and desire.

Eurymachus speaks for all of them.

'You look as if Pallas Athene had just wafted over you with her wand. If all the Achaeans in Ionian Argos could see you now, no palace in the world could contain the gathering of lovers that would compete for your hand, for there isn't a woman in the world to touch you.'

The fair Penelope, as modest as she is wise, brushes that compliment aside.

'Well, I don't know about that, but I do know I have just enjoyed a most refreshing sleep. And sleep, as we all know, is a great beautifier, so any beauty you may perceive in me must be the work of Morpheus and not Aphrodite. All the same, I could have wished that it had been the sweet sleep not of Athene but of Artemis, and that one of her gentle arrows had prevented me from wasting my days beyond today, sitting alone as always, and languishing in tears for the man who was the glory of Greece.'

Every man present at that moment wishes he could take that man's place, little realising that the man himself is sitting among them, watching their every move, weighing their every word, storing it all up to hold against them when their hour should come.

'In the meantime,' continues Penelope, 'I take a dim view of the maltreatment of that stranger sitting over there. What happened, according to the report that reached my ears, was a disgrace to this house.'

'It was, mother,' says Telemachus, 'and I was powerless to prevent it, but I can at least assure you that things did not fall out as Antinous had hoped and expected. That useless hulking bully, Irus, is even now propped up against the courtyard wall close to the gates. He's hanging his ugly head, and not because he's drunk as usual, but because he lacks the bones to support it. They've been crushed by a single punch from that same stranger, and I doubt if he'll even manage to make his way back out into the street, let alone live. And if he does live, begging's all that's left for him. I must say, I'd love to see your suitors scattered about the courtyard in a similar situation. That would cool their ardour.'

Eurymachus stands up.

'That was uncalled for, sir. It's an entirely unfriendly line of talk and an insult to your guests.'

'It would be – if I had guests. But I don't. I didn't ask for your company. As I recall, you're simply uninvited spongers, that's all.'

Eurymachus remains calm. 'Still, you must admit that you can't blame us for your mother's beauty. Here she is, a widow for all this time and in need of a husband to look after her estate, and she comes down tonight to grace us with her presence, looking like a goddess. A man's not made of stone, you know. And as I've said already, if every Greek man could see her, this house would be thronged with suitors, and we'd have to extend tomorrow's feast out into the courtyard.'

So speaks the silver-tongued lover, little knowing that tomorrow's feast will indeed turn out to be an extended one, but not in the way he imagines.

Meanwhile Penelope, wise as ever, uses this speech as an opportunity to make a cleverer one.

'Thank you again for the compliment, Eurymachus. I must say they are flying tonight. But one thing does concern me, and it's this. If you value me so highly as a prospect, and if your handsome young heads are really turned by the looks of a mature woman, it's a wonder you haven't done the proper thing by now.'

'Tell us what it is,' says Agelaus.

'That's right!' shouts Leodes. 'Tell us what it is, and by god we'll do it!'

'Well then,' said the wise Penelope, 'instead of just turning up here empty-handed, expecting free meals, I'd have thought you might at least have shown your ardour by bringing along your own beasts to the banquet instead of slaughtering mine. It doesn't exactly make you seem keen, does it, that sort of meanness? It's hardly an inducement. I mean, what is a woman supposed to think?'

'You're right,' says Eurydamas. 'We've not shown sufficient respect.'

'We'll change that!' cried Peisander. 'Anything else?'

'Well, there is one other thing, but I'm almost ashamed to refer to it.'

'No – tell us, tell us!'

Eurynomus and Demoptolemus are on their knees.

'Surely then, surely it's customary for suitors to woo a lady with gifts – I mean really valuable presents, to prove to her the degree to which she is adored and appreciated.'

'I'll be first!' roars Amphimedon, always first to get drunk. 'And I'll send out for them right now!'

Under his rags, Odysseus can scarcely contain his delight. A clever diplomat of a queen, wheedling gifts from her despised lovers and bewitching them by her beauty and her coquetry to provide tribute, which will go straight into her husband's estate and compensate in some measure for all the wastage and losses. These will be the last gifts they will ever give and will never be taken back. This is a queen fit for a king, the perfect spouse for the artful Odysseus.

The gifts are sent for and produced. The doomed fools fall over each other in their eagerness to impress. Antinous offers an embroidered robe, glittering with golden brooches, a dozen at least, with pins that clip into curving golden bars. Eurymachus presents a golden chain, elegantly made and strung with amber beads, each gleaming like a little sun. A pair of earrings from Eurydamas, lambent, lucent, lovely, each with a cluster of three droplets that fall like the tears of Niobe. And many many more follow.

Penelope's women carry all the gifts up to her apartments for her to assess in private and so appraise the relative worth of the donors, so she says, assuring them it will be a close-run contest. And the suitors, pleased with themselves, light three braziers in the hall and resolve to make a good night of it. Tons of logs are ferried in by the sweating slaves and left in piles by the braziers for the maids to throw on every so often and keep the firelight bright till dawn.

'You girls keep the brands in the braziers,' leered Antinous, 'and we'll keep our torches in you. They'll be well lit up!'

Raucous laughter.

He grabbed one of the girls called Melantho, gripping her by the haunches. She pulled her dress over her head, turned her back to him, propped both elbows on the table and stuck her arse in the air. Eurymachus kept her as his own regular mistress but apparently liked to show her off in orgies. He climbed onto the table facing her, kicked aside the plates and pitchers, and took her head in his hands, forcing it into his groin. She flipped out his prick and gave it the works while Antinous went at her like a little bull from behind. He came quickly.

'Your turn now, Pelias. Try this end.'

Pelias was well oiled by this time.

'Yes, Antinous, but not where your well-used knob has been, excuse me! Look, she's dripping – and she comes like a man.'

'Well,' said Eurymachus, 'so she's a squirter. If that bothers you, try the arse. But get on with it, for fuck's sake!'

The whore took the prick briefly from her lips.

'Yes, come on, Pelias, let's have a bit of buggery while I'm finishing off your mate. Ah!' and she gasped as Pelias obliged.

Most of the other shagging was going on in the shadows, but the quartet at the table were too drunk to care.

'When I own this palace,' laughed Eurymachus, 'I'm going to build a shrine where this table is, sacred to the nymph Melantho – the nymphomaniac!'

After they'd taken her fill of her and she of them, she stood up, still naked, and threw on a few logs. She swept up a wine cup and stood knocking it back, her behind to the brazier. Her face was flushed. I approached her, holding out her dress, which I'd picked up from the floor. She snatched it from me and threw it away.

'Keep your filthy mitts off my clothes, you old fucker!'

'Well now,' I said, 'I was only going to suggest that you and the other girls get dressed and go back upstairs to your mistress where you belong. And I'll look after all three fires. Even if the lads here keep on drinking till daybreak, I'm their man. I can carry on, I assure you. They won't see me out – I'll see them out first. I'm as tough as old rope.'

The whore spat out her wine in my face.

'There's your answer, bastard head! You see, I can squirt at both ends! Now fuck off before I piss on you as well. Who asked you to stick your old oar in? Has the wine gone to your noodle? Or do you think you're somebody now just because you happened to give a coward a thrashing? He was all mouth, and you're still nobody. A real man would have flattened you. Now vanish, you old fart, before I set the dogs on you!'

Eurymachus applauded her.

'She's quite a girl, isn't she, my Melantho? How'd you like to be my age again and have her cupping your balls, eh? She'll be in charge here when I'm the man, and Penelope will be her flunkey. As for you, old bummer, it's time you left town – unless you want to do some real work for me up on one of my farms, dyking or ditching or felling trees. That would sort you out. But you'd rather turn up here to fuck up our feasts and stuff your gluttonous stomach, am I right? Of course I'm fucking right!'

'Of course he's fucking right!' echoed Melantho.

'Is he?' I asked. 'I'll bet he doesn't know what real work is. Listen, my lad, I'd like to take you out at dawn in summertime when the days are long, out in some hayfield, just the two of us, a sickle each and a whole day's reaping ahead of us, and nothing to eat or drink till sundown. Or how about a four-acre field for the two of us to plough, with a pair of oxen apiece, beasts bursting with fodder, big buggers that don't wear out, that pull away from you all day. Then we'd see whose legs and shoulders would last out and who'd cut the straightest furrow. Then we'd see what's what. Then we'd see who's who. Or if I were to take you out into the front line with the arrows whanging and the spears whistling and the chariots thundering at you in the dust – then we'd see which one of us shat himself first. You think you're a big man, but you're small fry, you're a useless bully, and if Odysseus appeared in front of you right now you'd find even that nice wide exit over there a shade too narrow for you in your panic to abscond!'

Eurymachus finally boiled over.

'You old bugger! You really have lost your fucking senses, haven't you? Are you off your face? Or is Melantho right? Beating that arsehole Irus has gone right to your head. But you've gone too far now, even for a crazy old cunt!'

He whipped up his stool and hurled it at my head. I ducked quickly, and it hit the wine-steward on the back of the hand. He yelped in pain, sucking his knuckles, and the jug clanged on the floor, spilling the wine.

Furore in the hall. My position didn't look too good.

'Who the fuck asked him to stay on anyway?'

'He's caused nothing but trouble.'

'Ruining the atmosphere.'

'Setting us at each others' throats.'

'Is the steward all right?'

'Oh, let's call it a night – it's almost fucking dawn.'

Telemachus was quick to capitalise on the sudden lapse of energy and the descent into lassitude and drunken weariness, and he announced formally that the celebrations were at an end.

'What the fuck are we celebrating anyway?'

'That woman still hasn't made up her fucking mind.'

'And we're lots of gifts down with nothing to show for it.'

'She's fucking fleeced us!'

Grumbling and slurring, they shambled over the threshold like beasts to the slaughter and out and away into the thinning dark. Still cursing and stumbling, holding onto their whores, they went off in their various directions, staggering home.

FIFTY-FIVE

I was left in the deserted hall with Telemachus. We stood in the shadows and looked at each other in silence.

'It's time,' I said, 'to prepare the ground. Remember the plan: first get rid of the weapons.'

He went to feed Eurycleia the agreed story, that they'd been tarnished by the smoke over the years and he'd pack them away in the storeroom for cleaning and polishing.

'The old beggar will help me,' he told her. 'It's not work for maids, and certainly not for whores. I won't have any of them touching my father's weapons.'

'When the time comes,' I said, 'the women will be locked away too. Eurycleia will see to it that they're confined to their quarters.'

'Couldn't we have taken her into our confidence by now?'

I put a finger on his lips.

'It only takes one to spread the word, and then our only ally – surprise, remember? – is no longer on our side. You know what women's tongues are like.'

At that point, Melantho flitted out of the shadows.

'What, still here, old ogler? Cruising round the house at your age, looking for a piece of arse, no doubt. Who'd sleep with you? Or you thought you'd catch me again without my clothes, did you, you old weirdo?'

'Take care, missy,' I said. 'If Odysseus had caught you without your clothes earlier on, turning his house into a brothel in his absence, he might have hanged you in them, strung you up on the spot.'

'Odysseus my arse! He's a fucking myth! He's history.' She flounced towards the doors. 'And if you're still mooching about here tomorrow night, you'll be flung out into the street with a torch tied to your old balls! I'll have my lover see to it.'

'Your lover? You mean your whoremaster? Your little pimp.'

'Fuck off!'

Another ugly scene.

Easy to follow it with a woven one. Easy to bring down Penelope to apologise for her maid's behaviour, overheard by Eurycleia. Easy to bring her down at last to meet her husband. Easy to maintain the disguise and act out the impossible, as people do in art, where nothing's impossible and people are not their real selves.

Spread a rug then, spread it on the settle, close to the fire, and let husband and wife come closer, let them speak their first words to one another in nineteen years, tricked by the swindler time, and by firelight and the dissembling shadows into innocent talk, the disguise impenetrable, arranged after all by Pallas Athene, cleverer than any mortal wife, even the divine Penelope.

It all came out: the Trojan War, delectable, detestable Helen, the thousand ships, the mighty dead, the missing husband, the endless weary waiting, no news, the suitors from Dulichium and Same and wooded Zacynthus, the Ithacan lice, the heart worn out with longing, the loom trick, the exposure, the sudden unavoidability of marriage, her own parents insisting on a match, and not without reason, nineteen years and no returning. She was out of options. It was over. Penelope's story.

As for Odysseus, he had a tale to tell that would have filled up another web.

Picture Crete, rich and wonderful, washed by waves, a lovely island, a golden brooch pinned to the sea's azure robe. Picture its ninety cities, its many languages, its races, the Achaeans, the Cydonians, the Dorians, the Pelasgians and the proud native Cretans. Picture Cnossos, that great city, ruled for nine years by King Minos, the grandfather of the old beggar, no less, the royal vagrant, now seated with the Queen of Ithaca.

Time to identify this beggar of royal blood, give him a name. Call me Aethon, he says, son of Deucalion and grandson of Minos. Aethon will suffice. Any name will suffice, except Odysseus. And next, picture Odysseus himself – the real Odysseus – bound for Troy but driven off course at malevolent Malea and putting in at Amnisus, where he's made welcome by none other than Aethon, and is wined and dined while the wind howls hard about them. The northerly gale blew hard for twelve days out on the deep, but on the thirteenth day the gale abated and Odysseus put to sea. No man making for Troy knew whether he'd got there, and if he did, whether he ever came away again.

Picture too in passing the tear on Penelope's cheek, drawn there by the beggar's lying yarns and the hand of the queen herself. Picture the east wind melting the snow that the cold west wind brought to the high hills and the thaws causing the mountain rivers to run down in spates, soaking the steep slopes. So did the falling tears fall in floods, drenching Penelope's fair face, though her husband's eyes stared hard and dry as iron, so cleverly did he suppress his sorrow, his tender tears, the master of disguise, the lord of his emotions.

You may even picture the brooch Odysseus happened to be wearing when Aethon met him, seen by Aethon's own eyes, pinned to his purple cloak: a golden brooch bearing an elaborate design of a dappled fawn struggling in the clutches of a powerful hound. The fawn's little hooves were kicking desperately, but the dog ripped out the throat and throttled the animal brutally. That picture drew more tears from Penelope – not for the sake of the fawn, but because she recognised the brooch as the gift she'd given her husband before he left for Troy, and so she knew the old beggar was telling the truth, even as he lied.

And picture finally the story of Odysseus's return from Troy, all the troubles that followed from the Cicones and the Cyclops, because Polyphemus was the son of the nymph Thoosa, daughter of Phorcys, Warden of the Salt-sea Waves, and it was Poseidon who filled her belly with this child when he slept with her in her cavern, hollowed and hallowed by the sea. So Poseidon's hatred remained implacable, intensified by the anger of Apollo, leading to the loss of the last ship and all her crew, nineteen days in the sea before reaching the sea-kings, cousins to the gods, who arranged the voyage home, interrupted however by Thesprotia and by Odysseus's final trip – he'd gone to Dodona to discover the will of the gods from the sacred oak tree there, and to ask advice about how to approach Ithaca. When in doubt, go to Dodona. When you want to know something awful, approach an oak. When you need secret advice, ask a tree.

And when you're looking for truth?

Ah, so we're back to that, are we? What's truth? Whatever it is, you won't find it in the web. Don't look there, not when you come home from wars and wandering with all those women behind you, the women you slept with. You did it a thousand times, so why shouldn't she? Do her eyes give her away? The eye is the index to the soul, and the window to her chamber. You squint into them secretly but hard, the eyes of Penelope, and you try not to imagine them closed in contentment as she lies down with Amphinomous, the one she was fond of. How fond? She had a soft spot for him, so they said. How soft? And where? You know where, don't you? You can picture that soft spot precisely, can't you? And her eyes opening as wide as her mouth as Amphinomous gets it up, oh yes, very well, he thrusts and sucks and her nipples come up stiff and wet and leathery, like little pricks, and there's that tense little smile on her lips, she's pleasured but impatient, her knees are pulled right back now to allow him extra depth, her legs come up, her heels digging his ribs, she starts to buck, fuck me! fuck me! he turns her over roughly, her arse in the air, like Melantho's, like Calypso's, like she did it for you so many nights, and she moves the arse for him now, like Calypso used to do, shifts it back and forwards, travelling slowly along the whole length of the wet swelling member, faster as he gathers speed, till he reaches under and cups her swinging tits, and she reaches back and cups his swaying balls . . . Oh, come quickly! Oh, come quickly, sweetest love, and suck my soul to thee! He comes. She comes.

Over. No? Don't be in too much of a hurry. He turns her over again onto her back, climbs aboard, sits on her tits, his prick still spilling over. She grabs it greedily and stuffs it in her mouth. He's still pumping it out and she squeezes it tight, the Calypso trick, to arrest the release, to stop the flow, filling him with ecstasy, with pain. The seconds are centuries. Then she unclasps her hand and lets him finish. Her tongue comes out and licks the glistening tip, licks the wet purple clean, sucks it off and swallows. Amphinomous's sperm is like snow on her red lips. He throws back his head and howls at the ceiling.

I'll make him howl all right, I'll murder the bastard, I'll rip those fucking balls off, and the prick too, I'll stuff it up her cunt and then I'll tear her all to pieces . . .

No, no, calm down, old man, take time to pause, to contemplate, it's not true, none of it's true, look in the web and see. Oh yes, the web, the web. But suppose you look in the bed instead, the bed she contaminated with her lover, the favourite. Suppose you run up there right now and examine the linen, see if you sniff Amphinomous on the sheets. No, no need for that, look at her instead, look hard at her and see what you see – the faithful wife, the fuller bosom, the wider hip. She has a lot more middle now, that is true, more belly to romp on, more silver threads than I'd expected among the gold, more wrinkles round the eyes, the throat. They are still lovely eyes, though, and her mouth is still a succulent mouth. Has it sucked his cock?

'You'd better have a bath,' she said.

What – like Agamemnon?

'A bath?'

'Yes, first thing in the morning, the maids will see to it. Tonight they can see to your feet and spread a bed for you.'

Spread their legs for me. I'll fuck the arses off them, the bitches.

'Give you a good rub-down.'

Give them a good rub-up. A right fucking drubbing, before I murder them. A drabbing. A stabbing.

'Would that compensate for your foul treatment here?'

Foul thoughts, compensation.

'A foot-bath would be fine – except I'd hate those maids to handle me, even my feet. Especially my feet. But if you happen to have some respectable old woman . . .'

Penelope smiled.

'I have just the woman for you. She was my husband's nurse, held him when he was born, bathed him when he was a boy. She's well through now, I'm afraid, but she's one of the old faithfuls, the best in that respect, so I keep her on. She's a little rough, you know, but she's devoted to my husband's memory, and you have such news of him, she'll be delighted to do this for you, if you don't mind telling her your story and listening to her gossip. I'll ask her. Eurycleia!'

'You don't have to ask me. I heard.' She came hobbling out of the shadows.

'Heard everything you said about me. I'm never far away. And I'm far from through, I'll have you know, though I may have a coarse tongue. So what? I'll wash this poor old-timer's feet with pleasure. Small wonder he doesn't want those whores to touch him. He can see for himself where they've been.'

'Thank you, old mother.'

'It's a joy. I'll do it for you like I did it for my lovely Odysseus, so often that I knew every scrape and scar of his body's history. I could chart you his childhood from that body of his, every cut and bruise from his boyhood days, oh yes, every scrape and scar.'

Every scrape and scar. Fuck! I'd forgotten about the scar! She'd see it and recognise me.

Enter now the boar, the perfect web-fellow. What's a web without a boar?

I am visiting Autolycus, my grandfather, my mother's father, the best thief and liar of his age, consummate in craft. I know where my many wiles come from, and I know that my grandfather's gifts came from Hermes. Autolycus was the one who named me, named me after the story of his life, in which he'd made many enemies. So that's what he called me on the day I was born: Odysseus, the son of suffering, child of antagonism and distrust.

I'm out with the hounds on the woody heights of Parnassus, accompanying my uncles, Autolycus's sons, and the dogs are hot on the scent. We come to a thicket, and they go mad with excitement – it's clear he's in there, but they can't get in, it's so dense. He gets out though, instead of lying low, and comes at us on the charge, his back bristling, his eyes on fire, unafraid. He's a big one, a brute, but I'm keen to do my stuff and show my mettle, so I run at him with my spear and stab him in the shoulder, bringing him down –

But not before he's gored me. The lunging tusk catches me just above the knee, a long bright slash. It's a flesh wound and doesn't maim me, but it marks me for life, though the bone is spared, and it's this old scarred gash that Eurycleia's wrinkled hands now passed over as she reached my knee, not even seeing it. She didn't have to – the feel of it was enough.

She gasped and let go of my foot. The bronze basin rang and clattered, the water slopping across the floor. The old crone's eyes went wide. So did her toothless mouth. I put my hand over it.

'That's right, old mother, you're speechless. Stay that way. Keep your mouth shut, or by God it will be my hands on your throat, not your gob!'

Unable to speak, her eyes darting, she waved an arm in the direction of Penelope, sitting pensively over by the fire. I grabbed her by her scrawny old neck and kept my other hand on her mouth.

'Do you want to destroy me? Say a word to anybody, a single soul, including your mistress, and I'll throttle you. Understand?'

I took my hands slowly away from her face. There was no fear in it.

'I know you will. I know you would. But you won't have to. Not with me. As you well know. I'm made of iron. I'm as dumb as stone. Except when I tell you exactly which bitch is which. That's all you'll hear from me.'

'No need for that either. I've seen for myself.'

'There's a couple of others you should know about, when the day comes.'

'The day has come – almost. It's almost dawn. So finish this foot-bath and get yourself some sleep. Tomorrow is a busy day.'

The old gammer grinned – a ghastly grin, toothless, wicked. It frightened me more than the thought of what lay ahead. She hobbled off to fetch more water. When she'd finished and rubbed in the olive oil, she mopped up the spilled water.

'It won't be water I'll be swabbing up tomorrow,' she whispered, still grinning.

'It won't be you doing the swabbing.'

Penelope is never done. Still weaving in her head, night and day, and deep into the night. And into her web now flies a little brown bird, a nightingale. And yet it's not a bird really, it's the daughter of Pandareus, sitting among the green leaves of spring, perched in a tree. She's pouring her heart out, singing her song of sorrow for Itylus, whom she bore for King Zethus, and her little throat is throbbing because this is the son she killed so carelessly, so foolishly, and Penelope trills and turns and tosses, just like the nightingale, torturing herself with longings and indecisions. Should she remain in the palace, keeping her husband's estate intact and his bed inviolate? Or should she put an end to the suitors and leave now with the best of them, and the most generous with his gifts? Amphinomous has given the dress laden with pearls.

Was that all he gave you, then? And what about the golden chain with amber beads? That was a generous present. What about Eurymachus, the whoremaster? Who was the more generous? Who was better in bed?

Which of them fucked you?

The question filled my throat, like the song of the nightingale.

Did you fuck them both?

My mouth brimmed.

While I was fucking Circe? And Calypso? Did you fuck them both at the same time? Did you fuck all of them in the same bed? My bed? Our bed? Did you fuck them one by one? All together? Did you suck their cocks?

I ground my teeth.

'I can't sleep.'

I bet you can't.

'All my nights are restless now.'

Lack of cock?

'I have bad dreams.'

Not enough cock.

'I had one dream . . .'

One dream. One more for the web. Twenty geese string out now, stretching under her hand, her busy hand, her cunning hand. What has that hand been up to? A skein of twenty, leaving her hand, leaving her head, craning, stretching their long necks, stretching the web.

'I do keep twenty geese, as it happens. They swing by from the pond to peck up the grain. I like to watch them. I love their cries, like trumpets in the sky. Sometimes you can't see them, especially in the nights, and it's as if the stars were singing to you. It's as if the heavens had a voice. What are they, these geese?'

Your longings. Your lovers. I can hear them too, crowding out my head, filling it to bursting, to madness. I know all about their fucking trumpets.

'And in my dream an eagle came down and attacked them.'

You bet he did.

'I saw him. And he had my husband's eyes.'

Of course he did.

'Down he swooped from the high hills, all claws and beak, ripping into them, screaming, scattering them like snowflakes, the feathers flying, a blizzard of death. He took his fill of them, then up he soared, leaving them in heaps, and he was soon a speck in the sky.

'I wept aloud in my dream, and the ladies gathered round me as I sobbed over my slaughtered geese. Then I woke up and the women were standing round my bed, concerned by my cries. But when I looked out into the yard, there were my geese, perfectly unharmed, pecking away at the grain, as always.'

As ever.

'Can you interpret it?'

An eagle with her husband's eyes. It needs no genius to interpret that one, does it? If this is a burnished horn dream and not an ivory one that issues in emptiness and lies, then the suitors are doomed. Her lovers are dead men. They're like the geese.

'The suitors are the geese.'

They are the geese. They're fucked, and she knows it. Has she informed them already? Has she seen through the disguise? Has she tipped them the wink? One of them? The most generous? The best in bed? Remember Agamemnon. Take care now.

And you – you too take care, because they're all fucked. Mind you do not share their fate. Lady.

No, no chance of that. She's thought of one last plan, an escape plan, an exit strategy, a last attempt to wriggle out of her predicament and thwart the suitors. Well, that at least is what she says.

'Can I tell you? Can you keep a secret?'

Can I keep a secret! Little does she know.

'It's a trial-of-strength plan.'

Like any good old Greek story.

'And a test of skill.'

Aren't they all?

'Odysseus used to set it up.'

Did I really?

'Because he knew nobody could compete with him.'

That was cunning. Tell me about it.

'He'd set up twelve pierced axes all in a row, like the props under a new keel, you know?'

I know.

'And he stood a good way off – and shot a single arrow through all of them, dead straight, every single hole, right through.'

What a man.

'He was the only one who could do it.'

And the plan?

'The plan is, I'm going to have these axes set-up, just as Odysseus used to do, and I'm going to insist that the suitors compete with each other in the same test of skill. Whichever man shoots an arrow through all twelve axes –'

Will shoot his arrow into you.

'It won't be Cupid's arrow, of course.'

Of course not.

'Unless it's tipped with lead. Not gold – I'm long past that.'

Hmm.

'Except for my husband, naturally.'

Naturally.

'A good plan?'

A good plan. But what if more than one of them succeeds in pulling it off?

'Pulling it off? I doubt if any of them will get as far as pulling the string. Or even stringing the bow.'

It's that tough?

'It's a brute. They don't know it, but only Odysseus could string that bow. And that's the bow they've got to use. No other will be acceptable. Well?'

Well. It's incredible.

'And it will happen.'

Incredible.

'But now I'll leave you. I must withdraw aloft to my bed of sorrows.'

Shame.

'Watered by my perpetual tears.'

Perpetual Penelope.

'So many tears.'

See how they fall.

'Falling like rain.'

The rainy Pleiades.

'Falling every night.'

Night must fall.

'Night has fallen so hard, so hard on me every night, ever since the day my husband left me and sailed away to that – that awful place. I can't even bring myself to say its name.'

The doomed city.

'But you must make yourself comfortable by the fire, now that Eurycleia has refreshed you. You at least may sleep in the arms of Morpheus.'

What better?

'None better. Goodnight, stranger.'

Goodnight? I had no intention of sleeping. As for the suitors, snoring their heads off in their homes, little did they know that they were sleeping out their last drunken slumber, the last little sleep before the big one.

FIFTY-SIX

Two Odysseuses lie awake. One will fall asleep in the web of dreams, the other will plot black murder and call it revenge, wondering if he'll get away with it, if he'll still be alive afterwards to see another sun go down. He hears laughter, shrill and silvery, rippling through the dimness before the dawn. He lifts his head a little, watches through the glimmering slits of his eyes.

That was me, brewing a bloodbath in my skull, planning mass murder. That's when I saw them leaving the house, cackling through the hall and out into the courtyard, the whole troop of bitches, out on the prowl instead of looking after their mistress. Were they off to team up with their lover boys? I wanted to leap up and run after them, bar the gates, tear their heads off. I could hear the blood singing in my ears, behind my eyes, telling me to forbid their filthy cunts a final fuck. No, that was madness. Let them die the next night with the sperm still warm in their bellies – before both turned cold.

That's it then, stay cool, old man, it's not worth it, don't ruin it now, you're too close. Tomorrow you can do what you like to them, let Nemesis enjoy the fare. Remember that cannibal? His one eye was like a cunt. You fucked it, fucked it up. You got the better of the bastard by keeping calm. Keep calm now. You got through it. You'll get through this.

Would I? How to take them on, all of them, and not get killed? When to throw off my cover? Could I get more support? What about Eumaeus? He looked as if he could handle himself in a fight, but would he stick with it? Men in tight corners are notoriously liable to run. Or switch sides. I saw some of that at Troy, even among allies. Could he be trusted? Could I trust myself? Would Telemachus bear up? And what about afterwards, and the grieving families of those I killed? Even if I survived, I'd be targeted and I'd have an even bigger fight on my hands. How to hide on an angry island?

The other Odysseus didn't have these problems. Athene descended, hovered over him, and sorted it all out.

'Listen,' she said, 'I know what's going on in that sleepless head of yours. All your fears and frustrations are known to me and your worries are needless. Haven't I always looked after you? Have I ever deserted you? Am I not a goddess? Very well then, will this finally send you to sleep? Let me tell you that if they were fifty times as many suitors surrounding you, all armed and baying for your blood, you'd still scatter them like sheep. With my help you'll see them off. All right? Now get some sleep. Tomorrow is a busy day. And tomorrow will soon be here.'

The goddess closed his eyes in sleep and sped back up to Olympus. As easy as that.

In the web, while I sleep, Penelope awakes. As faithful wives do when their beds are empty and their husbands missing in action. Worn out with weeping, she tries a prayer.

'To Artemis, daughter of the greatest god: send me an arrow from your gentle bow, painlessly to penetrate my heart and pluck my spirit away. Or send the storm-wind to snatch me from my bed and vanish with me into the dark, drop me into the deepest sea, the ocean stream.'

The orphaned daughters of Pandareus appear in the web, illustrating her despair. Here are Artemis and Athene, making them lovely and wise and rich in womanly skills beyond compare, and when the time comes for them to put a cloth between their legs, Aphrodite arranges glorious marriages for all of them. But on that very day the storm-fiends snatch the girls away to the abominable Erinyes, to serve their every need.

'That's what I want to happen to me,' sighs Penelope. 'Life in all its sweetness left me long ago.'

Rather than serve a man inferior to the glorious Odysseus, she begs to be blotted out forever, to be stricken dead and sink deep into the bowels of the earth with her husband's image intact in her heart.

'And my belly will be spared the indignity of a breach of honour, for only Odysseus belongs down there.'

Dawn came and flooded the east with gold. I could hear Penelope's distress upstairs. I went out into the courtyard and stood in the thunder of the sunrise. Across the courtyard stood the handmills where the female slaves ground the grain into meal for the household bread. Since the suitors had been gathering at the palace, the rate of bread consumption had gone up a hundred times and the mills never stopped working. Twelve women toiled at them during the early hours, and this morning they had gone off to seek some sleep before the next shift, all except one who lacked the strength of the others, being old, and had failed to grind her share. She toiled on at her task, muttering and grumbling as she worked. I crossed over to her and stood in the doorway. The sky grumbled briefly along with her, though there wasn't a cloud. The last stars rusted away. She unbent with a groan, one hand on her creaking back, and saw me watching her.

'Hear that?' she said. 'That's a sign.'

'A sign of what, mother?'

'Don't you know? Any fool knows that. Thunder out of a clear sky – that's god, that is, speaking to the wicked.'

'And who are the wicked?'

She cackled and spat.

'Don't you know that, either? You haven't been here long enough to learn anything. They're the ones who've been breaking my back night after night till I've no strength left to stuff their gobs and fill their fat bellies with fresh new bread. I just wish this were the last meal, that's all.'

'You mean the last meal you have to grind?'

'I mean their very last meal – even better!'

'Well,' I said, 'let's hope the thunder's an omen. And I'll tell you this for nothing, old mother, beggar as I am – if Odysseus ever appears, I'm willing to bet one of the first things he'll do will be to free you from this toil and end your backache with a softer form of work.'

She laughed at that. 'Aye, that'll be right. Odysseus doesn't even know I exist.'

'You never know,' I said. 'He could be looking at you right now.'

The household came to life. Telemachus appeared, flanked by two dogs and swinging his spear. I signalled to him not to approach me yet and he went on his way. Eurycleia shouted her morning orders.

'Hurry along there, you've all last night's slops to clean up, and it's a public holiday today – the jackals will be early on the scrounge!'

Melantho, sleepy-eyed, scowled at her. 'Who gave you the right to gab about our guests? You'd better shut your old gob!'

Eurycleia made a face at her. 'You'd do better to shut yours, slut – and your fanny too! Though I don't mind betting they'll both be shut for you before you're much older!'

I threw her a furious look, and she winked at me. Could she be trusted to keep the early morning flies out of her mouth?

The women came back from the well. Eumaeus was with them, driving three fatted hogs.

'Tonight's meal.' He let them hunt and gruntle around the courtyard. 'Their last bite, poor buggers.'

I nodded. I was on the point of saying something but kept it to myself.

'How did they treat you after I left?'

I shook my head.

'They haven't a decent bone in their bodies,' I said. 'Not one among them.'

Eumaeus spat. 'They're cunts.'

Talking of which, Melanthius arrived on the scene with the choicest goats. He and his herdsmen tethered them under the echoing portico. He spotted me and went straight to the attack.

'What's this? Still mooching around here, you old bag of shite? Not dropped dead yet, killed off by your own stink? You'd better fuck off this time – otherwise you and I are going to come to blows before this day's out!'

Ah yes, I thought, I fancy we are. But I kept my tongue between my teeth.

He was still eyeballing me when the master herdsman came up and ordered him to get on with his work. Philoetius. I remembered him well. He looked at me curiously and came straight over, his hand outstretched, smiling. My heart beat hard. God, there were tears in his eyes. I shook his hand and waited. I could hardly breathe.

'You know, old friend, I don't know who you are, but right now you just happened to remind me of somebody.'

'Oh, and who might that be?'

'My old master. There was something of him in you, I thought, just for a moment – that's why the sudden tears. I'm sorry.'

He brushed them away.

'Anyway, welcome to Ithaca. You look as if you've come far.'

'Far enough. And on my travels I heard news about Odysseus. They say he's close.'

'They all say that. Odysseus is on everybody's lips. No lack of sightings either. But he's a dead man.'

We weren't being overheard as Melanthius had gone, so I persisted. I liked the look of Philoetius.

'It's not that I'm on the lookout for a free meal or anything – I'm being well taken care of as it is. But I have it on excellent authority that Odysseus is not only not a dead man but is headed for Ithaca and may even be here right now.'

Philoetius grimaced.

'You don't say. Well, in that case it'll be the jackals that'll be the dead men, when the lion gets in among them.'

'You don't think much of them, then?'

'Oh, I'd like them well enough – with their throats cut. Then they wouldn't be squandering all these beasts. You should see what they're doing to the herds. Odysseus employed me to look after them when I was out in the Cephallenian country, just before he went off to the fighting, and in a few years I don't mind admitting I worked wonders. These herds have spread like cornfields – only to be slaughtered as if there's no tomorrow. I'll tell you this much, if Odysseus appeared on the scene it would be the two-legged ones for the chop, and I'd be right in there lending him a hand.'

'Are you serious?'

'Serious? You can bet your old life I'm serious. What, slaughter these bastards? That wouldn't be work, it would be a fucking pleasure!'

The jackals did come early. And everybody got busy dancing attendance on them. Eumaeus put out the golden cups, Philoetius piled the baskets high with fresh bread, and Melanthius went about with the wine, filling every cup to the brim. He came over and sneered at me.

'Fuck all for you, Father Time – not till I need a piss anyway. Then I'll be over at the toot to fill your cup and force it down your neck. I'm telling you for the last time to shift your stinking arse out of here!'

Telemachus got rid of him and brought me an old stool and a small table which he placed by the threshold just inside the hall. He poured me my wine and helped me to a selection of meat. The suitors had pushed the boat out tonight – they'd killed the biggest sheep and the fattest goats and porkers as well as the heifer from the herd.

'I want none of the usual abuse,' Telemachus announced loudly. 'No brawls or quarrelling, not as long as you're under my roof.'

'As long as it is your roof!'

The yell came from an overweight lout called Ctesippus. Pallas Athene had no intention of letting things calm down. She wanted the anger to bite even deeper into my brain, until I was driven mad by the blood-lust and the quest for vengeance. So she put it into the head of Ctesippus, who was an idiot, to behave even more insolently than ever.

He was a slob from Same who had a fool's view of wealth. He thought his fabulous fortune would turn Penelope's head his way. It was a long time since he'd seen his own reflection in a wine cup. The queen would rather have slept with a donkey.

'Hey, lads,' he shouted. 'Telemachus wants this old fart of a friend to be properly looked after. Seems to me he's got plenty on his plate as it is. But to make sure he's not stinted, I'm going to give him a personal present straight from the table. I'd rather you choke on your own vomit, you old stinker, but if not, well, there you go, try choking on this!'

He picked up the heifer's hoof and hurled it at my head. When you've ducked the Trojan javelins in your time, a cow-hoof is easy. It hit the wall behind me. He grabbed another. It sailed straight through the open doorway and clattered in the courtyard.

Telemachus stood up.

'I asked you politely. I won't ask again. You're lucky you didn't hit him. If you had, you'd have felt my spear in your fat guts!'

Ctesippus clenched both fists.

'I ought to fucking kill you for that threat! Any more and I fucking will!'

Agelaus stood up. 'That's enough, Ctesippus. You were well out of order. But I have to point out, Telemachus, you can see what all this prevarication of your mother's has led to. We're all pissed off. She's pocketed her gifts and still no decision. No more shilly-shallying. Let her choose once and for all and have done with it. Then you can enjoy your own inheritance, and she can look after her new husband's house. Your father is not coming home. Face that fact and move on. Just let it go. My advice is kindly meant and I hope you'll take it. Is it fair?'

Telemachus raised both hands.

'It's fair – on the face of it. A good speech, Agelaus, and a reasonable proposal, and kindly taken too, I assure you. I have absolutely nothing to gain from my mother's procrastination. She shouldn't delay her decision a day longer, you're right. And I can tell you right here and now, I have actually urged her to get married. My father is not coming back. I weep to say it, but again you're right. On the other hand, for a son to say the final word, the word that would expel her from the palace, evict her from her own home and against her will – no, I'm sorry, that would be against my principles. It would be profoundly immoral. She'll have to make her own decision. Personally, I can't do it. I just can't.'

'He can't do it! He can't do it!' A few sneering echoes were taken up and followed by prolonged chanting, thumping the tables and banging down the brimming cups so that the red wine spilled from the gold and ran over tables and floor as they continued to roar in unison.

'He can't do it! He can't do it! He can't do it!'

And so like flies they fell into the web. They struggled to escape but couldn't. They were caught in their own hysteria and deafened to reason by the pealing of their own helpless, uncontrollable laughter, brought on for the occasion by Pallas Athene. She befuddled their brains faster than wine could have worked on them. Then she altered the expressions on their red spluttering faces to looks of incomprehension and terror. The food in front of them was suddenly spattered with blood, the gold cups brimmed with it, thick and dark, the tables ran with it, the floor was awash. They tried to drink away the fear but spat and vomited when they tasted not wine but black death. Their eyes filled up with tears and they broke down.

Theoclymenus the prophet stood up.

'You poor sorry little men! What's this I see on you, all around you? Night has fallen on your heads, and the funeral pall hangs about your knees. I hear a wailing in the air – it's your stricken families, lamenting your end. I see faces wet with tears, cheeks scarred by nails, heads white with ash. Your guilt runs in blood down the palace walls, the porch is thronged with ghosts, the whole court's a-glimmer, flickering crowds of phantoms hurrying down to Hades, scurrying into the dark. Your souls precede you, the sun is blotted from the sky, your end is nigh, catastrophe has come to you at last, you're dead men all and the mist surrounds you. I can see no more. I wish to see no more. I am leaving this house of the dead, while there is yet time.'

'Oh, fuck off then!'

They laughed and laughed. The tears streamed down their cheeks.

Eurymachus stood up. 'You won't have to leave – you'll be thrown out if you don't shut your mad mouth! Here lads, somebody chuck this drunken fucker out into the street, since he finds it so dark in here!'

'I'll do it!' yelled Melanthius.

'I'm on my way,' said the seer. 'As you'd be if you had a brain to share among you. Stay here and be slaughtered, then. This hall is a burial chamber. You're all corpses!'

Melanthius ran at him as he left, aiming kicks at his arse. Antinous applauded. They were over their fit.

'Yes, Telemachus, you really are unfortunate in your choice of friends. First you drag in this work-shy old fraud, who's done fuck all since he came here except eat – and cause trouble. And now we've had to put up with this gibbering imbecile. Where the fuck did you find him? Take my advice – and this is also kindly intended – clap them both in irons and send them to Sicily. They'll fetch a nice price there, and we can all share in the profits!'

Telemachus kept his head. He was watching and waiting for the moment of attack.

'Still the same old Antinous, eh? Look, why don't we all calm down and get back to our meal? After all, it's a holiday, and I'm paying for it, and I don't want good food to go to waste. Eat up, all of you, eat in style, forgive and forget. I expect to see the tables cleared. Eat, gentlemen, until you can no longer move.'

That's the spirit, Telemachus, nobly spoken. And they all swallowed it, along with an amount of eatables that would have made an elephant incapable. Even so they were still planning on a late-night supper to which this dinner was only the prelude. They had no idea what was being planned elsewhere, still less of the bronze in the bowels that awaited each man, the final portion of the great feast.

FIFTY-SEVEN

Time now for Penelope's last prevarication, the trial of strength and skill, of which the suitors as yet knew nothing. When the feasting was nearly finished, she left her apartments and entered the storeroom, where she still kept Odysseus's treasures, together with all the chests of clothes laid by and layered with scented herbs. Here among bronze and gold there hung on a peg the king's great bow and the quiver packed with death, both of which had been presented to him by the great Iphitus when they met each other in Lacedaemon.

Odysseus had left Ithaca for Messene to recover three hundred sheep stolen by the Messenians. He was still a young lad, and it was his first solo mission, entrusted to him by his father. Iphitus was also searching for animals, a dozen mares together with their foals, good muscular little mules, and it was in his quest for these missing beasts that he encountered the cruel-hearted Heracles, who first feasted him and then murdered him, as Aegisthus did Agamemnon, stealing the stock for himself, and for the enrichment of his own stables.

But some time before the dreadful end to his story, Iphitus came across Odysseus in Ortilochus's house in Messene and gave to the youth his great bow – which had been bequeathed to him by his father. Odysseus valued it so highly that he decided not to take it with him to Troy and stored it away with the rest of his treasures. This was the weapon that Penelope now took from the peg and removed from its shining case. She burst into tears when she saw it but brushed them away and carried it downstairs and into the hall to confront her suitors. The quiver bristled with pain for those proud lords – though as yet even she was unaware of who would fire its arrows. Her women followed her, carrying the additional arrows and a dozen bronze axes, all pierced. There was a stir of interest among the suitors. What was she up to now? What was her latest ploy?

'It's very simple, gentlemen,' she announced. 'I am declaring my intention to be married at last – but only to the one among you who can string this bow and shoot an arrow from it through these twelve axe-heads lined up in a row. Odysseus used to do it as a party trick – this is the very bow – and I think it's only reasonable for me to expect the same degree of strength and skill in my new husband as I admired in Odysseus.'

So spoke Penelope, hoping in her heart that none of the suitors would succeed in meeting the challenge.

She went on.

'If any man can display the necessary strength and skill, with that man I'll leave this house which I came to as a bride so many years ago, and I'll be his new bride, though I'll never leave behind me all the lovely memories of this house, for they'll stay with me in my heart. If you agree to this, I can be married to any one of you as early as tomorrow. What do you say? Is it a reasonable proposition?'

She passed the bow to Eumaeus and asked him to give it to the suitors. Antinous took it first into his effeminate hands and examined it carefully.

'It certainly sounds reasonable, though if my childhood memory is accurate, Odysseus was the only man who could even string this bow, let alone perform the feat you describe. You're asking quite a lot. But it's a powerful piece of work, to be sure. Quite a weapon.'

He was secretly hoping he'd be the one to string the bow and break the hopes of all the rest. What he didn't know was that he'd be the first to feel an arrow from it. If he'd seen these images in the web, he'd have fled the house and Ithaca too. But no man escapes his destiny, and by the time the web was woven, Antinous was no more.

He didn't notice Odysseus getting up from his seat near the door and making his way into the courtyard. None of them did; they were all so interested in the business of the bow, all wanting to run their hands over it and get the feel of it, all watching Telemachus directing the servants to help him dig the single long trench in the ground of the hall for the line of axes, stamping down the earth around each one. Everybody crowded round. They wanted to be sure the alignment of the axes was impeccable, and that it wasn't another of Penelope's tricks.

I went out into the deserted courtyard with Eurycleia, as arranged between us earlier. We stood in the dark by the well and washed away the worst of the grime.

'Now come up with me quickly, and I'll give you a proper bath – just like I used to do.'

I stood naked for her as she washed me thoroughly and got busy on my hair and beard, cutting and combing, trimming and untangling, examining every part of me.

'It's nothing to an old woman like me. I saw you often enough like this when you were a little boy, and not much has changed since then, except here and there. Mostly there!'

She cackled and applied the olive oil. Then she produced the new outfit I'd asked her for: sandals, tunic, cloak, every item one of my own, from the scented chests.

'Now you look the part,' she said. 'And you're yourself again. Now go and fuck the bastards!'

'Do you think they'll recognise me?'

'Of course they'll recognise you – you haven't changed that much. But muffle yourself up in the big cloak when you first go in, then throw it off and watch them tremble!'

'Would you have recognised me, seeing me now?'

'For god's sake, man, why do you keep worrying about it? A few years is nothing. You're still the same old Odysseus.'

'What about Penelope?'

'It doesn't matter. She won't be there – she's been sent back upstairs until the trial's over.'

'Telemachus?'

'Yes, he wants her safely out of the way. He knows there's going to be trouble. Is it all worked out between you?'

'All set-up. And remember your own instructions – all the women to be locked in and nobody to be let out, don't forget. And the door to the hall.'

'I remember everything. In you go.'

I took a few deep breaths and made my way towards the hall.

It would have been more startling to have stayed as the old beggar, more theatrical and thrilling dramatically to have cast off my rags at the right moment and turned them all to stone. The Medusa effect – that would have been something. Or better still if Pallas Athene had descended from Olympus and transformed me in a twinkling from the odious black bundle into the Odysseus of the imagination, the legend in his own lifetime. And I was thinking as I strode up to the threshold that if there was ever a time I could have used the help of a goddess, the time was now. I took another deep breath and stood in the doorway . . .

But let's play it that way, let's run it back, let's pretend. I'll step into the web and back into my rags.

They still didn't notice me. There was quite a stir going on. Antinous had proposed the order in which each man should take his turn – it should go from left to right, following the way the wine went round. He didn't want to be the first man up. So it fell to Leodes, son of Oenops, to try his hand first. He was a decent enough man, as it happened, better than the bulk of them. But his decency didn't make any difference. His decency wouldn't save him. He was part of the pack, he was one of them. Spare none was the plan. Keep it simple. Any inner doubt and debate about degrees of decency could have done for me, clouded the brain and given the enemy an edge. No, for this I had to stay sharp and keep a clear head. All these men had to die.

Leodes, with his dainty little fingers, never stood a chance. When he failed to string the bow and pronounced it unstringable, except by two men at once, Antinous got angry.

'Just because you weren't born to be a bowman doesn't mean the rest of us are incompetent. But I have a suggestion. This bow hasn't been used for years, not since it's owner went off to the war. It's too dry, see? Let's give it a good greasing before the next man tries, what do you say?'

Leodes put down the bow and went back to his seat. 'Believe me, this bow will break the hearts of many strong men. And perhaps it's better to die than live without the love that lures us all here in vain.'

Antinous exploded. 'Utter rubbish! Melanthius, get some tallow – we're going to do as I say and grease it before we go any further!'

Melanthius, eager to please, ran for the tallow, which he heated in front of the fire, and they greased the bow and gave it to the next man. And the next, and the next, and so on, following the way of the wine. It was while this was under way that Eumaeus and Philoetius saw me signalling to them from the doorway. They followed me outside.

'One question,' I said, 'but answer me quietly. If Odysseus were suddenly to turn up here right now and have a go at these lads, which side would you fight on, his or theirs?'

Swineherd and cowman looked at each other and back at me.

'Are you joking?' said Philoetius. 'You know my position already. I'd stand by his side though I knew I'd die for it.'

'And I'd stand on his other side,' said Eumaeus.

'In that case,' I said, 'here I am.'

Shock, astonishment, disbelief, belief, laughter, tears. Naturally belief would have been impossible without the disclosure of the scar. And even then, Pallas Athene found it necessary to produce a momentary metamorphosis, revealing the man beneath the rags, before turning me back again into the beggar for the benefit of the suitors and the success of the plan. And then Eumaeus and Philoetius realised that this was godwork. They stood with their mouths open.

'Better shut them,' I said, 'and keep them shut. And now listen carefully. In a moment, I'm going to go back inside. You two follow – not together but separately; leave a minute between you. Not too much movement either. Keep a low profile, nothing to attract attention until we're ready. I say *we* on the assumption you meant what you said just now. You're ready to stand with me and take on that lot?'

'We meant what we said.'

'We're ready.'

'Right. Now here's your cue, Eumaeus. I'm going to ask you for a shot at the bow. They'll tell me to get lost, of course, but bring it to me anyway. Bring it down the hall to the doorway and give it straight into my hands. Telemachus will back you up. Then check that the door to the women's quarters is definitely bolted. Your job, Philoetius, is to bolt and rope the courtyard gate.'

'So that none of the bastards can escape?'

'You've got it. This is a death-trap. Make it tight. I'll see you inside.'

Back in the hall, Eurymachus had just failed to string the bow and was mouthing off.

'Fuck the thing! Fuck it! Fuck it! Our names will be fucking mud!'

Antinous was offered his turn but was too crafty to accept.

'Hang on, lads, what are we thinking of? Today's the public holiday, remember? It's Apollo's Day. In honour of the archer god. Hardly a time to be arsing about with archery ourselves, as mere men. It's an insult to the Immortal Archer. Tell you what, let's drink a toast to Apollo and give the bow a breather. We've all drunk a bucket anyway. We'll be fresher in the morning, and every man can have another go. I don't recall Penelope saying anything about the number of attempts per person. By the law of averages, if we keep trying we're bound to succeed. And we'll get Melanthius to bring down the pick of the herd and give Apollo his due. Then we'll go for it again – and may the best bugger win!'

Huge approval, loud cheering and a general return to the tables, cups raised, glory to Apollo! After the libation I spoke from the doorway.

'Could I try?'

Silence for a moment. They all turned in their seats to look at me.

'I asked if I might make an attempt at stringing the bow.'

'What the fuck —'

'It's the old shitebag!'

'Who the fuck does he think he is?'

'Just because he whacked an even bigger arsehole!'

'Piss off, ancient arse, before you get hurt!'

That was Melanthius. I addressed him.

'Bravely spoken, goatherd, but I was addressing these gentlemen, not you, and I'd appreciate the opportunity to show off my own skill.'

'You what? Your what?'

'I told you, I'm an old soldier, a veteran. I fought at Troy.'

Laughter.

'Aye, fought off the flies, you mean, you old maggot!'

Antinous didn't find it so funny.

'Listen, I don't know what game you think you're playing, but you can forget it, old soldier or no. Nobody here gives a fuck what you did at Troy, if you were ever there, which I doubt. You're still a pile of pigshit and you're becoming too fucking familiar around here, let me tell you, worming your way into the household, browsing and sluicing and acting the part of the old salt. Last man I remember behaving like you got his nose and ears sliced off. And if you even think about trying to string that bow, if you even fucking touch it, the same will happen to you. You've had too much to drink — that's your trouble. Now fuck off and leave your betters in peace!'

Telemachus intervened.

'It's not up to you, Antinous, to be telling my guests to come and go. You don't give the orders around here. And I'm sure the old man is not suggesting for one moment that if he were to win the contest he'd have any intention of marrying my mother and taking her home with him.'

'He doesn't even have a fucking home!' yelled Melanthius. 'He's a fucking vagrant!'

'Well, exactly,' said Telemachus. 'So any idea of marriage would be preposterous. Out of the question — as my mother would be the first to agree. All he's proposing is a bit of fun. I mean, you're not imagining that he's actually going to succeed, are you, Antinous?'

'That's not the point. Or rather, it *is* the point. Suppose that by some fluke he did manage to string it — we'd never live it down. What, an old toe-ragger trouncing the flower of Ithaca? We'd be a laughing stock.'

'The laugh's on you already,' I said, 'since you've failed to string the bow. And if I do string it, that will be a story for centuries to come. They'll set you to song and dance — and it won't half be a funny turn!'

Antinous picked up his stool and hurled it at me. It slammed harmlessly into the wall.

'Get this fucker out of here! If you don't, Telemachus, I will! And I mean now!'

'You'll do nothing of the sort, Antinous. I'm in charge of this household and I've made my decision. I'm giving the old man a try. He's going to have his chance like the rest of you. And if he succeeds, I'll give him a new rig-out, and a spear and sword and a brace of dogs, and enough silver to take him on to wherever he wants to go. That will be his prize. Eumaeus, give him the bow.'

The swineherd picked up the bow and quiver and started walking down the hall towards me. Protests rang out.

'Hey, where do you think you're off to, pig-fucker?'

'Put it back!'

'Get back here with that fucking bow! Move your arse!'

Eumaeus stopped, apparently cowed. My heart dropped a beat. Was it an act? Would he cave in when I needed him? Was he up to it?

But then he dropped the weapon and everybody laughed. Telemachus put on his own act.

'Pick up that bow, you fumbling old idiot! You take your orders from me, not from that lot! And if you don't obey me then I'll throw you out! Got it? I'm beginning to think these lads are right. I've been too easy on you. And on you too, old man,' he said to me. 'You'll string that bow after all your boasting! And if you don't, I'll have you flogged!'

Hoots and cheers.

'Well said, Telemachus!'

'You've just grown up!'

'At last!'

The distraction had worked. Eumaeus completed his journey down the hall and handed me the bow. Then he went to see to the upstairs door as Philoetius slipped past me. Nobody paid any attention to either of them as I made my way into the hall. All eyes were on me.

I looked at the weapon, twisting and testing it, checking for worm-holes. There were none. I ran my hands along it and brought it up level with my eye. The inspection produced more laughter.

'What an expert, eh?'

'A great eye for a bow!'

'Look at him – you'd think he was a collector!'

'Just take your time, hot-shot!'

'The Trojans must have loved him! Slow as shit!'

'An easy target!'

'He thinks he's Apollo!'

As smoothly and easily as a musician strings his lyre, I strung the bow and twanged the string. It sang like a swallow.

'And who do *you* think I am?'

Silence in the hall. They sat like statues.

'I said, who do you think I am?'

Fear on all their faces now. And still they gaped.

'You should close your mouths, my masters — they make you into first-rate targets. Anybody could send a few arrows in your direction. They'd go right down your throats — and come out at the arse!'

All the colour left their faces.

'But that's too easy. Those aren't the targets, are they? These are!'

The quiver bristled with bronze. I selected an arrow and balanced it against the bridge, drew it back slowly, horribly slowly, slowly, aiming straight ahead — and shot. From the first axe-head to the last, through every one and out at the last, the arrow didn't miss a single ring. It thudded into the far wall.

'No, the Trojans didn't love me for that, I have to say.'

I nodded to Telemachus, who left his seat and sprang to my side. Antinous reached out for a gulp of wine.

'That's right, gentlemen, you can open your mouths again and drink up! And toast your own demise, why don't you? It's suppertime!'

I jumped back up onto the great threshold. See me on the web, and I am still in my rags. Or see me as I am – it makes no difference now. This scene was only ever going to end one way.

'Now there's a better target – a fucking beauty!'

Antinous was still gulping from his golden cup, little dreaming that the draught of courage was his death-drink. His head was tilted back, as I loosed the second shaft, aiming for the white, exposed throat. It struck him just below the Adam's apple. The point went straight through and reappeared out of the back of the neck. A shot that thrilled me to the balls. I was back at Troy, the throbbing song of the bronze music to my ears. The cup went flying and Antinous keeled over, his last words a few red bubbles on his lips. He tried to stand but lurched over, blood spouting from his nostrils in two thick jets, and his mouth spraying a mixture of blood and wine. His bread and meat were spattered with it, spoiling his place at the table. Theoclymenus had seen right. A messy feeder was Antinous. He fell on his back, half under the table, both feet beating out a brief tattoo on the floor. Then he was still.

They all stood up, cursing and screaming together. Eurymachus shouted louder than the rest.

'You fucking fool! You've only just gone and killed the son of the most powerful fucking family in Ithaca! You're for the fucking vultures!'

They still didn't get it, the morons. They thought it had been an accident. Or that I'd taken some sort of mad turn. There was no way of letting them down gently, the stupid bastards. I needed to tell them.

'The most powerful in Ithaca, did you say? Well, you got that wrong for a start. The highest in the land is right here. Take a good gander, goose-brains! Do you get it now? Surely you can't all be as stupid as you look – it's not fucking possible!'

Yes, they'd been afraid, but they thought they were afraid of the impossible. Now they knew it was real, and the green fear showed in their faces. And in their flickering eyes, as each man looked around for an escape route. But there was none.

'That's right, you cunts! You've got it at last! You didn't think I was ever coming back, did you? So you thought you could feed on a dead man, you flock of vultures, eat up my estate, insult my son, go after my wife, rape the maids and turn them into your whores, you immoral bastards! And you thought you could do it all for free and still get away with it afterwards. Well, I reckon that, unlike you lot, I'm a long way from being dead. And I've come back to tell you all that this is the last act. And the last act is always bloody, so it's time to litter the stage with corpses. Are you ready to die? Last man standing gets to speak the epilogue. Agreed?'

Now at last they moved. Or tried to. But there was still nowhere for them to go. And when they looked about them frantically for weapons, there were none. Some of them were wearing short swords, but otherwise they were defenceless. That other look came back onto their faces, the look I'd seen often enough at Troy on the face of a soldier looking for a funk-hole, a crapper, any sanctuary from sudden fucking death, the unavoidable terrible end of life.

And again, there was none — except of course for the old sanctuary of excuse, shifting the blame, whining for life. It was Eurymachus who tried that line, speaking for the spineless.

'Odysseus, if it's you — and I can see that it must be, that it is — everything you are accusing us of is true, and there's no excuse for it. But the man mainly responsible for it lies dead. He led us on, and we went along with him. We were wrong. He even planned to murder your son, the bastard. And I, for one, didn't agree with it. None of us did. He was the one, he was power-mad. Now you've punished him, let it rest there, and we'll stand with you against his family when they come after you, as they surely will. I know I'm speaking for every man here — and also when I say that we'll compensate you for all your losses, until you're satisfied. We'll carry on paying for the rest of our lives if that's what it takes.'

'Eurymachus.'

I said it quietly.

'Sadly that's not going to be long enough. Your lives will be too short, you see. They're ending now. You won't be seeing the sun tomorrow.'

'Wait, Odysseus! Twenty oxen each, and bronze and gold from all of us. And we'll see to it that Antinous contributes, even though the bastard's dead. His family encouraged him. They wanted to take over the island — they're the ones to blame!'

How can you feel sorry for a shit? Antinous was a cunt. Or had been. But this Eurymachus was the slimiest of the lot. I looked at him the way you look at what's been left in the crapper.

'You. You forget I've watched you and heard you. You thought you were first in line for my throne and my bed. You were no different from him, just a better hypocrite. As for atonement, all of your estates wouldn't save your skins now, not if you made them over to me. And how will you pay for my wife's shame? How will you pay for the whoredoms you've committed here? Can you give the maids back their virginities? Can you unfuck the sluts? If you can't, then you'd better start running!'

They were about to scatter, but Eurymachus stopped them.

'Right lads, you've heard him – he's merciless. He'll stand there and shoot until he's killed us all or run out of ammunition. Are you going to go like sheep? I'm not. Let's make a go of it, fight our way out of it if we can. We've got nothing to lose. Up with the tables – we can use them as shields and advance in a body. All we need is for one of us to get past him. One man through that door and into the town for help, and he's finished. Get the tables up, and I'll rush him!'

He came at me fast with his sword. I had to admit he showed some spunk. I whanged an arrow at him, and it stopped him before he'd even taken a couple of steps. He got it near the nipple and must have felt it in his liver. He screamed, dropped the sword, tottered, swayed over the table, crumpled up, clutching at the arrow, then went tumbling, table and all, sending the wine cups clanging to the ground. His forehead hit the floor, his feet drummed in agony. I aimed another arrow at his ear. It pierced the skull, and the feet stopped drumming.

'In one ear, out the other. He never listened, did he?'

They stared at me, shocked, and back at Eurymachus, his head like a spiked apple. Then they ran from him.

Amphinomous came next, sword out, hoping to force me from the door. Telemachus took him out from behind – he'd run back to get Eurymachus's sword. The spear hit Amphinomous between the shoulder blades and came out through the chest, ending the brief charge. He dropped the sword, both arms spread out, mouth opening soundlessly like a fish – an actor who'd forgotten his lines. His eyes gaped sightlessly and he crashed forwards, dead before he hit the ground, dead before he could feel his forehead splitting open. The dark pool spread out around his head. This was a good start.

Telemachus ran to recover his spear. I shouted him back. 'No – you're exposed! Get up here again beside me – quick!'

When he rejoined me, I hissed into his ear. 'Storeroom – now! Bring spears, helmets, shields, more arrows, anything you can! Fetch weapons for the other two as well – and be quick! I won't be able to hold them off for long!'

While he was away, I kept on shooting, picking them off one by one. They could have rushed me in a body, using the tables as a front line shield-wall. But the cunts lacked the courage. Each of them knew that whoever was in front was a dead man, and no one wants to be a dead man, even when he knows it's coming anyway. So they ran about like rabbits and hid and shivered as I calmly selected my targets. They'd have been fucking useless at Troy.

The corpses were piling up by the time Telemachus got back with the weapons. The swineherd and drover were with him, wearing armour and carrying the extra shields and spears. And that was just as well. The arrows gave out and there were no spares. And at that point, one of the group remembered the postern. It was higher up and had close-fitted doors, but it led up past the threshold into an outside alley. They only remembered it when I shouted to Eumaeus to guard it. I should have kept my mouth shut.

Agelaus pointed. 'Look lads, the postern! It's only the pigman guarding the approach. If somebody can take him out and get up there and into the alley, we can raise the alarm! Any volunteers?'

Melanthius screamed back at him from behind a table. 'Impossible! The opening to the alley's so fucking awkward, it's useless! I know that route – it takes just one man to hold us back from it, and that fuckpig can do it. But not if you've got some heavy armour – then you could get through. I'll bring you some. I know another way to the arsenal!'

He managed to clamber up the wall to a smoke-vent in the roof. An arrow would have brought him down, but I was out of them and the bastard was quick. Too late I hurled at him as he disappeared through the hole.

'It doesn't matter!' I shouted. 'The arsenal's locked! He can't get in!'

But suddenly he was back, hurling helmets and shields and spears down into the hall. I looked at Telemachus. He made a face.

'I thought I'd locked it – fuck!'

Fuck was putting it fucking mildly. I heard Melanthius shouting down.

'I'll go and get some more – the place is stacked out! He won't have a chance now. He's finished!'

I shouted to Eumaeus.

'Go and bolt that fucking door! Now! We don't want any more of those buggers armed. And kill that bastard up there while you're about it!'

He nodded and ran.

'Eumaeus – wait! On second thoughts, don't kill the cunt – leave him for me! Tie him up in the arsenal before you lock it. String him up if you can. Don't choke him, just enough to let him suffer for a while. Take Philoetius with you. Telemachus and I will take care of these lover boys.'

The lover boys were having a dust-up. There weren't enough weapons to go round, and they couldn't agree on who would be the lucky ones.

'It's either a shield or a spear – you don't get both!'

'Not till Melanthius gets back with more!'

'It's no good going against him unarmed!'

'One or the other – which is it to be?'

'Some of us have got fuck all!'

'There's more ammo on the way!'

'No there isn't!' shouted Eumaeus. He was fresh back from the arsenal. 'Your little goat-fucker has got plenty of weapons up there, but he's a bit tied up right now. You'll have to make do! What you see is what you get!'

They'd found Melanthius in the arsenal and lashed his hands and feet together behind him tightly – to the point of snapping sinews and breaking limbs. Then they'd hoisted him aloft against a pillar, all the way to the roof and left him slung there, the bones grinding in their sockets. His screams came tearing down into the hall through the light-holes. Eumaeus grinned.

'Hear that? Melanthius won't be serving you up your usual fare tomorrow! And when the sun comes up, she won't catch him napping either! At dawn, he's for the chop. You all are – the chopper and the slab!'

Bravely spoken, just like at Troy, the war of words, the dance of defiance, vaunting, daunting, keeping death at bay – for a time. But only for so long. Sooner or later you have to close and settle the issue, not with bravado but with bronze. Then all the fine words in the world won't help you. We were four men facing a still formidable unit, some of whom were now armed and armoured.

For a moment it looked like we'd get a fifth man.

My old friend Mentor broke away from the other side and started towards us, arms wide.

'I'll stand with you, Odysseus!'

He'd been a good man. Maybe he still was. Maybe it was a matter of weighing up the situation and, in spite of the odds, deciding against the suitors – he'd never had much respect for them. Maybe it was the sudden sight of me and the memory of past friendship. Maybe it wasn't even Mentor. Maybe it was Pallas Athene. Soldiers have been known to see gods in battle, appearing in the skies. Some have seen gods through blood and mud, though I never did. I didn't even know what a god was supposed to look like. Penelope knew all that.

It didn't matter. Agelaus was assuming command, and he bellowed at Mentor.

'Get back in line, you! These men are dogmeat! Join them, and you will you be too, and we'll see to it that your family suffer. After we've wiped out these four, your estate will be forfeit, your son won't live, your daughter will be raped, and your wife will be thrown out onto the streets to beg through life. That suit you? Is it enough?'

Mentor's fate was decided. He crept back into line.

🔲

Pity. Pity, pity, pity. Mentor would be among the dead at the end. Penelope chose the Athene interpretation. See the goddess in the web, assuming the appearance of Mentor and inspiring Odysseus.

'Stand fast, Odysseus, you who for nine unyielding years took on the Trojans for highborn Helen's sake, and devised the trick that toppled topless Troy! See now how Mentor stays loyal in the ranks of death!'

And after delivering this speech, Athene transformed herself into a swallow and sped up to perch aloft on the smoke-begrimed main beam of the hall, from which vantage point she had a literal bird's-eye view of the battle.

'Right!' shouted Agelaus. 'It's still just the four of them! I want six spears up front!'

And he called up five to join him: Eurynomus, Amphimedon, Demoptolemus, Peisander, Polybus. They all looked shit-scared, but they were going to make a stand. Agelaus was no fool, and he was showing some leadership. Good for him.

'All you other lads, now, hold your fire, for fuck's sake! Keep those spears close – you'll need them! Us six will fire together. Go for Odysseus, never mind the other three. Once he's down, they're a pushover.'

I laughed back at him. 'There's a brain in there somewhere! Shame it's about to say chin-chin to your skull! When did your lads last throw a spear at a man instead of a rabbit?'

'Ignore him, fellows, he's trying to put you off! Now altogether, fire!'

The whole volley went wide. One hit the doorpost, one the door, one the wall, the other three went nowhere, and we didn't even bring up our shields.

'Fucking pathetic!' I shouted. 'You wouldn't last five minutes in the line! Now we'll show you how it's done. Ready, boys? Left to right as we stand. Fire!'

Four hits. Down went Demoptolemus and Euryades, each with an eyeful of bronze. Elatus got it in the throat, and it came out the back of the neck further than any spear I'd ever seen.

'If I'd known you could throw like that I'd have taken you with me to Troy!' I called to Eumaeus.

Peisander fell flat on his back with Philoetius's spear singing in his skull and swaying like a sapling in the gale. The cowman also could have signed on with Agamemnon. The two men left out of the six who'd shot at us turned and ran with the rest all the way up the hall. We followed, but only as far as we needed to pull our spears from the still twitching carcasses. Never waste weapons on the dead. And we backed up to the threshold door again, keeping our shields raised. Agelaus tried to restore discipline, but the next frantic flurry of spears was frankly laughable. They'd have done more damage if they'd farted on us.

We discharged our next volley into the thick of them and scored another four hits: Eurydamas, Amphimedon, Polybus, and – oh, glory! – Ctesippus, the brainless bully. Philoetius hit him square in his barrel chest, and he started walking backwards like a complete fucking idiot, staggering and spitting.

'There you go!' yelled Philoetius. 'That'll pay you back for the cow-hoof!'

It was impossible to miss, but we were running short of spears.

'Don't throw any more!' I ordered. 'Get ready for the dash in!'

We ran at them, roaring and screaming. Most of the bastards turned and ran. Agelaus faced me, but I drove my blade straight into his belly and felt it stick in the bone at the back. He dropped to his knees, screaming. I kicked him hard in the face and he fell back, clutching at his belly.

'Something the matter down there? Let me help you out.'

I wrenched the spear with a twist, and the entrails came out on show. Telemachus brought Leiocritus down. We closed in together. The enemy – if you could dignify the wankers by calling them that – was in disarray . . .

. . . like the cattle stamping under the dancing gadfly, gone mad in the sudden spring-time, when the old earth heats up and the long days come in. Up aloft in the smoky roof of the palace hall, Athene raised her baleful aegis, and Odysseus saw the signal.

It was time to massacre the bastards.

The ones that remained alive were no fighters, just beggars for mercy. They got none. What they got were split skulls, slit throats, burst bellies, bronze between the teeth, through the eyeholes, up the arse. We hacked them down, sliced off arms, legs. The ground glittered with their innards and grew greasy with their blood. We started slipping.

Somebody ran at me and clutched my knees.

'Odysseus – I'm Leodes! I was their priest, that's all. I never touched any of the women, I swear, and I kept telling them their behaviour was reprehensible, but they wouldn't listen to me. Why should I be treated the same as them when I've done nothing wrong, I ask you? I'm begging you, let me live! You wouldn't kill a priest, would you?'

I looked down into the desperate eyes.

'No, I wouldn't kill a priest.'

The eyes filled with relief.

'But you're no priest!'

I kicked him away from me, and he came crawling back.

'Let go of my fucking knees!'

I kicked him again, this time in the teeth. He fell back into a sitting position, spitting blood and looking silly.

'You're no priest. You're just another fucking hypocrite!'

I picked up the sword that was still clutched in Agelaus's dead hand.

'Odysseus, I prayed –'

'Yes, prayed I'd never come back, and that you'd get your priestly prick into Penelope!'

He started to say something else as I struck him sideways on the neck, and the slashed head hit the dust still speaking, fuck knows what.

The next beggar to drop on his knees was Phemius. He was holding out his lyre.

'You see? No weapon. I'm only the minstrel, Odysseus. That's all I ever was.'

'I know you're the fucking minstrel – I've heard you entertaining the cunts! You'd better give us a song then before you die, and it had better be fucking short! Are you in tune?'

I grabbed his long hair and gave it a twist. 'Let's hear how you sing with your throat cut!'

A hand came over my sword hand. Telemachus. 'No — stop! This man's innocent. He never was one of them.'

'It's true, Odysseus!' He threw away his lyre and held my knees.

'I never wanted to come here. They forced me to sing for them. They didn't even pay me. Let me live, and I'll sing for you from now on — for nothing, like a bird does, like a bird for a god!'

'All right, I believe you. No need to make an epic out of it!' I laid my sticky hand on his head. 'I'm sorry about the blood.'

A wide smile from Phemius. 'On the contrary, my first song for you will be a song about this blood.'

'And,' said Telemachus, 'another one we have to save is Medon the herald. He's not one of them. They forced him like they forced Phemius. He'd no choice. But he always looked out for me and informed against them when he had the chance. I hope to god he's not among the corpses.'

'I'm not.'

An oxhide draped over a chair started to move, and out came Medon. Telemachus burst out laughing. I couldn't laugh, but I laid my hand on his head.

'At ease, man, you're safe. Now you and Phemius get out of here and wait in the courtyard. I may have more work to see to in here, and you're safer out of the way — unless you want to fight.'

They both shot out at the double, still half wondering if they'd really been spared. We raked around the hall for survivors and for anybody faking death or cowering under hides like Medon. I delivered the death-stroke here and there to stop the jerkings and the groanings. Then after all the noise there was this strange sudden silence. They were all dead.

All dead. So many open mouths and eyes, heaps of them, like fish gasping on the sands, soundless shoals dragged from the glinting surf and thrown from the net to end their lives on the beach, under the bright sun, still longing for the sea, their salty, life-giving, liquid element. That's how the shoal of lovers now lay, with gaping mouths and open eyes, some of them still quivering, fresh dead in the net that destiny had spread for them.

'Right,' I said, 'now it's the women's turn. Go up and tell Eurycleia to join me here. Nobody else is to come down, not yet, not one. Keep them locked in.'

When the old woman entered the hall I hurried over, thinking to steady her as she looked at the battlefield. Already the stench was terrible, and I was spattered with blood and gore from head to foot. I put out an arm for her, but it wasn't necessary. She looked at me, then at the pile of corpses. She took one of the drooped heads by the hair and raised it to see who it was, then dropped it with a hiss and a grin and lifted her bony arms high over her head. A weird cry came out of her. It wasn't fear or pity: it was exultation, a song of terrible holy joy.

I took hold of her and stopped her.

'They were scum. But maybe it's a bad thing to gloat too much over dead scum. They've paid the price. And we'll be dead ourselves soon enough. Now tell me, who are the good women in the house and who are the whores? I know one in particular already.'

She gave me her toothless grin.

'I'll run through the whole list, my boy. You've got fifty women between these walls. Most of them are making the best they can out of slavery, and some are bitches gone a bit wild but who can learn from their errors. The rest are first-class whores with no respect for themselves, let alone for me or your wife. There's a dozen like that, the ones who've turned really bad. They stick their fingers up at us and lift their skirts for that lot. Not anymore, though.'

She started to howl again. It gave me the shivers.

I cut her short. 'Bring them down. If they refuse to come, tell them they'll be burned alive.'

She hobbled off at full speed, and I called everybody together – Telemachus, the two herdsmen, the minstrel and the herald, the heart of a new household.

'When the women come down, start ferrying out the dead and make them assist you. I want them to take a good look at what's left of their playboys now. As soon as they've taken out the bodies, make them clean up in here – tables, chairs, the floor, everything. They'll need plenty of water and sponges. And once they've done their housework, take them outside. Take them to the area between the round-house and the courtyard wall, and use your swords on them, any way you like. Just make sure that none of them is left alive by the time you've done with them. They had a high old time here, fucking their lovers and pissing on the household. Now they'll piss themselves, all right. They'll beg. Don't listen. I want them all dead.'

Eurycleia didn't obey orders. The whores trooped in with the tears streaming down their faces, but so did Penelope. As the females bunched together in their terror, I saw the horrified figure of my wife standing behind them. She was staring at me. Eurycleia was screaming, out of control.

'It's him! I told you! I told you! It's him! You didn't believe me!'

Still she stared, still as a statue, white-faced, speechless. What should she say? What should I say? What can you say? How are you, my dear one? It's been a long time. Did you miss me? Aren't you glad to see me then? Shall we forget the war and everything? And resume our lives?

Odysseus stands among the corpses of the slain like a lion fresh from feeding after his killing spree. He has torn the bullock to pieces and dipped his jaws into its side. He lifts his head and glares, and the crimson gore drips from his mouth and mane. His eyes are on fire. He roars and shakes himself, scattering droplets of blood. Among the dead suitors, spattered with blood and filth, so stands Odysseus, the king of beasts, the King of Ithaca.

Is that what she saw? It's what's in the web. It's what she wove. But I'm willing to bet that what she saw, after the years of not seeing, was a madman, a killing machine that had done its work and didn't know what else to do, except kill. She saw an alien in her home, a brutalised being, drunk on blood. And she turned and ran.

That made it easier. We set the whores to work. First, as directed, they removed the corpses of the suitors. Where heads were missing, they were told to identify them correctly and stick them back on. I made them strip the men naked and pile up the clothes for burning.

'How d'you fancy them now, you sluts? Not so pretty, are they? And their pricks have gone soft!'

They washed down the walls and the furniture, cleared away the ruined food, the wine cups, the spilt bowls. They scraped the filth and slithers from the floor, piled up the scrapings and took them outside.

They put the naked bodies under the portico and propped them up against each other in a ghastly row. I hounded them on at their work.

'Come on, don't take all fucking day!'

Then we herded them into the narrow space between the round-house and the wall. There was no exit from there.

'That's it,' I said, 'slit their throats.'

They screamed and held each other.

'Wait!'

I thought Telemachus was having second thoughts.

'Wait,' he said. 'Why should we give them a decent death? They're not only whores: they also treated my mother like a whore. They fed the lusts of that filthy gang, slept with the little shits night after night. Opened their legs to all-comers. You saw how it was. It was a fucking brothel. Let's rip off their tits first.'

'No,' I said, 'stay calm. They'll die cleaner than they lived, but it will still be a dishonourable death. We'll hang the sluts.'

I got hold of a ship's hawser and fastened one end of it to one of the portico columns. The other end I sent snaking over the round-house and hauled on it till it was nice and taut. I made sure it was just high enough to stop their toes from touching the floor. Then I pushed them forwards one by one, still snivelling and twittering for mercy, like little birds that come to the coppice hoping to roost, but who fly into the net and find not sleep but death instead, the sleep of death, and they flutter for a while before they die, making tiny noises. That's how these women died. There was no way out for them. The net had closed. They stood in a line and held out their heads obediently, and we fitted a noose around each slender neck, all twelve of them, and we let them kick, their feet feeling blindly for the floor.

It didn't take too long. I couldn't help noticing how small all the feet were, and how delicate, how dainty, just like little birds', especially Melantho's, although she was the biggest whore of the lot. They kicked and quivered miserably. And when they stopped twitching, we cut them down.

'And now,' I said, 'that goat-fucker Melanthius. Bring him down.'

Eumaeus and Philoetius went and brought him from the arsenal, dragging him, still bound and screaming, across the courtyard.

'You'll be howling louder before I'm done with you!'

I dragged him by the hair and pulled him through the gate. Then I cut the knots and unbound him. Limbs cracked.

'Never mind. You won't have much use for your legs shortly. You won't need your arms either. You won't have any fucking appendages.'

We all got going on him. We sliced off his nose and ears and lopped both hands and feet. The screaming grew high-pitched, like a pig's in the first minutes of slaughter. Lastly we ripped off his prick and testicles.

'And now to stop your infernal fucking howling!'

I cut out his tongue, threw it away, and crammed his cock and balls into the red hole. It was gaping but quieter now.

'That's what happens to fucking loud mouths!'

After that, we washed ourselves at the well. Eurycleia was still around, watching us. She was everywhere, dancing her dance of triumph on legs like sticks, defying her age and sex.

'Eurycleia, enough of that. Do something useful, will you? Bring me sulphur and get a fire on the go. I'm going to fumigate this place. Bring down the decent females to help you. And tell Penelope everything's in order. She can come down now. Her husband is home. It's over.'

Over? It's never over, is it? It will be with you for the rest of your life. It will deprive you of your rest, it will provide you with your dreams. It will murder sleep.

Sleep's the word, but it's more like drowning, this nightly descent, like slipping into the sea, pulling the liquid blanket over your head and sinking down, down, deep down to where the monsters lurk, except that you don't actually drown, and the monsters prey on you until you wake. Until you die. Even when you're awake you're never sure where you are, or who you are. All that is solid melts into air, all that was holy is profane, all that was gold turns to rust. And all that you fought for is a lie. It was a lie from the start and you knew it, but you learned to live it. Out in the field, on the open sea, in the theatre of war. As if it were true.

What happens when the lie shifts to the bedroom? When you can't settle the issue with a weapon? Every man's Troy is followed by every man's homecoming, and the re-entry problem starts up another war, the war fought without arms. They're no use to you now, the spear, the sword, the good old bronze. Your shield won't protect you either.

What did she really see when she looked at me again? A butcher, a lunatic, a stranger. I don't know what she saw. I couldn't climb into her skin and look at me. I hadn't been standing there for all this time, waiting. I wasn't where she was, what she was. I wasn't the one lying in the bed. That bed.

And what did I see? What does any man see nineteen years on? Or nine. Or even nine months. Does he see the same woman, she the same man? It could happen in nine hours, nine seconds. He's changed, she's changed. They've lived apart. Even without a war between them, countries, fields, years, seas, the rawness and madness, the terror and nerves – even without all that, the two of them become different beings; they're no longer the same people who got married. Add to the equation of absence the heart's fondness, coldness, cruelty, unpredictability, and the difference may prove to be unbridgeable.

We may well possess some golden core of being: there may even be a soul, and it may even be forever. But the rubbish all around it doesn't last, the daily wear and tear, the dear old house of flesh, so frail, so palpable, so tender, trite, so transient and true. Even the mind itself runs on like a river, flows away from us, becomes somewhere else.

No, it's not over when the killing's over, when the living has to start, when it becomes clear at last, the solving emptiness, that what cohered across the years was absence, not Ithaca. Troy kept us comatose, or high. Troy kept us distanced from living, and even from dying, though we danced with death. Troy kept us free from self, from the sadness of home, from the endless tilling of fields and the going under. Troy was the ache and energy of love — of a kind. It was tough and kept us tough. It was the potency and pain of being young. Younger. Troy was the truth that will not come again.

So I missed it — missed it like I missed home, or thought I did, and I see them now, the same old scenes, turning over and over like clods under the plough that unearths the darkness. And I hear them too — the spears, glorious as geese in winter, whistling, and the javelins darkening the skies. Weapons that broke men and built barrows, monuments. Mounds to forgotten success.

Forgotten. What was it they said of me? A man whose white bones are rotting in the rain, or rolling in the waves. The dogs and the birds have torn him, flesh from bone, or the fishes have eaten him in the sea. His bones are embedded in some beach, the sands piled high above them. He's never coming home. None of them is ever coming home. Only ghosts come home. There are no returners. There are revenants but not soldiers. They're all dead now. They're the forgotten army.

It reminds me well enough of a piece of bullshit, spoken when Agamemnon was in an unusually lucid mood.

'Forgotten army? Forgotten, did you say? Well let me tell you something, lads, you're not forgotten! You're not the forgotten army! Forgotten? It's worse than that. Nobody has even fucking heard of you! But they're going to! Oh, fuck me, yes, lads! They're going to hear of you, because you're going to do glorious fucking things, great deeds! You're going to go down in history, you're going to bring down the towers of Troy and ride in triumph through streets of fire! Am I right?'

Yes. Easy, easy, lads. Easy to triumph, easy to die, easy to be forgotten. It's forgetting that's hard. And being remembered. And having to remember. Remembering is hard. What to do, what to say when you stand apart, facing one another, and nothing between you but the white bed, fresh as new bread, waiting to be torn, and tasted, like it was on your wedding night, yes, it's hard, that's hard.

Why? It ought to be easy, like eating and drinking are easy. Easy to approach her, to slip that robe from her shoulders and let it fall to the floor, to stare at it all over again, to be transfixed by the wonder of it, the conquest of the country of which she was once queen, and you the undisputed king, when those breasts pointed at you, a little proudly perhaps, and the belly pouted, urging you to hurry, and the hips that gathered themselves into your palms began to move, Penelope's knees up around you again, the belly pushing, the pelvis thrusting, the legs in the air, the feet facing the sky, after all this time, yes, easy, easy to be inside her again, to feel the cunt sucking up the sperm, the tongue sucking out your soul –

– and nothing between you.

Except Troy. And the Cicones, and the Lotus-eaters, the Cyclops, the Keeper of the Winds, the Laestrygonians, Circe, the Sirens, the Drifters, Scylla and Charybdis, Poseidon, Calypso, Nausicaa, the suitors, the ruined suitors, the Halls of Persephone, Agamemnon, Achilles, Hector, Helen, Hell. Hell, hell, hell. You've come home and it's not goodbye to all of that but welcome to hell, old boy. Yours is the House of the Dead, the mighty dead. You are the dead.

Eurycleia hurries upstairs as fast as her little old legs can carry her, legs like dry sticks, and her feet fairly twinkling in her mad dash.

'Wake up, woman, your husband's home!'

A yawn from Penelope. 'Have you gone soft in the head, you old fool?'

'Never clearer, I assure you – your husband is downstairs.'

'Here I was having a lovely sound sleep, the best in years, and you dare to wake me up with this nonsense. Away with you, now!'

Eurycleia sweeps back the bedcover and pokes her in the ribs.

'I'm telling you, he's back! He's the old stranger.'

'What old stranger?'

'The beggar, of course, the black rag-bag, the king in disguise, just like in the old stories, remember? Haven't you ever heard of kings got up as beggars? Haven't you listened to the songs? Well, this one's true. Your husband, King Odysseus, has come home. He's not dead. But all your lovers are. He's killed the lot. They're all propping each other up in the portico, as dead as can be. If you don't believe me, come and see. What do you think all the noise was about? Didn't it wake you? Well I heard plenty, and I came down for myself and saw him standing there like a lion among the corpses, all splashed with their blood. A glorious sight – it would have thrilled you. Why won't you believe it?'

'I do believe it, perhaps – that they're dead, I mean. But if that's the case, then it has to be the work of a god. They've been punished at last for their insolence and immorality, all that depravity and greed. But Odysseus will never know it. What you saw was not Odysseus but an avenging Immortal. Odysseus himself is long dead and far from here.'

'My god, you always were a stubborn one! I don't know how he put up with you! The patience of Penelope? Pig-headed Penelope, more like. You belong with the swineherd. What will it take to convince you? Wait a minute – I know, I've got the proof. I've seen it, felt it. You know the scar?'

Penelope's heart leaps.

'Scar? What scar?'

'Don't play your games with me, madam. I know you too well, and you know which scar. The one on his thigh, the one he had since he was a boy, the one he got from the boar. Last night when I washed his feet, I touched it accidentally and he nearly killed me, swore me to silence in case I gave him away and alerted the suitors. Does that convince you?'

'I don't know. But there's only one way to find out, isn't there?'

'At last!'

So they came down – and we barely even glanced at one another, it was such a moment. Mythical, unreal. Telemachus was shocked.

'How can you sit there like that, mother, away from him, saying nothing, not even looking? This is the greatest moment of your life! Your husband, my father, has come back from the dead after years of war and suffering, and you don't utter a word, let alone give him a hug. Are you so hard-hearted? This is the ultimate anti-climax. Has absence made you so cold, so cruel? It's inhuman.'

He was young, Penelope told him. He didn't understand. He couldn't. Nobody could. 'I just don't know what to say, what to ask, what to feel. To be honest, I feel numb. I can't even look him in the eye. But perhaps – '

'Yes?'

'Perhaps if the two of us could be left alone for a little while, we could work this out, put things to the test.'

I had to smile.

'Your mother's right, son. As always. Leave us alone for a little, and I guarantee she'll be smiling when you see her again. In any case, I need you to be busy. There's another problem I want you to deal with.'

'Another problem? I thought all our problems were dead.'

'Precisely. We've just plucked the flower of Ithaca. Which says little for Ithaca, by the way — they were black weeds. But that's not the way their families will see it. They'll be after our blood. We need to buy some time. So here's the plan. Get that minstrel going. He can thank me for his life. He promised to sing for me, remember? Well he'd better start now. A lively dance-tune, as loud and long as his lyre can make it. Get the girls to join in — plenty of singing, dancing, applause. Tell them to sing their hearts out and make it sound like a celebration — a wedding celebration. Penelope's getting married. At last. That's why the young lords are so long in coming home. They're drinking till dawn, drinking toasts to the winner among them, to the lucky man and to the darling couple. By the time the families realise it's a mass funeral they're facing instead, we'll have beaten a retreat to our farmlands up among the orchards, and we can plan our campaign from there, depending on how the people choose to stand on this issue.'

So the festivities filled the hall — the false festivities, the hollow lyre pouring out hollow melodies and the feet of dancing men and women stamping madly. While just outside, the propped-up corpses still stared open-eyed, open-mouthed at the moon. And in the long arcades, in the cool night air, the new-hung maids swung, with swollen eyes and bulging tongues and bare unsandalled feet.

People paused in the early morning streets, stopped and listened.

'Hear that? Know what it means? She's given in at last, the heartless whore. The empty bed proved too cold for her in the end. She fell at the final hurdle. She's gone and married after all — and her poor husband still out there somewhere in a foreign land, imprisoned or enslaved or still fighting, who knows? And her too faithless to honour the memory of a hero. But she was always a cool one, a hard-hearted bitch.'

Enter now Pallas Athene. Yet again.

Eurycleia had already bathed me, washed away the blood, rubbed in the oil, kitted me out with a gorgeous new set of clothes. But the goddess put the vital finishing touches to the business, enhancing the heroic king from crown to toe.

'I think we'll add some height,' she said. 'Give you those few extra inches. They'll make all the difference.'

And she caused the lush locks to cluster on my noble head as thick as hyacinths in bloom at the height of their growth. I stepped out of the bath like a god.

Was Penelope impressed? Did it make any difference? Not a bit. Still she didn't budge.

'Well,' I said, 'now I know you've a heart of stone. And the iron has grown into your soul over the years. Eurycleia had better make me up a bed just like she did in the old days, when I was a bachelor and a boy, since it looks like I'm not sleeping with my wife tonight.'

'That's right,' said Penelope. 'You're not sleeping with your wife, it seems, whoever and wherever she may be, and you're certainly not sleeping with me. I last slept with my husband nineteen years ago, and he didn't look anything like you. He was a lot shorter, for a start. Time changes us, but not that much, and not usually for the better. You're not Odysseus. But if you're so insistent you are, you can at least sleep in the marriage bed – alone. I'll allow that much. Nurse, bring out the big bed. Get the maids to remove it. They can make it up for this guest – outside the bedroom, if you please. You may provide him with plenty of rugs and blankets to keep out the cold after you've shifted the bed.'

The test.

'What are you talking about, woman? You know very well that bed can't be moved. And I hope nobody tried to do so in my absence. I built it myself, in case you've forgotten. I fashioned the big bed-post from the trunk of the olive tree that was still growing there, and I presume still is, though back then it had already grown to an impressive height, reaching all the way upstairs. You know full well I built the whole bedroom round it. You could say, in fact, that I built the entire palace round that tree, since our bedroom is the beating heart of the house – at least it was. I hope to god you haven't cut through the living tree and shifted the bed.'

Test passed.

And that's what it took to thaw the uncertain heart, to banish the fears of trickery and time, to bring the tears to her eyes at last, to make her throw her arms around my neck and kiss me hard, the husband who really was her husband because he remembered the bed. What woman wouldn't want her man to remember their bed? Many times I'd been wrecked and had felt the sweetness of the shore stroking my limbs, but this was the sweetest salvage of all, to feel beneath me the bay in which I now put in. And she wound her white arms round me and kept me anchored there all night long. Dawn would have come and lit up our love-making had not the tireless Pallas Athene added one more cosmic touch. She held up the universe for us. Slowing the horses of the night, she held them lingering in the west, while in the liquid east she kept Aurora waiting, so that Lampus and Phaethon, the nimble colts that pull the day's chariot, stood unyoked and wondered what was going on.

What was going on was the longest, most lyrical love scene in the whole human history of love, the most protracted and the most postponed. And only when she was sure that we had taken our complete fill of love, and more, in each other's busy arms, rounded off by a little sleep, did Athene of the flashing eyes finally tip the wink to the lazy dawn to leave her golden ocean throne and bring back daylight to the darkened world.

SIXTY

And while Odysseus lay entwined with the fair Penelope, still fair after nineteen years, Cyllenian Hermes was busy shepherding the souls of the slaughtered suitors, who still milled about their own corpses, mystified and adrift. Using his golden wand, the god summoned them sternly to the next world, and they answered the summons, squeaking and gibbering like bats, trailing after the releaser of spirits with their thin shrill voices down the dark mouldering ways, over the barren sea, past the White Rock and the Western Gate and the sphere of dreams until they reached the fields of asphodel, the chosen place for the burned-out wraiths of erring men, the whispering drifted dead.

And here they experienced the first great revelation: small fry as they were compared with the heroes of the past, they could now converse on equal terms with the souls of the most illustrious dead of all Achaea, the glory of Greece – Achilles, Patroclus, Antilochus, Ajax and Agamemnon, all equal in Hades, lacking rank in eternity and shorn by death of the last shreds of their former glory. They'd lived great lives, but now it was as if life itself had never been.

Agamemnon, nonetheless, had much to say, as ever, irrelevant as his words were now, his estate an illusion. The suitors' souls overheard him angrily bewailing his lot.

'Achilles, here we are together still in the House of the Dead, but you are the happier because you had the happier death. Men fought and died for you in the dirt-cloud that covered your corpse. There in the whirling white dust you lay in Troyland, from Argos far, but illustrious in your fall. Your mother, the goddess Thetis, rose from the sea, the deathless sea-nymphs round her, and a great wailing went up, unearthly out of the ocean. Thetis had left the depths to look on the dead face of her son, she and the daughters of the old sea-god, clothed in the robes of eternity and the scents of the salt sea. Many were the tears they shed for you then as they stood around your corpse, sighing with sea-voices bitter with spume, and all the nine Muses singing for you too, their threnody laced with such sweet sorrow that there wasn't a dry eye in the Argive army, so plangent was their song.

'And that was only the start. Seventeen days and seventeen nights of mourning we held for you, until on the eighteenth day we gave you up to the fire. You had all that a corpse could have wished for in the flames: the fatted sheep, the shambling cattle, the garments of the gods, ointments and unguents and sparkling wine, the honey, the infantry, the cavalry with chariots round the pyre, and the white bones gathered in the dawn.

'They were laid in sweetest wine and oil and placed in a golden urn, given by the grieving goddess herself, a gift, she said, from Dionysus, and crafted by Hephaestus. This is where your white dust lies, mingled with the dust of the great Patroclus, who died before you, and Antilochus after him, yet in your deaths you were not divided but brought together as you were in life. And, over you, the Argive army built a great memorial, a glorious grave-mound on a headland commanding the Hellespont, so that sailors of today and tomorrow will salute you as they pass. That was what I call a death, Achilles. That was an ending. Not like mine – murdered miserably in my bath by an adulterous wife and her ruthless lover, a wretched end for the man who won the Trojan War.'

Agamemnon's lament had been interrupted by the arrival of Hermes ushering in the shades of the suitors to their eternal abode, and he was amazed to see so many fresh arrivals all at once. The first he saw and recognised was Amphimedon, and Agamemnon tried to disguise the bitter joy he felt at finding an old acquaintance come to join him here in Hades, shared misery being pleasing to certain souls who abhor solitary grief. Above all, Agamemnon was eager to learn of the manner of Amphimedon's death.

'Do you remember, Amphimedon, the time I came over to Ithaca with Menelaus to ask Odysseus to join the expedition, and you looked after us so well before we left for Troy? At least your father did – you were very young then, and it was a long time ago. What's happened since then to bring you down here so early instead of living out your span, you who were so privileged?

'And why all these young men with you, the pick of Ithaca? It's as if Persephone had ascended and come back down with the flowers of the island, culled by her pale hand and specially selected to decorate these dark halls. Did some savage tribe surround you when you were lifting their cattle and raping their women? Or did Poseidon take you in a gale and drive you down the sea's white windpipe? Surely it must have been some catastrophe, or the work of a god? You weren't murdered in your bath by any chance, were you?'

A look of hope appeared in Agamemnon's dead eyes and faded fast as

Amphimedon shook his sad, blood-bespattered locks. For hope there is none in Hades.

Amphimedon's death-grin was the one left on his face after Telemachus had unlocked the doors of his belly with his spear.

'It was the work of a god,' he said, 'and a catastrophe too. They were both called Odysseus.'

He told him the whole story – the courting of Penelope, the play for time, the unravelling at the loom, the return from Troy, the king in disguise, the stratagem of the bow, the net that enmeshed them all, the terrible slaughter. Agamemnon heard it all eagerly, drank it up like blood.

'So Odysseus is still the same old fox – and a survivor. He survived all that, and still his shade is not yet coming to accompany us in Hades and recall sweet life with a tear. But it will come in time. Even the soul of the wily Odysseus must submit and appear at the appointed hour. In the meantime he's happy and can celebrate a wife who will go down in legend for guile equal to his own. And for loyalty and constancy – Penelope the faithful, the flawless, the patient. What would I have given for a wife like her! Men and gods will sing her praises for centuries to come. And they'll pour scorn on my married lot and what I got instead, a murderess and a whore. Penelope and Clytemnestra, the opposites of their sex, two songs that will never cease to be sung, and mine the bitter one that eats at the ear.'

While all that was happening, I went to visit another man in hell. It was time to see my poor old father, Laertes.

I found him in a hovel which passed as a cottage, a run-down set of walls up in the farmlands. He'd chosen to live out his last days among the serfs, with only an old Sicilian woman to see to his basic needs. Otherwise he'd have left off eating altogether. His old heart was broken.

Of course he didn't know me. He was too far gone. Too much time, too much heartbreak, ashes on his head, black holes for eyes. A husk. And a son? He didn't even remember he had a son, he had no memory left, he was barely alive. That was all that was left of him, a white wisp among the ashes. That husk.

Clasp him in your arms all the same? Oh yes, hug him hard, but not so hard as to hurt him. Show him the scar, enumerate the events, the places, the people, Autolycus and his sons, the boar's white tusk, everything you can think of that will stir the ashes, light a candle in those eyes, make the flame where the life went to flicker, somewhere inside, the life that got lost at Troy, like so many other lives that were ended by war when sons did not come home.

'And after your son was lost, old man? What then? What happened then?'

'Then? Then there was no then.'

It was hopeless. You can't bring back a son to a dead father. You can't bring back *then* to lost time, unless in art, as ever, which is long where life is short, as they say. And don't women prefer happy endings anyway? Penelope came up with the idea of the trees.

'Do you remember, father? This will surely bring it back to you. One day when I was quite a little boy, I trotted after you among these trees, the very ones, and you told me all their names and said they were all to be mine; they were to be my trees. You gave me thirteen pear trees, ten apple, forty fig, and you showed me the fifty rows of vines that were also to be mine, your gift to me, your little lad. You see? I even remember the exact numbers, from all those years ago!'

Did it work? Of course it worked — in the web, where everything is well worked and worked out, where life is as it should be, not as it is. In that happy country, my brain-dead old dad is given back his mind. He remembers me, accepts me, leaps up and hugs me, arises from his ashes and becomes a new man. And why? And how? Because Pallas Athene is at work again, ensuring that all is as it used to be, all goes back to how it was, all to what they were. The derelict becomes the soldier, the beggar the king. And an unremembering veteran stands up and salutes his dead son who is alive again, stands with him in the line, stands against the suitors' families and their friends. He even kills one of them. He can throw a spear again. He can hear the song of the bronze.

While I was kissing goodbye to the sad husk of my father, the news had got out, as it had to. The rumours began to fly, and the murmuring mourners thronged the gates. The murmuring quickly turned to shrieks and curses when they broke into the empty palace and found the corpses, their sons. The dead were ferried out and taken to their homes. Those that belonged outside of Ithaca were shipped back to where they'd come from and where they should have stayed, where if only they'd stayed they'd have stayed alive. From every town in Cephallenia the wails went up. And a sore sobbing was heard in Same, in Dulichium and over wooded Zacynthus.

Unsurprisingly, the chief speaker against me at the hastily called Assembly turned out to be Eupeithes, the father of the worst of the bunch, the dead Antinous. Like father, like son. It was quite a speech, as I heard later.

'I denounce Odysseus as the enemy of Ithaca. I accuse him on all counts. He took away the best young men of his generation, twelve shiploads of them, took them to Troy to fight a foreign war and came back without a single man. All perished, every boy lost, and every ship of the fleet. All those years of occupation, and for what? Not a foot of land, not an ounce of gold, not a drop of oil, not a woman, not a grape, not a cow. And then he comes home at last to slaughter the best of the next generation, our sons, and only because they were offering to occupy an empty throne and an empty bed. For doing their duty, he murdered all of them. A mass murderer. A butcher from the wars. What else could he have learned out there in those killing fields, after all? And he was away so long he doesn't even deserve to be called our leader. He's lost the right. He's no longer King of Ithaca. How can a man return after an absence on that scale and expect to pick up where he left off? How can a killer pick up the reins of good government? I say let's get him now, while he's exposed, before he has a chance to fly to Pylos or escape to Sparta, to his old chums, to make them allies against Ithaca. They ruined Troy, and they'll do the same to Ithaca unless we stop him. In any case, we'll stink in the nostrils of posterity if we don't pay him back for our murdered sons. Let's do it now, before he can seize a ship. Come on, he's killed all of ours. It's time for him to die as he's lived – bloodily.'

A demolition job. It would have convinced even me if I'd been there. I might have killed myself, it was so persuasive. At the very least I'd have turned myself in. And not one of them spoke for me in that spineless tribe.

Except for Medon, who'd stayed behind long enough to find out which way the wind blew. He told Eupeithes he pitied him in his anger and his grief, but that, like many others whose sons were despised in Ithaca, he had fathered a rotten apple. They'd never done a stroke of work, they'd lived off the handouts of an absent authority. Or rather they had filched from the authority, and now the authority had returned. He'd handed out punishments instead, payback for the years of sloth and slobbery, and much else. It was harsh, but things had been evened up.

'They were wasters,' said Medon, 'and a waste of space. Of no use to our society and a drain on its resources.'

'A damage to its standards as well,' chipped in good old Halitherses, reminding the men of how often he'd urged them to restrain their offspring. 'They plundered and they whored. They knew no bounds, no decency. They were a disgrace to you as parents and a disgrace to Ithaca. They got what they deserved.'

The oratory was too full of home truths. The fathers didn't fancy taking those bad apples home with them, to tell their wives that the fault lay not in the stars but in the rotten fruit of their bellies. There was uproar, and Eupeithes won the day. The meeting ended with a call to arms.

We were at the farmlands when the scouts came rushing into the house. They'd heard from Medon and reported that the force was on its way.

'Hundreds of the fuckers!'

I ran out and saw it for myself, a dust cloud in the distance. On my side there was Telemachus, Eumaeus and Philoetius, and added to the force of four that had seen off the suitors, there was Phemius and now Medon. That made six. The old Sicilian woman looking after my father did have six sons. They were serfs, not soldiers, but then the opposition was anything but soldierly. Even so, twelve against hundreds was desperate. The suitors had outnumbered us, but they'd been cornered and outmanoeuvred. I couldn't count on my father. He couldn't count on himself. He couldn't even count. There was no getting out of this situation. We were out in the open, and all they had to do was surround us. If we retreated, they'd hunt us down and pick us off one by one. It was only a matter of time till all of us died. If we holed up in the farmhouse, they'd smoke us out or burn us down. I didn't fancy a live funeral pyre. I didn't fancy running either.

Impasse. Old Odysseus out of options at last. What's left then?

⑤

What's left? What else are you left with when all else fails? Pallas Athene, of course. And Penelope. A goddess and a good woman. Quick, pick up the shuttle where the sword no longer suffices nor the spear prevails. The bronze age is over, sit down at the loom, throw away the shields. Flick, flick.

Athene zooms up to Olympus.

'Son of Cronos, Father Zeus –'

'Yes, yes, you can drop the titles – there isn't time. Get to the point.

I know what's on your mind. I am, after all, the great god.'

'And only you, All-thundering One, can save Odysseus this time and avoid a massacre.'

'I don't mind a massacre, but I don't want a civil war, and that's what it will be in Ithaca if this goes any further. Only war itself is necessary, inevitable, and even a joy to the gods. But civil war is not glorious. It's unsightly, and should be stopped.'

'And so?'

'So here is my decision. They must agree on a truce and make a peace treaty. Odysseus is the rightful king, and he and his heirs must reign in perpetuity, with an act of oblivion on the part of the gods obliterating the slaughter of their sons. We'll have goodwill brought back on both sides, the old order restored, peace and plenty to prevail. How does that suit you?'

'Perfectly.'

'Then let it be. One last thing, though – we'd better have a death. One will do. A sacrifice is always good. And it will show them we're serious.'

So Pallas Athene put the divine plan into action and stood by old Odysseus in his last stand. She breathed life into Laertes and whispered in his deaf ear to be a man again, the hero of the hour, to swing back his long bronze spear and let it fly –

'– at that man there. Aim it at him, the one right out in front, the one making the most noise. You can't miss him, and I mean that literally. You can't miss him!'

He couldn't. Not with Pallas Athene guiding the javelin, flying alongside it – see how she flies! See how it flies! Homing in on the target, seeking the heat of human blood! Oh, what a picture! Bronze meets bronze, the spear-point pierces the cheek-guard of the helmet and Eupeithes stops the noise he's making and makes another sound, a smaller one. Then he stops that too. Then he stops altogether.

He crashed to the ground and his armour rang about him.

'You see!' Odysseus roared at them. 'Even an old man is made into an Achilles when god is on his side! You're all going to die!'

Not that it really took a god. If that's all it ever took, the lists of the heroic dead would be shorter and the grave-mounds few. What it took was Eupeithes splashing his followers with his brains. My javelin crashed through his forehead and out the back of the skull. When they felt the spray on their faces and saw the pinkish-grey stuff spattering their sleeves, they turned a colour like the sea in spring when the wintry muddiness has gone and the water's green and clear. And it was clear enough to those who saw his skull spill that some of them were going to die, and that the manner of it would be something along those lines.

Better to stay alive? The ones in the front, the ones who got splashed, thought so. Sometimes when you're facing a pack of wolves, you only have to cut down the front runner to make the others scatter. And these men weren't even wolves. They were armed to the teeth but arms don't make the man. Balls make the man. And they saw that one man who had balls now had no brain, and they thought of their own firesides, and of their wives and maids laying the table and the stewards pouring the wine, and the chamber-women making the nice sensible beds . . .

Granted, they couldn't think of the grandchildren their sons would be giving them, because their sons were dead, but when they set all of the above, grandchildren aside, against speeches and politics and codes of honour, suddenly it didn't seem worth it after all.

And they stood and gaped. And we fell on them with a roar, whooping like the Trojan charioteers. We might even have wiped them out to the last man, our spears up their retreating arses, if Athene hadn't materialised over our heads for the last time and delivered the verdict.

'Ithacans! Enough! Enough blood has been spilt! Drop your weapons, all of you. You too, Odysseus! This is the time of peace!'

'Peace? Never! I know no peace! War is peace! Peace is war!' I came out with it again, the terrible Troy war-cry, and swooped down on them like an eagle.

It took a thunderbolt to convince me. Zeus, the old flame-thrower, let loose. The earth rose to meet the clouds and cratered between me and the enemy. Pallas Athene pointed to the huge hole in the ground.

'Don't cross that line, Odysseus – unless it's to shake hands. You've had your war. And you've had your revenge. A double whammy. Epic enough for one man, I should say. And for a lifetime, don't you think? No more soldiering for you, old son. And no more roving either. You can go home.'

Sometimes you do think you hear gods speaking to you. Sometimes you listen to the voices in your head. Other times you don't.

EXODE
THE LAST VOYAGE

Blue water and the four points — and the skylines all around, empty, alluring, inklings of adventure, impossible to abjure. That was the old life, the easy life, tough as it seemed at the time. Once it was all that mattered. Fill the benches, grip the oars, set a course for nowhere, pulling as one on the polished pine, bury the blade in the waves and feel the whole ocean suddenly make love to you, sweet as the first thrust, mysterious, deep. Nothing to equal it, the magic of that moment, not knowing where it will take you, but knowing it will be new, forbidden, forbidding, fresh as first love.

And now? Now I sit here on the hillside under the sun, waiting for death and thinking, thinking now of the dead seasons turning over like waves in my head. My head . . . Ah, yes, I had a head once like the ways of the sea. I was wily, I could slip through your fingers. They used to call me the old fox, the one of twists and turns, the man of many guiles, the talker, the thinker, the teller of stories. Thought and action make strange benchmates, but they teamed up, a fine match, a marriage for life, so I thought once.

Once there was no parting, no separating them, one from the other, the hand quick as the brain, the arm supple and strong, and the long blue straits and barren fields of the sea suddenly a bursting harvest — monsters, gods, women, wine, songs, the whole catastrophe, remember?

I remember, yes. And luck? Was there luck on my side too? No, there's no such thing as luck; there's only bad luck. Like losing your head. Hector's head once trundled in the dust and heaps of men keeled over. And the killers were killed in their turn. The difference between me and Hector or Paris or Achilles? I survived. Simple. That was the trick. Survival.

That meant keeping your head. It meant resisting the temptation to sleep, to forget yourself and your humanity. That was all too easy. The forgetters were everywhere; the sea swarmed with them — Aeolian incest, the Cimmerians in their oblivious mist, the Sirens in their specious fields, the Cyclops in his stoppered cave, Circe, Calypso, hidden deep in the sea's blue navel, the whole ocean their loom. Easy to have stayed. But I'd sooner have died where the spears flew thickest.

Except that I never wanted to be a hero, not me. Heroes are not survivors. Heroes are dead meat. They're losers. They get great big grave-mounds, huge ones on headlands. Sailors salute them on approach. Then they sail on, leaving them grinning in their graves, beneath the bluebell and the bee. Sailors are survivors. They've learned the trick of passing by, or of leaving islands, islands that incarcerate, incinerate, turn you to ash. Even Nausicaa's. And she was a good girl. Standing naked in front of her as she kissed my briny beard and saw a husband beneath the sea-scum – yes, that was thrilling, I admit. But not thrilling enough, not enough to keep me, not enough to beach the keel and leave the oar to flake and blister in the sun and rain.

The way home was strewn with thrills. But there was nothing to compare with that first night back, the night I spent with the swineherd in his hut, when the workers came home tired, and we all lay by the fire after supper with the rain pounding down outside and the winds howling and me telling stories of Troy, lies mostly. That was a lot more tempting. That, you could say, was the real thrill – returning to the world of hard work and sore rest and meat and drink, with the fire blazing and the wild weather rattling the roof.

Not that even that was enough to hold me, though it was poetry enough at the time, for a man like me. Not for me the poetry of heroes – all those proud captains who were the cocks of their own middens, the plumed glory boys. Where are they now? Hell's crawling with them. I had more *nous*, more brain than bronze. They were brilliant in action. But they never hunkered down on a hillside beneath stars, like me, and thought, and thought . . .

About Troy. And all that. I had to go back, naturally, as veterans do. Truth is, we never really left. Or we left something big behind us. Even so, it was strange to stand again on the site of all that conflict. So little to show for the suffering. Still some bones beneath the once high battlements. Small bones. And then there were the Greek war dead, the mounds, a cemetery under the clouds, cared for by lizards.

The sky stands empty over Troy. Looking at it now, you can't help thinking that there could have been peace. We all wanted an exit strategy. Instead, Greeks and Trojans and all their allies lay sprawled in the dust, face down, belly up, next to one another. Agamemnon was why. And he said Helen was why. But in the end, nobody needs a why. We go along with it because deep down war is what we need and it's what we do. Peace is what we put up with once we've done it, once we've held the funerals for all those shattered lives and all that waste of people.

I broke down in Scheria when I remembered it, and the pity of it, and I wept real tears. Penelope stitched them in threads of silver, big glittering beads and droplets on the web. If only she could see me now, she'd give me golden tears, more precious than greed or glory or the dreams of wine, and I'd cry all over again as I did years ago for my fallen friends, while the gods, fiery, flaky, elements of ourselves, sat on our prows and laughed, spat on by sea-spire, drenched with spray, laughing their old heads off and reaching out to us as we toiled at the oars, still laughing amid the spindrift, shaking their immortal locks, extending their easy, chiselled and indulgent arms.

Oh, I could have wept at many a revisited scene of past exploits, scenes that lacerate, as the poet says, simply by being over, and not because they meant so much at the time. Why would I wax sentimental, for example, about a cannibal? And yet the cave of the Cyclops was the scene of one of my best triumphs. And there I was friends with perished people. Can't a man enjoy his great deeds? And even make out of them some sweet philosophy? I could tell you, if you wanted to believe me, that I did go back to Crete and found Polyphemus still alive, and much changed.

'Ah, is it you, Odysseus? Or Noman, should I say? I thought I recognised your voice. Let me assure you, the volcano you made of my eye no longer troubles me. The eye is extinct. It's long plugged – only cold ash now, and silver scarring, rather like Calypso's loom and hearth will look like when you get there, as I know you will. I know many things now, which were forbidden to me in my ignorance and my brutality. So you see, I have to thank you. And I can promise you Poseidon will not be pursuing you. These days I'd find sight something of a distraction, I must confess. I'm content to sit and think.'

Believable? It's asking a lot, and I was always such a liar. That was another of my survival instincts. But I did go back to Circe's place, and I could have cried there too for the lady who learned to love me, the maker of spells who fell spellbound herself when she met her destiny, the only man who could set her free to love and not to conquer, not to subdue. I could have cried because I failed to stay with her. But I knew I was not in love again. If I'd cried I'd have been crying for myself, for lost life, for beautiful youth, not for the girl but for the passing of things, not just love and vigour and hope, but all things.

I came to Calypso's cave. The hearth was cold, the lyre strings shattered and tangled, the loom cobwebbed. Where was she? Gone was Eros, gone was Himeros, gone were love and desire for the nymph of the lovely locks. But I'd made that decision long ago. There was a price to be paid in her bed, and the price was forgetting. Even Argus didn't forget. And is a man any better than a dog? Some men are worth a lot less. While I slept there with Calypso, there on that very bed, Penelope was weeping for a pile of white bones, rotted by the rains, when the bones not only had flesh on them, and made passionate love, but had the chance to live forever, as we long to believe that bones will do. I was on an island of immortality which kept me from the mud and muddle of life, cut me off from flesh and blood, the fury and the mire. But what man wants the cool nudity of the sex goddess? I wept then because I wanted to return to real life — sweet simply because it ends, because it's fragile, precarious, unpredictable. And I yearned again for the trials and wanderings renewed time and again, the earth flinty beneath my feet and the slow ocean rolling underneath me as it has rolled under others for centuries, millennia, rolling me on to the next experience.

And Helen. What of Helen? Yes, I stopped there too, on my last journey, a fly on the wall in Sparta, because I needed to know what it all adds up to when a thousand ships are launched, and thousands die, and cities fall. Was it all for love? They said the long connubial years became a bore — to both, and to all who stayed, and to those who danced attendance on the pair. But I wanted to find out for myself if that was true.

It was. Menelaus out-Nestored Nestor in garrulity. He sacked a hundred Troys between noon and supper, and sacked each one a hundred times. He grew deaf to her nagging, she grew shrill to his deafness. Her golden voice cracked. And both were old. He sometimes asked himself why Paris ever came to Sparta. Or left with her. Or why he went to Troy, went after her. She wept a lot, wept for her wrinkles. Her eyes, viscous, sticky, dropped tears as fast as the Arabian trees their medicinal gum, as they say. They lay together through the useless years, trapped by time, dry-shanked and impotent. Sometimes he muttered in his sleep between the snores and whistles . . . Troy . . . Paris . . . and at his name her withered loins twitched and she cried in her dreams. And Paris slept on by Scamander side.

At last she came to die. A ghost sees all. They wove her white hair, washed her face, bathed the long crinkled eyelids in cool rosewater to let them open for the last time on the almond eyes, bleary now. Blonde-locked granddaughters bent over the fallen breasts, baring them a little to let her breathe more easily, while in at the opened window crept the old scents of the sea.

She remembered. She asked to see her shroud. They lifted the cedar-chest lid, inlaid with ivory, and showed her the work she'd woven so long ago, bent over the loom, not thinking then that the day would ever really come when she'd be wrapped in it, embroidered as it was with the scenes so lovingly recreated by her remembering hand: a blue sea crowded with ships, towers toppling, heroes cut down, children killed, women enslaved, all for her sake. Now the day had come. The years rushed back – and suddenly she was a young braided girl again, with buds for breasts, and Theseus was buggering her by Eurotas' green banks . . .

Was that her last memory? Even a ghost has no window into a dying brain, a dead, dreamless head.

The laments and lacerations start up, and the gem-covered corpse is borne away along the long lobby, subterranean, dark, except for the flickering lamps and torches. The dead tresses are strung with amber beads, the perished breasts bejewelled, the waist girdled with gold. Slippers cover the horny feet, and only one cold hand is on show, holding her favourite mirror, cold bronze clasped by colder fingers to the blind face, hiding the crow's feet, the shrivelled neck. Golden bowls are brimming all around the body, and the wine cups glimmer with mingled resin and wine, a bumper farewell, a generous pledge to toast the long journey into night. The lingering incense fades, the last lamps gutter, the last clang on the golden string echoes eerily, leaving the tomb a trembling memory, all sealed up. They leave her to herself and to the dark. Now she can gaze into the glass, admire herself again for all eternity. If only she could lift that hand. If only she could open her eyes.

Helen. The madness of love, without which life could not continue. Why did Medea fall in love with Jason? Why did she hack her own brother to pieces and hurl him into the sea? Why was Agamemnon axed in his bath? What made Ajax rape Cassandra and enrage Athene? What made Achilles love Penthesilea and murder Thersites? Who made Eros after all? Ares and Aphrodite, love and war. Eros subjugates the heart, assaults the intellect, breaks the will, kills the soul. It lures sailors to sirens and litters the meadows with their rotting corpses, rolls their bones in the ocean. It's what bewitched the suitors when they saw Penelope and listened to her siren talk, so that the palace hall could be strewn with dead. It's the madness that caused the most famous war in history. Helen was the cause but the sexual roots of the carnage at Troy plunged deeper into history, humanity, hell. Zeus lusted after Thetis, Eris sowed strife, Aphrodite cheated. Helen loosened men's balls, spilling sperm. She loosened their knees, spilling blood. Cupidity made love to Cupid, and Persephone waited in her halls. The war was born of betrayal, sex, intrigue. Sex and death – how can you part them, after all? Troy was rooted in the pain of their marriage, the madness of desire.

I tried to leave that madness and go home, and found that I couldn't until I'd found myself again. Who was I? What was I? Beggar, wanderer, outcast, lover, warrior, god. There's a god in every man. And a beggar. And returning soldiers need mending. Drugs can't heal them; that's for sure. Circe offered drugs, Helen had drugs, lotus drugs that eased the suffering memory, the pain of remembering. But that's not the way home. There's no identity without pain, and it's pain that helps you in the end to snatch what you can from the dark. Otherwise you're a dead man.

I came home on a sea of death – it was my element. Each island was deadly because the islands were my own failings, my muddles. And in each encounter I met only the monsters of myself. The true traveller tours death, sees the sights of Hades. I went to the House of the Dead, I spoke with ghosts. I was a dead man, not only to myself but also to those who loved me. I was the white bones on the shore. I was the hole where the hearth was, where the heart was. I longed for life and couldn't find it, not after Troy. War, like love and death, changes everything. When I heard stories about myself, I buried my head in my sea-blue cloak and cried for all I'd lost and could never recover.

Out on the sea I learned to live again, to stay alive. Then I came home and found insular, intolerable Ithaca – the land of peace, the land of the suitors, men of the land. Me, I was always a ship man, though I farmed. The sea brought me up, a good rough nurse of youth. It gave me dreams, sea-dreams, some of which came true, including the bad ones, the monsters of the unconscious. I was, after all, the child of unhappy anger, or whatever else Autolycus meant when he named me. I keep thinking about him, my grandfather, my disreputable mentor, the one who taught me archery.

'The big boys despise the bow,' he said. 'They think bowmen are cowards and softies. And it's true that some weaklings like to fight that way and only that way, and they're afraid of the front line. But just you do a body count of all the dead heroes. You won't find many bowmen among them. How you stand up, how you fall down – it doesn't matter. Staying alive is what matters. It's all that matters.'

He sent me to Thesprotia once to root out a particular poison for my arrows, one that was awkward to come by. I learned early to get in and out of tricky situations.

'And don't think you have to escape everything with honour,' he said. 'Just get out with your life, that's all. What's the use of being an honourable dead man?'

He was a cattle-thief and a rationalist. I took my realism from him. Monsters, narcotics, women who swallow you, the vast loom of the sea – all irrational, all to be overcome. The challenge was the thrill. It gave meaning and purpose to the voyage, not to the arrival, not to Ithaca. It was the beauty and the burden of the journey that counted, the process, the exploration, the taste of life in all its forms, and death on board every hour, every foot of the way, to make the taste seem sweeter, to whet the appetite for life over and over, so that when Persephone finally came for me and held out her pale hand, I could tell her there was nothing she could take because I'd nothing left to give. I'd squandered the lot, done it all, drunk the cup to the dregs and thrown it to the ocean. There wasn't a drop left for her to pour out onto the embers and ash of my existence on earth. All dross burned away.

And that last journey – carrying my oar and all that? Well, I see it now, clear and simple. This is it, right here and now – it's started, I'm on my way. Into that desert country where they've never heard the sea, or even heard of it. That's death, to be separated from the scents and shapes and sounds of the sea. Death is the desert. And the oar planted in its sterile earth, the oar in the mound, is the sailor's only monument. The hauling days are done. The long trick's over.

Am I wandering? I expect I am. I'm entitled to. And, except in debate, I always was a wanderer. I never set a straight course; sometimes I think I lost my way on purpose. Well, now the spirit's free to wander off eternally, wherever and whatever that might be, but somewhere somehow out on my own element, absconded from ash, shaking away the last embers underneath the oar, slipping quietly back to sea, utterly engrossed by the opulence of ocean. The spirit can do all that, can't it? Maybe I'll be that white gull you see, a flash of wings, high in the blue emptiness. Maybe I'll put in from non-time to noontime, come ashore with the flowergirl wind on a day when the first petals are sparking the grasses and the lambs are sucking their mothers' milk, when being surrounded by such simplicity in this beautiful brutal world is much more precious, as a bard once sang, than Pylos or Sparta or Troy or any gathering of metal from slaughtered enemies or the raping of their wives.

And so I'll be the croak of the frog in the empty well, the lone drone of the bee, the dry grate of the grasshopper, the limestone's white, burned voice. I'll be yellow as gold, I'll be stonecrop on tumulus, cool under cumulus. Maybe I'll hear the gods talking in the sun, their chatter heady with absinthe, their archaic smiles brightening the sullen sea, the misty olive woods, the weak congenial moon. And I'll see the tall blue irises again in green fields, and the red geraniums shedding their blood on the old stones of Troy. Or what was once Troy, its marble monuments turned to dust, like the white fistfuls of kings that lie scattered among the ruins, dribbled on now by poppies and rain, mocked by the hills, cold-shouldered by the sea.

The sea. I'm starting to catch it now, the smell of it, the pull of it. The sea, the sea. That feeling you get when you walk through cities, settlements, and you're impatient to leave, can't wait to see the back of them. You come to farmsteads, villages, you cross fields. Your pace quickens. The last scattered houses fall behind you, and you're almost running now, hurrying over scrubland, still lugging your life along with you, the big burden, hungry to purge yourself of it, to unclog your soul.

Suddenly a surge of gulls, the sting of salt, and the roar in your ears – and you're really running now, stumbling over tussock and boulder and beach-grass until you arrive at the sea's seaweedy edge and see it spread out before you like uncharted existence, unfenced emptiness, and you understand what you're smelling now, it's the scent of adventure, the old aroma of the unknown, the unexperienced, the outermost edge of the landsman's life, and you lose your loamy gravity and grow light, shedding the past as a swimmer peels off his clothes, and out you go . . .

I'll meet them all there, I expect – Ajax, Agamemnon, the sailor lads that roved with me and lost their lives, our oar-blades an eternal chorus to the ocean, sweeping through the lee-long blue. And when I'm dead at last – and I think now I am – let the flames lick me all over, consuming all, all except this grey old head. Keep that. But take the oar, and carry it to that last country, where I'm lying. You know the place; it's not far. The oar is the ferryman's now. Charon, the lone rower. Maybe he'll hand it to me one last time, and I'll be one with the gulls again, back with that garrulous old washerwoman, the sea, like Eurycleia, never done scrubbing.

And set the skull at the window, out on the sill, eyeholes to the ocean, where it can collect the lichens, leprous as a stone. And hush then, hush . . . just listen, listen awhile, and you'll hear what I'm hearing, what the child hears when he puts the shell to his head and the sea talks to him, the whole ocean in one ear, the same old roar, muted for the moment to the soft shoom and sough of the eternal element, deaf wars at either side, Ilium and Odyssey, bone become beach, and deaf seas inside the skull, where the mind once worked, niftily, shiftily, where the brains were, the heroes of the corps.